FREE BORN SAGA
BOOK 2
ELYSIA

BENJAMIN SANFORD

STENOX PUBLISHING
Clarksburg, MD

ISBN 979-8-9890221-2-0 (pbk)
ISBN 979-8-9890221-3-7 (digital)

Printed in the United States of America

ASTARIA

POR-SHADA
MOUNTAINS

UPPER VELO

LORTAIA
CAREGA

PICERAN

ASTARIS
PLEXUS

UPPER TORLIN

VECTA

VETCUS

TORLIN

LOWER VELO

LAROSE

SABOL

TALESIA

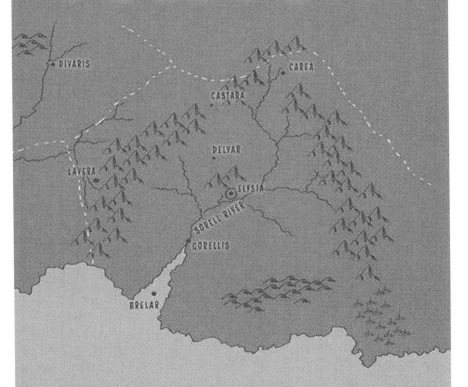

CHAPTER 1

He stood alone upon the upper battlements of Astaris, watching the Vellesian caravan cross the Torlin, before disappearing over the horizon, his mind a maelstrom of emotions twisting him into a tortured relic. Bronus denied the tear struggling to break free, a pitiful reminder that he was just as human as any other, but he'd be damned if he'd give that *woman* the satisfaction. His heart broke for his son, thinking of what life he was being led into.

He gave his freedom to spare my life. The thought pained him with guilt for his stupidity. How could he have been so blind to Valera's intentions? She simply walked into his home and stole his son, in full view of every mage king in Elaria. The House of Blagen was now a source of laughter and ridicule. His kingdom stood upon the precipice, one misstep, and they were doomed. It was obvious now that they were surrounded by enemies, not one realm in all the land willing to ally with them against the greater threat. For all his life, he proudly believed himself invincible, the mighty Bronus Blagen, the first Elarian in five hundred years born a lightning Lord. How wrong he was, and how truly weak he felt.

"Lightning Lord," he nearly spat, shaking his head. If what Amanda said was true, the power to cast lightning was as useful as spit in the wind against the Vellesian queen and princess. Only Ethan's obedience kept them from using their vast powers against Astaria. He wondered why the other mage kings couldn't see that Ethan's protection in no way extended to them. Were they fools, or were they being manipulated?

Blast it! He cursed to himself, his anger welling up again. It was a constant torrent of rage followed by calm and then depression before giving way to rage all over again. He felt like smashing something and came up here before venting his fury on his *guests*, the very mage kings who betrayed Ethan to Valera.

"You are not alone in your sorrow, my love," Gabrielle said softly, stepping to his side, touching a hand to his thick shoulder.

He looked over to her, losing himself in her light green eyes that stared back at him with knowing grief. She never failed to calm his raging heart with the slightest touch, a power no one but her exerted with the Astarian king. He spoke not a word for the longest time, drawing her close with his left arm around her as they looked east, where Ethan rode away somewhere over the horizon.

"I think of all the years I wasted fighting with him, trying to make him into something he is not," he lamented.

"Not wasted, my love. Every instruction helped mold Ethanos into the man he is, a man we both admire. It is not in shame he rides away, but in love, love for you and I and our people. Take hope in that," she said, leaning her head against his thick chest, savoring the comfort of his strong embrace.

"All he ever spoke of was his freedom, though he could've claimed it anytime he chose. All he had to do was walk away, forsaking Astaria to live as he wanted. He didn't require a royal request to do so. He is immune to magic and any hold it had on him. He stayed because he wouldn't accept his freedom without my consent, knowing he would have to forsake our family to do so. His love for us forged his chains. His royal request merely allowed him to remain in our family and embrace his freedom. And now..." his words died in his throat, barely able to utter them.

"And now his love for us forges his chains anew," Gabrielle finished his thought.

"Aye," he sighed.

"Your guilt is less than my own, my love. It was always my wish for him to wed and gift me grandchildren. How the fates have thrown that wish against me. He shall sire me a mighty grandchild that I shall never likely see and will be used as a sword against us, if what Amanda says is true, a child of my namesake."

"And you believe they mean him no harm?" He asked, doubting Valera to keep her word.

"Amanda claims they shall not kill him," Gabrielle sighed.

"Placing him in a cage is worse than death, as far as Ethan is concerned."

Gabrielle sighed, knowing the truth of that.

"Have faith in our son, Bronus. If anyone can circumvent mage law, it is him." She smiled at the countless memories of his mischievous youth.

"Something amuses you?" He looked down at the smile stretching her lips.

"I just envisioned Ethan reshaping Valera's crown." Gabrielle laughed, recalling their son's first attempt with Bronus's regal headdress when he was six years, molding its top into an unseemly shape.

"You weren't laughing with his first attempt if my memory is correct. It looked like a giant teat resting on my head," Bronus snorted, recalling Ethan's face at the time without a shred of shame on it.

"How could I with so many in attendance," she recalled the looks of the court when his crown was placed upon his head without inspection after sitting his throne. She recalled the assemblage suppressing their laughter so as not to incur the king's wrath. Unfortunately, her father was present to commence the uproar, laughing loud enough to wake the dead and drawing Bronus' ire.

"He had the temerity to claim it was a spear tip," he shook his head, wondering how a child of six could not only take his crown unseen but work a forge and reshape it without anyone noticing.

"He was only a child, Bronus. He said since you were a mighty king, your crown should be adorned with a weapon." She smiled.

"A teat?"

"He meant it as a spear tip," she defended their son's innocence.

"Hah! You give the lad too much trust. He knew well what he was doing. Any child knows the difference between a spear tip and a breast, especially one with his appetite the first two years of life," he growled, drawing a playful slap from his queen.

"A spear tip," she insisted, maintaining Ethan's purity.

"Maybe you're right. If he wanted to adorn my crown with a weapon, there is a better part of a woman's anatomy he could have chosen."

Another playful slap followed, causing him to smile, drawing his beloved into a tighter embrace.

"The boy was a handful." Bronus shook his head.

"That was my mother's opinion when he gifted her the fish he caught, storing it in her baggage." Gabrielle sighed, recalling her mother's face upon discovering the source of the smell afflicting her carriage. He was only four years at the time, celebrating his first catch by gifting it to his grandmother, much to Dragos's amusement, placing his catch atop her gowns.

"Hah! Dragos enjoyed that antic as well. I would have liked Ethan to subject your father to one of his idiotic misdeeds for once. No wonder he always humored Ethan's misadventures, sitting back and reveling in our misery."

"Father did enjoy his company," she reflected, recalling all the times Ethan spent in his grandsire's tower or at his palace at Plexus.

"Bah! Like two wayward criminals conspiring to make my life difficult." Bronus snorted.

"And you enjoyed every moment," she reminded him, knowing he was secretly proud every time Ethan confronted him.

"The boy's no coward. I'll give him that."

"And you miss him dearly." She closed her eyes, tucking her head into his shoulder.

"Aye, I miss the rascal. May he give Valera as much grief as he gave me."

"I have little doubt that he shall." She sighed.

"I should see to our guests. Give them a proper send-off as befits their treachery," Bronus snorted, thinking of other things he'd like to do with his royal guests.

"Tristan is already attending to that task," she said.

"He is?"

4

"Yes. He thought to spare you the bother. He is a fine man and worthy heir," she reminded him, admiring their dutiful second son.

"Aye, he is. I should be helping him and giving our guests their rightful due," he growled.

"They are suffering his rebuke, which is no less severe as your own, I assure you."

"They are?"

"Yes. Tristan has always been protective of his brother and is admonishing the mage kings for their folly. Amanda is with him, sharing in his reproach."

"Truly?"

"Does it surprise you?" she asked.

"Not really. She seems a fine girl, considering who her mother is."

"She tried to warn Ethan to leave the palace, but alas, it was not to be."

"She did?" Bronus wondered how Gabrielle knew so much, and him, so little.

"Yes, and suffered dearly for it."

"Her thigh." He remembered Arian healing her burn.

"Her mother gifted her that for warning Ethan."

"What kind of mother would do such a thing?" He shook his head, fearing what awaited his son in her keeping.

"Perhaps Amanda shall enlighten us."

"Yes. I have many questions for her," he said, drawing forth the mysterious stone she gifted him, holding it aloft in his free hand.

*****

"This is preposterous!" Magnus Delmarin, king of Relusia, protested. The Relusian monarch stood in the center of the great hall, staring up at Tristan, who sat his father's throne. King Marvo of Meltoria looked equally upset, standing off to the side, surrounded by his royal retinue.

"The king's word is law, Your Grace," Tristan reminded him.

"My daughter's betrothal—" he further protested before Tristan cut him off.

"Rests within the purview of Astaria, as per the treaty of Astaris, Your Grace," Tristan reminded him of the terms he and King Marvo swore to upon their defeat at the Velo.

"She is too young," Magnus pleaded.

"She is recently flowered, my prince," Lord Celembar, steward of the inner palace, advised, standing at his left.

"Yes, thirteen years, if my memory serves me," Tristan said, giving Magnus a knowing glance.

"Flowered but dangerously young for the birthing bed!" Magnus protested.

"Perhaps for the birthing bed, but not a betrothal, one that can be extended if the crown is merciful, Your Grace," Tristan reminded him.

"To whom shall she be wed?" The Relusian monarch asked. Whomever the Astarian prince declared would father his realm's future king.

"The crown has chosen Geoff Jarvo, heir of house Jarvo and cousin to King Bronus to wed the Princess Shandara," Lord Celembar revealed the crown's choice.

"She is worthy of a prince, not an Astarian Lord!" Magnus argued, aghast that his eldest daughter and heir would wed an Astarian Lord.

"The crown might have considered your objection, King Magnus, had you not sided with Queen Valera over Prince Ethanos in regard to his royal request. It is the opinion of the Astarian Throne that Lord Jarvo's heir be compensated, as he was originally chosen to wed the crown princess of Vellesia, and shall now be given the crown princess of Relusia in her place," Amanda said, standing to Tristan's right.

"And steal my throne by proxy!" He growled, envisioning Jarvo's get ruling Relusia. He wanted to curse Valera for her false promises of freeing him from the contemptible treaty he was forced to agree to after the Velo, binding his realm to Astaria. She assured him that Bronus and his fool of a son would break their agreement with her, severing all bonds of magic linked to the Astarian Throne, including his and the Meltorian king. But alas, it was not to be, with Ethanos choosing slavery to Valera over death for his mighty sire. And what did Magnus gain from any of this? By taking Ethanos, Valera left him at Astaria's mercy. *Curse that woman!* he thought bitterly.

"Your heirs shall still sit your throne, oh King. If you are displeased, you have none to blame but yourself. King Bronus dealt with you fairly, and you rewarded his mercy by conspiring with my mother to steal his son. Now you shall suffer the full terms of the Treaty of Astaris," Amanda reminded him, reading his thoughts so clearly.

Magnus regarded her warily, withering under her intense glare. Her mental powers were overwhelming, forcing him to look away.

"The Princess Shandara shall remain in Astaris until she is wed, whereupon she and Lord Jarvo shall return to your capital of Aridin, and assume her rightful place as your heir. The Astarian crown shall find suitable matches for your remaining five daughters from the noble houses of Astaria. So it is decreed!" Tristan declared, effectively binding Relusia to Astaria, dismissing the ashen-faced monarch.

"King Ortovan Marvo!" Lord Celembar summoned the Meltorian King hither.

And so it went, with Tristan relaying his severe judgment upon the Meltorian king, binding his heir, Prince Orvonit IV, to a loyal highborn lady of Astaria, Lady Viola Luciel. It was Lady Viola's father who fell in battle, charging the Meltorian host at the Velo. His sacrifice was rewarded with the placing of his blood on the Meltorian throne. An added boon to Meltoria was that the lady Viola was a gifted mage healer, a precious gift to any realm. For his subterfuge conspiring with the Vellesian queen, King Marvo's realm was subjected to severe tariffs on all goods traversing the lower Velo and an annual tribute of one hundred thousand gold coins for the following six years.

Unfortunately, Astaria had no such hold on the Sarcosan and Estasan kings. With the Vecara Mountains shielding them from the former and Relusia and Meltoria separating them from the later, neither was in the position to threaten Astaria. With that, King Ectus and King Lorga made a quiet exit, leading their retinues from the palace, leaving the king of Gorgencia the last monarch remaining.

King Gregor Vorhenz stepped before the throne, curious about what the boy would say. He planned to leave immediately after Valera, needing to reach his native Gorgencia ahead of the Vellesian Royal party, to properly receive them, but couldn't help himself, savoring this triumph over the hated Astarian king and his brood. His son and heir stood farther back, surrounded by his retinue of household knights and retainers, his arms crossed with a pompous smirk painting his face. Prince Borcose's smug airs did not go unnoticed by Tristan, who fumed at their complicity in the Vellesian plot. Amanda revealed the extent of their collusion with her mother, going back before the battle of the Velo.

"What words have you for me, *boy*? Any edicts you would like to decree condemning my house?" King Gregor taunted. "I am not bound by the absurd terms of the treaty you forced upon Relusia and Meltoria. You sit friendless, surrounded by enemies, and your greatest asset forever removed to never threaten us again. I am surprised with the ease with which Queen Valera was able to remove the troublesome Ethanos from under your sire's nose. Of all the fates I dreamed up for Ethanos to suffer, I never thought he'd be bound to woman's skirts, groveling at her feet like a beaten pup!" Gregor's laugh was chorused by his son and retinue, causing the Astarian royal guards posted around the chamber to put their hands to their sword hilts, ready to draw steel.

"I would not be so quick to celebrate, Gregor," Tristan omitted his title just as the Gorgencian King omitted his. "Astaria is fully aware of the extent of your subterfuge. You may boast of your strength, but that is all it is, Gregor, a boast, and a false one at that. How many shield and shade mages did you lend to the Meltorian and Relusians at the Velo?"

Gregor's smile faltered.

"Nearly every noble house of Gorgencia lost a member there in some fashion, mages all," Amanda said, unnerving the Gorgencian King. "Prince Tristan is aware of all your dealings with Queen Valera, King Gregor. The House of Blagen knows how you conspired with

Vellesia, supplying Relusia and Meltoria with both shield and shade mages, as well as numerous fire casters and combat mages. Estasa and Sarcosa are equally culpable, filling out the ranks of shields and shades, with promises of rich rewards, all dividing the spoils of Astaria among yourselves. Do you deny it?"

Gregor stood dumbstruck, confounded by her power and the revelations of Estasa and Sarcosa, of which he was ignorant.

"You were unaware of the other's involvement?" Amanda asked bemusedly, knowing the answer as she was privy to much of her mother's machinations. "And what did she demand from the plunder?"

Gregor stared blankly, never thinking to ask that of her.

"Did you not find it strange that she asked for nothing?" Amanda smiled knowingly, enjoying seeing the pompous fool twist in the wind.

"She wanted Talesia," he answered, not at all certain.

"No, King Gregor. She lured you, Sarcosa, and Estasa to gift Relusia and Meltoria much of your mage power to draw Prince Ethanos back from across the barrier from Red Rock. Only a threat upon Astaria could accomplish this, as their prophecies foretold. Had you defeated Astaria, she had agents in place to retrieve Prince Ethanos, but she knew you would fail. And now you are without much of your strength, the strength needed to stand against a lightning lord. Only House Loria can defeat such a power, and House Loria has sworn not to do so to ensure Prince Ethanos's fidelity. Astaria may not have Prince Ethanos to protect it from the enemies that surround it, but neither do you possess the shield mages needed to contest a lightning lord. Nor can you rely upon Meltoria or Relusia to draw away Astaria's strength while you attack from the east. Astaria's might is now fixed upon you, King Gregor, and Queen Valera shall not intervene on your behalf, I assure you. You have kindled the wrath of King Bronus Blagen, and a wiser ruler than you would tremble before such folly!" Amanda's voice reverberated throughout the storied chamber, unnerving Gregor.

"We also know of your legions waiting upon our eastern border, waiting to strike if we had faltered. You have severed any bonds of friendship with Astaria, conspiring with those who would doom all of Elaria to slavery and conquest. You are forewarned, King Gregor, that any act committed against Astaria, our people, or any agents of the crown in Astaria or abroad shall be met with total *war*. Forthwith, you shall remove all foreign ministers, merchants, and citizens of Gorgencia from Astaria, never to return again. All bonds of cordiality are now severed. Take your men and *go*!" Tristan proclaimed, causing the Gorgencian Monarch to storm out of the Great Hall, his dark cape billowing in his wake.

"Well done, my Prince," Amanda said, watching the Gorgencians exit the chamber.

"Well done with a great deal of assistance from you, Princess," he regarded her, admiring her fierce strength and intellect.

"Your Highness, if I may. I should see that our guests are under-way." Lord Celembar bowed, Tristan waving him off with a polite nod.

With that, Tristan stood, offering Amanda his arm, escorting her to the family's private sanctum.

"My father and grandfather have many questions, Princess," Tristan said, giving her a sympathetic smile that set her at ease.

"I shall answer them to my utmost, my Prince, but please, call me Amanda. I am no longer a Princess, despite your mighty Sire's kind words."

"I shall honor your wishes, Amanda, but you are still a princess, as my father so adamantly declared. But in fairness, if I am to refer to you so informally, I would ask the same in return," he said, unable to stop thinking of her enchanting beauty.

"That would be seen as presumptuous on my part considering the crimes of my family against Astaria," she sighed.

"The crimes of Vellesia are not crimes of Amanda," he smiled.

"You are very kind, Tristan," she couldn't hide her own smile breaking across her face, finding it strange to feel so accepted by people who had no reason to do so. She had just forsaken everyone she had ever known, taking refuge in a palace of strangers, yet felt at home, as if she had known them all her life.

"It is you who is kind. You and your brother," he said.

"Raymar?" she asked guardedly.

10

"Yes, though I dare not speak his name too loudly. Your mother may still have spies about," he stole a cursory glance around them as they traversed the wide-lit corridor, his guards far to his front and rear.

"You can freely speak of him in my presence, but your family can never know. Their thoughts are not protected as yours or mine, and should my mother learn of his warning you..." she left unsaid the terrible implications.

"Would she kill her own son?" he asked.

"There are things worse than death, Tristan," she regarded him knowingly.

*****

The entire royal family was waiting for them when they entered the sanctum, a modest and cozy chamber set in the upper portion of the Queen's Tower, with cushioned settees lining its periphery and mage lanterns bracketed high upon its walls. Arian and Felicia greeted Amanda warmly upon her entrance, embracing her like another sister, while Queen Gabrielle brought her into a warm embrace.

"Welcome to Astaris, my child," Gabrielle greeted as they drew briefly apart. Amanda felt comforted by the queen's acceptance, the stain of dried tears reminding her of what the Astarian Matriarch had suffered this day.

Ceresta received her cordially, her reputed fiery temper subdued as she withdrew to her thoughts, her mind trying to work out the problems before them as she sat off to the side. Dragos had no such reservations, drawing the Vellesian Princess into a fearsome hug, twirling her about before setting her down, his surprising strength taking her aback, considering his age.

"Thank you, Dragos." She smiled, remembering what Tristan told her as to how his grandsire liked to be referred. *It makes him feel young, so humor him*, he told her on their walk here from the Great Hall.

"Ah, my grandson taught you well," Dragos gave her a flirtatious wink, his mischievous smile setting her further at ease. Tristan's family was nothing like her own. Though she loved her many grand-mothers and her grandfathers, they were too steeped in formality, protocol, and propriety to ever feel welcoming.

"Prince Tristan has been very instructive on the preferences of his family." She gave Tristan a knowing look.

"He is a fine young man, if I dare say, and very handsome, like his grandfather." Dragos ruffled Tristan's hair like he was a wee tot, which caused her smile to widen.

"You mean his other grandfather." Bronus snorted, shaking his head as he stood at the sole window of the chamber, looking out over the city from these airy heights, his back still to her.

"Never mind him. He can be a tad grumpy at times, but it is all bluster," Dragos whispered in Amanda's ear, just loud enough for Bronus to overhear.

"Father!" Gabrielle gave him a stern warning, lifting a reproach-ful brow over a green eye.

"Now, Gaby, you know better than to refer to a strapping young fellow as myself by that appellation," Dragos gave Amanda a mischie-vous wink before stepping away, his azure robes swirling in his wake, silver crescent moons and stars emblazoned throughout its rich folds. He very much reminded Amanda of her great-grandfather Corbin, though years of confinement dulled much of her great-grandsire's spirit. She couldn't help but wonder if he would be much the same as Dragos if he hadn't been taken as a consort to her great-grandmother Caterina.

As Gabrielle and Dragos backed away, Bronus turned from the window, regarding her briefly, his stormy gray eyes a maelstrom of conflicting emotions. She swallowed nervously, staring back at him, the chamber growing silent as a tomb. She felt Tristan take her hand in his, giving it a reassuring squeeze as if to say she was not alone.

"Forgive my grave countenance, Amanda, I am never good company when my anger is roused, as my children can well attest," Bronus said, which all his children, save Ceresta, nodded their heads, disagreeing with that charge, their false nods almost comical if things were not so dreary.

"You are always pleasant with us, Father." Felicia smiled all too sweetly. As the youngest, she was always the peacemaker in their household, using her large expressive eyes to disarm him any time his ire was raised.

"Let Father speak, Felicia," Ceresta scolded her younger sister, tucking her hands within the large sleeves of her black gown. Amanda recalled her aunts describing each member of house Blagen for her mother and grandmother, as her house was obsessed with every detail of Astaria's royal family. Ceresta was told to them as responsible, logical, and protective of her father. Though third in birth order, she assumed the duty of a firstborn, ever serious and vigilant. Her aunts' description proved prescient.

"I have many questions, Amanda. I hope that you can answer them," Bronus lifted the stone Ethan gifted her for all to see. He could feel it interrupting his mage power, if ever so slightly. The others looked on curiously, as Amanda had not as yet explained its significance.

"I shall answer them, as far as my limited knowledge can attest, my King," she said, lifting her chin in preparation for all she was to reveal.

"In private, you may call me Father, for I acknowledge you as my own. Ethan chose you of all the Vellesians in your mother's retinue to set free. You accepted his gift of freedom and forsook your mother's house to remain here with us. As an orphan in our land, I offer you our home, if you accept it," Bronus said.

"I humbly accept, oh King—Father," she corrected, overcome with their acceptance.

"Welcome, Amanda," Gabrielle again stepped nigh, drawing her into a warm embrace, as did the others. After a lengthy exchange of pleasantries, they again stepped away as Bronus asked his first question, one of many that they were all anxious to have answered.

"This stone that Ethan gave you, you knew he had it, but your mother seemed unaware, at least until you convinced Ethan to give it to you. How did you know he possessed it, and what in the blazes is it?" Bronus held it higher for all of them to see before passing it among them to examine.

"The stone is the rarest of treasures, invisible to human eyes, save for your eldest son. In his hand, it glows, revealing itself to him. In our hands, it looks like a simple gray stone. Only its unusual effects confirm it is so much more," she began.

"But what is it?" Felicia made a face as she received it, looking at it strangely.

"It is pure anti-magic, though a very small amount. It can disrupt your magical powers if it is near you or interrupt Ethan's anti-magical power, if ever slightly. It can block a weaker mage's power completely. I only first noticed it when Ethan entered the Great Hall to confront my mother. Alesha sensed it as well, as she was able to briefly probe his mind, though not deeply before he forced her out. That was when I knew he possessed it. House Loria has been obsessed with finding anti-magic for centuries but have gained no more than the amount in this stone," Amanda explained.

"For what purpose?" Gabrielle asked.

"It has many uses, my Queen. It can blunt the power of any mage, even a lightning Lord, if they can gain enough of it. Though House Loria is not concerned with the power of any mage in all of Elaria."

"They should fear a lightning Lord. There is no greater power in all of Elaria. Bronus wields the power to strike down armies. He can…" Dragos argued before Amanda silenced him with a nod of her head, refuting his belief.

"This is not so, Dragos. The firstborn female in my mother's line has wielded power to cast lightning for a thousand years. They do not fear King Bronus or the power any of you possess. If all the mage lords of Elaria were arrayed against them, House Loria would dispatch them as easily as you dispatched the Relusians and Meltorians at the Velo after Ethan removed their shields," Amanda said sadly, hating to reveal how weak they truly were.

"I don't understand. How do they all possess the power of lightning?" Gabrielle asked.

She turned to Tristan, who gave her a reassuring look before continuing. He was unable to reveal much of what Raymar told him to his family, lest Valera learn of Raymar's betrayal. Now it was time for all of them to learn the full and terrible truth.

"The true power of House Loria lies with one very *unique* mage gift, a gift that goes back thousands of years, before recorded history. It is the power of magical unification, the passing on of all magical powers and advantageous physical attributes to the firstborn child of our house from *both* parents. The child has always been female. Eventually, one from our house wed a king of ancient Vellesia, gifting him a daughter so powerful that she superseded her younger brother in succession. Since that time, house Loria assumed the throne, garnering more mage power with every passing generation. They would seek out those with powers they lacked, taking them as consorts for their crown princesses, passing their power to the next generation. They continued this until they possessed every mage ability, even powers as innocuous as changing the pitch of one's voice or as powerful as casting lightning," she regarded Bronus briefly before continuing.

"For a time, they even wed those with special skills, such as artists and sculpturers, passing on those abilities as well. Even Ethan's special ability to learn rapidly is a trait they mastered long ago, as well as his impressive strength. This gathering of power culminated with the marriage of my mother and father. My father was the heir of the second greatest house in Vellesia, House Menau. Like House Loria, House Menau passed on all mage gifts from both parents but to *all* their children, but only those pertaining to the mind, especially foresight, telepathy, and prophecy. Those of House Menau can mask their appearance by manipulating what others see, which is why my aunts were able to dwell in Astaris unseen for many years."

"Your aunts?" Ceresta asked, uncrossing her arms.

"My aunts Sarella and Selendra. It was they who foiled your attempt to wed Ethanos to Lady Elenna, conjuring the false marriage contract between House Estasa and Vellesia," she explained, the revelation taking them aback.

"What of poor Elenna?" Arian asked.

15

"She is wed to a Vellesian Lord. Whether she is happy, I am uncertain. But considering, so few find happiness there, I do not favor her chances," Amanda sighed.

"They have been spying on our house for years?" Bronus growled.

"They have been spying on your house for centuries," Amanda said, her words furthering their collective unease.

"Why?" Gabrielle asked, her heart beating emphatically as if to burst from her chest.

"Prophecy," Amanda said, letting that single word hang in the air as she looked at each of them before continuing. "It was long ago foretold to House Menau and House Loria that a lightning lord would be born to a king of Astaria, and the firstborn son of that lightning lord would be born immune to magic."

"Ethan." Gabrielle closed her eyes, sitting down on a settee.

"Yes, Ethan," Amanda lifted her chin, bracing herself for all that portended.

"Why Ethan?" Felicia asked. "If he is immune to magic, what help can he give them?"

"Is it not obvious? He is the only one who can stop them, so they remove him from their path." Dragos shook his head.

"If it were merely that, Dragos, they could have arranged Ethanos's death many times. No, they have waited for his birth for more than a thousand years to fulfill their destiny," Amanda said.

"What destiny?" Bronus growled. "From what you have said, they already have the power to sweep away the other six mage realms and make themselves masters of Elaria. What more can Ethan give them?"

"Ethan is the final piece to their complete ascension. In Alesha, they have gathered every mage power in known existence. From Ethan, they shall gain immunity to magic. Both powers shall pass onto their daughter. It is she that shall conquer the world, *all* the world. It is foretold that she will have the power to restore magic in the Mage Bane and extend her power to the wilds. There will be no limit to her reign. All of Elaria will bow to her throne." Amanda lowered her head.

"Ambitious bunch, aren't they," Dragos said dryly, his dark humor failing to lift the dour faces in the room.

"Amanda, once Ethan sires a child on Alesha, what shall they do to him?" Gabrielle asked, unable to raise her eyes, lest they see her tears.

Amanda could feel the grief pouring off the Astarian queen, like waves crashing you into the shore. She stepped nigh, taking a knee before Gabrielle, placing her hands in hers. "They shall not kill him if that is your fear. Their prophecies are very explicit that Ethan must be sworn to the throne for all his days. He cannot serve them if he is dead."

"Truly?" Gabrielle asked, looking into her golden eyes for reassurance.

"Truly."

"Serve them? Serve them in what way?" Bronus asked, his anger flaring at the thought of his son humiliated in that way.

Amanda kept hold of Gabrielle's hands while looking over her shoulder at Bronus.

"The prophecies are unclear as to why he must be bound to the throne, only that the realm will suffer dearly if he is not. The prophecies of House Loria are far weaker than House Menau, but even my father's house believes Ethan must be bound to the throne."

"You mention your father's house, but what part do they play in all this? If they hold great power, why were they not absorbed into House Loria long ago?" Ceresta asked, trying to make sense of all that she said.

"Because House Menau did not allow it. My father's House is *very* powerful and has aligned itself with House Loria for centuries, guiding them to fulfill their destiny. Their houses were to remain apart until a lightning Lord was born to the Royal House of Astaria. Once Bronus was born, they arranged the unification of their houses, ensuring the heir born of their union would be aligned with the birth of Ethanos."

"If Ethan is so important to them, why did they treat him so poorly? Why humiliate him?" Dragos asked.

Amanda lowered her head briefly, collecting herself before gaining her feet. "It is difficult to explain the magic of House Loria without suffering its curse. I can only speak to what I feel through my mother and grandmothers to poorly describe what they suffer."

"Suffer?" Gabrielle asked.

"Their immense power has a cost. Since the birth of house Loria, our first ancestor was born with the power of unification. For all we know, she might have had no other mage gift. She might have been a peasant woman, a wild dweller or a woman born of a noble house. We are not sure of her origin, only that her marital union would pass on all positive attributes of herself and her mate. With this power came an insatiable hunger for any mage power she did not possess, an overwhelming desire for something she could never have. This craving forced her to choose a mate with a power she lacked, passing that gift on to her firstborn daughter. That daughter would share this hunger for every power save for those she inherited. As much as I despise the actions of my mother, I pity her also. Imagine a craving that can never be sated, an all-consuming hunger that drives you to the brink of madness? It was this desire that drove house Loria to gather such power unto it. They logically believe it is for the fulfillment of their destiny, a destiny to rule all of Elaria. They believe Alesha's daughter will fulfill that destiny and end their pain," Amanda said.

"But why treat Ethan with such vitriol?" Arian repeated Dragos's question.

"It is complicated. For one thing, imagine this insatiable hunger for the slightest power you lacked, and then think of Ethan, who is uniquely more powerful than your entire house. My Grandmother Caterina said that when Ethan was born, they felt his presence in Vellesia, like a cavernous void calling to them, driving them to madness. Be thankful you were not in Elysia when Ethan disappeared across the barrier. As painful as that year was for each of you, not certain of his fate, it was infinitely worse in my mother's palace. Only the prophecies of my father's house reassured them of Ethan's eventual return and what was needed to make it so. It was they who arranged the Meltorian and Relusian invasion to draw him back from Red Rock."

Not all of them were yet aware that Vellesia orchestrated the war, causing an immediate uproar until Bronus demanded silence for Amanda to continue.

"Once Ethan returned and managed to free himself from the throne, my mother was briefly overjoyed, seeing an opportunity to seize him outright, but he foiled their plans at Cordova, and then the disastrous interference of Luke Crawford and his men sent Elysia ablaze. Imagine the horror my mother and grandmothers endured when Alesha was taken captive in the Mage Bane. Instead of capturing Ethan, they were faced with the death of their treasured heir, without which, Ethan was useless to them. All their hopes rested on the very boy they conspired to capture, rescuing Alesha from that foul place. It was utter madness and intolerable for those of us who suffered my mother's presence."

"If they owed Ethan so much, then why treat him thusly?" Gabrielle again repeated Dragos and Arian's question.

"Because they fear him, and partly out of petty spite for his speaking so rudely to my mother upon arriving at Astaris. She does not suffer such insult kindly. If it was anyone but Ethan speaking thusly to her, they would already be dead or wished that they were," Amanda said.

"But a collar? I wouldn't do that to a man awaiting the block. It is for slaves, and slavery is forbidden in Astaria. The only slaves in my realm are those pulling an oar on visiting ships, and yet that woman placed one on *my* son!" Bronus growled, causing everyone to startle.

"My mother insisted upon it to demonstrate her power and for revenge of his insult. But there is more to this than her pettiness. House Loria has long used collars imbued with their magic upon their consorts. It serves two practical functions. With everyone except Ethan, it binds their power, preventing them from using it against our House, especially their wives. The more important function is it dulls the cravings of their wives, greatly reducing their all-consuming hunger. In that regard, it is more a blessing than a curse for the consorts of our house. Imagine being wed to someone whose mere

19

existence drives you to madness? The collars block much of that, allowing each royal couple to coexist, though the hunger remains to some extent."

"Alesha did not seem troubled when in Ethan's presence," Ceresta recalled their many interactions at Astaris and thought of the times they shared before then.

"Ethan is different in many ways," Amanda sighed.

"Well, that strikes the mark," Bronus exclaimed, nodding in agreement.

"Bronus!" Gabrielle reproached, which only drew an innocent shrug from her husband.

"It was always difficult to suffer Alesha's presence, her mind consumed with Ethan's power. Strangely, whenever she was in his presence, all her yearnings seemed to lessen, as if he was a balm to her hunger, his unique aura driving it away from her. As far as the collar, it has no power over him and is merely a symbol of his place as a royal consort," Amanda explained, though the others did not share the trivializing of the humiliation.

"So Ethan is to fulfill the ascension of House Loria," Dragos opined, rubbing his chin as he paced the floor.

"Yes," Amanda sighed.

"Why then did Valera not just claim him when he was born? Clearly, she wields enough power to have done so. What stayed her hand?" Dragos asked.

"For the same reason, no one from Astaria has ever wed a Vellesian queen or even a Vellesian vassal. My father's house long counseled House Loria that they must not interfere with Astaria in any way, lest they disrupt the Blagen bloodline that would lead to Ethan's birth. They prevented their lords from wedding anyone of Astarian blood, keeping the intended timeline pure. Whenever a kingdom threatened war upon Astaria in its storied past, House Loria intervened in secret to thwart them. There were many times a Vellesian queen thought to seize Astaria to make a vassal of house Blagen, and thus control Ethan before he was even born, but House Menau intervened, tempering their zealousness, reminding them of the magic binding them from interfering with Astaria."

"What magic?" Dragos asked.

"It is the magic bound up in the prophecy. The prophecy that foretold of Ethan's birth, also protected Astaria from direct Vellesian interference. When King Bronus refused my mother's offer to wed Ethan to Alesha when they were children, the magic prevented her from taking him outright. The magic protected Astaria from Vellesia until Ethan forsook the throne, then all protections were dropped. But by then, House Loria realized that any direct confrontation with Astaria was doomed if Ethan took the field, especially after the Velo. The results of that battle affected every mage king in Elaria, all fully aware of what Ethan is capable of. My mother used their fear to further her aims, aligning them against you, placing swords on your necks from every direction as she plotted Ethan's capture. Ironically, it was Alesha's capture by Luke Crawford that revealed how she might seize Ethan," Amanda shook her head.

"What did she learn?" Gabrielle asked, thoughts of Ethan entering the Mage Bane fueling her inner rage.

"His love of his family was greater than his love of freedom. That was when she began to plan the events that led to our coming here during the winter festival and trapping Ethan by a simple trick, where he had to choose between his father's life and his own freedom. It was never truly a contest, for Alesha knew which he would choose. The only setback for my mother was Ethan setting me free, for which I shall be eternally grateful," she regarded Gabrielle appreciatively.

"They were willing to kill your uncle to arrange this entire affair?" Dragos asked, referring to the queen's uncle Alexar, who perished with the destruction of his ship at Talesia.

Amanda gave Dragos a look that dispelled that assumption.

"What?" Bronus growled.

"My uncle lives. My mother is many things, but killing members of her own family is something she would not consider, though she is not above other means to torment us." Amanda sighed.

"It was all a farce?" Bronus's temper was about to break.

"All a means to trap Ethanos. A simple matter that you overlooked when my mother asked for so little in compensation. When a member of a royal family perishes on his flagship in one of your port cities, and all his queen asks to make amends is a consort from one of your vassals, why would you investigate further? She knew, as we all did, that Ethan would be coming home during the winter solstice and planned our trip here accordingly."

"Valera must think me a fool!" Bronus wanted to smash something, turning back toward the window, looking out over his capital city, but seeing nothing, his mind consumed with his failure.

"She thinks everyone outside her maternal line to be fools, my King," Amanda tried to assuage his failure.

"That is all well and good, but what now?" Ceresta asked the most pertinent question, their list of options looking sparse.

"Eventually, we shall be confronted with Alesha's heir, whom we have no defense against," Tristan said.

"You mean our granddaughter?" Gabrielle reminded them all their connection to the child.

"Which means naught if she intends to topple our House," Ceresta argued.

"Whether she is reminded of your kinship or not, we have time to prepare for it. As for this present time, we have other threats to consider," Amanda reminded them before looking at Tristan.

"Amanda is right. We are surrounded by enemies. Valera bribed each of the other mage realms with vast amounts of gold and promises to assail Astaria from all sides had they failed to take Ethan. Amanda was very helpful in my dealings with the Meltorian and Relusian kings, putting them in their place. The one great benefit of Ethan submitting to Valera is that it preserved the magical bonds we placed on those two realms. It still leaves the others for us to deal with, however, especially Gorgencia," Tristan said.

"Estasa is too far afield and will not attack you without Relusia and Meltoria aiding them," Amanda said, understanding much of that far kingdom's workings through her mother.

"And Sarcosa?" Ceresta asked.

"They will not attack alone. King Lorga is a coward!" Bronus said over his shoulder, still looking out the window.

"A fair summation of the Sarcosan King. My grandmother has repeated that opinion for many years now," Amanda said.

"Then our current focus should be with Gorgencia," Dragos reasoned.

"With father's leave, I shall return to our army camped along the upper Morow. Lord General Brax should be wondering when I will return," Tristan said.

"What caused you to leave for Astaris, to begin with, my boy?" Dragos asked, wondering what drove him to abandon their army and seek out Ethan.

"I cannot say, Dragos, for none of your minds are shielded from Valera's spies. Only Amanda and I have sufficient shields to guard secrets," Tristan said, not willing to reveal that it was Prince Raymar that warned him. Should Valera learn her own son betrayed her, he would suffer greatly, and Ethan would lose his only ally in Elysia.

"You believe our minds are so weak?" Gabrielle asked indignantly.

"If it was merely my mother or any of her grandmothers, then your mental shields would be strong enough, but Alesha possesses all the power of House Menau, and they can read your mind like clear parchment. And even if my aunts Sarella or Selendra are not here to spy on house Blagen, there are other members of their house who may, many of them I am unaware of."

"Our powers are that weak?" Dragos asked, the revelation a blow to his pride.

"Your powers are very strong, Dragos, but House Menau has had nearly as long as House Loria to gather great power unto itself. Where you wield several mage gifts with great skill, their House holds many fold that number and can use them simultaneously and longer lasting. It is not just the power of their mage gifts but their duration and intensity. This is true of House Loria as well. Where a common blinder mage can block someone's sight for a brief period, Alesha and all her forebears six generations back, can hold someone in a sightless state almost indefinitely, with little strain upon them. They can cast fire in endless streams without respite or heal a person with a mere touch of their finger without cause or worry. Against such power, even a mighty lightning lord is a small obstacle to be overcome." Amanda's revelation further dampened their spirits.

"You spoke of your grandmothers, Amanda. Just how many still live, and if so, why are they no longer queen?" Gabrielle asked.

Amanda released a breath, knowing this question would arise and wondering where to begin.

"There are always two queens in Vellesia, a queen mother, who oversees the affairs of House Loria, and a queen daughter, who oversees the affairs of the realm. And then there is the crown princess, the firstborn child of the queen daughter. Once the crown princess begets an heir, she ascends to become the queen daughter, and the queen daughter ascends to become the queen mother. The queen mother then joins her mother and grandmothers in the coven of House Loria, where they guide the new queen mother in all things." Amanda paused, gauging if they were following what she had said.

"We have heard rumors through the years on the structure of the Vellesian Royal Family but never thought to investigate," Dragos said, scratching his chin.

"And how large is the current coven of your mother's house?" Ceresta asked.

"Twelve," Amanda said, bracing for the questions sure to follow.

"Twelve?" Bronus growled.

"Twelve?" Gabrielle gasped.

"Twelve?" Arian and Felicia shared a look.

Dragos just shook his head, waiting for further explanation.

"Long ago, one of my distant grandmothers wed a mage who shared Ethan's ability to self-heal. All of you believe Ethan has no magic as he is immune to it, but this ability is a mage power, one that is as rare as a lightning lord. The same is true of his great strength and his uncanny ability to learn things quickly or master a skill in a brief time. These gifts have long been acquired by House Loria, but it is his ability to self-heal that also causes long life, *very* long life," she emphasized.

"How long?" Ceresta asked.

"From what we have experienced, almost 300 years. About that time, their body just passes, often in their sleep. My eldest grandmother Evalena is 292 years old. She is the head of their Order, and by the nature of House Loria, the weakest as well."

"Ethan will live three hundred years?" Ceresta shook her head.

"Three hundred years bound to Valera," Gabrielle closed her eyes.

"We don't have three hundred years," Tristan stated the obvious.

"And each of your grandmothers is powerful mage, I assume," Ceresta said.

"Any of them are more powerful than any mage in all of Elaria, and most could defeat all the mage kings combined by their lonesome," Amanda said.

"With Alesha, Valera, the Queen Mother, and the twelve others, that pretty much sums up our chances," Dragos shook his head.

"Which is why Ethan surrendered," Felicia wiped a tear from her eye.

"Lest we forget the vast armies our neighboring realms were prepared to launch at us if he refused. Father would have been slain at the outset and most of us with him. Ethan would have slain many of the mage kings, and perhaps Valera or Alesha, but not both. Astaria would have fallen and fallen quickly," Tristan said.

"But we are fallen all the same if what Amanda says is true," Bronus said.

"No, we have time, precious time that Ethan bought us. Our priorities are threefold in order of importance," Dragos began. "One, we must prepare for war with our neighbors, or at least come to terms with them. Two, prepare for a way to counter the Vellesians power. Three, and this is one thing each of us has forgotten, and that is dragons."

"Dragons!" Felicia asked in alarm.

"Ethan saw them in Dragos's visions. He saw them laying waste to Astaria," Tristan said.

"The barrier would have to fall," Arian said. The barrier stones were imbued with anti-magic, bound with the magic of the mage lords of old.

"If they falter, we would need massive sources of anti-magic to repair them, and that was if we knew how to do it in the first place," Bronus explained. Amanda meant to refute this assumption but thought better of it for now.

"And this stone Ethan gave us is not enough, and we have no means of acquiring more," Arian said, holding the stone aloft.

"The stone is key, but in what way I am not yet certain." Dragos walked across the chamber, taking it in hand, holding it before his eye.

"What should we do?" Felicia asked, looking around the room for any sign of hope and direction.

"It is too late in the evening to make important decisions. Let us retire for the night and think on it," Gabrielle said, stepping toward Bronus, touching her hand to his shoulder.

"Aye, you have the right of it, my love. I am too angry and too tired to think straight." He drew her into his arms, hugging her tightly.

Amanda looked at them with profound admiration and a hint of jealousy, wishing her parents could have shared such affection. The Astarian king and queen genuinely loved one another and all their children. If only her own family were thus, most of the world's strife would be set aside. Just as she was admiring their devotion, a distant conversation touched her mind, the look passing her face catching Ceresta's attention.

"What ails you, Amanda?" she asked, stepping nigh, as if she expected Amanda to fall.

"Someone is speaking with the lord steward, something about Ethan," Amanda said, the others all looking at her.

"Where?" Bronus asked harsher than he intended.

"The courtyard," Dragos said, already finding them with his mind.

*****

"Can this not wait until morning, Master Torg?" Lord Celembar, the palace steward, asked, the two men standing in the middle of the courtyard, knights and men-at-arms moving about around them.

"Aye, it can, but I thought the king would like to know," Torg Larios, the master blacksmith of Astaris conceded, preparing to step away when a thunderous voice called out from the palace steps.

"If you have something to say of Ethan, Torg, I will hear of it!" Bronus bellowed, walking briskly in their direction.

"My King," both men greeted, beginning to bow.

"None of that now. I am in no mood." Bronus bid them to remain afoot. "What news have you of Ethan?" he asked, stopping before Torg, as Gabrielle and the rest of the royal family gathered behind him.

"Well, sire, it is just that he asked of me a favor, which I agreed, but with him now gone, I do not know what I should do with them?" Torg said.

"Do with what, Torg? Blast it, man. Spit it out!" Bronus growled.

"The toys, sire," the weathered-faced blacksmith said.

"Oh, Ethanos," Gabrielle read Torg's thoughts so clearly, seeing what he was referring to.

"Toys? Speak sense, man!" Bronus growled.

"Prince Ethanos asked me to help him forge toy soldiers and dolls for the children of the palace, mainly the children of the palace servants. He mentioned a holiday his friends across the barrier celebrated in which they gave children gifts. He wanted to do that here. I offered to help, providing my other duties were attended first. The lad went and found me a large source of metal for the forging by way of the Gorgencian Prince and his lot," Torg grinned.

"Aye, I remember. Hah, wish I could have seen the look on that little—"

"Bronus!" Gabrielle warned, stopping him from whatever curse was about to follow.

"Bah!" He waved off her reproach. "Show me what you have," he said, following Torg to his smithy.

CHAPTER 2

"We must return. We are past our allotted time," Sergeant Jordain cautioned.

"Shh!" Ethan quieted his companion, lifting his Winchester to his shoulder. Further upstream along his line of sight, a mountain buck lapped the cool water of the shallow stream. Ethan's breath held in the cold winter air as the deer lifted its head, staring in his direction with its ears erect when he squeezed the trigger.

The sound of the rifle echoed through the vale as the bullet struck the deer's throat. Tall pines lined the north bank of the stream, the midday sun playing off their highest boughs. Long matted grass covered the south bank, where Ethan and Sergeant Jordain sat atop their mounts some seventy yards downstream. The sergeant was taken aback by the strange weapon, awed by its power.

"Come on, Sarge!" Ethan shouted, with Bull galloping off to retrieve his kill.

Sergeant Ander Jordain reluctantly followed, hoping Ethan would heed his advice and return to camp. Within moments, Ethan dismounted and dressed the deer, spilling its innards upon the grass with Ander looking on.

"What sort of knife is that?" The sergeant asked.

Ethan looked up at the sergeant after wiping the blood off the blade on the grass. "Jim Bowie invented this knife. They say he died with one in his hand at the Alamo, though a smaller knife is better to dress a deer."

"Jim Bowie?" Ander made a face.

"Just a legend from a different world. At least he died free, which is more than I can hope for," Ethan said, lifting the carcass, tying it down behind his saddle.

"You speak as though you were a prisoner or slave?"

"That's because I am," Ethan grunted, wiping his hands in the grass.

"You are a royal consort. The crown princess honors you with title and position."

"What's your given name, sarge?" Ethan asked as he climbed into his saddle.

"Ander," he answered warily. The giving of his first name felt out of place, but he answered. The queen's guards were unsure how to interact with Ethan. He was unlike anyone they ever knew. He was irreverent and did not hide his disdain for authority. The sergeants and other guards quickly noted that when they were alone with him, he spoke to them as their equals. He was not mean or petty, like so many born to the royal houses of the seven kingdoms. He wanted to like Ethan, but the boy's previous disrespect toward the queen and the crown princess cautioned him against such sentiment.

"Ander, can I go home to Astaris?" Ethan asked.

"No," he answered, confused by the question.

"Can I hunt all day if I wish?"

"No."

"Can I go fishing, or must we hurry back to camp?"

"We must return. We are long overdue."

"Why? Why must we return?"

"The queen was adamant that we…"

"Ah! The queen said I had to return when she said."

"I do not understand," Jordain said.

"It's simple. I cannot go where I want, when I want, and I must obey the orders of the queen and her daughter. That makes me their slave or prisoner or vassal."

"But…you are a royal consort," Sergeant Jordain explained as if such a statement should put everything to right.

"Did I ask to be a consort?"

Ander had no answer as they rode back to camp along the vale.

"But the princess is the most beautiful woman my eyes have ever beheld. Most men would risk death a thousandfold for the chance to wed her. Were you not smitten when you first beheld her? You begged the queen to win her freedom, did you not?"

The bitter memory of her betrayal was fresh in his mind. "Yes, I loved her, Ander. But then she betrayed me," he growled.

"You must feel some affection? Are you not pleased that of all the men in the seven kingdoms, it was you she chose?"

"You don't know much about women, do you?"

"My wife might disagree with that assessment, Consort," Ander said.

"Do you think Alesha chose me for my fair looks?" He gave him a look that he believed just the opposite.

"You are a handsome fellow."

Ethan gave him another look. "Remind me not to place my bedroll next to yours."

"I did not mean…"

"I know what you meant, so relax. What I was saying is that Alesha…"

"Princess Alesha," Ander corrected.

"All right. Princess Alesha did not choose me for my face and certainly not for my wit."

"Then why did she choose you?"

"Power. I'm immune to magic, and she desires it. That is why she chose me."

Ander reflected on Ethan's words, knowing they were not entirely true. The Princess was in good spirits since their party departed Astaris nine days before. She radiated a warmth that matched a happiness within. She certainly did not seem a woman consumed with power alone. Ethanos was a fool not to see it.

Ander Jordain was the epitome of a queen's guard. His ebony black hair fell below his polished helm. His square jaw was cleanly shaven, and bright silver mail hung about his solid build. His smooth deep olive skin radiated perfection. He served for two decades as a queen's guard, and Valera placed great trust in him. He took affront of any criticism of his queen or princess. This was why he kept Ethan at arm's length, and not any closer. The queen could read his thoughts, and he would never compromise her trust by befriending her critic.

Ander also reflected on how differently they were dressed. He was clade in bright mail, polished and resplendent in the midday sun. Ethan wore his buckskin trousers, with their frayed sides that matched his moccasin boots. His simple tan leather shirt had no adornments. His belt was bedecked, with his holster on his right hip, and a sword on his left. His large knife was sheathed behind his sword. He wore a fur-lined cloak and his strange hat. Any casual observer would easily confuse which of them was born a prince and which was common. The boy dressed like a barbarian and didn't seem to care.

"At least we can eat well tonight," Ethan said, fishing an apple from his cloak and taking a bite.

"Eat well?" Ander thought their food was quite good.

"Venison steak. Venison stew. That should bring a smile even to you," Ethan grinned, but Ander found little humor in it.

"I have never tasted venison. Is it good?"

Ethan pulled on Bull's reins, circling in front of Ander's mount. "You never tasted venison?"

The sergeant shrugged his shoulders, wondering if he committed some offense. "No, I have not."

"Come by my cookfire tonight, Sarge, and we'll rectify that," Ethan smiled.

"That would be improper to fraternize with one of your station, Consort Loria."

"Don't call me that," Ethan despised that title and name.

"That is your title."

"Look, no one else is around but you and me, so just call me Ethan."

The sergeant shook his head negatively. "Queen Valera is adamant as to how we are to address you."

Ethan let out an annoyed breath. "No one else is around, Ander. What difference does it make?"

"A good soldier follows orders, Consort Loria. I vowed to serve the throne of Vellesia. The queen's orders may seem trivial to you, but we in Vellesia hold them sacred. Besides, the queen can read my every thought."

He left unsaid that he reported to the queen of every word Ethan uttered.

"Well, if you're insulted by being seen eating in my company, it is your loss," Ethan pulled on the reins, redirecting Bull to their return path.

"It is not I that would be offended, but you," Ander said, riding at Ethan's side.

"Why would I be insulted? You're a sergeant in the queen's guard while I'm just her slave."

Ander shook his head. "You are of the royal house of Vellesia."

"If I'm so high and you're so low, then why was I put into a collar back in Astaris?"

"It was a symbol of honor, not bondage. Every man in Vellesia would eagerly take your place. You should be proud that our crown princess favors you, just as you should be proud of your royal blood."

Ethan gave him a look. "There's nothing royal about blood. Blood is blood."

"You speak blasphemy, Consort."

"Only petty minds relegate truth to blasphemy. All these titles we live by are artificial creations passed down through time to justify the mage-born's grab for power. By claiming the natural superiority of body and mind, they justify their right to rule. Look at me, Ander, I am mage born. I am the firstborn son of a king, and I am dumber than many a common man."

"That is untrue."

"How would you know? You believe what you're told. I've seen the mageless world and the inventiveness of common men. They are better than us. They are smarter, better armed, and more sophisticated, and they do it without magic."

Ander had no counter to Ethan's logic. He rode with his jaw clamped shut.

"Take a good look at me, sarge. I dress like a barbarian. I am not very smart. I have a foul tongue and poor manners. Despite all that, I can best any mage in the seven kingdoms, even our mighty queen. So tell me, Sarge. If an uncouth simpleton like me can best all these powerful mage lords and ladies, what does that say about their superior royal blood?"

Ander said nothing.

"No answer? It shows they are as common as dirt."

"If you are better than Princess Alesha, why did you wear her collar instead of her wearing yours?"

"Because I'm an idiot, and she's sneaky."

Ander shook his head. He never met anyone like Ethan before. He thought different, spoke different, and acted different from everyone else. His ideas were so alien Ander thought him mad. His complaints were irrational and tiresome. Ethan spoke of being a slave or prisoner, yet he had more freedom of movement than anyone within their caravan. The princess allowed him to go on patrols to hunt and fish and to practice in arms whenever he wished. Even his clothing was of his choosing. No other consort would have been allowed in their regent's presence dressed so informally. When he first encountered him outside the royal chambers in Astaris, Ander despised him. His arrogance and disrespect for Princess Alesha stirred him to swift anger. Now he found the Astarian Prince more tolerable. When Ethanos wasn't complaining about his captivity, Ander found his company enjoyable. Since that night in Astaris, the queen and princess ordered them to ignore Ethan's barbs and ramblings. They need only report his off-color comments.

*****

The Vellesians were encamped on high ground on the west bank of the upper Morow, overlooking a sharp bend in the river below. A long line of tall pines covered the rolling foothills north and west, like towering green soldiers standing post. A winding stream cut through a narrow vale to the north, merging with the Morow. For two days, they waited in camp for their Gorgencian escort to guide them across the Astarian border. Tall pavilions of silver and blue dotted the high ground. Amidst this cluster, a crimson and gold pavilion rose to the height of five men. Atop its highest point blew the banner of house Loria, a golden rose upon a field of black.

Ethan descried the banner from afar as he and Ander rode south along the Morow. The sight of the queen's sigil filled him with apprehension, as if the Collar was still affixed to his neck. Fortunately, Alesha allowed him to busy himself away from the royal pavilion. He would go there when summoned and at night for bed. Perhaps he should thank her for this small kindness, but the anger coursing his veins prevented that.

The crisp winter air gave way to warmth as they passed through Valera's mage spell that circled the camp. Sergeant Jordain welcomed the change in climate, though Ethan felt little effect.

"I shall give our report on our patrol, Consort Loria, unless you would like to."

"Go ahead, Sarge. I'd rather stay clear of the queen's company if I can help it. Besides, you'll need to inform her of all the rotten things I said." He smiled.

Sergeant Jordain bristled uncomfortably. "You know?"

"Of course, I know you tell her everything I say. She can read your mind anyway, so what difference does it make."

"And you are not angry with me?"

"For what? Doing your duty? I know you obey your oath to Vellesia. I don't begrudge you for that, Ander. I do know the sacredness of vows."

"But you forsook your throne. You were bound to House Blagen, and you walked away."

"I earned the right to walk away from the throne, but I never foreswore House Blagen until Alesha…"

"Princess Alesha!" Ander corrected him.

"All right. I never forswore House Blagen until *Princess* Alesha forced me. Now I have to honor the vows I made to her and Vellesia, or she'll kill my father," Ethan's mood soured whenever he thought about it.

"You honor House Loria with your choice, Consort."

"No. I honor my father with my sacrifice. I do not honor my mistress or her mother. I merely obey them."

Ander understood Ethan's animosity but could not tell him that. "When I report, I'll provide two soldiers to accompany you."

"To guard me," Ethan said.

"To *protect* you, Consort. We are tasked with the safety of all members of House Loria."

"And I thought I was protecting you," Ethan smiled.

"We are the trained guards of the queen. Our skills with sword, lance, and spear have no equal in the seven kingdoms," Ander said defensively.

"That's because you never faced Luke Crawford."

Ander gave him a look.

"He was a gunslinger, one of those men from across the barrier I told you about. Allie didn't mention him to you?"

"Allie?"

"My apology. Princess Alesha did not speak of him?"

Ander nodded negative.

"Why am I not surprised? Luke Crawford was a dangerous man and nearly my equal on the draw. He was the one who took Your crown princess captive, dragging her and her mage healers to the mage bane. Fortunately for Crown Princess Alesha, an unwitting moron came to her rescue, killed Luke Crawford, and returned her to the safety of her people so she could plot against her brave rescuer."

"She did speak of your bravery, and as her sworn protector, I thank you."

"You seem more grateful than she is. Anyway, Luke Crawford is dead, but he has a few comrades still out there. Emmitt Cobb is nearly as deadly as Crawford. If he shows himself, I'm the only one who can protect you."

"We are the ones charged with your protection, Consort."

"All right. After you report to the queen, you can *protect* me while I cook this venison. Then you can taste some."

"You still desire my company even though I must report your words to the queen?"

"You swore an oath to obey her. I know that. Besides, Queen Valera knows how I feel. It's no secret that I hate her."

*****

Ethan skirted the encampment, leading Bull as he walked, keeping to the perimeter and avoiding any proximity to the royal pavilion. He passed the Astarians assigned to escort the queen's caravan to the Gorgencian border. Marco was charged with leading the contingent. He regarded Ethan from afar. Ethan was forbidden to speak with them or to be within twenty paces of them. The guard's Sergeant Jordain assigned him, followed close behind. They were well-built youths with wide eyes and quick swords. Neither said a word or looked him in the eye. Ethan found them a nuisance.

Ethan found a place along the perimeter to his liking. It was flat and dry and faced the river below. He dropped the carcass on the ground and prepared a cook fire with tools from his pack. His guards stood several paces away, wondering what he was doing.

"There are servants who can prepare your game, Consort Loria," they said.

"I don't want anyone waiting on me. I'll do my own work."

The guards shared a look as if he were mad.

After a time, Ethan had a fire going and the deer roasting on a spit. He stood with his right hand resting on his holstered colt as he gazed at the lands beyond the river, Gorgencia. War would soon come between that foul land and his beloved Astaria, and he could do nothing to stop it nor help his father if it did. He was bound to Alesha and could only venture where she allowed. The sun was drawing to the west, with dusk soon to follow. He would be expected at the queen's pavilion after dark, but he still had some time. He turned as several more of the queen's guards approached, smiling to see Sergeant Jordain among them.

"Some of the food is ready, Sarge. Come and try some," Ethan waved them over.

"Come," Ander called out to his men. "The princess consort has prepared some strange meat and requires our testing it for poison," he explained, justifying their partaking of it.

"Eat up, fellas," Ethan said, passing his fork around with slabs of venison hanging off the end as he sliced the meat off the carcass. They were tentative at first but, after a time, returned for second, third, and fourth helpings. Ethan thought about their miserable lives. The drudgery of standing guard over the queen from dawn to dark to dawn every day seemed unbearable. As time continued, he sensed them becoming more comfortable in his presence. He couldn't hate these men for doing their duty, and as he came to know them, he couldn't help but like them, most of them anyway. Sergeant Bourvelle despised him, still angry over the words they shared at Astaris, but Ethan was working on repairing that. He noticed the ornery fellow approaching them, his dour face matching his purposeful gait.

"Sergeant Bourvelle, the next serving is yours," Ethan invited him into their growing circle, holding out another fork with a slab of steaming meat toward the hesitant fellow, who reluctantly took it. After a few bites, his scowl eased. Ethan invited him to help himself to however much more he would like.

Ander drew Ethan aside as the others happily partook.

"Your venison is quite tasty. It was very kind of you to offer it to us," Ander said.

"Hah! I knew you'd like it. There's plenty more if you like. Maybe rotate those on post duty and invite them over too," Ethan slapped him on the shoulder.

"Perhaps we shall, Eth...Consort," he corrected himself.

"You were going to call me Ethan," he smiled.

"My apologies, Consort Loria."

"No. I like it. I'm wearing off on you, admit it, sarge."

Ander gave him a fearful look. "I should be leaving," he started to turn.

"Ander, wait. I'm sorry. I shouldn't encourage you to be like me. If I do, it will only land your head on a pike by the queen. Just stay. Enjoy the venison, and I promise not to disparage the queen, the princess, or your beloved Vellesia while in your presence. Fair enough?"

"You will hold your tongue in my presence?"

"I will," Ethan held up his hand like the oath he swore when Sheriff Thorton deputized him.

"Why?"

"I can vent about the queen elsewhere. I just enjoy your company and don't want you to suffer the queen's wrath because of me."

"Very well," Ander said, the two of them coming to an agreement as they returned to the others.

Soon, more of the queen's guards joined them, with Ethan putting several to work helping carve the carcass, gathering more wood for the fire and rotating the spit. He shared his adventures as they listened attentively, captivated by his telling. He asked them about their experiences in serving the crown. Even if their stories were of little note, Ethan listened as if they were grand adventures. They lost track of time in the waning daylight. For the first time since leaving Astaris, Ethan felt at ease, almost forgetting where he was going.

Ethan's calm was short-lived as a hush fell over their small gathering. The crown princess approached, walking across the grassy field with Leora Mattiese beside her. The guards quickly knelt as they drew nigh, bowing their heads with deep reverence as if Alesha were a goddess. Ethan noted the stark transformation in the men's demeanor whenever Alesha, Valera, or a high minister of the court was near.

"Princess," Ethan greeted her as she entered their midst, kneeling before she could admonish him for his lack of protocol. He mentally shook his head before lowering his eyes.

"Ethanos," she said, not unkindly. "I see you are ingratiating yourself with my guards."

"Just sharing my game with the men, Princess. I hate to see it wasted. Would you like to have some?"

"You may lift your eyes, Ethan. Everyone else may rise," she said.

The guards came to their feet as Ethan knelt alone before the Princess. She knew how much he hated bending his knee to anyone, let alone her or the queen, but thought it prudent to remind him of his place at times, especially before treating with her mother or grandmother, which he was about to experience. Ethan possessed many wonderful qualities that she admired, but he did lose his temper at times, especially when forced to do something he didn't want to.

"Sergeant Jordain," she called out to Ander.

"Yes, Your Highness," he bowed his head.

"How is Ethanos's cooking?"

Ander was briefly taken aback by the question before answering. "Quite good, Highness. I never tasted this Venison before, and it exceeded my expectations."

"Ethan's culinary skills are impressive for a man." She turned her golden eyes to Ethan's upturned blue. "He once cooked me a snake, and it, too, exceeded my expectations."

The guards could ill imagine their crown princess eating a snake, seeing it as an insult to House Loria. Offering a snake to Vellesian Royalty? Such an affront could not go unpunished.

"Of course, no offense was intended on my consort's part. We had a choice between snake and hunger. We wisely chose the snake." She smiled, setting her guards at ease.

"Shall I fetch you a morsal, Your Grace?" Ander asked.

"Nay. Do not trouble yourself, Sergeant. It is not your place to wait upon me as if you were a maid. My consort can serve me. You may rise, Ethanos. Bring me a sample of your catch."

Ethan glared at her as he came to his feet, retrieving a piece of meat with one of the forks, offering it to her.

"Mmm. This is very good, Ethanos," she smiled sweetly.

"I'm glad you like it," Ethan said, biting off his anger.

"Your Highness," he added as she gave him a reproachful look for his informality.

"Sergeant Jordain!" She called him forth.

"Your Grace?"

"Have one of your men tend my consort's mount. Bring his saddle pack to the queen's pavilion, and then take the beast to the stable pen."

"Yes, Your Grace."

"You and Sergeant Bourvelle may see to your other men and invite them to partake of Ethan's generous offering."

"That is very kind, Your Grace."

"Ethanos!" she commanded.

"Yes, Princess," he answered quietly.

"Attend me!"

*****

He followed her across the field, walking toward their encampment, with Leora holding back, allowing Alesha to speak with him privately.

"Walk beside me, Ethan," she invited as he fell in beside her.

"Making friends with my servants?" she asked.

"I was just being kind to your soldiers. I have no friends. Not here, anyway."

"Your anger is growing tiresome, Ethan."

"I didn't know my happiness was required. Was that one of the vows you made me say?"

She stopped abruptly, slapping his hat off his head.

"I've allowed you much freedom within this camp. Shall I take that away?" she warned.

He stared at her with the setting sun playing off her face. There was so much left unsaid between them, but Ethan could barely utter a word as his anger tightened his throat. "Allie, I...I...," he struggled to speak. "Agghh!" he shouted, releasing his pent-up rage. He drew his father's sword and struck the ground repeatedly for several moments until his anger eased. He finally relented, catching his breath.

"Feel better?" she asked.

"Allie, I can't do this." He lowered his head. "I can't live like this. For a time, when I was with the men, I felt like my old self. The stories, the cookfire, then...then you walked into our midst, and—"

"And what?" She placed a warm hand upon his cheek.

"I am so angry inside, Allie. I can't stand it. When I see you, I see the woman who betrayed me, but I also feel a burning desire to love you."

"To love me?" She smiled lasciviously. "That is a welcome change."

"How are you able to place an enchantment on me, Allie? I'm immune to magic, but you are doing something to me. I can feel it."

"An enchantment is a power over the mind. Your affliction is one of the heart, Ethan."

"You're not doing it?" he asked, doubting her truthfulness.

"I am not like the other women you have known, Ethan. You claim women only desire power. They often feign interest to entice a suitor to chase them, or they provide false praise to strengthen a man's resolve to pursue them. I play no such games. I am bereft of such feminine weakness. I see what I desire, and I claim it. For my mother, it is about your magical immunity. For me, it is so much more. As difficult as this is for you to live within the bounds that I have placed you, you must suffer it, for I shall not free you. Not ever."

"Allie, I—"

"Enough!" She placed a finger over his lips. "I shall allow you as much freedom as I can, as you have taken advantage of throughout our trek. These coming days, however, you are expected to attend me at all times, conducting yourself as a consort should. Do you understand?"

"Yes," he answered dejectedly.

"Very good. Now, follow me. Mother is waiting..."

Ethan grabbed her shoulders, drawing her close, before crushing his lips to hers. Alesha's heart pounded emphatically, startled by his bold advance. Before, she was helpless in his arms, her powers muted by his own, but now...now their unborn child gave her full use of her power. Part of her wanted to resist, that part of her mind fueled by pride. But a greater part of her, the part buried deep within her, only feigned resistance, secretly yearning to be in his arms. It was this greater part of her that was long buried that Ethan drew out with such ease. Though she had access to her mage power, she never felt so helpless being in his arms, so vulnerable, so alive. Every part of her flesh sparkled with life as his lips placed their claim. It was then that she wondered how long had it been since she felt the hunger for his power that consumed her since birth. Ever since they first met in the Mage Bane, she hadn't felt the overwhelming desire for his power. She remembered thinking at the time that it was the effect of that mageless land, but when they escaped, the hunger never returned. Ever since that day, the hunger was obscured by her desire to be with Ethan, but she hadn't realized that it was gone forever. She no longer desired his power but Ethan himself.

"Ethan…," she gasped once their lips parted.

"My body may be in love you, Alesha Loria, but my brain hates you. If you are going to drag me back to Vellesia, then I might as well make the best of it," he said with that intense gaze that seemed to pass through her, stripping her bare.

She stood statue still, transfixed by his touch and his piercing blue eyes.

"You assume much, Ethan," she whispered.

Ethan reached down to retrieve his Stetson, brushing it off before setting back on his head. "I don't assume anything, Allie, except a cage and a leash. Now let's go see what your mom wants."

*****

The familiar visage of Sarella Menau received them before the queen's pavilion, her beguiling purple eyes staring intently at Ethan as they approached before shifting to her niece, bowing reverently.

"Your mother awaits you, my dearest Alesha." Sarella smiled, lifting her head.

"It is good to see you again in camp, Aunt Sarella," Alesha greeted. Sarella had returned from the border, treating with their Gorgencian hosts before they crossed over in the coming days.

"I am joyed to again be in your presence, my dearest. All the years we have labored have finally born fruit," she smiled, her gaze resting on Ethan.

"The last time I saw you, you and your sister sent a mob of free swords after me in Cordova. That wasn't very nice of you," Ethan reminded her, crossing his arms.

"Simply another failed tactic we employed to attain you, Ethanos. You were in no true danger, though I cannot speak the same for the poor brutes we sent against you." Sarella kept her smile, looking at Ethan with a sense of wonder the others did not exhibit.

"It still hurt!" He growled before Alesha put a hand on his shoulder to calm his ire.

"You are no stranger to pain and suffering, my dearest Ethanos. I lost count of the times I have watched you in the training yards of Astaris, matching steel with your father's knights. How many blows would you suffer in a day? Too many to count. My dearest Alesha would receive our missives on your reckless behavior with deep concern." Sarella shared a knowing look with Alesha.

"At least then I believed you felt no pain from your wounds. I still think of what you suffered at the Velo," Alesha said, looking at Ethan with sincere empathy, which took him aback.

"Or his near-fatal wound across the barrier, that he never shared with his family. It was Nate Grierson, I believe, that shot you in the back," Sarella said, her intimate knowledge of his times in Red Rock, sending alarms off in his brain.

"Yes. He experienced a similar wound at Crepsos, foolishly meeting Luke Crawford in the streets of that port city, giving Emmitt Cobb opportunity to murder him," Alesha recalled, another reminder of his recklessness.

Ethan just shook his head, knowing there was little point in arguing. They would use his supposed recklessness to justify the cage they were placing him in.

"We shall speak at a later time, Ethanos. There is much we have to discuss." Sarella smiled before stepping away.

"Come," Alesha said, leading him into the pavilion, the royal guards bowing deeply as they entered.

No sound issued from the dimly lit chamber, which Ethan found unnerving, as he removed his hat, following her in. The chamber was bathed in mage light, which Ethan could not see. Two basin torches were alit for his benefit, which they didn't know he didn't need. They were placed in the vast tent's center, each flanking a massive orb floating freely above a kneeling Valera, with her back to them.

"Kneel beside me, Ethanos," Alesha whispered, kneeling several paces behind her mother.

Ethan felt uneasy, noting the glazed look in Alesha's eyes, guessing they were partaking in some strange ritual, the nature of which conjured his darkest suspicions. They were alone with the queen, another fact fueling his unease.

"Allie, what is this?" he whispered.

"Shh!" she chided.

The orb above Valera grew murky as if traversing a foggy sea. The angled lines of a beautiful feminine face emerged through the swirls of mist, her silver eyes fixed upon Queen Valera, projecting a stern countenance. She appeared in her fourth decade with hair like obsidian, and light olive-hued skin, that radiated perfection. Her high cheekbones and full lips projected a feminine grace rivaling Valera and Alesha, though Ethan saw none of this.

"Queen Mother." Valera bowed, placing her forehead on the ground.

"Queen Mother," Alesha followed, pressing her head to the ground in awed reverence. She snapped her fingers, pointing to the ground beside her, directing Ethan to bow his head. He reluctantly obeyed, disgusted by such groveling. He never expected to witness Valera bowing to anyone. Whoever the Queen Mother was, he couldn't imagine she was worse than Valera, but his record to date on such things was not very good.

"Arise, Queen Daughter. Let me see my child's face," the Queen Mother said.

Valera lifted her dark almond eyes to her mother.

"*Have you brought him?*" the Queen Mother asked, for she could not see Ethan through the orb, just as he was blind to her.

"We have, Queen Mother," Valera said triumphantly.

"*Alesha, lift your eyes so I might see my daughter's daughter,*" the Queen Mother commanded.

Alesha did so, directing Ethan to lift his head as well.

"You have sealed your bond to the first son of Astaria?"

"I have, Grandmother," she said proudly. "He kneels beside me as you have commanded."

"And his seed has taken hold?" the Queen Mother asked.

"It has, Grandmother. The child grows within, a union of his powers and ours." Alesha smiled, reaching out her hand toward Ethan's, squeezing it briefly before letting go.

Alesha's words rang through Ethan's mind. The news that he was to be a father sent scores of emotions racing through his brain. The fact she did not tell him sooner did not surprise him.

"Then all is proceeding as our visions have foretold," the Queen Mother said. *"The greatest joy of any Queen Mother is the birth of her granddaughter's child. But our Alesha's child is far more. House Loria has prepared for this day for a thousand years when our visons first revealed the rise of a lightning lord in Astaria and the unique nature of his first-born son. I look with joy to this birth, Alesha, so I might see my beloved daughter Valera rise to Queen Mother, and you to Queen Daughter. Then I can join the coven of our ancestors, where my mother, grandmother, and great-grandmother await me. They shall witness the birth and oversee the ceremony of ascension. The rule of Vellesia falls to each of you as the future Queen Mother and Daughter. I have prepared you for that day. Take what I have given you, and pass it on to our future crown princess. You have selected a name for this beloved progeny?"*

"Yes, Mother. Alesha shall name her Gabrielle," Valera said wordlessly, so Ethan might not overhear.

"In honor of the Astarian Queen?" the Queen Mother asked.

"A small boon for her helpful prodding," Alesha said.

"The binding of Ethanos proved difficult, Mother. He is rebellious, even now. His anger has proven problematic," Valera continued to speak to her mother's and Alesha's minds, so Ethan could not hear.

"And you wish to dispose of him, Valera?" Queen Mother Corella asked.

"He has given his seed. He has fulfilled the highest duty of a royal consort. Perhaps it is wise to release him, perhaps across the barrier. He can live a life of his choosing. We can seal the boundary, trapping him there so he will not interfere.'

Alesha's eyes narrowed severely, enraged by her mother's suggestion.

"*No!*" Corella declared. "*Our visions reveal he shall be of great service to Vellesia. You have always known this, as have we all. He MUST be brought back to Elysia.*"

"*He is wild. Unless he is properly broken, he is unsuited to life in court. Alesha refuses to employ the tactics I have suggested. Only the threat to his father's life ensures his obedience, and that is not enough, not in the long term.*"

"*He belongs to Alesha. In time, she will break his spirit as I have foreseen. That time is not now. Unlike our consorts, he shares our power of regeneration. His life and vitality are as long-lasting as our own. Alesha has many lifetimes to bind his will.*"

"*His mind is closed to us. We cannot see what dangers lurk behind his veil,*" Valera warned.

"*His power can be bound in time. We only lack the anti-magic to do so. Even without it, he is still just a boy, despite his impressive abilities. Once he enters our domain, he shall never return to Astaria.*"

Ethan grew impatient waiting for them to speak. He couldn't read Valera's thoughts or hear Corella's voice echo through the orb. For all he knew, they might be partaking in some form of meditation or just talking about the weather.

"Allie, what's going on?" he whispered in her ear.

Alesha shot him a dangerous look.

Valera turned her head, fixing Ethan with a terrible gaze, her eyes burning like embers.

"Be still your tongue, Ethanos!" Valera warned.

Ethan glared at her, wondering how she heard his faint whisper. "Forgive my insolence, my Queen." He bowed his head. He was bound by the vows he swore to always speak to Valera with respect and deference. Any violation of his vows, and the magic would consume his father. Ethan had warned them, however, that if his father died, he would kill them all. Even their guards couldn't save them from his wrath, or so Ethan believed.

Valera knew that Ethan might be defeated, but not broken.

"*The boy tests you?*" Corella asked.

46

"He has proven more difficult than we anticipated," Valera said.

"Yet he still knelt before Alesha and took his vows," Corella said.

"Not before doing us great harm."

"Such as?"

"He angered Alesha into revealing many of our powers before the assemblage of kings. They now know of the threat we pose, something we wished to keep secret until it was too late for them to unify against us. He managed to free Amanda from her vows to Vellesia, freeing her to tell the Astarian king our plans. I cannot silence her for he tricked me into pledging that the Vellesian throne would do no harm to the person he freed or their descendants. Then he freed Amanda, and she betrayed us by accepting his offer!" Valera bitterly answered.

"My dearest Valera, did you expect to simply enter Astaris, fasten a collar around the neck of its king's firstborn, and drag the boy back to Vellesia without protest?"

"Mother, I meant to…"

"No, daughter! Do not begrudge the boy for resisting his imprisonment. In time, he will be brought to heel. Until then, do not allow your emotions to trump reason. Everything is nearly in our grasp. The empire we shall establish shall encompass ALL the world. It shall endure eternal, an endless reign of House Loria, as befits or divinity. It shall be a world without war, hunger, or infirmity. A world without ugliness, where beauty is common. A land where motherhood is revered, queens are worshipped, and the grand empress is acknowledged as the goddess in a monotheistic world. Gabrielle Loria shall be that first empress. Alesha shall bear many daughters, and each shall be queens of the seven kingdoms, the Mage Bane, and the wilds. All shall come to pass as long as the first son of Astaria is delivered into our realm. Do not allow his childish rants and boyish mischief to easily offend you, my child."

"Yes, Queen Mother," Valera bowed her head.

"Alesha," Corella addressed her granddaughter.

"Yes, Queen Mother," Alesha answered.

"We look with anticipation to your coming home. A great wedding feast is planned for the day you return to Elysia. You shall preside over the Queen's Ball that follows."

"*That sounds lovely, Grandmother.*" Alesha lifted her golden eyes to Corella's glowing face.

"*My dearest Alesha. You may now reap the rewards of your years of preparation and sacrifice. All that we promised you shall now come to pass. For you, the pleasures of this world are beginning to blossom. Once in full bloom, they need not end.*" Corella smiled lovingly at her beloved granddaughter.

"Thank you, Grandmother," she answered, again reaching out for Ethan's left hand, intertwining the fingers of her right hand with his left. Merely touching him before would have caused her grandmother's visage to falter, but she was immune to his aura, their unborn daughter's power radiating through her. His touch, however, kindled something far more potent than their magical union. It was a physical spark that sent torrents of euphoria throughout her body, stimulating her mind beyond anything she could have ever imagined. She could feel by his touch, the similar effects manifesting in him. His touch was becoming addictive, an all-consuming desire to be near him constantly.

"*Hasten your return, my children,*" Corella's final words drifted with her face fading in the cloudy sphere.

Valera slowly gained her feet, turning to face her daughter, who remained kneeling beside Ethan.

"You may retire to your pavilion, Alesha. I shall send Ethanos along shortly after I have spoken with him."

"Of course, Mother." Alesha released his hand before standing and stepping without.

"Remain where you are," Valera commanded as Ethan started to rise, gazing down at him with cold, appraising eyes.

"I guess I should congratulate you on becoming a grandmother, my Queen," he said.

"Be still your flippant tongue, child. Even when your words are respectful, your eyes betray the venom of your heart. Have you so quickly forgotten your vows, Ethanos?"

"No, my Queen," he answered while dreaming of snapping her neck.

"You vowed to speak with deference and respect when addressing myself, Alesha, and members of my court."

"Am I not kneeling before you, my Queen? How more *respectful* can I be?" He fought the anger welling up inside him.

She took a dangerous step closer, fixing her terrible gaze upon him. "You prostrate yourself in my presence, but you preach blasphemy when left to your own counsel. *Blood is blood*, you have told my guards. Denying the divinity of House Loria is the greatest violation of your vows."

"Divinity?" Ethan scowled. "You think yourself a God? Now who's the blasphemer?"

"I could take your father's life for such insolence," she warned.

"If you take his life, then I take yours!" Ethan stood, towering over her, his intense stare stripping away her defenses. He caught for the briefest moment, a look of fear crossing her eyes. Then it was gone, replaced with a fierce stubbornness to match his own.

A dozen queen's guards flooded the chamber, dressed in silver mail and white kilted tunics. They circled Ethan with spear tips leveled to his throat.

"Kneel, Ethanos!" she commanded.

He stood unmoved.

"For your offense, I can claim your father's life, and yours as well. Alesha may favor your company, but I already have what I need from you."

"Their spears won't stop me from killing you," he growled.

"Perhaps, but your father's life would be forfeit. His life is in your hands, Ethanos. Kneel!"

Ethan relented, dropping to his knees.

"Lower your eyes!"

He obeyed.

"Heed my words, Ethanos. You vowed to serve me in all things. Do you remember that vow?"

"Yes...my Queen," he answered quietly.

"Very well. You shall no longer speak despairingly of the Mage Born or the equality of mage born and commoners. Am I clear?"

"Yes, my Queen."

49

"You shall only speak fondly of House Loria."

"Yes, my Queen."

"The crown princess allows you certain liberties in her presence. As your mistress, she may do so, but you are *not* to say her name without title in the presence of others. I will not tolerate such disrespect. Am I understood?"

"Yes, my Queen." Ethan wanted nothing more than to die and be done with it, and if he couldn't escape, old age was his only means to such an end.

"Bring me his pack," she ordered her guards. Two of them quickly bowed before hurrying to retrieve his saddle pack just outside the pavilion, bringing it to the queen, setting it at her feet. She ordered them to empty the pack, setting each item on the ground before her. She regarded the rifle, bow, hundreds of rounds of ammunition, two knives, arrows, bags of gold and silver, cleaning kits for his weapons, fishing lines, books, hammer and nails, an axe, a box of spices, spare moccasins boots, horse brush, cleansing powders, buckskins trousers and shirts, and bedroll, all spread out before her.

"You seem to have many weapons in your pack," she observed.

"Yes, my Queen."

"Gold as well. What purpose does it serve you, Ethanos? As a royal consort, you have no need of coin."

"I earned it, my Queen. It belongs to me."

"Belongs to you?" She laughed, raising an eyebrow. "Nothing belongs to you, Ethanos. You belong to Alesha. Therefore, anything you possess belongs to her. Your horse, your weapons, even the clothes you wear, are adornments that she allows you."

Ethan felt his chest tighten, wondering what sort of life awaited him in Elysia.

"Tomorrow, we shall treat with emissaries from Gorgencia, who shall usher us across the Morow, and into Gorgencia proper. I expect you to show them proper respect. I should guess that King Gregor and Crown Prince Borcose shall await us at Torval, their capital city. I know that you and the crown prince have made each other's acquaintance at Astaris. Of course, you were equals then. I need not remind you that you are no longer a prince of Astaria or even a free man of

Elaria. You are a consort of Vellesia and shall show our host his due respect. Am I clear, child?"

"Yes, Your Highness."

"Very good. Though Alesha has allowed certain liberties of late, your presence shall be required in the coming days, where you are expected to attend her at all times, as befits the duties of a royal consort. As such, you are required to wear the golden collar, that Alesha has generously removed. Should you prove sufficiently dutiful, she will be permitted to remove it as we progress into the Gorgencian heartland. Perhaps you might even be allowed to partake in hunting or fishing forays into the countryside where time and location permit." She dangled his favored activity as a reward for his obedience.

Ethan closed his eyes, hating the thought of that foul device wrapped around his neck. It was nothing more than another means to torment him as if his current slavery wasn't enough.

"When Alesha does not require you, you shall be instructed by my chief minister on the protocols of the Vellesian Court and the expectations of a royal consort."

Any thought of sharing the company of Leora Mattiese filled his mouth with bile.

"Leora," Valera called out before drawing forth the hated collar, fastening it about his neck.

"Queen Valera," the queen's first minister appeared at the entrance with her hands folded before her, overtop her dark dress.

"Leora, please escort Consort Loria to the princess' pavilion."

"I shall, my Queen. I believe she desired that he bathe before presenting himself."

"See to it."

"As you command, oh Queen." Leora smiled before regarding Ethan's kneeling form. "Come, Consort Loria!"

*****

Leora led Ethan to a black tent set near Alesha's gold pavilion. Stepping within, he found a large silver tub with steam pouring over its sides.

"Disrobe, and step within!" Leora commanded.

"Are you going to stay and watch?" Ethan couldn't help himself.

"My coming and going is not your concern, Ethanos. You need only obey," she said humorlessly.

"Just asking." Ethan shrugged, unholstering his pistol belt, setting it aside before stripping off his shirt. If Leora wasn't offended by his nakedness, then neither was he. He sat down to work his moccasin boots from his feet, then stood before taking off his trousers and undergarment, which caused her to turn away as he finished disrobing.

"You can look if you want to. I'm not completely naked. I'm still wearing my collar." He smiled, stepping in the tub.

She waited for the sound of him stepping into the water before turning around. "A collar hardly constitutes clothing," she chided him.

"Everyone says it's a great honor to wear the collar of a royal consort. Who needs clothing when I can cover myself in honor."

"You needn't attempt to stir my anger, Ethanos. Your boyish mischief is hardly original. I've dealt with your ilk before."

"I doubt you ever dealt with anyone like me, Leora."

"My proper appellation is first minister. You may also refer to me as Lordess or Lady Mattiese."

"Well, Lady…"

"Lady Mattiese," she corrected him.

"Well, Lady…Mattiese. Since I forsook the throne of Astaria, my title is deputy of Red Rock. Once I return to Texas, I might even become sheriff someday or even a US marshal. But I really like the sound of Texas Ranger Ethan Blagen." He smiled, leaning back in the tub, pretending he hadn't a care in the world as he faced her.

She shook her head, dismissing his childish fantasies. She snapped her fingers, signaling a young maid to enter and gather up his clothes and weapons.

"Where's she going with my things?" Ethan asked warily.

"You needn't fret, Consort. She will merely wash your detestable garments and return them by morning. Your weapons will be placed within Crown Princess Alesha's pavilion."

"She shouldn't trouble herself."

"She isn't troubling herself, Consort. She is doing as she is bid."

"If you insist that I refer to you as your lordship, lady, first minister, or whatever ridiculous title you give yourself, then I insist you refer to me as deputy, not consort. At least that is a title I earned and was not born to." Ethan knew it was pointless, but couldn't resist raising her ire.

"Your Mistress awaits," she stated flatly, unfazed by his banter. "Be thankful for her leniency. If it was my decision, I would burn your dreadful attire and clap you in irons until we attain Elysia."

"You wound me, Lady Mattiese. And here I thought you were growing fond of me."

"Oh, I am fond of you, Consort Loria. We have awaited your coming with anticipation. We look for you to assume your proper place in the Vellesian Court."

"My proper place?"

"The proper place for any prince of Astaria, kneeling before the queen of Vellesia."

"You're a charming woman, Leora. Your husband must be one lucky fella," Ethan gave her a stupid grin before climbing out of the water and donning a robe set aside for him. "Lead the way, Lady Mattiese."

*****

Ethan paused at the entrance of Alesha's pavilion, noting the rich details embroidered along its golden folds. It was not mage crafted but produced by a skilled seamstress, who no doubt spent endless hours to produce such work. The mage born would little note the labor and craftsmanship of common people, but he knew. Allie probably didn't appreciate the work of others. How could she when all her needs were satisfied by her many gifts?"

He noticed that no guards were posted on either side of the entry flaps, as an enticing perfumed scent beckoned him to enter.

"You are to enter and disrobe!" Leora commanded, directing him toward the entry.

Ethan gave her a look and entered. He felt the thick furs beneath his naked feet, covering the entirety of the chamber. A large bed was centered in the pavilion, with red silk covers. A basin torch at the pavilion's side, softly lit the spacious chamber, its shifting flames casting dancing shadows across the walls. Ethan removed his robe, tossing it aside. He waited for her to approach from behind, running her soft hands up his back, and over his shoulders. She lightly glided her fingers over the tingling hairs of his flesh. Electricity sparked between them, heightening the sensuous caress they shared.

Ethan swiftly turned, scooping her into his arms, crushing his lips to hers. He carried her to the bed, gently setting her down as he lingered on her lips, savoring every taste they proffered. He briefly withdrew, staring into the golden pools of her eyes. He wondered how she could elicit such passion in his heart when his mind despised her. As lust and hatred vied for dominion, a more powerful instinct overwhelmed him. He sat upright, looking down at her perfectly feminine form with a new thought consuming him…protecting her.

"Why do you stop?" she asked, taken aback by the strange look passing his face.

He reached out with his hand, smoothing her hair behind her ear, his gentleness surprising her. Even before she betrayed him, he had never shown tenderness this deeply.

"What troubles you, Ethan?"

"Why didn't you tell me you are with child?"

"Does it please you to know?"

"Yes, it pleases me."

She smiled widely. "Then kiss me and finish what you started."

"Allie, I…"

She lifted her hands, cupping his cheeks. "Why do you tarry?"

"We shouldn't do this if your…well…in your condition. We might harm the baby," he said, looking down at her stomach.

She laughed, admonishing his foolish notion. "Nothing will harm our child, Ethan, especially this. Now, as your crown princess, I order you to kiss me and finish what we started," she playfully commanded.

He kissed her softly as if she might break if he pressed too hard. They made love each night since leaving Astaris. The other nights he was torn between lust and hate and treated their marriage bed accordingly. Now his mind was consumed with their unborn child. His brother warned him of the child's danger to the world, but he couldn't help the protective instinct taking hold of him. He ran his right hand gently over her taut olive skin, from the swell of her breasts to the flat of her belly. He pressed his lips to her womb as she stared at him oddly.

"Are you well?" she asked, nearly laughing at his behavior.

He positioned himself overtop of her, his hands on either side of her head, staring intently into her golden eyes.

"It was on our first night together in Astaris?" he asked, guessing the answer of when they conceived.

"Yes," her sultry voice whispered.

"That is why we glowed that night and not the nights since?"

"Yes."

She was instantly aware of the moment of her conception that night. It was another of her many mage gifts. The women in her family also possessed the power to control their fertility, and never suffered menstrual cycles, their first egg preserved for their firstborn heir. She should have control of the egg's fertilization, but Ethan's seed would not be denied, claiming its prize without her control. Of course, that was what she wanted, but the fact she couldn't control it was both thrilling and disconcerting.

"You knew that night?"

"Yes. In the small chance that you might escape your vows, I ensured that I would at least leave Astaris with your child."

"You can control your cycles?"

"Oh, Ethan." She smiled, pressing her hands on his cheeks. "I don't have cycles. I only deposit an egg when I will it. The first egg is the most sacred, and that is the one that now grows within me."

Understanding washed over him at the realization of her power, fearful of what other powers she possessed. What were the limits of her mage gifts?

"What can't you do, Allie?"

"My powers are nearly without limit, Ethan, except for...you. In your presence, I am simply a woman...your woman, your wife." She failed to reveal that this was no longer so, their child protecting her powers in his presence. "Outside of this pavilion, I am your mistress. In here, upon this bed, I am your slave. Must I beg for your touch? Must I beg for you to finish?" She reached up to kiss him, pressing her lips fiercely to his. Ethan held some unknown power over her, consuming her waking thoughts, filling her with an unquenchable desire for his touch. She was certain that he possessed some untold power to command her love. Since that first night in Astaris, when they consummated their passion, the bond between them grew exponentially. Yet he claimed that it was she who was bewitching him. It made little sense. Her mother never shared such a bond with her father. Her mother found little attraction to her father other than his unique mage gifts. With Ethan, it was different. Alesha felt an overwhelming desire for him. Physically, he was the epitome of male perfection. He was tall, incredibly strong, handsome, and confident. He carried himself in a way that bespoke pride without arrogance. Her mother despised his rudeness, but Alesha had seen his gentle manner with the way he treated those she considered beneath him. Children gravitated toward him, men respected him, and women swooned at the sight of him. If he loved the children of strangers, how much more would he love his own? On a deeper level, she was drawn to Ethan's mind and heart. She came to know him in a way that she knew no other. Before her betrayal, he was her friend, her only friend. They shared so much more now, yet she missed his friendship. Such weakness felt strange and alien to her.

"Ooohh!" Her back arched severely, responsive to his intimate ministration. The erotic sensations quickened, building in unbearable intensity before bursting. Waves of euphoria rippled her flesh, washing over her extremities and back again. The process repeated itself over and over, a timeless joining of two souls.

*****

She rested her head upon his chest as he stared at the ceiling of the pavilion. They spent most of the night making love, as they had every night since leaving Astaris. Ethan never knew such pleasure. He hated admitting to her how much he longed for each day to pass so they could spend the night together. He still hated her for her betrayal but felt an invisible bond connecting them, a bond that grew stronger every time they were intimately joined, a bond that he could not explain or comprehend. It was clearly some sort of witchcraft of House Loria, meant to enslave him to her will. Very little frightened Ethan, but the thought that Alesha could bind his heart filled him with trepidation. Even if he could break free of the vows they made him swear, the thought of living without her seemed as forlorn as living under their yoke. His desire for freedom and his passion for her vied for dominion of his heart. For the first time since her betrayal, he pondered if he might have both.

"What are you thinking of, Ethan?" she asked dreamily, resting her chin on his thick chest, gazing into his sea-blue eyes.

"Nothing," he lied.

"You are a poor liar, Ethan. What can I do to make you happy?"

"You can take this blasted collar off my neck." His words came harsher than he intended.

Her eyes darkened with his rebuke. "You shall wear that collar to your dying day. Then you shall be buried with it," she whispered just as harsh, rolling of him, turning her back to him, and falling asleep.

CHAPTER 3

Ethan tugged at the collar of his shirt; its constricting material tightened miserably around his neck. The shirt was deep red, with traces of gold sewn into its folds. He wore black trousers that fit so snugly he might as well have worn the short puffed pantaloons and hose that Alesha threatened to make him wear.

"Stop fussing!" Leora warned as several maids finished his final touches. They sprayed him with scented perfumes and fixed a foppish golden hat upon his scowling head. The only item he was allowed to wear from his gear was his father's sword on his left hip.

"You know, Leora—oh, my apologies—Lady Mattiese," he corrected himself. "You know, Lady...Mattiese, I've been pondering the fate of my predecessor, our queen's husband. I never hear mention of his name, or if he still lives. Is he still among the living?"

"Consort Travin Loria has unfortunately expired."

"So what was the cause of his demise?"

"He met an unfortunate mishap," she answered curtly.

"Hmm," Ethan doubted it. "You know, Lady Mattiese, I think I know what might've happened."

"And what great revelation have you discovered, Consort?" she asked humorlessly.

"He probably died of embarrassment from wearing the clothes the queen picked out for him."

Leora simply glared at him, trying to ignore his juvenile remarks. "Now that you look presentable, Crown Princess Alesha awaits you at the river."

"You are truly a vision of loveliness, Leora. I used to know a man named Hank Grierson. You two would've made a charming couple. Well, I best be going. Don't want my mistress scolding me for being a tardy slave." Ethan stepped without, leaving Leora and her scowl behind.

*****

Ethan found Bull saddled and waiting outside the pavilion. Save for his sword, all his weapons were removed from his pack. Obviously, Valera was concerned that he might kill Gregor Vorhenz if granted the opportunity. He climbed into the saddle and rode toward the river.

*****

Valera rode south along the riverbank, astride a black mare, with Alesha beside her upon Glynderelle, and a score of royal guards trailing them. They wore light mail over bright riding leathers of crimson and gold. A rider before them bore the standard of House Loria, a golden rose upon a field of black. They descried the Gorgencian sentries lining the far bank of the Morrow, awaiting their arrival.

"Today we can at least be gone from this dreadful land." Valera smiled.

"Gorgencia is no better," Alesha said. In truth, Astaria was one of the most beautiful kingdoms in Elaria while Gorgencia was the dreariest.

"Ahh, but Gorgencia is no threat to Vellesia. Astaria is."

"Astaria? Astaria is neutered, Mother. Without Ethan, they are mere bugs beneath our boots."

"Perhaps. But if your consort should slip his collar, then Astaria shall be a greater threat than Vellesia has faced in a thousand years."

"Ethan is not bound by his collar, Mother. He is bound by *me*. He shall never return to his precious Astaria. Vellesia is his home now," she said, stroking Glynderelle's snowy mane.

"Speaking of your troublesome mate, here he comes now," Valera said.

Alesha shifted her stare, descrying Ethan galloping down the grassy hilltop off their right. Her heart sang at his approach, noting the black trousers and silken shirt of crimson and gold that melded to his masculine form. His short dark hair framed his chiseled face and square jaw. She preferred his hair longer, but it would eventually grow to a length she desired. He attempted to shorten it after leaving Astaris, but she ordered him to leave it be. She was certain that he hated the clothing she selected for him, but his buckskins were inappropriate for treating with royalty. She would allow him his things when his presence wasn't required if he behaved himself. If he was miserable, he did not show it, presenting a cheerful disposition as he drew nigh.

"Queen Valera, Princess," Ethan greeted them with a slight bow of his head.

"Attend us, Ethanos," Alesha commanded, inviting him to ride beside her.

He circled Bull around, coming up along her right.

"You look quite handsome in that attire, Ethan." Alesha smiled. To her, he could be wearing sackcloth and still be the handsomest man in Elaria.

"Since wearing whatever you tell me to is part of my vows of obedience, I don't have much choice in the matter, do I, Princess?" He gave her a fake smile.

She pursed her lips, tempering her anger. Every attempt to compliment him or ease his transition was met with vitriol. "You would do well to remember that I need not return your things to you, Ethan. I've allowed you to wear your buckskins and pistol for much of our journey because I know they are comfortable and familiar to you. I desire to cause you as little anguish as possible with your new life. I have also removed your collar whenever protocol does not require it. Be mindful that I need not be so accommodating. Am I understood?"

"Yes." He sighed.

She gave him a reproachful look.

"Yes, Highness," he corrected himself.

She was weary of his childish antics. She had hoped he would accept his role with grace and deference but scolded herself for such fanciful optimism. "Where is the hat I selected for you?" she asked, suspiciously noting its absence.

"The wind blew it off my head, Princess. The last I saw it, it was fluttering somewhere off to the west. Do you wish me to fetch it?"

"Must you test me, Ethan?" She sighed.

Valera held her tongue, allowing Alesha to deal with his insolence.

"Since you act as a child, so shall I treat you. One more act of petty defiance, and I'll burn your things. If, however, you behave yourself, I shall return them after we pass into Gorgencia. Am I understood?"

Ethan stewed in a maelstrom of rage, struggling to tame his tongue.

"Am I understood?" she asked more firmly.

"Yes, Highness," he relented.

"Very well. Let us proceed to the crossing."

*****

Queen Valera could conjure an ice bridge across the Morow with a simple wave of her hand but instead adhered to protocol while entering Gorgencia, by way of a stone bridge further downstream. The bridge was built into the hillsides upon opposite sides of the Morow. The bridge spanned six hundred meters, supported by a series of arches of gray stone rising from the riverbed like the outstretched arms of giants. The bridge was wide enough for six wagons to ride abreast, with each end guarded by a stone fortress. The west end was garrisoned by Astarians and the east by Gorgencians, the two groups keeping constant vigil upon the other.

Expecting to be ushered across the Morow by the ranking Astarian commander, Valera was surprised to see the tall standard blowing freely upon the ramparts above the west end of the bridge, a bolt of yellow lightning upon a field of black, the royal seal of the

House of Blagen. Two figures rode out to meet them, followed by a score of Astarian cavalry. One was a tall, slender man with sand-colored hair blowing beneath a gray helm, wearing a wolf fur cloak over his dark mail. Valera recognized him immediately—Prince Tristan. He was accompanied by a beautiful woman with a lush auburn main blowing freely in the wind. She wore yellow armor over red riding leathers. She rode forth headstrong with golden eyes that stared through Valera's mind, unnerving the Vellesian queen with their intense power.

"Amanda," Valera whispered, recognizing her wayward child approach. She was nearly struck dumb by the power emanating from her. Amanda possessed all the powers of House Menau and the few gifts given her by Valera, but they were never directed at Valera... until now.

Ethan's heart lightened watching his brother riding to meet them. Never had he so longed for a friendly face as he did now. Though Marco had escorted them to the border, he was forbidden to speak with him or be in his presence. He noticed Valera and Alesha stiffen as they drew near.

"Ethanos!" Alesha called out to him.

"Yes, Highness."

"Fall back to your proper place behind me and lower your eyes. Do not lift them unless I tell you."

"As you wish." He shook his head, weary of her need to control his every interaction with anyone not of her house. He withdrew as Tristan and Amanda stopped short of Alesha and the queen, the four of them observing each other for a moment.

"Crown Prince Tristan. We are honored by such a prestigious escort across the border." Valera smiled sweetly, refusing to acknowledge Amanda's presence.

"Captain Marco shall escort your company across the border, Queen Valera. I am here on behalf of my father, the king."

"What troubles your Lord Father that he should send his only son to treat with me?" Valera asked, omitting Ethan's place in the House of Blagen.

"I've come to speak with my *brother*. Send him forth!" Tristan said firmly.

"Mind your tongue, child. No one makes demands of me!" Valera scolded.

"I am not your child, Valera. Send Ethan forth!"

"Ethanos is a member of my household. He is forbidden to treat with anyone unless I allow it. Members of your House may visit him in Vellesia but not here."

"The Mage Laws of Elaria allow mage kings or their designees, to freely speak with anyone within their realm. The law overrides any other bonds that bind the individual. Unless you wish to violate sacred Mage Law, Queen Valera, then I suggest you send my brother forth."

"Very well. Ethanos!" Valera called out to him.

"Yes, my Queen," he answered.

"Come hither. The crown prince of Astaria wishes to treat with you."

"Wait, Ethan!" Alesha commanded, her eyes fixed on her sister. "She is not to partake in your counsel," Alesha said to Tristan.

"Princess Amanda is a ward of House Blagen. She and I are designees of the king. She and I *will* treat with Ethan. Is that understood, Princess?" Tristan returned her stare with a look matching her seething glare.

Amanda smiled inwardly. No one had ever spoken to her sister like that except Ethan. All her life, everyone she encountered lived in her family's shadow, fearful to offend Valera or Alesha in any way, lest they incur the wrath of House Loria. House Blagen held no such reverence for her mother's house. She was finally free of her mother's and Alesha's tyranny and owed that wondrous gift to Ethan. She owed Tristan and his parents, sisters, and even Dragos for welcoming her into their family. She felt as if she truly belonged among them, a true home, something she had not felt since her father died. She rewarded their kindness by informing them of all the subterfuge of House Loria through the centuries, and their vast powers and plans for domination. Beyond this, she placed her own significant powers at their disposal and would use them to protect the House of Blagen unto death.

"The world is not yours to command as yet, Sister," Amanda said.

"You have betrayed your blood, Amanda, our very House."

"I would rather betray a House bereft of kindness than betray the man who loves me."

"I chose duty over the wants of my heart, Amanda. There is more at stake than such fanciful sentiments. Ethan has a destiny also, one he is long past shirking," Alesha said. She regretted attacking her sister at Astaris, but the sight of her in Ethan's arms triggered her basest inclinations. She loved her siblings dearly, even if Amanda did not believe so. Perhaps it was the years consumed with attaining Ethan, where all her other relationships were overlooked or ignored, her hunger for his power all-consuming.

"No." Amanda shook her head. "You are a fool, Alesha. You threw away Ethan's love for a cold throne. He will never love you after such betrayal, and without love, life is empty and joyless. I pity the way the hunger consumes you, for what joy is in a life where it can never be sated? I took Ethan's gift and shall embrace life to its fullest. And if Astaria should one day fall under your tyranny, I shall rejoice in the years of freedom his gift afforded me," Amanda said, lifting her chin in defiance.

"No matter Astaria's fate, your freedom from Vellesian rule is permanent, by Valera's own decree. She swore that the throne of Vellesia and her royal House, would bring no harm to whomever I freed with my royal request. That vow extends to your decedents as well," Ethan said, reminding Alesha and Valera of that vow.

"Be still your tongue, Ethanos!" Valera hissed.

"You do plan to honor your vows, Queen Valera?" Tristan asked sternly.

Valera's eyes narrowed severely. "Of course, Prince Tristan. Affording my daughter and her descendants' freedom from Vellesian...interference is a small price to exchange for Astaria's *true* crown prince. Amanda is only a second daughter, as you are a second son. Her loss is of little note."

Alesha cast her mother a disapproving look with that remark.

"From what Amanda tells, every life is of little note in Vellesia, save for yours and Alesha's. I will speak with my brother now," Tristan said.

Valera waved Ethan onward as Tristan and Amanda drew him aside, while she and Alesha observed them intensely from afar. Tristan ordered his guards to back away, lest Alesha overhear their discourse through the guards' ears.

"You are a sight for weary eyes, little brother," Ethan smiled.

"So are you, Ethan."

"I see you're keeping better-looking companions these days." He gave Amanda an approving look.

Tristan ignored the innuendo. "Amanda has been very helpful. You were wise to free her, Ethan."

"Amanda, you should be flattered. That is the most praise my little brother has ever given any woman. He must hold you in very high regard." Ethan smiled even wider, much to Tristan's annoyance. Tristan was always a deep thinker, paying little heed to the fairer sex. Ethan thought Tristan might blush with embarrassment, but his face held its color.

"I am flattered and humbled by the kind treatment of your entire family, Ethan," Amanda said softly, her affection for each of them evident in her tone. "You have a wonderful home, and parents that love and adore you. I envy your upbringing, and pity you for what awaits you in Vellesia. I know well my sister's true nature. I beg of you to not incur her wrath. Other than their inner council, my mother and sister view everyone else as dirt. You are different, though. They need you, Ethan, but they are uncertain of how to control you. I sense great unease in my mother's thoughts. She despises you but also fears you, a dangerous combination. She has never known such fear. She desires to be rid of you, but my grandmother insists on you being brought to Vellesia. Alesha shall never allow my mother to dispose of you or even free you, which she has contemplated. Alesha's behavior regarding you is most peculiar. Since she and I share such powers of clairvoyance, her mind is shielded from me. Though you may not believe so, she has shown you great leniency. If any other chosen consort spoke to her so rudely, as you often do, they would be cinders. Such benevolence will most likely cease once she is with child. Any flippant remark would most likely mean your death, though you might slay her as well."

"She's already with child," he said.

Amanda's face went ashen. "And so it begins. Ethan, I know what your freedom means to you. Remember it fondly and take pride in all the good you have done, but you must stay alive. Do not offend Alesha. Grant her no reason to kill you. Until we can find another way of stopping her child from destroying Astaria, you are our only hope. There may come a day when you must strike down your own flesh to save us all."

Ethan paled. He knew in his heart he could never harm his own child. The very thought was impossible. He didn't know why, but he felt a powerful bond with the child growing in Alesha's womb, a bond that transcended paternal affection. It was equal to the over-powering bond he shared with Alesha.

"Find another way. I could never harm my child or Alesha. Valera, I could kill without regard, but Alesha…" He couldn't explain the hold she had on him.

Amanda and Tristan shared a look.

"Are you well, Ethan?" Amanda asked. "Alesha cannot enchant you. Your immunity protects you."

"I…I can't explain it. All I know is…I can't allow her to be harmed. I must protect her, even if I hate her." His voice trailed as if it were being drawn away.

"Then we are doomed," Tristan said.

"No! I'll find a way. I promise. I'll find a way," Ethan said, his voice regaining its strength.

"I believe you will, Ethan," Tristan gave him a heartfelt smile. Only Tristan and Amanda counseled such extreme measures to stay the inevitable, but they did not reveal such intent to King Bronus or Queen Gabrielle. Bronus and Gabrielle would never sanction the sacrifice of their unborn granddaughter, even if her birth foretold their doom. Tristan knew well his brother's character, knowing he could never commit such an act. No, Ethan had to find another way.

"Let me worry about Alesha and our child. You both have more pressing matters if what I saw in Dragos's vision comes to pass," Ethan warned.

"Dragons." Tristan sighed, wondering how they would counter such a threat.

"Dragons are anti-magic, like yourself. How we may counter that, is beyond us," Amanda lamented.

"Maybe not. I gave Tristan my twin pistol holster, with matching colts, and plenty of ammunition. Krixan has plenty as well. Since they're from across the barrier, maybe they can hurt a dragon."

Tristan and Amanda shared a look, wondering if it would work. Maybe it could, but two guns might not be enough, but it was something to ponder.

"Speaking of Krixan, I miss the big fella. When he finally shows himself at Astaris, tell him…well, tell him I miss him, and that… well, he is my best friend, and I couldn't imagine any of our adventures without him beside me," Ethan said, trying to keep his composure, while fishing a folded parchment from his saddle pack, handing it to his brother.

"What's this?" Tristan asked, taking hold of it.

"Just something I wrote for Krix. Give it to him, would you?"

"I will," Tristan smiled, tucking it away.

"Thank you."

"Father desired to come bid you one last farewell, but Amanda urged him to remain in Astaris. His mind is open to Alesha's probing. You should know that he has found other matters requiring his involvement," Tristan said, changing the subject to brighten his mood.

"What other matters?" Ethan asked, concern knitting his brows.

"The day you departed Astaris, Torg sought an audience with father. The smith relayed a fanciful tale of a former crown prince of Astaria, and his intent on giving out toys to all the children in the palace," Tristan smiled wryly.

"I was planning to until Alesha locked this collar around my neck and dragged me away," he growled.

Amanda shook her head in disbelief. She never imagined a crown prince placing such value on the happiness of children. Alesha would never think of such a thing. Ethan and her sister were so different in so many ways. He desired freedom where she sought power. He saw all men as equals where she saw herself as supreme. He sought friendship while she sought subjects. Amanda never felt so ashamed of her House as she did now. This was a time Ethan hoped to spend with his family, and he was stripped of all the things he cherished and forced to serve a wicked queen because of Alesha's betrayal. *You deserve far better than to be wed to my sister*, she thought sadly.

"When father heard the full telling of Torg's tale, he nearly wept. He quickly ordered all his smiths to finish what you started but on a much grander scale. He ordered *every* child in Astaria to be given such joy."

"Every child?"

"Yes, to honor you, Ethan. He pays homage to your sacrifice by honoring what you value."

Ethan closed his eyes, a stubborn tear escaping his left eye, trying to picture their father as Tristan described. Bronus was always rough-spoken, projecting a fearsome image, though each of them witnessed his many acts of kindness.

"Tell him thank you," was all Ethan could manage to say without breaking.

"And Mother?" Tristan added. "She has been his equal partner in the endeavor."

"Tell her I have given her what she desires, a grandchild for her, and a cage for me." He regretted saying the words as they slipped his tongue.

"You needn't punish her further, Ethan. She did not forge your chains, my sister did," Amanda said.

"She did not forge my bonds, but she doesn't lament them either."

"She weeps for you every night, brother. She cries out your name, beseeching the spirits to bring you home. She'd rather you be free, even if to do so you might never look upon her again. Do not begrudge her for sharp words spoken in hurt and anger," Tristan said.

Ethan lowered his head in shame for his self-pity. His mother did not spare Alesha's life in the Mage Bane or invite him to attend the Queen's Ball with the Vellesian Princess. No, he forged his own chains, not her.

"Tell her I am sorry, and I forgive her. Tell her...tell her I love her."

"We shall, Ethan," Amanda smiled, reaching her hands to each of them, Ethan with her left, and Tristan her right, squeezing them tightly. "The Brothers Blagen. You are the finest men I have ever known." She smiled.

*****

After treating with Ethan, Amanda and Tristan withdrew to a hillside overlooking the bridge, watching as the Vellesian column began to cross over into Gorgencia. They were surprised to see a hooded figure pass freely through their ring of guards, riding a gray palfrey, wearing a red blouse over leather riding trousers. Tristan drew his horse in front of Amanda, shielding her while his hand went to his sword hilt.

"You need not fear me, Prince Tristan." Amanda recognized the sultry voice of her aunt Sarella as the woman lifted her hood, dark lush hair spilling out over her shoulders, purple eyes fixed to Tristan's gray.

"Aunt Sarella," Amanda greeted, easing her horse up alongside Tristan, revealing her name for his benefit.

"Your aunt? The spy?" Tristan asked, eying the woman warily.

"Spy, is it? A rather crude description of my role in Astaris, crude and most assuredly false," Sarella said dryly, stopping just in front of them, her spirited gray shifting slightly beneath her until she touched a hand to its head, calming the beast.

"What else would I call someone who spent her lifetime *spying* on my family?" Tristan stated flatly, raising a skeptical brow.

"You may think of it as spying, but a more accurate description is *protector*," Sarella answered.

"Protector? Of what?" Tristan was weary of Vellesians and their subterfuge.

"Of destiny, both Alesha's and Ethan's, and protector of Astaria as well."

"Protector of Astaria?" Tristan almost laughed.

"Mind your tone, child. Your kingdom only stands because of House Menau. It was we who shielded you from enemies through the centuries, guarding your secret destiny," Sarella admonished.

"Secret destiny, Aunt? 'Tis no secret now. All you have done is assured our mutual destruction by delivering Ethan into their hands," Amanda said.

"Foolish girl. Ethan and Alesha share a far greater destiny than you could possibly imagine, and your meddling will cause naught but grief for them and you. Between you filling Ethan's mind with nonsense and your brother interfering with Tristan, we are compelled to correct your meddling. You can stop this childish tantrum and return quietly to Astaris. Prepare the kingdom to deal with the troublesome Gorgencians and dragons, should they appear. You have nothing to fear from Vellesia. House Menau has been the shield of Astaria through the centuries and shall continue to do so, so long as we are not distracted by your antics. Even now, your aunt Selendra is busy protecting your fool of brother, covering his absence while he makes his return to Elysia," Sarella scolded her.

"But Ethan is our only hope to defeat mother..."

"Ethan's destiny has nothing to do with stopping your mother, Amanda. Nor is it his destiny to wander through the world as a free spirit, lending a helping hand to the downtrodden, as he is wont to do. He was not given such power for so little a purpose," Sarella said.

"Then what purpose does he serve?" Tristan asked.

"Only House Menau knows his true destiny, my dear Prince, and I shall not give that to you so carelessly. You need only safeguard Astaria from the threats I told you of. Leave Ethan, Valera, and Vellesia to me." And with that, Sarella rode off as inconspicuously as she came.

*****

The Vellesian caravan crossed the expansive stone bridge, Valera riding in the center of the procession, with Alesha beside her. Ethan rode just behind them as they crossed onto the west end of the bridge, with scores of Astarian soldiers lining their flanks as they passed, crowding nigh. The Astarian soldiers pressed their fists to their hearts, their eyes fixed proudly to Ethan when one cried out with a deep voice, "ETHANOS!"

Others quickly took up the call, drawing their swords, pounding them upon their shields, chanting his name, until the entire garrison lining the battlements of the fortress joined in. Ethan's moist eyes swept the line, trying to commit their faces to memory, pressing his right fist to his heart, returning their cheer with a salute. Many of the faces were those of his light cavalry. They came to see him off, and pay homage to their former commander. He saw Xavier Murtado and Vancel Torrent among them, standing beside Captain Marco, each here to honor their friend, Prince and brother-in-arms. He shared with them a knowing look, each a good friend he would dearly miss.

Valera shared a look with Alesha, before looking back to Ethan, her displeasure painted clearly upon her face. Alesha bowed, reluctantly acquiescing to her mother's command. She turned her mount, circling back to Ethan.

"Drop your fist, Ethan!" she ordered.

"I am merely extending a courtesy to my countrymen, Highness," he answered.

"It is not your place to acknowledge them. Lower your fist and your eyes. I forbid you to look at them!" she commanded over the sound of the soldiers cheering his name.

He reluctantly complied, taking her rebuke as another dagger to his heart. She took hold of his reins, leading him across the bridge like a child. Tristan and Amanda looked on from the near embankment, observing Alesha's poor treatment of Ethan.

"Why?" he asked bitterly. "He bent his knee as she asked. He has given her everything, and she still treats him so? Why?"

"Because...he is hers. She needs to bend his will to hers. The adoration of your people is a reminder of his former glory. She will

71

not tolerate the love of his people to occupy any part of his mind. Nothing must distract him from his devotion to her." Amanda sighed.

Tristan felt ill thinking of the life his brother was bound to. For anyone else, it would be miserable, but for Ethan, it was so much worse.

The Astarian soldiers chanted louder, undeterred by Alesha's cowing of Ethan.

A far different greeting awaited Ethan on the east end of the bridge. Scores of Gorgencian soldiers in brown mail and dark red trousers stood in disciplined ranks before the entrance to the stone fortress built over their half of the bridge. The fortress towered over the eastern bank of the Morow with its jagged ramparts of gray tortured stone jutting above. Ethan lifted his eyes skyward as they neared the raised portcullis centered on the east end of the bridge. There atop the highest battlements, blew the standard of House Vorhenz, a white stallion upon a field of green. He felt the intense stares of the Gorgencian host upon him. He prepared much of his life for a war with Gorgencia, as these men did likewise with Astaria. He sensed the mixture of curiosity and hate as they gleefully observed the hated son of Bronus Blagen dragged into captivity. The sound of his countrymen shouting his name dulled as he passed through the gate, following a short tunnel, before the path opened into a large courtyard of smooth black stone. The Vellesian columns broke left and right, forming a semi-circle along the perimeter as Queen Valera and Princess Alesha rode forth to the center, where a tall, broad-shouldered man with rust-colored hair awaited them. He stood with a small entourage of Gorgencian nobles, standing behind him. He wore thick mail over a black tunic and trousers, with a blood-red cape, draping his shoulders. A long sword graced his left hip, and his face bore a striking resemblance to King Gregor.

"Follow, and attend," Alesha said, casting Ethan's reigns behind her, before riding forth with Valera to treat with the Gorgencian envoy. A thousand Gorgencian troops lined the battlements above, each staring intently at the spectacle below. Ethan noted two snow leopards sitting on either side of the Gorgencian dignitary, each licking their paws, apparently disinterested in the proceedings. House

Vorhenz were known for their power to control animals, the vicious predators little more than house pets in their presence, though that could change with any threat to their master.

Valera and Alesha stopped several paces before the envoy.

"Ethanos!" Valera snapped her fingers.

Ethan dismounted, stepping between the princess and the queen, offering his hand to Valera.

"Lower your eyes, child," she reminded him.

He seethed with her rebuke but wisely kept it to himself as she took his hand, allowing him to help her dismount. He knew this was for show, for she hardly needed his help with anything. He repeated the same ritual for Alesha, then followed two paces behind them as they approached the envoy. The Vellesian caravan knelt in unison, as did the Gorgencian nobles behind the envoy, before Alesha directed Ethan to do the same.

"Welcome to Gorgencia, Queen Valera, and Crown Princess Alesha. I am Duke Torz Vorhenz, brother of King Gregor, and your guide to the imperial city of Torval, where my kingly brother shall await us. He and Prince Borcose have already crossed over the Oclovar, and shall precede us to the capital," the duke greeted, trying desperately not to leer at their disarming beauty. The Oclovar was a reference to the bridge fifty leagues downriver, where the main road connecting Astaria to Gorgencia passed over. Ethan wondered why Valera chose this more northerly approach but guessed it was for reasons she would never tell him.

"We accept your generous hospitality, Duke Vorhenz. We look forward to a new age of Vellesian and Gorgencian cooperation and friendship," Valera smiled sweetly as Alesha emptied his mind of its secrets.

"As does House Vorhenz, oh Queen. You have lifted from our people a heavy burden by collaring the son of Bronus Blagen. My king speaks well of the ceremony at Astaris and the pleasure of seeing Prince Ethanos so humbled in his father's house," Torz sneered, steeling a gleeful glance between them, where Ethan knelt on the unforgiving black stone.

"Humbled, Duke Torz?" Alesha lifted a dark brow over a golden eye.

"Yes...well...I meant..." Torz fumbled his words.

"Prince Ethanos took his vows of affirmation as my consort. I have honored him by accepting his affirmation."

"Yes, Princess," the Duke conceded. "Of course, we must insist that Prince Blagen be disarmed and restrained while traversing Gorgencia. "We have smiths here at the fortress able to forge chains strong enough to hold him. Such is the wish of King Gregor."

"There is no Prince of Astaria in our company, Duke Vorhenz. Ethanos!" Alesha beckoned.

"Yes, Highness," he answered without lifting his eyes.

"Come hither."

"What is your name?" She asked as he stepped beside her.

"Ethan..."

"Ethanos," she corrected.

"Ethanos Loria," he said evenly, trying to keep his tongue.

"What is your loyalty to House Blagen?" Valera asked.

"None, my Queen. My loyalties are to House Loria, the throne of Vellesia and my queen and princess."

"Very good, my son." Valera smiled, returning her eyes to Torz. "You see, Lord Vorhenz, Ethanos is of my house. Should he be armed or restrained, it shall be by my leave and mine alone."

"Of course, oh Queen," Torz bowed, fumbling over himself to please her.

"Let us proceed," Alesha whispered, which Ethan was certain the Duke could not overhear.

"Let us proceed. I trust the matter to your keeping," Torz smiled warmly, his mirth clearly out of place.

Ethan gave Alesha a strange look, which she returned with a flirtatious wink.

"Let us proceed, husband," she whispered in his ear, leading him into the fortress proper.

CHAPTER 4

"What troubles you, Allie?" her father asked, squatting before her with his elbows on his knees, his gentle purple eyes staring into her gold.

"Mother was unkind to you today," she said sadly, placing her small hands on his cheeks.

"My dearest girl, you must not worry over such things. Your mother is afflicted with the hunger, and it is maddening at times. Since I do not wear her collar, it is even more pronounced," he said, pushing the flaps of his collared shirt apart, revealing his naked throat.

"If you wore one, would she love you? Would it bring you both happiness?" she asked, her little eyes filled with hope.

"I am afraid that can never be, my dearest. When you are older, I shall explain." He sighed.

"When?"

"After you and Prince Ethanos are wed, I shall tell you everything." He ran his hand over the side of her head lovingly. That would be many years, but knowing her mind, she would never forget his promise. His House insisted that he would be unlike any other Consort of House Loria, in that he would not be collared, lest Valera read his thoughts, laying bare the secrets of House Menau. Of course, this had the consequence of fueling Valera's hunger for his power, causing constant strife in their family.

"Why doesn't she love you?" Alesha asked with the saddest eyes.

"Of course, she loves me. Just as one day you will love Ethanos." He ruffled her hair.

"*Mother says love is an amalgamation of lust, desire, and reciprocity. That it is not real.*" She lowered her eyes. Her father thought those were awfully big words for a child to use.

"*That is not true. I love you and feel none of those things toward you. I would love you if you hated me. You are my dearest little girl, our firstborn. One day, when you and Ethan are wed, you will understand the true meaning of love, as well as the love you will have for your children.*"

"*He might not love me.*"

"*Of course, he shall. You are the prettiest girl in all the world.*" He smiled.

"*That's what you say to Amanda, father.*" She gave him a look.

"*You both share that distinction, my dear girl. Every girl is the most beautiful in their father's eyes. As far as Prince Ethanos, only you will find such favor in his eyes.*"

"*What if I hate him because of his power? Mother says our collars will not contain his power. What if his anti-magic drives me mad? What if I hate him? What if he hates me?*"

"*Now you are speaking silly. He will adore you. Remember, you are of House Menau as well as Loria. We have foreseen your destiny, and Ethan's. They are intertwined. You will not need a collar to curb a madness that shall never claim you.*"

"*Truly?*" She smiled.

"*Truly. My House has seen your future, Allie, and it is wonderful. Think of how you feel about your mother, myself, Raymar, Amanda, and all your grandparents. You love them, don't you?*"

"*Yes.*"

"*What you feel for each of them will be even stronger with Ethanos.*"

"*But Mother says love is not real. Does that mean she does not love us?*"

"*Do you love me?*"

"*Yes.*"

"*Of course you do, just as I love you. Sometimes mothers say silly things, Allie. Pay it no mind.*"

"*Thank you, Father.*" She hugged him.

"There now, it's time for bed, little one." He smiled, kissing her forehead before tucking her in.

"Good night, Father. Maybe if you tell mother how much you love her, she will say it too," Alesha said as he stepped toward the door.

"All right, my little Allie, perhaps I shall."

*****

Alesha took a sip from her goblet, the memory of her father fading in the noise of the great hall of the Gorgencian holdfast. She found the austere surroundings unimpressive, with barely adequate lamps lining its stone walls, with most of their fellow Vellesians seated at the long tables stretched across the floor below. She found herself sitting at the high table, between her mother and Ethan, who constantly tugged at the collar of his shirt while shifting in his seat.

"Sit straighter, and stop fidgeting," she admonished, hating how she had to constantly remind him of proper behavior. She couldn't miss the way he looked out over the crowd of Vellesians and Gorgencians, their bemused looks at his predicament fueling his anger. She knew he wanted nothing more than to run them through with his sword. She reached out under the table, taking his hand in hers, and squeezing, soothing his rage. She hated how her mother constantly tormented him, and even more so when she forced Alesha to do so. She knew he was at a breaking point. There was only so much a person could suffer before they exploded. One born a peasant or slave learned to curb that prideful rage early in life, but someone like Ethan held no such restraint. She recalled the stories Sarella and Selendra shared with her throughout their years of watching over Ethan in Astaris. Even as a child he was constantly challenging his father, causing all sorts of mischief, and taking his punishment without complaint. It was ironic that the love for his father kept him from causing similar mischief here.

She wanted nothing more than to reach Elysia, her home. Only there could she greatly loosen his chains, giving him enough freedom to make his life with her bearable. Her mother thought it a useless endeavor. She wanted her to break him, humble his spirit, but she could never do that, not after what they shared in the Mage Bane. Ethan was not who she expected. He was so much more, and she truly admired him. At times, she cursed her duty and destiny, which forced her to betray him. Touching a hand to her womb reminded her that there was more to her destiny than slavish duty forcing her to do things she would rather not. Their unborn daughter was worth all the things she had to do, and if she had to choose between Ethan's friendship and their daughter's existence, it was an easy choice. That didn't mean she couldn't help him, however, and once they were into the Gorgencian countryside in the coming days, she would allow Sergeant Jordain to take him exploring whenever they set camp.

"To our honored guests, Her Most Royal Highness, Queen Valera, and her daughter, the Crown Princess Alesha," Duke Vorhenz declared, lifting his goblet high into the air, as he stood from his chair, sitting Valera's other side, at the high table's center.

"To Queen Valera and Princess Alesha!" The gathered host saluted, lifting their goblets into the air.

Valera observed the Gorgencians seated below bemusedly. They were saluting her victory over Ethan more so than anything else. She could read the relief in their minds, that they would never have to contend with the troublesome son of Bronus Blagen. They looked upon him gleefully, thinking his new life would be one of humiliation and bondage. *They think themselves his superiors now*, she marveled at their stupidity. *The meanest of my slaves is higher than these fools.*

Valera lifted her goblet, regarding the meager assemblage with false interest, before sipping her wine. She thought to address them but found them little worth her time while taking mild delight in Ethan's misery. She regarded him out of the corner of her eye, two places to her right, seated uncomfortably between Alesha and Leora. This would be the first of many official feasts on their long journey to Elysia. His father was remiss to excuse the boy from so many functions of state. He was terribly unrefined in the protocols of a royal court, or he simply didn't care. This task would have been far easier if she could have raised Ethanos herself, molding him into a proper consort. Though he already fulfilled his primary function of siring her future heir, her mother insisted he held some greater purpose, thus burdening her with correcting his insufferable behavior.

Ethan resigned himself to making the best of his situation. There was little for him to do but sit and eat and smile like an idiot, as was expected of a royal consort. He emptied his goblet, gulping it down without stopping, before setting it firmly on the table. A serving girl hurried to his side, refilling it as was expected of her. Palace table servants were ever charged with never leaving a guest's cup empty. The girl looked no older than twelve years, with homely features. Gorgencian nobles were renowned for filling their halls with fetching servant girls of proper age. This girl was obviously selected to appease Queen Valera. Nothing offended most women more than seeing men ogling their servants with lustful stares. The girl filled his goblet with downcast eyes, holding a pitcher far too large for one so small. She wore a gray coarse wool dress, and a steel collar gracing her neck, marking her a slave, her tired shoulders and hunched back reflecting her broken spirit. Her plight enraged Ethan. He wondered how anyone could treat a child so callously. She bobbed a curtsy and withdrew to the end of the table, where she waited to attend to the next guest.

Alesha did not require magic to read Ethan's thoughts. Had the incident happened a fortnight past, she well knew his course of action. He'd have snatched the girl and carried her to freedom, after breaking her master's neck. He always sought to help the downtrodden, despising injustice, and especially bullies. This, coupled with his fondness for children, challenged his restraint. That he was not allowed to vent his fury only fueled his resentment of her. Alesha sighed, taking no joy in his frustration. She hated seeing him in such a state, longing to return to her native Vellesia and share the wonders of her home with him, to let him see for himself how her people were cared for. No child was born a slave in Vellesia, for the queens of old forbade such vile practices, reserving that designation for debtors, criminals, and prisoners of war. A child could only be enslaved if it fell within one of those parameters.

Alesha again placed her right hand over his left, tempting to calm his ire. He stiffened at her touch, reminding her of their broken trust. Would he ever tire of hating her? Perhaps, or perhaps not, but she knew she had little choice in the matter. She always planned to wed him since she was a child, and her mother's prophecies demanded that it be so. She often thought of little else, consumed with the fulfillment of their shared destiny, and whatever means were required to fulfill that end. But then she met Ethan, and her heart was filled with other longings, other dreams, other…possibilities. How tempted she was before the Queen's Ball in Astaris to forsake her throne and follow him wherever he led. The cravings for mage power, which ran so strongly through her veins, were dulled by her love for him. Never had a Vellesian princess forsaken the throne for the love of her mate. What was different with Ethan? Why did she long for more than his mere obedience? She was prepared to throw all she had labored for, to the wind, and flee Astaris with him.

Alas, fate was a cruel mistress, dangling fanciful possibilities before our eyes, then taking them away. All she truly wanted at that eternal moment was a life with Ethan, far from royal courts and false flatteries, just the two of them and their children. She could visit Red Rock and meet the friends that he was so fond of. They could dwell in the Astarian countryside, or in Cordova, building a life for themselves without her mother's interference. But it was all an illusion, her vision proved it to be so. Without her intervention, Ethan would die, and then what hope or joy would she have? Left to his own devices, he would tempt fate once too often, dying beyond the barrier, beyond her means to save him. As she told him that night when they became one flesh, if his hate was the price she must pay to protect him, then she would pay it gladly. Only by following through on her mother's plan to trick him, and bring him back to Vellesia, would he be saved.

She would never allow his father to be slain, but needed him to believe the threat to be true, though her mother held no so compunction in carrying it out, for what else could compel him to obey? In order to make her false threats believable, she had to play the part of a cruel mistress, who would not hesitate to punish him, when all she really wanted was his love. She longed for his friendship. A single kind word from him would be a balm upon her broken heart. Such affection was a luxury she could not suffer, for her sake and his.

She regarded the collar about his neck, hating that her mother demanded he wear it for this occasion, for the Gorgencians amusement. It was another reminder to the hosts of their shared interests, keeping the Gorgencians eyes fixed upon Astaria, and ignoring the true threat of Vellesia. It was a game House Loria played perfectly, pitting kingdom against kingdom, but never allowing any of them to gain dominion over the others. All the while, Vellesia husbands her strength for that one day when her heir would strike out in force, shattering the weakened, disunited kingdoms in one fell strike. Alesha thought it all unnecessary, especially this humiliation of Ethan for the Gorgencians entertainment. She could play with their minds with ease, pitting lords against one another, and the Prince against the king. Her mother, however, wanted a strong Gorgencia to keep Astaria occupied, and thus have little time to plan for the inevitable rise of Vellesia.

"Come here, girl!" Lord Jadiv Galmar, castellan of the fortress, called the slave girl forth to fill his cup. He sat two places to Ethan's right, boasting a prominent forehead and a narrow, clean-shaven jaw, with cruel blue eyes. Ethan thought his face looked like a triangle, a very ugly one at that.

"Yes, my lord," the girl answered, hurrying forth, hoisting the heavy pitcher in her skinny arms, managing well enough, though a few drops fell over its lip.

"Clumsy girl. Be gone with you!" Lord Galmar ordered her back to her place. She took no more than a step when a Gorgencian knight standing below the high table, outstretched his hand, tripping the girl. She fell face first upon the raised platform, the sound of the pitcher breaking echoing off the stone walls.

A chorus of laughter followed, the smirking knight wallowing in the praise of his fellows, while the head steward reprimanded the poor girl for her carelessness.

"Ethan, wait," Alesha softly commanded, touching a hand to his shoulder, before he could rise.

Come here! Alesha whispered, the offending knight ascending the dais as she placed a glamour upon the crowd, none taking notice of the knight until she touched a finger to his forehead.

Strike the duke! she whispered. The glamour lifted as the brash knight approached the duke, reaching out to strike him before the duke's nearest guard struck off his hand.

"What is the meaning of this?" Duke Vorhenz bellowed, rising from his seat, the stricken knight now held by several of his guards, nursing his severed hand, his eyes darting back and forth in a dazed stupor.

"An assassin, no doubt," Valera said, as Alesha manipulated the would-be assailant's memories, memories believing the duke dishonored his mother. Soon, the pitiful wretch began babbling, accusing the duke falsely, before he was dragged off to the dungeon, his life forfeit. Valera regarded Alesha knowingly, internally shaking her head. Within moments the guests returned to their revelry as if the incident never happened.

"Thank you," Ethan said to her, looking at Alesha the way he used to, if ever so briefly.

"You are welcome, Ethan." She returned his gaze, gifting him the slightest of smiles before calling the head steward to her.

"Princess Alesha, how may I serve you?" the pompous steward asked, bowing his head reverently from the opposite side of the table. He was a nondescript man, with a gaunt, humorless face, wearing a mustard tunic over green hose, with the pointy shoes Ethan found ridiculous.

"Our serving girl, what is her name?" Alesha asked, though fully able to read his pitiful thoughts.

"Kia, Your Highness. I apologize for her clumsiness. She will be sternly dealt with, I promise," the blubbering fool assured her.

"That is not necessary. To whom does she belong?"

"Lord Galmar. As castellan, he owns all the slaves of the palace staff."

"I will speak with him. We have need of another slave attending us on our journey. See that she is properly attired and given to Lady Sarella," Alesha said, pointing out her aunt seated at the end of the table off her right. "She shall assign her, her new duties. My consort shall oversee the transfer."

"Of course, Your Highness." The steward bowed, hurrying off to help the girl to her feet.

"You bought her?" Ethan gave her a look.

"Yes. Her fate is in your hands, Ethan. Should you wish to free her, I suggest you wait until we are safely in Vellesia. Setting her free in Gorgencia will not prevent a second cruel master to replace her collar with another once we are gone."

"Thank you, Alesha." He again smiled.

"Keep smiling like that, and we shall have to retire earlier than I planned from this feast. Now go oversee the transfer of our new charge, but hurry back, for I'll not long suffer your absence."

"Fair enough." He smiled again.

*****

Little Kia was surprised to learn she had been sold, fearing her new master or mistress to be as cruel as her last. The steward dragged her into the outer corridor connecting to the upper apartments of the castle, delivering her to Ethan and Sarella, before hurrying back to his duties. She kept her eyes trained on the floor, her hands shaking from her earlier ordeal, wondering what punishment she must suffer.

"Kia, look at me," Ethan said kindly, squatting before her with his elbows resting on his knees.

"Yes, my lord," she trembled, barely able to look at him.

"None of that lord nonsense. My name is Ethan."

"Ethan?" she asked, wondering if that was what she should call him.

"Yep, just plain ole Ethan."

"Are you a lord or knight?"

"No. I am only a slave, like you," he said, tapping his golden collar, which drew a sigh of disapproval from Sarella, who stood over them, looking on.

"You don't look like a slave," she said.

"He isn't, child." Sarella gave Ethan a disapproving look.

"I'm not?" He shrugged, giving Sarella that stupid innocent look he mastered since he was a child.

"Do not mind his nonsense, child. Ethanos is the consort of our princess. It was his wish and hers to free you from your master. You will wear that collar until we reach Vellesia, where you shall be formally freed, and offered an appropriate apprenticeship. You may thank Ethanos for this, and later, you can thank Princess Alesha," Sarella said.

"Free? You would do this for me? Why?" She asked, her expressive brown eyes melting his heart.

"The knight in there was mean to you. I didn't like that. My mistress didn't like it either. We are going to take you away from here unless you don't want to," he said.

"I'll go. Thank you, my lord."

"Ethan, just call me Ethan." He ruffled her hair.

"Come, Kia. You shall go with Leisa, Princess Alesha's head maid in our entourage." Sarella directed her to Leisa, who waited behind Sarella, with her hands tucked into the billowy sleeves of her dress, who took her in tow, disappearing into the adjoining passageway.

"I'm not too proud to say thank you, Sarella. When I see a child mistreated like that, I…I can't control my anger," he said, stealing a glance at the opposite end of the corridor, which opened to the great hall, preparing to make his return.

"Perhaps, but you are too proud for correction," she reproached, circling him.

"What's that supposed to mean?" He followed her with his eyes, losing her briefly as she passed behind him, emerging at his opposite shoulder.

"You whine like a child with everything asked of you. What happened to your vows of obedience?"

"I am here, aren't I?" he stated the obvious.

"True. You are following the legality of your oaths but not the intent. Before you open your mouth and spit out some childish rebuke, consider this important point, Ethanos. Whether you despise your situation or embrace it, you are still going to Elysia."

"Thanks for stating the obvious," he said.

"I could ask you to mind your tongue but needn't bother. My point, Ethanos, is you are going to Elysia, and you are bound to Alesha. You can do so miserably and lament the loss of your precious freedom, or you can do what Ethanos Blagen has always done and embrace your situation."

"Embrace my situation?" He made a face.

"Yes. Do you truly believe that you were meant to wander the world, living free as you will, righting injustice wherever you found it? To what end?"

"To what end? It's my life, and I should be free to decide its course!"

"You may believe you were doing good when left to your own devices, Ethan, but you are very selfish."

"Selfish? I've spent my life putting things to right wherever I've gone. If you want to see selfish, have a look in a mirror, the whole lot of you. Who are you to judge me? I'm not the one who spent her life spying on me since I was born, manipulating events to suit your own purpose. That was you, Sarella. You and your sister. You are as guilty as the rest of them, and I wear this because of you!" He tapped his collar.

"That ornament will be removed when we depart this region. You can thank your wife for that. She defends you before her mother constantly, and what does she get from you in return? Nothing but vitriol. And when I say you are selfish, you react as a child and ascribe all of us thus. Before you open your mouth, look no further than young Kia, and you will know what I am speaking."

"We freed Kia," he said, wondering what she was talking about.

"No. Alesha freed Kia. All you could do was watch or throw a tantrum. Do you know why she freed her?"

He couldn't answer.

"Because of you. Because you were about to do something foolish, and she stopped you, and then she intervened, punished that cruel man by turning him into a failed assassin, and then freed Kia, all because it made you happy."

"Shouldn't she want to do what is right because it is right and not to make me happy?" He hated how that sounded.

"You have eyes, but they do not see. Do you care to know how many children like Kia are enslaved in this fortress? Or this region? Or this kingdom? Or all of Elaria? The Mage Bane? The Wilds?"

He said nothing.

"More than you could count in a lifetime. And what of Kia's replacement? Shall we free her as well? And if we do, and move along our merry way, another shall be taken to fill that absence, when we are no longer here to stop it. Such is the nature of our world, Ethan. And here you stand in judgment of us, the boy who wishes only to be left alone, freeing everyone he encounters from their cruel bondage, but answer this, how many could you free in a lifetime?"

"Thousands. Tens of thousands, maybe more," he said defiantly.

"A pittance. And what would become of the world after your passing? Oppression, slavery, and war would merely fill the void left in your wake. Your many deeds would be little more than notations in history tombs, forgotten by nearly all. Alesha, however, can bring about lasting change, saving many times your pitiful numbers."

"Then why hasn't she? You Vellesians have more power than all the other kingdoms combined. Nothing is preventing you from invading Gorgencia and setting their slaves free? Or what of the slaves you hold yourselves? I don't see much good you are doing."

"You saw it tonight," she said, looking briefly down the corridor where Kia went.

"You said yourself, that is just one slave."

"Yes, and Alesha is capable of so much more but is not moved to do so of her own desire but to please you. You, Ethan, are a catalyst, the catalyst, that can transform the world."

"How?"

"How? Is it not obvious, you stupid boy? With her!" She pointed toward the opposite end of the corridor, toward the great hall and Alesha. "Don't allow Elysia to change Ethan Blagen. Let Ethan Blagen change Elysia, as he has done everywhere he has ever gone. And in turn, perhaps the good things of Elysia shall change you in some ways. Was this not so in Red Rock? In Cordova? With the light cavalry you trained, who proved their worth at the Velo? All those you encountered were better off for knowing you, Ethan. Do the same for your next adventure and for the woman who loves you, no matter how much she tries to deny it," Sarella said, leaving him to think on her words as he returned to the great hall.

CHAPTER 5

"I must advise against this," Sergeant Jordain cautioned as they stood beside the creek bed, watering their horses. He felt out of place without his armor and warhorse, dressed in brown wool trousers, and leather jerkin, with his long sword riding his left hip.

"Come on, Ander, this will be fun," Ethan said, looking all too comfortable in his buckskins and pistols with his strange-looking hat, his neck free of the accursed collar he complained about for three days after departing the Morow.

"Queen Valera was very clear that we were not to wander far afield, Consort Loria," Ander said futility, his words having little effect in convincing Ethan to turn back.

"Alesha said—"

"Princess Alesha," Ander corrected him.

"Princess Alesha granted me permission to explore the Gorgencian countryside. She didn't mention any limitations."

"Queen Valera…"

"Isn't here. Forgiveness is always easier than permission, Sarge. I learned that lesson at an early age as a son of Bronus Blagen." Ethan smiled.

"I surmise you were a difficult child." Ander snorted.

"Did you just make a joke?" Ethan nearly fell off Bull.

"I do not jest, Consort Loria," Ander said indignantly.

"So you think I was a troublesome child?" Ethan challenged.

Ander attempted to answer but thought better of it.

"I was, actually," Ethan shrugged, recalling the fits of rage he sent his father in. "I once dyed my father's favorite war horse lavender, just before a tourney." He chuckled at the memory.

"Why would you do such a thing? And to the king?" Ander gasped.

"Because children are idiots, and I wasn't an exception." He shrugged, not thinking the affront was that bad.

"The royal children of Vellesia would never act with such disrespect."

"They would if they could, Sarge. Allie was no different from any other child."

"Princess Alesha," Ander corrected him for what seemed the thousandth time.

"Yes, Princess Alesha," Ethan rolled his eyes.

"She serves her house as is expected of her," Ander affirmed.

"Yes, she serves her house very well, even if she has to enslave a friend to do it." Ethan shook his head.

"You are no slave, Ethanos," Ander retorted, weary of this same conversation they had every time they left camp.

"Slaves wear collars."

"You haven't worn one for many days now," Ander pointed out.

"Oh, that's right. It's only for *Special* occasions."

"Would you prefer it to be all the time?"

"Fair enough. But slaves have to go where they're told and do as they're told."

"That describes the duties of everyone," Ander wondered what his point was.

"Everyone else receives compensation for their labor. I don't."

"But you don't do any labor," Ander pointed out.

"That's not what I mean."

"Then what do you mean? You have plenty to eat and fine clothes to wear, and you sleep with the most beautiful woman in the world, who carries your child. Every man would love to be enslaved as you."

Ethan didn't know how to counter that argument.

89

"Beyond this, the princess has given you the liberty to see the countryside and to wear your…outfit that you love."

"Yes, my mistress has been most generous. Let's not waste a moment of freedom talking about it." Ethan clicked his tongue, urging Bull to gallop ahead, with Ander following after. They passed over lush hillsides and open meadows along the west bank of a stream. Ander protested in vain as Ethan angled left, ascending a hillside.

"Consort Loria, I…"

"Sarge, how many times have I asked you not to call me that?" Ethan asked, cringing every time he did so.

"The queen will know if I address you otherwise," he panted, drawing his spirited charger up alongside Bull.

"That's only around others. Take a look around, Sarge. Do you see anyone else?" Ethan waved his left hand in a wide arc across the open valley below, and the sparse countryside stretching to their west. Other than a few trees and a dozen saplings, the rolling hills along either side of the vale were covered in dry, waist-high grass, their brittle stems rippling in the wind like a golden sea.

"Very well…Ethanos, though I must inform the queen of my impropriety."

"Ethan, just Ethan. Besides, I'll speak with Mom on your behalf. She knows what a stinker I am."

"Mom?"

"Oh, I'm sorry, Sarge. The Texans call their spouses' mothers by that appellation. It's less formal than saying mother." Ethan smirked to himself, imagining Valera's reaction if he started referring to her as *mom*.

"I know you don't value my opinion, Ethan, but I would advise against addressing our queen thusly."

"You don't think it's a good idea, huh?"

"No, I do not."

"Hmm, you may be right." Ethan shrugged. If only his father's life wasn't at stake, he could have a lot of fun tormenting his new queen.

They continued for a while, seeing little of note. He wondered if their Gorgencian host didn't provide an escort because this area was mostly barren. He discarded that thought upon seeing an antelope grazing near the stream below.

"That looks tasty," he whispered, easing Bull down the near slope to get a clear shot.

Sergeant Jordain knew to keep still, lest he spook Ethan's game. As a royal guard, he never needed to hunt, with all the meat in Vellesia farm-raised, but he learned much on the subject after spending so much time with Ethan.

The harsh sound of the rifle pained Ander's ears. He would never get used to its awful noise. He wondered why Ethan seemed so unaffected by it. He had to admit that the Earth weapon was quite devastating, especially in Ethan's hands. The Astarian prince tried to teach him to use it, insisting really. He found it rather simple to use but would require endless practice to reach a base level of competency.

Ethan cursed as the buck shifted just as he fired, the bullet striking its midsection. The antelope stumbled briefly, before bounding up the far slope.

"Come on, Sarge. We have some tracking to do."

Off they went, down the near slope, and up the far one. By the time they crested the opposite slope, the beast was nowhere to be found, but Ethan picked up its trail rather quick. Sergeant Jordain simply followed his charge, riding swiftly through the tall grass.

"How are you able to find its blood trail so easily?" he asked.

"It's pretty simple once you get used to it. I learned a lot by making a bunch of mistakes, and I've been hunting since I was about knee-high. Did quite a bit of hunting with ole Judge Donovan. That man's forgotten more about tracking than I'll ever know."

"Yes, he was the magistrate you befriended across the barrier," Ander recalled Ethan's fanciful yarn. He certainly didn't believe any of it but found the tale entertaining. Of course, he had no explanation for Ethan's strange weapons or the magical immunity of the outlaws that took the Princess hostage.

"Sheriff Thorton is a good hunter too, but good luck getting a word out of him. He ain't one for idle chatter," Ethan further explained, reverting to his Texas drawl. Ander noticed Ethan was happiest whenever he recalled his times in Red Rock. Real or not, if it kept him happy, then Ander was more than happy to listen.

They found the antelope dying under a lonely pine, where Ethan mercifully finished it. Before Ander could dismount, Ethan was halfway through gutting the animal.

"I got it, Sarge. You don't want to get your good clothes all bloody." Ethan waved him off, finishing the carcass, before tossing it over his horse as if it were a sack of straw. Ander heard rumors of Ethan's strength and quickly learned the truth of it.

They followed the opposite ridgeline back to camp, able to see a bit more of the countryside. An impressive river valley rested off their left, where they could see spirals of smoke from the chimneys of homesteads spread out along the vale. Some distance south, a sharp ravine cut across the face of the ridgeline, forcing them deeper into the vale. Ethan would rather avoid contact with the Gorgencian people but not at the cost of going leagues out of their way. Finding a narrow path along the west bank of the river, Ander urged Ethan to follow its course, sparing their horses the uneven ground along the ridge. Ethan agreed, not wishing to risk Bull breaking a leg, while fishing an apple from his saddlebag, giving it to his trusty mount.

"You like those, don't you, boy?" Ethan patted Bull's neck. Apples gave Bull terrible gas for some reason, but the palomino liked them, and Ethan liked making him happy, considering the journeys they shared. Thinking of Bull breaking a leg gave Ethan cause for worry. Since Bull came from across the barrier, he was immune to magic, but unlike Ethan, he could not regenerate, and he couldn't be healed, making a broken leg a death sentence.

"Why do you always talk to your horse? He can't answer back, can he?" Ander asked.

"He's my friend, Sarge. He knows what I'm saying."

"Perhaps if you could read his thoughts, but you do not possess such a mage gift." He reasoned.

"You don't need magic to understand love. You should speak to your horse. Let him know that you are his friend," Ethan advised.

"It's a mare."

"Oh." Ethan shrugged, wondering how that escaped his notice. Such things were not easily missed on horses, especially that.

They soon came upon a hamlet of homesteads scattered along either side of the stream. They were little better than thatched huts, constructed with mismatched timbers with small chimneys. They spotted dozens of peasants in the fields stretching along the slopes of the vale. There was little flat land along the stream to exploit, and not enough forest nearby to build sturdier homes, despite a few lonely pines along the river bank. The ground looked difficult to work, and the stream was not navigable, dooming these people to poverty. Judge Donovan once explained the importance of geography, and how it condemned some nations and people to poverty, and others to prosperity.

"It's easier to float things, Ethan, than to move them overland," the judge said one evening, explaining that most of Earth's rivers were not navigable but were useful in irrigation. He spoke of the Yellow River in a far-off land called China and the Ganges in India. Neither was navigable but fed very fertile river valleys that supported a large population doomed to poverty. Wherever rivers were navigable, however, and overlayed arable land, goods could be easily moved along their length, allowing trade and specialization, and wealth formation.

"It wasn't until the railroad went through Kansas that the people there could use timber for construction. It was too expensive before then to move it by wagon. They were forced to use sod for their homes. That's where the term sod buster originated," the judge explained. He went on to explain how the greater Mississippi and its countless navigable tributaries, guaranteed America's prosperity, no matter how much the *fools* in Washington mismanaged the nation. Ethan chuckled at the memory, missing all those nights when Ben and the judge imparted their wisdom on the young deputy.

It was the first home they came upon where Ethan saw a young girl, no older than six years, struggling with a bucket of water near the stream. The bottom of her brown wool skirt was wet, and coarse dark hair fell all around her dirty face. She looked up briefly, startled by their presence, before dropping to her knees.

"Beg pardons, my…my lords," she whimpered, pressing her head to the cold ground.

The sight tore at Ethan's heart. He stepped down from Bull while keeping the elk from slipping off the saddle. He approached the girl, taking a knee in front of her, lifting her head with his hand.

"You don't have to be afraid, miss." He smiled, examining her gaunt face. He thought she might be quite lovely if she were better fed, groomed, and cleaned, but such was the state of the Gorgencian peasantry.

"I…Mother…Mother says we must bow to lords and knights, my…lord."

"I'm not a knight or a lord, miss. My name is Ethan. What's yours?" He smiled easily, trying not to frighten her.

"Cora, my lord. That is my name," she managed to say, though her heart was beating rapidly. Men on horses were never good news, so her mother often said, but Ethan looked friendly and had a nice smile, she thought to herself.

"Cora? That is a pretty name. Now, tell me, Cora, why is a little pretty girl like you, carrying this heavy bucket? It looks way too big for someone your age."

"Momma asked me. She needs help, and I have to help her," she explained with expressive blue eyes that melted him.

"Where's Momma now?"

She pointed up the embankment toward a small cottage, where a woman was threshing grain on a large flat stone. The woman suddenly froze, finally aware of their presence. Even from this distance, they could see her tremble.

"Momma works hard since papa got hurt," little Cora explained.

"How did your papa get hurt?" Ethan asked.

"Fell off our roof." She pointed to the top of the makeshift cottage, where a large rag flapped overtop of some missing slats, a poor attempt to plug a leak.

"Consort Loria!" Sergeant Jordain cautioned as the woman dropped to her knees, a frantic look transfixing her face.

"Yeah, I see her. Go tell her to stand up and that everything is fine while I help Cora with the water."

94

"Consort Loria, that would be improper," he warned.

"Improper?" He made a face.

"A royal consort cannot be seen attending the menial chores of peasants. It reflects poorly upon the House of Loria."

"Sarge, just tell her to stand up, and I'll be right along." Ethan shook his head at the stupidity of it all.

"Very well." He sighed, knowing there was no talking Ethan out of whatever he was about to do.

Ethan grinned, turning his attention back to Cora. "Have you ever ridden a horse before?" he asked, touching a finger to her nose.

She just nodded, her eyes as big as saucers.

"Would you like to? I'll walk right beside you. It will be an adventure," he reassured her, his smile winning her over. He ruffled her hair before picking her up, sitting her in the saddle as he pulled the antelope carcass off, throwing it over his shoulder, picking up the bucket in his free hand.

"Whoa," she said, excited and frightened all at once.

"It's all right, Cora. The horse is named Bull. He's one of my best friends. You can pet him along his neck. He likes that," he coaxed her along as they walked back to her home.

"Cora!" Her mother greeted nervously, her frightened blue eyes drifting between Ethan and her daughter. "My lord." She curtsied, uncertain of Ethan's station. He was dressed rather strangely, his garb primitive but unique. He carried himself with confidence, meaning he was no peasant. At first, she would've thought him the other man's servant by their attire, but the way the older man regarded him proved otherwise.

"Sorry I frightened you, ma'am." Ethan lifted his Stetson, paying her his respect, before setting the bucket down.

Ander was dumbstruck by Ethan's deference toward the peasant woman. Was this the same irreverent boy that insulted the royal houses of Elaria with impunity? It made little sense.

"I am well, my lord." She curtsied again. The poor woman looked far older than her years, her dark hair graying sooner than it should, probably from her labors and diet. Her face was as gaunt as

Cora's, with heavy lines around her eyes. Her dress was little more than sackcloth, its coarse wool chaffing her skin.

"Just Ethan, Ma'am. I'm no lord or knight. Just plain ole Ethan," he said, dropping the antelope carcass on the ground before helping Cora down.

"Ethan," the woman tested his name, though sensed he was more than what he claimed.

"Sorry again for scaring you, ma'am. I know I would be concerned in your place if some strangers accosted my daughter. We just saw poor Cora carrying this heavy bucket and thought she needed some help."

"That is kind of you, sir." She bobbed another curtsy, obviously uncomfortable with their presence.

Under different circumstances, Ethan would oblige her and move on, but even a blind man could see the sorry state this poor woman was in. Her roof was leaking. She was still threshing grain from her harvest when it should already be done and stored for winter. She had no barn for storage or livestock, only a small shanty beside her home to place her harvest. No animals meant they had to plant their crops by hand. A steel plow and team of oxen would do wonders for this poor family, but steel was not available in such quantities in this world. *Where's Andrew Carnegie when you need him,* he thought of the American steel tycoon whose mass production techniques revolutionized the steel industry, making steel cheap and plentiful.

"Cora says your husband fell fixing your roof," Ethan said, the woman giving her daughter a wary look, concerned that he knew she was alone.

"He is inside." She sighed.

"Papa's back is hurt real bad, Ethan. He can't move his legs no more," Cora said sadly.

"He's alive?" Ethan thought he had died by the way Cora first spoke of him.

"He lives but not well." The woman sighed.

"Might I see him?" Ethan asked. He knew this made her even more uncomfortable, but he had to ask. "Please, ma'am, it's very important."

"Very well," she relented, more out of fear than want.

He was greeted by a foul stench entering the pitiful shelter. The home was only four walls with a chimney on the far wall. A small table was off his right and a straw bed his left. He found her husband in the middle of the dirt floor, laying on a gray woolen blanket, wearing naught but a long tunic, his head resting upon a pillow. A small girl sat in the corner, holding a straw doll. She looked no older than two years, sharing her mother and sister's dark hair and blue eyes.

"Who...," the man uttered, staring at Ethan with frantic eyes. He looked desperately weak, his pale legs little more than thin sticks peaking below his garment. He was missing his front teeth, slurring his words as he spoke.

"Easy, friend." Ethan put his hands out, palms wide, meaning he meant no harm, before taking a knee beside the man's head. "The name's Ethan, sir. What is yours?"

"Caleb," he whispered, his voice dry.

"Your daughter mentioned that you hurt your back. Can you feel anything below your hips?"

"No." He shook his head weakly.

"How long ago did this happen?" he asked the woman, who stood at the man's feet.

"Two moons ago." She sighed.

"Two moons?" He shook his head, wondering how much suffering the man had endured. His sorry state was a burden on his poor wife. Just cleaning his waste took precious time she could not spare. "And you've been tending the harvest on your own and caring for your home," Ethan marveled at the woman's strength.

"Our son helped finish the harvest but couldn't finish the threshing before our lord took him." She sighed.

"Took him? Why?" Ethan's eyes flashed dangerously. Sergeant Jordain nearly flinched looking at him from the doorway. He had never seen Ethan this angry, not even in Astaris when he discovered the queen's subterfuge.

"After harvest, every household must offer up one member to work in the lord's holdfast throughout the winter," she explained.

"Doesn't your lord know of your husband's injury? And why doesn't he arrange a mage healer to tend him?"

"We are bound to our lord no matter our plight, sir. And a mage healer would never be bothered with landed peasants," she said.

"A lord is responsible for his people. Your state reflects poorly on your lord," he spat.

"Cons…Ethan," Ander warned, knowing it unwise to speak ill of the local nobility. He needed to understand he was no longer a prince of Astaria or even a free man who could do as he pleased. Nobles were not questioned, especially in their homeland.

Ethan backed off, knowing the look Ander gave him. Stirring up trouble with some local twit lord would bring no good to these poor people. Once Ethan was gone, they would be at said lord's mercy. But that didn't mean he couldn't help them in some way, perhaps in a very *big* way if he played his cards right. He chuckled at the thought of playing his cards right, considering his poor poker skills.

"If you care to make a bargain, ma'am, my friend and I just killed an antelope. If you agree to cook it, we will split it with you and repair your roof," Ethan offered. He knew these folks rarely ate meat, their diet consisting of grains and whatever vegetables grew in summer, or fish caught in the stream.

"We…we couldn't accept such generosity, sir. We are forbidden to hunt our lord's game," she said, clearly frightened.

"Well, we caught the game, so that shouldn't be a problem. We had permission to do so. There isn't any law about cooking it, is there?"

"No, sir." She twisted her skirts in her hands.

"Ethan, ma'am, I'm no sir or knight."

"Very well, Ethan. I am Sara. I am certainly no ma'am," she said tiredly.

"Can't help it, Sara. A good friend of mine named Ben Thorton always said to pay the ladies respect. In Texas, they call the women folk ma'am, and I reckon to do the same," he winked, tipping his hat.

Ander scratched his head, never recalling Ethan referring to any of the ladies at court as ma'am.

"Very well, Ethan." She blushed shyly.

"Then let's get started. Rest easy, Caleb," Ethan gently patted the man's chest before whispering in his ear, a message the others couldn't hear.

*****

Ander marveled at how quickly Ethan went about setting things to rights. He skinned the antelope carcass in mere minutes before sending him off to gather kindling for a cook fire.

"*We really must be going, Ethanos. We are expected back at camp,*" Ander pointed out before they began.

"*Aw, they know where we're at Sarge. There's nothing important going on tonight anyway. If you lend me a hand, the sooner we'll be on our way,*" Ethan had said.

Ander simply sighed and shook his head. There was no talking Ethan out of something once he put his mind to it. He thought a more appropriate moniker for Ethan would be Consort Mule, considering his stubborn nature.

Once they set up the spit and carcass, Ethan fished a small box from his saddle pack, lending it to Sara. Inside were a variety of spices for the meat. Sara's eyes bulged from her head, never having seen such a luxury, and here Ethan was offering their use for free. Once he got her sorted out and the fire blazing, he went to work building a ladder to fix the roof. Once again, Ander looked on in wonder as Ethan fished an axe, hammer, and nails from his saddlebags, half expecting him to next pull out a forge and a team of smiths. In no time at all, he found a pine tree near the riverbank and chopped it down. He had to admit, the boy was handy with an axe. He cut the tree up in good fashion, forging a ladder with two long pieces and nailing cross steps along their length. He fashioned the leftover wood into planks, leaned the ladder against the front wall of the home, and went about repairing the roof.

Little Cora stood at the bottom, staring in wonder as Ethan went up and down the ladder. At one point, he took off his Stetson, setting it on her head, giving her a wink with several nails between his lips while carrying more planks in his free hand. The sound of hammering nails echoing along the vale, coupled with the smell of meat cooking, quickly drew attention. Before long, a number of their neighbors appeared, staring curiously at the goings-on. Ethan offered to share his bounty with the interested onlookers if they were willing to thresh Sara's grain. Before long, others appeared, and Ethan put them to work clearing the filth out of the cottage, washing Caleb's clothing and blanket, and bathing the poor man. Despite Sara's best efforts, Caleb suffered bed sores down his back and legs.

No sooner had Ethan finished with the roof, he then set about repairing other parts of the home. The back wall had several loose boards, and the soil footers were thinning along its length, with gaps of sunlight peeking through. He sent several of his new recruits to shovel fresh soil to reinforce the footers. Others used a proxy mix Ethan concocted to fill in the seams where the chimney met the wall. They brought dozens of large flat stones from the river bed, spreading them out over the dirt floor, spreading Ethan's mortar proxy between them.

Poor Ander had long given up trying to coax Ethan back to their own camp. He now found himself busy replacing several rotten boards on the home's front wall. It wasn't long before some of the meat was finished cooking with several of the women folk ferrying sizable portions to those working around the homestead.

"Here, Ethan," little Cora offered him a large slab of meat on a clay plate.

"Why, thanks, Ms. Cora." He smiled, tearing off a piece in his mouth with his right hand while his left hoisted a massive flat stone over his shoulder.

"You're strong," she marveled, her eyes drawn wide.

"It's just a little rock, Cora. These will help your mother with all the dust her floor has been kicking up," he said with his mouth full, wondering why they hadn't thought of it before.

It wasn't long before their activities were discovered by less welcome visitors. A dozen riders in gray chainmail over scarlet tunics and trousers came riding north along the riverbank. Ethan's new workforce immediately scrambled in front of the cottage, dropping to their knees as the armed men rode into their midst.

"What is the meaning of this?" A large boisterous man shouted. He sat tall in the saddle, with a thick black beard and cruel green eyes.

Ander set his hammer down, stepping forth to address the man when Ethan put a hand on his shoulder.

"I got this, Sarge," Ethan said, his words doing little to put Ander's mind at ease.

"How can we help you fellas?" Ethan asked innocently, his right hand resting on his holstered colt, his strange attire making the armed men a mite wary. Though he was dressed like a barbarian, he carried himself with an air of confidence that gave them pause.

"You can *help* us by explaining where you came about the meat you are eating?" The black beard pointed at the roasting spit off Ethan's right.

"Oh, that? That's an antelope I shot earlier. Would you like some?" he offered.

"You shot?" the black beard asked, thinking he meant with an arrow. "Hunting on Lord Moosin's land is forbidden!"

Did he just say Lord Moosin? Ethan snickered to himself. His lord should be more concerned with changing his name than worrying about hunters on his property.

"Sorry, friend, don't know this Lord Moose you're speaking of," Ethan said.

"Lord MOOSIN!" The black beard corrected him, his green eyes now glaring at him, his men spreading out, several taking up position to Ethan's sides.

"However you pronounce it, I never heard of Lord Moose. I was given permission to explore your countryside by Duke Torz Vorhenz. He is the emissary of King Gregor charged with escorting our caravan to Torval, where the king awaits us."

"Duke Vorhenz would never allow anyone to hunt Lord Moosin's lands without informing us. And even if he did, he would never condone you interfering with our peasantry. What business do you have with Lord Moosin's vassals?"

"We were returning from our hunt when we came across Ms. Sara, and her family, only to discover they were in pretty rough shape. Her husband is laid up inside with a broken back, and her son is working her lord's lands, leaving her with a great deal of work. We just couldn't bring ourselves to leave her like this without pitching in and helping her."

"Ms. Sara?" The man sneered, dismissive of the high-born appellation Ethan bestowed upon the miserable peasant.

"You know, it slipped my mind to ask her her surname, so Ms. Sara will do," Ethan added, ignoring the man's derision.

"It will, heh?" The black beard shook his head.

"Sure," Ethan ignored the man's challenge. "She agreed to cook our game, and we helped fix things up a bit. We managed to repair her roof. Sarge here has been hard at work replacing a few rotten boards. A number of the neighbors showed up right before you, and I offered them a share of the food if they helped out. This place is coming along fine. Your lord should be pleased that we restored one of his homesteads to an acceptable state."

"You talk too much. I don't know who you are, but you have broken our lord's law."

"And what law is that?" Ethan tried to hold his temper. He didn't want any trouble. Allie let him go on these little excursions as a *kindness*. If he stirred up any trouble, whether it was his fault or not, she would confine him to camp for the rest of their journey. That was a fate he wouldn't wish on Luke Crawford, let alone himself. Of course, the thought of Luke trapped in camp with Leora Mattiese made him smile. Ethan needed this time away from Queen Valera and her court. Even his time as a prince of Astaria was not as confining. His parents knew when he needed to clear his head, whether it was hunting, chopping wood, or learning some new skill. He always longed to be truly free, beholden to no one, and no one beholden to him. He wondered if Alesha truly understood what she took from him.

Quit your complaining, Ethan, he scolded himself, thinking of the suffering poor Caleb and Sara have endured. If any trouble arose over this, they would suffer the most. At least Alesha cared for him in her own demented way. These people lived under the tyranny of their lord, with no recourse. Whenever a person held unchecked power over another, they eventually abused it, and these people had no means to defend themselves against an unjust lord, their very lives depending fully upon his *mood*.

"The crime is poaching," the black beard said, directing his men to move forward.

"I already told you—"

"SHUT! UP!" the man snarled. "We've been hunting two poachers in this area for weeks now. And here we find you two, and you insult my intelligence with a wild tale that you are part of a Vellesian caravan. The crime is poaching. The punishment is dismemberment. What shall it be? Your hands, your feet, or your eyes?"

So much for diplomacy. Ethan shrugged. He backed a step, trying to put all of them in his view, as those to either side eased their mounts forward. The one off his left shook out a rope, with a noose on the end to lasso him, like he was one of Bill Lawton's ranch hands.

"My good sir." Ander stepped forth, trying to salvage the situation. "I am Sergeant Ander Jordain, of her majesty Queen Valera's royal guards. This man is the royal con—"

"I said shut up! I can see that you are a Vellesian by your dusty skin. That doesn't make you a royal guard," the man sneered at the audacity.

"Get back, Sarge," Ethan snatched him by the collar, pulling him behind him.

"Take them!" the black beard shouted, drawing his sword.

Ethan went for the draw, the sound of his pistol ringing through the air, the bullet shattering the fellow's right hand.

"Agghh!" the black beard screamed, dropping his sword, bone fragments and blood spewing from his ruined hand.

"The next bullet goes in your brain!" Ethan warned, shifting the barrel to the man's head. It was for naught, for the others were already moving. He shifted his aim, shooting the man's good arm in the shoulder as the lasso dropped overhead. Ethan ducked, the rope sliding off his back as he dropped to his knees, with two horses closing from both sides.

Ander rushed to his left, taking a knee, and thrusting his sword outward as the hooves drew nigh, guarding Ethan's flank.

Ethan paled at his friend's gesture. He could heal from any wound, but Ander could not.

This is gonna hurt. Ethan growled, turning his back to those approaching from the right, emptying his colt into the horses approaching Ander, braining the beasts, before a spear tip punched through his chest from behind, driving him to the ground.

Ander's jaw slackened as the horses dropped, throwing their riders into the dirt, one dropping at his feet. Ander spun his sword upside down, driving the blade into the man's breast, his spell-forged blade piercing the fellow's mail. He pulled the blade free as others closed upon them, with the sound of hooves echoing behind him, where Ethan had stood.

"Ander!" Ethan warned.

Ander turned, his heart rising in his throat as a spear drove Ethan into the ground, his pistol falling from his grip. He jumped back as one horse continued straight for him. He jumped clear, parrying the rider's spear as he passed.

Pain shot through Ethan's chest, the spear skewering his right lung. The rider twisted the shaft, the horse's hooves clapping the ground near Ethan's head. Ethan shifted, thrusting his elbow backward, snapping the spear off as he rolled away. The rider's grin soured as Ethan ripped the spear from his chest, before springing to his feet, apparently unharmed, snatching his pistol from the ground, returning it to his holster.

"How…" The rider gasped as Ethan ran to Ander's side, snatching the sword from the man his friend had slain, having left his father's sword back in their camp.

Ethan darted left and right, cutting the legs out from under another horse, jumping upon its back as its rider tumbled over its head, before springing onto the back of another. Ethan shoved that rider to the ground with his free hand, commandeering his mount. Ander shifted around the fallen horses, using them to shield himself from the other mounts shifting all around them. He caught sight of Ethan knocking another from the saddle, his blade spinning in his hand, cutting and slashing with abandon, men and horses giving way to panic, fleeing his sword. The black-bearded man fixed his eyes upon Ethan's mount, focusing his magic upon the beast's mind, planning to cause the beast to throw its rider.

Nothing.

The black beard grunted his frustration as if his magic hit a blank wall surrounding the beast. His eyes drew wide as Ethan turned toward him, his horse running at full gallop.

"No...," the black beard cried out, unable to move with both arms crippled, sitting helpless in the saddle as Ethan drew near, his blue eyes staring into his own.

Ethan rode past, kicking the man from the saddle, sending him to the dirt. He circled about, springing from his mount, his sword in hand, towering over the fellow, who looked up in disbelief, wondering who this man truly was. Ethan grabbed him by the throat, lifting him into the air with his left arm, the man's right arm striking his elbow.

"Tell me why I shouldn't kill you right now?" Ethan spat, his tight grip preventing the man from answering. He tossed him to the ground as if he were a child.

"You...you are ma...mage born," the black beard coughed, regarding him with newfound respect, and a healthy dose of fear.

"Not quite," Ethan said, spinning the sword in his right hand, before setting it down. Drawing his holstered colt and reloading it.

"Not a mage?" the black beard asked, not believing it.

"I'm far more dangerous than a mage," Ethan gave no more than that, his eyes following the three mounted men still in the fight. They rode a distance away before circling back, deciding among themselves whether to attack Ethan or Ander, before settling on Ethan.

"Idiots." Ethan shook his head as they lumbered forth, leveling their spears as he shrugged, raising his pistol, catching sight of Ander rushing to his defense. He didn't want that. His guardian couldn't heal himself like he could, and any mortal wounds might kill him before they could get him to a mage healer. Even though Ander demonstrated impressive sword handling, he didn't like his chances against charging horses. Ethan didn't hurry his first shot, training his sights on the lead horse, knowing it wasn't the ideal use for a pistol, but his rifle was unfortunately on Bull's back, and Bull's leads were tied off on the other side of the cottage.

The horse's skull grew large in his sights when it suddenly reared into the air.

What? Ethan made a face, as all three horses threw their riders, rearing into the air as if running into an invisible wall, rising so far into the air nearly throwing them on their backs. Ethan's gaze swept the area as he lowered his pistol. The thrown riders lie dazed on the ground. They were lucky to be alive. Several others still afoot, dropped to their knees, raising their hands in surrender. The black-bearded ruffian who started all this mess was looking behind Ethan with ever greater apprehension if that was possible. Ethan wasn't sure he wanted to know but turned around anyway.

There, astride her horse, was Queen Valera, with her right hand outstretched, having thrown a kinetic punch of some sort that knocked the three horses back. Alesha drew alongside her, with dozens of royal guards fanning out around them. Both of them were dressed in black leather tunics and trousers, with silver mail and helms. Ethan released a heavy breath as they stared back at him.

Crap, he thought sourly, knowing this wasn't going to end well as Ander stepped to his side, taking a knee with his head bowed in deep reverence.

*****

The Vellesian royal guards quickly went about setting things to right, gathering the wounded Gorgencian warriors for Valera to heal. Ironically, none were slain, though some were near death. They collected the peasants in front of the cottage, where they knelt, fearful of what might become of them. The Gorgencian warriors were disarmed and placed further afield from the peasants. They knelt shame-faced as Duke Vorhenz berated them as an emissary from their King.

"It never takes you long to find trouble," Alesha said, stepping around him, inspecting him for damage.

"This wasn't my fault," Ethan said, turning to face her as she lingered at his back, touching a finger to the hole punched through his shirt.

"What happened here?" she asked in a dangerous tone as he turned to face her, causing her hand to fall. He found it irritating how she was inspecting him.

"Just an accident." He shrugged as she discovered the other hole on his chest, that aligned with the one in his back.

"Don't lie to me, Ethan. You're not very good at it. Sergeant Jordain!" She called Ander forth where he stood a few paces off.

"Highness." He bowed, stepping forth.

"What happened here?" she asked, pointing out the damage to Ethan's shirt.

Ander began to answer when she put a finger to his lips, having already read his thoughts.

"Remain here, both of you," she commanded so coldly as to send a chill down Ethan's spine.

"Allie, wait," he called after her as she strode toward Duke Vorhenz, ignoring his plea.

"No, Consort Loria," Ander put a hand on his shoulder, stopping him from following her.

"What is she going to do?" he asked, shrugging off Ander's grip.

"Her duty," he said, handing him his Stetson that he dropped in the battle.

Alesha stormed over to the Gorgencian warriors, pointing out the one that drove his spear through Ethan's back, to the duke, explaining what he had done.

"My apologies, Highness, I didn't...," the man pleaded, his hands going to his throat as Valera stilled his voice.

"You assaulted and attempted to murder a member of the Vellesian royal family. Stand!" Duke Vorhenz ordered the man to his feet. "He is yours to do with as you please, Queen Valera," Torz stepped back, waving an open hand toward the soldier in question.

"Thank you, Duke," Valera said, outstretching her hand, levitating the soldier into the air, drawing him away from the others. A burst of fire emitted from her other hand, engulfing him in flames. Silent screams issued from his throat, his burning corpse floating in midair. The peasants and Gorgencians stared in horrific wonder at Valera's immense power.

Alesha walked back to Ethan as the soldier's corpse dropped to the ground, his flesh charred beyond recognition.

"Allie, you didn't have..."

"He touched you, Ethan. He meant to kill you. You are my husband, an extension of my own flesh. Anyone raising a hand against you is to be punished by death." She caressed his cheek with her right hand, her golden eyes staring into his sea blue.

"I can heal myself. You didn't have to kill him."

"If you care for others not to suffer as he did, then be mindful of the consequences of your actions. Had you not come to help these people, the soldier would still be alive," she reminded him.

"Sarge, can you give us a moment?" Ethan asked, drawing Alesha away. She nodded to Ander, acquiescing to Ethan's request.

"What is it you wish to say?" She lifted a brow after Ander bowed and withdrew to fetch their horses.

"I can handle myself. I wasn't in any danger. Not by that bunch anyway."

"You're not invincible, Ethan. Don't let your pride give you a false sense of security. There might be a wound you cannot heal from, and we dare not test those limits. And in case you have forgotten, your life is *mine*!" she said in a deathly whisper. "The soldier's death is a warning to any that would try to take you from me."

"Allie, I…"

"Enough! Gather your things and your horse and prepare to leave. I needn't remind you of the consequences of your actions for this mess. You will be confined to camp for the duration of our journey. Am I understood?"

"There is…"

"Am I understood?"

"Yes." He sighed angrily.

"Check your anger, Ethan. It serves you poorly. If you don't like me treating you as a child, then don't behave as one."

"That means a lot coming from you," he growled.

"Ethan!" Her eyes narrowed severely.

"Check my anger? What about yours? Since we left Astaris, you've spent half the time furious with me."

"Furious? You think I've been furious with you?" She took a bold step toward him. "Woe is the day that you ever see me truly angry at you."

He swallowed his pride and backed away, knowing this was a battle he couldn't win. Then he remembered what brought him to this place, to begin with…little Cora and her family, a family he could only help a little, but Allie could help a whole lot.

"Alesha." He sighed, his eyes looking softly into hers. "I am sorry for…this." He waved a hand around their surroundings.

"If you are truly sorry, you will learn from your mistakes," she said guardedly.

"I…I didn't start all this to cause trouble. I was just trying to help…"

"Help Cora and her family, I know, I read Sergeant Jordain's thoughts."

"Well, if you know, then could you…"

"Could I what, Ethan?" she asked, knowing what he was going to say, but wanting him to speak it.

"Cora's father is laid up in their home with a broken back. Their poor mother is killing herself caring for him, their children, and working the land. Could you help him?"

"Are you asking me to help him, or asking if I can?"

"Will you help him?"

"Gather your things and wait with Sergeant Jordain," she said before turning around and walking toward the cottage.

*****

Caleb winced, his aching back granting him little respite, despite the attention the others had given him. He knew there was trouble outside but couldn't move to investigate. He could only lie still like the invalid he was. His eyes were suddenly drawn to the doorway when the most beautiful woman he had ever seen entered therein. His eyes drew wide as saucers as she stood over him as if her piercing golden eyes could see into his soul.

"You are a healer." He gasped.

Alesha lifted a curious brow, reading his thoughts.

"Ethan told you I might come," she said, kneeling at his side, touching his forehead, before brushing a stray hair out of his eyes. If this poor peasant could grow his hair out, why couldn't Ethan? That thought miffed her.

"He said…," he began before she finished for him.

"That the most beautiful woman in the world could heal you, and he might be able to arrange it," she smiled inwardly at his flattery.

"If you are the healer he spoke of, then he was not lying, my lady." He couldn't stop staring at her. She was the loveliest woman he had ever seen.

"Be careful, Caleb, for I know your thoughts." She smiled warningly as other thoughts entered his mind.

"My apologies, my lady," he said red-faced, lowering his eyes shamefully.

"You are a man, Caleb. If every man apologized for their lustful thoughts, they wouldn't have time for anything else. Now be still," she commanded, touching a finger to his forehead, a burst of orange glow bathing his flesh in an ethereal light.

"M-My lady," he gasped as she withdrew her hand. It was over in a blink of an eye. Having never seen a mage healer, Caleb would not fully understand the immense power Alesha possessed, healing him with so little effort. Most mage healers were severely drained after healing smaller wounds than Caleb suffered. She restored him completely with a touch of her finger. He smiled, feeling his toes wiggle. He sat bolt upright, joy spreading across his formerly weathered face, her touch repairing the damage the sun had wrought.

He opened his mouth to speak but stopped as his tongue moved along his restored teeth.

"You are healed, Caleb. Be mindful of the gift I have given you, for I shall not be around to fix you a second time," she warned.

"My lady." He knelt.

She was a princess, not a lady, but felt no sense in raising the issue. She frowned as his gratitude transformed into uncontrollable affection, images of her beauty flashing through his mind. She recalled the time before she revealed her true self to Ethan at the queen's ball. She masked her beauty to everyone but Ethan, lest she draw undo attention to herself. That would've hindered her interaction with Ethan and spoiled her plans. She often masked her beauty whenever she grew weary of the lecherous thoughts that flooded the brains of nearly every male she ever knew, save for those able to shield their minds from her. It usually didn't bother her, knowing it to be the expected male reaction. But her mother wisely pointed out that once some men gazed upon her beauty that they might never find satisfaction in another. That would not serve the stability of the realm or endear the House of Loria to their female subjects. And so Alesha masked her true self more and more, except in recent days, since leaving Astaris. Perhaps it was petty, but she enjoyed seeing Ethan's reaction to the attention she received from others, a not-so-subtle reminder to him that his wife was truly beautiful and worthy of his adoration.

She gave Caleb one last gift before departing.

"You will forget my face." She touched a finger to his forehead, her magic washing away his memory of her beauty, before casting a shroud of distortion over her countenance and stepping without.

*****

"My gratitude, Queen Valera," the black-bearded Gorgencian groveled at her feet after she restored his hand and shoulder.

"Remember this mercy when treating with your lord's subjects. You mistakenly assaulted a child of my house. Your man forfeited his life for driving his spear into my son's back, but you gave the order," she regarded him sternly, looking down into his pathetic eyes.

"My apologies, Queen Valera. I did not know," he blubbered.

She shook her head internally, disgusted by his weakness. He was brave when facing peasants and *supposed* outlaws that his men outnumbered ten to one, but against an even greater power, he crumbled into a spineless knave. She thought to make an example of him, but he was mage born, though a low-born one at that. She could still do so if she wanted, but he was not worth her time. The world was full of mindless brutes. Such men needed a strong master to control their excesses or a strong mistress, she reminded herself. Eventually, Gorgencia would fall under her dominion but not yet. She did find their king and nobles rather easy to manipulate, with their intense hatred for Astaria blinding them to the true threat her queendom posed.

"You are forgiven, Sir Blanchar. Attend your men." She bid him to rise.

"Thank you, Your Grace," he bowed repeatedly while backing away.

She caught sight of Alesha emerging from the peasant's home, her daughter regarding her briefly before walking back to where Ethan and Ander waited with their horses, the brief exchange allowing Alesha to share her thoughts with Valera.

*****

Ethan leaned forward in the saddle, flanked by Alesha and Ander, watching the peasants and Gorgencians disperse. Alesha hadn't said a word since stepping from the cottage, her silence not a good sign.

Nothing good ever comes from a quiet woman. It means she's thinking of ways to make your life difficult. His father once told him when he, Tristan, Kraxen, Krixan, and Dragos sat around a campfire one night. It was one of his fondest memories of his father. The six of them would spend a night hunting in the foothills north of Astaris on occasion. Krixan's father would join them whenever he visited the palace. He, Tristan, and Krixan would listen to the older men's stories or their complaints about their women, who thankfully remained in the palace.

Truer words were never spoken, Dragos seconded his father's opinion.

I'd welcome silence over a wooden spoon against my skull. Kraxen chuckled. Krixan's mother was known to strike her husband whenever he raised her ire.

Ethan wished they were with him now, here for him to share his own stories and complaints with. While he was wallowing in self-pity, he didn't notice little Cora standing at the doorway of the cottage, staring at him with watery eyes. The brave little girl ran toward them, stopping beside Alesha's horse. A guard meant to stop her, but Alesha waved him off.

"Can I help you, Cora?" Alesha smiled at the child. Ethan couldn't tell if it was genuine or not, never truly knowing what she was thinking.

"You are Ethan's friend, my lady?" Cora stared up at her, nervously clutching her skirts.

"Yes, child, I am Ethan's friend." She stretched her smile, her white teeth sparkling with perfection.

"You healed Papa. Thank you, my lady," Cora curtsied deeply, tears pouring from her eyes.

"You are most welcome, Cora. Now run along and mind your mother. There is still much to do to put your farm to rights," Alesha said as Cora waved goodbye to her and Ethan before running back to her home.

"Thank you," Ethan said, breaking the silence between them.

Alesha regarded him briefly. Though she couldn't read his thoughts, they weren't difficult to guess. He truly cared for the plight of these people. There was a kindness to him that most nobles and royals did not have. As much as she wanted to be angry with him, she couldn't, not really. That didn't mean she would let him off easy for placing himself and Ander in the danger she found them in.

"We shall see how grateful you are." She smiled.

*****

It was a long ride back to camp. Alesha and Ander were far up ahead, leaving poor Ethan in Valera's company. The queen ordered him to ride beside her, an order that made his blood run cold, imagining the dressing down she was certain to give him.

"You acted foolishly today, Ethanos," she began, her almond eyes fixed straight ahead as they rode.

"Things didn't go as well as I hoped, my Queen," he said, hating addressing her so reverently.

"When we are alone, Ethanos, you are to call me Mother."

Mother? he thought, making a face.

"Don't give me that look, Ethanos. You are a child of my house and my son by your marriage to Alesha. You are now my child, my son, and therefore you will address me properly when we are alone."

"Very well, M—"

"And don't think of calling me mom," she warned him.

"How did you know I was going to say that...Mother?"

"My dear boy, I do not need magic or clairvoyance to read your mind. You are as predictable as the sunrise."

"You got me there." He shrugged, finding this whole discussion surreal. Was she actually having a real conversation with him?

"Indeed, I do. Right now, you are wondering why I am speaking with you so informally."

"Wow, you are good. But this isn't exactly that informal," he quipped.

"My dear Ethanos, this is as informal as anyone can expect when treating with me."

"That explains a lot." He didn't mean to say out loud but couldn't help himself. He cringed waiting for the blowback. That flippant remark would surely put him in a cage for the duration of their journey. Instead, she just laughed, which was nearly as unsettling.

"Oh, my child." She smiled, looking over at him. "You have much to learn before we reach Elysia. That is why you and I are having this discussion."

"You know, whenever I upset my father, he would voice his displeasure by yelling, screaming, and striking me. But then he would calm down and we would be fine. We usually finished emptying a few kegs in the palace cellar."

"Yes, where your immunity to inebriation helped you to drink your mighty sire under the table. I know all your tricks, Ethanos."

"How'd you know about...never mind." He shook his head, knowing she read someone's mind for that information.

"We have had spies in Astaris long before you ever born and not just Sarella and Selendra. Every detail of your childhood and upbringing was relayed to us in splendid detail, including every little prank and mischievous behavior you practiced with regularity."

That's kind of creepy. He kept that thought to himself. "Well, now you got me." He smiled.

She returned his false smile with one of her own.

"I was wondering, though. The reason you needed me was to pass on my power to Alesha's baby, your heir. Since Alesha is pregnant, why do you still need me?"

"I have asked that of the Queen Mother, and she insisted that you must serve House Loria in perpetuity."

"Why? What good am I to you?"

"You mean what use have I for an ill-mannered boy who is more suited to the wilderness than a royal court? The simple answer is that our prophecies foresee your importance to Vellesia and especially House Loria. For your sake and mine, I advised our Queen Mother to set you free, sending you across the barrier where you could do us no harm, but she refused, reminding me again of your prophetic importance to our house and realm."

Across the barrier, he thought sadly. He would be mortal there but would be with his friends. Red Rock always felt like home. "I'm surprised you suggested it. I thought it was your personal quest to make me miserable?"

"You are referring to the humiliating ceremony in Astaris," she said dryly.

He didn't have to answer that.

"It served two purposes," she continued. "One was for you to formally acknowledge me as your rightful queen and to confirm your bond to Alesha. The second reason was recompense for your rude behavior toward me and the Vellesian throne. A few of the more humiliating touches like the collar were added for my amusement. I believe you have suffered enough for your transgressions. Our little talk here can commence a fresh start if you wish. We need not be enemies, Ethanos."

"We're not exactly friends, either," he shrugged.

"You desire your freedom, the one thing I cannot grant you. That will always place a wall between us, child. In time, you will grow accustomed to the life we have planned for you. In time, you will see that what we will achieve is far more significant than anything you could manifest on your own."

"I thought I did quite well on my own. You can ask the good people of Red Rock or the now free citizens of Cordova what good I accomplished in a short time." He couldn't help refuting her nonsense.

"And if I set you free, where would you go? Back to Red Rock? Cordova? The Mage Bane? Earth and the Mage Bane impair your gifts. Both locations would lead to your death. As reckless as you are, I would give you one year in either place. That leaves Cordova. How long until your free spirit infected the small isle, leading them to war with one or more of their neighboring mage realms? You could simply travel the lands, protecting the peasants you come upon, protecting them for a time. Protecting them from the injustices visited

116

upon them by their masters. Of course, once you moved on, which you would do considering your restless spirit, what would become of them?"

"I—"

"They would suffer their lords' wrath. All because you made them believe they could live free as you do," she cut him off. "Who is crueler, Ethanos, you who fills their hearts with false hope, or we who work for their long-term benefit?"

"You make them contented slaves but slaves all the same. People weren't meant to have all their needs and wants provided by another. People should be free to choose their own path."

"Freedom? Freedom to starve, freedom to suffer? Freedom to murder their neighbor? You speak with such reverence for this concept of freedom but are ignorant of its true nature. Freedom requires individual responsibility. Where has this played out to a positive end? People are inherently unable to manage their affairs without an iron authority keeping them together."

"The Americans do quite fine without such authority," he corrected her.

"Your friends across the barrier," she quipped, unimpressed. "Here, you can have this back." She removed a book from her saddle pack, handing it to him.

Ethan gave her a look as she handed him one of his books on the history of the United States, that Judge Donovan had given him.

"Don't give me that look, Ethanos. It was among your belongings in your tent. I told you before that everything you possess belongs to the throne."

"Including me." He shook his head.

"Including you. Especially you," she affirmed. "I read that book, partly to better understand you and the friends that you idolize."

He wondered how she could read it since it was in English, and she didn't know the language. Then it dawned on him...Allie. She learned the language during her time as Luke's captive. That meant she could learn things as quickly as he could. Of course, she could. It was a gift that he didn't realize was a mage gift that he possessed all along, a gift she inherited as well. Tristan did tell him that House

Loria gathered every mage power, passing them down to their heirs. That meant *every* power, including his. They only lacked his immunity to magic. He recalled that morning in Astaris when he taught her how to shoot, and she picked it up as quickly as he had. That meant she shared his ability to self-heal and his physical strength. The thought they possessed such power made his heart quicken.

"I read the others as well, the ones detailing the Earther's history and scientific achievements. They are quite interesting, but I must question your devotion to a people who seem to commit such cruelty upon each other. Even your precious American friends held other men in bondage and irradicated indigenous peoples."

"No men are perfect, but as far as slavery goes, they went to war with themselves to end it. No people are inherently more moral than others, that is the point, really. The one thing the Americans understand is that power corrupts, and no one person can be trusted with it. Power must be diluted and restrained to protect the individual."

"Interesting," she purred. He expected her to declare his words blasphemy or treasonous, but she simply listened. Was it a trick? Did she actually consider his radical beliefs, or was she merely humoring him?

"They are doing quite well without a monarchy or noble class, just free men and women choosing their own path."

"Yes, but monarchies are the norm for this mageless world, are they not? And your American Republic benefits from the isolation from the other great powers. This allows them to make mistakes that are fatal to other realms. Should one of our mage kingdoms devolve into civil war, the other mage kingdoms would take advantage. Your friends' isolation greatly reduced that possibility. It is also a world without magic. Magic is the foundation of our right to rule. Magic, my son, is the means by which we make this a better world."

"It can be used for the greater good, but from what I've seen, it's simply an instrument of power, forging unbreakable chains for the masses. Because of magic, you can never have a revolution, no matter how oppressive a king or queen becomes, and that, *Mother,* is what makes magic so terrifying."

"Mortal men are often small-minded, abusing their power for petty reasons. Magic should be entrusted to those who respect its potency."

"And I guess that is you." He shook his head.

"It is," she stated flatly, ignoring his sarcasm.

"Wasn't humiliating me in front of my family and countrymen petty?"

"No. I already told you it was recompense for your rudeness. As long as you behave, I see no reason for you to suffer any more indignities. Of course, you are expected to adhere to royal protocol, as befits your station, but as Alesha has told you, we will do our best to shield you from these duties."

"Yeah, I was never much one for kneeling and bowing."

"You were poorly raised," she quipped.

"I was not poorly raised. I was taught to respect my parents and elders, and to protect my siblings and the people of Astaria."

"If you truly respected your sires, you would not have forsaken your birthright."

"I didn't forsake my birthright. I simply earned my freedom from it. There's a difference. I saved my father and Astaria, and all I asked for in return was my freedom." He was tired of explaining this to those who could never understand.

"You cheapened your great deeds by robing your father of his true heir."

"That's not true. My brother will make a better king than I. By stepping away, I forced my father to accept this fact. Tristan is far wiser than I, and it freed me to serve the greater good."

"Greater good?" She regarded him curiously. "Your freedom wasn't for the greater good, child, it simply served a selfish desire to be free of responsibility, free of duty, and free of the authority that truly protects the greater good."

"If it wasn't for my *selfish* choice to be free, I wouldn't have been in Cordova when Alesha was taken by Luke Crawford. She would've died in the Mage Bane if Krixan and I didn't follow them there against my mother's warning. I thought you of all people would appreciate that," Ethan growled. Who was she to judge his choices?

"Oh, I appreciate your intervention, Ethanos, and I am thankful that you kept her safe, but that doesn't make your decision to forsake the throne virtuous. If you remained your father's heir, it would have made it far more difficult for us to capture you."

"You mean trick me."

"If you prefer to see it thus. It matters not, really, for you ended up where destiny preordained for you to be all along, a son of House Loria."

"Destiny had nothing to do with it. My father's life is why I'm here. Without the sword you hold at his throat, I would ride out of your camp and never look back."

"Then it serves us well to keep the sword in place."

"And it wasn't destiny that I fell into your hands. My destiny is to be free."

"You are immune to magic, child, thus blind to it as well. House Loria has looked for your coming for a thousand years. Your destiny lies with us. It was always meant to be. You were not born to be free, my son. You were born to serve my house."

"I was born to be free." He couldn't bear listening to any more of this drivel. Who was she to decide his destiny or to call him son?

"I hoped to acquire you when you were a child, but your father refused. It would've been more merciful if I had."

"Merciful? To take a child from its home?" He made a face. The thought of being raised in her household made him ill.

"Yes, merciful. We would have disavowed the foolish notions of freedom and independence that have taken root in your mind. You would have been raised as a dutiful, obedient child, grateful for his place in House Loria. To you, this sounds manipulative and cruel, but the end result would've made you content and happy serving as Alesha's consort."

"If you believe that, then you haven't really learned anything about me," he said, though doubted if he could've resisted their manipulations as a child.

Valera smiled at his prideful defiance, his words not matching his doubt. No child could've resisted her *guidance*, not even one with his unique gifts.

"You needn't let it upset you, child. It was but one possible path your life might have taken. The course of any life contains countless branches one might take. It matters not in your case, for all your branches led to the same conclusion, as a son of House Loria, where your destiny lies."

"I have no destiny, not anymore. You've seen to that."

"You are mistaken, my son. Your destiny lies with Alesha. The greatest part has already been fulfilled. The child she carries will one day rule all of Elaria. She will bring about a golden age of peace and plenty. No peasants will go hungry, or soldiers die in pointless wars. The gifts bestowed upon her through her ancestors will grant her unchallenged power to manifest such change."

"Doesn't it sound dangerous to place such power in the hands of a child? If our daughter wields such power, then what is stopping her from using it against you?"

Valera gave him that knowing smile as if amused by his idiocy, privy to something he overlooked. "There is more to the sacred power of House Loria that you are unaware. Besides our unique power of our firstborn heir inheriting all the mage power of both her sires, our heirs are bound to the ascension of House Loria, bound to obey our mothers. You see, Ethanos, Gabrielle will not only wield unlimited power, but she will enforce her mother's will upon the world."

"Gabrielle?" He made a face.

"Oh, were you not told?" She smiled, knowing full well that he was not. "Alesha promised your mother to name the child in her honor."

Giving the child a name made it all the more real. His heart pounded in his chest, thinking of her. He loved her already but was torn by what evil she might portend. No matter the love he might have for his unborn child, could he doom the world to her tyranny? Perhaps he could whisk her away, raising her with his values, making her an instrument for good rather than evil. The problem was Valera believed her cause just. How can you argue with someone who believes they are right, and you are a fool? Their plan was madness, but how could they believe otherwise when everything has transpired as their prophecies foretold? The short answer was, he couldn't. He was trapped and couldn't see a way out of it.

"There is more to your purpose than siring Alesha's heir, my son, a purpose that will reveal itself in time, as our Queen Mother reassures me. Ride up ahead with Sergeant Jordain. I need to speak with Alesha. I found our conversation enlightening, Ethanos. We must speak again."

"You can speak with me anytime you want. It's not like I'm going anywhere...Mother." He tipped his hat and rode on up ahead, passing Alesha going in the opposite direction. She simply gave him a cold look before passing on, the same look his mother gave him whenever she feared for his life after first expressing concern for his well-being.

To hell with her, he thought miserably. After all the crap she pulled, she didn't have a right to be angry with him. The only problem with that was that she held the power to make his life miserable.

*****

"And?' Alesha asked, her eyes trained on Ethanos, riding several hundred paces ahead.

"We had an interesting conversation. The boy is rather complex on one level and hopelessly simple on another," Valera said, following Alesha's gaze to the source of their discussion.

"Did you learn what you wanted to know, Mother?" she asked guardedly.

"Unfortunately."

Alesha didn't like the sound of that.

"You would think someone so naive on the machinations of court, would be easy to manipulate, but he holds deeply held beliefs that run counter to the foundations of our rule. These beliefs have been strengthened by his experiences, so much so, that we will never convince him of the righteousness of our cause."

"Ethan will honor his vows to serve our house, mother. He is a man of his word," Alesha lifted her chin defiantly.

"You may control him physically, but his mind will always be at war with us."

"His mind will come around, Mother. He is still angry over what transpired in Astaris. He bound himself to us to protect his family, his love for them greater than his desire to be free. We are now his family, and once Gabrielle is born. We will be bound by blood."

"He must be broken." Valera sighed tiredly.

Alesha froze.

"You know this to be true, Alesha. He is too wild. If we raised him from childhood, we could have tamed his wild nature, but now it is too late."

"I will not do that to him," Alesha said coldly.

"Better to do it now than later, but it must be done. You know this. You have always known this. What has changed?" Valera thought it more merciful to send him across the barrier, over breaking him, but Alesha refused that mercy as well, not willing to part with him.

"I..." Alesha paused, unable to put her true thoughts into words. 'Twas a strange affliction for one of her power. "I didn't know him then." Since she was a child, Alesha's mother and grandmothers regaled her with tales of her destiny, of the crown prince of Astaria who would one day be hers, of the heir promised of their union. Ethan was just a name and a destiny bandied about, not someone she actually knew.

"*Is he handsome?*" she once asked her great-grandmother.

"*We are told he is exceptionally attractive, my dear,*" Mother Caterina told her one night at her bedside.

"*When can I have him?*" she asked, studying the former Queen Mother's eyes curiously, awaiting her answer.

"*When it is time, child.*" Caterina smiled, brushing a stray hair behind Alesha's ear.

"*How long must I wait?*" Alesha asked impatiently.

"*As long as it takes, Alesha. Perhaps soon, perhaps when you are grown. Be assured, the prophecies are clear that the son of Astaria will one day be yours.*"

"*What if he doesn't like me? What is he refuses to come with us?*"

"Of course, he will like you. You are the most beautiful girl in the world, and boys love beautiful girls. And it matters not if he comes willingly or not, he will come, even if we must break him."

The memory sent a chill down Alesha's spine. It was the first mention of the cruel practice that the queens of Vellesia often used to tame their mates, breaking their spirit. As the years went on, and Ethanos evaded the traps set for him, the Queen Mother spoke increasingly more often of the need to break Ethan once they had him. She, too, thought it a practical course of action considering his willful spirit. Her aunts relayed stories of Ethan whenever they would visit Elysia. They devoted their lives observing the boy and guiding his path when necessary. They would tell her all about the handsome prince who loved to learn new things, whether it was smithcraft, swordsmanship, riding a horse, carpentry, and countless other tasks. He was reportedly very strong and could heal himself as she could, but it was his immunity to magic that thrilled her, the very power her family coveted for thousands of years. None was ever born immune to magic until Ethan. He was the one they waited for since the founding of their house. Though that detail excited her, she savored every detail her aunts provided of him. Her favorite stories were of him helping others, or performing tasks that other noble children found beneath them. She thought it funny, imagining him doing such things. It was completely out of character of who she thought he was. When they relayed tales of his willful nature, and desire for freedom, she grew afraid, and knew her grandmother and great-grandmother were correct in the need to break him.

But then came that fateful day in Cordova when she first set eyes on him, and everything changed. She had a face for the name, and it was far more handsome than she could have dreamed and strangely familiar. Then came her capture by Luke Crawford when Ethan followed her into oblivion to rescue her. She recalled the first words he spoke to her.

"Are you all right, miss?" Ethan asked, squatting in front of her with his elbows on his knees, holding his bowie knife in his right hand after killing one of her captors.

"It's you," she whispered.

"Yeah, it's just me, Ethan..."

Those simple words pierced her soul, forever changing her carefully constructed world.

"You love him," Valera hissed, unable to mask the venom in her voice.

Alesha pursed her lips, sorting her emotions before answering. "Love is merely an amalgamation of attraction, lust and reciprocity, nothing more," she repeated the mantra her mother said time and again to her and Amanda.

"Which perfectly describes your state of mind, daughter. I see the way you look at him, and it has nothing to do with his power." The heirs of House Loria always held an insatiable hunger for mage powers they did not possess, the hunger forcing them to seek out mates with gifts they lacked. Though the gifts would pass onto their daughters, they would never possess it themselves, always looking to their husbands with jealous hearts, hungering for their power knowing they could never have it. The power of House Loria was also its curse, for every heir was consumed with this jealousy, even as each generation grew stronger than the last. Valera came to despise her husband Travin, whose power was immense as a son of House Menau. Looking at Ethan was even worse, the boy's power greater than her own, a power rendering all of hers moot. Did not Alesha hunger for his power? Her daughter seemed oblivious to its implications. She didn't hunger for Ethan's power, she hungered for Ethan himself. Despite the boy's anger, she saw that he was similarly affected, drawn to Alesha like a lovesick fool.

"Madness." Valera shook her head.

"I am not bound by the hunger that consumes you, Mother. Ethan has already passed on his power to our heir, and I see no reason to break him, as you and grandmother repeatedly demand."

"I thought you could not read my thoughts?" Valera growled.

"I never said I couldn't. I only told you that I couldn't manipulate your memories and thoughts as you are a mage regent. Just as we could not manipulate King Bronus to simply give Ethan to us," Alesha said calmly, not revealing that even that was no longer true, as the baby she carried allowed her to ignore all the rules of magic.

It was exhilarating, a mere foreshadowing of the immense power her daughter would wield. Unfortunately, once Gabrielle was born, this power would leave her. Strangely, sharing Gabrielle's power made her feel closer to Ethan, and protective of him in a far deeper way than she could imagine.

"So be it." Valera sighed. "I will leave Ethan's correction to you, as is your right. I only hope you know what you are doing."

"Have faith, Mother. Was it not my machinations that brought him into our keeping?"

"Was it not Ethanos's manipulations that stole Amanda from under our noses? Do not underestimate the boy. One of such power could blindly stumble upon the means of our ruin."

"The prophecy…"

"Is magic as well. And Ethanos could destroy the prophecy whether he intended or not," Valera warned. There was something about Ethan that gnawed at the back of her mind. Finally obtaining him should be a joyous victory, but she couldn't help but feel something was awry. Despite this, she had noticed that her sleep was strangely peaceful as late, growing more restful with every passing day.

"All is well, Mother. For once, put your heart at rest and bask in the glow of your victory."

"He will betray you, so the visions have shown," Valera finally declared, reminding her of Alesha's own vision that haunted her. It was a vision shared by every member of Alesha's father's house, their gifts of prophecy and foresight far beyond House Loria's ability. 'Twas a fact that irked Valera and her mother to no end, this immense power that Alesha possessed and they did not.

"The vision is gone." Alesha sighed. The vision, a minor prophecy as her aunt would explain, was vivid in detail, revealing everything but Ethan's visage, which was a blank silhouette in her memory. The vision depicted Ethan betraying her, though she could not see the nature of the betrayal, only that he did so. She never revealed to her mother the vision that accompanied it, the one she could see Ethan's face so clearly. The second dream was after the Mage Bane, where she could recognize his face. After she beheld the vision, Ethan's countenance faded frustratingly from her sight. But now both visions were gone.

"What do you mean it is gone?"

"It is gone."

"Since when?"

"Since Astaris. Since our…physical union."

"And you are only telling me now? You should've spoken of this earlier."

"I thought it might come back, but now I know differently."

"What makes you believe so?"

"Before, the vision was always the same. Now it is either clouded or branching into many possibilities. Many are crowded simultaneously, occupying the same time line, as if Ethan was in many places at once, or others were sharing his power. As far as his betrayal, I cannot see it."

"And you think the future has been changed?"

Alesha shrugged. "Perhaps. Perhaps not. I cannot know."

"Very well. It bears watching, and do not delay telling me of any changes should they appear, Alesha. I do not like you keeping this from me."

If only you knew what I keep from you, Mother, Alesha mused.

"We will be reaching the crossroads of Tal-Kar in a few days, and Torval soon after. Tell Ethanos he is to be on his best behavior and that he is confined to camp for the duration of our journey."

"As you command, Mother." Alesha bowed her head.

CHAPTER 6

Astaris

Bronus swung the axe, splitting the block of wood in one blow, venting his frustration, then tossing the two halves toward Yance, who stacked them. Laris Yance struggled to keep pace with the king, who came here every morning since Ethan was taken away, raising blisters while attacking the wood pile. The first morning the king appeared, he ordered his guards to stay at a distance while tossing his thick fur cloak aside, snatching Yance's axe and getting to work. He didn't say a word until the end of the first morning, simply telling the old woodcutter that he'd see him tomorrow. And so it went, with the king rising at dawn to help old Yance chop wood, the two sharing stories about their youth, with Bronus boasting of his drinking prowess, and Yance of his legendary flatulence.

"It was my wife's sister's third wedding," Yance recalled while stacking the pieces Bronus was tossing his way, the pile at his feet growing quicker than he could keep up. The king was no slacker when it came to chopping wood. At least Ethan went at a pace Yance could match.

"Third wedding? What happened to the first two?" Bronus grunted, setting another piece on the chopping stump.

"Well, sire, it happened perchance the first one went missing along the headwaters of the Vecta a few days after their nuptials. Some say a bear got the best of him, others think he drowned. I think he just collected the dowry and headed out for the high country. The second husband couldn't hold his liquor. He drank one too many and fancied himself a bird. Climbed atop the amphitheater in Larose, and jumped off the top, flapping his arms. 'Twas the craziest thing I ever saw." Yance chuckled at the memory.

"You saw it?" Bronus said, his next swing catching most of the way through the wood. He grunted, kicking it free, before flipping it over to finish it.

"Yes, sire, saw the entire thing from the street below."

"Why didn't you stop him?"

"No one could talk him out of anything once his mind was made. It's like my pappie used to say, *sometimes you have to let the bird out of the nest.*"

"Yes, but that bird didn't have any wings." Bronus shook his head.

"No, I guess you're right." Yance scratched his head.

"All right, woodcutter, you were saying something about your wife's sister's third wedding," Bronus said, tossing two more pieces his way.

"Aw yes, lucky number three. Well, as it happened, they served up turlo pudding at the wedding feast. As you may know or not, I dearly love the taste of turlo pudding, but it does leave me a mite gassy, and that wedding was no exception. Didn't take long to clear away the guests and send the bride and groom in opposite directions before my wife struck me about the head with a cooking pan." Yance chuckled.

"The lady folk can be a mite testy. My dearest Gabrielle has awoken me more than once with a bucket of ice water after a night of drinking. I would holler louder than a fox in heat but couldn't stay angry when I looked up at her beautiful face. A good woman will do that to you, make you forget all the trouble they cause you," Bronus split the next one in one swing.

"Aye, sire. I do miss my late wife. She was a good woman." Yance sighed, recalling her lovely face, ignoring the wrinkles that time had painted there before she passed. She would always be as he first saw her, young and beautiful. He remembered telling Ethan about her, talking more about her than anything else. To the boy's credit, he always listened, always making Yance feel as if he was the most interesting man in the world. King Bronus was rougher and loud-spoken, but he could see the similarities with Ethan. Neither was shy to raise a blister or speak his mind.

"Sire, Lord Celembar seeks audience," Captain Clovis of the king's royal guards, declared, stepping from the tree line of the small forest that was set behind the inner palace but within the walls of the outer city. The king kept his guards at a distance, not wishing to be disturbed. He used these mornings to work up sweat and vent his frustrations. Visiting Ethan's old stomping grounds made him feel closer to his son as if a part of him still lingered there.

"Ah, send him forth," Bronus grunted, driving home his next swing, taking satisfaction in the wood splitting. No wonder Ethan enjoyed this, it felt invigorating. Bronus felt like a young man again, working his muscles like in the days of old.

Captain Clovis returned with Lord Celembar, the steward of the inner palace, the man looking aghast at the sight of his king doing manual labor, staring dumbstruck with his hands tucked into the sleeves of his fine robes.

"What ails you, Celembar?" Bronus said, setting another piece on the chopping stump.

"The lords of the great houses are inquiring when they might leave, sire. Or should you have them stay when you plan to call them to council?"

"Bah!" Bronus shouted, driving his ax into the wood, his grunt causing the lord steward to flinch. "Tell them we wait for Tristan and Amanda to return. Then we will hold council."

"As you command, sire," Lord Celembar bowed while remaining in place as if he had something else to say.

"If you have more to say, Celembar, then toss aside your robe and lend a hand. This area is for work," Bronus said, tossing the split pieces to Yance's feet.

"I shall inform the lords, sire." Celembar bowed and withdrew before the king's suggestion became an order.

"He was never one to favor hard work." Bronus shook his head as Celembar disappeared between the trees.

"Perhaps not, sire. He sure dresses pretty, though." Yance chuckled.

"Yes, he certainly does. Looks like some fool thing my queen would have me wear." Bronus snorted, realizing that was something Ethan would say.

They continued working for a little longer, with Bronus helping the old woodcutter finish stacking.

"Tomorrow again, sire?" Yance asked.

"Yes, but I'll see you tonight in the palace tavern. Torg and his fellow smiths shall be there and hundreds of knights and a few prissy lords. You'll fit right in Yance."

"That is most kind of you, sire," Yance bowed, taken aback by the king's invitation. A commoner drinking with his king was unheard of.

"I'll have the kitchens make you some turlo pudding."

*****

Bronus spent the rest of his day with Torg Larios at his smithy, going over their progress. Ethan's once small idea was now a fully manned operation, with Torg's men working dawn to dusk forging toy knights, horses and princesses from the molds Ethan first provided. Bronus soon replaced those molds with ones richer in detail. He recruited Arian and Felicia to organize the ladies of the court to sew outfits for the princess dolls, and ordered Dragos to oversee the painting of the toys. Eventually, he drew nearly everyone into the endeavor, even royal knights were pitching in gathering iron scraps to give to the smithy. Local merchants organized lists of all the children in greater Astaris, by name and gender. Queen Gabrielle was more dumbstruck than opposed to the whole idea, wondering if her kingly husband had gone mad. Soon, even she was drawn into the madness, finding herself sewing a doll's dress, with her ladies in waiting and palace maids gathered around her, joining in.

Bronus already ordered each of his high lords to prepare similar operations in their respective regions. Whenever one would ask why they were doing this, Bronus simply said one word, Ethan. The entire realm knew what Ethan did for them at the Velo, and the sac-rifice he made by bending his knee to Alesha. Had he not done so, Astaria would have been overtaken by its enemies, its people slain or enslaved. What they at first did for his memory, was now enjoyed by all, the idea of making children happy spreading like a contagion through the realm.

Another evening found the king deep in his cups in the palace tavern, surrounded by his knights, guards, Laris Yance, Torg Larios, and dozens of high lords and court officials. Each night was a bois-terous affair, with games, songs, and merriment. Even Dragos and Gabrielle would stop in from time to time.

Ceresta, however, was aghast, trying desperately to curb her father's excesses, the troubles of the realm consuming her waking thoughts. This night found her atop the palace battlements, looking off to the east where her brothers were somewhere beyond the hori-zon. She wanted to be angry at Ethan for leaving them again, but this time, he did so for unselfish reasons.

"You should be abed, Ceresta," Queen Gabrielle's voice drew her from her brooding, stepping to her side upon the causeway.

"Sleep has not been welcoming for many days now, mother."

"You are thinking of Ethan, I suppose," Gabrielle said. It was decided that Ceresta would be the one to visit him once Alesha gave birth as the official envoy of Astaria.

"For once, no. It is Father. He is ignoring the threats to the realm to honor Ethan with a silly gesture. Such folly." Ceresta shook her head.

"Do not mistake kindness with weakness or shortsightedness. Your father is many things, but a fool he is not, nor is he blind, or a blind fool. He knows well the crisis we face."

"It doesn't seem so." Ceresta sighed.

"We can do naught until Amanda returns. She knows her moth-er's plans more than we. I agree with her that Valera will not move against us until Alesha's heir takes the throne. Ethan's bending the knee keeps the magic binding our western neighbors. We need only concern ourselves with Gorgencia for the short term, and they are in no hurry to cross a lightning lord with so many of their own mages dead at the Velo," Gabrielle said.

"There are still other threats—"

"Threats that are not pressing at the moment. Your father needs time to grieve, and I do not begrudge him this. Besides, this business with the children is giving everyone a boost of morale, which is sorely needed, and an act of kindness is never a foolish endeavor."

"I didn't mean to say it was, I just..."

"I know, Ceresta, you are worried for the realm. You may be your father's favorite, but you are more like me than any of my children. It is a burden holding to duty when those around you act more like children than responsible adults. I found it endearing how Ethan caused Bronus such angst growing up, yet Bronus is just like him."

"Father's favorite?" Ceresta questioned that.

"Do not deny it. He always looks to you for answers, over even myself or Dragos. For proof, look no further than who he brought to the Velo with him. Only you."

"Ethan was there."

"Ethan was there by his own accord. Where was he at the outset? Across the barrier and unavailable. It was you that your father trusted most and brought with him to battle."

Gabrielle's words brought a rare smile to Ceresta.

"You are smiling now, and I thought only Ethan could do that." Gabrielle smiled too, smoothing Ceresta's hair behind her ear.

"Ethan only made me smile by doing something stupid or saying something moronic."

"Just like his father," Gabrielle said, causing them both to laugh.

*****

Two days hence

At midday, Astaris was abuzz with the arrival of Kraxen Kraglar and four of his sons, including Krixan. Few men in the realm stood out like the giant patriarch of House Kraglar and his even larger son, Krixan. They were spotted many leagues out when King Bronus sent out the royal cavalry to give them a proper escort. Bronus awaited them in the Great Hall, sitting forward on his throne, eager to see his old friend, and Krixan, who watched over Ethan through all their travels. It was heartening to know that Krixan and Ethan were the best of friends, much like Krixan's father and he were. His only regret was leaving Kraxen behind when he called his banners to war at the Velo, but as commander of the city guard of Vectus, Kraxen was needed at his post.

The Great Hall was filled with hundreds of courtesans, nobles, and mages, each gathering to see the arrival of the king's good friend, as well as the famed Krixan, whose legendary journeys with Ethan were the source of wonder and gossip. Gabrielle joined him, taking her seat on her throne beside him, with Felicia, Arian, and Ceresta standing behind them. Bronus's heart skipped as the herald announced their arrival, ushering them into the Great Hall, Kraxen and his sons towering over the assemblage. Bronus grinned when his eyes met Kraxen, his familiar face bringing back such memories. He wanted nothing more than to bring his comrade into his embrace and invite him to the cellar tavern for a tall tankard of ale and rehash old times.

Bronus's grin faltered as Kraxen and his sons took a knee, formally greeting their king. It was no longer Kraxen's face he saw, but Ethan's, bowing before Alesha and Valera.

No! he shouted in his brain, shaking his head, reliving that horrible scene time and again. It tormented his dreams and now his waking hours, driving him to the brink of madness.

"GET UP!" Bronus shouted, startling the grand assemblage, all eyes riveted to the king, who now stood from the throne.

"Sire?" Kraxen asked, wondering what ailed his friend.

"Get up, Kraxen, and all of you! Especially you, Krixan. You are a free man now, by royal decree, unless you have forgotten. You kneel to no man and no one kneels to you."

"Aye, I remember, my king, but Ethan is gone and I still remain. You are still my king, and I serve Astaria!" Krixan declared, his loyalty bringing a tear to Gabrielle's eyes.

"You are always welcome at my table, boy, now and forever, but you will not kneel. None of you will kneel to me!" Bronus declared, his voice nearly shaking the stone walls. "Not you Kraxen!" He pointed to his friend. "Or you, Lord Jarvo! Or you, Lord Murtado! Or you, Yance!" He called out the old woodcutter who he had invited to all his recent court appearances.

"Sire?" Lord Celembar asked, confused by his strange declaration.

"I have sat this throne for many years now, as every lord and commoner knelt in my presence as if I were a God, paying rightful homage to their king. Such things do not make a king. I never took pleasure in it, and unfortunately, some men do. I spent the better part of the last twenty years berating my son for his hatred of this practice, this foolish protocol to which we religiously adhere. It wasn't until I saw him..." Bronus paused, his emotions overcoming him. "It wasn't until I saw him dropping to his knees to that...woman, that these blind eyes of mine finally saw. He knelt before her, doing the thing he hated most in this life, for me. No more! My son's sacrifice will not go in vain. Let the word go forth, from this day until the breaking of Astaria, no man or woman shall ever kneel to another. No head shall bow or eye lower. Whether peasant, noble, prisoner, or king. Let Astaria be known forever more as the kingdom where *all* men stand!"

The crowd stood there in silence, their eyes looking at one another for a response.

"A salute then, sire!" Kraxen shouted, his deep voice even louder than Bronus. He thrust his fist to his heart, the proud gesture returning the smile to Bronus's broad face.

"Aye, old friend!" Bronus saluted in kind, pounding his fist to his chest.

"To Astaria!" Lord Murtado declared, pounding his fist to his heart, acknowledging his king.

"Astaria," Bronus returned the salute.

"To King Bronus Blagen!" Lord Chartes saluted.

"Aye, Lord Chartes!" Bronus saluted.

"To the king!" old Yance hollered from the back.

"To the king!" others joined in chorus.

"To Ethan!" Krixan finally said, pounding his large fist to his chest.

"To Ethan," Bronus whispered before descending the dais to embrace his friends.

CHAPTER 7

"'Tis a beautiful night," Amanda said, looking at the clear starlit sky through the wavy boughs above. They set camp within a copse of pines, forgoing the settlements to their east for the countryside, placing them many leagues closer to Astaris. She sat on her bedroll, warming her hands toward their cookfire.

"I agree," Tristan said, sitting off her right, his eyes looking at her rather than the sky.

"Tristan Blagen, are you flirting with me?" She playfully reproached, keeping her gaze on the stars above.

"Not very well, by the looks of it." He smiled.

"Hmnn," she mused, continuing to look up, twisting her head slightly to watch a shooting star pass between the swaying pines. She reflected on how her life had recently changed. It seemed ages ago when she suffered her mother's madness, laboring for the ascension of her house. Now she was part of a grand adventure, helping House Blagen against her mother's realm. Her time with Tristan was the happiest in her life. Though most maidens found Ethan the handsomest man in Elaria, she thought of him more as a brother than a romantic interest. Tristan, however, sparked something within, igniting a passion she never felt before. He was charming and witty yet studious and reserved at times. She enjoyed his company, as time seemed to pass so easily in his presence. Here they sat, exposed to the elements, and she couldn't feel more at peace, more alive.

"My father brought Ethan and me here quite often when we were boys, camping under the stars, fishing in the Torlin which rests yonder to our west," Tristan recalled fondly. "I spent most of the nights shivering though, except in high summer. Father always brought extra blankets just for me. I remember one time, I lost Father's favorite knife somewhere on the trail. I was so frightened that he would be angry. Ethan took the blame in my place, suffering his wrath," Tristan said, losing himself in the memory as he stared into the fire.

"You have a wonderful family, Tristan." She smiled, now looking at him with the gentlest smile he had ever seen.

"Thank you. They are all stubborn and strongheaded, but I wouldn't have any other." He leaned back on his bedroll, using his pack for a pillow.

"Yes, you are very fortunate."

"What of you? Surely they were not all so awful?" he asked.

"It's complicated." She sighed. "When my father lived, things were different. He protected us in his special way, drawing all of Mother's madness to himself. He always brought the three of us together, Alesha, Raymar, and I. He said families are to stand by each other, and love each other. Alesha was so kind then. After he died… well, she was different. And so was everyone."

"She was mean to you?"

"Yes and no. She was singularly focused on Ethan, so much so that we were an afterthought, an annoyance, really. Mother was another matter. She could be cruel one moment and loving another, but in a more prideful and protective way, not with the tenderness most mothers possess. Considering my grandmothers are much the same, I can ascribe it to the madness of House Loria, the all-consuming hunger for mage powers they did not possess."

"What of your grandfathers, those on your mother's side? You mentioned two in passing. What of them?"

"Grandfather Darius and great-grandfather Corbin." She smiled fondly. "They are kind but very reserved and quiet. They have spent all their adult lives in the palace, wearing the collars of consorts, their mage powers bound by those foul devices. Their powers have been bound so long that their wives are no longer afflicted by the hunger in their presence. Nor are they affectionate with one another, either.

It is sad, really. When I look into their eyes, I sense their loneliness. I would rather die than live such a loveless existence."

"I could ill imagine." Tristan sighed. "I always knew I would have to wed for the betterment of our House, but as the second son, hoped I might find an agreeable match. Now I know what Ethan felt when he resisted the marriage noose. Without the right one, life would be intolerable."

"Have you considered which you will choose?" she dared ask, regretting the question as soon as it slipped her lips.

He smiled, looking over at her for a painfully long moment. "There is one I am contemplating."

A long silence passed between them before two of their traveling companions stepped into their midst, setting their bedrolls across from them, Xavier Murtado and Vancel Torrent. The two young lords accompanied them to the Morow, along with Captain Marco and a contingent of royal guards.

"When is the wedding, Highness?" Xavier smirked, taking a seat on his bedroll.

"Wedding?" Tristan lifted an unamused brow.

"With the looks you each have been sharing, we cannot be blamed for asking." Xavier smiled as Vancel fumbled around in his pack, looking for something.

Amanda blushed, pretending not to listen while looking at the tree trunk off her left. Tristan tossed a pine cone at Xavier's head, which the young lord failed to dodge, striking him in the chest, which only widened his grin. Only Vancel grunting in frustration distracted them as he continued to search his pack, before opening his right hand, light emitting from its palm, illuminating his pack.

"What are you looking for?" Xavier asked, wincing from the blinding glow.

"I have a bag of jerked meat in here somewhere," the large-built lord said, looking in vain for it.

"You ate that yesterday, don't you remember?" Tristan reminded him.

"Not all of it, I am certain," Vancel grunted before giving up after a few more moments of frustrating search, his hand dimming.

"Is that all you think about is food?" Xavier shook his head.

"We have been riding too fast to eat adequately," Vancel lamented their arduous pace, which limited their food options.

Tristan and Xavier both tossed pine cones at their big friend, both bouncing off his head.

"Must you both act like children," Amanda scolded them before giving Vancel a sympathetic smile. "You are a very gifted light mage, Vancel. It is very useful in the wilds, where we now find ourselves," she complimented him.

"Tell that to my father. He was most disappointed that his eldest was born with such a gift over those more useful to the heir of a great house." Vancel shook his head.

"You're also a shield mage, Vancel. That kept you alive during the fated charge of the noble cavalry at the Velo," Tristan said, recalling the fire mages that decimated the Astarian noble cavalry, killing Lord Luciel.

"Yes, you were very brave that day. Tales of that battle were the talk of court in Elysia for many days when we learned of it," Amanda complimented.

"Light magic is good for a daughter or a cave explorer. Not much use on the battlefield." Vancel shook his head.

"Not when sent into an enemy's eyes," Xavier said.

"Perhaps afoot but ahorse?" Vancel practiced that technique with uneven results.

"Alesha can do that quite well," Amanda said. "And if she can master it, so can you."

"I don't think she would be willing to teach me, Princess," Vancel pointed out the obvious.

"She doesn't have to. Do you know any who has mastered their light casting?" she asked.

"Lord Varo's eldest daughter, Lady Constance. She is very adept with its use," Tristan said.

"And is she still at court?" Amanda asked.

"I believe so. Father said he would keep all the high lords at Astaris until we returned."

"Very good. I will demonstrate what a member of House Menau is capable of." She gave them a knowing smile.

"And what is that, Princess?" Javier asked curiously.

"Transference." Tristan smiled, her reaction proving his guess correct.

"What is transference?" Vancel made a face.

"A very rare gift. One of the mind and uniquely useful. Dragos can do so, but his is very limited and singularly focused on language. If one is powerful enough, they can transfer all sorts of knowledge and skill from one to another," Tristan explained.

"Very good, my Prince." Amanda bowed her head, impressed with his insight.

"Of course, sharing someone's knowledge doesn't give you their physical experience. You must still practice what you are given, building memory within your muscles and reflexes," Tristan said.

"But you can gain their knowledge?" Vancel asked, sitting up straight with the possibilities.

"Yes. Amanda, would you care to demonstrate?" Tristan asked.

"As my prince commands," she flirted shamelessly.

"Xavier is a much better jouster than Vancel. Can you help our large friend out," Tristan directed her toward his friends.

Amanda approached Xavier, touching a hand to his forehead, and another to Vancel. Images and knowledge flooded Vancel's mind, including all the tricks and techniques Xavier had used in all their bouts. The feeling was pure rapture, filling him with overwhelming confidence. When she removed her hands, Xavier felt no worse for the wear, but Vancel sat there with a stupid grin on his face.

"When we reach Astaris tomorrow, I want to meet you on the tourney yard, Xavier." Vancel nudged his friend.

"You'll still lose," Xavier japed.

*****

They entered the gates of Astaris the next afternoon, met by a cohort of the king's royal cavalry outside the city walls. The captain of their escort relayed the king's new decree to Tristan and Amanda, who shared looks of disbelief, before breaking into laughter. Amanda rode proudly at his side as they led their small procession through the city, waving back at the throngs of people emptying into the street to greet them. She was coming to love the people of Astaria and especially her new family. A selfish part of her was glad that things unfolded as they did, or else she would be in Elysia, suffering her mother's failure. Because Ethan failed to free himself, he freed her instead, a gift she could never repay him. She looked up to the northern end of the city, where the great palace rested like an azure mountain rising into the heavens, its many towers jutting like jagged peaks piercing the clouds. It was foreboding and inviting in equal measure, and for now, it was home.

Upon reaching the inner palace, Amanda and Tristan were immediately ushered into the king's private sanctum, where the royal family, Krixan, and his father awaited them. Amanda was again taken aback by their warm reception, especially Tristan's sisters and mother, who embraced her upon entering. Even King Bronus brought her into a fierce hug, which she felt might break her in half, but found endearing.

"All right, out with it, boy!" Bronus began as soon as they exchanged greetings, wanting a full report on the happenings at the border.

"We first met with Ethan at the upper bridge along the Morow," Tristan began.

"Why are they going that far north? That pompous Gregor and his whelp took the direct route across the Oclovar," Bronus asked.

"She will inspect the barrier along the Kieran Divide, perhaps even extract anti-magic from the stones there, if she is able and foolish enough to try," Amanda guessed her mother's intentions.

"Is she touched? That would weaken the barrier. Should Dragons breach the barrier there, they will not be contained in Gorgencia," Dragos's said in alarm.

"More arrogant than touched, but I agree, Lord Mortune," Amanda addressed Dragos properly.

"Simply Dragos, my dear. Lord Mortune makes me sound old," Dragos insisted.

"As you wish, Dragos," she smiled.

"Never mind him. What of Ethan?" Bronus asked.

"He is well, considering his plight," Tristan said as diplomatically as he could.

"Truly, Tristan?" Gabrielle didn't believe it.

"He sends his love, Mother, to everyone, but especially you. He knows it was his choices that led him where he is, including not heeding your warning of the Mage Bane," Tristan said.

"There is more you are not saying, brother," Ceresta crossed her arms, knowing when Tristan was holding back.

"Alesha is with child," Tristan revealed.

"That was quick." Bronus snorted.

"A child?" Gabrielle asked, unsure how to feel about that now.

"That gives us the time frame to go by," Dragos said, doing the math in his head. "Of course, we still don't know at what age her conquest of Elaria shall commence."

"Five years at most, if I were to guess," Amanda said.

"Asking a five-year-old to conquer the world is bit much, don't you think?" Krixan asked.

"Perhaps, but if you knew Alesha at five, you might think differently," Amanda said.

"How does Ethan feel about this news?" Gabrielle asked.

"He is torn. On one hand, he is concerned as we all are, but on the other, he is strangely protective of the child." Tristan sighed, sympathetic to Ethan's dilemma.

"Are they treating him well?" Arian asked.

"As fair as can be expected. They will not harm him as long as he obeys them," Amanda said.

"Did he have anything else to say?" Bronus asked impatiently.

"He said to focus on the dragon he saw in Dragos's vision. That should be our immediate concern," Tristan said.

"Which might be sooner rather than later if Valera interrupts the barrier stones, fool woman," Dragos shook his head.

"But what can we do? Dragons are anti-magic, like Ethan, but larger and more dangerous," Felicia pointed out their problem.

They collectively sighed, stumped with what they should do next.

"What about those?" Kraxen finally spoke up, pointing to his son's twin holstered colts.

"I wonder," Tristan thought aloud.

"Well, spit it out, boy!" Bronus growled impatiently.

"Ethan gifted me a similar set. Krixan, you have a rifle as well," Tristan recalled.

"Aye," the big men affirmed.

"And your horse, that is the one you brought from Red Rock?" Tristan asked.

"Aye," Krixan said.

"And what of Ethan's pack animals he brought with him? Dragos sent them here from Plexus when Ethan left for the Velo," Tristan looked to his father, who simply shrugged, not understanding where he was going with this.

"They are still in the stables," Felicia confessed. She searched each of the beasts when they arrived, looking for anything Jake might have sent along.

"Amanda," Tristan turned to her, as she realized what he was asking.

She reached out with her mind toward the stables, feeling the waves of energy pass around the beasts, blind to everything within several feet of them.

"They are there, the same as Krixan's horse," she affirmed.

"What are you two babbling about?" Bronus growled.

"There is a chance we might defeat a dragon, Father," Tristan wanted to smile but wouldn't risk overpromising with something that was still a theory.

"Tristan, are you certain?" Gabrielle asked.

"We have four pistols and a rifle and several animals immune to magic. If dragon fire is magic…"

"You don't know that," Ceresta warned.

"True, but we can speculate," Tristan said. "Our weapons will not avail us against a dragon, but those from Earth might penetrate their anti-magical protection," Tristan said.

"Maybe hurt them, but their hide is too thick for a pistol or even my Winchester unless we shoot the blasted beast through the eye," Krixan said.

"What if we had more rifles and heavier munitions from across the barrier?" Amanda asked.

"That would help, but only Ethan can open the barrier," Tristan said.

"What of Krixan's horse and the pack animals? They must be able to open it," Felicia said.

"They are immune to magic, but they are not anti-magic. Only Ethan is or the barrier stones, or so we believe," Tristan said.

"I am not certain about the barrier stones. House Menau believes they are forged of something different," Amanda said.

"What makes them believe so?" Gabrielle asked.

"Because House Loria attempted to extract anti-magic before from a barrier stone in one of our northeastern regions. They found nothing and severely weakened its integrity. Dragons have been seen testing it of late."

"Why in the blazes would they do something so stupid?" Bronus snorted.

"Is it not obvious?" Amanda looked knowingly into Bronus's steel-gray eyes. "With enough anti-magic, they might be able to bind a dragon to their will or forge a collar able to bind Ethan's power."

The room fell silent with that grim possibility.

"Since they could not find any anti-magic there, they believe the stones might be forged with a different material strong enough to ward off dragons. Mother, of course, does not believe it, and persists in her quest."

"You said that she only has a handful of anti-magic. How much more would she need to bind a dragon, or bind..." Gabrielle couldn't finish her sentence, not wishing to even contemplate Ethan suffering further humiliation.

"Many times more. You must understand that anti-magic flows through Ethan, to every part of his flesh. Even a dragon might not possess his equal," Amanda said.

"We are focusing on the wrong thing. There is no point in repairing the barrier unless we have access to it, and from what Amanda claims, the likeliest breeches are in Gorgencia and Vellesia. Neither of those realms will allow us near their vulnerabilities. We must focus on dealing with the dragons *when* they cross through the barrier, not *if*," Ceresta rightly pointed out.

"Which brings us back to Tristan's plan, but how do we get more rifles if we can't access the barrier to Red Rock? Only Ethan could open it," Bronus said.

"There is one possibility, though I doubt it is strong enough to open the portal," Dragos said.

"And?" Bronus said impatiently.

"Ethan's stone. Ethan was able to not only open the portal but keep it open for some time after passing through. The stone may not be able to do that, but…" Dragos paused.

"It might open long enough for a single person to pass through." Tristan smiled.

"Two would be better. In fact, two is all we would need," Dragos scratched his chin before rubbing his hands together excited by the possibilities.

"If you're thinking what I think you're thinking, I want a large contingent going this time, not just two," Bronus said.

"I should have no shortage of volunteers," Dragos grinned.

"Aye. And since I'm the only one who knows his way to Red Rock, I'll be leading this expedition," Krixan said, crossing his arms.

"How well do speak their native tongue?" Amada asked.

Krixan's lack of words confirmed her suspicion. When he departed Red Rock, he could hold a conversation with the locals, but it was a constant struggle if they started speaking fast.

"We are fortunate that my sister learned much of their language when taken captive by Luke Crawford. We transferred that knowledge to many of our border and port officials, should they encounter any of Luke's surviving men trying to enter Vellesia. Every member of the royal guards at Elysia and all my kin know much of it as well," Amanda said. She could transfer what she knew to everyone they planned to send through the portal.

146

"I'm going," Felicia said firmly.

"No!" Gabrielle shook her head.

"Mother, let me do my part in all this. None of us are truly safe anywhere with the threats now looming," she pleaded before looking at her father.

Bronus felt his heart torn, imagining his youngest suffering some ill end across the portal, but he saw the desperation in her eyes. His brain was saying no, but his instincts felt differently.

"A *very* large contingent," he repeated his order to Dragos, bringing a smile to Felicia's face.

"Very well," Gabrielle sighed, knowing when the tide was against her.

"It's time I speak with our lords and apprise them of our plans for the Gorgencians. Tristan will attend me and share what he learned from Lord General Brax," Bronus said. "As for the rest of you, you have work to do. And Krixan, if all goes well, you'll see your friends in Red Rock soon."

"Krixan, Ethan told me to give this to you," Tristan handed him the parchment before following his father out the door.

CHAPTER 8

"I've spent a good part of many winters in my grandfather's tower, studying maps of Elaria, and Gorgencia in particular, Sarge," Ethan said, their horses following along an ancient road that had seen little use in recent years by appearances. A barren, uneven terrain rested to either side, stretching to the horizon.

"Go on then, Consort Loria." Ander sighed, knowing Ethan always followed up a comment like that with a question.

"It's just you and me here, Sarge. You can call me Ethan."

"Alone?" Ander gave him a look, pointing out with his gaze the riders to their rear, flanks, and up ahead. Not to mention Queen Valera, Leora Mattiese, and Alesha further ahead, just beyond earshot.

"Well, as alone as we've been in recent days," Ethan pointed out. The nearest rider was at least three horse lengths ahead. Ethan spent the past two days at Alesha's side, never given leave to wander afar since the incident with Sara and Cora.

"If you stopped causing mischief, the queen might loosen your shackles," Ander said, sounding more like Ethan with every passing day.

"She might be angry, but it was worth it to help Caleb and his family. You were doing pretty good work back there, Sarge, fixin' up their place. Maybe someday, Alesha will let us venture on our own. We can travel from village to village in Vellesia, fixin' up cottages and such." Ethan thought it a wonderful idea.

Ander snorted, giving him that look like he had grown a second head.

"You were speaking of maps." Ander redirected him back to his original point.

"Well, I'm no traveling expert, but I know which direction Torval is, and it isn't north, which is where we are headed. Not to mention we left most of the queen's entourage a day ago," Ethan said. It was a day after leaving Caleb's house, their caravan stopped at the crossroads of Tal-Kar, when Valera left most of their people camped beside a grove along the west bank of a stream, before heading straight north. Equally confounding was the blank looks of their Gorgencian escorts, who appeared out of sorts.

"The queen must have a reason for delaying our entering Torval," Ander stated.

"A reason for heading north? You do know what lies ahead, don't you?"

"It matters not. If the queen asks that we accompany her, accompany her we shall," Ander stated firmly.

"And if she told you to jump off a cliff, you'd do that too?"

"Yes," Ander said without pause, which made Ethan wince.

"At least you're loyal. That's probably why she put you with me."

"Undoubtedly, Consort Loria." He smiled proudly.

"I'm not complaining, Sarge. You're starting to grow on me. Just a few weeks of riding with me and I got you telling jokes," Ethan laughed.

"You are a corrupting influence, Consort. I hope our benevolent queen will forgive any lapses in protocol should I falter." Ander sighed.

"Oh, come on, Sarge, Queen Valera is very fond of you. Besides, with me around, all her anger has a singular point of focus. She's probably up ahead telling Alesha that I'm a moron that needs to be punished."

"Which is within her prerogative, Consort Lo—"

"Would you stop calling me that." Ethan hated that appellation.

"That is what you are," Ander pointed out.

"All right, but you don't have to say it with every sentence. One time for each conversation is enough."

"As a sergeant in the royal guards, I would be remiss to conduct myself as you suggest…Consort Loria." Ander hide his smile under a practiced frown.

"Now you're just messing with me, Sarge, hiding behind protocol to keep calling me that, knowing how much I hate it."

"I must confess, it is quite empowering to simply utter a phrase, seeing its effect on you, Consort Loria." Ander couldn't hide his smile any longer.

"You know something, you and Krixan would get along like Bull and a bag of apples." Ethan shook his head.

"Your large friend, how so?" Ander recalled the stories Ethan shared, all of them involving Krixan in some way.

"Like you, Krixan always blamed me for all the trouble I got us into. He also took great pleasure in anything that annoyed me, like my mother making me wear ridiculous outfits for court, or whenever Ben and the judge beat me at poker."

"He sounds like a reasonable fellow."

"He is. He put up with me dragging him all over creation, without killing me, which should count toward his character," Ethan smiled.

"You are fond of him," Ander said.

"He's my best friend, and I never got to say goodbye." Ethan's smile faltered.

"Perhaps you shall meet again one day."

"Only if he comes to Vellesia. My mistress is very insistent that I'll never leave there."

"Your mistress?" Ander scowled at that remark, weary of telling Ethan that he wasn't a slave. "At least you no longer wear your collar."

"For now. Alesha said that I have to wear it for ceremonial purposes, whatever that means."

"There will be numerous galas you are required to attend upon our arrival at Elysia. That is what the crown princess is likely referring."

"Wonderful. It's bad enough I have to wear this getup," he complained, tugging at the collar of the tight silver shirt he was forced to wear, and the matching britches. At least he was afforded his fur cloak to protect him from the biting cold. He still retained his father's sword, his guns and buckskins locked away in the queen's carriage, which was now sitting with the rest of their party leagues south. Being separated from his firearms was even more concerning, considering their direction of travel. The Kieran Divide rested somewhere up ahead, and he could only wonder why Valera was leading them there.

*****

"My queen, the way is blocked," Sir Dougaris reported, the visor of his crimson and gold armor lifted, his heavy war horse shifting below him. Valera easily read his thoughts, the visage of snow and ice piled upon the road ahead vivid in his mind.

"Shall I, Mother?" Alesha asked, sitting her mount beside her, their pathway reduced to a narrow road winding through a winter vale. A gray overcast shrouded the sun, a grim reminder that winter was ever present in these northern regions with higher elevations.

"Remain here, Alesha. I shan't be long," Valera ordered, easing her spirited black mare up ahead.

A short distance beyond the next bend, she was greeted by a wall of snow and ice blocking their way. Her guards held position beside her expectant of what would follow as Valera outstretched a hand, waves of heat bathing the frozen obstacle. Her other hand sent a fierce wind, pushing the melting snow and ice off the side of the road. She removed the heat after opening a large portion of the path before refreezing the soil to firm up the trail. She repeated the process further ahead, removing a second obstacle.

"Bring up the column!" she ordered, pressing on.

*****

Ethan rode beside Leora Mattiese the rest of the climb through the vale. She spoke not a word, ordering him to silence. This was obviously Valera's means to torment him. Of all the women he met in his life, none was as miserable as Valera's chief minister. She would be attractive if she possessed the slightest bit of warmth. Riding beside her felt like riding beside a lizard. If he wasn't in enough trouble already, he'd tell her so, but irritating her was hardly worth it. The road suddenly ended atop the valley, disappearing into an endless open expanse. Tall mountain peaks dotted the horizon to the west and others beyond their line of sight to the east, cradling the vast open land before them, the Kieran Divide.

"Now what are we doing here?" he whispered under his breath, the column coming to an abrupt halt. He saw Valera and Alesha in a heated discussion up ahead and decided to listen in.

"Consort. You are to remain with me!" Leora ordered as Bull trotted up ahead.

"Just having a look, Leora. You never know what danger is lurking in the wilds." He pointed north toward the great unknown.

"Regardless, you are to…," she protested as he rode off, forcing her to follow. She looked forward to the day when the queen gave her leave to whip the insolence from his flesh.

Ethan rode past Duke Vorhenz, the Gorgencian Lord sitting saucer-eyed in his saddle, staring aimlessly in the distance. Several royal guards were further ahead, and three knights, each reacting immediately to his approach.

"Far enough, Consort!" Sir Dougaris warned, leveling his spear.

Let him pass, Rodero, Queen Valera spoke directly into the knight's mind.

"You may pass," Sir Dougaris lifted his spear.

Alesha gave him a disapproving stare as he drew nigh, standing beside her mother, her horse's reins in hand. Standing apart from the rest of the column, who waited patiently behind them.

"Ethan, go back until called for," Alesha commanded, irritated with his presumption.

"The boy can stay. I will hear his counsel," Valera surprisingly belayed Alesha's orders.

"You are most kind, my Queen," Ethan said, wondering how he and Valera found themselves on the same side of anything.

"I have decided to inspect the boundary since our route of travel passes so near. We must ascertain its strength considering the troubling visions you beheld in your grandfather's tower," Valera said all too sweetly.

"The Wilds are dangerous, my Queen. Dragons dwell there, and are drawn to magic, especially magic as powerful as yours," Ethan pointed out, not believing her nonsense about paying a casual visit to this place, as it was so near. It wasn't *that* near, and Valera didn't do anything by mere chance. She planned to come here all along.

"There have been rumors swirling about that the Gorgencian boundary stones have grown weak. A break anywhere along the boundary threatens *all* of Elaria. Are you not worried for your native Astaria, my son?" She gave him that condescending smile he hated so much.

"How do you intend to test its strength? The boundary stones are forged with anti-magic, or so we believe, and nearly all are invisible to the naked eye, hidden by the wizards of old, my Queen," he asked. Unless she entered the barrier, there was no way for her to confirm its power, and that would expose her to the dangers lurking beyond.

"There are ways to locate the stones and test their fortitude if one has the correct combination of mage powers at their disposal, and we have all of them," she said with unnerving certainty.

"I don't know if I'd go tampering with those ancient stones. What if you break them, can you repair them before a dragon makes a snack out of you?"

"Mind your flippant tongue, child, and leave the barrier stones to your betters," Valera warned.

Ethan raised his hands in mock surrender.

With that, Queen Valera lifted into the air, gliding forth across the open expanse of the Kiernan Divide, hovering just above the ground. Lightning erupted from her fingers, striking out northward across the open space. Ethan and Alesha watched as the bolts of electricity swept unbroken in an endless stream, an awesome display of her immense power. Ethan paled staring at the magical strength of the woman, lightning flowing off her fingertips with greater authority than his mighty sire demonstrated at the Velo. A triumphant smile graced Valera's lips, watching as her lightning struck an invisible barrier, the bolts of energy flowing around a nondescript patch of ground.

She eased her lightning, gliding swiftly toward the area in question, before cutting her lightning altogether, circling the ground where her power was nullified. Only the most intense display of mage power could reveal the barrier stone, which must be buried in that patch of ground. She hovered dangerously nigh, her power faltering some distance away. She lowered herself to the ground, sending a telepathic link to her soldiers, ordering them forth with spades and shovels. Her magic wouldn't work here, forcing her to rely on mortal labor.

'Twas a dangerous game she played, attempting to extract anti-magic without significantly compromising the stone's integrity.

"Roar!"

The terrible scream rent the air, driving men to their knees. Valera collapsed to the ground, her body shaking uncontrollably as if torn asunder. Alesha and Ethan winced, hearing inhuman anguish in their brains. Gazing skyward, Ethan caught sight of dark wings drawing close. In the sky flew a dragon, covered in green scales from snout to tail, leathery wings pounding the air below it, dust swirling in its wake. Fierce blue eyes fixed hatefully upon Valera as she lay helpless, gazing up in stupefied horror as its maw opened, flames swirling in the recesses of its throat.

Ethan shoved Alesha to the ground, catching her off guard. Before she could voice her displeasure, he was gone, racing toward her mother.

Valera struggled gaining her feet, stumbling backward where the barrier stone blocked her power. She collected herself, knowing the beast would devour her if she lacked the power to flee. She stepped forward, feeling her magic restored, preparing to lift into the air and speed southward around the barrier, and beyond the dragon's range.

Alas, it was too late, the beast hovering just above her, its mouth drawn widely open, slather dripping from its jowls. She was helpless, caught within the beast's anti-magical aura, much like Ethan's but to a greater scale. She gazed up into its cavernous throat, flames spewing from its recesses. She winced, closing her eyes, feeling the heat of the flames sweeping over her. Strangely, she felt no pain, nor burning.

"Roar!" The dragon's deafening howl pierced her ears. She opened her eyes, finding Ethan standing over her, facing the dragon, its flames funneling around him, shielding her from their scorching fire. The beast hovered in the air, howling as if in pain, its eyes fixed on Ethan, who stood defiantly, wielding his father's sword, the blade alit in otherworldly light.

"Get up, and back away!" Ethan said, keeping his eyes on the beast hovering above, the creature unnerved by his presence.

Valera managed to gain her feet, backing carefully away behind the barrier, her eyes drifting between Ethan and the dragon, the beast's anger strangely waning as she withdrew, its expression changing to strange curiosity as it briefly gazed at Ethan before lifting high into the air and flying off.

Ethan lowered his sword, its mysterious glow dimming as the dragon disappeared into the northern sky, the garbled voice that echoed in his head fading away. He sheathed his sword before turning back to the others, finding Valera and Alesha staring at him.

"You all right?" Ethan asked Valera, stepping south of the boundary where she stood beside Alesha, her armor marred and cape soiled, and half torn from her left shoulder.

They spoke not a word to him, an unsettling quiet passing between them as if seeing Ethan in a new light, with a dangerous mix of awe and trepidation.

CHAPTER 9

It was a quiet ride back to Tal-Kar, where most of their entourage awaited them. Ethan rode behind Valera and Alesha, neither speaking a word to him since the incident with the dragon. The beast obviously upset them, neither having seen one with their own eyes. Dragons were known to attack mage born, drawn to their magic with unrestrained hatred. To know of such things was nothing compared to experiencing them for oneself. Valera meant to extract anti-magic from the barrier stones, just enough to not diminish its potency. Only now could she the folly in such thinking. Ethan wasn't told why she undertook such a risk but could guess. Though neither mother nor daughter spoke, he could tell they were communicating through their thoughts. He could tell they were not entirely pleased with him but were grateful for his intervention, or at least they *should* be grateful.

Idiot, he scolded himself for expecting any sense of gratitude from either of them. It just wasn't in their nature.

He also wondered why he interfered to save her at all. If the dragon ate Valera, it would be one less problem for him to worry about. Then again, Alesha had many grandmothers still living, if what Tristan said was true, any one of which was more powerful than any mage in all of Elaria, including his father. The more he thought about it, the more depressed he became. If there was a way to escape the cage that they had prepared for him, he didn't see it.

He looked off to the west, thinking how wonderful it would be to just ride off into the sunset, disappear into the wilds, and never look back. What would it feel like to wander freely, setting his own course, without the lives of so many he cared for resting on his obedience to Valera and Alesha?

After a while, Alesha rode on ahead, Valera easing her horse's gait, allowing Ethan to ride alongside her. She spoke not a word for what felt like an eternity but was only a few moments. Any moments in her presence felt like eternity, he reminded himself. Ethan was never much for protocol, and certainly never one to suffer painful silence in quiet solitude, so decided to open things up.

"Pretty scenery around here. Kind of reminds me of the New Mexico badlands. I spent many a night there with a posse chasing one of Crawford's friends, a right ornery fella named George Spencer. When we finally found him, it took the better part of a day to root him out and kill him," Ethan began, forgetting to add any of the queen's useless titles.

"Spare me your childish attempts to ingratiate yourself with me, Ethanos. Your homespun tales on the glories of your misadventures across the barrier will not loosen your leash," she said, knowing full well there was nothing *Pretty* about their surroundings.

"That's a little harsh, don't you think? I was just trying to start a friendly conversation with my wife's mother rather than suffer in silence. We don't have to be enemies, you know," he said.

"Enemies?" She gave him a look, a bemused brow lifting over a curious eye. "No ONE has ever spoken so brazenly with me as you. Are you even cognizant of your disrespectful tone?"

"I've always spoken my mind, as Sarella and Selendra probably told you after all those years spying on me. I can shut up if you want, but figured you wanted to talk since you're riding beside me. I'm guessing it has something to do with our big green friend back there." He jerked a thumb over his shoulder.

"Our green friend." She shook her head at his simple description. "You will speak not a word of it to anyone, am I understood, child?" She gave him a dark look.

"If that's what you want, but I'm not the only one who saw it. Most everyone here…" He stopped, realizing Alesha already erased it from their memories… "I won't say a word."

157

"Excellent. As for your timely intervention, I am pleased you have honored your oath of loyalty."

"I gave my word." He sighed, recalling the painful vows of obedience they made him say back in Astaris.

"Yes, you did, but you could've let me die, and no one would be the wiser. The troublesome Valera would no longer trouble you, slain by a crazed dragon because of her own brazen act. And yet Ethanos interceded."

"Like I said, I swore an oath."

"An oath holds great meaning for you, as you once said to Alesha about your oath to Red Rock."

He recalled their conversation in the Mage Bane, discussing his oath as deputy, and why he must uphold it.

"You also made a promise to your mother, and broke it," she mused, weighing his conflicting actions.

"To save Alesha. Would you have preferred me to have kept my promise instead?" He challenged.

"Do not use that flippant tongue with me, child. No, I am obviously pleased you broke your promise to your mother, but it proved you were willing to do so if certain conditions arose."

"Since my father's life depends on my upholding my oath to you, then you have little to fear when it comes to my loyalty, my Queen," he said.

"Fair enough," she conceded.

They continued for a time before something suddenly came to him, an oversight that nearly slipped his mind.

"You know, Your Highness, as I figure it, shouldn't I receive a royal request for saving your life from our green friend back thee?"

"Alesha and I were discussing that very thing, Ethanos." She gave him a knowing look, as if she knew exactly what his next words would be.

"Well, you know what I want, and I think the life of the *great* Queen Valera is at least worth the freedom of one pitiful slave, or consort, for that matter." He shrugged innocently.

"Oh, Ethanos, sometimes your humor is most entertaining. Alesha and I expected you to claim ownership of the royal request in question."

"The request I earned, you mean?" He didn't like the way this was going. Valera had an irritating way of turning any setback in her favor.

"It is not for debate whether you earned a royal request or not, Ethanos, but who is entitled to it. As you are by Vellesian law the property of Alesha, it is she who owns you and all that you possess, including your royal request," she smiled.

"That's not how royal requests are supposed to work."

"Perhaps in Astaria but not in Vellesia."

"We aren't in Vellesia," he said.

"True. Do you care to petition our Gorgencian host?" she asked, knowing King Gregor and Prince Borcose despised him.

"Not particularly."

"I thought not." She lifted her chin proudly.

"You know, I gotta hand it to you, Queen Valera, no matter what I do, you always come up with some way to make sure I lose. It's like playing poker with Sheriff Thorton and the judge." Ethan shook his head.

"In all fairness, Ethanos, House Loria has awaited your birth for more than a thousand years. We have spent countless generations forging your chains. No matter your efforts, you will not slip them, not even for saving my life."

"Other than Alesha's baby, what use am I to you? It seems a great deal of effort just to cage little old me?"

"As I have told you repeatedly, our prophecies are very specific on this. The one born immune to magic *must* be bound to the Vellesian throne for all his days."

"Why? If our daughter is going to be as powerful as you all claim, what good am I?"

"If I knew that answer, Ethanos, I would tell you." She sighed in all honesty, a rare moment of weakness he hadn't seen before.

It was then Ethan realized how truly trapped he was, knowing how committed they were to keeping him caged. Only death would free him, and he might have to wait fifty more years for old age to take him. *No*, he thought. *If I don't find a way to slip their chains soon, all of Elaria will fall under their dominion.*

"As for your royal request, you can speak with Alesha to see how she wishes to spend it," Valera said as Alesha came galloping back from the front of the column, Glynderelle kicking up a small cloud of dust in her wake. Valera turned about, riding off to the rear of the column, leaving the two of them alone.

They rode for a while in silence, Alesha looking over at him from time to time, as if searching for something, but not knowing what. Ethan could tell she was troubled by what happened but could hardly blame anyone but her and Valera. They risked all their lives, including their unborn daughter, just to pilfer a barrier stone.

"All right, spit it out! I know you got something to say, so might as well get it over with," he said.

"You could have died," she gave him an icy glare.

"So could of you. That's why mages shouldn't be loitering near the border."

"It wasn't I that threw herself in front of the dragon. You had no right to risk your life without my consent."

"I did it to save your mother. Would you rather I let her die?"

"Mother knew the risk and knows your importance to our house, which is far more important than her own life."

"That's pretty cold, even for you, Alesha." He shook his head.

"Do you think my love and devotion to my mother is any less than yours to your father and mother? As the future queen of Vellesia, I cannot place sentimental affection above duty. Your life holds greater value than hers for our house and realm. That is a fact, just as our daughter's life holds more value than you or I. Great leaders must make decisions based on logic over emotion. As fond as I am of you, Ethan, you would have made a poor king."

"Fair enough. Next time one of you looks about to die, I'll just watch."

"That's not what I meant." She looked away.

"Then what do you mean? I'm a little confused here, Allie. First, you make me swear to those humiliating oaths back in Astaris, and the first time your mother's life is threatened, you chastise me for helping her. You aren't making much sense."

"My mother knew the risk at the border if a dragon was nearby. As much as her death would grieve me, her greater purpose has been fulfilled, yours has not."

"What purpose has she fulfilled?"

"She has born me. That was her purpose."

"And I have given you a baby. Wasn't that my purpose?"

"Your primary purpose, yes, but there is more."

"Your mother keeps saying the same thing, but can't say what that purpose is."

"Neither can I."

"You can't or you won't?" He didn't believe her.

"I cannot because I know not. As I told you before, our prophecies claim you must be bound to our throne for all time, for a need we cannot foresee."

"Sounds like a good excuse to rob me of my life." He shook his head.

"I am sorry you believe so, Ethan."

"To be truly sorry means to make amends for what you did, and there is only one thing that can do that."

"I am not setting you free, but I can lessen your burden," she said.

"How so?" He wouldn't look a gift horse in the mouth, as Judge Donovan would say.

"Though you deserve punishment for risking your life…"

"Hold on a minute, Allie. I deserve punishment for saving your mother from the dragon, but you receive my reward for saving your mother? That doesn't make any sense!"

"Of course it does. As my consort, your life belongs to me, and by risking it, you risk destroying a life that is mine. By saving my mother, your body is rewarded with a royal request. Since you are mine, so is your reward."

"Unbelievable." He shook his head.

"Do not pout, Ethan. It is unbecoming. Now, as I was saying, though you deserve punishment for risking your life, I intend to ease your burden."

"How?" He might as well take whatever crumb she was willing to cast his way.

"As you are aware, our Gorgencian hosts, their monarch and heir, are looking favorably to your humiliation, looking to see you humbled in their esteemed presence."

"I figured. We didn't really see eye to eye on all that much."

"No, you didn't." She rolled her eyes with that understatement.

"Let me guess, they were looking forward to my kneeling and groveling in their presence and calling me stupid names like Ethan Loria or Consort?" He couldn't help himself.

"Stupid names?" she asked, unamused.

"All right, don't take offense. So are you going to get me out of it or not?"

"Let us say that your presence will be less ostentatious."

"What's that mean?" He pretended not to know.

"Feigning ignorance is unbecoming, Ethan," she reminded him, able to see through his falsehoods.

He shrugged innocently.

"I know all your little tricks, so don't try them with me," she warned.

"Tricks? What tricks?" He gave her that hurt look.

"Right there, that hurt look of yours. You like to play the fool, allowing others to underestimate you, only to catch them by surprise later on. You will find I am aware of such tactics, as are my mother and grandmothers. We know of your deep intelligence and clever cunning."

"Deep intelligence and clever cunning?" He rubbed his chin as if in deep thought. "I like the sound of that. After playing me for the fool back in Astaris, I thought you might give me a moniker like *Ethan the Gullible* or *Consort Dumb Dumb.*"

"Would you prefer *the Devil's Deputy*?" She smiled, recalling the name Crawford's men referred to him.

"I kind of liked that one, so did ole Skeeter."

"So did my grandmother Demetra, when I told her of your adventures across the barrier, taking particular interest in your battle in the streets of Red Rock when you slew bobby Crawford and Hank Grierson."

"She did, huh?" Ethan asked, wondering how many grandmothers Alesha had.

"Yes. All my grandmothers hungered for any information about the wayward Astarian prince since they anticipated your birth for all their lives."

"Hope I didn't disappoint them," he quipped, though actually finding it a little uncomfortable with them being obsessed with him.

"Hardly." She rolled her eyes. Of all the things one could say about Ethan, boring wasn't one of them.

"Let's get back to my reward. You are going to keep me out of sight from Gregor and Prince Moron?"

"Not completely, but their hatred for you will be somewhat dulled."

"I reckon you'll do one of your mind tricks on them. Shouldn't be too difficult considering they're both idiots."

"You might wish to speak respectfully of our host if you wish to escape their attention. And yes, I will help dull their interest in you."

"Wait up, I thought your powers didn't work on kings?" He recalled their inability to sway his father to their will.

"Very good, Ethan, but there are ways to bend the perceptions of the simpleminded," she would not say their child's power removed such impediments to her magic.

They continued, with each recalling the dragon's terrible screams that echoed in their minds during their encounter. Since Alesha erased the dragon from everyone else's memory, they did not know that only the two of them heard it.

CHAPTER 10

Torval

The Gorgencian capital of Torval straddled the confluence of the
Ka-Kelpar and Dor-Par rivers, with thick curtain walls circling the
city for miles, rising two hundred feet into the air, connected by massive turrets nearly sixty feet abreast. From afar, Ethan could see men
lining the battlements, clad in polished steel helms and bright silver
mail, an obvious display of strength for the queen's visit, vainly trying
to impress Valera with Gorgencia's might.

Didn't they learn anything at Astaris? Ethan thought, wondering
how any force of arms could compare to the power Valera and Alesha
wielded.

"Hail, Queen Valera!" Hundreds of people shouted, gathering
along their route of travel, taking a respectful knee as the Vellesian
column passed. The road they traveled was a wide, stone causeway,
meandering the north bank of the Ka-Kelpar, winding through the
lush countryside dotted by peasant homesteads surrounding the
larger palatial estates of the Gorgencian aristocracy. The closer they
drew to Torval, the more impressive these settlements became, with
the richest lands nearest the capital. Ethan noted the stark contrast
of the arid plains straddling the Kieran Divide with the rich greenery of the Torval region. The local peasantry appeared better dressed
than those they encountered throughout their journey, the men clad
in bright-colored tunics and thick hose, and the women in woolen
gowns with touches of lace, a rare luxury for many in their caste.

Ethan regarded the men with sympathy, despising tunics and hose with a passion, favoring trousers and a plain shirt himself. He tugged at the collar of his gray shirt, the garment tighter than he liked, but Alesha insisted he wear with matching trousers and tall black boots. His favored buckskins and weapons were stored away until they departed Gorgencian lands. Valera did not want any incident between Ethan and their host, thus removing his easiest means of causing mischief.

"Stop fidgeting," Alesha said, riding at his side, unable to ignore his obvious discomfort.

"It's just tight," he commented, unable to hide his displeasure.

"There are other outfits I would have preferred." She smiled, recalling the dark pleated kilt and doublet that she first recommended.

"Think I'll stick with this," he said before she changed her mind.

"Come now, Ethan, you would look most fetching riding beside me, attired so," she teased.

"I thought my reward was not drawing undo attention while visiting Torval?"

"Only you think it strange to dress so. I warn you that, as my consort, you will be required to dress in many outfits you consider scandalous in Astaria." She smiled, enjoying seeing him squirm.

"Be careful with that, Allie. There may come a day when our roles are reversed."

"Oh? And what would you have me wear, husband?" she asked, enjoying this playful banter.

"That short tunic you wore in the Mage Bane was the first thing to come to mind," he recalled the brevity of the garment that displayed her legs perfectly.

"Truly?" She smiled lasciviously, remembering her wantonly teasing him throughout their trek to Crepsos.

"Yep. Or I could order you dressed like a dancing girl from Near Polantis." He smiled, recalling the provocatively clad Polantis girls performing in a tavern in Cordova, wearing naught but a strip of silk through a belt low upon their waists and another binding their breasts.

"Interesting." She smiled slightly, entertaining the thought.

"Stinker." He shook his head, unable to embarrass her with his lewd suggestions.

"Yes, I am a stinker, and if you behave yourself during our stay here, one night I might entertain your Polantis dancing girl fantasy."

"Easy boy," Ethan said, with Bull taking that opportune time to snort loudly.

"Be still, Glynderelle, lest you excite Ethan's horse," Alesha stroked her Martel's lush mane, giving Ethan a mischievous look.

Harroom!

Horns sounded from the city walls, heralding their approach, bringing a swift end to their playful exchange. Ethan's eyes went instantly to the city gates ahead, rising forty feet high, with a raised porticus in front of them. To each side of the open gates were massive statues cast in the visage of a cave bear and lion, each the height of ten men standing head to foot. The bear stood to the left, its massive paws raised, standing upon its hind legs, gray fur cast from stone as if rippling in the wind. Sapphires set in the bear's eyes circled a fist-sized onyx stone, projecting a deathly gaze. The lion stood to the right, its large maw drawn open, with fangs cast from ivory, jutting sharply from its mouth, standing upon all four legs as if to pounce. Citrine stones were set in its eyes, circling fist-sized Onyx, giving the beast haunting yellow irises.

"The Gorgencians may be mindless blowhards, but I commend their artistic talents," Ethan commented, gazing up at the towering statues.

"An overly ostentatious display meant to impress their subjects," Alesha dismissed their artistry.

"They look pretty impressive to me." Ethan shrugged.

"Because you have a fondness for animals, my dear husband. Come, Mother beckons," she said, quickening her horse's gait to the head of their column, Ethan following close behind.

Her mother awaited her before the gates of the city, greeted by the governor of Torval and his retinue. The governor was dressed in a red doublet and puffed trousers, sporting a trimmed beard and a thick black mane framing his thin face.

"Oh, great Queen, welcome to Torval, fortress city of Greater Gorgencia, and capital of kings," Governor Ledera greeted her, bowing in the saddle with a sweep of his hand outstretched to his side.

"We are welcomed, Governor Ledera. Duke Vorhenz has been a most gracious host and guide and has delivered us safely into your capable hands," she briefly regarded the duke, sitting her left.

"You are most kind, oh Queen," Duke Vorhenz bowed, passing the Vellesians onto Governor Ledera.

"Lead on, Governor," she ordered, following his procession through the gates of Torval with Alesha at her side.

Ethan trailed them, with Leora Mattiese drawing up beside him, her stern gaze a warning to him to be on his best behavior. He never met a more insufferable woman in all his life than Leora Mattiese, Valera's chief minister and his personal tormentor. Her overall dislike of him was borderline irrational, which was why Valera probably chose her to shadow him. Why couldn't she just keep Ander as his chaperone?

*****

They traversed the wide avenues of Torval, with throngs of people kneeling as they passed, their heads pressed to the ground. Ethan noted the impressive stone edifices lining either side of the street, set far back, surrounded by tended greenery and exotic gardens. Most had pillars lining their fronts and were the palatial estates of lesser nobles and wealthy merchants. Nearly half the people he saw were slaves, dressed in brief tunics with collars adorning their throats. The foul practice was outlawed in Astaria, but thrived here unchecked, especially in the larger cities of Gorgencia, though landed serfs were used in the deeper countryside, like poor Caleb and his family.

The Sarcosans were even worse, their entire peasant class reduced to chattel slavery. If the slaves could lift their faces from the street, he could see the hopeless desperation in their eyes. Ethan wanted nothing more than his freedom to begin setting things right. He knew he couldn't free all of them, but he could save many, and strike a righteous blow to their masters, letting them taste a true sense of fear. No man should live above the consequences of his cruelty. He recalled something ole Judge Donovan once said. *There is no greater sound than slaves striking their chains to rise as free men, or for powerful evil men to hear a brave man say NO!*

"You are brooding again," Alesha said, now riding at his side.

"Just keeping quiet, like you suggested."

"That scowl you're wearing is louder than any shout."

"This better?" He gave her a ridiculous grin.

"For someone who has finally won a measure of my mother's favor, you are trying awfully hard to ruin it," she said.

"Her favor? How could I tell? She does nothing but give me that disgusted look every time she sees me."

"You did save her life, and for that, she is grateful."

"And gives you my reward for doing so." He shook his head.

"Oh, but you are being rewarded. King Gregor and Prince Borcose fully expected to see you humbled in their presence. Now you shall simply blend into your dutiful role as my consort and not be the source of derision they desired."

"You would've subjected me to that?" he asked darkly.

"Probably not. I so hate that hurt look you wear so pitifully.

"My hurt look?"

"Yes, it's quite pathetic but effective. Just don't overuse it, or it will no longer serve you. I may have a soft spot for you, but Mother and Grandmother do not."

"You can say that again," he mumbled, looking ahead as they drew near the royal palace, not liking the look of it. A towering curtain wall circled the place, skirting the northwest confluence of the Ka-Kelpar and Dor-Par rivers, rising 250 feet into the air. Beyond this outer barrier, rose another wall, some 500 feet high, with a massive inner keep beyond it, reaching high into the firmament. The palace was spell forged, its impossible engineering crafted by mage lords of incredible power hundreds of years ago, with its utmost citadels spiraling eight hundred feet above the city. It was a monstrous mountain of sand-hued rock, towering over the surrounding city.

"Shall we?" Alesha asked, following her mother's lead through the massive gates of the palace.

*****

King Gregor awaited them upon a raised dais just beyond the inner walls, with his wives, concubines and ninety-four children gathered behind where he stood, with his heir and eldest son, Prince Borcose, at his right. Sitting at the base of the dais were twelve leopards, staring blankly ahead like watchful sentinels, spellbound by King Gregor.

Ethan felt Borcose's eyes upon him as they approached, an arrogant smirk painting his childish face that didn't fit his large body.

Wonder if he still holds a grudge? he asked himself, the sneering look the pompous prince gave him answering that fool question.

Valera smoothly dismounted with effortless grace, her entire entourage following in kind as she ascended the dais. Everyone assembled upon the palace green took a respectful knee, save the two monarchs and their crown heirs, Alesha and Borcose. Ethan was the last to kneel, the humiliating act just another insult he must endure. As protocol dictated, Alesha and Borcose knelt last, their heads bowed in respectful supplication.

"Queen Valera, welcome to Torval. I hope you find my hospitality a more inviting experience than what we each suffered at Astaris," King Gregor greeted, his voice laced with derision at the mention of Ethan's homeland. He couldn't mask his glee upon seeing Ethan brought low. There was hardly a great noble house in all of Gorgencia that didn't lose at least one precious son at the Velo, that disastrous battle slaying two generations of shade and shield mages throughout the realm, and many more kingdoms as well. Had Ethan not intervened, King Bronus would be dead, and Astaria partitioned among the victors.

"Your kind words honor me, King Gregor. We must not disparage our previous hosts, however, for our visit there proved most profitable." She cast a glance toward Ethan, which pleased Gregor.

"Indeed," he agreed with a booming laugh. "Come, you and your lovely heir are my guests of honor. Tonight, we feast, and tomorrow you shall be my guest for the Grand Review. There shall be a melee, archery and horse races, and a jousting tourney, where one fair maiden shall be named our queen of beauty."

*****

"I thought you weren't going to make me wear something ridiculous?" Ethan growled as Leora ushered him into Alesha's chamber. The day was growing late and they were expected in the grand feasting all.

Alesha turned, the maids attending her, drawing briefly away, a bemused smile painting her lips. There he stood, dressed in a silken silver tunic and hose, with a long black cape draping his large shoulders, looking miserable. She directed the maids to continue setting her dress, a voluminous, emerald gown with a snug bodice and billowing skirts, its long sleeves, and neck trimmed with Brelaran lace. She was breathtakingly beautiful, enough so to cause his frown to briefly falter.

"Mother insists that you be appropriately attired, as befits a consort of House Loria. You do look quite fetching." She tried biting her smile but failed miserably.

"So much for not humiliating me," he growled, stepping toward her chamber's large bay window, the view of Torval breathtaking from the airy heights of the upper palace. The sun was setting in the western sky, as Ethan gazed in the direction of home.

"Only you consider being properly dressed as humiliating. You needn't fret, Ethan. If you behave yourself tonight, I will reward you tomorrow," she said as the maidservants finished, freeing her to step toward him.

"And perhaps I shall reward you tonight as well," she whispered seductively in his ear.

"Maybe I can endure this for a few hours," he said, entertaining the possibilities.

"Good." She smiled, making a lazy motion with her left hand, her jeweled crown lifting off its open box beside a table on the other side of the chamber, levitating into the air. She summoned it across the room, setting it upon her head.

"Cute trick." He shook his head, thinking of all times that power would've been useful.

"It's simply power, Ethan, incredible power," she said, levitating her sword from its scabbard beside her chest. A twirl of her finger spun the blade above her bed with dizzying speed before returning it to its place.

The maids looked on with practiced indifference, their heads bowed in deep reverence for their mistress, save for Kia, who stared dumbstruck before lowering her head, the former Gorgencian slave mesmerized by Alesha's power.

"Princess Alesha could just as easily have twirled a dozen blades, Consort," Leora coldly reminded him, standing at the doorway, giving him a condescending smirk.

"Perhaps a hundred blades, but even that would not impress Ethan. What is such power when compared to what he possesses? The power to negate all the strength I wield." Alesha caressed his cheek, the thrill of his presence causing her heart to race. She felt vulnerable and invigorated simultaneously, but mostly, she felt alive. Of course, it wasn't completely true, his power not affecting her while she carried their daughter. If this was an inkling of what their child would feel like, she should be envious, but she wasn't. All her life, she hungered for Ethan's power, desiring to possess it by possessing him, but knowing she could never have it for her own. She could only pass it on to their daughter. Such is the paradox of all the firstborn in her family line, to crave powers they did not possess, and seeking mates who did, passing on their combined strength to the next firstborn daughter, ever strengthening their line. The paradox lay with the insatiable craving for their mate's power, a craving never sated. It was the practical reason royal consorts were collared, the magic of the collars binding their powers, thus dulling the hunger, allowing queen and consort to dwell in relative peace.

171

Alesha was struck, however, by the complete lack of hunger in herself whenever in Ethan's presence. What should have been insatiable hunger was replaced with euphoria and an overwhelming desire to be with him in every way. It was like invisible bonds wrapped themselves around her and him, drawing them together with a power she could not understand or refute, or even want to refute.

"Come, we are expected." She smiled, lowering her hand for him to take.

They were greeted by a palace steward in the outer corridor of her chambers, along with her own royal guards, attired in ceremonial uniforms of silver mail over white tunics with pleated kilts. Sergeant Jordain commanded Alesha's personal guard, greeting her with a deep bow, before lifting his gaze, bemused by Ethan's attire.

"Don't even say it, Sarge. Your outfit isn't any better," Ethan growled, regarding the skirted garment Ander was wearing.

"Fair enough, Consort Loria." He grinned, stepping aside, waving them forth, his men forming a protective circle around them, with Leora preceding them.

*****

They were escorted to the great feasting hall, joining King Gregor and Queen Valera, each sitting on massive thrones overlooking the chamber. The two monarchs were sat side by side upon a raised dais, with a long table before them, presiding over the prestigious assembly. A large saber lion sat beside the king, its massive fangs curved menacingly over its lips. Gregor treated the fearsome beast like a house pet, its will bound to his own. The chamber was square-built, with rows of tables upon each side resting on raised tiers, overlooking a large open floor below. The open floor was spacious enough for melees, entertainers, and even horses to parade in full review for the amusement of the king and his court. Valera sat beside king Gregor, with their respective houses and retainers seated along the adjoining walls, facing each other. It was along the east wall Ethan found himself, sitting at the high table beside Alesha, with Leora sitting on his right. The members of Valera's entourage occupied the three rows of tables resting on the lower tiers below them. King Gregor's many children, wives, and concubines lined the tables along the west wall, with the seat of prominence opposite them still empty, awaiting the arrival of Prince Borcose.

Looking to his left, Ethan eyed a sizable host of palace courtesans and Gorgencian nobles seated along the south wall, many giving him sneering or hateful looks. He caught a few maidens coyly smiling, which didn't go unnoticed by Alesha, who quickly removed such thoughts from the maidens' minds with a subtle wave of her hand.

Ander stood behind them, ever watchful, standing his post like a sentinel cut from stone. Ethan had to commend the man's sense of duty. He was growing to like the man he loved calling Sarge.

A sudden cheer erupted from the congregants along the south and west walls, heralding the arrival of Prince Borcose and his favored companions, each a noble son and knight of great renown. They marched into the chamber through the archway positioned at the southwest corner, like strutting peacocks, arrayed in bright mail, over black trousers and tunics, Borcose with gold mail and his six companions in silver.

Borcose waved to his adoring crowd, whose cheers seemed more forced than genuine, his smirking gaze stopping briefly at Ethan, before softening as he beheld Alesha, struck by her beauty. Quietly collecting himself, he led his companions toward his father's dais, stopping in the middle of the chamber, taking a knee.

"Father, I present the Crown's defenders in the Grand Review," Borcose declared proudly, each of his knights beaming proudly to represent the crown in the contests before the eyes of the noble houses of Gorgencia.

"I see Sir Galbor behind you. I expect him to partake in the melee," King Gregor said, calling out a red-haired, bearded giant of man.

"Aye, sire. And the joust!" Sir Galbor's booming voice answered.

"I look to it with heady anticipation, Sir Galbor. I also see Sir Lanzer. Is there any jouster as skilled as thee?" Gregor asked as if taunting the other houses daring to take the field against his chosen favorites.

"If any dare to tap my shield, I shall answer their challenge, sire!" Sir Lanzer declared. He was black of hair, with cruel sharp features and piercing dark eyes. Slender of build, he stood slightly shy of Ethan's stature. His carriage reminded Ethan of his friend Xavier Murtado and wondered just how good this Gorgencian knight was in the saddle.

King Gregor called out the other four knights by name, lauding them with undo praise, impressing upon his noble houses the futility of any of them attaining victory in the Grand Review. Sir Venton stood seventy-two inches, with long blond hair and a trimmed beard, framing bemused blue eyes. He was lean and agile and was favored in the archery contest and the horse race. Sir Colben stood seventy inches, powerful of build with brown cropped hair and a prominent jaw. He was an excellent jouster. Sir Bouton was seventy-four inches, portly, with shaggy brown hair and beard. He wielded a heavy war hammer and was entered into the melee. Sir Cragar stood seventy inches, with a medium build, and black hair, framing pale green eyes. He favored the mace and was entered in the Joust and melee.

"Should any of our Vellesian guests wish to enter the field come the morrow, they would be most welcome, Queen Valera," Prince Borcose politely offered.

"You are most gracious, Prince Borcose. Should any of my brave knights wish to partake, they may do so with my full blessing," Valera said, all too sweetly.

"As long as they hold the proper writ of knighthood, of course, oh Queen, unless my mighty Sire should wave such legalities." Borcose looked to his father.

"In the spirit of greater competition, I would be remiss to douse the hopes of any aspirants who wish to test their metal. So let it be known that all free men are welcome to enter the lists!" King Gregor declared, his proclamation sitting poorly with his nobles. Most of their household knights wanted nothing to do with challenging the king's champions, but by opening the competition to all comers, they would be shamed to forgo the lists while commoners filled the ranks. They were forced to lose face or risk their horses and armor to the victors should they lose.

"Very generous of you, Your Grace." Valera smiled sweetly, taking a sip from her jeweled goblet.

With that, Borcose withdrew, he and his companions taking their seats at the high table on the west wall.

"More wine, my lord?" A briefly skirted slave girl asked, drawing Ethan's eyes away from the pompous Borcose, to the shy maid attending him. She was shy and recently flowered, far too young to be serving dressed in such fashion. He couldn't miss the thick silver collar gracing her throat, marking her as a palace slave.

"Water please, my lady. Wine is wasted on me." He smiled gently, his politeness taking her aback. She curtsied before calling another slave forward, bearing a water pitcher, a boy dressed in similar garb as her.

Ethan shook his head, disgusted by the sight of men and women in bondage, let alone children.

"Thank you, sir," Ethan said, taking the boy aback by addressing him respectfully. The boy and girl again bowed and moved along.

"My lady and sir?" Alesha smiled, sipping from her goblet.

"Just being polite, Alesha," he said, taking a generous gulp of water.

"Oh, you were far more than polite, my love. You enjoy exalting peasants and slaves, addressing them with deep respect. I've seen you do so in the Mage Bane, at Astaris, with little Cora, and now here. Conversely, you loath to address those of royal birth, let alone nobles, with such courtesy."

"Hmm, I never noticed." He shrugged.

"You're a lousy liar, Ethan."

"Not surprising, I'm lousy at a lot of things."

"Except humility. You have mastered that," she said before noticing his expression suddenly harden, anger flashing dangerously in his eyes. She followed to where he was looking to the opposite wall, where Borcose struck the servant filling his goblet, a slave boy not older than fifteen years. The boy stood beside the crown prince upon trembling knees, blood oozing from a split lip. Borcose stood from his chair, towering over the slave, his hands glowing, preparing to brand the boy's flesh with his hands.

"Be calm yourself, Ethan." Alesha touched a hand to his shoulder.

"He's an animal!" he growled, cursing her for stealing his freedom. He would never stand aside in Astaria in the face of such injustice, but here he sat, helpless to intervene without disobeying his Mistress, and incurring the consequences for doing so.

"*Release him!*" Alesha ordered with a beguiling whisper, that hung briefly in the air, before fading.

Ethan watched as Borcose dismissed the servant, retaking his seat as if nothing happened. Ethan looked at her, awed by her incredible power. He should be angry with her for binding his ability to act but appreciated her intervention.

"Thanks," he acknowledged her good deed.

"I had to before you did. I know you are struggling to restrain yourself from our insufferable host, but we are guests here, and another altercation between you and Borcose would be...unfortunate." She moved her hand to his knee.

"I wouldn't have to intercede if you did it for me. You intervened, whispering two simple words, resolving the entire matter with ease, no one the wiser. If I had such power, I wouldn't hesitate to use it to help these people."

"And how would you help them, Ethan? Would you set that slave free? Would you kill his cruel master? And after you departed this land, what would become of the freed slave or the vacant seat of his master?" she asked, his silence reaffirming her point.

"I wouldn't regret it," he finally answered.

"Of course, you wouldn't, but what would you accomplish other than a brief respite of injustice? Nothing. The freed slave would fall under a new master, and another tyrant would replace the one you slew. Nothing would've changed, except you would feel good for your kind deed, your actions doing naught but fueling your pride."

"My pride? I thought you said I was humble?" He shook his head.

"Humble with peasants, but prideful when treating with royals. And you would be wise to not shake your head when addressing your crown princess in such a formal setting," she warned.

176

"As you wish, mistress." He bowed his head, wishing to be gone from this place.

"Mistress?" She raised a dangerous brow at that appellation. Was he truly seeking her ire?

"Your Highness," he corrected himself, wondering what difference it made. Wasn't he truly her slave? What was the point in pretending otherwise?

"Come! You're not going to spoil this evening!" she ordered, grabbing his hand, preparing to stand.

"Go where?"

A mischievous smile touched her lips as King Gregor again addressed the assemblage.

"My good people. I would be remiss not to formally introduce our guest of honor, the Crown Princess Alesha!" Gregor declared to hearty cheers.

"You are a most gracious host, King Gregor!" Alesha inclined her head, awaiting his next utterance with knowing guile.

"We are most pleased with the great service you have rendered Gorgencia, Princess. Never again shall our people be threatened by the war-mongering former crown prince of Astaria. We are heartened by the sight of him properly cowed by your majesty, and the gentle chains of his consortship!" Gregor added, his eyes fixed on Ethan.

"Be assured, oh great King, that Ethanos will no longer pose a threat to your mighty realm. Let peace reign between all peoples, and may Gorgencia partake the fruits of said peace, now and forever!" Alesha proclaimed.

"Well said, Princess. As my most esteemed guest, the first dance is yours, as is the floor!" Gregor waved a hand to the open space below.

With that, Alesha led Ethan onto the floor, as musicians began a gentle melody.

"You're enjoying this, I see," Ethan said, pressing his right palm to hers as they moved across the floor, keeping a respectful distance befitting their station.

"Immensely." She smiled devilishly.

"This is how you reward me for saving your mother's life?" he asked, wanting to shake his head, but thinking better of it with every eye upon them.

"Oh, you shall be rewarded, Ethanos, but not here." She smiled knowingly, enjoying this a little too much.

"Then when?"

"As I told you earlier, you shall receive a part of your reward tonight," she whispered seductively.

"Oh." His eyebrows happily raised with that.

"And tomorrow, you are excused from the formal activities until the grand feast in the evening. You are free to tour Torval in disguise if you wish but with a proper escort, of course."

*****

It was late in the evening when they retired to their chambers, Alesha leading him by the hand through the entrance, leaving her guards outside.

"Oh!" she gasped as he swept her into his arms, carrying her across the chamber, setting her upon their spacious bed, diaphanous curtains surrounding it. A glowing hearth upon the far wall illuminated the cozy stone chamber, the crackling fire the only noise besides their breathing.

"Your reward, husband," Alesha said, drawing her gown below her full breasts.

Ethan pressed a finger to her lips, before stripping off the hated tunic and hose, climbing back onto the bed in all his natural glory.

She gasped as he ran a finger around her breasts in seductive circles, each pass smaller than the last, drawing nearer the sensitive center. A sudden quiver rippled her flesh, her heightened senses alive with glorious rapture. Every touch from Ethan grew more intense, every part of her flesh sensitive to his ministrations. She lay there as he undressed her, giving herself into his power. Her eyes opened slightly, taking in his beautiful face, losing herself in the mysterious depths of his sea-blue eyes. Imagining a lifetime of sharing her bed with this man brought a coy smile to her lips.

"Why are you smiling?" he asked, his finger stopping alongside her left nipple.

"Just admiring your work, Ethan. Continue!" she commanded, flicking his nose.

"None of that," he said, taking both her hands into one of his, pinning them above her head, before crushing his lips to hers.

*****

The next morning found poor Ander following Ethan through the streets of Torval, with Sarella observing them from the shadows, informing Queen Valera of the misdeeds and mischief he was bound to cause and mitigate any problems that might arise. The streets of the Gorgencian capital were alive with vendors hawking their wares, the avenues overflowing with people traveling from afar to attend the Grand Tourney. Nobles and knights from as far as Sarcosa journeyed to partake, drawn by the large purse rewarded to the winners of each event.

"Is this necessary, Consort Loria?" Ander asked warily, following him through another seedy side street, the foulest stench tormenting his senses, likely a healthy dose of horse droppings piled somewhere nearby.

"Just a shortcut to the next street, Sarge. We're bound to find something interesting. In my travels, I discovered incredible things in the most unlikely places," Ethan said, though, in truth, he only took this route to irritate Sarella, whom he pretended not to notice following them. He wished he could see her wrinkle her nose as she followed them through one foul-smelling alley after another. Ethan was thankful to be out of the foppish outfits he was tortured with in recent days, donning simple black trousers and shirt, with his father's sword riding his left hip, concealed by a heavy hooded cloak. He hid himself within the cowl of his hood, not wanting to be recognized. Ander was similarly attired, forgoing his impeccable uniform for Ethan's nondescript appearance.

"Why is it when you speak of interesting, you really mean trouble?" Ander rightly pointed out as they turned the corner onto a busy thoroughfare, a wide set avenue with scores of specialty shops along its length.

"Careful." Ethan put his hand on Ander's chest, just as he was about to step in a warm pile of horse shit.

Ander nodded his gratitude, wondering how he missed seeing it.

"I didn't want to smell it on you all day." Ethan shrugged.

"You are most kind." Ander shook his head.

"Come along, Sarge, let's have a look around the city," Ethan said, leading the way.

Ander sighed, following after Ethan and hoping nothing would go wrong. To the boy's credit, they kept off the center of the avenue, avoiding passing wagons or the many knights parading along the street on horseback. They went out of their way to avoid passersby, stepping aside whenever possible, drawing little attention to themselves. Ethan kept looking about as if searching for someplace specific until his eyes found it. To Ander's dismay, Ethan led him into a toy makers shop, with miniature knights in full regalia and dolls displayed in its broad windows. Of all the places they could visit, this wasn't what he expected. Ethan took his time exploring the many items the shop offered, inquiring if the shopkeeper had molds for the dolls or knights, offering enough to purchase them outright.

"How old is your daughter, Sarge?" Ethan asked, recalling their many conversations about his only child.

"Five years," Ander said, recalling have spoken of that in at least one of their conversations.

Ethan slapped him on the shoulder before picking out one of the finest dolls from the main display for him to give her, as well as three others. He noticed a young servant girl working alongside the shopkeeper, discovering she was from a poor family who worked there to help feed her ailing mother. Ethan fished extra coins from his pouch, purchasing the finest doll the shop had for the girl and gifting her and the shop owner an extra gold coin, much to their dismay. They were soon on their way with his purchases in tow.

"Ethan, I..." Ander didn't know what to say, touched by the gesture.

"Calling me Ethan instead of Consort is all the thanks I need, Sarge." Ethan smiled, noticing Sarella standing across the street, pretending not to see him. He decided it was silly pretending she wasn't there.

"You might as well walk with us, Sarella. I already know you're there," Ethan said, upon approaching her.

"I know you can see me, Ethanos. If I so desired, I could have watched you from afar. I was merely allowing you the courtesy of not suffering my presence." She fixed him with those piercing purple eyes of hers.

"What difference does it make, Sar. We planned to find a place to eat, and I can't enjoy my food if I know your standing around all hungry like," he said.

"Hungry like?" She made a face.

"Come on, food will do you some good, and you can help carry these." He handed her one of the dolls he purchased, wrapped in decorative cloth.

And so they went, visiting a local pub, and partaking in the cuisine and ale, though Ander and Sarella kept their consumption within reason. He spoke of his adventures in Cordova and Red Rock, asking them of their own tales. Ander's, he heard sparingly in their travels, the man usually tight-lipped about his past. Sarella spoke mainly of observing Ethan over the years, notably his many antics as a child.

It was late morn when they continued on their way, coming upon a gaggle of men making sport of another, with many more looking on. Ethan held his tongue, observing the exchange within earshot at the back of the crowd.

"You haven't much chance, Dolus, but I shall welcome taking your horse and kit!" A massive Gorgencian knight bellowed, mocking a much older fellow who stood before a smithy, surrounded by the knight's comrades. Ethan recognized the boisterous knight as Sir Galbar, one of Prince Borcose's champions.

"He won't challenge you, Galbar. He will test his luck with lesser contestants, hoping to draw a tie, forgoing the cost of greater loss, and certain humiliation," another of Borcose's champions sneered, the one called Lanzer.

"What is this about?" Ethan asked Sarella, deciding to make use of her power.

She drew him away from the crowd, where they could speak freely.

"Three of Prince Borcose's champions are deriding the lesser knight named Dolus. He is a lesser knight sworn to House Daylom, their fiefdom located south of Divaris. It seems Lord Daylom ordered his heir and household knights to not participate in the tourney, fearing defeat at the hands of the king's champions. The duty to represent their house falls to Dolus," she explained.

"Why did the heir fear losing? There is nothing wrong with doing your best," Ethan asked.

"Gorgencian law of jousting differs from Astarian. The winner in any bout claims the horse and armor of the loser. For this reason, many noble houses of Gorgencia have offered up their lesser knights to the tourney, lesser knights who fear disobeying their lord."

"And this Dolus will likely lose everything he owns." Ethan now understood, shaking his head at the stupidity of it all. Such tactics did little to improve the overall skills of the realm's knights.

"Unless he draws a tie, which will cost him half the loss of a full defeat, the purse going on to the overall tourney champion," she explained.

"And these champions are that good?" Ethan asked.

"They are impressively skilled, but—"

"But what?" Ethan asked.

"They tend to benefit from their king's…blessing."

"The king is impartial," Ander pointed out the letter of the law.

"Knowing Gregor, I doubt it. Let me guess, he messes with their opponents' mounts?" Ethan asked, reminded of Gregor's mage gift of controlling animals, her silence confirming his suspicion.

An unusual hush fell over the crowd, the source of the sudden quiet none other than three Vellesian knights wandering into their midst. Sarella drew Ethan and Ander further away, listening in from afar. They recognized Sir Dougaris among them, Leora's future son by marriage, and one of the queen's most notable protectors. They were dressed in their distinct gold and crimson armor with a golden rose emblazoned on their chests. They passed the smithy, suffering the quiet stares of their Gorgencian host for not entering the lists for any of the events.

"What is it?" Ethan asked Sarella, noticing the restrained anger testing her resolve.

"We best be going," she advised as the Vellesian knights passed from sight, none of them seeing them in the back of the crowd.

"Well, something raised your hackles. Mind telling me what?" Ethan asked, Sarella's silence undone by the voice of the large Gorgencian knight.

"Their queen granted them leave to enter, yet none have chosen to do so. They are craven." Sir Galbor laughed after Sir Dougaris and his comrades disappeared down the avenue.

"It would've been a pleasure to knock about that prissy lot. They are much too pretty to be knights," Sir Cragar sneered.

"Pretty enough to be ladies in waiting," Sir Colben added for good measure, drawing more guffaws from those standing around.

"Their armor would have been a pricey boon, though It couldn't fit me." Galbar chuckled.

"The tourney is hardly worth our effort unless more high lords fill the lists," Colben complained. The poorer and lesser knights' armor and horses were worth far less than the upper castes. The king opened the tourney to all comers, as a means of shaming more lords to participate, lest they be upstaged by commoners.

"Plenty have, including the heir to House Nolvar," Sir Cragar said.

"The one with the pretty slave girl?" Colben asked.

"Aye," Cragar affirmed with a devious smirk.

"I shall trade his armor and horse for his wench," Galbar boasted.

"That is a heavy price for one slave. Perhaps for a noblewoman," another knight Ethan didn't recognize, pointed out.

"Is there a difference? You put fine silks on any woman, and she'll moan just as prettily on your furs. You put rags on any of the wealthiest crones, and she'll look no different from a peasant," Sir Galbar said.

"Not the Vellesian princess. What I wouldn't give to celebrate my victory by mounting the wench!" Sir Cragar crowed.

A long silence passed between Sarella and Ander, each waiting with bated breath as Ethan's countenance transformed to stone.

*****

Alesha sat between Leora and her mother in the king's box overlooking the palace green, the midday sun signaling the commencement of the Grand Review. The king's box presided over the tourney grounds, with viewing stands circling the field of competition. The box held twenty guests, with the high lords and the king's many children seated in the lower stands to either side, followed by lesser lords, merchants, and commoners seated opposite the king.

"*Ethanos's absence has gone unnoticed. Why is that?*" Valera spoke to Alesha's mind, with King Gregor blissfully unaware sitting her other shoulder.

"*His reward, mother. Why torture him with this farce of a tourney. Allow him this time to explore the city and avoid the silent taunts of our host. 'Tis a small boon considering he saved your life,*" Alesha countered.

"*That did not answer my question, Alesha. Why has he gone unnoticed?*"

"*I did not manipulate the king's mind, mother, just his heir and closest advisers. They each believe Ethan is confined to his chambers,*" Alesha said.

"Very well," Valera voiced aloud just as King Gregor stood to address the crowd.

"My good people and esteemed guests. By tradition, the Grand Review begins with a melee and ends with the joust, with archery, spear toss, and the horse race set between them. In a break with tradition, we shall reverse the order of events, beginning with the joust!" King Gregor declared to thunderous applause, as the contenders entered in the lists, paraded onto the tourney green.

Each contender circled the field, parading before the spectators, displaying their house colors, or the sigil of their lord. The king's champions were arrayed in silver armor, with capes of forest green draping their shoulder, with a white stallion emblazoned upon it, the sigil of the king. Each rode matching white destriers, the horses trotting in perfect unison, almost too perfect. Other houses were represented in a myriad of colors and sigils, from the falcon of House Nolvar to the desert owl of a Sarcosan knight of House Beltara. It was the last contender that immediately drew Valera and Alesha's attention, a man clad in simple boiled black leather cuirass and trousers, bearing a heavy wedge shaped shield and riding a midnight black charger. His helm and lance matched the black of his entire ensemble, an austere display of simplicity.

"*What is he doing here?*" Valera scowled, noticing right away the complete lack of magic permeating the man.

"*What Ethan always does, Mother…the unexpected,*" Alesha sent that thought back to her, an intrigued look in her eyes.

After once around the field, each contender stopped beside their designated post, setting their shields upon them, before taking position behind them as the king commenced the tourney.

"With our contenders prepared for battle, let the Grand Review begin!" Gregor proclaimed to even louder cheers as he outstretched his hands. "The JOUST!" he shouted.

With that, the contenders were free to begin, yet all waited briefly to see who would place the first challenge. By the tourney rules of Torval, any contender could challenge any other by tapping their lance to their opponents' shield, upon which they would proceed to the jousting line, facing one another across the field, with the dividing fence separating them as they traversed its length. The King's Champions sat below the royal box, Sirs Galbar, Colben, Lanzer, and Cragar, each smugly waiting for any brave enough to challenge them. They expected to wait for the list to thin as the challengers knocked one another out, building their purses before risking their armor and mounts to the favored champions. If no one made a move, they would take it upon themselves to challenge the foes with the most enticing worth. And so, it began with the heir of

House Gustiv parading around the field before tapping the shield of Sir Hosutte, the sworn vassal of Duke Vorhenz, who sat behind his brother the king. The two men retrieved their shields, taking up position upon the Jousting field as King Gregor gave the honor of commencement to Queen Valera. She stood from her seat, extending a scarlet ribbon over the wall of the king's box, releasing it.

With that signal, the two men spurred their mounts onward, The heir of Gustiv's heavy destrier against Sir Hosutte's gray charger. They broke their lances upon each other's shields with the first pass, circling about as squires hurried forth, replacing them. The second pass found Sir Hosutte knocked from the saddle, the heir of Gustiv claiming his prize. Sir Hosutte gained his feet before saluting Gustiv, acknowledging his defeat. He walked off the field to strip his armor and gift it to Gustiv. The young heir lifted his bright crimson visor, showing his winsome smile to the crowd who cheered his triumph. Emboldened by his victory, he paraded before the royal box, tapping the shield of Sir Colben, much to the surprise of the crowd.

Colben lowered his visor over his square jaw, riding forth to the starting position.

Valera felt the power emanating from King Gregor, directed at the heir of Gustiv's mount, causing her to smirk at his subtle interference. She forbade her own knights from participating in this farce, despite her public proclamation contradicting it. She cared not for the vanity of kings, wishing to conceal what her own knights were capable of. Let the Gorgencians think them flowered weaklings. When the time came, Vellesian knights would sweep these fools from the field, but in war, not games.

With the release of the ribbon, the two men charged, their horses' hooves kicking up the soil as they drew nigh, lances leveled. Gustiv's horse shifted unnaturally before he centered his lance, sending it astray as Sir Colben struck him clean in his breast, unhorsing him. The crowd roared as the young heir of Gustiv tumbled to the ground. A mage healer hurried forth to tend Gustiv, the boy suffering broken ribs and a sprained knee, which she restored in moments. Sir Colben retook his place, setting his shield again on his post.

"That should quell the fervor of any daring to challenge our champions, Father." Borcose smirked, sitting Gregor's opposite shoulder.

"Yes, but hopefully not for long. We have another thirty contenders and we cannot allow their cowardice to draw this out too long," Gregor said, just as the knight clad in black started circling the field, his lance held loosely in his right hand.

"Our mystery knight," Duke Vorhenz leaned forward. whispering into his brother's ear.

"No mystery, brother, his name is on the lists," Gregor answered back.

"And what name would that be?" the duke asked.

"Steward! What name does our knight in black herald?" the king asked his steward, standing behind his opposite shoulder.

"He is no knight, sire. He gave only a name, a Jake of House Thorton." The steward politely bowed.

"A most peculiar name." Gregor shrugged, watching the lightly clad fellow continuing to circle the field, turning the near bend, approaching the royal box.

Alesha and Valera shared a look, both familiar with the name Ethan chose. Valera considered putting a stop to this, but Alesha convinced her to stay her hand, especially after seeing her aunt Sarella across the field, sitting among the commoners, speaking to her across the tourney green.

Allow him this, my dearest, Sarella advised.

Gregor and Borcose's bemused smirks turned to dismay as Jake of House Thorton rode past the royal box, tapping every shield of the king's champions, the sound of ringing metal echoing strongly in the still air, the crowd stunned in silence.

Sir Galbar roared his displeasure with Ethan's arrogance, retrieving his shield and lowering his visor, as his shield was the first one tapped. The crowd roared as the largest and most powerful of King Gregor's champions paraded forth, his heavy destrier clopping the soil as it moved into position.

Valera shook her head before releasing the ribbon, Sir Galbar's horse exploding out of its stance. She could feel Gregor reach out to

Ethan's mount with his power, expecting to cause it to falter. Alesha masked her worry with her stoic countenance, her *Queen's Face* as her grandmother would call it, watching as Ethan maneuvered his lighter mount with uncanny grace. She could only guess where he purchased the horse or how he built such rapport in so little time. He obviously didn't want to risk Bull in this tourney. Gregor's confident smirk quickly soured, realizing his power had no effect.

"Surely not," Valera gasped.

She stared in disbelief as Ethan flipped his lance into an overhand grip, rising in the saddle, driving the tip of the shaft overtop of Galbar's shield. It was an unorthodox, impossible act, requiring incredible strength that no human should have. Ethan twisted away from Galbar's lance, while his blow struck true, taking the giant man in the shoulder, unhorsing him. Galbar tumbled backward off his saddle, impacting the ground in a painful heap. Ethan sped past his foe as mage healers rushed to attend to the listless Galbar. Ethan paraded before the silent crowd, tossing his splintered lance aside, before retrieving a new one from an attending squire. He spoke not a word, his horse cantering across the tourney field, stopping on the opposite side, facing the royal box, pointing the tip of his new lance at Sir Colben.

Alesha was sitting fully erect, leaning forward in her seat, spellbound by his mastery of horse and lance, as he and Colben took up their positions after Galbar and his horse were cleared from the field. The contrast between the two men could not be more distinct, Colben in heavy plate armor, designed for jousting with Ethan, who was lightly clad, making him vulnerable to severe injury even with the blunted tourney lances. Even their choice of mounts couldn't be more different, Colben's heavy white destrier and Ethan's light black charger.

Valera dropped the ribbon, shaking her head as the two men charged. Once again, King Gregor grunted in frustration, unable to confound Ethan's horse as Ethan repeated his trick, sending Colben flying. Ethan raced past the Gorgencian knight, tossing his lance aside, catching a new one before parading across the field and pointing to Sir Lanzer. The process repeated itself, this time Ethan holding position in the saddle, breaking his lance upon Lanzer's shield, receiving one point for the strike, Lanzer's lance going astray. The second pass sent Lanzer tumbling, Ethan's lance catching him square in the chest, somehow avoiding his shield altogether. By now, the crowd was dumbstruck, watching as three of the favorites fell to this mysterious black rider as Ethan called out the fourth, pointing his lance to the bull-necked Cragar.

Cragar snorted derisively, lowering his visor as he moved into position, determined to send this upstart a lesson, rules be damned. At the drop of the ribbon, the two horses exploded out of their stance. Preparing to receive the blow with the first pass, Ethan held firm, but Cragar lowered his lance, leveling at the neck of Ethan's horse.

Alesha stared with cold fury as Cragar's lance struck true, punching the horse in the neck, the beast dipping head first into the soil, sending Ethan sailing overtop, smashing into the ground. Cragar lost hold of his snapping lance, parading to the end of the field, celebrating his victory. Striking the opponent's horse was outside the rules of tourney chivalry, but the king could allow it by royal decree, which Gregor did with an uplifted hand, granting Cragar grace. The match was ended if the fallen could not rise. Cragar raised his hands in triumph, ignoring the warning from the crowd with his back to Ethan, who was already standing.

Whenever a knight was unhorsed and managed to gain his feet, he remained afoot, vulnerable to a mounted charge, his fate likely doomed to defeat. Cragar sensed something amiss by the crowd's reaction, circling his destrier about. He barely turned about before Ethan was upon him, running across the tourney field, sunlight playing off the blade of his sword, illuminating its blue steel in otherworldly light. Cragar drew his mace, twirling it as Ethan drew nigh, his destrier shifting beneath him.

Gregor's smirk died on his lips, watching as Jake of House Thorton caught Cragar's mace with his sword, twisting it free, the weapon sailing harmlessly away, nearly pulling Cragar from the saddle. Ethan followed with a strike at the wrist of Cragar's strong hand, the Sword of Starlight cutting through the vambrace like wet parchment. Cragar screamed, trying to urge his horse to flee, before Ethan yanked him from the saddle, tossing him through the air. Gregor and Borcose looked on in horror as the mystery knight stood over their last remaining champion, his sword pressed to his neck.

"Do you yield?" Ethan asked, pressing the tip of the blade to Cragar's throat.

"Aye," the defeated knight conceded. The crowd roared as Ethan helped him up, with the remaining contenders tossing their lances to the ground, yielding to the mystery knight.

With a heavy sigh, King Gregor stood from his seat as the mysterious Jake of House Thorton approached the box after sheathing his wondrous blade.

"In the annals of Torval, never has there been such a grand display of knightly virtue and martial prowess. As Champion of the tourney, you are rewarded the armor and horses of the defeated, a place of honor at tonight's feast, and can name any maiden or lady as queen of the Tourney. Name your queen and remove your helm!" King Gregor ordered.

A royal page hurried forth, presenting a single long-stemmed rose to Ethan, to use in declaring his choice for the queen of the Turney.

Valera raised a bemused brow as Ethan tossed the rose to her, before removing his helm. Gregor's displeasure turned into restrained rage as Ethan stared back at him, the reason for his inability to affect his horse now laid bare. Borcose looked to be apoplectic, a deathly silence sweeping the royal box.

"King Gregor, I am humbled by the majesty of your court and mighty city. In the spirit of friendship between my queen and your great kingdom, I return the armor and horses to their masters. I have little use for them, or the gold they would bring in ransom. Please receive them as a token of peace between our two great peoples!" Ethan bowed, his politeness taking Valera and Alesha aback, forcing Gregor to grind his teeth.

The Gorgencian king snarled inwardly, forced to act gracious by Ethan's apparent humility, and his acknowledging the Vellesians as *his* people.

"I am surprised by your appearance, *Consort* Loria. I was told you were confined to your chambers, and yet, here you are, bathed in glory," Gregor said.

"My apologies, oh great King! I managed to slip away, wishing to honor my queen as no other of Vellesia was entered into the lists. One day, perhaps you shall visit Elysia, and we would be remiss if you were unable to place a strong representative upon our tourney field." Ethan again bowed before addressing Valera.

"Oh great Queen! I stand humbly in your presence, naming you the queen of the Tourney as befits your beauty and charm, which is unmatched in all of Elaria, except perhaps your lovely daughter who sits beside you!" Ethan bowed his head briefly to her in turn, disarming Valera with his ostentatious display.

Valera smiled, not believing the drivel spilling from his lips. The boy impressed her with his clever ability to soothe their anger, forcing them to be lenient with him. Alesha simply shook her head, amused by his antics. Once again, he did the unexpected.

*****

"My Queen." Sarella bowed, greeting Valera upon entering her chambers, bearing an object wrapped in decorative cloth in her hand. The queen stood at the large bow window of her room, looking out over the city from these airy heights.

"Sarella," Valera said, swirling the wine in her goblet, watching as the sun dipped below the horizon. She waved her sister by marriage to come hither, her gaze lingering in the distance before turning to her. "You were to watch over the boy and keep him from mischief. Do you care to explain how he was able to enter the lists?"

"He would not be turned once his anger was roused, my Queen." Sarella shrugged, briefly regarding the breathtaking view of the window.

"And what roused his anger? Did some Gorgencian mock his status as consort? Or berate a peasant he thought more worthy than their betters?" Valera asked skeptically.

"Words were spoken by certain Gorgencian Champions, disparaging the worth of our Vellesian knights, questioning their manly virtues when their backs were turned. That alone tested his resolve to defend their honor," Sarella said, gauging Valera's response before continuing.

"I am to believe Ethan cared for the honor of our knights?" Valera shook her head.

"Does that surprise you? Ethan despises authority but despises braggarts and bullies far more. He likely would have intervened on our knights' behalf if given longer to consider it, but the Gorgencian fool's next utterance removed any hope of calming his ire."

"Do continue, sister. What foolish thing did they say?" She sipped her wine.

Sarella's pause spoke volumes.

"Sarella?"

"A certain Gorgencian Champion…"

"A name, Sarella! I have no patience for ambiguities!"

"Sir Cragar."

"And what did he say?"

"He spoke his desire to bed the Vellesian princess."

The room turned suddenly cold, Valera's eyes blazing with restrained fury.

"Ethan responded much as you, my Queen. He has meted justice to the guilty and those who found humor in the boast. Perhaps you can forgive Ethan now, for doing as you would in his place."

"It is not enough. Cragar must die," Valera said with a cold voice.

"I already removed the memory from the minds of those who overheard, as well as Sir Cragar. All has been set right. There is no need to exact further retribution. You should look to the good in this than dwell upon the bad." Sarella smiled.

"The good?" Valera lifted a brow.

"Ethan. He did not hesitate to protect Alesha and defend her honor. Is this not what you desired from him?"

"I desire obedience. We are capable of defending our honor by ourselves."

"The bonds that you hold over Ethan are easily breakable, sister. His obedience is only ensured by the tenuous hold you have upon his father's life. Coercion is a weak method for controlling him, as I have warned repeatedly after observing him for so many years. The strongest chains holding him in place are the bonds he forms with those around him. He forms friendships easily, especially with those of good character. Once formed, he is loathed to part ways. Think of his great desire to be free. All those years in Astaria, he could have chosen his own path and forsaken the throne, and none could stop him. He did not do so, and you know why? Because he would lose his family, those whom he loves. He would gladly give his own life for his friend Krixan. His time in Red Rock was no different, forming strong attachments to the sheriff and judge. Or Cordova, and his friendship with Lord Darcannon of Valconar. These are the bonds that hold him, not threats to his sire."

"Perhaps in time, Sarella, but we have no such bonds to hold him at this time."

"Don't you? He was prepared to defend your knights' honor; knights he barely knows. What of Ander?"

"Sergeant Jordain?" Valera wondered her point.

"When first assigning Ethan a handler, you thought to select Leora, your staunchest loyalist and confidant who despises Ethan intensely. Your second choice was a knight from your retinue, your third was captain Tolliver of your royal guard. Any would have served you well, observing Ethan and curbing his wild independence. Though fine people all, they were unsuited for what was needed. Ander Jordain is loyal but also thoughtful and kind. He is the very type of man Ethan could form a friendship with. Ethan loves genuinely decent people, and of all your guards and knights, there is none more decent than Ander Jordain. Ethan is growing very fond of him, which is but one small bond tying him to Vellesia."

"Ethan needs obedience, not friends, Sarella."

"Only if he is broken, and as I have told the Queen Mother, Ethan is useless to you broken. His destiny requires his spirit as much as his abilities, a spirit you must cultivate and bend. Friendships are important in achieving this."

"And what proof have you that he feels any bond to Sergeant Jordain?" Valera asked skeptically.

Sarella handed Valera the wrapped item she was holding.

"What is this?"

"It is for you. Open it."

Valera carefully removed the decorative cloth, revealing a large doll, carved from ivory, with lifelike facial features, and dark hair springing from its head, dressed in an emerald lace gown. It was a beautiful lifelike toy any young girl would adore.

"Very lovely, but what is the point of this?" Valera asked.

"Before we overheard the Gorgencian knights' boasting, Ethan purchased four of those dolls from a toy makers shop. One is for Gabrielle, one for Alesha, one for you, and the last for Sergeant Jordain's daughter," Sarella revealed.

"But what is the point of this? I have little use for such."

"Can't you see, my Queen? It means something to Ethan. He put much thought into this, looking for a way to please you in his unique way. By giving one to Ander, he reveals his fondness for him. It proves the bond is strengthening."

"Where else did Ethan visit while in the city today?"

"Just the toy shop and the tavern where we ate, before the incident with the Gorgencians. After that, we visited an armorer, tailor, and corral to purchase a kit and horse for the tourney."

"Had he not overheard the insults of our host, you are saying he would have been content with visiting a toy maker and eating a tavern meal?"

"Yes. He seemed happy enough," Sarella explained.

"He is a child, a very complicated child." Valera shook her head.

"After observing him for so many years, I would agree with that summation. He is overly simple when discussing complex matters and over complicated with simple ones. Of course, the bonds he builds go both ways, my Queen."

"You think he is gaining Ander's loyalty?" Valera asked warily.

"To a certain degree, but none that would supersede Ander's loyalty to you. No, I was referring to Alesha and to…you."

"Me? Speak sense, Sarella."

"You are changed. Not greatly but ever slightly. I sense an easing of your burden. Am I remiss to believe so?"

Valera took another sip from her goblet, swirling it in her mouth for the longest time before swallowing. "My hunger has eased. When I look at Ethan, it is not as pronounced as before, almost dulled, and even more so with every passing day. It makes little sense."

Oh, it makes a great deal of sense, Valera, Sarella thought gleefully.

"Whatever the reason, it matters not, for my mother and grand-mothers are still afflicted. I can feel them now, staring back at us from Elysia with insatiable hunger, their every thought consumed with Ethan and the untold power he brings us. I fear what their madness will become when he is brought into their midst. We are on uncharted ground, and any misstep could end us," Valera voiced a rare doubt.

"Things are not so dire, sister. Every day brings you closer to home, and every day Ethan's bonds to Alesha and to all of you grow ever stronger."

"I hope you are right, Sarella."

"Speaking of Ethanos, what punishment shall he receive for his little adventure today?" Sarella bemusedly asked.

"Since he is an honored guest after his victory today, we can hardly hide him away as Alesha was willing to do to reward him. As for punishment, I have chosen a most entertaining means of tormenting the boy," Valera smiled wickedly.

*****

"Quit your pouting, it is unbecoming," Alesha teased as Ethan led her across the dance floor of the great hall, suffering hundreds of eyes upon them.

"So much for my reward," he growled inwardly while giving her the fakest smile of his life.

"You threw away your reward to be left alone when you won the joust. You are now a guest of honor as the champion of the tourney," she smiled gazing into his sea-blue eyes.

"Then why am I dressed like an idiot?" He smiled back, spinning her away from him, before returning her to his embrace.

"I think you look quite fetching," she regarded the black pleated kilt, white shirt, and black doublet he wore.

"I am glad you are amused." He shook his head.

"It is only proper punishment for your willful disobedience. Be on your best behavior or you shall wear that every day until we reach Vellesia." She smiled, enjoying this far too much.

"I disobeyed to defend your honor, you know," he reminded her, stealing a glance around them, suffering the scowls of the fallen champions and their crown prince. They should be grateful that he hadn't entered the melee and claimed that prize as well, Sir Galbar earning first place, while Sir Ventin took archery and horse racing.

"And you were rewarded by our host as his honored guest," she reminded him.

"That's not a reward to me."

"Oh, you shall be rewarded later tonight." She smiled as they finished, enjoying their last dance until they reached Elysia.

CHAPTER 11

Red Rock, West Texas

Sheriff Thorton looked over his desk with a dozen wanted posters spread out across it. The names read like a rogue's gallery of Texas' most dangerous outlaws. Luke Crawford stood out in the center, the picture capturing his likeness better than most posters Ben looked at over the years. The reward on Crawford was now up to $4,000 since no one heard hide or hair of him for over a year. The same could be said for most of the others, including Emmitt Cobb, George Middleton, Colm Conroy, and George Carson. It was almost as if the earth opened up and swallowed them whole.

The sound of the church bell ringing up the street signaled the end of the school day, where Judge Andrew Donovan acted as the town schoolmaster. Ben was still looking over the posters when the judge entered the jail, after sending the last of his students off. The judge took off his coat and hat, hanging them beside the door before pouring himself a shot of whiskey and taking a seat across from Ben.

"How long you fixin' to look at all these?" the judge asked, picking up the poster of Colm Conroy, examining it.

"Until I know they're dead. Men like Luke Crawford don't just give up. Reminds me of Bill Wilson, the Ozark Bushwhacker. Union guerillas burnt down his house and he declared a one-man war against the union. They say he killed a hundred men." Ben scrubbed his jaw, burning Luke's face in his mind.

"Crawford taint likely to kill a hundred men, Ben. He might be dead already, fallen in a ditch off some beaten path. If coyotes got to him, you'd never find the body," the judge reasoned.

"That might explain one man gone missing, Judge, but all these fellas were last seen riding with Luke, and no one's seen a hair of 'em for over a year. They didn't all slip on a rock, or get lost wandering the desert. No, they're out there somewhere and will show themselves when we least expect it."

"If you still got a bur up your saddle over it, send out a wire to El Paso, and see if the sheriff there has heard anything," the judge advised.

"Already did, Abilene too. No one's heard a thing. It's the damndest thing I've ever seen." Ben shook his head, pouring himself a drink as well.

"You don't fool me, Ben. There's someone else you haven't seen in over a year that you're really worried about," Andrew said, emptying his glass.

"Not much I can do about that. Ethan needs to come to us. What I can do is find these men, and bring them to justice."

"That's a job for the rangers or US marshal's, not a sheriff from a small west Texas town with only one old deputy backing his play."

"What else do I have to do? Town's quieter than a funeral this past year."

"That's what poker is for, Ben. The Lucky Star looks a mite dead, mayhap John is up for a game. Where's Skeeter?" He asked. Poker was always better with four than three.

"Across the street at the mercantile buying tobacco. Been there an hour now."

"George is talking his poor ear off," the judge surmised. George Adams, the mercantile owner, could talk all day and night, asking question after question without listening to the answer. Most town folk walked out of their way if they saw him coming down the street, lest they lose half a day trying to say goodbye.

"Sounds fair enough since Skeeter can't hear so good." Ben shook his head.

"He heard me well enough to call my raise in our last game." Andrew snorted.

"When money's involved, his hearing improves," Ben said, just as the man in question entered the jail with young Billy Wells on his heels shouting excitedly.

"Come outside, Sheriff! There are people coming. Lots of 'em!"

"Whoa, slow down, son." Ben raised an open palm, tempering the boy's zeal. "Who's comin'?"

"Up the street! A whole train of people. Krixan is with them!" Billy grinned, pointing excitedly out the door.

Ben and the judge jumped up at the mention of Krixan, out of their chairs as if they were still young men and through the door, with Skeeter and Billy right behind.

Of all the sights Ben Thorton and Andrew Donovan had seen in their long adventurous lives, nothing compared to seeing the large red-haired giant leading a hundred riders into town, most clad in armor, bearing long swords, with some clad as locals, though they looked a bit too clean for the trail. Beside Krixan rode an elderly gentleman wearing what looked like a blue overcoat of some sort with stars and moons sewed into it, riding a large gray palfrey. A young woman rode Krixan's other side, a right pretty gal with long blond tresses and bright green eyes, wearing some sort of riding leather blouse and trousers. With a sword upon her left hip.

Their eyes fixed on Krixan, who headed the odd column, wearing his broad Stetson, and his six-shooters. Neither Ben or the judge would ever get used to the sheer size of the man, with his great height and girth. Ben recalled sending Krixan to break up a brawl one night at the Lucky Star. One sight of Krixan sobered up the boys right quick. By now, half the town spilled out into the street to have a look-see. As pleased as they were to see Krixan, the one question running through Ben's mind was where was Ethan?

"Hold!" Krixan held up a hand, halting the column, using clearer English than Ben or the judge remembered, stopping short of the jail.

"Krixan! Get down here son, and say hello!" Ben said with a rare smile.

Krixan smiled in turn, a rarity as well for the giant. Dragos and Felicia looked on amusedly as the two men shook hands before sharing an even rarer hug.

"Good seeing you, laddie!" Judge Donovan embraced him next. Krixan was the only man to ever make Andrew look small.

"I think you know what we're going to ask," Ben said.

Before Krixan could answer, Felicia already dismounted and embraced Ben, planting a kiss on his cheeks, looking at him like a long-lost relative.

"You are Jake's father, aren't you?" she asked, an infectious smile playing across her lips.

Before he could answer, she was attacking Andrew with a hug and a kiss as well, much to the old Judge's delight.

"Well, young lady, of all the greetings I've had in my life, that was the most extraordinary." Andrew grinned.

"And you are Judge Donovan." She smiled.

"That is correct, miss. Might I ask your name? I would have remembered meeting a lass as pretty as you." Andrew grinned.

"Felicia would be my guess if I were placing a wager on it," Ben said, causing her eyebrows to raise happily.

"Yes, how did you know?" She smiled even wider if that was possible.

"A certain US marshal won't stop talking about Ethan's kid sister with the sparkling green eyes and hair as gold as a Texas Rose," Ben said.

"Jake remembers me?" She couldn't hide her glee.

"He's not like to forget you, lass. Looking at you now, I now know why," Andrew said, causing her to blush.

"A proper introduction would be appreciated, Krixan," Dragos said, dismounting in a grand flourish for a man his age.

Krixan quickly introduced them to Ethan's eccentric grandfather, who mentally matched each man with the stories Ethan shared of them. Vancel Torrent drew up alongside them, dismounting as well, wearing crimson armor with a white cape, which looked as out of place as anything Ben or the Judge had ever seen. Ben noticed the proper English each of them was speaking, even Krixan, who struggled mightily with their language when he last visited. It was one of many questions he had.

"We can rightly guess you each have many questions, but a street is hardly a place for the answers," Dragos said, regarding the curious onlookers filling the street, and their own men lined up behind them.

"Let's talk inside," Ben directed them toward the jail, while Krixan ordered Captain Marco to hold tight, before leading Felicia, Vancel, and Dragos inside, joining Ben, Skeeter, and Judge Donovan.

*****

"Where's Ethan?" Was Ben's first question as soon as the door closed, their looks giving credence to his instinct that something was wrong.

Felicia and Dragos shared a look, wondering where to begin.

"He was taken," Krixan blurted, cutting to the heart of it.

"Taken? By who?" Ben growled, wondering who was able to do that considering Ethan's power if half of what Jake told him was true.

"It would be best if we start at the beginning," Dragos suggested.

And so it went, with Krixan, Dragos, and Felicia relaying all that transpired, with the battle of the Velo, Ethan claiming his freedom, the hunt for Luke Crawford and Alesha's betrayal at Astaris. They explained the use of Ethan's stone, which gave them enough power for a few at a time to pass through the portal, where they ferried their people across. They also explained how Amanda was able to transfer all knowledge of English to everyone sent across the portal, as well as many of those still in Astaria. He was surprised to learn that another two hundred Astarian soldiers and knights were encamped on the Texas side of the portal, and another four hundred on the Astarian side. The judge and Ben shared a look when the discussion shifted to the threat of Vellesia and Dragos's vision of dragons. It was all surreal, but for some reason, they believed it.

"And that is why we are here. We need your help to procure weapons to fight the dragons," Felicia implored.

"The only reason?" Ben asked, doubting her father would send his youngest daughter to a far off dangerous land.

"And perhaps help us retrieve Ethan," she said, chewing her lower lip, hiding her own reason for being there.

"I will do all I can for Ethan, but we're just three men and old ones at that. I can put a bullet in this queen your talkin' 'bout, but from what you're saying, she will kill your father if I do," Ben said, frustrated by the whole affair. If Ethan was merely being held some-place, they could plan a rescue, but all this magic business meant he was bound by the threat to his father, and Ben had no means to fix that.

"But you are immune to magic, and that's a start," Dragos opined.

"So you will help us?" Felicia asked, looking up at him with those beautiful green eyes and thick lashes.

"If you're Ethan's kin, then you are mine as well, Felicia. Same goes for any kin of the big fella here," Ben said, jerking a thumb toward Krixan, who stood beside the judge, his thick arms crossed over his chest, with a large grin on his face.

"If Ethan needs help, this old man will do whatever you need, young lady," Judge Donovan winked, drawing a beautiful smile from the Astarian princess.

"Count me in as well," Skeeter added, his voice whistling between his missing teeth.

"As for your dragon problem, just how big are they?" Ben asked.

"They can be many times the size of this structure," Dragos said.

Skeeter's whistle pretty much summarized Ben and the judge's opinion on the matter.

"Might need heavy artillery to bring down a beast of that size," Judge Donovan said.

"I doubt the darn thing would sit still for that. Might need a Gatling or two," Ben said, scrubbing his hand over his chin.

"Or three or four." Skeeter grinned.

"They're a bit pricey, not to mention ammunition," the judge said.

"We have gold," Felicia said.

"How much?" Ben asked, doing the math in his head.

"More than enough to buy an army." Krixan snorted.

"And extra for each of you, and the people of Red Rock. We brought many gifts, courtesy of the king and queen of Astaria for your friendship with Ethanos," Felicia smiled.

"Ethonost?" Skeeter made a face, wondering to whom she was referring.

"Ethanos. It's Ethan's true name," Ben corrected his deputy.

"He prefers Ethan, Sheriff, especially from you, the man he respects more than any other, except his father, and you as well, Judge Donovan," Felicia said, looking proudly at each of them, her words having a profound effect on the two men.

"You as well, Skeeter. Ethan told a mighty tale of his brave friend who held off the nefarious Sam Shade and his outlaws by himself until the sheriff and Ethan could come to his aid," Felicia added, mindful to include the old man that her brother was so fond of.

"Here that, Judge, Ethan's been tellin' stories on my heroic gunfight." Skeeter chuckled.

"Very well, let's get your people settled in," Ben said. One thing was certain, and that was their lives would never be the same.

*****

They spent the rest of the day setting camp on the outskirts of town. Doc Wilson offered Felicia and Dragos the use of his home while he bunked with Judge Donovan. Krixan took up his duties as deputy, staying in the jail with skeeter. Captain Marco and Vancel Torrent organized their encampment, established a perimeter, and set up around-the-clock watch duty. The town folk looked on curiously at the strange pavilions propped up alongside the town, most of which were black with gold lightning sewn into their folds, the sigil of House Blagen. Vancel shared a pavilion with two of his brothers Arosh and Cadar, adorned in the red and white of House Torrent.

Throughout the day, the locals began to introduce themselves, with Felicia offering gifts on behalf of Astaria. She took particular delight in meeting the Adams sisters, gifting them many yards of silk and lace, upon the insistence of her mother the queen. The Adams sisters were heartbroken to hear that Ethan was wed but were quickly distracted by the hundred potential suitors that flooded the town. They immediately started cooking up food to serve to the Astarian men, winning them much favor from Vancel, who took an immediate shine to Sara Adams. Marco delivered fifty kegs of Astarian ale to the Lucky Star, much to the delight of John Custis, its barkeep and proprietor, compliments of the king. More silk and cloth of exquisite taste were gifted to all the ladies of the town, compliments of Queen Gabrielle. Doc Wilson was given a finely crafted looking glass from Sabol, its cylinder lined with gold. Skeeter was given a leather overcoat lined with mountain wolf fur. Each of the local ranchers was given ten Martel-bred horses from the royal stables, five stallions, and five mares to begin their own herds. No one was overlooked, the good people of Red Rock receiving the spoils of Astaria. Even Long Paws' village was included, with gifts of horses, blankets and cookware with mountains of food. Judge Donovan was given richly detailed tomes of Astarian history and maps, though the script was in their native Elarian. Parson Green was given a new church bell, and fresh timber for a new steeple, with enough Astarian volunteers to build it.

Last, and certainly not least, Sheriff Thorton was given a beautifully crafted long sword, forged by Torg and Bronus, the king using lightning to strengthen its milky steel. Ben drew it from its jeweled scabbard, holding it aloft before noticing the distinct script in his native English upon the blade.

To Ben Thorton, sheriff of Red Rock, for protecting my precious son during his time in your fair land. I am forever in your debt for being his father in my place. Your friend from afar, Bronus Blagen, king of Astaria.

To say Ben was touched was without question. He stood there for the longest time, staring at the blade given to him by a man he never met, but one he knew through the boy he thought of as a son. It was Felicia who gifted him the blade, insisting to do so alone as the night grew late. She did so in the jail, after Skeeter and Krixan took a patrol around town, leaving the two of them alone.

"Ethan spoke so well of you, Sheriff. He planned to come here before he was taken. He wanted you to know he killed Luke to set your mind at ease. But mostly, he used that as an excuse because he wanted to see all of you again, especially you. He spoke glowingly of your wonderful land and people, trying to replicate it in some way while in Cordova. He gave up his crown to be more like you. He loves you very much, but would never say such a thing because he is too much like father and too much like you. Men." She shook her head, wondering why they didn't share their emotions.

"He's a good man, your brother. Just like my own son. Jake spoke well of you as well, Felicia. He told me about his ambush and how Ethan came and rescued him, taking him to your land. He spoke of waking to the most beautiful sight he ever beheld, a golden-haired, green-eyed beauty staring down at him after nursing him back to health," Ben said.

"And he is the most beautiful thing I ever saw as well. He, too, is a good man, that son of yours."

"I would agree. I am very proud of him."

"Does he ever visit?" she asked guardedly, trying to shield her heart, and failing miserably.

"Perhaps twice a year, if his journeys take him into western Oklahoma or Texas. But you might be interested to know that he will be here in two weeks' time," Ben said.

"Two weeks?" She couldn't hide the smile spreading across her face. She knew that translated to fourteen days in Astaria. Fourteen days seemed so soon and yet so far away. She couldn't help kissing Ben on the cheek for telling her.

*****

Luke Crawford is dead. One of our long-lost friends has returned.

Jake Thorton read those words from the telegraph over and over since leaving Abilene, making his way to Red Rock, with his two guides, Long Paws, and an old friend from his childhood, a colored gentleman he hired named Jerimiah Hanson. Jerimiah's father was a member of the Ninth Cavalry Regiment of buffalo soldiers serving in West Texas. Jerimiah was also an acquaintance of Jake's good friend Marshal Bass Reaves, who wanted to follow in Bass's footsteps in becoming a US marshal but was blocked by former confederates in the marshal service. Jake shook his head at such bigotry, considering Bass was the finest lawman he knew and was himself appointed deputy marshal by a former Confederate general turned US marshal, James Fagan.

"How much further have we got, bossman," Jerimiah asked, riding alongside Jake on a white mustang, his Stetson drawn down over his eyes.

"A few miles, Jerimiah. How's your back?" Jake asked, his friend having been thrown the day before when a rattler spooked his horse.

"Still a mite sore," he moaned, rubbing his hand behind his left hip.

"Lucky you landed in sand. I got ambushed along the Pierna Mala a couple of years back, landed in the creek bed and it busted me up right good," Jake recalled.

"Bass spoke of that, said you were hurt real bad and it kept you laid up a while, but still was able to join in the shootout in Red Rock," Jerimiah said.

"I had a lot of help, especially from a friend of mine," Jake thought of Ethan.

"The one with the pretty sister I always hear you speaking of?"

"That's the one." Jake smiled.

"She must be one heck of a girl?"

"That she is." He half smiled, half frowned, wondering if he'd ever set eyes on her again.

"What sort of town is Red Rock?" Jerimiah asked.

"Small, quiet for the most part." Jake couldn't think of much more to say about it.

"What of the people? Are they difficult?" Jerimiah asked warily, knowing the town's confederate leanings, except for Jake's father and the judge he often spoke of.

"Let's just say slavery wasn't a revered institution in that part of Texas. The locals are friendly enough, and any friend of mine will be accepted. This ain't lower Arkansas," Jake said, recalling Jerimiah's experiences back in his home state once the federals removed their soldiers from the south, ending reconstruction, causing many colored folks to suffer at the hands of corrupt southern governments.

"I'll be takin' yer word for it." He sighed, not having much faith in white folks' words.

"Give folks a chance, Jerimiah. I know most you've met aren't worth rattle spit, but when you meet good ones, the rest don't mean a damn," Jake said, sounding more like his father every day.

Jerimiah took his words to heart, reminding himself that Jake was one of those good ones. Then again, he was a quarter Kiowa, and not fully white to begin with. After a while, Long Paws broke off, heading toward his village while they continued on their way.

*****

The early evening found Felicia, Krixan, Dragos, and Vancel joining Ben, Skeeter, and the judge gathered around Ben's desk playing poker. After two weeks, they made steady progress, even erecting proper shelters to house the Astarian soldiers. Orders were arranged for the first shipment of firearms to be delivered, the locals providing instruction to the Astarians on their use. They managed to construct impressive fortifications around the portal opening, with the anti-magic stone heavily guarded, and used each day to bring men and supplies back and forth. Local tailors were put to work, sewing clothes for the Astarians to blend in, including the Adams sisters who helped sew Felicia a pretty blue dress, which she was currently wearing while dealing out the cards. Their poker games were becoming a nightly ritual, gathering in the jail enjoying drink, song, and Dragos and the judge's stories. Felicia now understood why Ethan loved it here. It was not the land, which was harsh and brutal, but the people, his friends who were the most interesting and endearing people she had ever known.

"I'll match your call and raise you ten," Ben said, calling Dragos on his bold move, counting on his three jacks to carry him.

Dragos kept a stone face, throwing in the ten, before each of them held at that, revealing their cards. Ben's face soured with Dragos dropping a flush in clubs.

"That puts you in the lead, Dragos, and you already won three times in the last five nights. Are you sure you're related to Ethan?" Judge Donovan asked, puffing on his cigar.

"Where do you think the boy got his good looks from?" Dragos said in all seriousness.

"His other grandfather." Vancel couldn't help himself, their hosts' good humor rubbing off on him.

"Shouldn't you be calling on that pretty gal from across the way? You need to do your part and have her keep that food of hers coming our way," Dragos scolded him.

The others chuckled, still recalling how all the baked goods the Adams sisters used to make for Ethan and them, dried up once he departed. Now the good times were back with Vancel and his brothers.

"She's at the Wednesday prayer meeting." Vancel sighed, thinking about joining her next time.

"She's a right pretty gal, that Sara," Judge Donovan said, passing a cigar to Dragos, who didn't mind if he did, lighting it up as Krixan dealt the next hand.

"Ethan wasn't very good at poker?" Felicia asked, never recalling his struggle with anything before.

Ben, Skeeter, and the judge broke out in raucous laughter, with Ben nearly spitting up his whiskey, and Skeeter's teeth whistling with the guffaws escaping his throat.

"You might say that, Felicia," Ben managed to say, once their laughter died down after so many minutes.

"Ethan was masterful at many things, but cards weren't among them," the judge said politely.

"He was worse than a blind archer with missing fingers." Krixan snorted, sounding too much like Ben and the judge, the two men rubbing off on him as well, now that he better spoke their language.

"He was that bad?" Her eyebrows knitted together.

"Never won a single hand in the year he was here." Skeeter chuckled.

"Truly?" she asked.

"Yep. The worst card player I've ever seen, even worse than lucky Ned Johnson," the judge said.

"Who is Lucky Ned Johnson?" Vancel asked.

Ben sighed, knowing this story was coming, the judge's face lighting up as he told the tale again, just as he told Ethan that one night here in the jail, and a hundred other times before. Ben had to admit, Andrew could tell a good yarn.

"Ned's lame horse spared him a sinking ship and a crazed bride," the judge finished, causing Felicia and the others to laugh.

"I hope I am not as poor at cards as my brother or Lucky Ned." Felicia smiled.

"You are fine, my dear. You even managed to bluff me twice now, if memory serves me right. You are no Nettie Roberts, I assure you," Andrew said, puffing his cigar.

"Nettie Roberts?" she asked.

Here we go again. Ben shook his head.

"The widow Nettie Roberts, married and widowed six times. She was a bit of a legend in east Kansas, an unlucky legend if the demise of her six lovers can attest." The judge took a deep puff on his cigar.

"The poor woman. How did she lose that many?" Felicia asked.

"It wasn't that she was wed and widowed six times that earned her notoriety, mind you, but the way each of them met their demise," Andrew leaned back in his chair, before continuing, drawing his words out to build anticipation like any good storyteller would do. "Her first husband was Hiram Jones, a right nice young fella as most folks attested. He died on their wedding day, at the post-service feast. It seems he didn't take well to peanuts and fell into a seizure of some sort, and died right there."

"Peanuts?" Vancel asked, hanging on the judge's every word.

"Some folks can't abide them, young Vancel, and we can count Hiram Jones among that number. Now, as I was sayin', he died right

209

there on their wedding day, making poor Nettie a widowed virgin, as strange as those odds are. After some time, she was courted by George Tipton, an adventurous fella who was smitten by her beauty upon first meeting her. They were wedded, and bedded, and seemed quite happy, but the war came upon them, and young George went off to fight for the Union. He was with General Grant at Shiloh, where he met his end." The judge paused, taking another puff, waiting for the inevitable question to follow. Ben shook his head, knowing what question would follow, having heard this tale more times than he could shake a stick.

"He died bravely in battle, didn't he?" Felicia asked, expecting that to be the answer.

"Unfortunately, no, my dear. It seems George avoided every bullet and cannon shell sent his way, surviving the battle only to die in the privy." Andrew let that sink in for effect.

"Died in the privy?" Vancel made a face.

"Yep, visited the privy ditch late at night, tripped and struck his head on something, falling to the bottom, where he drowned in a puddle of waste," Andrew said, the others looking a little green from the revelation, save for Dragos, who simply grinned.

"How terrible," Felicia said.

"Yes, indeed, but Nettie was a resilient lass and put her misfortune behind her, catching the eye of a strapping young man named Luke Morris, who stood near the height of our good sheriff here," Andrew pointed his cigar toward Ben, before continuing. "They had a July wedding, and it happened that four weeks after, Luke was driving a fence post and was set upon by a crazed woodchuck, of all things. He bashed it over the head, killing it, but not before taking a bite of his left leg. It came about that the fool thing was rabid. Poor Luke died a terrible death sometime after, howling like a madman."

"A rabid woodchuck?" Vancel found that peculiar. Even in Elaria, they were aware of rabies, ever mindful of it in the heat of summer.

"Yep, not the sort of animal one associates with that affliction. Poor Nettie was in mourning for a spell, until meeting husband number four, one Dalton Green, who was struck by lightning six months after they wed. A few years passed by, with Nettie's reputation for bad luck spoiling her chance of finding husband number five, but eventually, her patience and prayers were rewarded with the arrival of a Mr. John Leyton, a railroad engineer who discounted poor Nettie's luck as superstition. A month after they wed, he was in a saloon in St. Louis and drank some bad liquor and died right there. Some say it was Tarantula Juice, others claim it was something else, all they could agree on was that Nettie was bad luck, and no man was fool enough to be number six. Well, a few more years passed, and unlucky number six arrived in the name of Harlan Smith, an older farmer who longed for a wife, especially one as fetching as our poor Nettie. They were wed for two years, and she bore him a daughter, but Nettie's bad luck continued when Harlan bent over to pick up something in his barn when their goat rammed its head into his backside, knocking him flat. His head happened to strike an anvil sitting on the ground, killing him on the spot. The last I know there was never a number seven. Some in those parts say she killed more men than Generals Lee and Grant combined," the judge finished, taking a well-earned puff on his cigar.

"Is that story true?" Felicia asked, her smile making her doubt so.

"Oh, it's true about her losing six husbands. But did they all die in the matter I said? Who truly knows." Andrew shrugged. "Your turn, Dragos," he said, Dragos always following one of the judge's stories with one of his own.

"There was a queen, a jester, and a two-headed cat," Dragos began. And so it went, the two men trading stories as the night progressed, downing bottles of whisky and Astarian ale. It seemed the drunker they got, the better at cards the judge and Dragos became while poor Vancel looked green around his gills, as Ben would say.

Felicia was spellbound by the entire scene, loving the camaraderie of this odd mixture of characters. She could imagine her father joining them, drinking heavily into the wee hours of the night, his booming voice waking the dead. After a night in Red Rock with the sheriff and the judge, her father would understand why Ethan stayed here so long. She was so caught up in the atmosphere she didn't notice the door opening until her eyes found Jake's staring back at her.

The room grew suddenly quiet, everyone looking at the two of them staring at one another for the longest time, neither able to move, until the Judge had had enough.

"Get yourself in here, Jake. Bring your friend too before you freeze us all to death," Andrew said, making room for them.

A round of introductions followed, with Jake sharing hearty handshakes with Dragos and Krixan, and a kiss on the hand of Felicia, causing her to blush. And so it went, with everyone sharing their news. Jake was relieved with the death of Luke Crawford and most of his men, but Emmitt Cobb still lived, along with Colm Conroy, Ned Stiles, and George Carson, each dangerous in their own right. He was grieved hearing of Ethan's capture, sharing sympathetic looks with Felicia and Dragos. He was pleased by everyone accepting Jerimiah into their midst. Any friend of Bass was a friend of Ben and Judge Donovan, and the Astarians accepted any friend of his.

*****

It was only after everyone retired for the evening that Jake had a moment alone to speak with Felicia, escorting her to Doc Wilson's house, where Dragos was already waiting. She slipped her hand into the crook of his elbow as they walked, enjoying the crisp winter air and starry sky.

"I am pleased you haven't forgotten me, Jake Thorton." She smiled.

"That would be a tall order, Ms. Felicia. I haven't stopped thinking of you since I woke up in Dragos's castle."

"A selfish part of me is glad things turned out as they did, for if Ethan wasn't taken, I doubt my father would have permitted me to come here."

"It is a dangerous journey, and I am surprised he did. West Texas ain't very hospitable or civilized. What changed his mind?"

"Once Ethan was taken, my father was greatly saddened, regretting all the times they argued, and wishing he shared more happy memories. He knew I wished to see you and would never force marriage upon any of us we did not agree to, especially after doing so with Ethan through the years. It was always a source of strife between them, and considering how things came about with Alesha, Father could not bear any of us to suffer someone we wish not to wed. Mother is displeased, I warn you, but not with you, just with the danger of coming here. That is why my father sent so many soldiers."

"To protect you." Jake smiled. "I agree with him. I would have sent a thousand if you were my daughter."

"Just a thousand?" she teased.

"Do you have more than a thousand?"

"Many times that."

His laugh caused her eyebrows to rise.

"Something humors you, Jake Thorton?" she asked.

"Sam Houston won Texas with just eight hundred."

"Truly?" She found that surprising.

"Truly. Of course, a generation later, and Texas fielded many thousands in the Civil War."

"That was the war to end slavery?" she asked, recalling some of what she recently learned of their history.

"For some, that was the aim. The town folk here thought differently. To them, it was about the right of Texas to secede."

"And what do you think?"

"I love Texas. This is my home, and always will be, even when I live somewhere else, but..." His voice trailed, trying to put words to his thoughts.

"But?"

"As much as I love Texas, no man has the right to enslave another, especially for no reason more than the color of his flesh."

"You are fond of your friend. Jerimiah is his name?"

"Yes. He is a good man, and I wish his path was easier. He has all the makings of a good marshal but will never get a chance with some of those now coming on. I took him on so he can learn the territory. That is half the job if you want to know the truth. My friend Bass was the first man of color to be named a deputy US marshal in the Oklahoma Territory and only after having ten years of experience scouting the land. It didn't hurt any that Bass was a large man and was an excellent shot. Jerimiah is a bit smaller than Bass and I, but his gun handling is improving, as is his tracking skill."

"If you speak well of him, that proves his worth. Our neighboring kingdom of Sarcosa is populated with men like Jerimiah, particularly in its southeastern regions. The great port city of Flevum is there, its sea lord very similar in appearance to your friend."

"Flevum is a funny-sounding name. What is it like?"

"I have never been there, but it is rumored to be the jewel of the Aqualania Sea, with towering marble structures circling crystal blue waters. Statues of sea maidens grace the entrance to the harbor, rising the height of thirty men, with sapphires set in their stone eyes, casting their wanton stares across the sea."

"That sounds right beautiful." Jake could only imagine the world she spoke of.

"Perhaps you might visit there one day." She smiled.

"Perhaps I will. I need only a proper guide to show the way." He smiled too, both knowing who he was referring to.

Their brief discourse came to its end as they reached Doc Wilson's home, where Dragos could be seen peeking out the window at them, a devious smile painting his lips.

"We shall talk more tomorrow?" she asked, losing herself in his green eyes.

"I would like that very much, Ms. Felicia." He kissed the back of her hand.

CHAPTER 12

They entered Vellesia west of Lavera, the people filling the streets of every village they passed, receiving their queen and crown princess with deep reverence. Ethan was struck by the quiet beauty of the land, with rolling hills, rich farmland, and rivers so clean that you could see to the bottom. The people looked well-fed and industrious and almost too perfect. Their teeth and skin proved they were frequently visited by mage healers, likely one of Lady Thela Corval's mages. Ethan recalled the Arch Mage from Cordova that he rescued with Allie in the Mage Bane. She was just one of many who played him for a fool, hiding their true intentions for visiting the tropic port. Despite that, he had to admit, she and her guild served their people well. Even the people's clothing was of fine quality, with bright-colored tunics and dresses, and capes of various hues. He noticed all the men were clean-shaven, and their bodies void of hair, wondering if it was a genetic quirk or a grooming etiquette of the realm.

As soon as they passed into Vellesian territory, Alesha permitted him to explore the countryside whenever they set camp, returning him his favored buckskins and weapons, with Ander as his guide, of course. Ethan found good hunting grounds along the Lavera Gap, bringing down a good-sized elk on his first foray. The queen's guards became accustomed to helping him cook his game, each taking turns at the spit, and sharing in the bounty. Sometimes, Alesha would join him as he and the men gathered around their cookfires, sharing stories and adventures. Ethan would play his guitar on occasion, teaching them the words to the *Yellow Rose of Texas*. Most nights, however, found them lodging with local lords and ladies, requiring him to dress formally and attend Alesha as was expected of her Consort.

Several times during their journey across Vellesia, the queen would have him observe the protocols of judgment as she and Alesha held court. It was then the local prisons were emptied; their occupants brought before them for judgment. One area that mage rule excelled over any other was the accuracy of justice, as long as the residing mage was honorable. The prisoners were brought forth one at a time, with their accusers, whereupon Alesha would touch their forehead, binding them to speak the truth. Most were guilty as believed, but occasionally, some were innocent, falsely accused. Nearly all those falsely accused stood alone, their accusers failing to show themselves, fearing being caught. Most were eventually brought to justice, suffering the queen's wrath. One young woman falsely accused a man of rape, out of jealousy for him choosing another. The queen judged her severely, enslaving her to her victim, who in turn sold her to a local lord as a maidservant. Another judgment fell on a man for actually raping a woman. He, in turn, was enslaved and given over to his victim, who ordered him castrated and sold as a galley slave. Theft was dealt with by forced labor equal to the value taken. Murder was dealt with by death in the same manner as the victim. The queen's justice was measured and fair, he had to admit, and resulted in very little crime throughout the land. Of course, it also meant peasants couldn't rise up against an unjust or cruel lord, suffering at his mercy.

He would spend each night in Alesha's arms, her power over him growing with every passing day. The closer they drew to Elysia, the stronger her hold became, consuming his waking thoughts. Strangely, the closer they came to Elysia, the kinder she became, freeing him from as much tedious protocol as she could, allowing him and Ander to wander from their encampment or whatever holdfast they occupied that night. Even Valera treated him fairly, his saving her life and naming her queen of the Tourney at Torval, earning him a measure of freedom, providing he restrained his negative comments. For once in his life, Ethan learned to keep his tongue.

Eventually, they visited the holdfast of Lord Mattiese, Lady Leora's father, who held dominion of the lower Sorell River Valley.

Ethan found the man as miserable as his daughter, his clean face and thick black hair masking his true age. Leora's daughter Teresa resided in the palace with her grandfather, awaiting the arrival of Sir Dougaris, her betrothed, who rode in the queen's company. Ethan recalled the story of the knight loving another, before the queen interceded, ordering Alesha to strip him of such memories, to preserve his betrothal to Lady Teresa. Looking at the man, he looked smitten by his betrothed, a testament to Alesha's power. They resided in place for several days for the wedding ceremony, overseen by the queen herself. Sir Dougaris would remain after they departed. As a second son to his house, Sir Rodero Dougaris would take the name Mattiese, as Teresa was heir to their great house.

It was late in the evening of their first night in the Mattiese palace, that Alesha led Ethan to the upper battlements. They gazed northeast where the road to Elysia fell under the shadow of the Salnar Mountains that dominated the horizon. Ethan found the view breathtaking, the towering peaks of the Salnar rising through the clouds, with thick evergreens circling the mountain range.

"Within that circle of mountains, rests Elysia, my home, and soon to be yours," Alesha said, taking Ethan's hand in hers as they stared off to the northeast.

"It is beautiful, I'll give you that," he said politely, though it would never be his home.

"I have dreamed of the day when I would finally bring you to my home, Ethan. I know your feelings and resentments with your situation, but please see Elysia with an unprejudiced eye. You may come to love it here, if given a chance."

He didn't really have a choice, but wisely kept that to himself.

"I will try, Alesha," was all he could promise, before taking her in his arms.

*****

Astaris

Gabrielle stood upon the lower battlements of the Queen's Tower, looking below as Tristan and Amanda entered the court-yard, their mounts lathered from their morning ride. She watched as Tristan dismounted in a flourish before helping Amanda down from her silver palfrey while stable servants hurried forth to attend their horses. Gabrielle smiled watching the two of them, Tristan escorting her into the palace, with Amanda tucking her arm inside his elbow.

"They seem happy," Ceresta observed, standing at her mother's side, her face a mask of indifference.

"Yes. The eyes reveal all. Your father and I were like that once." Gabrielle smiled at the memory.

"You are still like that now," Ceresta reminded her.

"In a way. I have always loved your father, and every day that love grows stronger in a deeply meaningful way, but nothing compares to when true love first ignites," she thought wistfully.

"True love, Mother? Be careful not to see what you desire over what is there," she warned.

"Oh, my dearest Ceresta, one day you will know what I speak of. A handsome boy will enter your life and sweep you away like a river cresting its banks."

"Not likely." She rolled her eyes, never one to humor the romantic fantasies like her younger sisters.

"If you believe so." Gabrielle smiled inwardly, knowing her headstrong daughter would change her mind one day, or at least she hoped she would. She wanted grandchildren from all her children and wasn't above any method that ensured that would happen. She would work on Ceresta once she finished with Tristan, and seeing the boy in recent days made her feel that that task was nearly complete.

"I know you favor a match between them, Mother, but I would caution, that as much as I admire her, she is still Valera's daughter," Ceresta warned.

"By blood, and nothing else. Her attributes far outweigh that one detriment. She is a princess by blood and quite lovely. She is also the most powerful mage in the realm, far greater than Dragos or I, or even your father. That alone makes her an excellent choice. But most importantly, your brother is smitten. One must never overlook the benefit of a match both parties desire on a carnal level."

"Mother!" Ceresta gasped at her impropriety.

"Oh, hush. You are not a child that I must curb my tongue. Marriages where a man and a woman desire each other are far stronger than loveless arrangements, I assure you. Besides, there is one other matter we mustn't overlook, one that even Valera hasn't likely considered," Gabrielle said knowingly.

"And that is?"

"Should Amanda wed Tristan, the protection from Vellesia that Ethan forced Valera to grant to Amanda, would extend to him as well, and their children," she said, referencing Ethan's Royal Request that freed Amanda.

Ceresta's silence proved she hadn't considered that reluctantly agreeing with her mother's summation.

"Ethan couldn't have known Amanda and Tristan would be drawn to one another, could he?" Ceresta made a face.

"No, just his usual dumb luck. After so much dumb luck, we have to consider it isn't dumb or luck, but something else," Gabrielle thought aloud.

"Such as?"

"Destiny."

CHAPTER 13

The Queen's Road wound through the Salnar Mountains, sunlight swallowed by its black surface. A deep vertical drop rested off the left side of the causeway, with sheer mountain slopes rising upon its right. Ethan craned his neck skyward as the jagged snow caps rose all around him. The air was strangely warm even though he was immune to the mage-spelled atmosphere that surrounded the causeway. The magic was useful in keeping the road clear of snow and debris, as it snaked perfectly along the base of one mountain, before passing over a bridge to the base of another. The road was wide enough for a dozen wagons to ride abreast, a marvel of engineering only possible with mage craft, or so his *beloved* wife reminded him as he rode at her side.

"Not much farther," Alesha remarked, gifting him a flirtatious smile. She could see that he was in awe, the dangerous beauty of the Salnar Mountains towering menacingly above.

"You are speechless." She smirked, pleased with his reaction.

"And I thought Astaris was difficult to approach," he said.

"Astaris can be approached from several directions. Elysia can be approached by *one*," she stated firmly.

"And this is the one." He sighed heavily as if invisible walls were closing about him. Even if he could get around the magic binding his father, he doubted he could escape Elysia.

"The mountain up ahead is Kagara. You can tell by the massive gouge near the summit's east face." She pointed at the misshapen peak, silhouetted by the clear afternoon sky. The road would soon pass under the mountain's shadow, after crossing a bridge that spanned the deep chasm separating the line of mountains. Ethan eased Bull to the side of the bridge, his old friend wary to be near the edge. The air caught in his throat as he stared over the precipice at the Elysian River flowing along the valley floor, two thousand feet below, passing underneath them, with a series of waterfalls along its course.

"Beautiful, isn't it?" Alesha said, easing Glynderelle to his side. "Come. We mustn't tarry," she said, drawing him away.

The road passed over the base of Kagara, with the deep chasm to their left. They were in the center of the vast column, their once sizable entourage growing exponentially since crossing into Vellesia. Ethan lost count, guessing their escort to be over one thousand mounted cavalry, four hundred knights, and thousands of nobles and their retainers. This was in addition to their original host, with the queen's personal retainers, courtesans, servants, and royal guards. Queen Valera rode up ahead, adorned with shimmering golden armor, and a large gold crown set upon her brow. Alesha wore silver armor, sunlight playing off her cuirass, with the sigil of her house emblazoned upon her breast, a golden rose upon a field of black. Her raven black hair flowed below her silver crown, sunlight shining off the diamonds embedded along its surface. She was beautiful beyond imagining, and he couldn't help staring, shamed by the power she held over him. She was his jailer, his betrayer, his mortal enemy, and all those facts meant nothing compared to the beating of his heart.

A wicked smile stretched across her face as she caught him staring, reveling in the power she held over him.

"Something catch your fancy, Ethan?" she asked playfully.

"Stinker," he mumbled under his breath.

"I can hear you." She smiled.

"You'd look better in a dress," he said.

"So would you," she teased him.

"No thanks. This is bad enough," he complained, tugging at the collar of his silk shirt. It was black, with the sigil of House Loria upon its chest. His trousers were of the same color and fabric and, like the shirt, were tight, conforming to his every curve. It was almost sinful the way it displayed his assets whenever he moved. His father's sword rode his left hip, with his pistols and buckskins packed away.

"I think you look quite fetching. The fabric is far more flattering than your buckskins." She ran her eyes up and down his muscled form.

"I guess it could be worse," he said, observing the ridiculous attire of the queen's footmen standing upon the back of the queen's carriage, each wearing a tight doublet over a ruffled blouse with short puffed pantaloons that came well short of the knees with a green hose. They each wore floppy red hats that topped their atrocious attire.

"Oh." She smiled, seeing what he was looking at. "You don't favor what my mother's footmen are wearing?"

"Not on a man, that's for sure."

"But it is fine if women are forced to wear such things?" She raised a brow, warning him he was on dangerous ground.

"You always twist my words around," he growled.

"I am not twisting anything, Ethan. You were commenting on the attire of the queen's footmen."

"Forget it." He shook his head.

"I will do no such thing. You commented on their *ridiculous* attire, insulting the queen's servants. For someone who constantly ridicules the pretensions of the mage born, I find it ironic that you are just as conceited as them."

"Conceited? I just said no man would dress that way by his own choice."

"Dress in what way?" she asked, masking her enjoyment of this exchange, with a practiced frown.

"Those puffed…trousers or skirt, or whatever they are, and the ruffled shirt thingy. Men shouldn't wear that stuff."

"They look little different from what the men in Astaris wore during our visit," she pointed out.

"Never mind."

"No, you are saying you don't favor the short pantaloons, is this right?"

"Or tunics, hose, anything with ruffles, floppy hats, kilts, or any of that stuff," he added.

"And what you are wearing now meets your satisfaction?"

"It's a little tight, but better than that." He lifted his chin toward the coach ahead.

"Then you better be on your best behavior going forward, my love. I get to decide your attire, though there are times when the Queen Mother and Queen Daughter will select what you will wear, as they do with myself and our entire household. Tonight, we shall be attending a gala in our honor, and the outfit you shall wear will reflect that, including some of the items you abhor."

She must be joking, he thought miserably.

"I am not jesting," she said.

"How did you know what I was thinking?" he asked warily, wondering if she could truly read his thoughts.

"It's not too difficult, Ethan, since you repeatedly complain about the same things. Just prepare yourself to be miserably attired over the next few days. The Queen Mother has prepared numerous celebrations that we must attend."

"Wonderful," he grumbled.

"If you behave, I will do my utmost to see you have some time to yourself after."

They continued along for a short while, passing the far side of Kagara, where the road jutted into an expanse, ringed by mountains. There, in the center of the great expanse, rested Elysia, the great capital palace of Vellesia, its outer walls rising a thousand feet, with massive battlements silhouetted against the clear sky. The walls were pristinely white, sparkling intensely in the sunlight. A ring of towers rose imperiously above the outer walls, each three hundred feet higher than the outermost battlements, one was silver, one red, and the other black as a moonless night. A large citadel rose even higher from the center of the palace city, its lowest ramparts overlooking the surrounding towers. A golden tower jutted above the massive citadel, its minarets rising twelve hundred feet above the outer walls.

"The tower of Glyndera," Alesha said, following his eyes to where the standard of House Loria graced the golden tower's summit, a golden rose upon a field of black. The massive standard stretched the length of twenty men, and the height of twelve, large enough to be seen miles distant.

Ethan paled at the majesty of Elysia, the fortress city dwarfing his native Astaris. Even Dragos's tower would barely break above its lowest walls. The road jutted across the open expanse, leading straight to the city gates, where a massive drawbridge was lowered, connecting the road to the palace, crossing over a deep chasm that circled the palace, its sheer cliff dropping thousands of feet below. The road jutted into the chasm, with the drawbridge overlapping its lip. The grandeur and power the palace impressed upon Ethan were suffocating, its overbearing presence reminding him of the futility of escaping this place.

"Welcome to your new home, Ethan," Alesha said proudly.

*****

A thousand trumpets sounded as the royal procession entered the city. Tens of thousands lined the streets, greeting their return, dropping to their knees as Valera passed, a golden glow alighting her countenance, bathing their faces in otherworldly light.

Ethan's eyes narrowed suspiciously as he and Alesha followed in Valera's wake, the city coming into view once they passed under the city gates. They traversed a wide avenue that ran from the city entrance to the massive citadel resting in the palace's center, its towering walls looming ominously several miles ahead. Towering evergreens lined the sides of the streets, their green needled branches contrasting the marble structures looming behind them. The street was pristine and spotless, its cleanliness matched by the symmetry and perfection of every edifice in sight. The people kneeling as they passed were richly attired, the women dressed in beautiful gowns, the men in doublets and pantaloons, or tunics with a hose. Thousands of soldiers lined the avenue in silver mail over white tunics with pleated kilts. A bright glow emitted from Alesha's countenance, proclaiming her eminence as she passed, the people shielding their eyes against the blinding glare.

Ethan made a face, wondering the reason for this strange behavior, before realizing its source. Though he saw nothing, Alesha's glowing flesh was another mage gift inherited from her ancestors. He couldn't see the waves of euphoria Alesha sent to the crowds, elating their spirits with a wave of her hand. They passed the base of the black tower, its surface as dark as a starless night sky, its base hundreds of feet across, supporting the structure rising into the heavens. The silver tower rested off their left, and the red on the other side of the city. The road rose in elevation as they drew nearer the inner palace, its white walls looming ominously ahead, its open gates akin to the jowls of a great beast meaning to swallow Ethan whole.

"The people love you, Ethan," Alesha said as they passed the cheering crowds. Ethan caught more than one face staring happily at him, their smiles seeming more genuine than he thought logical.

"They don't know me." He sighed warily.

"They know all about the former crown prince of Astaria. Bards sing of your great deeds throughout Elysia, their crowds growing with each telling."

"And how is it they learned of my exploits? I didn't think your mother would allow her people to grow fond of her troublesome sl—son," he caught himself from saying *slave.*

"You misjudge your queen, Ethanos. Your glorious victory at the Velo and journey to the Mage Bane to rescue me reflects favorably upon the House of Loria. The Queen Mother has allowed these truths of you to reach the ears of our people."

"Why?" He made a face.

"You are a prince and a hero, a worthy consort for their crown princess. It allows our people to celebrate our union with the significance it deserves."

"With the significance it deserves but not the true significance of our union. They don't know the secret of House Loria, do they?"

"And what secret is that?" She gave him a dangerous look.

"Just who exactly knows that our child gains both of our powers?" he whispered, leaning close so others couldn't overhear.

"Very few, and I expect you to make sure that list doesn't grow."

"What does it matter? By now, everyone in Astaria knows, and how long will it take before that rumor crosses the seven kingdoms?"

"It won't pass into Vellesia, and Vellesia is all that matters. Am I understood, Ethan?" she warned.

"As you command, mistress." He gave her a mock bow.

"I thought you gave up whining. It doesn't become you."

"I'm entitled to a little whining now and then. Don't worry, my love. I won't embarrass you in front of your people. I can play the part you set out for me." He smiled at the crowd, waving his hand. "Not that it matters. Even if I do something foolish, you can always wave your hand and make their unwanted memories disappear."

"That is hardly a thing done lightly."

"Relax, Allie. I'll do what you ask. I'm here, aren't I? Playing along like the lap dog you've made me. You won, I lost, and now we are here. So go on, lead me to my cage."

She pursed her lips, biting off the anger he so easily invoked. She looked forward to showing him her home, where she grew up, hoping that he would take interest in an intimate part of her life. It was a foolish hope, a sentimental weakness her mother would scorn. Why did she yearn for his approval? Why did he hold such sway over her heart? Why did it feel as if his callous disregard was a rejection of her? Had not her ancestors expunged such feminine weakness from their bloodline? Was it the child growing within, that brought about such sensitivity?

No! She would not do this. A lesser woman would take his words to heart, guilting him into an apology, or build walls of ice between them. Alesha Loria was not a lesser woman. She was the crown princess of Vellesia and the conqueror of Ethan Blagen.

Very well. To your cage, I shall lead you, she prepared to say when he surprised her once again.

"I'm sorry, Alesha. Your home is beautiful. Never mind me. I do complain a lot. I'll get over it. Just bear with me," Ethan said in all sincerity. "And it was kind of your grandmother to let the people know my history. I do appreciate their fond greetings."

"Apology accepted." She gifted him a smile for once again surprising her.

*****

The inner palace of Elysia towered over the city like a mountain of stone overlooking a low plain. Massive bulwarks and turrets jutted prominently around its face. The base of the inner palace rested nearly four hundred feet above the base of the outer walls, with the road following a steep ascent from the outer gate to the entrance of the inner palace. The inner palace rested on a central rise, with the city proper circling it in a series of concentric rings, sloping in each direction. This provided the inner palace with a commanding view of the city, even from its lowest levels. Ethan craned his neck skyward, the jagged battlements above, obscuring the citadels that spiraled into the heavens behind them. It pained his neck looking up, searching for the summit of those towering walls as they drew nigh. No army in the world could breach this fortress. If the other six realms united against Vellesia, he doubted they could win, even with the combined might of all their mage born.

A grand entourage awaited their procession at the gate of the inner palace, led by Prince Raymar astride a spirited black charger, wearing a scarlet doublet over a white silk shirt and black trousers.

"Mother," he greeted with a bow, after the head of the procession parted, allowing Queen Valera to make her way to the front.

"Raymar." She smiled at her handsome son, who stood nearly a height to Ethan, with long coal black hair framing his smooth masculine jaw, and deep olive skin.

"You are a welcome sight, Mother. The palace has been painfully dull in your absence." Raymar smiled, his pure white teeth sparkling with perfection.

"And your charm was lacking on our journey." She drew her horse alongside his, reaching a hand out to his cheek.

"You should have brought me along, Mother."

"Perhaps. You might've kept Amanda from betraying our House," Valera quipped.

"Yes, Grandmother was most displeased. We mustn't despair, Mother. I may have lost a sister but have gained a brother. Where is the mighty Prince Ethanos whose legend precedes him?" He looked past her shoulders, searching for the man in question.

"None of that now, my child. There will be time for introductions later. The Queen Mother is expecting us, and even I dare not keep her waiting."

"True. Very well then, my Queen." Raymar smiled, waving a hand through the open gate. "Elysia is yours."

*****

"Who is he?" Ethan asked as they followed her mother through the gate.

"My brother," Alesha whispered, identifying Raymar, who rode up ahead alongside her mother.

The one who met with Tristan, trying to warn me, Ethan recalled. He wondered how he was able to sneak away from Elysia without being missed. His journey to Astaria must have taken a very long time. Amanda did mention that she and her brother wielded powerful mental mage powers, including the ability to shape memories and thoughts. Since they inherited these abilities from their father, it meant Valera and her mother did not possess them, only Alesha and her siblings. *At least I have one potential ally here*, he thought, latching hold of any good news he could.

The outer walls of the inner palace were over one hundred feet thick. They passed through a large tunnel behind the gate that ran under the massive wall. He could see daylight bathing the open courtyard up ahead, where the tunnel led. The further they entered Elysia, the grander the palace became. The tunnel opened up to a large palace green, with an expansive parade field and courtyard. Beyond this was the inner citadel, a mountainous structure stretching to the heavens, its massive battlements jutting prominently overhead, with the Tower of Glyndera resting behind these ramparts. A large, wide stair rested at the base of the structure, stretching fifty yards abreast, with hundreds of courtesans and royal guards standing statue still to receive them.

Queen Valera dismounted upon the place green, with attendants rushing forth to retrieve her horse bowing low as she strode forth. Prince Raymar did likewise, followed by everyone else. Another army of servants hurried forth to attend to their mounts, leading them to the stables off their left, a large, gray circular structure, that looked as large as a small palace itself.

Ethan paused as an attendant reached for Bull's reins, reluctant to trust his horse to anyone else's care.

"Come, Ethan," Alesha urged, wondering about his hesitation.

"Give me a moment to settle Bull in his stall," he said.

"The Queen Mother awaits us. Leave Bull to the servants."

"What about my things?" he protested.

"They will be delivered to our chambers. Come!" she ordered, offering her hand.

*****

Ethan and Alesha followed Valera across the palace green, with Raymar falling in step behind them, their entourage trailing further back, with their military escort breaking off to stable their horses. Ethan counted hundreds of court officials, mage lords, and palace guards crowding the wide stair ahead, forming a semicircle around an open space in their center. He caught sight of two women amidst this assembly, standing side by side with matching purple eyes, Sarella and Selendra, Alesha's aunts who spied upon him through the years in Astaris. He hadn't seen Sarella since they entered Vellesia, as she rode on ahead to treat with the Queen Mother.

Wonderful. He rolled his eyes, adding them to his list of obstacles to overcome. He could feel the eyes of Leora Mattiese boring into the back of his skull from wherever she was behind him. She was the sourest woman he had the displeasure of ever meeting. He knew Valera and Alesha possessed almost unlimited power, but he hadn't a clue what Leora was capable of. She was powerful enough to hold the favor of the queen. In all fairness, she was no worse than the other ministers of Valera's court, who all stared at him with pure loathing. He guessed they didn't take to his opinion of Valera back in Astaris. It didn't matter, he reminded himself, for even if they did think kindly of him, Alesha could just replace those pleasant thoughts with the ones they now had.

Alesha and Valera's powers were unsettling enough, but when he thought about their many grandmothers, all with nearly as much power as them, he grew depressed with the futility of his situation. Even if he could free his father of their magic and escape this place, neither of which looked possible, he couldn't prevent them from destroying Astaria. Though he could defeat any one of them, he couldn't be in every place at once, and they would attack Astaria from every direction. If he countered Alesha at one border, Valera or Corella would overrun another. Besides that, how could he stop Alesha without hurting her? He was overcome with a driving need to protect her, as the very thought of her being harmed sickened his soul. Every day, this feeling grew, binding his heart and free will to hers.

He was so lost in his thoughts he hadn't noticed that they had come to a stop before the palace, the crowd silent as a tomb as if waiting for something or someone. His eyes drifted up to a massive outcropping jutting from the palace some three hundred feet above, where stood a dozen women adorned in golden robes, overlooking the assemblage below. One stood out from the others, wearing an ornate crown resting in her midnight black hair. The crown was twice the height of her head, with fist-sized diamonds embedded on its golden surface. To his utter dismay, the woman lifted into the air, easing over the parapet of the outcropping, hovering above them before slowly descending into their midst, setting down upon the center of the semi-circle of courtesans.

The entire assemblage dropped to their knees in unison, even Alesha, who tugged on his sleeve, drawing him to kneel, before pressing his head to the ground. He found bending one knee humiliating enough, but this was beyond the pale. Even Valera prostrated herself before the Queen Mother, indicating the power Corella held over House Loria and the realm. He hoped his intervention with the dragon where he saved Valera, might garner him some points in his favor, but what did Valera's life matter in the grand scheme? It was Alesha that bore the future heir, and Corella who held final authority of the realm. Valera was only the Queen Daughter, a simple middleman in the chain of command. If Valera was intimidating, Corella was downright frightening, or at least he expected her to be.

"Arise, my children," Queen Corella commanded, her mage-projected voice echoing across the assemblage like gentle thunder, though Ethan only heard her quiet utterance.

This is gonna be a long day, Ethan thought miserably, gaining his feet, feeling Corella's gaze upon him. He was taken aback by her piercing silver eyes that stared right through him with terrible intensity, before shifting to Valera.

"Come hither, daughter," Corella beckoned her forth, reaching out her hands to her as Valera floated through the air, setting down before her.

"Mother." Valera bowed her head slightly to where Corella stood, overlooking the crowd.

Ethan cringed at the power they displayed, first observing this mage gift when Valera floated above the barrier stone before the dragon attacked. *We never stood a chance*, he thought miserably, that thought repeating in his brain, making him wonder why they even needed his power. They could topple all the mage realms with ease, and there wasn't a thing they could do about it. He made a face whilst looking at the two of them, confused by Corella's youthful appearance. If Valera looked no older than thirty years, then Corella appeared only a year or two older. They could be sisters if he didn't know better. They were exchanging pleasantries that he couldn't hear until they summoned Alesha forth. She took Ethan in hand, dragging him along. Alesha decided to walk beside him rather than float through the air like her mother. He figured she felt the need to lead him personally to her grandmother like a prized stallion or lamb heading to the slaughter.

"Queen Mother." Alesha bowed her head after ascending the stairs. Ethan stood at her side, looking around like an idiot as they greeted one another.

"My dearest Alesha." Corella pressed her hands to her granddaughter's face. "Welcome home, child."

"Thank you, Grandmother."

"And this," Corella cooed, pressing her palm to Alesha's womb. "You bring a wondrous gift."

"A child of prophecy," Valera beamed, standing beside them.

"The fulfillment of House Loria," Corella added before bending down, placing a kiss upon Alesha's stomach, blessing her womb.

Alesha blushed with the queen's reverence.

"We have such plans for you, little one," Corella whispered to her unborn grandchild, before straightening.

"It has been a long journey." Valera sighed tiredly.

"Indeed, a long and legendary trek halfway across the seven realms and back. Nearly as arduous as Alesha's journey to Cordova and the Mage Bane but not nearly as perilous, though there were dangers," Corella gave Valera an admonishing look.

"It was a necessary risk, mother," Valera said.

"Dragons are not necessary risks, my child. Thankfully, my new grandson was there to intervene on your behalf," Corella regarded Ethan, who was caught staring at the ramparts above.

"Uh, sorry about that." He shrugged, noticing a slight twitch at the corner of Corella's lip, and the others staring at him.

"Ethan," he said, offering his hand. "You must be Alesha's grandmother. Pleasure to meet you, ma'am," he said with a Texas drawl that caused Valera to cringe and Alesha to nearly face-palm at his lack of decorum.

"Ethan," Corella, to her credit, greeted in kind, taking his hand as he shook it, before kissing the back of it.

"I see where Alesha and Valera get their looks from. They never mentioned your astounding beauty," he decided to lay on the charm. It wasn't a stretch of the truth, either, for Corella was stunningly beautiful. Her skin was fairer than Valera, which led Ethan to believe Valera's darker coloring came from her father.

"I am delighted you find me fair to look upon, Ethanos. I am also delighted that rumors of your beauty were equally founded." She ran her eyes easily over his comely form. She thought to put the boy in his place, reminding him of who he was speaking to, perhaps having him kneel and kiss her feet. That would establish his true place in her house, but that could always be done later. Instead, she used a different tact, repaying his comment with one of her own. He clearly didn't like to be called beautiful, and it delighted her to see him trying to smile at that.

"Pretty." Corella's smile stretched painfully wide as she caressed his cheek. "And brave. You have done a great service to your house by saving my daughter from that dreadful dragon. Such a deed warrants the granting of a Royal Request."

Royal request? He shook his head, knowing what she was going to say next.

"As Alesha's consort, your life belongs to her and therefore any boon you earn passes rightfully to her."

No kidding, he thought sourly. They were as predictable as they claimed he was. Why did he even bother? He should've let the dragon eat Valera and have one less of them to deal with. No, he thought bitterly, he couldn't do that. As much as he hated her, he still wasn't ready to kill her. It would only hurt Allie the way his father dying would hurt him, and for some reason, he cared about her.

"Thank you, Grandmother," Alesha said, touching a hand to Ethan's shoulder. "I would like time to think on the matter before deciding. Perhaps something to make Ethan's stay here a little more to his liking, as long as it is appropriate."

Well, that rules out just about everything, he thought.

"Take your time, dear one. You have truly earned it," Corella cooed, addressing Alesha while her hand still lingered on Ethan's cheek. "We have awaited this day for centuries, Ethanos. You didn't make it easy, but the greatest treasures are never cheaply won."

It seemed pretty easy to Ethan. They strolled right into Astaris, tricked him and his father, and strolled back out with Ethan in tow.

"Come. The pleasures of Elysia await you. We have prepared a great feast to honor your union, and a grand ball. The nobles of all the great and lesser houses of Vellesia have gathered to partake in our celebration. In two days, all shall gather in the throne room to witness the formal wedding of Alesha and Ethanos," Corella said.

Formal wedding? He made a face. He thought they were already wed when she put that damn collar around his neck.

"The royal seamstress has produced the loveliest gown for your nuptial. You will look stunning, and I am certain Ethanos will look forward to seeing you in it." Corella smiled.

Alesha placed her hand in his, squeezing it tightly.

"Armor and trousers are not appropriate until the child is born," Corella admonished, regarding Alesha's attire.

"The…," Valera spoke up in Alesha's defense before her mother interrupted.

"It was a wise precaution on the road, I know, but you are home now, thank the spirits of our ancestors. Come, the pleasures of Elysia await."

*****

"I'm not wearing this again," Ethan growled, tugging at the tight green doublet and white silk shirt with puffed sleeves he found himself attired. A black pleated kilt and sandaled boots completed the dreadful ensemble. He stood in the center of their spacious chamber, staring miserably into a large mirror held by doting servants.

"You look very handsome." Alesha smiled, standing beside the mirror, facing him. She donned a floor-length silver gown, with diamonds sewn into its tight bodice and long billowing sleeves and skirt. A slender silver crown rested upon her head, her long black hair framing her beaming smile.

"I'm not wearing this, Allie," he warned, ready to tear the garments off.

"You will, or Mother will burn your precious buckskins and Stetson."

"Allie…I look ridiculous."

"You look handsome. I've always wondered how you would look dressed as a proper noble or prince. You put the crown royals of the seven realms to shame. Besides, the Queen Mother selected this outfit for you especially, and she is not to be trifled with, I assure you."

"The Queen Mother? You mean your grandmother. You can forgo the fancy titles. It's just you and me here, Alesha," he said, overlooking the dozen servants attending them, spread throughout their private chamber like a small army. There were eight women and four men, all attired in formal clothing, the women in shimmering gowns, and the men in tunics with hose. The men were not of hardy stock, each a full head shorter than Ethan, with dainty builds. He doubted they could lift a hairbrush, let alone a sword. He wondered if they were selected for their unusually diminutive size. The men attended him, and the ladies Alesha, fussing with their attire and setting their hair. He hated how much longer his hair was now, dipping below his collar, Alesha refusing to let him cut it.

"Come sit, Consort Loria," one of the men said, indicating a plush stool near the chamber's far wall.

Ethan grumbled, taking a seat as the fellow unfurled a cloth with a dozen combs and brushes arranged in their allotted places.

"What has befallen your hair, Consort Loria?" The fellow gasped in a voice far too loud for a man.

"It's getting far too long for my taste. Why do you ask?" Ethan grumbled.

"Too long? This will not do. Not do at all, I am afraid," the fellow tutted and tsked.

"Ethan has always cut his hair close to his scalp, Fabin. I have ordered him to grow it out, though he protests doing so," Alesha explained to the man tending his hair, as the ladies knelt before her, settling the hem of her gown.

"My apologies, Your Highness. My work may not meet your expectations considering the state of his hair. Might you lend a hand?" Fabin asked, wondering if she might lengthen his hair through her magic.

"Ethanos is immune to such ministrations, Fabin. Even I am powerless to do so." Alesha hated admitting to her limitations. Though their child's immunity to magic passed to her, she still could not affect Ethan. At least his presence no longer interrupted her magical abilities, but that would likely change once the child was born. That meant their child's powers could not affect Ethan but would affect her. That realization would be ill-received by her mother and grandmothers.

"Enough." Ethan stood, fed up with Fabin's fussing.

"My apologies, Consor..." Fabin backed a fearful step.

"Ethan, just call me Ethan. And stop trying to fix my hair!" he growled, taking a comb and running it twice over his head before tossing it back on the table. "See, that's all you needed to do."

"That will not do," Fabin protested, aghast at the state of Ethan's hair.

"It'll do. Where I come from, men don't pamper their hair," Ethan dismissed his concern.

"Truly, Ethan?" Alesha crossed her arms. "Every high lord in Astaria has well-tended locks, even your father."

"Not in Red Rock." He let slip.

"You're not from Texas, Ethan. You were born a crown prince of Astaria and will die a royal consort of Vellesia. To pretend otherwise is childish. Fabin is only doing his duty as a royal hairdresser. You need not torment him," she scolded.

"The only one being tormented is me," he countered.

"Everyone, leave us!" she ordered the servants out before taking Ethan's hand, leading him to her bay window overlooking Elysia.

"Alesha, I...," he started to say before she placed a finger to his lips.

"Ssh," she hushed. "I know this is difficult for you. If the choice was mine, I would not force all this upon you. You must understand, my family has looked to this day for many centuries. They are eager to see you and see you with me. Just do as the Queen Mother asks for the next few days. All of Vellesia is gathered here to celebrate our union. Once the pomp and ceremony are passed, you can partake of all the things you enjoy." Her golden eyes gazed pleadingly into his sea blue.

"I enjoyed being free."

"Ethan, don't." She shook her head.

"Yeah, I know, I won't bring it up." He threw up his hands.

"You will always bring it up. It is an invisible wall that will always lie between us."

"And whose fault is that? If you hadn't tricked me in Astaris, we'd still be together but happier."

"Together?" She shook her head.

"Together. I would've built a home for us, just you and me, and no one else. No queens to please, no protocols to follow. No one but you and I, living free from the world and its problems. Does that sound so awful?" He took her in his arms, pressing his forehead to hers.

He told her this before, on that eventful night in Astaris when her true identity was revealed. She sighed, nearly losing herself in his embrace. Part of her wanted to give in to him, to run away and live as they chose, just the two of them. Whenever Ethan held her, everything felt right with the world, as if she found her missing half. Since she was born, she was consumed with the insatiable hunger for the power she did not possess, for Ethan's power. 'Twas a hunger that every heir of Vellesia felt for thousands of years, a hunger that was all-consuming, driving every crown princess to seek a consort with a power she lacked, a hunger so powerful that would not lessen even after the new power passed on to their heirs. It was a hunger she could see in her mother and grandmother, whenever they looked at Ethan, a jealous fervor of seeing his immense power, and never being able to possess it. Valera explained that this hunger would never abate. Even after his death, her mother could never overcome her jealousy of her father's power. Strangely, Alesha's hunger began to lessen the moment she first met Ethan, eventually disappearing altogether, replaced with a new hunger to simply be near him, to hold him, to…touch him. She loved the sound of his voice, and the beating of his heart whenever she rested her head upon his chest.

Is this love? she asked herself, but nothing she heard of love could explain a feeling this strong. What she felt for Ethan was beyond such a simple word. It was to a point now, where she did not think of his power at all, and if she did, it was something she admired in him, a thing to cherish and not envy.

You have a duty! another voice whispered in her ear.

And so she did. She was the heir to Vellesia, the crown princess of the realm, and duty bound to rule and pass on to her unborn daughter all of hers and Ethan's powers.

"It is beautiful scenery. I'll give you that," he said, staring out the window at the snow-capped mountains ringing the palace in the distance.

She turned, pressing her head to his chest, staring out the window. Her royal apartment was high in the central citadel, overlooking the jagged ramparts of the inner keep and the outer walls of the inner palace. They could see people moving along the city streets below, like small insects from these airy heights. They could even see over the outermost walls of the palace, and the mountain road, where it snaked between the towering peaks, disappearing in the distance.

"I have missed this," she whispered, recalling the times they shared before her betrayal, the times he was her friend, the only true friend she ever knew. To admit such was unlike her. It was a weakness her mother and grandmothers could never understand. But they never shared with their husbands what Alesha shared with Ethan. He risked his life for her in the Mage Bane, not for the crown princess of Vellesia but for a mage healer he didn't even know. He thought her ungrateful for what he did, but how could she ever forget? For the first time in her life, she was helpless, captive in the Mage Bane, surrounded by dangerous men. She, the most powerful mage ever born, was helpless against Luke Crawford and his men, men each immune to magic as Ethan, but without his good heart and honor. If they wielded swords or arms native to Elaria, she might have overcome them, but guns? Guns she was unfamiliar with at that time. It seemed hopeless until Ethan appeared like a hero in a story. He was a hero, her hero. What she felt for him at that moment only grew as she came to know the boy behind the name and face. No, not boy, man. He was a man in every sense of the word, the kind of man men were meant to be. Every day from that moment until her betrayal rent her heart for what she had to do. There was no other way. She had to trick him, to bring him back to Vellesia and bind their fates as destiny and duty demanded. Finally, now, here in her bedchamber overlooking the Salnar Mountains, she finally felt what they shared in the Mage Bane. Oh, he was still angry with her, but he cared for her and loved her. For now, that was enough.

*****

"We had these built for you in mind," Alesha said as they stepped into the lift. It was the size of a large closet, constructed of sturdy oak, and operated on an extensive pulley system. The lift was manually operated with a team of men working a massive crank to lower and raise the platform through the length of the golden tower. A second manual lift ran from the top of the inner palace to the ground level, a short distance from the base of the golden tower. They were the only manual lifts in all of Elysia, built specifically for Ethan. The other lifts throughout the city were operated by magic, completely useless for Ethan to ascend with, but for some reason, he could use them to descend. It was another peculiarity that was worth investigating.

"It's a good thing, or I'd spend all my time here taking the stairs," he said.

"I am certain you would manage." She smiled, slipping her arm around his elbow before stepping out at the base of the golden tower, where it opened to one of the upper levels of the inner palace. They entered a broad, well-lit hallway with basin torches liberally spaced for Ethan's benefit, as the corridor was also alit with mage lanterns, which he could not see. Unbeknownst to everyone, Ethan could see in the dark, a fact he never shared with anyone. Royal guards stood post along the corridor, dressed in bright silver cuirasses, helms, and greaves over white tunics with pleated kilts. They stood rigidly to attention, dipping their spears as they passed.

"Are we the only ones attending this thing?" Ethan asked, noticing the empty corridor. The hall was impressive in scale, with life-size statues of former queens spaced along its length, with beautifully painted frescos decorating the high walls between them. Alesha pointed out the names of each of the queens as they passed.

"Everyone is already there waiting for us," she said as they neared the end of the corridor, where a massive archway rested, light from the adjoining chamber bathing the end of the passageway.

"Your Highness." Leora Mattiese bowed stiffly, greeting them at the archway.

"Minister Mattiese, you look stunning, I must confess," Alesha commented on her floor-length emerald gown, and coifed hair pinned high upon her head.

"You are most kind, Princess." She smiled before turning to Ethan, her eyes alit with his ensemble. "I commend your attire, Consort. It is very becoming."

"Yes, it is quite fetching," Alesha agreed before Ethan said something flippant.

I'll show you becoming, witch! He kept that thought to himself. There wasn't a woman in the world he despised more than Valera's lickspittle. The way she smirked with her eyes lingering at his bare knees before returning to his face, made his blood run cold.

"The queens await, Your Highness." Leora curtsied, stepping aside, her open hand waving them through the archway.

*****

"Crown Princess Alesha and her Consort, Ethanos Loria!" The herald announced upon their entrance.

Ethan was taken aback by the scale and grandeur of the Great Hall. The chamber was more than one hundred yards square, with large stone columns bending toward its domed summit. The floor was mirrored jade stone with speckles of gold flickering when the light hit it. The walls and ceiling were cast in sky blue, with clouds painted along their surface. Lanterns running across the ceiling, alit its surface as if the open sky rested above. The entire scene was breathtaking and disorienting when seen for the first time. Ethan's head was spinning as he followed Alesha through the chamber. They crossed the center floor, with thousands of guests seated at the tables that circled the floor. The guests rose to their feet as they passed, each a high lord or lady of Vellesia, hailing from each of the twenty-three provinces of the realm. Some of the men were attired in flowing robes, others in doublets and pantaloons. Some wore silk shirts with trousers, while others donned colored hose and tunics. Most were clean-shaven, with few boasting full beards. He noticed a few with thick jerkins and fur-lined trousers, likely from the northern mountain provinces by their coarse hair. The ladies were more uniform in their appearance, with flowing gowns and obscenely tight bodices, though in an extensive variety of colors.

They walked across the open center floor, approaching the front of the Great Hall, where Queen Corella awaited them upon a raised dais. She sat on a majestic diamond throne, its high back sparkling like a thousand stars. She wore a pristine white gown with her large crown resting upon her brow, her silver eyes staring intensely as they neared. Upon her right, sat Valera, upon an onyx throne, its black stone swallowing much of the light Corella's gave off. Valera wore a black gown, matching the hue of her throne, a silver crown nestled in her dark hair. As they approached, Ethan could see that Valera's throne was set lower upon the dais, denoting her subservience to the Queen Mother. He noticed an empty sapphire throne set even lower and to Corella's left. It was likely Alesha's by its placement.

Stopping short of the dais, Alesha tugged Ethan's sleeve as she knelt. He lowered himself beside her as they pressed their foreheads to the floor in supplication.

A satisfied smile played evilly across Corella's lips, savoring this triumph. All her life was centered upon this singular goal. The crown prince of Astaria was finally brought to heel, bowing to her in humble obedience. The only piece upon the gameboard of Elaria capable of contesting their dominion now belonged to them. And soon, his wonderous powers would belong to her heir. The ascension of House Loria was now inevitable. Once Gabrielle matured, all the kings of Elaria would bow at their feet. She could feel the power radiating off Ethan like the sun breaking a morning sky. Oh, how she wanted it, wanted all of it. His power was beguiling, driving her envious heart to the brink. She wondered how Valera managed to keep her wits about her during their return journey. How could Alesha survive a lifetime wed to him without losing her mind? How could she share a bed with him while tortured by hunger that could never be sated? 'Twas a hunger ten thousand times as consuming as any their house has ever beheld.

"Arise, Alesha!" she commanded, keeping Ethan on his knees.

Grandmother, please! Alesha spoke to her thoughts, pleading for Ethan to rise. She had come far in rebuilding her relationship with Ethan and did not wish to see it undone by this petty demand of obeisance.

He needs reminding of his place, child, Corella warned, keeping him where he knelt for a long moment before bidding him to rise, displaying her authority over him before all of Vellesia. Once Ethan gained his feet, she stood to address the assemblage.

"My lords, ladies, and esteemed members of my House, I welcome you to the grand ball and banquet to celebrate the wedding of my granddaughter Alesha and her Consort, Ethanos, former crown prince of Astaria!" Her magical voice echoed clearly through the chamber, like gentle thunder, though to Ethan it was but a quiet utterance. "Let the festivities commence!" she proclaimed, descending the dais, taking Alesha's hand, leading her to their table.

"Come, Ethanos." Valera held out her hand, following several paces behind her mother.

"Where are we going?" he asked as she tucked her hand around his elbow.

"To our table. The feast is about to commence, and then you and Alesha will begin the ball with the first dance. All the high lords and ladies of Vellesia are here to celebrate your union. Be sure to be on your best behavior, my son," she said while nodding to a lord dressed in a dark silk shirt and serge cape, who bowed his head as she passed his table.

"Who's he?" Ethan asked, the fellow's eyes betraying his true age, despite the youthful sheen of his shoulder-length black hair and youthful boyish face. It was a disturbing trait in many Vellesian nobles as if aging stopped at thirty.

"That is Lord Lar Daravon of Baetala," she revealed. The Baetala Province rested along the eastern half of the Brelar Bay, with vast trading networks and rich vineyards and farmlands, making it one of the wealthiest provinces in all the seven realms. A man of such wealth and power was certainly a powerful magic wielder as well. Ethan thought to ask what mage power he possessed but doubted he'd receive an answer. The man was surrounded by two sons, three daughters, and a woman of similar age, a dark haired beauty who sat his left, his wife no doubt. They each bowed their heads with deep reverence as they passed.

They continued on, passing between the two rows of round tables that circled the chamber, Alesha and Corella receiving the deepest bows from the gathered nobles, though Ethan received the most curious stares. Every noble of Vellesia knew of his many adventures, especially his victory at the Velo, and his journey to the Mage Bane to rescue Alesha. The men regarded him with the deepest respect for his fell deeds, and the ladies swooned with a romantic sigh, imagining his courtship of Alesha. Valera pointed out each noble, denoting their lordship and kin, educating Ethan on the vassals sworn to House Loria.

"Why are they so happy to see me?" Ethan whispered, the looks of the Vellesian nobles, sounding alarms in his brain.

"Your legend precedes you, my son. They know of your fell deeds and that you forsook the throne of Astaria so that you might court and wed your true love." Valera smiled sweetly, regarding Lady Constance of Galea.

"What?" He made a face.

"That is what they believe, and what you shall say should anyone inquire. Is that understood, Ethanos?" She regarded him with a raised brow and a false smile for the benefit of the crowd.

"If they really knew anything about me, they would…"

"They know what they are told, Ethanos. Instead of the stubborn prince who Alesha dragged off against his will, you are the heroic prince who fell in love with their crown princess, rescued her from the Mage Bane, and forsook his crown to wed her, pledging his undying love to her for all time."

"Why spread such a lie so that your people would like me?" It didn't make sense.

"It is a gift from Alesha."

"A gift?"

"A gift. Alesha wished to share the love of our people with you, and they do love you, Ethan." It was the first time he recalled her ever referring to him as Ethan instead of Ethanos.

"Love? Why would they love any of us?"

"My poor, deluded child," she tsked, shaking her head at his naivety. "Our people love the House of Loria. It is our house that safeguards the realm. Of all the mage realms, none has known such peace as Vellesia. That is due solely to the power of House Loria. Our people do not go hungry or lack access to a mage healer if one is needed. Their every need is provided."

"The same could be said of Astaria. Our nobles respect and fear House Blagen, but I doubt they love us. Besides, I thought love was merely a combination of attraction, desire, and reciprocity?" He threw her words back at her.

"There are two kinds of love, as you well know, my son. The kind you are referring is the supposed feeling between lovers. The kind I am referring to is akin to the love a child has for a parent or a pet to its master. The people's affection is not necessary, but it is useful. I can read the affection in their minds."

"And if you read discontent?"

"Then Alesha has the power to erase it." She shrugged, as if it were a small thing, just as House Menau had done on behalf of House Loria for centuries.

She could see he did not approve by the look he gave her.

"But that hardy is necessary as the affection of our people is quite genuine. Now that affection extends to you, Ethan," she said, stopping at the base of a broad stair, centered upon the east wall, which led to the royal dining area overlooking the Great Hall. "You won the tourney of Torval, naming me Queen of the tourney. You also saved me from the dragon. You didn't have to do either of those things, Ethan. You did them out of your own sense of honor. All Alesha has done is allow our people to know this truth. Besides, we hardly require their hostility toward you to enforce your obedience. That could be done with a wave of our hand. Come, our family awaits." She smiled, waving an open hand up the stair, where Alesha and Corella ascended, floating above the wide stone steps with effortless grace.

"Aren't you going to take the easy way too?" he asked, expecting Valera to fly to the platform above like the others.

"My legs work just fine, Ethan." She tucked her arm through the crook in his elbow, continuing up the stairs.

An army of servants flooded the main floor, bearing pitchers of wine and steaming platters of cooked food. Ethan cringed as the monotonous sounds of harps and flutes echoed through the chamber, played by a bevy of musicians cloistered in the northwest corner of the hall. It was the stale, soulless music played routinely in all the mage realms. At least the Vellesians weren't perfect in everything, he thought reassuringly.

Atop the stair was a large expansive outcropping overlooking the main floor below, with a massive round table centered upon the dark stone floor. Standing before the table were Corella, Alesha, and Prince Raymar, who was dressed similarly to Ethan, and did not spare him the slightest acknowledgment. What took Ethan aback were the twelve women already seated at the table, dressed in shimmering golden dresses. They were incredibly beautiful in an ancient and haunting way. They each stared at him with keen interest, as unsettling as when Valera first stared at him upon the palace green at Astaris, or Corella when she first saw him at the castle entrance. They looked strikingly similar in the aura that seemed to surround them but were from varied racial and ethnic groupings. One of them was very dark of skin, like those from lower Sarcosa or the Africans of Earth. Another was of a far eastern extract, hailing from southeastern Vellesia, akin to the China men who worked for the railroads that Jake Thorton told him about. Some shared similar traits to either of the women while others were of medium complexion. Most were of olive skin, like most native Vellesians. Two were blond of hair, and another bright red, with very fair skin, like the Irishmen Ethan encountered in his travels across the barrier. Despite their differences, there was something odd about them, something that bound them together in a way that made the hairs on the back of his neck to rise. None looked older than their fortieth year, but their eyes looked ancient. There were two men sitting at the table, each dressed in similar attire to his own, with doublets over puffed white shirts. He could not see below their waists as they were seated but correctly guessed they were wearing the same black kilt that he was. One was very pale, with gray tinting his dark brown hair. Ethan could only guess his age to seventy or eighty years, though he looked much younger, his body obviously manipulated by their mage powers, by his clean-shaven face and glowing skin. The other man was of darker complexion, with very deep olive skin, akin to the Tejanos he knew in Red Rock, and the commonest racial grouping in Vellesia that populated the coastal regions along the Aqualania Sea. What was disconcerting were the golden collars gracing their necks, the exact style and make of the one Alesha placed on him at Astaris, and required it of him on occasion.

One of the blond-haired women rose from her seat on the opposite side, circling the table to greet the Queen Mother, her eyes never leaving Ethan's as she drew nigh. To his surprise, Corella and the others dropped reverently to their knees, forcing him to do like-wise. Whoever this woman was, the Queen Mother deferred to her, sending more alarm bells ringing through his brain.

"Rise, my children," the woman said, bringing Corella into her embrace.

"Mother Evalena," Corella greeted the woman.

"And my sweet Alesha," the woman reached out to embrace her.

"Mother Evalena," Alesha beamed proudly as they parted, the woman running a hand affectionately over Alesha's womb.

The woman, Evalena as they referred to her, embraced Raymar and Valera, before stopping at Ethan.

"Mother Evalena, may I introduce Alesha's Consort, Ethanos." Valera bowed reverently.

Evalena stared intensely at Ethan with emerald eyes so bright that their luster seemed to bleed into their whites.

"Ethanos," Evalena whispered his name hypnotically.

"Er...ah...hm," he said, losing his train of thought as the woman continued to stare at him like some strange novelty.

"Ethanos, this is Mother Evalena, the head of the Order of Loria," Valera warned, reminding him to be respectful.

"You are Queen Corella's mother?" he asked, recalling what Amanda and Tristan explained to him of Alesha's many grandmothers still living.

"No, child. I am not Corella's mother. I am the head of the Lorian Order, the coven of sorceresses that protect Vellesia and House Loria," she cooed, touching a hand to his cheek. Any woman who commanded Valera, Corella, and Alesha's deference was not one to be trifled with, but why they all deferred to this woman was another mystery to be solved. She was obviously more than she seemed, as well as the other *witches* gathered about the table, each staring at him with the same keen interest.

"We have foreseen your coming for hundreds of years, Ethanos. To see the prophecy fulfilled in my lifetime is a sight to behold, though you have given us many frights through the years with your antics." Her intense stare eased as she guided him to his seat at the table, where he was seated between Evalena and Queen Mother Corella. Alesha was seated opposite him, across the massive table, flanked by Valera and one of the witches of the coven, a strikingly beautiful woman with piercing purple eyes, rich ebony hair, and fair skin, who was later introduced as Caterina. Beside her sat the older gentleman, who was pale of skin. The other gentleman with deep olive skin, sat two places to Ethan's left, beside Queen Corella. Prince Raymar sat several places to his right, lost in a sea of the golden-clad witches, who seemed to ignore the hapless Prince, though he seemed to take it all in stride. Raymar had yet to acknowledge Ethan with little more than a nod. He really wanted a chance to speak with the man and learn what was really going on in the palace, and the true role of the Lorian Order in relation to the crown.

Evalena rang a small bell placed in front of her, signaling an army of servants who hurried through a large archway behind them, that led to the palace kitchens. They bore pitchers of wine and platters of bread and fruits. These servants, unlike those serving on the main floor below, were exclusively male, dressed in fine livery to match the richest of lords, with matching silk shirts and puffed short pantaloons over thin hose. Ethan wondered how anyone could think such clothing looked good. He'd rather die than wear that, but then he looked down at what he was wearing, sadly shaking his head.

"Ethanos, as this is your first night in Elysia, I think it proper that introductions are in order," Evalena began. "Of course, I am Mother Evalena, head of the Lorian Order." She touched a hand to her heart before continuing.

247

"This is my daughter, Mother Zelana," she indicated the woman to her immediate right. Zelana looked strikingly similar to Evalena, though with slightly upturned eyes and dark hair, meaning her father was of far eastern descent.

"The daughter of Zelana, Mother Veriana," Evalena next introduced her granddaughter, who sat to Zelana's right. Veriana looked completely of eastern descent, proving her father originated from that region as well, with their distinct eyes, and light-olive skin.

"Mother Ametria, daughter of Veriana," who looked similar to Zelana, with subdued eastern features.

"Mother Clarisa, daughter of Ametria," she introduced a woman with golden hair with the slightest of eastern features, and pale skin.

"Mother Demetra, daughter of Clarisa," she said of a woman with a very dark complexion and features akin to the Africans of Earth and the southern Sarcosans of Elaria.

"Mother Porshana, daughter of Demetra," who appeared completely of African or Sarcosan descent, with piercing silver eyes, bursting with power. She was strikingly beautiful and exotic, and Ethan had to guard himself against falling under her hypnotic gaze.

"Corbin, Consort of Caterina," Evalena introduced the elder of the two gentlemen sitting across the table. He had long, brown hair with strands of gray betraying his true age, with few wrinkles gracing his countenance. Corbin's blue eyes regarded him briefly, before looking away.

"Mother Caterina, daughter of Vetesha, and mother to Queen Mother Corella," she introduced the wife of Corbin, whose rich black hair and fair skin complemented her vibrant purple eyes. Ethan noted they were now out of sequence, wondering what happened to the family line after Porshana. Alesha sat beside her, staring at him from across the table, slightly shaking her head, sympathetic to his suffering, knowing he had no idea who each of these women was. She gifted him a smile, a small encouragement to soldier on. Valera was next, followed by Inese.

"Mother Inese, daughter of Porshana," Evalena introduced her, reestablishing the direct line of succession. She was an exotic blend of Porshana's dark skin and features and Valera's light olive hue.

"Mother Mortava, daughter of Inese," she said, introducing a woman with deep olive skin and alluring golden eyes that matched Alesha, like two burning suns blazing in a clear sky.

"Mother Elesha, daughter of Mortava," she introduced Elesha who had flaming red hair, styled high upon her head. Prince Raymar sat quietly beside her, taking a sip from his goblet, though Ethan wondered if he was supposed to, considering the disapproving look Valera gave her son. Raymar shrugged innocently, setting the cup back down.

A nonconformist. I like him already. Ethan kept that happy thought to himself.

"Mother Vetesha, daughter of Elesha," Vetesha sat beside Raymar, with reddish black hair, and bright blue eyes that glowed like sapphires.

"Darius, consort to our Queen Mother Corella," she regarded the younger of the two consorts, whose brown eyes and dark olive skin masked his true age. His teeth were sparkling white, like everyone else seated at the table. Ethan couldn't miss the golden collar gracing his throat. Ethan was taken aback, realizing that Darius was Alesha's grandfather and Valera's father. He recalled that the collars were more than decorations. They were mage forged to bind the magic of those wearing them. He wondered what power Darius passed on to Valera.

"You are Alesha's grandfather?" he asked, the others taken aback that of all those that were introduced, Ethan would deign to address him first.

Darius was equally taken aback, looking to Corella for direction, the Queen Mother granting him permission to speak.

"Yes, Consort Ethanos," he finally answered.

Consort Ethanos, not Consort Loria? Of course, for Darius was a consort of House Loria as well, and only their first names would differentiate them. Ethan felt the others staring more intently at him, if that was possible. Was he not supposed to speak to the man? He was Allie's grandfather after all, and Ethan did what he always did, be true to himself.

The others stared dumbstruck as Ethan stood up and stepped around Corella, patting Darius on the shoulder, extending his hand.

"It's an honor to meet you, sir. You have a beautiful granddaughter. You should be proud." Ethan grabbed hold of Darius' hand, shaking it vigorously.

"Ah...Tha...thank you," Darius looked gob-smacked, not certain how to respond to such rare praise and respect.

"Actually, I forgot about your other granddaughter, Amanda. She is very lovely also," he added, the mention of Amanda kindling expected angst among the others.

"You are very kind, Ethanos. Please come sit," Mother Evalena softly ordered, patting his empty chair beside her.

"Of course, Mother Evalena, I didn't mean any offense. It is customary in Astaria to honor our spouse's grandparents," he explained, retaking his seat. "My Texan friends must seek out a woman's father for permission to marry her or her grandfather if the father is absent," he threw that tidbit out there, just to rankle their feathers. He caught Alesha shaking her head, staring at him with a smirk on her lips. Valera, however, was not amused. Nor was Corella, who sat stiffly between him and Darius.

"An interesting tradition, though a but quant," Evalena remarked before lifting her goblet for a toast.

"Tonight, we honor the union of Alesha and Ethanos!" she declared, taking a sip.

"To Alesha! Long may she reign!" the others chorused in unison.

"And Gabrielle," Corella said, lifting her goblet.

"To Gabrielle, daughter of prophecy. Long may she reign!" Evalena said proudly.

"Long shall she reign!" the others chorused.

What if it's a boy? Ethan chuckled to himself. They couldn't even fathom that possibility, but he wondered what sort of panic it would instill. The House of Loria was built upon a defined order, guided by unfailing prophecies. Introducing any level of uncertainty, created chaos in their ordered world. Unfortunately for Ethan, he was chaos in the flesh, a wild, untamed tempest sweeping into their midst that they fought to control.

After the servants served their meal, they began to eat. He was surprised by the size of the table, expecting a smaller affair since it was reserved for the royal family until the introductions revealed who all these women were…Alesha's ancient kin. This Lorian Order was the true power of the realm, commanding even Corella's obedience, the Queen Mother bowing to them with deep reverence. The question he had to ask was how they lived so long. Evalena must be hundreds of years old, and each of the others only less so than their mothers. Would Alesha live that long? He also struggled trying to determine who actually ruled Vellesia. Did the Lorian Order serve the crown, or did the crown serve them? If it was the former, then Evalena was the true Queen Mother, and all the rest princesses, fourteen generations of them, and Gabrielle making fifteen upon her birth.

The women were now engaged in conversation, asking Valera about their journey, and her treating with the Mage Kings at Astaris. Valera asked of the state of the realm in her absence. They discussed matters of state, betrothals of the high lords of Vellesia, and their heirs, requiring approval of the crown. Unlike Astaria, House Loria held complete authority in arranging nuptials for all the noble houses of Vellesia.

"How is your food, Ethanos?" Mother Zelana asked from her place to Evalena's right.

"Very good, great actually," he said in all honesty. "I never had seasoning on vegetables before. They taste better than dessert, and the fish is delicious."

"It is Alesha's favorite delicacy. Our fisheries are well-stocked with a variety of tasty species," Zelana said.

"Alesha spoke glowingly of your culinary skills when she returned from the Mage Bane," Evalena said.

"Yes, we were quite surprised. No other prince of Elaria is so inclined," Corella added.

"Most consider such tasks beneath them," Mother Porshana opined, torchlight playing off her pure silver eyes.

"I don't favor cooking, ma'am, but when you're on your own, it's either that or starve." Ethan shrugged, using his Texas drawl.

"We must reprimand Sarella and Selendra for not mentioning your culinary skills, though they spoke of your many other *unique* activities growing up in Astaris," Mother Mortava said.

"I have partaken Ethan's cooking during our journey. His venison was quite good," Valera added.

"I can cook what I kill in the wild, but I'm not much use in the kitchen," he pointed out, not liking the direction this conversation was going.

"I am surprised you didn't learn since you made it a habit to master every other menial task in Astaris, such as blacksmithing, grooming hooves, sweeping chimneys, chopping wood, to name a few," Corella pointed out.

"I'm a quick learner, my Queen, but then again…so are you." He took a generous sip of wine.

"Indeed," she regarded him coldly. Being this close to him was suffocating, his magical immunity impairing her power whenever she leaned too close. Evalena suffered much the same, enduring his presence with practiced grace.

"You also cook snake, as my dearest sister can attest," Prince Raymar finally spoke, swirling his wine in his goblet before taking a sip.

"Actually, Alesha did most of the cooking that night if I recall." He could feel the tension at the table when he spoke of her so informally. It wasn't lost on him that he was introduced to them more as an exotic pet than their newest kin. Despite this, he pushed his bounds, nonetheless.

"Truly? Alesha?" Mother Porshana lifted a curious brow over a sharp silver eye.

"I did and confess that it was quite tasty," Alesha quickly came to Ethan's defense, lifting her chin proudly, with a smile that reached her eyes while looking at Ethan sitting across her.

"What you must have suffered in that dreadful place, with your mage gifts impaired," Mother Veriana tsked, shaking her head.

"Not true, Mother Veriana. I recall fondly my time in the Mage Bane." Alesha thought of her and Ethan's first meeting on that wondrous night he freed her from Luke's men, and the endless conversations they shared throughout their journey. Looking back, she recalled how quickly time passed whenever they were together, like rain slipping through her fingers. She remembered how they would talk throughout the night and never grow tired. She would gladly suffer all she endured a thousand times over to relive those first magical days with Ethan. He was with her now, but not like before, and she missed their friendship, desperately so.

The others smiled politely, though Valera stiffened at Alesha's remark, knowing the truth of it. Her daughter was rather fond of her consort, in a dangerous way they had not foreseen. In time, the others would come to see it as well, as Alesha grew closer to Ethanos with every passing day. Regrettably, she knew what would have to be done and wondered why it was starting to bother her so. She looked across the table to where her mother, Queen Corella, sat, recalling the old proverb of the blessing of unfulfilled wishes. She demanded that Ethanos be brought to Elysia, as prophecy foretold, and so he was here, bound to them by oaths, and now by walls. Despite his immense power, he was still hopelessly within their grasp, but as she was beginning to learn, Ethanos presented a far greater danger than his physical power and magical immunity. Everything he believed and represented was in conflict with their house. She kept her own misgivings to herself, not sharing her suspicions of Alesha's growing fondness for Ethan, fearing how her mothers would react. Alesha was growing protective of Ethan as well. Despite her magical bonds to House Loria, would she break those bonds to protect Ethan? No, Valera shook such doubts from her mind. Alesha understood her destiny and duty. Besides, Ethan wasn't going anywhere, and if he must be broken, Alesha would have to stand aside.

The mothers asked Ethan about his time in Red Rock, horrified to learn how many times death almost took him. His adventures in the Mage Bane were little better, the boy courting death with painful regularity. They were quite aware of the happenings in the Mage Bane as Alesha witnessed what transpired there, especially the showdown between Ethan and Luke Crawford. What happened in Red Rock, however, was mostly a mystery other than what Alesha gleaned probing Krixan's mind once they escaped the Mage Bane.

"You were shot in the back by Nate Grierson, is this not so?" Mother Evalena challenged his omitting this fact.

Ethan felt all their eyes upon him, like a parent asking a child to explain their misdeeds.

"I took a bullet, but it missed anything vital, and I quickly recovered. It actually turned out in my favor, giving me time to read dozens of Judge Donovan's books. I managed them pretty well for a dummy like me, so it all worked out for the best." He smiled, his attempt to make light of it failing miserably.

"There will be no more of such foolishness. Are we clear, child?" Mother Porshana admonished, her silver eyes blazing like white fire.

Ugh, which one is in charge here? He asked himself. Porshana might have been the one to say it, but they were all thinking it. "No arguments from me, ma'am. Not getting shot seems like a good idea." He shrugged innocently with a half grin that was given a quick death by the sea of scowling faces. The situation was intolerable, like being a child again with his mother scolding him for something he probably did, except here, it was fourteen mothers scowling at him.

"As long as we are clear, child. And you are to address me as Mother Porshana, not ma'am. Are we clear on this as well?" Her glare intensified.

"Yes, ma'am, I mean Mother. Mother Porshana." He nodded in her direction, downing his goblet, wishing it could make him drunk. *And what if there's a dragon threatening your queen again, should I just step aside?* He wanted to say.

The tempo of the music suddenly shifted, the sound of trumpets heralding the commencement of the grand ball.

"The people await their crown princess." Mother Evalena smiled, urging Ethanos to his feet, directing him to circle the table and take Alesha's hand.

Alesha smiled, placing her hand in his as he helped her to her feet, leading her to the top of the stairs.

"What are we supposed to do?" he whispered, leaning close to her ear with thousands of eyes staring up at them.

"You are going to dance with your princess." She smiled at the crowd seated below.

"CROWN PRINCESS ALESHA AND HER CONSORT!" the court herald announced as they descended the stair before stepping to the center of the floor. The trumpets grew silent, replaced with the sounds of harps and flutes echoing serenely through the Great Hall.

Her golden eyes glowed like vibrant flames as she stared into his. All her life, she dreamed of this moment, dancing with her handsome consort in this very chamber. The eyes of the court followed them across the floor. She held up her left palm, directing Ethan to press his to hers.

Does he not know this dance? She made a face.

"Place your right hand over your heart and follow my lead," she whispered as they circled one another in rhythmic steps.

As much as he hated dancing, he found himself lost in her eyes. The swell of her breasts against her bodice enflamed his desire.

This damn kilt, he growled to himself, knowing the garment wouldn't conceal what she was doing to him.

"Why isn't anyone else dancing?" he asked. Looking back, he never suffered this affliction in Elaria until he met Alesha. Only across the barrier did he first experience such longings. He long feared he might be a eunuch, void of lust or desire, unable to please anyone, even himself. He was too embarrassed to admit such to anyone, not Krixan or his kin. It was another reason to stay in Red Rock to feel the longings that everyone else enjoyed. Why was he able to feel such on earth, but not here? But then he met Alesha, and those stirrings returned a thousandfold. It was nothing like he felt on earth. It was so much more powerful, more vibrant. Why was she the only one in this world who could invoke such passion in him? Was this a mage power she somehow invoked, denying him to anyone save her? He was immune to magic though, so what could explain it? He laughed at her jealousy whenever a girl in his past was mentioned. He couldn't do anything with anyone else if he wanted. Even if he escaped Elysia, he would doom himself to a life void of passion, a life void of love. Was his freedom worth that? Yet if he stayed, he could feel himself being bound with invisible cables, growing stronger each day. Every day he became more trapped.

"The first dance is ours, and ours alone, so all the people can see their crown princess and her consort on this joyous night," she explained as they circled about the floor, their eyes fixed intensely from one to the other.

"Well, you are easy to look at. I'll give them that."

"As are you." She smiled. He was strikingly handsome in a way that made her ache for his touch. Just touching his hand sent an electrical thrill coursing her flesh. No other man kindled such a passion in her. In fact, no other man kindled any passion in her at all. Her entire life, she felt no such longings, wondering what all the fuss was about when others spoke of love. But then she met Ethan, and all that changed in a blinding instant. He invoked such passion that it overwhelmed her, consuming her waking thoughts and dreams alike. There was no escaping him. Before the Mage Bane, she needed Ethan to fulfill her destiny. After the Mage Bane, she needed him to sate the yearnings of her heart. Her desire was now all-consuming. Destiny or not, she could not live without this man. All her ancestors were driven by an insatiable hunger for mage powers they did not possess, adding one after another, passing them down to their heirs. Her birth was the culmination of their efforts, a complete mage with all mage powers bound in one person. All that remained was Ethan, and the hunger that drove her to wed his immunity to her immense power. Yet once she met him, that hunger was replaced by a much stronger hunger. A simpleton would call this hunger love, but what she felt was beyond such a primitive concept.

"Enough of this," he said, drawing her close with his hands resting on her waist.

"Ethan?" she warned as they moved across the floor, their bodies pressed obscenely close.

"This is more like it." He winked as she rested her hands upon his thick shoulders, the crowd gasping at his audacity.

"Perhaps, but hardly appropriate." Her lips reproached, though her body spoke the opposite.

"Who cares what others think." He shrugged, giving her that mischievous smile she hadn't seen since before her betrayal.

"You're incorrigible." She rolled her eyes.

"I know, aren't I?" he grinned.

"That smile is very dangerous, *husband*." She lifted a bemused brow.

"I'm sure it is, *wife*."

"That's hardly the proper appellation for addressing your crown princess, Consort Loria," she teased.

"Don't worry, Your Highness, they can't hear us." He cast a glance around the cavernous chamber, enjoying the shocked looks painting the nobles' faces.

"They don't need to hear us," she pointed out.

"They're just jealous that I'm dancing with the prettiest girl in the world."

"Dancing most inappropriately." She smirked.

"I don't see you pushing me away. Besides, I kind of have to stay close to you, considering this damn kilt you made me wear."

She made a face, confused by his claim until realization struck her, followed by a devilish grin spreading across her lips.

"Oh." She smiled, pressing her body briefly to his, confirming his obvious state.

"Yes, very funny." He rolled his eyes.

"And how is dancing this close helping with that problem?" She smiled.

"It's not reducing my condition, but it is hiding it from everyone else's view. You should have considered that before making me wear this."

"I don't know. I find it quite fetching. Besides, it allows me easy access to my favorite assets," she could see him turn painfully red. Oh, how she delighted in this power she held over him.

"We need to shorten your skirts so I can return the favor," he smiled, moving her slowly across the floor.

"Promise?" she flirted shamelessly.

"Oh, that's a promise all right," he said in all sincerity. He could hardly keep his hands off her as it was.

"We shall have to confine such wanton behavior to our private chambers. The queens and mothers would disapprove of such in public view."

"Yes, your mothers." He cast a suspicious glance to the terrace above, where they were all now standing, looking down at them with intense interest. "Evalena is the oldest, and the others are her direct descendants, that much I guessed."

"Mother Evalena," she corrected.

"Fine, Mother Evalena. What I don't understand is who is in charge. If Corella—"

"Queen Mother Corella." She rolled her eyes, wondering how many times she'd have to correct him.

"If Queen Mother Corella rules the realm, why does she bow to Mother Evalena and not Evalena bow to her?"

She wanted to laugh at such a silly notion, but he wouldn't understand why. "The crown and the Lorian Order are one and the same, Ethan. Do not let the protocols of the court confuse you. Mother Evalena and Queen Corella, speak with the same voice. You cannot separate one from the other."

He made a face, even more confused than before he asked. "If each of them is your direct ancestors, which is Mother to Queen Corella? I didn't hear that mentioned," he asked.

"Mother Caterina bore our Queen Mother. She is the youngest member of the Order. Her husband, Corbin, still lives, further proving her younger age."

He recalled her black hair and vibrant purple eyes. "She is very beautiful, as they all are, but none of it makes sense," he said.

"How so?" she asked, the hem of her gown sweeping the floor as they danced.

"How are they all so young?"

"They are not young," she said.

"Young-looking," he corrected.

"Yes," she said.

"Mother Evalena must be hundreds of years old if what you say is true."

"Two hundred and ninety-two," she said matter-of-fact.

"Two hundred and ninety-two? Is this another mage gift you inherited along the way, some type of eternal youth?"

"Not eternal. There is a limit. We usually pass, nearing the end of our fourth century. And yes, it a mage gift, one you are familiar with."

"I would remember hearing of such a gift," he said.

"It is a familiar gift if you truly consider it. It is the gift of self-regeneration, your gift, Ethan." She smiled, wondering why he never considered the implications of his power.

"Wait," he pondered the implications but missed the greater point she was making. "Everyone in the order is your grandmother to some degree," he whispered as if searching for something.

"Yes."

"And each wields incredible power, but everyone a little less than their daughter, but even Mother Evalena wields incredible power, and hers would be the weakest." His mind was trying to sort it all out.

"True," she marveled that he missed the greater implication.

"Two hundred and ninety years." His jaw nearly hung open. He counted twelve mothers in their Order, plus Corella and Valera, each possessing immense power. He again scolded himself for his stupidity and for thinking he only had to account for Valera and Corella to counter the Vellesian threat to Astaria. That would be difficult, if not impossible in itself, but there were twelve mothers to account for as well, and any number of powerful mages that were offshoots of the royal line, each possessing power as great as his own family. It was hopeless. Oh, he could destroy most of them if he had to but couldn't shield Astaria from their collective wrath. Another point to consider was Evalena's vast knowledge considering she lived for nearly three hundred years. It was ample time to prepare for any contingencies he might throw their way. Accepting defeat, however, wasn't his nature.

Who am I fooling, they've been planning this for hundreds of years, and I've been thinking about it for a few months, he bemoaned his sorry state. He was truly caged.

"I know that look," Alesha reproached. "You were planning something but are now resigned to your fate."

He brought his eyes sharply to hers, confirming her suspicion. He hated how transparent he was.

"Whatever it was, put it far from your mind, Ethan. I warned you in Astaris to never betray me in matters of state or matters of the heart," she said with steel in her heart.

"I will never betray your heart. I avowed such before my family in Astaris. You are my wife, Alesha, and I will have no other," he said it and meant it.

"You vowed to serve House Loria for all your days. You swore to obey your queen and princess in all things. I will have your heart along with your mind and body as well, Ethan. You swore those vows."

"And I've kept them," he reminded her.

"But you would forsake them if you could."

"I would choose to be my own master, but you seem to find that offensive," he growled, weary of the whole thing.

"You cannot be free and serve House Loria. I am a jealous woman, Ethan. I don't want just your heart. I want it all. Every part of you belongs to me."

"You're fighting a battle you already won, Allie. I'm yours. I'm here with you, aren't I? Dancing in your palace, under your mothers' watchful eyes." He spared her family another glance. "Not to mention that I'm wearing these ridiculous clothes. What more do you want?"

"You would escape if you could," she scowled.

"Would I? I'm not so sure anymore. I would leave this place if I could, but I wouldn't leave you, and that scares the life out of me." He sadly shook his head, confessing his heart.

"Is my heart any less your slave? You are a millionfold more dangerous than my mother prepared me for. I never knew my heart could be so fragile, so weak, so…human. I thought I was above such yearnings. I was wrong. Your mere existence lays false such notions. I can no more live without you than the air that I breathe, and *that* scares the life out of me," she too confessed.

"Fair enough. I guess we are in this together." He smiled, trying to change this serious mood he foolishly put her in.

"Yes, we are, husband, *three hundred years together.*"

Her words froze him in place. "*Three hundred years?*" The question repeated in his brain until he comprehended it. How could he have overlooked the obvious? He was so wrapped up in the long age of the Lorian Order, he forgot he shared the gift that caused it. Panic suddenly took him, realizing he was bound to serve House Loria for life, a life that would last hundreds of years. He also considered that his father would not live so long, and they must have contingencies to keep him obedient once he passed away. His breath caught in the narrows of his throat, his chest contracting as if plunged into cold water.

"Ethan?" she asked, drawing him from his stupor.

"I..." He paused, bereft of words, mind-numbed by thoughts of three hundred years trapped in Elysia. He thought to make a jape or quip to make light of the situation, but for the first time in his life, he had nothing. Alesha had beaten him in every way possible. They held a royal flush while he couldn't even boast a pair of twos, as Judge Donovan would say. Alesha's grandmothers alone could conquer the mage realms. Only he stood in their way, and he was only one man surrounded by their armies in this mountain prison, trapped here for all eternity. He could endure any torment for a time, so he thought, but not for three hundred years, even to a beautiful captor like Alesha.

"Is three hundred years with me so awful a fate?" she asked, shaking her head, wondering how it took him so long to figure this out.

He regarded her, staring intently into her golden eyes that sparkled like twin suns. She was so breathtakingly beautiful it almost hurt to look at her but even more so to look away. If he was doomed to live three hundred years, there were far worse companions for him to share it with.

"You know better than to ask me that." He managed to smile.

"Do I?"

"If you don't, you should. I'm here, aren't I, dancing with my wife after being blindsided yet again with another surprise you manage to spring on me."

"Surely you knew you would live far longer than mortal men?" she asked.

His silence answered that question.

"Then you can't accuse me of springing this surprise on you when your own ignorance is equally to blame."

"And how could I have known I would live so long? I never knew anyone who could regenerate. You, on the other hand, were surrounded by them your entire life," he pointed out.

"Fair enough, but now you know." She smiled, enjoying the back and forth between them as they danced. Three hundred years with someone dull of wit would be unbearable now that she knew Ethan.

"Are there any other surprises I should know about that you haven't told me?"

"Oh, I'm full of surprises, Ethan." She winked wickedly, her long lashes fluttering shamelessly.

There, upon the dance floor in the Great Hall, in full view of the Vellesian court, Alesha kissed her husband.

CHAPTER 14

Ethan backed a step, blocking the thrust with a powerful riposte, nearly disarming the Vellesian Prince. Ethan slipped around Raymar's side with deadly speed, catching him by surprise with the blunted training sword pressed to his neck.

"I yield...again," Raymar grunted, not shaking his head until Ethan withdrew the blade.

"You're getting better," Ethan said encouragingly, returning to his starting position.

"You're not good at lying, Ethanos," Raymar quipped.

"How would you know, we just met two days ago." Ethan spun the training sword in his right hand before banging it against his shield, signaling the start of their next bout.

Raymar struck first with a flurry of blows, forcing Ethan on the defensive. The Vellesian prince could tell Ethan was holding back, revealing little of the sword skill he was famous for. The queen's guards spoke glowingly of Ethan's prowess, and his knightly skills were further demonstrated at the joust of Torval. Naming his mother the queen of the tourney was a brilliant move to ingratiate himself in her good graces, putting the bitterness of Astaris further in the past. Ethan was more clever than his mother gave him credit, or so Raymar believed.

The Vellesian prince regretted not warning Ethan sooner of his mother and sister's betrayal at Astaris but was fortunate to attempt it in the first place without raising the suspicion of the Queen Mother and the Lorian Order. When his mother and Alesha departed for Astaris, it allowed him to slip away under the guise of visiting his paternal kin of House Menau. It was all he could do to travel to the Astarian border and draw Tristan away to treat with him. It was all for naught, as his warning reached Ethan a day late. Prince Tristan was delayed in relaying his message by the elements, and a myriad of strange occurrences that made him believe another force interceded on his mother's behalf. It was either that, or dumb bad luck, and Raymar wasn't one to believe in dumb luck or coincidences. Someone or something conspired to ruin his plans, and Ethan was now a captive in this cursed palace.

"Ugh!" Raymar groaned, landing painfully on his rump, though having no idea how he got there. *By the spirits, Ethan is quick*, he winced.

Ethan held out his hand, helping Raymar to his feet.

"You are awfully polite for someone who is beating me senseless," he japed as they reset to try again.

"You're doing fine, just need to improve your footwork a little, that's all," Ethan encouraged.

Raymar shook his head and smiled. Ethan was nothing at all what he expected. Crown princes were arrogant and cruel, not helpful and kind, at least most weren't. Knowing this made him feel even worse for failing to warn him of Alesha's betrayal. He wanted to speak with him when he first arrived but didn't have the opportunity with the whirlwind of activities his mother planned for them. It wasn't until the night before that he invited his new brother by marriage to spar the following morn. Alesha surprisingly thought it a grand idea, as she was occupied throughout the morn preparing for the ceremony.

Alas, another ceremony, he bemoaned the celebrations that had no end in sight. Of course, he should've expected this as House Loria planned for this occasion for centuries. They were parading poor Ethan before the nobles and people like a prized stallion. He could see Ethan growing weary of it all, but there was no recourse. Like the rest of the mere mortals of their house, Ethan would learn to endure whatever whim or fancy their queens and crown princess inflicted upon him.

"I haven't thanked you for saving my sister, Ethanos," he said, parrying another strike of Ethan's blunted sword.

"At least someone's grateful." Ethan shrugged, again slipping around Raymar's shield, touching his blade to the Vellesian prince's throat.

"I was referring to Amanda," Raymar whispered with Ethan close enough to shield others from listening.

Ethan lowered his sword, regarding Raymar as he backed a step. He was waiting for some sort of confirmation that Raymar did in fact send him a warning through Tristan, that it was Raymar and not just a trick of Valera.

"Yes, it was I," Raymar whispered after stepping nigh, taking no chance of discovery. The palace had ears in every corner and little if nothing escaped his sister. Other than a few servants, the training arena was empty, but little was beyond Alesha's capability. She didn't even need to read the servants minds; she could merely tap into their consciousness and listen to what they heard.

"Then why…," Ethan began to ask before Raymar warned him to silence.

"We can only speak freely when I am close enough to touch you, else we can be heard. Why else would I take up sparring as an activity in recent months? This is an excellent place for us to interact and draw close enough for others not to overhear."

"You've only been practicing swordplay for a few months?" Ethan asked as they briefly drew away, the question, if heard by others would not raise suspicions.

"What better way to bond with my future brother? Of course, I am not very good as these bruises you are generously giving me can attest," he japed.

"Oh, you're very good. Don't sell yourself short."

Raymar gave him a look. Ethan had beaten him in every way imaginable, despite holding back. He shuddered to think what he was truly capable of. They reset and began again, Raymar driving him back with a flurry of thrusts that he knew Ethan allowed, either to encourage him or conceal what he was capable of by prying eyes.

When his sword found purchase in Ethan's side, he knew he was being humored, Ethan lowering his sword in defeat.

"You are as lousy an actor as you are a liar, Ethanos." Raymar shook his head.

"What?" Ethan gave him a hurt look that only proved his point.

"If you're trying to make me feel better, I know you let me win. If you're trying to conceal your capability, you needn't bother." He smiled, helping Ethan to his feet. "Your reputation precedes you."

"My reputation?"

"House Loria is well aware of your capabilities, Ethan. Did you not consider that your routine bouts with the royal guards at Astaris were observed by my aunts? Every royal guard of Vellesia is equally aware and has been drilled thoroughly in tactics to subdue you, if necessary."

"What tactics?" Ethan growled.

"Easy with that frown, Ethan. We don't want to arouse suspicion." Raymar backed a step, a false smile painting his lips, encouraging Ethan to reciprocate.

"How's this?" Ethan's lips stretched painfully, causing Raymar to roll his eyes.

"Forget the smile. Just don't frown so hard." He sighed hopelessly.

Raymar found himself again on his back after a devastating riposte that sent his training sword flying from his grasp. Once he was close to Ethan, he answered his question concerning tactics.

"The tactic that I am referring to is where your father's soldiers learned to work in concert, each pinning their swords into your body, and holding them there until enough were placed to subdue you. Our royal guards have been proficiently trained to execute that tactic."

"They can practice all they want, but they're forgetting a key point," Ethan said calmly.

"And that is?"

"I never used killing strokes on my father's men. I have no such hindrance with your mother's guards."

"You are a fine swordsman, perhaps the greatest in all Elaria, but you should know that every mother in the Lorian Order is nearly as deadly with a sword. EVERY ONE OF THEM," Raymar emphasized.

"Deadly? How deadly?"

"Nearly as deadly as you, some might be better. They train constantly, though we mere mortals rarely see them do so. Remember, most of them have been training for more than a hundred years."

"Wonderful." Ethan lowered his sword. The situation was beyond hopeless, with every day him discovering another thing stacked against him. "All this effort to restrain little ole me." He shook his head.

"Yes, little ole Ethan, the most dangerous man to have ever lived. They are cautious for good reason, my friend."

"What are they worried about, they already won?"

"Have they?"

"I'm here, aren't I? And I've already given Alesha the child they need."

"Their prophecies are specific. They need you bound to Alesha for life."

"I've heard all this before, but why? Nobody can answer that."

"They've already told you."

"What do you mean they told me? All they said is that I need to serve House Loria!" Ethan growled.

"Shh!" Raymar scolded as quietly as he could manage. "Yes, serve House Loria, but you don't know why, and...neither do they," Raymar whispered.

"That doesn't make any sense."

"Of course, it does." Raymar smiled. "The prophecies imply that you will perform vital service for House Loria beyond siring the all-powerful future queen of the world."

"What service?"

"If I knew that answer, I would tell you. The point is, they need to keep you here and will do so by any means necessary."

"My father's life is all the means they need."

"Your father's life..." Raymar's words died on his lips as Leora Mattiese appeared at the entrance with her arms crossed.

"Minister Mattiese, a pleasure as always," Raymar greeted her, his strong voice carrying across the large chamber.

"Prince Raymar." Leora bowed her head with deep reverence as they approached, their armored boots kicking up sand as they crossed the floor.

"Minister Mattiese," Ethan greeted as politely as he could manage. He'd prefer a different greeting, something along the lines of *witch* or *bitch* but didn't see the benefit of kicking the hornet's nest.

"Consort," Leora greeted him with all the warmth of a glacier.

"Ethan was kind enough to instruct me in swordcraft. My first lesson has been quite educational," Raymar japed, regarding the bruises covering him head to foot.

"A prince of Vellesia hardly needs to wield a sword." She raised a disapproving brow.

"True, but learning a new skill stimulates the mind, and things have been insufferably dull before you and Mother returned, Minister," Raymar said.

"It has hardly been dull, Highness, especially with the preparations you undertook to receive us," Leora acknowledged, though Raymar himself arrived at the palace just before them, using the guise of visiting his paternal grandfather's holdfast, while actually traveling to Astaria in his failed attempt to warn Ethan.

"Pffft. 'Twas hardly a bother." Raymar waved a dismissive hand.

"It was a bit more than that, Highness. Regardless, I apologize for interrupting your session, but I have come to retrieve the crown princess's consort. He has much to do before their nuptials today."

"Very well." He politely nodded before turning to Ethan. "I look forward to our next lesson, Ethanos." Raymar regarded him formally, giving no indication to Leora of his fondness for his new brother.

"Sounds good, Ray." Ethan slapped his shoulder, already giving him a nickname, undoing all of Raymar's subterfuge, his familiar gesture causing Leora to gasp.

"Prince Raymar Loria is to be formally addressed at *all* times, Consort Loria!" She reproached, her eyes boring into his. "A bow of the head is offered at the commencement and conclusion of every interaction between a consort and a prince of the realm. Am I understood, Ethanos?"

"Give the poor fellow time, Leora. I am certain he is unfamiliar with our protocols, which are too numerous to count," Raymar interjected before giving Ethan an expectant look to comply.

"Prince Raymar," Ethan growled, bowing his head in disgust.

Bear with me, Ethan, Raymar wished to say aloud. He could tell by the look in Ethan's eyes that he understood the need for this apparent wall between them.

Ethan took Raymar's training sword, carrying it to the rack where it belonged, passing a servant that tried to receive them.

"My lord?" The young man gasped as Ethan walked past, putting the weapons and his shield on the rack in their proper place.

"No worries, sir, I got it." Ethan patted the man's back before returning to a furious Leora and a bemused Raymar.

"We have servants for such menial tasks, Consort." Leora's eyes narrowed cruelly.

"If I use something, I put it back where I found it. I don't need a servant for that," Ethan dismissed her protest. Before he took one step away, Leora raised her hands, levitating the swords from the rack, sending them across the chamber, dropping them on the sand floor.

"Pick them up!" she commanded the servants.

"Yes, Minister Mattiese." The servants bowed, hurrying to obey. Ethan noted their rich attire, with soft pastel tunics, hose, and pointy shoes that he found atrocious. Even the lowliest of servants were formally attired. It was all ridiculous and unnecessary. What else could one expect with women in charge, forcing everyone to dress their best at all times?

"Come, Ethanos," Leora ordered, turning abruptly about, her skirts swirling in her wake.

"Good luck," Raymar worded silently as Ethan walked by, following Leora out of the chamber.

"Three hundred years," he mouthed silently back, shaking his head, the gesture causing Raymar to smile.

*****

"What is it exactly I have to do?" Ethan asked, catching up to Leora as she hurried along the corridor.

"Prepare you for your nuptials." She stopped to brush the sand off his sleeve.

"Prepare how?" He didn't like the sound of that.

"A bath and suitable attire to begin with. What you're wearing is filthy and unsuitable." She tsked, regarding the thick black wool trousers and shirt he wore for sparring.

"Doesn't look so bad," he thought aloud, looking down at his clothes.

"Perhaps not for training with Prince Raymar in the arena but certainly for anywhere else in the palace," she continued on her way.

"I'm more than capable of choosing my own clothes."

"No, you are not. Left to your own devices, you'd present yourself in that detestable Texan garb with that ridiculous hat."

"What's wrong with my hat?" He gave her that hurt look he used all too often.

"It has no place in the palace."

"Why all the emphasis on attire, anyway? Everywhere I look, people are over dressed in one way or another. Even your lowest servants are dressed better than Astarian nobles."

"The Queen Mother demands everyone in the palace to be impeccably attired, especially her servants and members of her house, for each is a reflection of her authority."

"Is this because of the festivities, or is this how it will always be?" he inquired. He wasn't sure how much more he could endure. Since his arrival, the outfits they were picking out for him were getting progressively worse, from pleated kilts to silk tunics and hose, to puffed pantaloons and floppy hats. Each time, he dutifully put on the ridiculous garb, to his utter shame, and Alesha's amusement. He swore he would return the favor one day.

"The Queen Mother's expectations are the same whether there is a special occasion or not. You will just have to comply with her wishes." Leora smirked, knowing attire was a point of constant contention with Ethan.

"Wonderful," he mumbled. "You know, Leora, I am curious why the chief minister is assigned as my handler? Isn't that beneath your station?" he asked, knowing how she hated when he referred to her by her given name.

"The fact that I am personally directing you should demonstrate how important your presentation is to the Queen Mother."

*****

"Wonderful," Ethan muttered under his breath, tugging the collar that was reaffixed to his neck awaiting his entrance into the throne room. Alesha did warn him he would have to wear it for this occasion, reassuring him that she would promptly remove it after. He spent the better part of the day being bathed, clothed, and primmed. True to her word, Leora oversaw his preparations with a religious zeal. His face was clean-shaven along with most of his body, his hair combed, set, and scented, and his clothing, what there was of it, was pitifully scant. He was miserably clad in a shimmering pleated, blue kilt that fell above his knees, made of a lightweight material he was unfamiliar with, much finer than silk. Other than gold bands gracing his wrists and ankles, his chest, arms and legs were bare. He wasn't even afforded an undergarment. Was he expected to enter the throne room nearly naked? Alesha did warn him that today would be difficult, and she would reward him for suffering it without complaint or protest.

If Ben, Jake, or the judge ever saw me like this, I would never live it down. He shook that dreadful thought from his head.

Three hundred years, he groaned inwardly until realizing that he was only bound to them as long as his father lived. That would reduce his sentence to fifty years at most, depending on how long Bronus Blagen endured. Even if his father's life wasn't in the balance, escaping Elysia was no simple task.

No simple task indeed. He looked up at the high arches spanning the width of the corridor, some fifteen meters above, and the ten arches running endlessly in opposing directions. The corridor was finely decorated with bright peach-hued walls, with frescos painted along its length in rich detail. The doors to the throne room were forged from pure silver, with gold inlays in the symbols etched into their face.

A dozen royal guards stood post around him, wearing their distinct silver cuirasses over white tunics with pleated kilts. Sergeant Jordain was among them but paid Ethan little heed, his eyes scanning the corridor for threats. Leora stood impassively before the doors, dressed in an elegant burgundy gown.

"It is time," she declared, reaching out her hands, magic flowing from her fingertips, opening the massive doors.

"ETHANOS LORIA, CONSORT to Crown Princess Alesha!" the herald announced upon their entrance, Leora preceding him, and the royal guards flanking him.

The throne room was massive. Tall columns lined either side of the chamber, forged from pure gold, and stretching imperiously to the arched ceiling above. There were five along each of the east and west walls. The south wall rested at the far end of the cavernous chamber, with massive windows running in a semicircle, behind three large thrones set upon a raised dais. The windows were obviously spell-forged by their unique curve and size, stretching twenty meters high, allowing a breathtaking view of the Salnar Mountains in the distance. Pillowy clouds gathered at the bottom of the windows, making the large chamber appear as if it were placed in the heavens. The clouds were obviously mage induced for aesthetic purposes but were impressive nonetheless.

A thousand pairs of eyes followed his advance across the mirrored stone floor. The chamber was crowded with dignitaries, nobles, and courtesans, gathered to either half of the throne room, with a broad aisle between them where he trod. He caught sight of the familiar faces of Thela Corval and her sister mage healers, the women gifting him their grateful smiles for rescuing them from the Mage Bane. He waved back politely, his gesture causing a slight stir in the assemblage. His anger at the healers over their role in Alesha's subterfuge had waned, and he guessed they had no real choice in the matter. Ethan wasn't one to hold grudges long after his initial anger passed.

Upon the dais, Queen Corella sat on a diamond throne, half a size larger than the one she sat in the great hall. She again wore a pristine white gown with a high collar and long billowing sleeves. Her silver eyes followed him across the throne room. Valera sat on her right, upon her onyx throne, its caliginous surface devouring the light emitted from Corella's. Valera's black dress draped her throne in billowing folds of obsidian. She, too, followed Ethan's approach, her eyes boring into him like burning embers. To Corella's left rested the empty sapphire throne, set lower than the others. Behind the thrones stood the Mothers of the Lorian Order, Alesha's grandmothers many times removed, all arrayed in shimmering golden dresses, their eyes fixed upon him.

Leora stopped short of the dais and knelt, bowing deeply, before lifting her head.

"I present the groom, my Queen!" Leora declared.

"Present him!" Corella gestured with a slight lifting of a finger, bidding Leora to rise.

"Proceed and present yourself to your queen," Leora whispered, backing a step to address Ethan.

It's gonna be a long day, he thought tiredly, stepping forth and kneeling where Leora directed him, unnerved by their eyes upon his nearly naked form.

"Head to the floor," Valera reminded him, lowering her left hand, mimicking the motion.

Ethan sighed, placing his forehead on the floor in complete obeisance and humiliation.

"You may lift your head, child!" Corella said, her silver eyes glowing with zealous glee.

Ethan lifted his gaze as Corella rose from her throne, her eyes sweeping the assemblage.

"The nuptials of a Vellesian crown princess and her chosen Consort is a momentous occasion, done only once in a generation," Corella addressed the court, her mage-projected voice echoing through the chamber like gentle thunder, though Ethan only heard her mortal tone.

"Though the wedding of a crown princess is a grand spectacle to be shared with the entire realm, symbolizing the strengthening of the Vellesian Throne, this occasion represents something more. Far more than the joining of two rich bloodlines, the union of my granddaughter Alesha with Prince Ethanos of Astaria completes the destiny of House Loria and ushers the dominion of Vellesia over all the mortal realms," Corella declared, her eyes briefly regarding Ethan before returning to the gathered Lords and Ladies.

"Each of your houses shares the bloodlines with my own, each taking a royal child to wed your heirs through the ages, or offering one of your own sons to wed ours. Each of your houses shares in our glorious ascension and shall reap the bountiful rewards of our kinship. To Vellesia!" Corella proclaimed triumphantly.

"Hail Vellesia!" the lords, ladies, and courtesans cheered.

"Hail House Loria!"

"Hail Queen Corella!"

"Hail Queen Valera!"

Their cheers reverberated through the chamber.

Ethan cringed. These people truly believed what they were saying, each house devoted to their monarchy. He had to hand it to Corella and Valera. They held the absolute authority in their realm and received the blind obedience of their lords. Though all the mage lords were bound by magic to obey their king or queen, the Vellesian nobles were true believers in the divine authority of House Loria. Only those with mental shields, such as Raymar, could resist their influence.

"As a royal consort, Prince Ethanos has forsaken all other titles and allegiances, to pledge his loyalty and devotion to House Loria and his bride, Crown Princess Alesha." Corella smiled, the crowd cheering her declaration.

"Though his vows were taken in Astaris, witnessed by the kings and queens of the seven mage realms, it is required that he repeat his vows before the Vellesian Throne, to include vows of obedience to myself as the Queen Mother, and to the authority of the Lorian Order!" she proclaimed, her eyes again meeting Ethan's with a devious grin.

Ethan just sighed and shook his head. He should've known this wasn't going to be easy.

"You shall begin with your vows of denunciation!" Valera said, gaining her feet to stand beside her mother.

"And with a voice loud enough for all to hear, my child," Corella added.

"I foreswear all loyalties to Astaria, my native realm! I forswear the name Blagen, and all loyalties to that house!" The words rang bitterly in his voice.

"Now you shall proclaim your vows of submission to House Loria!" Corella commanded.

This vow was new, but at this point, he wasn't surprised by anything they ordered. He didn't fully understand what they wanted him to say but could guess, and if he misspoke, they would correct him.

"I submit to the authority of House Loria," he said, looking to Corella to see if that would be enough.

"And promise to serve…," Valera added with barely a whisper.

"And promise to serve…," he repeated.

"House Loria in perpetuity," she said.

"House Loria in perpetuity."

That meant *forever*.

"You must now pledge your vows of affirmation," Valera declared, her eyes sweeping the assemblage as her mother descended the dais to stand before Ethan, looking down upon him with triumphant glee. "Your first vow of affirmation is to the Queen Mother."

"Take my hand, Ethanos," Corella offered her left hand, which he reluctantly held with his right.

"Use both hands, my son," Valera gently corrected.

"Now, swear eternal loyalty, devotion, and obedience," Corella said dryly.

"I accept…," he began.

"You submit!" Corella corrected him.

"I submit to Queen Mother Corella. I vow to honor her as my Queen, and obey her in all things."

"Now, kiss my hand," she softly ordered, and he did so.

"And now you shall pledge your vows of affirmation to the Lorian Order!" Valera continued as Corella ascended the dais, retaking her place upon her throne, watching with satisfaction as Mother Evalena stepped to her side, touching a hand affectionately to her shoulder, before taking her turn at the base of the dais.

Ethan took her hand in his, pledging eternal loyalty and obedience to the Grand Sorceress of the Order. Evalena smiled, her green eyes staring down at him with satisfaction, as if a great burden was finally lifted. Mother Zelana came next, followed by Veriana, then Ametria. Ethan repeated the vows of affirmation one after another. Mothers Clarisa, Demetra, Porshana, Inese, Mortava, Elesha, Vetesha, and finally Caterina. It was a seemingly endless parade of former queens, each very much alive and a direct ancestor to Alesha. They each stood before him where he knelt, receiving his vows of loyalty before returning to their place behind the throne, each receiving his sacred oath in order of age, from Evalena the eldest to Caterina the youngest.

After her grandmother Caterina received Ethan's oath, Valera addressed the assemblage.

"My lords and ladies thus concludes the vows of affirmation to the Queen Mother and the Lorian Order. Though I and the crown princess have received oaths of loyalty from Ethanos, he shall renew those sacred vows for all of Vellesia to witness!" Valera descended the dais, extending her long slender fingers to Ethan, who took them in his hands and repeated his vows. She regarded him strangely, searching his sea-blue eyes for something she could not explain. All her life, she struggled with an insatiable hunger for any mage gift not her own, the same hunger that afflicted her mother, grandmother, and every direct ancestor before them. It was a hunger that was all-consuming, driving them to the brink of madness. It was the same hunger that drove them to seek consorts possessing powers they lacked. Though these unions could never bring them peace, their hunger remained, driving their jealousy toward their mates. Only the collars binding their consorts dulled this hunger but could never cure it.

Valera sighed, thinking of her own husband, the eldest son of House Menau, Travin. He was the only consort to not wear a collar, the gesture a symbol of respect for House Menau to honor their age-old alliance with House Loria. How she despised him for this privilege her mother granted him, his immense power paining her mind with endless torment. Even his death could not sate the madness.

Valera thought about the collaring of Ethan at Astaris and the anger it invoked in King Bronus. True, it was a means to humiliate the boy in retaliation for his many slights of her person, but it was symbolic as well, the ceremonial binding of a consort's power, rendering him harmless to House Loria. With Ethan it was only a symbol, for only a collar laced with anti-magic could bind his power, and there wasn't enough available to them to forge one. And so Ethan's power went unchecked, a constant reminder of what they did not possess. They knew his presence would be maddening but had to bring him to Elysia regardless, to fulfill their destiny.

Ethan's mere presence should drive them mad, but strangely, the opposite was occurring. It started during their journey, the hunger that consumed Valera all her life slowly abated. By the journey's end, it was but a faint echo. As long as Ethan was close to Alesha, the hunger shrank. Conversely, any physical distance between them caused the hunger and madness to grow.

"I avow…," Ethan repeated his oaths to Valera as she continued her musings.

Have you noticed something Mother? Valera asked, linking her mind to Corella's, feeling her mother's eyes upon her back.

Other than this victorious day? Corella smiled triumphantly.

The hunger, has it lessened?

A pregnant pause followed; Corella suddenly cognizant of the fact. Valera could hear the internal sigh of relief.

I feel it now. How did I not sense it before? Corella gasped, though it was only slightly diminished, yet noticeable.

I feel it as well, Mother Caterina joined in, a sense of euphoria spreading to their mothers until each of the Lorian Order realized the significance.

Ethan looked warily at the assembled faces upon the dais staring back at him with unnerving smiles.

Now what? he thought miserably. Every time one of them smiled at him, they followed it up with another humiliation of some sort.

"HER ROYAL HIGHNESS, CROWN PRINCESS ALESHA!" the palace steward heralded.

All eyes were drawn to the back of the chamber where royal guards entered the throne room, followed by a retinue of maidens dressed in flowing silken gowns of scarlet and green. The maidens tossed golden rose petals upon the floor, the symbol of House Loria.

Ethan grew weary of craning his neck, and gained his feet, ignoring the displeased look he received from the Queen Mother for breaking protocol. Corella's ire quickly waned as her eyes fell upon Alesha entering the chamber, her slippered feet following the trail of rose petals to the throne. Ethan's heart quickened as their eyes met, a smile blossoming across her beautiful face. She wore a shimmering blue gown, her ample breasts straining against its bodice, its voluminous skirts swirling about her ankles as they swept the floor. A thin silver tiara graced her black hair, which was styled high upon her head. His mouth went dry, her beauty consuming his every thought, sweeping away her betrayal and the humiliations that followed. At that moment, all he ever wanted was walking across the throne room toward him.

She blushed, feeling his eyes so intently upon her. Though thousands of eyes greeted her entrance, 'twas as if she and Ethan were alone, losing themselves in the other's gaze. The way he was staring at her at this moment was unlike any other. It was all-consuming, driven by some otherworldly omnipotence that she could neither explain nor comprehend. Her legs felt strangely weak, the tingling sensation of standing upon a precipice coursing her flesh. Alesha surrendered to her magic, floating over the floor, lest her feet betray her.

The royal guards and maidens stopped at the front of the assemblage, fanning out before the dais, making way for Alesha. Alesha forced her eyes from Ethan upon reaching the dais, her golden eyes sparkling with mirth as they met the Queen Mother's. She stepped past Ethan, dipping into a deep curtsy.

"Rise, Granddaughter," Corella commanded with a subtle lifting of her finger.

Alesha straightened, drawing to her full height before turning to face Ethan.

"You...you look good," he stupidly said, a complete loss for words.

"Oh, Ethan." She smiled, shaking her head, taking a step closer, touching a hand to his cheek, feeling his warmth through her fingers. She could lose herself in his eyes, eyes as blue as the sea. "You look good also," she whispered his words back to him, words that were simple and honest, just like the man who stood before her.

Corella looked on with knowing disbelief, Alesha and Ethanos's intimacy a soothing balm to her soul. She felt the effect it had on her mothers and daughter, each similarly impacted, a warmth permeating their entire being.

It was rapture. She shared a look with Valera, before returning her gaze to Alesha and Ethanos, unable to look away.

"Your vows, Consort!" Leora growled a whisper from her place behind him, horrified by the trance that seemed to afflict the queens, Alesha, and the entire Lorian Order if the looks they were giving were anything to go by. Her admonishment didn't go unnoticed, bringing Corella from her thoughts.

"Yes, your vows, Ethanos," Corella ordered, shaking her head as if waking from a dream.

"Kneel," Alesha softly commanded, running her hand along his jaw and throat, stopping at his naked chest, feeling the thick muscles beneath her fingers.

Not much longer, my love, she wanted to say, to answer the look of annoyance crossing his face.

He sighed as he knelt, taking her outstretched hand in his, repeating his vows of fidelity, obedience, and loyalty, swearing to a lifetime of devotion while looking up at her smiling face.

"Now, kiss her hand, binding your soul to hers for all eternity!" Corella commanded, her voice echoing like gentle thunder.

As soon as his lips touched her flesh, she caressed his cheek with her free hand, staring lovingly into his sea-blue eyes. Her smile eased upon seeing the annoyance on his handsome face. Knowing how much he hated kneeling, it was little wonder. She once had an exciting thrill picturing him kneeling at her feet, swearing his eternal loyalty. Now it just felt…wrong. Why did she now hate seeing him like this? What had changed? All her life was directed toward this one triumphant moment, the moment he knelt in the throne room of Elysia, binding himself to her for all time.

"Stand." She smiled, shaking her head. "You weren't meant to be on your knees."

He made a face as she helped him to his feet. *Not meant to be on my knees?* He wanted to laugh. That's all he's been doing since Astaris.

Don't be a fool, Ethan. If she's going to lighten up a little, let her, a voice of reason echoed in his brain.

"Thank you," he mouthed quietly.

"As Queen Mother, I proclaim the union of Crown Princess Alesha and the former crown prince of Astaria, Ethanos Blagen, in full witness before the Lords and Ladies of Vellesia, and the royal family of House Loria. From this day forth, let it be known that the former crown prince of House Blagen shall be known only as Ethanos Loria, consort to Crown Princess Alesha Loria!" Corella proclaimed.

"You may claim your prize, Alesha," Queen Valera added, a smile blossoming across her face.

Alesha cradled Ethan's cheeks with her hands, pressing her lips to his, kissing her husband before the assemblage.

"Come." She smiled, placing her hand in his, leading him up the dais. She fluffed out her billowing skirts before sitting the sapphire throne, its blue surface sparkling like a tropical sea. She directed Ethan to stand beside her, keeping her hand in his, as she surveyed the assemblage, staring proudly at the sea of familiar faces. Her free hand found itself upon her womb, the power emanating from her unborn child growing more potent every day. She told no one that the child's immunity to magic was transferred to her, at least until birth. At first, it was being able to use her own power in Ethan's presence. Now it began to interrupt the mage power of others.

She recalled the surprised look earlier that morn, when Aisley Fabren, one of her ladies in waiting, and youngest daughter of Lord Fabren of western Corellis, attempted to levitate a hairbrush when Alesha interrupted her. She was startled when the brush dropped to the floor of their dressing chamber, the girl uncertain of the cause of her power failing.

Alesha's gaze found her aunts Sarella and Selendra in the front row of the assemblage, their purple eyes staring happily back, the joy of this day not lost on her father's sisters. Like all members of House Menau, her aunts were exceptionally powerful, mastering all mage gifts of the mind. Like her siblings, Raymar and Amanda, the members of her father's house were able to shield any probe of their thoughts or manipulation of their minds. Of course, Alesha shared these wonderful powers, where her mother did not. This gift often created a measure of distrust between their houses, with House Loria only placated by the promise that one of their heirs would one day wed a son of House Menau, thus adding their powers to the throne. Alesha often wondered if there was any subterfuge with her father's house, weighing the possibility that House Menau had other motivations.

Whatever are you thinking? Alesha mused, staring into her aunt Sarella's purple eyes.

Beautiful dress. She looks so lovely... Alesha could hear her aunt's thoughts before noticing her wince as if a dagger twisted in her skull. Alesha withdrew immediately, taken aback by the revelation. She could tear through their mental shields. She decided against any further attempts, lest anyone discover what she was now capable of. As her baby grew, perhaps she could probe her aunt's mind further and undetected. Perhaps Raymar's also. The idea her daughter would one day wield such power both frightened and excited her. She then regarded Ethan standing by her side, the catalyst of all this power, the man who saved her from certain death, and protected her even after her betrayal. It was then she knew there was no one, save their daughter, that was more important to her than him.

"You will rule beside me, Ethan. Your place is at my side. It always has been and I will share all that I have with you." She squeezed his hand fiercely.

Rule beside her? He'd be happy to just rule his own life.

"Let us proceed with the wedding feast!" Queen Corella declared, concluding the ceremony.

*****

The wedding feast consisted of twenty-one courses, with exotic delicacies brought from as far as the western reaches of the Aqualania Sea. Thankfully, Ethan was allowed to change his attire, trading in the scandalous thin kilt for plain black trousers and a pullover shirt. True to her word, Alesha removed the collar before the feast. Throughout the feast, the noble houses approached the high table one at a time, bestowing gifts upon the royal couple. Ethan's ears perked as one Lord Valnar of Vecaba, was introduced, with his lady wife, Elenna, his former betrothed. He scolded himself for forgetting the house she was pledged.

"My princess." She curtsied to Alesha, not daring to look in Ethan's direction. It was surreal seeing the woman his parents had arranged for him to wed, here at his own wedding. The way she ignored him made him uneasy. It was as if she didn't recognize him at all.

"You have our thanks, Lady Valnar." Alesha smiled in kind as the noble couple returned to their table.

"She doesn't remember me, does she?" he asked once they stepped away.

"No," Alesha confirmed, not unkindly.

"Did you do it? Did you steal her memories?"

"Yes." Alesha sipped her wine.

Ethan shook his head with her pettiness.

"And you are disappointed, I presume." She didn't look at him.

"Just because you *can* do something, doesn't mean you have the right."

"Did you love her?" she asked, knowing that he didn't.

"You know I opposed the betrothal."

"I do, and I know you didn't love her, but you would have wed her all the same, at your father's insistence."

"Yes, when I was bound to the throne of Astaria like you are to the throne of Vellesia. I didn't want to marry her, but I didn't wish her ill either. Playing with people's memories is cruel and unnecessary."

"Cruel?" She turned to him with a raised brow. "Cruel is seeing that poor girl besotted with the impossibly handsome Ethanos Blagen, only to be forced to wed a lord as old and foul as Lord Valnar. Removing her memories of you was a *kindness*."

"You could've sent her back to her people. There was no point…"

"Send her back?" She looked at him incredulously. "Her uncle, King Evor, would see her as tainted. Such is the fate of women throughout the other mage realms, Ethan. Tell me you know this? Women are bartered and sold to forge or strengthen alliances and bloodlines. They are little more than pieces on a game board."

"Like me."

"Yes, you, the most important piece on the only game board that matters. Now you know how she felt, as all women feel throughout your precious Astaria, to be sold off like prime stock."

"Not all. My sisters will have a say in who they wed." He knew his father would place their happiness above any other considerations.

"Yes, because your family is different, Ethan. They truly love each other. It was something that took me aback when I first arrived in Astaris. It was one thing to hear of it from my aunts after years of observing your family but quite another to see for myself. I was taken aback by how much they loved one another and were especially worried about you."

"If you're trying to make me feel guilty, it's working." He downed his goblet as another lord and lady approached. Once they exchanged greetings and stepped away, she continued.

"It wasn't meant to make you feel guilty, Ethan. It was to remind you that they love you. All the choices you made and the dangers you faced, were done for a reason. They shaped the man you are, the man I admire. I wouldn't change any of the things you have done even though I, too, feared for you when you were doing them. The only difference is that I feared losing your power, they feared because they love you. Now I understand what that fear is like."

"What do you mean?"

"The fear of losing someone you love." She looked down at her plate sadly.

"I thought love was an amalgamation of lust, desire, and…"

"I know what I said, and I was a fool." She looked up at him, staring deeply into his eyes. "I am so sorry for bringing you here against your will, Ethan. I am sorry for betraying your trust. And I am so sorry for all the indignities you have endured for me. If I could do it all over again, I would want nothing more than to run away with you before that fateful night in Astaris and live in a small home far away from everyone."

"You would've done that?"

"No. I would've *wanted* to do that. I would want to do that to make you happy. But I couldn't. There is more to our choices than our happiness. We have a duty, you and I, to serve the greater good. You may not see it, but it is there all the same. Our daughter must be the queen of Vellesia. The mage realms, the Mage Bane, and the wilds are full of injustice, cruelty, and unbearable hardships. She can change all that, and we must be by her side to guide her. Her life is too important for me to place our happiness above her needs."

"If our daughter is to be as powerful as you believe, she doesn't need a throne to shape the world."

She gave him a look. "The throne is an instrument, a tool to help her fulfill her destiny. The more power she has, the less bloodshed will be necessary to unify our world. And only with absolute power over the world can she better the lives of everyone. No more petty wars, no more cruel lords abusing their peasants for their own greed, and no more injustice."

"And what if she is the tyrant? Who can check her power? Absolute power is corrupting. Tell me you have thought of this?"

"Our daughter will not be a tyrant!" She glared; aghast he could think it possible. "She will be a light to the world as our prophecies have foretold for thousands of years. To believe otherwise is heresy."

"It is only logical to point out what might go wrong with your plan." He shrugged, taking another sip from his goblet.

"Not in this matter. What you are suggesting is heresy, and you will not speak of it again. If my mother or grandmother heard what you said, I..." She shuddered to think of the consequences. "Just do not speak of it."

That's not very reassuring. He shook his head. *No wonder Amanda and Raymar are so worried for the future.*

"I'll keep it to myself, Allie, but I hope you are right about all this, and may the fates help us all if you are wrong."

The feast concluded with the celebration continuing in the Great Hall for the wedding ball, where each of the lords and ladies shared the dance floor with the royal couple, each taking turns dancing with the bride and groom. With twenty-one major provinces and numerous prominent vassals within each one, there was no shortage of partners to share a dance with. With many lords bringing multiple sons and daughters, the numbers ballooned to over a hundred and fifty pairings Ethan and Alesha would share. Before the first dance commenced, he was taken aback as Alesha brought forth a young girl no more than five years, wearing a lovely emerald gown, and holding a familiar doll tightly in her arms.

"Ethan, this is Shae Jordain. She has something she wishes to say to you." Alesha couldn't hide her smile, bringing the girl forward.

"Hello, Ms. Jordain, you are very beautiful," Ethan said, squatting low to her level, as she shyly bit her lip.

"Thank you for my doll, my lord." She bobbed a curtsy.

Ethan shared a look with Alesha, realizing the girl was Ander's daughter. The fact Alesha invited her to the grand ball was surprising considering the number of lords that could not attend. He spared a glance to the side of the chamber, where Ander stood guard, the sergeant looking warily back at his daughter.

"You are most welcome, my lady." He smiled.

"I am not a lady, my lord. My father is..."

"He is a very good man. Do you know he saved my life?" Ethan said.

"He did?" Her eyes drew wide.

"He did. Some very bad men wanted to run me over with their horses and spears, and your father stepped in front of them to protect me. He was very brave that day. You should be very proud of him," Ethan recalled their skirmish in front of little Cora's house.

"Papa did that?" Shae's little voice rose three octaves in disbelief.

"He did, Shae. Ethan never lies." Alesha shared a smile with her husband.

"Do you know how to dance, Shae?" Ethan asked, looking around as if frightened.

"Not very good, I am afraid." She shrugged.

"I don't know how to dance at all, and you see all these ladies throughout this Great Hall?" Ethan asked, pointing out the many faces looking at them.

Shae followed the direction of his eyes, swallowing a lump in her throat at the people staring at them.

"Maybe you could help Ethan, Shae. Maybe you could teach him what you know, so he isn't afraid when he dances with everyone else," Alesha encouraged, giving Ethan a playful wink.

"I don't know, I..." she stammered.

"Sure you do. I know you can teach me because you are very brave like your father. Can the Princess hold your doll for you, while you teach me?" Ethan asked, as she handed it carefully to Alesha, who promised to safeguard it with her life.

And so Ethan let Shae lead him onto to floor, commencing the ball with the first dance. Alesha couldn't hide the smile gracing her face, watching him dance so gently with the child. Some of the nobles were aghast that a commoner was taking the position of honor, but most followed Alesha's example and smiled at the scene. She called Ander over from his post along the near wall, surprising him when his wife, Emily, appeared, dressed in an emerald gown that matched their daughter's.

"You may have the next dance, Ander." Alesha smiled, placing his resistant hand in Emily's.

"Your Highness, it is not my place to...," he stammered.

"Are you refusing your crown princess's order on her wedding day, Sergeant Jordain?" Alesha asked.

"No, Highness, it is just not proper for..."

"Nonsense. You have done a great service to my family throughout our journey home, guiding and protecting my husband, for which I am grateful. Your wife suffered your absence and should be rewarded for her sacrifice. Besides, Ethan is so very fond of you. This would please him." Alesha smiled, using a bit of magic to push them onto the center floor.

Alesha stood there for a time, observing Ethan and little Shae, touched by him, letting her lead him across the floor, making her feel special. She imagined him doing the same with their daughter, dancing with her, guiding her, protecting her. She could feel her mother's and grandmother's eyes upon her, neither knowing what to make of this but remaining quiet for Alesha's sake. This was a part of Ethan that her family would come to appreciate as she has, his genuine caring for those most would consider below them. He loved honest, hardworking people, and honored them whenever he could. This was her way of pleasing him, by honoring a man he respected, Ander Jordain. Eventually, the dance came to its end, and she returned the doll to Shae and greeted Ander and Emily as they collected their daughter.

"Take your beautiful wife and daughter, Sergeant, and enjoy the ball. You are excused from duty for the day," she said, drawing surprised looks from them both, raising a hand to still their protest.

"Go on, Sarge, enjoy the gala. Your princess commands it." Ethan nudged his shoulder.

A grateful Emily thanked Alesha, drawing her husband and daughter away.

"That was kind of you," Ethan said, watching Ander disappear to the far side of the chamber.

"It was just a small part of my royal request for your action with the dragon. A small gesture that I thought you would appreciate, Oh great champion of the common people." She smiled.

"A part of the royal request?" He made a face.

"Yes. I have decided to ask for a thousand small favors rather than one large reward, which the Queen Mother has agreed. I have decided to use most of them for small things that will make you happy, like honoring Ander as you would have done if you could."

A wane smile graced his lips, touched by her kind act.

"Shall we?" he asked, offering her his hand for the next dance.

"We share the last dance, not the first or second," she reminded him, directing him to the waiting arms of Lady Thela Corval, their old acquaintance from the Mage Bane, and Arch Mage Healer.

And so they danced with every lord and lady in attendance, finishing in the early evening, with the final dance in each other's arms.

"Finally." Ethan gave her an easy smile, leading her across the floor, the guests gathered along the periphery to watch.

"I am worth the wait." She smiled back after spending the entire ball dancing with everyone but each other.

"Yeah, I reckon you are, Ms. Allie," he said with his Texas drawl, which was completely out of place for where he stood.

She just shook her head. Despite all that happened between them, he was still the same old Ethan. The same boy she met in the Mage Bane.

"Something amuses you?" he asked.

"Nothing." She smirked.

"And you call me a lousy liar." He rolled his eyes.

"Despite everything, you are still you," she said, losing herself in his sea-blue eyes.

"Was I supposed to be someone else?"

"That's not what I meant. You still have your humor and easy nature. I like that about you."

"You do?"

"It took a little adjusting at first, as I have never known a prince of royal blood to speak or act so not like a—"

"Like an ass?" He smirked.

"Like a prince of royal blood." She shook her head at his coarse language.

"That's what I said."

"Not all princes are asses," she corrected him with feigned annoyance that he could see right through.

"Yes, they are, though I'm an ass as well, so I guess it doesn't matter."

"Now you listen, Ethan. I won't have you calling yourself an ass, no matter how cute you think it sounds. It's a bad influence on our daughter. She will only know that her father is the finest man in the world."

"Cute?" He made a face.

"Of all that I said, that's what you remember?" She would've swatted his shoulder if it wouldn't make a scene.

"Men don't like being referred to as cute, just so you know. It's almost as embarrassing as what I was wearing earlier."

"You needn't be embarrassed. Every royal consort has endured the same ceremony for a thousand years. Besides, I found you most fetching," she teased.

"I'm sure you did." He rolled his eyes.

"You needn't fret, for tomorrow you can dress as you please, except your buckskins, which you must only wear outside the palace."

"Really?"

"Yes. I've already informed my mother and grandmother that you deserve a reward for your good behavior and of course for your deeds with the dragon, which is part of my request."

"Thanks," was all he could think to say.

"I will be treating with the high lords of the realm for much of the day tomorrow. I shall expect you to join me for a meal in the afternoon. Until then, you are free to explore the palace and find some activities to occupy yourself. Raymar has volunteered to guide you, and Sergeant Jordain will be at your service as well."

It was too good to be true. He was already planning half his day.

"Just remember to behave. Grandmother will allow you to indulge in such things as long as you follow the rules," she warned.

"I'll be good."

"I know you will, or else you will be dressed as you were on our first night in Elysia and given lessons on etiquette with Minister Mattiese," she warned, recalling the black kilt and doublet they forced on him.

"Eeggh!" he moaned at such a horrible thought.

"It was Mother who recommended it should you misbehave. So be mindful that she knows what truly makes you miserable, or that will be your punishment for any rebellious act." She almost laughed, picturing him suffering so.

"Thanks for the warning."

"You are welcome."

He tried to shake the strange feeling of everyone's eyes upon them, which was nigh impossible. The lords regarded them studiously and the ladies with blushing smiles. Far too many looked at him like grinning idiots as they danced.

"Gabrielle will be a good queen, I promise you," he said, reassuring her after their earlier conversation.

"She will because her father is a good man, and she will learn from him." She smiled, touched by his sincerity.

"I'm a good man?" He lifted a bemused brow.

"You heard what I said." She rolled her eyes.

"We'll raise her to be a good queen, together, you and I," he said before having her put her head on his shoulder as they slowly danced, breaking all protocol as they swayed with the music.

CHAPTER 15

"Welcome, Duke Alose," Valera greeted the high lord of Brelar, the rich port city that guarded the mouth of the Corellis bay, and Jewel of the Aqualania Sea.

"My Queen." Duke Alose stepped into the queen's sanctum, kneeling with his head bowed.

"Arise, my lord, and please sit." Valera waved an open hand to a high cushioned chair across from her.

"My princess," Duke Alose bowed his head reverently as he stood, regarding Alesha, who sat her mother's right.

"My lord," Alesha extended her hand where the dark-skinned, silver-haired Duke kissed it upon taking his seat. The queen's private sanctum was a spacious, richly adorned chamber, with a high domed ceiling and stone pillars supporting its weight. Frescas of exquisite quality adorned the curved walls, each depicting historical events of Vellesia's past. A large bay window rested off Alesha's right, providing a scenic view of the Salnar Mountains ringing the palace. Rich furs covered the dark marble floor. Duke Alose found the chamber warm and inviting, very suitable to interact with the queen less formally.

"I hope this morning finds you well, cousin?" Valera asked, her eyes softening, her familial acknowledgment setting him at ease. The duke's mother was Princess Glyndera, the second daughter of Mother Vetesha, who wed his father the Lord of Brelar, raising their lordship to Dukedom.

"Very much so, my Queen. The hospitality of Elysia has been most agreeable," he said.

"And you have visited with Mother Vetesha?" Valera asked.

"I have, my Queen. My grandmother was pleased with again meeting my daughters, as was Mother Caterina." He smiled graciously, acknowledging his aunt, who always treated him kindly. It was his house that fostered Prince Alexar, Mother Caterina's second child and brother of Queen Mother Corella. Alexar and Arose, though cousins, were as close as brothers, and Arose was most grieved when he believed Alexar had perished when his flagship met its fate in Astaria. Only recently was he informed of the truth and harbored Alexar in his holdfast, keeping his fate secret from greater Elaria.

"Did you enjoy the wedding feast?" Valera asked. Though she and Alesha spent the better part of the morning treating with one high lord after another, she still took time setting each lord at ease before addressing pertinent matters of the realm. It was a courteous and diplomatic way of treating with her vassals when they were alone, an important lesson she instilled in Alesha long ago, preparing her for Queenhood.

"Of course, my Queen. My daughters especially. "'Twas all they spoke of all night and at fast this morning. It was a lovely ceremony," he said.

"Your daughters are both quite lovely, my lord," Alesha said, the remark having the desired effect.

"You are most kind, Princess." A grateful smile graced the older man's thin face.

Valera smiled inwardly at Alesha's practiced charm. She knew Alesha could just as easily manipulate their lords into believing or saying anything she wanted, but such power should be used sparingly. It took more than mage powers to make a good queen, and Alesha understood that.

"We have spoken with several of your lords in recent days. They shared their concerns about the state of their holdfasts. They spoke well of you, of course," Alesha stated.

"My lords are loyal to House Alose and House Loria, Princess."

Indeed they are, for Alesha could read that in their thoughts.

"Their loyalty is beyond reproach," Valera said knowingly. "And their concerns are of a local variety that they can redress without bothering their Lord Paramount."

"I am pleased, my Queen." The duke bowed his head.

"Your place as a duke in good standing is reassured, my lord." Alesha put him at ease.

"There are those other matters, however, we wish to discuss," Valera added.

"The matter with Prince Alexar has been attended with utmost secrecy, as you commanded, my Queen," he said, regarding his harboring the queen's uncle until they decided to return him to court.

"A most delicate matter, that you have handled astutely," Valera said. With Amanda's betrayal, much of Elaria would soon learn that Alexar lived. Her primary concern was that Ethan not learn of this in the near future. Of course, when he did learn of it, there was naught he could do. Alexar's apparent death was the reason for the treaty with King Bronus, which led to Ethan's capture. To learn it was all a hoax would rouse Ethan's anger, and with things progressing between them, that was the last thing Alesha wanted. There was always the possibility that Amanda already revealed this truth to Ethan during her and Tristan's meeting with him before they crossed into Gorgencia, but she doubted it, for Ethan would have let them know, such that his anger would be.

"And the second matter, my lord?" Alesha asked.

The matter in question was four mages of significant skill, who were given safe passage through Brelar, and transported to Cordova by way of ships loyal to House Alose. They were to join the free city's Mage Council. Each was of an eastern race, hailing from the easternmost province of Vellesia, Celovar, claiming to have fled from unknown eastern lands to join Cordova's Mage Council. Their true loyalties, however, would always be with Vellesia.

Ethan's friends dwell in Cordova, Mother, Alesha once said when this plan was implemented, long before they set out for Astaris.

And our mages will protect his friends and are powerful enough to safeguard Cordova's independence, Valera explained.

Alesha knew well what that meant. Cordova would be safe as long as Ethan remained loyal to Vellesia. It was another chain binding him to Vellesia.

"They boarded ship without incident, traveling under the guise of wine merchants. The latest reports claim they were well-received and are now placed within Cordova's Mage Council," Duke Alose said.

"You have done well, cousin," Valera said.

"It is my honor to serve you, my Queen," he again bowed.

"And do you remember their names, Duke Alose?" Alesha asked, her mother surprised by the question. Of Duke Alose's many mage gifts, his perfect memory was the most well-known.

"Of course, my Princess," he claimed, his smile slowly dying on his lips, his renowned memory failing him.

"Something troubles you, Duke Alose?" Valera leaned forward, wondering about his affliction.

Alesha withdrew the anti-magic from his mind, his memory returning as he blinked his eyes, quickly rattling off the names. Alesha released a measured breath, startled by her baby's growing power. No matter how powerful Alesha was, no power she possessed could remove magic. Only anti-magic could do that, and she now possessed the power to project it, impairing the mage powers of others. Even the mage collars worn by royal consorts required trace elements of anti-magic to impair their wearer's powers. The collars were imbued with potent magic, coupled with anti-magic to bind the wearer's powers. She knew full well, if they possessed enough anti-magic, they could forge a collar strong enough to bind Ethan's powers, as the trace amount used in the collars they now possessed did nothing to him. It seemed only free-floating anti-magic could impair Ethan, not the anti-magic she was able to project. She contemplated this, wondering why it was so. She could only conclude that the power she now wielded came from their child, and its anti-magic came from Ethan, thus making him immune to it. Whereas the anti-magic in the small stone he gifted to Amanda, was not from him, and thus, could harm him. Though the power she could project still had no effect on Ethan, it shielded her from being impaired by him as well, which only validated how truly powerful he was. She kept this a secret from everyone, for it would raise more questions than she cared to answer. She was entitled to some secrets, she reasoned. Just as well, for if her mother and grandmothers knew, they would insist she use her ability to project anti-magic to forge a collar that could bind Ethan, which she knew would not work, and if it could, she wouldn't do it anyway. She betrayed Ethan once and would never do so again, no matter what the Queen Mother insisted she does.

Why do you vex me so, Ethan? she asked herself, not able to bear the thought of him being powerless. She thought of her grandfather Darius and great-grandfather Corbin, each a shell of their former glory. Darius possessed great speed, magic enhancing his mobility to run several times faster than normal men. The day her grandmother Corella discovered him when she was crown princess of the realm, she fixed the collar to him, binding his power forever. He once told her how wonderful it felt as a young man running through the forests of Celovar, moving far faster than any horse in the royal stables. She recalled the sad look in his eyes, remembering the days of his youth, and the power he could no longer touch. She would never let Ethan suffer such humiliation.

"Of course, you will keep us informed of any happenings in Cordova, Duke Alose," Valera commanded, drawing Alesha from her musing.

"Most certainly, my Queen, and any happenings of consequence along the Aqualania Sea that reaches my ears," he assured her.

Valera smiled, dismissing the dutiful lord.

"Something vexes you, child?" Valera asked once the Duke stepped without.

"What are your intentions with Cordova, Mother? Ethan would be most unhappy if we interfered with his friends there."

"I've instructed our mages to support the ruling council there. Without my intervention, the city would be doomed. Only Ethan kept the greedy mage realms from moving upon the free port. They were helpless when Luke Crawford slaughtered their mage council. Without Ethan arriving when he did, they would have quickly fallen."

"So we sent our mages to protect Cordova, their support for the city dependent upon Ethan's obedience to us," Alesha stated obvious.

"Yes. Though protecting the sovereignty of Cordova is in our interest as well. Having Cordova fall under the dominion of another mage realm would not be to our benefit. And...if it makes Ethan happy to know his friends have kept their tenuous autonomy, then so much the better. I know his happiness is important to you."

"I see no benefit in him being unhappy." She shrugged.

"Fair enough, and Mother Caterina agrees with you."

"Truly?" Alesha found that surprising.

"Yes, and Mothers Porshana and Veriana as well. In fact, they are all quite pleased with Ethan's presence."

"The hunger is gone, isn't it?" Alesha said, a slight probe of Valera's mind revealing the truth.

"Strangely, yes. I noticed first during our journey from Astaria. The longer you and Ethan were together, the weaker the hunger. My mother believes the first effects were felt when you and Ethan first met in Cordova. Looking back at that time, I believe she is right. I recall the dreadful day when we learned that you were taken captive. As you well know, that was not foreseen. But the strangest thing..." Her voice trailed, a faraway look passing her eyes..." The strangest thing was that I felt at peace."

"The prophecy is fulfilled. Of course, you are at peace, Mother."

"No, the prophecy mentions nothing of our hunger for mage power abating. When you returned from the Mage Bane without Ethan, it actually felt painful, almost cripplingly so. It went beyond the lust for mage power that has consumed our house since its inception. It was a pain that afflicted the entire Lorian Order and my mother as well. It persisted until Ethan arrived in Astaris, joining you there. Whenever you were in each other's company, the pain was swept away. Along our return journey, the hunger faded as well."

"It is not Ethan, Mother, but the child I carry. She is the reason why Ethan and I were destined to join. She is..."

"No." Valera shook her head gently, softly touching Alesha's cheek. "It is you and Ethan together that brought this about. Whenever you allowed him to explore the Gorgencian countryside or hunt, the hunger returned, if ever so slightly. The further the physical distance between you, the greater the anguish I felt. Had you probed my mind as freely as you do everyone else, you would have sensed this. Even now, I am less at ease because he is at the base of the palace doing whatever it is that he is doing, while you are here."

"That makes little sense." Alesha made a face. She was rarely, if ever, confounded, but this revelation was unexpected.

"If you deeply think about it, it makes all the sense in the world. Our prophecies were adamant that Ethan had to be bound to Vellesia. You couldn't merely couple with him. No, he needed to be brought here and *remain* here. We oft questioned why this was so, often asking your father's kin that very question without a suitable answer. Your father's kin were advisers to House Loria for hundreds of years, always guiding our house to fulfill our destiny, a destiny that eventually joined our two great houses with my marriage to Travin. The reason is now clear, Ethan is needed here to quell our hunger, removing this madness that has forever plagued our house. It is a gift from the spirits to reward our dedication to the fulfillment of the prophecy. We are now free to enjoy the fruits of our labors."

"That is wonderful news, Mother." Alesha reached out her hand to Valera's knee, squeezing it tightly.

"It is indeed, my love, as you also have felt the hunger abate."

"The hunger for Ethan's power abated long ago, Mother, but my hunger for his companionship only grows," she sighed.

"And he is equally afflicted. That I have seen so plainly upon his face," Valera observed.

"It makes me wonder if all our efforts were for naught." Alesha let her gaze wander to the window, lost in thought.

"Whatever do you mean?" Valera thought it absurd.

"If we were destined to be together, it would've happened regardless. Did I really need to trick him, earning his scorn? What if I told him the truth in the Mage Bane? I knew even then that he was hopelessly smitten. In time, he might've come here on his own," she lamented, still staring out the window, where the white caps of the Salnar Mountains peaked through the clouds.

"And if he did so, you would never have had to suffer his hate."

"He never hated me, Mother. It's not in his nature." She sighed, keeping her gaze toward the horizon.

"His disappointment then. You believe you could've avoided all that, leaving all we gained to chance?"

"If it meant not hurting him…then yes." She shifted her golden eyes to her mother's doubtful face.

Well, this is new. Valera was taken aback. "Alesha, destiny is a fickle thing. It must be nurtured. Our prophecies were given to us to prepare, each generation sacrificing for the greater good, sacrificing all else so that you would be born and Ethan brought to you. After so much has been spent, we couldn't let it all fall to chance just to spare his feelings."

Alesha shook her head.

"He would've come, Mother. He would have come for me to be with me. I know this. I know this as deeply as I know anything."

"He is wild, Alesha. Wild as a mountain wolf. You cannot know what he would've done."

"I do know. Don't ask me to explain it, but I know."

"Oh, my dear child. Guard your heart well, lest he break it," Valera said with all sincerity.

*****

Alesha walked along the corridor, her mind a whirlwind of worry. Matters of the realm never bothered her before but felt strangely burdensome for some reason, whether it was Duke Alose's watchful eye upon Cordova or Duke Thandor reporting of suspicious activity along the Ionia Divide, the northwest corner of the realm that separated Vellesia from the Wilds. She spent a lifetime preparing to assume the duties of Queen Daughter, savoring the power she would wield, but now it only felt tedious. There was little joy in directing affairs of the state, which unfortunately was the primary duty of the Queen Daughter, whereas the Queen Mother handled matters pertaining to House Loria.

She sighed tiredly. All she really wanted was to spend time with Ethan, the realm paling woefully in comparison. She shook her head, realizing that Ethan ruined the throne for her. After spending time with him, the throne was just…boring.

"Highness," guards greeted, bowing as she passed. The corridor ended just ahead, where the entrance of the training arena rested.

"Looking for your consort, Alesha?" Mother Porshana asked as she drew nigh, waiting for her at the entrance.

"You wouldn't ask if you didn't already know, grandmother," Alesha said, regarding the dark-skinned woman with a respectful bow.

"Grandmother, is it?" Porshana smiled at the appellation. Alesha always referred to her by the formal title of mother.

"Would you prefer *mother?*"

"No, I kind of favor Grandmother. To be accurate, you would have to place six greats in front of it, but that would be a mouthful to say. Grandmother it is then."

"You are not offended?" Alesha asked. Porshana well earned the title of Mother in the Lorian Order, her reign as queen regarded well in Vellesian history.

"My dear child, you are simply stating fact. I am your grandmother, and nothing I have accomplished as queen can compare to that." She drew Alesha into her embrace.

"Thank you, Grandmother. I've come to realize that life is too precious to place these formal walls between us."

"Very well, Alesha. If you prefer it thus, I will be honored to have you call me Grandmother. I sense the influence of your consort in your change of thinking," she smiled.

"Perhaps, or he simply has made me realize what I have always known but was too blind to see."

"And what were you too blind to see?"

"That family is what truly matters. You, Mother, Grandmother Corella, all my grandmothers in the order, Grandfathers Corbin and Darius, Raymar, Amanda, and Ethan are my family."

"Family can be a weakness as well. When you learned how important his family was to Ethan, you used that against him," Porshana pointed out.

"To my dying shame." She sighed. "Ethan knew more than I what was truly important."

"You judge yourself harshly, child. You also knew that Ethan would die if left to his own devices. By bringing him here, you have prevented that dark possibility. But you didn't come down here to bemoan your choices. You are looking for your husband, and he is waiting behind these doors," Porshana stepped aside, waving an open hand through the entrance. Porshana meant to comment on Alesha's lack of royal guards but received a mental reassurance from her granddaughter that she had no need of them.

Alesha paused at the entrance, sensing her grandfather Darius' presence within, as well as Raymar and her great-grandfather Corbin. "Why are all our menfolk with Ethan?"

"Spare a glance." Porshana rolled her eyes toward the arena.

Alesha was not surprised to find Ethan and Raymar sparring in the loose sand, the sound of clashing swords ringing in the air. What was surprising was the sight of her grandfather and great-grandfather clad in training leathers and armor, watching the two younger men exchange blows.

"Don't let me win, Ethan," Raymar grunted in annoyance as Ethan feigned a stumble, allowing Raymar to nearly tap his leg with his blunted steel.

"I wasn't faking, Ray, that was a good strike. You're getting better."

"I'll take you at your word, brother," Raymar grunted before Ethan again knocked his sword from his hand, leveling the blade at Raymar's throat.

"Your turn Grandpa Darius." Ethan stepped aside, exchanging places with Alesha's grandfather as the dusty-skinned man faced off with his grandson.

"I say the same to you, Raymar. Don't let me win. I will earn my victories," Darius said as he thrust forward, taking Raymar by surprise.

"He's getting better," Ethan said to Corbin, placing a hand upon the elderly man's shoulder.

"Yes, but we had large margins to improve," Corbin stated honestly. He felt young again training with swords, something that hadn't happened since he was collared and wed. As a royal consort, it was deemed unbecoming and unnecessary to be trained in martial skills. How Ethan was able to gain the queen's permission for this exercise was beyond him.

Alesha shook her head in disbelief, watching her husband interact so familiarly with her grandfathers and brother.

"They have been at it all morning," she heard Porshana say. "That husband of yours convinced your great-grandmother Caterina to allow this, taking Corbin in tow along with Darius. They both required little convincing by the enthusiasm they have shown like children let out to play."

"And the Queen Mother?" Alesha asked, stepping back into the shadows to observe them unseen.

"She is unaware and presently discussing other matters with Mother Evalena."

Of course, she doesn't know or she would have put a stop to it, Alesha mused, smiling as Ethan stepped back into the fray, this time with her great-grandfather Corbin. Corbin had little formal sword training in his youth, hadn't touched a blade since he wed her great-grandmother Caterina. She looked on as he came alive, displaying moves a man of his age had no place making. He was no match for Ethan, however, but she loved how Ethan balanced gentleness and respect, exchanging blows at a pace equal to Corbin.

"Better," Ethan encouraged, his blade touching Corbin's neck.

"Better is a kind way of saying I shall never master the sword with the years left to me." Corbin sighed.

"You've come a long way in just a few hours, Grandpa. Give me another year of training you, and you'll match swords with the best of them."

Grandpa? Alesha stifled a laugh at that moniker. It certainly didn't take Ethan long to ingratiate himself with some of her kin.

"Shall we?" Porshana asked, preparing to announce their presence.

"Wait, this is interesting." Alesha touched a hand to her grandmother's shoulder.

"Ethanos, I'll count it to my good fortune if I live to see another summer." Corbin laughed.

"Don't listen to him, Ethan. He said the same thing last winter," Raymar remarked, lowering his sword.

"And the winter before that." Darius snorted, taking advantage of Raymar's lowered sword, his thrust nearly catching his grandson unaware before Raymar parried the blow.

"He almost had you, lad." Corbin grinned as Darius backed Raymar several paces.

"Distractions will get you killed, Ray. Stay focused," Ethan reminded him as the men circled each other in the sand.

Alesha kept to the shadows, watching their exchanges for what felt like hours. She never saw her grandfathers like this, acting like carefree young boys. It was endearing. Eventually, it was time to end, and Ethan saw them off, promising to continue their lessons the following morn. Alesha stepped briefly away, allowing Raymar, Corbin, and Darius to leave without seeing her.

"I'll leave you alone." Porshana smiled, before slipping away, as Alesha entered the arena, the hem of her gown sweeping over the loose sand.

"We have servants for that," she said, catching Ethan putting away their sparring gear.

He froze briefly at the sound of her voice, before turning around.

Catching Ethan by surprise was a rare feat indeed, she smiled at the thought as she strode forth. She frowned as he started to kneel.

"Don't." She waved him off. For some strange reason, she had come to hate seeing him on his knees.

"As you wish." He sighed warily, not expecting her there.

"Did you have fun?" she asked, stepping nigh.

"Yes. How long were you watching?"

"Long enough," she said, brushing loose sand off his shoulder.

"We got permission if you're wondering," he said defensively, expecting her to disapprove of dragging her grandfathers along.

"No need to worry. Mother Porshana informed me," she said, setting him at ease, though by his posture it was a vain attempt. She was taken aback by his standoffishness. Hadn't she told him he was free to do such activities last night?

"I didn't hurt them if you were worried."

"I know, Ethan. You were very gentle, and I appreciate what you did."

"You do?" His eyes lifted in surprise.

"Of course, I do. My grandfathers have spent most of their lives sheltered in Elysia, rarely venturing from the royal apartments, let alone the palace walls. My grandmothers mostly forget about them since their duties of siring heirs have long passed."

"I noticed when they seemed pleasantly surprised when we asked them to join us."

"They were. No one has asked them to do much of anything for many years. Grandfather Corbin hasn't lifted a blade in over sixty years."

"Why not? What else is there to do here to pass the time?"

"It is frowned upon by court etiquette. Royal consorts are not expected to know such things. They are protected and have no need to protect others."

"So we are violating court etiquette?"

"Ethan, you are a living violation of court etiquette." She laughed. "You needn't worry. We have granted you much leniency to ease your transition here. You may practice swordsmanship with my grandfathers and brother all you like, as well as other activities that pique your interest, as long as they are within reason, of course."

"Fair enough." He reached down, gathering up another training sword to put back on the rack by the near wall, when she stopped him, lifting his chin with a lacquered finger.

"Of course, if you wore less clothing, I might take more interest in your training." She smiled deviously.

"You could always join me if you're willing to do the same."

She smiled mischievously, hiking up her skirts, and tying them off high above her knees before taking the training sword from his grasp. "Shall we?" she asked, levitating a shield from the ground, calling it to her free hand.

"Maybe this isn't a good idea with you being…pregnant." He looked warily at her stomach.

She answered with a sudden strike, knocking his sword from his hand, driving him to his back.

"Do you yield?" she asked dangerously, the point of her sword pressed against his throat.

"First bout goes to you, it seems." He snorted, pushing the blade away while gaining his feet.

"The first of many," she taunted, returning to her starting position while he fetched his sword and shield.

"Me and my big mouth," he mumbled under his breath as she came at him again. She was a dervish with a blade, moving with blinding speed, speed that was mage gifted, and didn't let up near his presence. All magic died when it came near him, but not hers, not now anyway. *How was she doing this?* he asked himself as she drove him back with a series of thrusts. He stopped her with a devastating riposte before tapping her knee with the toe of his boot, simulating a crippling blow.

"What was that?" She lifted a curious brow.

"I broke your knee," he explained, wondering her point as he lowered his sword.

She thrust forward, knocking his sword out of his hand before he stopped her follow strike with the flat of his shield.

"You can't do that with a broken knee," he growled, picking up his sword before fending off her next strike.

"You didn't break my knee. You only tapped it. You can't use simulated strikes with me, Ethan. Hold nothing back."

"And break your bones? I won't do that," he said, blocking another deadly thrust that nearly missed his left ear.

"You won't hurt me." She smiled before lifting into the air, floating far overhead, while circling him.

"Nice view." He smirked, getting a sight full beneath her skirts.

"Only for you." She smiled back, discarding her shield while calling a spear from the weapon's rack, the object flying across the chamber into her outstretched hand. She threw it at him with terrifying speed, the shaft bouncing harmlessly off his shield.

"That's kind of cheating you know." He shrugged.

"It's not cheating using all my abilities, just as you did at the Velo," she reminded him before calling a dozen more spears off the rack, hurling them at him from all directions.

Ethan lowered his shield, shaking his head as they dropped at his feet as if striking an invisible wall.

"They are powered by magic, Allie. They can't hurt me," he said before hurling his shield at her.

A beam of energy emitted from her outstretched hand, shattering the shield into a thousand pieces.

"You can stay up there all day or we can fight," he shook his head.

"I can stay up here all day and hurl objects at you until you grow weary and then strike you at my leisure. Or...you can yield."

"Do your worst." He shrugged.

"I shall." She smirked, dropping down upon him before he snatched up a second blade. She called a second blade as well, their blades clashing as soon as she touched the ground. She spun swiftly around him, her mage-enhanced speed outmaneuvering him, cutting him across his right thigh, but she was driven to her back as if she hit a wall. His blade was at her throat as soon as her butt hit the sand.

"You used magic to harm me, it backfired," he reminded her, helping her to her feet. "This bout goes to me."

"Now we're even." She snorted, returning to her starting position.

"We're far from even, Allie." He thought of all the crap she's put him through.

"Are you going to *punish* me?" she asked in a seductive whisper.

"I'd like to, but those vows of obedience you made me swear sort of rules that out."

"But if you could, what would you do to punish me?" She asked, twirling her swords hypnotically.

"I'd take you over my knee like your parents should've done long ago."

"Sounds exciting if you ask me. Perhaps a friendly wager."

"What kind of wager?" he asked suspiciously.

"The best of eleven. You win. You can take me over your knee and punish your cruel wife for all the things she has done to you."

"And if you win?"

"You spend the night rubbing my feet."

"You can make me do that anyway with those vows you made me take," he pointed out.

"Oh, I could, but it wouldn't be as satisfying if you had to do it because your wife defeated you in combat. I don't think you would ever put such humiliation from your memory. The mighty Ethanos Blagen, hero of the Velo, fighter of dragons, former crown prince of Astaria, beaten by his wife," she teased.

"I've already been beaten by my wife."

"In a battle of wits, yes, but not physically. What say you, husband?"

"You really shouldn't be doing anything, Allie, when you're pregnant. It is my job to protect you."

"That's a poor excuse for not wanting to be embarrassed, Ethan," she taunted.

"All right, girl, you're on," he came at her in a flurry, their blades clashing in a whirlwind of steel. They moved across the floor, their feet shifting deftly in the loose sand, their steps precise and economical. Neither made a mistake, their feet and hands working in concert.

Ethan pressed his advance, surprised by her strength and skill, wondering how his anti-magic no longer dampened her magic. He finally backed her to the wall, finding an opening when her left hand drifted too high, exposing her wrist to his steel. His sword shattered touching her flesh, the blow sending a shock wave toward his chest, knocking him from his feet. No sooner did he blink an eye, then her steel was at his throat.

"I hope your hands are more careful rubbing my feet than keeping your sword." She smirked, helping him to his feet.

"How...how did you...what happened?" He looked at her gobsmacked. It was similar to her strike on him.

"You used magic to harm me, Ethan. It backfired." She threw his excuse back at him.

"Only anti-magic could stop that." He gave her a look.

"Is that so?" She shrugged.

"The baby!" He suddenly realized the source of her new found power. The baby's anti-magic transcended to her, protecting them both. Magic couldn't hurt her, just as it couldn't hurt him. But they both wielded magic as well, though his was pitifully small compared to hers.

"Two to one now, husband. Four more wins and I shall claim my victory," she came at him, her two swords to his one.

He thought of something and lowered his sword, allowing her blade a free strike to his right arm, her sword shattering like his. The follow blast threw her back, her eyes out of focus as she fell. He rushed forth, catching her in his arms, easing her to the sand.

"We can't hurt each other, Alesha," he said, cradling her in his arms.

"Three to one, Ethan," she said, touching her remaining blade to his neck.

"Two to one, Allie. If you push that blade any harder, it will break like the other one. We obviously are not allowed to harm each other," he realized.

"But my blade still touches your neck, so I win." She smiled wickedly at him, ignoring his revelation.

"Fine, you win." He stood, scooping her into his arms, pressing his lips to hers before carrying her back to the royal chambers. With a flick of her wrist, she returned the armaments to their proper place as they disappeared into the outer corridor.

*****

Raymar sat in deep meditation within his chamber, visions sweeping through his mind like leaves in the wind. They were a myriad of possible futures, some dark and some light, each unfolding in the strangest of ways. His visions were always one of two stark outcomes opposing each other with their implications. Whenever they grew murky, his meditation would bring them into focus, guiding his actions toward the favored outcome. Alas, this was no longer the case. Ever since Ethan's arrival, his visions were convoluted, with nonsensical outcomes and paths that even a great seer could not follow, let alone guide others through.

He opened his eyes in frustration, rising from his settee, and walking to the center of the room where his mystical orb rested, the surface of the cloudy sphere a maelstrom of shifting vapors. He outstretched his hand, setting it upon the orb, the vapors clearing, revealing its secrets to his curious eyes.

"Your worries are for naught, and your meddling is most unhelpful, Raymar." His aunt's voice echoed from the shadows.

Raymar gave Sarella a look of annoyance, wondering how she was able to enter his private sanctum without his knowledge? Her mental mage powers were his equal, the gift passing down to every member of their house, so it should not have been a surprise for her to do what he did all the time.

"My worries should be yours as well, Aunt Sarella." He sighed, placing his hand firmly on the orb, the magical item focusing his clairvoyance, the visions it conjured unalterable no matter his machinations.

"The orb can deceive you," she warned.

"The orb reveals hard truths. It is pure prophecy requiring no guidance," he said as the vision materialized.

"A truth that is easily misinterpreted," she warned, tucking her long fingers in the billowing sleeves of her gown.

His trained eyes drew wide as red scales stretched over taut flesh rippling within the orb, shrinking as the full picture came into focus.

Dragon! His mind screamed as he drew away before she placed her hand over his, keeping it on the orb.

"Do not flinch, nephew. Face the vision you desired to know."

He tried closing his eyes, but the orb drew him in, slather dripping off its slackened jaw, wars and dragons filling his vision. Terrible carnage swept over lands far and near, and in the center of this stood Ethan, his sea-blue eyes staring back at him.

"Enough," Sarella said, pulling his hand away.

Raymar stumbled briefly, as if he were a puppet with half his strings cut. "How?" He gasped, his purple eyes meeting hers.

"How could you see Ethan, you mean?" She completed his question. Ethan's anti-magic shielded him from mage-summoned visions, his visage cast in shadow or a darkened void. His face could never be seen.

"Yes."

"Through this," Sarella said, opening her left hand where a simple black stone rested in her palm, no wider than two finger widths.

"Is that..."

"Anti-magic," she answered. Such a stone was precious, worth more than most royal treasures. Anti-magic was rare, very rare, and nearly impossible to discover. To anyone mage born or of common blood it looked as any other stone. Only Ethan could see them by a mere glance. Its discovery by anyone else was blind luck. One might not even know they had it unless it would be used in a certain way, or it disrupted their mage powers, though it would be very subtle.

"With that we can see Ethan in our visions," he said excitedly.

"We could, but we won't." She closed her hand.

"But why? I need to see his future so I can help him!"

"You and Amanda have interfered enough," she warned.

"If anything, we have done too little. Had we moved sooner, Ethan would've been warned."

"Ethan is where he belongs."

"He is the Free Born. He is the only one who can stand against this tyranny."

"He cannot stand against them. He could only destroy them from within. I have foreseen this," she warned.

"How? By siring upon Alesha a child that could doom the world?" he asked incredulously. "Their child shall wield unchecked power, so much so that we will be but bugs in her presence. Even the kindest child would turn into a murderous tyrant if their every wish was granted."

"The child is pure. It is her destiny to topple House Loria. That is Ethan's true purpose, to raise her with his heart."

Raymar shook his head, denying such optimism. "I, too, have foreseen the future, dear aunt. The child will conquer the world, her power reigning over the mage realms. The visions reveal the mage kings trembling in fear, the realms falling one after another by her and her progeny."

"Then your visions are false. House Menau has foreseen her coming for centuries, and she will deliver us from the tyranny of House Loria."

"A fool's hope," Raymar said, receiving a slap across his face for the offense.

"The only fool is you, nephew. Your meddling nearly drove Ethan and Alesha apart. Their union is essential for the prophecy to be fulfilled. Beyond this, you are risking your life and ours by continuing this path."

"I've done nothing yet to oppose Alesha," he retorted.

"You have in your thoughts, and now they can betray you."

"No one can read my thoughts, not even you with that stone. Its anti-magic is too weak to tear through my mind."

"Who said anything about me?"

"Then who?"

"Alesha," Sarella hissed.

"Alesha? How?" His eyes narrowed suspiciously.

"The child. Her unborn daughter carries her father's anti-magic, and Alesha has use of it until she gives birth."

Raymar drew back, fear filling his eyes. Why had he not foreseen this possibility?

"Oh, yes, nephew, she can read your treacherous thoughts if she cares to. If so, then your head will grace a pike, or worse, you'll be a guest in the dungeon."

"Has she already read my thoughts?"

"If she had, you wouldn't be here. She hasn't thought to question your love and loyalty. Don't give her reason. Be the dutiful brother you have pretended to be all your life and leave the prophecies to me."

"What if you are wrong?" he asked.

"I'm not."

"Ethan *is* the Free Born. The prophecy says this is so. I know you have kept this from House Loria, never revealing Ethan's true destiny. The Free Born must be *free*, that is his purpose. He must be free to deliver Elaria from being enslaved by House Loria. They brought him here to enslave him, forever binding him to the throne. Every day he losses more of himself to Alesha. In time, he will accept his cage, dooming the world to oblivion. His good heart that you are counting upon to temper his daughter's power will be long gone before his daughter is old enough to emulate him."

"Ethan will not succumb. Look to your own survival, Raymar, and trust Ethan and his daughter's lives to me."

"If what you say about Alesha is true, then you too are helpless against her. She will discover your perfidy and pass judgment on your house."

"And what path would you choose, Raymar? If you believe the child is a threat, what choice would you have but kill it."

"No!" Raymar refuted, disgusted by the insinuation. "I could never kill my blood."

"Very good. I would be disappointed in you otherwise as our house has always been loyal to its own."

"I am loyal to my blood and would never harm Alesha's child."

"Then how would you stop her if she is destined to become a tyrant?"

"I would take her to the Mage Bane, to live peacefully where her powers would be muted. Lord Darcannon is a friend of Ethan's. Surely, he would accept Ethan's daughter as his ward. I am certain he has sons or even grandsons she could wed," he explained, hoping that Sarella could see the logic in his thinking.

"Foolish boy. You will have to go farther than the Mage Bane." The prophecies were clear that Alesha's child would overcome the magical inhibitors of that dreaded place.

"Then I'll go further, to the ends of the world if need be."

"And it would be for naught."

"We have to at least try," he pleaded.

"Try? You would be helpless against that child. She might kill you by mere accident once you were alone. That is if you could escape with her in the first place, which you cannot."

"No, but Ethan can."

"He will never harm his own child."

"Who said anything about harming his child? He can take her far away and raise her without the queen's influence."

"He won't do it."

"Why? He hates it here. Only the threat on his father's life keeps him here, and there is a way around that."

"Yes, and you are foolishly thinking of telling him."

"I am. As soon as we are alone with no prying eyes around."

"You will do no such thing! You will not speak of it to him."

"Why? He has a right to know he can finally be free of them."

"His place is here. Besides, he cannot leave, even if he desires to. He is now bound by a force far more powerful than magical bonds."

"Bound by what?"

"Love," she said matter-of-fact.

"Love? For Alesha? She betrayed him, betrayed him in a most hurtful way. He cannot love someone like that."

"Regardless, he does. It is his destiny. There is magic at work here, magic that we are woefully unaware."

"He is immune to magic."

"Not this magic. She consumes his waking thoughts, driving him with mad desire. She is equally afflicted. There is no separating them now, and I pity the one that tries."

"No, he will leave once he knows his father is safe."

"He will never know, for you will not tell him."

"And how can you stop me?"

"I shall inform the queen of everything."

"What?" he asked in alarm. "You would doom yourself and House Menau?"

"Yes, I would. The safety of my house and my life I would sacrifice for the greater good."

"Greater good! Keeping Ethan ignorant serves the greater good?"

"Keeping him here does. Only here can he achieve his destiny and topple House Loria from within. To make sure that happens, I am prepared to do *anything!*" she said in a deadly whisper.

"And if your visions are wrong, you will take away our only chance."

"Visions are faulty. Prophecies are not."

"Prophecies require guidance."

"Yes. And we have guided this prophecy to its fulfillment and will not be turned at this late hour by a foolish boy who hasn't the slightest inkling of what he is doing."

Raymar stared at her with calculating eyes, weighing his options rapidly in his head. Fight or acquiesce? Those were his only options, each bearing a terrible cost. Family was very important to him, as it was to everyone born of House Menau. Despite this, he was willing to see his mother's house destroyed to save the world from tyranny. Was he equally willing to murder an aunt from his father's house to see it through?

"Do not even think it!" Another voice whispered deathly in his ear as a knife pressed to his throat from behind. He knew that voice, for it belonged to his aunt Selendra.

"It wouldn't have been a choice made lightly." He didn't attempt to hide his murderous intent. His aunts were far too clever to believe otherwise.

"Of course, for you serve the greater good, a trait that runs in our family veins. We also have considered such extreme measures, including killing you to make sure you didn't interfere, but we hope it is unnecessary by this demonstration," Sarella warned.

"Do you vow not to interfere, Raymar?" Selendra asked coldly, pressing the blade tighter against his throat.

"I will share nothing with Ethan concerning his father, nor will I interfere to aid his escape," he agreed, closing his eyes with a defeated sigh.

"Swear it upon a magical vow," Sarella said.

"How can I make such a vow when I do not trust your prophecy? Your plans could come to ruin in the blink of an eye."

"Prophecies properly guided always come to fruition. Is your knowledge of Mage Law so faulty?" Sarella countered.

"Avow it, or you force our hand," Selendra commanded, pressing the blade harder against his throat.

"Very well." He sighed. "I will avow it upon an oath-bound in magic, but I hold you to lift this oath should House Loria move against Ethan."

"We can agree to that," Sarella said, receiving a nod of agreement from her sister.

*****

Alesha rested against the headboard of their spacious bed, her eyes staring lovingly as her husband sat at the end of the bed, rubbing her feet. Though magic could remove any discomfort, it could not equal the electric thrill his touch invoked.

"You're enjoying this too much." He shook his head, taking the other foot in hand.

"The rewards of victory are always sweetest," she teased, lifting her free leg, rubbing her toes along his chest. Oh, how she loved to touch him, whether it was a slight caress or the height of passion. Nothing in the world felt righter than being with him.

"And if you lost?" He lifted a dark eyebrow, his sea blue eyes making her flesh tingle as they stared directly into her golden pools.

"Either outcome would've been a victory." She smirked.

He shook his head, not believing her.

"Shall we test my sincerity?" She smiled wickedly, turning onto her side, patting her posterior invitingly.

"You're serious," he acknowledged in disbelief.

"Unless you are scared?" she challenged.

"Oh, I'm not scared of swatting your backside, girl. Come here." He smiled, inching closer on the bed, running his hands up her left ankle.

"You'll have to make me!" she challenged, making a weak attempt of withdrawing her captured limb.

He was upon her in an instant, pinning her hands in his, forcing her to her back, staring intently into her eyes.

"You're supposed to spank me," she whispered seductively, her eyes sweeping the length of his face that lingered inches from her own.

"I've got a better idea." He smiled, crushing his lips to hers.

CHAPTER 16

Red Rock, Texas

"I'll call, and raise you three more," Judge Donovan Said with his cigar clenched in his teeth, tossing a $3 chip on Ben's desk.

"All in." Dragos smiled, shoving all his chips forward, before taking a generous puff of his own cigar.

"I'm out." Sheriff Thorton threw down his cards, reaching for a bottle of whiskey from the drawer in his desk.

Krixan simply looked on, having tossed his hand in at the outset. He sat at the side of Ben's desk with his chair turned backward, resting his giant forearms on its back, with his Stetson pushed back on his head. Skeeter sat next to him, tossing in his cards as well.

Andrew Donovan looked across the desk at his nemesis, Dragos and himself waging a nightly battle of wits, having shared the winnings almost down the middle since he arrived in Red Rock.

"All right, you varmint," the judge called, pushing in his chips.

Their cigars about fell out of their mouths as Dragos laid down a flush of clubs, queen high, with a ten, nine, five and deuce, while the judge dropped a flush of spades with the exact same cards.

"Never saw that in all my days." Ben shook his head, topping off everyone's whiskey glasses.

"Me neither." Skeeter whistled.

Krixan just let out a deep breath, shaking his head.

"Dragos, I ain't seen that but one time in all my years playing this game. Here's to number two." He tapped his glass to Dragos, the two men removing their cigars to down their drinks, before splitting the pot.

"You sure you're related to Ethan?" Ben asked, gathering up the cards to deal out the next hand.

"The boy has many talents, Ben, but this ain't one of 'em," Dragos said with a perfect Texas drawl, taking another puff of his cigar.

"He wasn't much for smoking either. It made him go green in the gills." Skeeter grinned.

"Aye, but the lad made up for it with the attention he drew from the ladies," Andrew said, receiving the first card Ben dealt.

"Now that's a trait he gets from me," Dragos said in all seriousness, though the look Krixan shot him dispelled that theory.

"I wonder how he is managing?" Ben said, finishing the deal.

"One can only guess what tortures he is enduring," Dragos said, picking up his cards.

"You mentioned she was a pretty lass," Andrew said, examining his cards, arranging them in no particular order to throw the others off.

"Very pretty," Krixan said, keeping a straight face, spotting a pair of kings while lifting his hand.

"Don't know if I'd complain if a good-looking gal dragged me off to bed," Skeeter added, the others' silence proving they had to think on that for a moment.

"Aye, the best lasses always have a little fire in their belly. I recall a good friend of mine, a trapper named Gus Franklin. He married himself a Shoshone Squaw. The girl would gut him if she caught his eye wandering. Kept him on the straight and narrow. She could skin a deer in a minute flat, and shoot the eye out of an elk at a hundred yards. She birthed him twelve children, with seven surviving. She was quite a woman," the judge said, recalling his friend with a bandage wrapped around his skull where she once hit him with a frying pan.

"It doesn't make much sense." Krixan snorted.

"Which part?" Dragos inquired.

"Allie. The girl hovered over him like a mother hen when we was in the Bane. She risked her own neck more than once, following after him whenever she thought he was in danger. Why do all that just to betray him later?" Krixan shook his head.

"It's like Amanda said, she needed him for their prophecy," Dragos pointed out.

"What use is the prophecy if she died herself?" Krixan asked, trying to make sense of it all.

"Don't go figuring what's on a woman's mind, Krix, it'll just make your head hurt," Ben said, raising his bid fifty cents.

"Ya might wanna give that speech to Vancel. Ms. Sara's got him wound as tight as a mule's…"

"All right, Skeeter, I don't need that image in my head," Ben cut him off.

"Where is our new deputy tonight, anyhow? It ain't like him to miss a game of cards?" Judge Donovan asked.

"Mrs. Adams invited him and his brothers to their place for one of her home-cooked meals. Seems all her girls have taken a likin' to the Torrent boys," Skeeter said, hoping Mrs. Adams would send along some of that food to the rest of them.

"Their father won't be pleased when Felicia's party returns without any of his sons in their company," Dragos said before asking Ben for three cards, not liking the state of his sorry hand.

Of all the things Dragos expected when he came to Red Rock, having Lord Torrent's three oldest sons smitten with three sisters of the good town, wasn't one of them. If things progressed much farther, he wasn't sure how the ornery Lord would receive three daughters by marriage that couldn't wield magic. Whether they could sire heirs that could was yet unknown. It would be the same for Felicia and Jake, who was accompanying his granddaughter back to Astaris. If Bronus raised any objections, he'd be sure to give his own high opinion of the man. Dragos held all of Ethan's friends in high regard, especially his present company. He wondered how his sweet Gaby would react seeing him decked out in what he was now wearing? He and Ben looked like a matched pair, with dark trousers and tan collared shirts, each with brown vests and cream colored Stetsons. Throw in tied down holsters and you had a good picture of what he looked like. Ben even gave him a star, making Dragos an honorary deputy. He was inclined to return the favor to Ben and Judge Andrew, by knighting them both, but they weren't the kneeling kind. They would still be his most honored guests when he invited them to Plexus.

"And how will your King feel when Felicia reaches Astaris with Jake in tow?" Ben asked, wondering his son's reception, which should happen any day now, as their party passed into Astaria a few days back, with their first shipment of guns.

"Jake's Ethan's friend, that's all you need to know." Dragos leaned back in his chair, releasing a puff of smoke, admiring the pair of Jacks Ben dealt him.

"The bigger question is how your son-in-law will receive his first shipment of rifles?" Andrew asked, picking up the two cards he asked for, another six to go along with the three in his hand.

"If he is clever, he'll keep it quiet, as I suggested. Whether he listens to my sage advice is another matter altogether. Our good Captain Marco has earned Bronus's respect since the Velo, and if he won't listen to me, he might him," Dragos said, examining the improved state of his hand, with two pairs, jacks high.

"He'll have enough rifles to outfit a company, with plenty of ammo to boot. It might not be enough to stop these dragons you're fretting over, but it's a start. That should hold him over a mite until Gus returns with the next shipment," Ben said, referencing Gus Lawton, who was waiting in Abilene for the delivery of two Gatling Guns and three artillery pieces they ordered. Ben was worried a shipment of that nature might raise suspicions somewhere but weighed secrecy against the Astarians urgent need and leaned to the later.

"Should we send more men to him, to safeguard the shipment?" Dragos asked.

"He's got three Lawton ranch hands with him and two of Caleb Miller's boys. All are good guns. Too many guards might raise more attention than you'd like. If too many folks hear tell of what they're picking up, they might think there's a gold strike in Red Rock or even silver. Last thing we need is folks from all over the country flocking here and snooping around," Ben reasoned.

"Point taken," Dragos said, raising everyone $2.

"The Gatlings and artillery will help with the dragon, but you need men to teach 'em how to use 'em," Skeeter said.

"Jake's got a man for that," Ben said.

"What they could really use is one of Phil Sheridan's Cavalry officers to instruct them on mounted tactics with repeating rifles. I wonder where they could find such a man?" Judge Donovan asked, giving Ben that harmless look that didn't work on the old sheriff.

"I'm too old for that, Andrew. Heck, I might not be able to last a week in the saddle at my age," Ben snorted, calling Dragos's raise.

"Bah, you were born in the saddle, Ben," Andrew said, calling the raise.

"I have a job, in case you hadn't noticed, Judge," Ben countered.

"Skeeter can fill in for you, for a while at least. If Jake can excuse himself from his duties for a bit, why can't you?" Andrew reasoned.

"Jake's got himself an excuse," Ben said.

"The same excuse you can use," Andrew pointed out. Jake sent a telegraph to Fort Smith, informing Judge Parker that he was pursuing witnesses that could confirm the death of Luke Crawford and other fugitives of *Interest*. It might be a stretch of the truth, but was factual to a degree. At least two of the men Ethan killed in Luke's band, had outstanding warrants in the Oklahoma territory.

"It's something to consider, Ben. King Bronus would be most grateful for your help. Couldn't hurt to share a few kegs from the palace cellars and exchange war stories. I'm sure Bronus would like to hear tell about your battles in the Shenandoah and Shiloh," Dragos said.

"Or the Comanche wars and your time with the rangers," Andrew added.

"Not much to tell of any of that. Just a whole lot of awful," Ben snorted, never one to fondly recall such horrors. If there was one thing General Sherman ever said he wholeheartedly agreed with, it was his summation of *War Is Hell*.

"Such was the Velo, so many brave lads falling in battle," Dragos recalled.

"And you led the coup de grace, if what you said is true, Dragos, your cavalry charge finishing the Meltorian Army," Andrew said.

"After Ethan and Bronus did the hard part, but yes." Dragos shrugged.

"You see, Ben, if Dragos can lead a cavalry charge at his age, you could at least teach cavalry tactics to men who are all experienced riders," Andrew said, pushing all his chips in the middle of the desk, going all in.

"Very well." Dragos smiled, pushing his in as well.

Skeeter folded, and Krixan and Ben followed the others, calling them all in. Ben just shook his head, his pair of aces going for naught as Dragos flipped two pair. Andrew Donovan threw down four sixes, ruining Dragos's night, which was short-lived when Krixan turned over four kings, collecting his winnings.

"Good to see someone other than you two idiots win for once." Ben shook his head, giving Krixan a respectful nod.

"Well played, my boy," Dragos patted the big man on the back, as did Skeeter.

"When we do see Ethan again, I will surely love to tell him how you fared this night at poker," Andrew lifted his glass to Krixan, the others chuckling, knowing how that would gnaw at Ethan.

"So what have you, Ben? Will you help train our cavalry?" Dragos asked.

"All right. I don't have many years left anyhow, might as well lend a hand," Ben said tiredly.

"Excellent, since I already said you would be coming in the letter I sent with Jake." Dragos smiled, leaning back in his chair, taking another deep puff from his cigar.

*****

Astaris

Of all the things Jake Thorton had seen in his life, nothing prepared him for the palace city of Astaris, its towering outer curtain walls rising imperiously upon their approach, only to give way to more impressive sights within. The broad avenue that ran from the city gates to the inner palace was widely set, with stately structures lining either side, most cast in marble, with towering pillars and statues lining their flanks and rooftops. Jerimiah rode along his left, the look on his face as mesmerized as his own. Felicia rode upon his right, waving to the throngs of people lining the street to greet her.

"Welcome to Astaris, Marshal Thorton," Felicia said, gifting the most beautiful smile while waving to the crowd.

"This is your home?" He shook his head at the wonder of it all.

"Up there, yes." She pointed ahead at the towering citadels jutting above the mountainous inner palace, rising hundreds of feet into the air. Nothing on Earth could rival such a structure. She could see him working out the impossibility of the palace in his mend.

"It is spell forged, built many centuries ago by the sky lords of old," she answered his unspoken question.

He laughed, shaking his head.

"Something amuses you, Jake Thorton?" she asked.

"Ethan was to be king of this great realm, and he gave it up to wander freely in the world, to live like me," Jake said.

"He didn't like to kneel. Would you kneel in exchange for this kingdom?"

"No, I wouldn't. On that, I agree with Ethan," Jake shared a look with her, which caused her to again smile, something she couldn't stop herself from doing whenever he looked at her.

"Something humors you, Ms. Felicia?" Jake asked, unable to not smile in return, equally smitten.

"You are a very attractive man, Marshal Thorton." She kept smiling, feeling no shame with her blunt honesty.

"Judge Parker would never believe it." He shook his head.

"Believe what?"

"That the prettiest girl in the world finds me attractive."

"Which world?" She chewed her lower lip.

"Both," he said, causing her to smile again, even wider than before.

"Is he a friend of yours, this Judge Parker?" she asked.

"In a way. I work for him. They call him the Hanging Judge, though that's more a matter of the men we have to deal with. Oklahoma is a dangerous place."

"I would like to meet him, and your other friends as well, especially Bass."

"Not likely to meet Judge Parker. Fort Smith is too far away. Bass is a possibility, should he ever come far enough west. Something tells me, though, I'll be held up in Astaria longer than we planned."

"Perhaps." She shrugged, already planning how to keep him here longer, if not indefinitely.

"Now, your father, what is he like? Does he look like Ethan? Or does...," Jake asked.

"Nothing like Ethan. He is a little bit taller, heavy build with a thick, black beard. He acts grumpy and rough but is quite gentle when he thinks no one is looking," she said.

"Sounds like my father," Jake said, remarking on his father's demeanor.

"What of you, Jerimiah, how do you like our city?" she asked Jake's companion.

"It's right beautiful, Ms. Felicia," Jerimiah said, craning his neck as they passed within the shadow of the grand bazaar, a massive, multi-layered structure with hundreds of vendors hawking their wares. It was not just the size of the city that impressed Jerimiah, but the order and cleanliness, each a product of their mage craft. Felicia noticed his eyes draw wide as they passed several food vendors, the aroma of fresh cooked meats permeating the air.

"I am pleased it is to your liking, Mr. Hansen," she addressed him properly as he had done with her. She found him a man of good character, which she would expect from any friend of Jake Thorton. "If you can resist the enticement of our local vendors, a grand feast awaits us at the upper palace."

"That would be right neighborly of you, Ms. Felicia," Jerimiah said, taken aback by their hospitality. He was uncertain of his reception in this land, not accustom to white folks treating him with equal respect. He used to be able to count on one hand the white folks he thought were worth a spit. That changed the day Bass introduced him to Jake Thorton. Coming to Astaria only magnified that number a thousand fold.

"It is you that is neighborly, Jerimiah Hansen. You and Jake will be guests of the king and rightfully so with the wonderous gifts you bear," she added, sparing a glance over her shoulder to the many wagons in their column, loaded with weapons, ammunition, and various goods that will be useful to the realm.

"Gifts your father paid for with Astarian gold," Jake reminded her.

"Gifts we could not even purchase without your help and the good people of Red Rock," she added.

Their column was soon met by Captain Clovis of the king's royal guards, who escorted them the final leg to the inner palace.

*****

Astaris throne room

King Bronus sat his throne, eagerly awaiting his youngest daughter and her companions. Queen Gabrielle sat her throne beside him, with Tristan, Amanda, Ceresta and Arian standing beside them to receive Felicia. He was most heartened to see his beautiful daughter enter the regal chamber, fearing for her since he agreed to let her join Dragos and Krixan on their expedition. He knew the leanings of her heart, and any other king would have forbidden its pursuit, but after what happened with Ethan, Bronus couldn't deny her. Here she came, clad in dusty brown trousers and a collared shirt, with a tied down holster like Ethan favored, wearing the same ridiculous hat that Ethan never parted with. Of the three men that accompanied her, he only recognized Captain Marco Valanus, Ethan's trusted friend, who distinguished himself at the Velo, earning his place among the royal guards. The other two men were obviously of Earth, by their matching garb and six guns, one of a darker white coloring, and the other very dark like a Sarcosan. They also held no magical aura surrounding them, as if their very essence was a magical void.

"Remain standing, Marco, no man of Astaria ever kneels again!" Bronus warned his loyal captain, who attempted to take a knee as they stopped short of the dais.

"Sire," Marco greeted with a fist to his heart, an acceptable substitute for kneeling to the king.

"It is good to see you returned safely with my daughter, who looks much changed by her attire." Bronus couldn't help but smile at her.

"Father." She bowed her head briefly, matching his smile with one of her own. They were still speaking in their native Elarian with Jake and Jerimiah oblivious to what was being said.

"Perhaps you should introduce your companions, Felicia, though I might guess one of them," Queen Gabrielle said in near perfect English that Amanda had imprinted, her eyes falling to Jake, who wore the buckskin trousers and moccasin boots that Ethan mimicked. He was of a size to Ethan, with a deeply tanned complexion, midnight black hair, and the narrow eyes like a hawk.

"Mother, father, this is US Marshal Jake Thorton, Sheriff Thorton's son, and Ethan's very good friend. And this is his friend, Mr. Jerimiah Hansen, a great gunmen and tracker. They have come to deliver the first shipment of weapons to aid us. They shall also instruct us in their operation and upkeep," Felicia introduced in clear English as well, the others using that tongue from that point on whenever speaking in their guests' company.

"Jake Thorton, I have heard many good things about you, mostly from Ethan," Bronus said, rising from his throne before descending the dais, offering Jake his hand.

"It is my honor to meet the father of the man who saved my life," Jake said, shaking Bronus's hand, surprised the king was familiar with the Earth greeting of a handshake.

"And you returned the favor, as Krixan and Ethan explained. I would very much like to hear of the battles in Red Rock from your perspective tonight during dinner. Jerimiah, it is my pleasure to meet any friend of Jake Thorton," Bronus greeted him in kind, as Gabrielle and the others joined him to receive their guests.

Gabrielle exchanged a heartfelt embrace with her daughter, and Jake as well, understanding why Felicia was so taken with the man. He was very handsome, sharing Ethan's unique balance of rugged wildness and good manners.

"Jake, how unfortunate that it wasn't I who nursed you back to health." Arian smiled as he kissed the back of her hand, playfully jealous of Felicia.

"I have to say, Ethan's family has no shortage of beautiful ladies," Jake said, looking from Arian, to Ceresta, then Gabrielle and Amanda, the last of which held her embrace with Felicia far longer than the others.

"We have news," Amanda whispered in Felicia's ear.

*****

The evening found Jerimiah and Jake as guests at the royal table, set in a modest chamber high in the inner palace, with large curved windows on its south face, providing a panoramic view of Astaris, and the lands beyond. Both men were overwhelmed with the visual feast, each sight more impressive than the last. It was all surreal, with towers citadels and magic they couldn't see, or feel. Ever since he awoke in Plexus after Ethan saved him, Jake felt his life caught up in a current of which he was helpless to direct. His doubts and misgivings were instantly washed away whenever he looked across the table, finding Felicia's smiling face staring back. The table was segregated, with men on one side, and the ladies the other, with Captain Marco and Tristan seated beside them. Arian, Ceresta, Amanda, and Felicia sat opposite them, with Queen Gabrielle and King Bronus presiding at opposite ends of the table.

"Marco, Jake, and Jerimiah, welcome to our table," Gabrielle said once everyone was seated, tapping her cup, signaling the servants to commence.

After an initial round of drinks and offerings of bread and fruit, Bronus began.

"Marco, I would have your report first. How fares our men at Red Rock?"

Marco spoke at length of their crossing the portal, and the securing of the site on both the Astarian and Texan sides of the opening. He detailed the layout of Red Rock, and the positioning of their soldiers, and interactions with the locals, leaving the rest for Felicia to continue.

She spoke of the gifts they bestowed upon the people, and of their first meeting with Sheriff Thorton and Judge Andrew Donovan, both men living up to the stature that Ethan described. Bronus looked forward to meeting both men, though felt a jealous tinge when mention of Ben Thorton, considering he was a surrogate father for Ethan during his time there. Bronus scolded himself for such self-pity, recalling the many men he looked up to other than his own father in his younger years. He should be grateful that Ethan found men of such character to emulate. It was Jake that drew him from his thoughts.

"My father was deeply grateful, king Bronus, for the sword you gave him. In return, he sent you this," Jake said, standing from his place at the table to retrieve a long package he placed along the side of the chamber, presenting it to the king.

"What is this?" Bronus asked as Jake drew a rifle from its leather sheath, handing it to Bronus.

"That is a custom made Henry rifle, 1866 lever action, .44 caliber. It is an older model than the Winchester '73s we brought, but my father thought you should have his preferred weapon," Jake explained.

To Bronus Blagen, king of Astaria, the father of the man who saved my life. Your friend, Ben Thorton, Sheriff of Red Rock.

Bronus read the inscription several times over, touched by the man's words.

"Thank you, Jake. I will treasure this always, and look forward to your instruction on its use," Bronus said, as Jake retook his seat.

"That was very gracious of you, Jake. If you would oblige a mother's curiosity, would you share with us Ethan's adventures in Red Rock, from your perspective. Ethan's version is woefully inaccurate, and Krixan went to great lengths protecting Ethan from our learning the dangers he was in," Gabrielle said.

"Well, ma'am, I can only attest to what I saw, and my time with Ethan was very limited. I was there, however, when he was shot, and the confrontation with the Griersons," Jake said.

"Tell it true, all of it," Gabrielle said, recalling much she learned from probing Krixan's mind when he returned to Astaris after Ethan was taken. That was the first she learned of Ethan being shot.

And so Jake recalled the events from his ambush where Ethan and Krixan saved him, to his arrival in Red Rock, and helping nurse Ethan back to health after he was shot. Gabrielle closed her eyes at that part of the tale, her heart racing at the thought of Ethan almost dying. They were all surprised to learn how Ethan spent his time recovering, reading the many books Judge Donovan lent him. The shootout in the streets of Red Rock piqued Bronus and Tristan's attention, captivated by Ethan's exploits, and the others as well. Jake spoke of Ethan's other gunfights after he departed Red Rock, learning of them from his father and the Judge. Bronus recalled how he reacted upon seeing Ethan just before the Velo, wondering where he had been for so long, and berating the boy. Now he knew fully what he had been doing. It didn't excuse Ethan's long absence, but how Bronus was proud of him.

Jake continued with more recent events, particularly the first shipment of weapons, including eighty Winchesters, and an equal number of Colt .45 pistols, and ninety thousand rounds of ammunition. It was a staggering amount, and Jake knew they would need it, especially for practice when training the men who would wield them.

"And you will be staying for a while to help us?" Arian asked, receiving a pinch on her thigh from Felicia for her subtle flirting.

"I will, if you'll have me. It is a debt I owe Ethan. He helped my father when I could not, now I would like to help his, where he cannot," Jake said, receiving an appreciative nod from the king and queen.

"Of course, I came here under the assumption I was looking to confirm Luke was dead, and Krixan and Felicia have given me a list of names of four of Luke's men that got away. From what Krixan said of their battles in the place you call a Mage Bane, I have to ask, how do you know the names of those fallen from those that got away? Neither Ethan or Krixan met Most of the men in Luke's company," Jake asked.

It was Amanda that answered.

"After my sister returned from the Mage Bane, my mother obtained many prisoners from the Palacians that helped Luke and his men. From them we extracted a great deal of information. Beyond this, my mother sent numerous agents to the Mage Bane, under many guises, adding their discoveries to what she learned from the prisoners. Ethan and Krixan confirmed that two of the men that fled from Crepsos were Emmitt Cobb and Colm Conroy. We believe the others were named Ned Stiles and George Carson. Among the dead were Luke Crawford, John Fuller, Terrance Wheeler, Jeb Cullen, and Logan Curry, as well as several others we have not identified. Do you recognize any of these names, Jake?" Amanda asked.

"All of them. There should be three others. Last rumors put George Middleton and Hank Evans in Luke's company. If you're certain on the names you gave, I'll need three of you to sign a witness statement claiming it to be true. I'll send it on to Fort Smith when I return to Red Rock. Many folks will rest easy at night once word of Luke's death spreads," Jake said.

"That still leaves Emmitt and the other three to deal with," Jerimiah pointed out.

"Our last reports still place them in the Mage Bane, guests of a Palacian warlord," Tristan said.

"And if they are fool enough to stick their necks out, we'll lop them off!" Bronus growled, downing his goblet.

"It would be nice to have at least one of their bodies as proof, but Judge Parker will take my word either way," Jake said, before fishing a letter from his satchel resting near his chair, passing it over to the king.

"What is this?" Bronus asked, unfolding it.

"A letter from Dragos, but I can't read your Elarian Script," Jake said.

"How is that old scoundrel faring in your land?" Bronus asked, looking the letter over.

"Bronus?" Gabrielle scolded his coarse tongue, calling her father a scoundrel.

"Yes, Father, it is unbecoming referring to Dragos as *old*," Tristan quipped, pointing out the one thing Dragos would have taken offense to.

"Bah, the old cuss gives it back to me tenfold. So, how fares he?" Bronus again asked Jake.

"He seems content, he...," Jake tried to explain before Felicia interjected.

"He is like a pig in mud. He and Judge Donovan have become as inseparable as they are incorrigible. They spend every night in the jail playing poker with Jake's father, deputy Skeeter, Vancel, and Krixan. Sometimes the town Doctor joins them as well. I do not know if he will ever return." Felicia shook her head.

"Felicia!" Gabrielle scowled, admonishing her harsh words for Dragos.

"You weren't there, Mother. Grandfather is quite taken with the place. Of course, I would gladly make the exchange, Dragos for Jake." She gave him a mischievous smile.

"That won't be necessary. His letter says he will return soon and that Sheriff Thorton will be coming here to train our cavalry with our new weapons," Bronus said, setting the letter down while raising a toast. "Let us welcome our new friends!"

"Our new friends!" Tristan chorused his father's declaration, the others following in kind.

"Thank you for your kindness," Jerimiah said, taken aback by their graciousness.

"You are most welcome, Jerimiah. Any friend of Jake's is always welcome in our home." Gabrielle smiled.

"Speaking of Jake, what is the state of your courtship?" Bronus looked first at Jake and then Felicia, his stern countenance casting a frigid pall over the chamber, affecting everyone save Felicia, who looked her father straight in the eye with a steel fortitude that made him proud.

"Jake is an honorable man and will be my husband. On this, there will be no compromise," she firmly declared, causing Jake's eyebrows to raise.

"Is that so?" Bronus asked, keeping as neutral a face as he could.

"It is so, Father."

"Jake?" Bronus looked over to the young man, who reminded him so much of his own missing son.

"I haven't made our courtship official until I asked for your permission, sir," Jake said, caught between Felicia's flirtatious glances and Bronus' unreadable expression.

"Is that a Texan custom, asking the girl's father to begin courtship?" Bronus asked.

"It is," Jake said, his proud carriage earning Bronus' respect.

"My daughter is an Astarian princess. Every noble house with sons has asked for her hand. I have refused them out of deference to her wishes. I have watched her for nearly two years walking about the palace tormented by a young man she never expected to see again. I knew nothing of this, the source of her pain, until Ethan was taken from us. Ethan left us that simple looking stone, which in turn opened up a world of possibilities. A few moons ago, I would never have consented to her journeying across the barrier, but what happened with Ethan…well, that changed things, especially for a cantankerous old bear like me. Ethan spoke fondly of you, Jake Thorton, and that is all I need know. If you wish to court my daughter, you may do so. You both have one cycle of the moon to complete this courtship. If by then you wish to wed, you must do so at that time. Are you agreed?" Bronus asked sternly.

"I am agreed, sir, and honored," Jake said, sharing a look with Felicia, her smile as bright as the sunrise.

"Welcome to our family, Jake," Gabrielle said.

"My thanks, ma'am," he said.

"The boy's polite, I grant him that," Bronus remarked, admiring Jake's manners.

"My father would tan my backside if I didn't show proper respect for my future wife's parents or anyone else's parents for that matter. Any self-respecting Texan does the same," Jake said.

Bronus looked at Jake for the longest moment, admiring the lad, and seeing so much of Ethan in him that it made him want to cry. He might not be a lord or even a knight, but he had honor and was a good man, one worthy of his daughter. If there was anything about the Texans that stood out, it was that they backed down from no one and respected their neighbor as they did themselves. It was little wonder why Ethan took such a liking to them, and they him.

"Your father sounds very much like our own," Ceresta said, pleased to finally have a face to go with the name of Jake Thorton. She was pleased to learn that her sister's affections were well-placed and not just a girlish infatuation.

"We have other wondrous news to share this evening," Gabrielle said, looking first to Tristan and then Amanda.

"Tristan?" Felicia asked, her eyes alit, guessing what he was to say.

"I have asked Amanda to be my wife," Tristan said, looking across the table to his beloved.

"And I have accepted," she said proudly, looking back at him.

"Two weddings!" Bronus said with his booming voice. "You desired grandchildren, Gabrielle, and now they will be coming faster than you can manage."

"I can manage quite well, husband." She smiled back, overcome with joy. Looking around the table she looked proudly at her children, admiring the people they had become. Her joy was tempered by the obvious empty chair, her dear Ethanos, hoping one day they could bring him home.

CHAPTER 17

The following weeks passed quietly in Elysia after the flurry of activity that followed Queen Valera's return. The palace resumed its ordered and quiet state. While Alesha prepared for her upcoming ascension to Queen Daughter, her days were filled with matters of the realm, under her mother's close tutelage. Valera seemed to float on air, a calm serenity permeating her entire being. She also looked forward to her ascension to Queen Mother, where her duties could focus on matters concerning their House, leaving the realm in Alesha's capable hands.

With every passing day, the burning hunger for mage power slightly abated until it was a mere quiver. The mothers in the Lorian Order were overcome with newfound joy and a passion for things that felt trivial to them before. It was all due to Ethan's presence, they came to realize, or more to the point, Ethan and Alesha. Once they discovered the connection, they encouraged them to spend more time together, though Alesha's duties oft interfered with those ambitions. Mother Caterina suggested Ethan attend to her during her duties, remaining constantly in her presence, but Mother Evalena refused entertaining such a notion. A royal consort held no power in ruling Vellesia, and his mere presence would lend to that perception.

Fortunately, Ethan never learned of that proposal, wanting nothing to do with matters of state. Instead, he spent his days learning the layout of the palace and its people. He spent his mornings with Raymar and Sergeant Jordain, sparring in the training arena. Sometimes Raymar's grandfathers would join in, displaying their improving skills with every session. Raymar noticed their changing spirits as if they were different men from those he knew all his life. They were more relaxed, even making jokes at times. Ethan referred to them as Dar and Corb, each accepting their nicknames as badges of honor.

Ander Jordain would give a resigned sigh whenever Ethan spoke of them so familiarly, but Raymar waved off his concerns, assuring him that Alesha would not hold him to account. Ander did take advantage of these opportunities to improve his sword arm, though he accepted he would never be able to match Ethan's skill. Ander would never admit to how much he came to enjoy Ethan's company or the friendly banter the former Astarian prince engaged with him constantly. There was always at least one mother of the Lorian Order overseeing their bouts, often sitting on the observation platform overlooking the arena. Ethan grew accustomed to their presence, eventually forgetting they were even there. Mother Caterina appeared regularly, watching Corbin with keen interest, her husband surprising her with his acumen, considering his age. Ander wasn't one to assume, but even a blind man could see the look they shared, proof of a rekindled romance.

Raymar didn't miss the looks his great-grandparents shared either. It was beyond strange. His great-grandmother Caterina was always consumed with a hunger for mage power, obsessed with the ascension of their House, just like her fellow mothers. Ethan's arrival somehow swept away those obsessions, causing her to discover the other pleasures that life offered. His grandfather Corbin was equally changed, from an elderly man who was constantly on edge and sickeningly deferential to his wife, to a man with growing confidence, looking upon his wife with renewed passion.

"Well done, Corb," Ethan praised as the elder consort disarmed Dar with a devastating riposte, a move Ethan had been drilling him in for days.

"I am shamed by the strenuous efforts you have expended on this poor pupil, Ethan, but I am glad for your encouragement." Corbin bowed graciously while Darius recovered his fallen sword.

"What are you talking about, Grandpa? You're a great student. That little tactic took me far longer to master, I assure you," Ethan encouraged.

"And how old were you when you did so?" Raymar knowingly asked.

"What difference does it make?" Ethan gave him a look to shut him up.

The others stared at him expecting an answer that forced his hand.

"Four," he mumbled, though the others heard him clear as day.

"Four?" Ander nearly choked, though he shouldn't have, considering what he already knew of Ethan's history. Ethan was a quick learner, the same as the heirs of House Loria, a mage gift passed down through their line.

"Dar, toss me your sword," Ethan said, catching the hilt in midair, while tossing him an axe in return, Alesha's grandfather giving him a strange look, wondering what he was to do with it.

"There's more to fighting than just swords. Every foot soldier in Astaria trains with a sword, axe, and spear," Ethan explained as Dar tested the weapon in his grip, slapping it gently against his shield.

"Why not master one, then spreading your focus on all three?" Raymar asked.

"Most of our enemies use one of those three weapons, and if you are going to combat them, you should know their strengths and vulnerabilities. There is the added benefit of using the enemies' weapons if you happen to lose your own in battle."

That makes sense, Raymar conceded.

A servant boy hurried forth, taking Darius's sword from Ethan to return it to the rack, handling the weapon nervously in his hands.

"Wait!" Ethan commanded, stopping the boy where he stood.

"Yes, my lord." The boy dipped his head reverently, his bright green eyes trained on the ground. Ethan looked the lad over, guessing his age to be ten or eleven. He was a good-sized lad, with long brown hair that reached his shoulders, wearing a leather tunic over a gray hose.

"Why are you holding the sword by the blade?" Ethan asked.

"'Tis how we are taught to carry them, my lord," he blurted nervously. He was clearly uncomfortable speaking with nobility, fearing he had offended Ethan in some way.

"Carry it by the hilt, the way a sword is meant to be held. Though it's only a training blade, you should handle it the way you do a real sword. That should've been your first lesson in sword handling."

"Apologies, my lord. I have not had lessons in warcraft."

"Ease up on the *my lord* business. My name is Ethan, what's yours?" Ethan asked gently, sensing the boy's misgivings by the fearful tone in his voice. Ethan squatted in front of him, resting his elbows on his knees, so the boy didn't have to look up so far at him.

"Jered, my lord."

"Jered," Ethan tested the name. "That's a good, strong name. I like it. Jered, I'm Ethan." He stuck out his hand, motioning the boy to shake it.

Jered shifted the sword to his left hand while shaking Ethan's with his right.

"You have a strong grip for a boy, Jered. Now why haven't you had a sword lesson yet?"

"I...I am a palace servant, My Lord. We are not taught such things."

"Would you like to learn?"

"I..." Jered struggled answering, torn between what he wanted and the fear of overstepping his place.

"Of course, you would, what boy wouldn't. Here, give me that." Ethan took the sword and escorted Jered back to the others, who were giving him mixed looks.

"Dar, Corb, Ray, Ander, this is Jered. He's going to train with us," Ethan patted the gob-smacked boy on the back, the other's faces appearing as surprised as his.

"Consort, I do not think it appropriate..." Ander started to protest when Darius interjected.

"It is a pleasure to make your acquaintance, Jered," Darius greeted politely.

"Thank you, my lord." He bowed.

"Welcome to our little gathering, Jered." Raymar smirked. The very idea of training a servant to wield a sword was absurd, and he found it most entertaining. One thing he could say about Ethan was that he was never boring.

"When you train with us tomorrow, lose that tunic, and wear trousers. If you don't have a pair, we'll fix you up with a new set of clothes," Ethan said, causing Jered's eyes to draw wide, surprised that he would be training with them tomorrow as well.

"My lord, what of my duties?" he nervously asked, his eyes drifting warily toward the arena entrance, expecting his superiors to fetch him, and fearing the consequences.

"What duties are you responsible for, lad?" Ander asked, not too pleased with the situation.

"I am to attend to your Lordships in the arena...," he began before Ethan cut in.

"And you'll be doing that while training. We will help you clean up, won't we, fellas?" Ethan gave each of them a look that brokered no compromise, followed by some enthusiastic nods and one reluctant one by Ander.

"Then I must report to the royal armory for my duties there."

"Which are?" Raymar asked.

"Polishing armor mostly, my Prince," Jered said sheepishly, ever conscious to whom he was speaking.

"We can help you with that as well, can't we, fellas?" Ethan generously offered up their services.

"Consort, that would be inappropriate." Ander finally had enough. Helping a servant attend to his duties sorting equipment in the arena was one thing but to continue with this charade in other parts of the palace was quite another.

"Nonsense, Ander. I spent an entire winter when I was only wee high, working in an armory," Ethan dismissed his concerns, holding out his hand about waist high, indicating the age he was referring.

"Why not? 'Tis a small price to pay to learn from the world's greatest swordsman." Raymar smirked, as Ander sighed, shaking his head in defeat, knowing when he couldn't reason with Ethan.

"Well, all right, Ray, let's get started." Ethan slapped his brother by marriage on the back before beginning Jered's first lesson.

*****

Four days hence

Young Jered made impressive gains in his short time training with Ethan and the others, displaying a sound starting stance, and a vicious thrust. His blocking and ripostes were much to be desired but showed increasing improvement with every lesson. Corbin and Darius took a special interest in the boy, each taking turns showing him different things they learned. Raymar noticed that even Ander was warming up to the boy, taking him aside and demonstrating whatever lesson Ethan was teaching.

Ethan regularly mixed up their regimen, working with various weapons such as axes, spears, arrows, and maces. He showed them how to properly engage two opponents simultaneously, sliding his feet and stacking them one behind the other. The key was movement and footwork, each requiring practiced repetition. They would finish their sparring, then put the arena back the way they found it, before proceeding to the armory.

Raymar sat in disbelief, again finding himself sitting at a workbench in the armory, sharpening swords, using one of his many mage gifts to aid in the task, namely his glowing hands, which emitted a fearsome heat.

"That's sort of like cheating, you know," Ethan commented, watching Raymar pinch the edge of the longsword between his glowing thumb and forefinger, running them along the blade.

"Using magic is not cheating, Ethan. It is simply being practical," Raymar pointed out.

"If you say so." Ethan shrugged.

"You are not one to cast aspersions, my friend. Your enhanced strength and recuperative powers are both mage gifts that you use to great effect in our bouts."

"Guilty," Ethan confessed as he picked up a vambrace from the rack, taking a seat across him, running a cleaning rag over it. Corbin, Darius, and Ander sat at the other end of the workbench, cleaning various pieces of armor, while Jered ran a whetstone over the blade of a knife. The armor master stood nervously at the weapons rack, uneasy with their presence. It was unusual for nobles of any sort to visit the armory, let alone members of the royal family.

"Davin?" Ethan called out to the armor master, drawing him from his thoughts.

"Yes, my lord?" He hurried forth.

"It's just Ethan, Davin. I'm no lord."

"If you insist, my lord," Davin answered, wary of following that suggestion.

"It must get awfully boring down here attending to all this all day, every day. What do you usually do to pass the time? Do you sing songs? Share stories? Do you tell jokes?" Ethan asked.

"Jokes, my lord?" Davin made a face.

"Oh, come now, Master Davin, surely you must know a bandy pun or two?" Raymar asked bemusedly.

"Have a seat, Davin, and I'll tell you a few I picked up while I was a deputy in Red Rock," Ethan said, drawing the unsuspecting fellow into their circle of confidants. "There was a sergeant, a captain, and a quartermaster walking across the desert..."

And so it went, for the next few hours, with Ethan telling them of his adventures, and sharing Judge Donovan's best jokes, though some were a bit inappropriate for a boy of Jered's age, but the lad didn't seem to mind. Raymar smiled inwardly as Jered sat there polishing a steel helm with renewed vigor, a smile painting his face as he listened. It was probably the most fun the boy had in his whole life, all because Ethan took the time to care.

Why didn't I ever take the time to make someone's life a little better? Raymar scolded himself. He spent his entire life thinking of the grand picture, saving the world from his family's tyranny, that he never considered the plight of the servants around him. True, they were fed, clothed, and cared for, but what of their spirit? There was more to helping your fellow man than providing their base needs. Men and women needed fellowship. They needed a sense of belonging, and Ethan saw this so clearly. Ethan probably didn't even understand or know what he was doing, because it came so natural to him. These weeks he spent with his new brother, were the best times of his life.

Curse you, Alesha, he bemoaned, wishing they could simply continue on as they were, living peacefully in Elysia. He needed to tell Ethan the truth that his father's life would soon be free of the magic binding him, but his aunts forced his silence. A selfish part of him didn't want Ethan to know, so he would stay. Life without him would be insufferably dull.

"Let me tell you fellas about Lucky Ned Johnson...," Ethan began another story, recalling the tale Judge Donovan told him one night back in Red Rock over a game of cards.

*****

"This needs to end now!" Queen Mother Corella stated firmly, her silver eyes flaring intently, staring out the window to the Salnar Mountains in the distance while sitting upon her settee in her private sanctum.

"Please, Grandmother, let them be," Alesha pleaded, sitting opposite her, her hands folded neatly in her lap.

"Let them be?" Corella lifted a dark brow, her eyes shifting smoothly to Alesha's. "I have humored your husband's outlandish antics since your nuptials, letting him lead our menfolk in their ridiculous training, though Darius is far too old and frail for such exertions. Now he is training alongside servants as well. Will he invite the kitchen staff to join them next or our handmaids?"

"Is it truly causing such harm?" Alesha reasoned.

"Yes," Corella stated firmly. "Allowing some of our lessors to believe they are our equals, sows rebellion in our midst."

"I can read the boy's thoughts, Grandmother, and there is no such presumption there."

"What has become of you, child? Has your fondness for Ethanos softened your mind? You indulge him far too much."

"We have taken so much from him. I have taken so much from him. What harm is there in allowing him this small pleasure?"

"Taken?" she asked incredulously. "We have taken *nothing* that wasn't ours by right. You haven't taken anything that wasn't yours by right."

"Ethan doesn't see it that way." Alesha sighed.

"It doesn't matter how he sees it. He is bound to Vellesia now and will act accordingly. I'll have a talk with your brother as well and end these silly get-togethers they have indulged in. Perhaps they could partake activities more becoming of royal consorts, perhaps the harp or poetry."

"The *harp?*" Alesha nearly laughed out loud. "I would have to force that on Ethan to gain his compliance, and I've forced enough other things on him already," she recalled the tunics, kilts, and floppy hats he had worn at her insistence. It was cute at first, but now she grew to loath seeing him suffer.

"If you must force him to act according to his station, then do so," Corella argued.

"I don't want to force him, Grandmother, not anymore!" Alesha retorted angrily, gaining her feet and stepping toward the window.

Corella was stunned by the outburst. Alesha had never raised her voice to her. She was ever the dutiful child, always serving the interests of their house.

"I never thought it possible," Corella said in disbelief.

"Never thought what was possible?" Alesha asked, her eyes fixed on the mountains in the distance, unable to face her grandmother.

"You are in love with him." The revelation was as absurd as it sounded but true nonetheless. She taught Valera and Alesha that such notions were merely an amalgamation of lust, attraction, and reciprocity, nothing more. Love was the false hope of dreamers, a deluded concept peddled by poets and singers.

"What Ethan and I share is far beyond any such notion. He and I are of one flesh, one soul, joined by omnipotent bonds that can never be sundered," Alesha said, running her hand over her growing womb.

Corella's eyes narrowed severely, contemplating all that Alesha shared. The situation was becoming unbearable. Alesha might as well give Ethan free reign of the palace. Making matters even worse, her own mother was acting like a lovestruck girl, rekindling her feelings for her husband. Caterina went so far as to ask Corella if she had invited Darius into her bed. Once a consort had given his queen children, he served little purpose. Darius had not shared her bed in ages, until now, and that frightened her. He was still a handsome man, despite his advancing years. His dusty brown skin and brown eyes were wickedly enticing, stripping her of her practiced indifference to such things. Since training with Ethan, Darius had grown so bold as to seduce her, and she let him. She was so overcome by suppressed desire and lust, that his mere offer was too much to resist. The insatiable hunger for power was replaced by carnal urges that she was powerless to resist. For a woman such as Corella, this was unacceptable. She felt a slight shudder ripple her flesh as she felt Alesha's eyes upon her.

"So that's what this is about," Alesha said accusingly.

Oh, how she hated that her granddaughter could read her thoughts while she couldn't reciprocate.

"You dare search my thoughts?" Corella asked dangerously.

"Oh, please, Grandmother, I can hardly not read them with how loudly you are thinking." She rolled her eyes.

"Perhaps, but you could at least have the decency not to point it out."

"Regardless, it wouldn't change the fact that this is all about your own doubts. What is so wrong about grandfather Darius bedding his wife?"

Slap!

Alesha backed a step, surprised by her grandmother striking her face.

"You will not speak of this!" Corella warned.

"What does it matter? How many years do you have left to share them with Grandfather? Look to the other mothers of our order. All their husbands are long dead. Only you and great-grandmother Caterina have spouses to share your beds. She is not wasting the precious time he has left, arguing over his effect on her power. She and great-grandfather Corbin look happier than I ever remember. He loves her, even if he still wears that damnable collar that binds his power."

"A consort has no need of mage power and should be rightfully bound. One day, we shall have enough anti-magic to forge a proper collar for Ethanos, and his threat to our house will be removed."

"That will *never* happen." Alesha raised her chin.

"It will, and you will place it around his neck as our visions have foreseen once he has served his purpose. Then you can do with him as you please."

"Just as you can do with Darius as you please. I am not saying this to raise your ire, Grandmother. I am pleading with you to accept this gift from Ethan. Accept the removal of the insatiable hunger that has driven us to the brink of madness all our lives. Ethan has lifted the madness, and you are now free. Embrace this freedom! Embrace life! Embrace the years that Darius has left to live, for once he is gone, you will have another two centuries without him to lament your choices."

Corella turned away, overcome with emotion as Alesha's arrows struck true. She did feel the persuasive tendrils Alesha sent to her mind, easing her doubts and fears. 'Twas something that was impossible before Alesha was with child, the anti-magic flowing through her veins granting her untold power.

"You are right, child. I've been a fool." Corella turned back to face her, tears glistening on her cheeks. "Your grandfather and I have been...closer of late, and it frightened me that he had such power over me even though he is helpless against me."

"Oh, Grandmother," Alesha embraced her, sending tendrils of affection through the Queen Mother, further setting her at ease. Corella would relent and let the *boys* have their fun...at least for now.

*****

Three days hence

"Perhaps it would be wise to have a mage healer attend us during our morning sessions," Ander moaned, walking stiffly to the weapons rack, replacing the sword he just polished. The afternoon found them again in the armory, helping young Jered with his chores.

"We don't need their help managing a few scrapes and bruises." Ethan waved off his concern while pounding out a dent in a steel cuirass, the sound of his hammer echoing painfully off the stone walls.

"Says the man who can self-heal." Raymar snickered, running a cloth over a longsword.

"Yes, he is quite generous with our bruises," Corbin pointed out, moving gingerly back to their workbench with a rapier that needed attention.

"Come on, Gramps, you got me pretty good with your cross guard this morning." Ethan ran his left hand over his right shoulder, recalling the emphatic blow.

"That would be great-gramps to you, you insufferable brat." The old man snorted.

Ethan just grinned, enjoying the back-and-forth with his new friends. Every day, Dar and Corb opened up a little more, coming out of the shadows they dwelt in since coming to Elysia. Who would've thought that Corbin was a prankster? The old man laced Dar's trousers with an itchy powder of some sort one morning. He laughed so hard he almost wet himself watching Dar hop around the arena cursing out Corb. As soon as Ethan brought up jokes, Corb paid a visit to the palace library, finding a large tomb filled with thousands of anecdotes and puns. They hadn't been able to shut him up since.

Young Jered just sat there most of the time, with a face-splitting smile, taking in the stories and banter as if he went to sleep and woke up in a whole new world. He reveled in the praise the older men gave him for his improving skills. The idea of becoming a knight was something he never dreamed possible, but now such thoughts were taking root, all thanks to Ethan. He didn't miss the disapproving looks of the nobles he came across, each jealous that a servant boy was gaining such attention when their own children belonged training with members of the royal family. He didn't care. He would train with Ethan until he was ordered not to.

Davin, the armory master, still felt nervous in their presence, but his misgivings eased with each passing day, though he kept most of his thoughts to himself.

"How about a song, Master Davin? I've heard tell that you have a handsome voice," Dar asked, causing the armory master to stutter in denial until Ethan and Raymar cajoled him to display his skill.

There was a crofter's daughter
A lass of nineteen years
With hair gold as the sea…

Davin sang as the others hummed along with the merry tune until their tasks were finally complete. Ethan could see the sad faces as they finished, meaning they were done. It wasn't putting the armory to rights they enjoyed but the fellowship. They all slowly gained their feet to leave, but Ethan was having none of it.

"Now that our work is done, how about a game?" he said, fishing his last deck of cards from his pocket.

"A game?" Corbin asked curiously.

"What sort of game?" Raymar asked as Ethan began shuffling the cards.

"Poker." Ethan smiled.

"Poke her? That sounds most inappropriate." Ander made a face, reminding Ethan he went too far.

"Poker, not poke her. Give me a little credit Ander, I'm not a degenerate."

"What is poker?" Corbin asked.

"Have a seat, and let ole Ethan show you."

And so it went, with Ethan teaching them the game over the next few hours until all had a grasp on its rules and strategy. Even Jered took to the game like a fish to water, managing to bluff Ander into folding a pair of kings. Ethan gathered a bunch of iron nuggets to use as chips and would play until one of them won them all, where they redistributed them to play again. Ethan was forced to sit beside

Raymar, so his magical immunity would block the prince from read-ing everyone's thoughts.

Ethan's hope that his luck with cards would change with new players was quickly squashed as he went on to lose every hand. He was brought low calling Jered with a full house when the little brat held four jacks.

"You're not very good at this," Darius pointed out the obvious.

Ethan just sat there dumbfounded, recalling all the nights in Red Rock when Judge Donovan and Sheriff Thorton picked him clean hand after hand. Then there was Cordova, where Lord Darcannon and his deputies beat him time and again.

"Unbelievable." He just shook his head as he was once again the first one out.

They quickly lost track of time, playing cards well into the eve-ning until Mother Caterina and Alesha came to fetch them. Ander stuttered an apology, quickly taking a knee while Darius and Corbin sheepishly lowered their eyes, realizing they overstayed their allotted time.

"Welcome, ladies," Ethan greeted them as they entered the chamber, rising from the bench, giving them a polite bow as the others took the expected knee.

"Ethanos," Alesha said formally, her displeasure evident with her raised brow and folded arms.

He released a resigned sigh and took a knee as the two women advanced into the chamber, their gaze stopping at the cards spread across the workbench.

"Poker again, Ethan?" Alesha commented, shaking her head.

"How…" He meant to ask how she knew about the game since he never spoke of it in her presence.

"Your mind is shielded from me, but not Krixan's," she answered, circling the table while Mother Caterina lifted a king of hearts, exam-ining it curiously.

"I assume each of these symbols represents different valuations?" Caterina asked, examining several more cards.

"Yes. It is a game based upon luck, strategy, and intimidation," Alesha answered dryly. "A game Ethan is woefully inept," she added, looking him directly in the eye, a slight smirk playing at her lips.

"Rise, gentlemen," Caterina commanded, touching a hand to Corbin's shoulder, helping him to his feet.

"Care to join us?" Ethan offered. Maybe if he acted like there was nothing wrong with playing cards all day, they wouldn't either.

Truly? Alesha shook her head, reading through his attempt to downplay their actions. "I actually came here to fetch my husband." She reached out, snatching his hand, taking him in tow.

"Good luck," Raymar mouthed silently as they passed him.

"Are you coming, Grandmother?" Alesha asked over her shoulder upon reaching the door.

"You go on, dear. I think I will stay," Caterina said, taking Ethan's place at the table. "So how do you play this game?"

*****

They walked silently, side by side through the halls of the palace, Alesha holding Ethan's hand tightly.

"Am I in trouble?" he voiced warily.

"Oh, you're in trouble," she said as the guards posted outside her chambers knelt as they passed. She closed the doors behind them with a flick of her finger, leading him to their bed, pushing him onto the large feathered mattress, and climbing atop of him.

"I thought I was in trouble?" He smiled as she ran her fingers through his lengthening hair, which was still shorter than she preferred.

"Very much so," she hissed, crushing her lips to his.

*****

Alesha lay her head on his chest, snuggling comfortably as he ran his fingers through her hair. She ignored the morning sun shining brightly through her window, wanting nothing more than to lay in bed beside him all day. Another night of blissful sleep following unbridled lovemaking only strengthened this desire. Every day, her bond with Ethan grew. The thought of spending her day attending matters of the realm dampened her spirit. She just wanted to spend her day with Ethan.

"What has become of us?" She sighed, her eyes still closed as his chest warmed her cheek.

"What do you mean?" he asked tiredly, his eyes closed as well. He, too, wished to sleep all day.

"All I want to do is stay here in bed with you. Nothing else interests me in the least." She sighed dreamily, running her hand over his stomach.

"What's wrong with that? It sounds pretty good to me."

"What's wrong, is that I am losing all interest in the realm, in my duty."

"The realm can handle itself. You have more than enough grandmothers to run it for you. Hell, it's hard to determine who's actually running the place as it is."

She opened her eyes, lifting her head to look at him. "The Queen Daughter rules the realm. When Gabrielle is born, the title falls on me. I've been raised all my life to assume my rightful place, and now I hardly care. Don't you think it odd?"

"Sounds pretty good to me," he said, cracking one eye open before closing it.

"No. It sounds frightening. I'm losing interest in everything except you and our baby. And before you utter one more flippant remark, the same affliction is affecting you as well."

"You got me there, sweetheart. I've lost all interest in you ruling the realm." He smiled, unable to help himself.

"Idiot," she mumbled neath her breath, playfully slapping his chest. "You're losing interest in your precious freedom, the very freedom you've been pursuing all your life."

"How do you know that?"

"Because, husband, you haven't complained about in some time."

"Maybe I just learned to keep my mouth shut."

"You haven't kept your mouth shut your entire life, and I doubt you just learned to now. As much as you treasure your freedom, and wandering as an aimless spirit, you would rather spend time with me."

"I don't really have a choice," he mumbled.

"True. At first, you were forced to come with me, but now you actually enjoy it. And don't think to deny it, for you are a terrible liar."

"Maybe I like spending time with you lately because you're acting more like Allie than Alesha, did you ever think of that?"

"I wasn't a different person then, Ethan. The girl you met in the Mage Bane, is the same one looking at you right now. I always knew we were meant to be wed. Destiny brought us together as our prophecies foretold, but I never thought to consider how powerful those prophecies were until I met you. Unlike you, I never as much as danced with another man other than my kin. I had no such longings. Passion and desire were as foreign to me as the stars and sky. You have seen the men of Vellesia. They are handsome beyond compare to men of other lands."

"I guess." He shrugged, though he wasn't one to judge male beauty.

"They are exceptionally attractive, and do you know what I felt growing up surrounded by such beauty?" she asked, waiting for a flippant remark.

Ethan closed his mouth.

"*Nothing*. I felt nothing. All my life, I knew I was to have you, but the concept was merely one of destiny, not passion or desire. I felt nothing for all those years until I first saw you in Cordova. The mere sight of you awakened longings I didn't know I possessed. These feelings grew more powerful with every interaction. When you first spoke with me after your brave rescue in the Mage Bane, I swooned like a lovesick maiden. At first, it angered me how you could stir such passion in me. I felt helpless in a way I could neither understand nor control. The passion is now a raging fire, wild, and untamed, driving me mad with desire," she said, matter-of-fact, trying to temper her emotions.

"You sound like that's a bad thing." He smiled.

"Weren't you listening?" She wanted to scream.

"I was listening. You find me irresistible." He chuckled lightly, earning another playful slap.

"More like insatiable. My passion is constantly inflamed around you. I went from nothing before we met, to this. How could I have no carnal urges all my life, and upon meeting you, be so enflamed?"

She felt him stiffen with that comment, a knowing look passing his eyes.

"What?" she asked, knowing he was hiding something.

"I…" He released a breath, running his free hand over his head. "I never felt anything either until I went to Red Rock."

A stab of disappointment drove into her heart at the mention of that place affecting him so. What was he about to confess would waylay those fears.

"It was like I was seeing girls for the first time. Growing up in Astaria, I felt nothing for anyone in that way. I could not even pleasure myself as most men do in private. Nothing. I feared I was a eunuch, unable to perform as a husband or man. When my parents arranged a marriage for me, I wondered how I could perform my husbandly duty. Crossing the barrier was like breathing air for the first time as if a pall was lifted from my natural yearnings."

"You felt nothing in Elaria, but in Red Rock, you were aroused?" She breathed heavily.

"Yes, but let me finish before you get bent out of shape."

"I am not *bent out of shape*, whatever that means."

"It means angry, and I can tell you're getting angry by that look in your eyes, and that twitch of your nose."

"I am not angry."

"Okay, and you say I'm a lousy liar. Anyway, as I was saying, I felt nothing sexually until I crossed the barrier. Though I felt attraction for some of the women folk there, it only seemed overwhelming compared to feeling nothing in Astaria. When I returned home, however, my urges dried up again. Nothing! It was little surprise why I wanted to return to earth, which I thought was the only place I could ever consummate a marriage."

"So why didn't you?"

"You know why. Luke Crawford followed me back, and I had to hunt him down before returning to Red Rock, but that led me to you." He gave her a knowing look.

"And?" She needed to hear him say it.

"What I felt upon seeing you that first time was a thousandfold more powerful than anything I felt for any woman in Red Rock."

"Truly?" Her golden eyes lit with wonder.

"What I feel for you is…overwhelming. Like I said, I was basically a eunuch until I met you. I was sexually dead."

"Well, you are certainly not dead." She smiled, recalling her ravishment the night before.

"Only for you." That comment made her heart sing.

"So what explanation is there? Is it fate? Magic? Destiny?" He was never one to believe in destiny but now had reason to believe otherwise.

"Is it not obvious? We were born for one another. No other can take our place," she said before a thought came to mind, making her laugh.

"What's so funny?"

"My mother and grandmother were certain that you would wed or bed another before we could consummate our union. I believed you were smitten with Jennifer Murtado, and yet all that time, you couldn't have done anything, even if you wanted."

"It didn't seem all that funny to me. More like embarrassing."

"That's because you belonged to me." She kissed him fiercely, pinning him to the bed. She devoured him, her lips crushing his, a tingling sensation coursing their flesh, electric yet soothing, drawing them one to the other. Ethan flipped her onto her back, straddling her, gazing into her misty eyes as she ran her fingers along his face.

"Destiny, huh?" He lifted a skeptical brow.

"You still doubt our prophecies? We are living proof of their validity. We were born for each other, and no other. The magic doesn't lie."

"We may be born for each other, but that might not have anything to do with your prophecy or the dominion of House Loria."

"Why else would we be drawn together?"

"My grandfather was convinced my destiny was to be the Freeborn, destined to..."

"Destined to bring freedom to all who live in greater Elaria, I remember you speaking of it."

"Who's to say his prophecy isn't the right one?"

"The fact you are here in Elysia, bound to the Vellesian throne, proves that prophecy false. How can you be free when your heart belongs to me?" She whispered in a sultry voice.

"I never said I believed in that prophecy either."

"Then what prophecy do you believe in?"

"None of them." He smiled, pressing his lips to hers. "Or all of them," he added, their lips parting to catch their breath.

"They can't all be true, for one disproves the other," she said before kissing his chest.

"It doesn't really matter, Alesha, for I don't care about either prophecy or any other one that's out there regarding us. We have free will to choose our own path, destiny be damned, and if our child is as powerful as you claim, she will probably do as she damn well pleases, no matter how you try to explain your prophecy to her. The only destiny that seems to be fixed is us. You and I obviously can only be intimate with each other, everything else is meaningless."

Perhaps he was right. Perhaps everything else was pointless except for them. If she dared to think that, it would force her to regret all that she did to him. No, he had to be wrong. Gabrielle had a destiny, and Ethan was bound to her, which bound him to Vellesia. The two are intricately linked. Of course, it didn't matter if he believed it, as long as he was here...here with her. There was only one thing she needed to say.

"Whether you believe your grandfather's prophecy, or not, never speak of the Free Born prophecy to anyone. Promise me!" she said fiercely, cupping his handsome face in her hands.

"Why?"

"It doesn't matter. You are sworn to obey me, and on this, you shall." Her eyes glowed so dangerously it sent a chill up his spine.

"All right, my lips are shut, but can I at least ask why?"

House Loria had long known and feared the prophecy of the Free Born, whose existence was a dire threat to their house. They hunted those who proselytized the prophecy, exterminating them wherever they were found. If any of them still believed in the prophecy, they were driven so far underground that none could find them. Since Alesha inherited from her father the ability to read anyone's thoughts, no one who held such beliefs could hide from her, except her father's house, who shared that ability. But with her newfound power, Gabrielle's power, she could even read their thoughts, if she chose to.

She sighed, contemplating telling him this or not, before reminding herself that Ethan was subject to her, not her to him. He would not react well learning that the adherents of the Free Born prophecy were persecuted by her family.

"I could tell you, but I will not. You will not speak of it to anyone. Do you understand?"

He nodded, taken aback by her insistence.

"Then say it?"

"I understand, Your Highness," he submitted in disgust. Whenever he thought she had changed, the old Alesha returned, putting him in his place.

She closed her eyes, steadying her breath, lest her anger take her places she would regret. *I'm doing this to protect you, you fool!* She wanted to scream but couldn't. That would only lead to more questions, and he would drag the truth out of her if she wasn't careful. When she opened her eyes, he was already out of bed and getting dressed.

She hadn't given him permission to leave, and thought to say so, but didn't care to see the disgust on his face whenever he submitted to her simplest request.

"Mother is expecting us for breakfast," she reminded him, hoping to change the subject.

"I don't have to dress up, do I?" He made that face like a little boy who didn't want to eat his vegetables.

"Wear what you like." She sighed, not wishing to hear his complaining. She was thankful he had the good sense to put on the thick black trousers that he trained with, rather than his buckskins. The black outfit wasn't really appropriate for breaking their fast with the queen but didn't look too bad, considering it was Ethan she was talking about.

*****

Alesha was surprised to find her mother's table empty, and the servants unable to say where she was. She could hear Ethan's stomach growl from the other end of the spacious chamber. It was unlike her mother to not be where she said. She didn't see any of her grandmothers either, which was equally strange.

"Should we wait for her?" Ethan asked, eyeing a platter of food the servants brought from the kitchens.

"Truly?" She lifted a disapproving brow, shaming him not to ask again. She closed her eyes, reaching out with her mage awareness, locating her mother, grandmother, great-grandmother, and three more of her grandmothers gathered in the…armory!

"What is it?" Ethan asked, noticing the odd look on her face.

"Come!" she said, walking briskly out of the room.

*****

"Raymar?" Alesha caught her brother in the outer corridor of the armory with a tray of steaming food in his hands. He turned, staring back at her with bloodshot eyes.

"What are you doing with all that food, Ray?" Ethan asked over Alesha's shoulder, eyeing the freshly cooked meat and warm bread.

"Where am I going?" He glared daggers at Ethan. "You created a monster, Ethan."

"Of what are you speaking?" Alesha asked impatiently. She could read his thoughts if she chose to, but did not wish to take such liberties with her brother.

"See for yourself." Raymar lifted his chin in the direction of the armory.

Alesha didn't know what to expect when she entered the armory, but never in her wildest imaginings could she have envisioned this. There in the center of the chamber were her mother, Grandmother Corella, Grandmother Caterina, Grandmother Porshana, Grandmother Inese, and Grandmother Zelana, playing poker, along with Darius, Corbin, and Ander. Young Jered was curled up in the corner of the chamber fast asleep.

"Alesha, my darling, come join us!" Mother Caterina shouted delightfully, beckoning her forth, as the others looked in her direction.

"How long have you been playing this silly game?" Alesha was aghast. Her grandfathers and Ander looked far worse than poor Raymar, their bloodshot eyes struggling to stay open.

"ALL NIGHT!" Raymar said, stepping around her to place the platter on the table.

"You've been playing all night?" she asked Raymar.

"Oh, not I. Since I can read everyone's thoughts, I was sent to fetch food, drinks, and whatever else they fancied," Raymar snarled.

"Yes, such a dear boy. Now you can serve," Mother Porshana ordered her grandson as she dealt the next hand, the large pile of nuggets in front of her indicating her success. Ethan noticed large piles in front of Caterina and Valera as well as Ander. Corbin and Dar were already out by the look of things, each sitting dutifully beside their wives.

"What of our talk yesterday, grandmother?" Alesha asked Corella.

"What of it, child?" she retorted, sitting close to Darius while ordering her cards.

What of it? You made your disapproval of the boys and their activities quite clear, and now you're joining them? she spoke directly to her mind.

"I am spending time with my husband as you advised, child." Corella smiled up at her while running her free hand possessively along Darius's shoulder.

Alesha was dumbfounded. Here sat six queens of Vellesia, gathered around a dirty workbench, playing one of Ethan's stupid games with a sergeant, a servant boy, and their husbands like they were a band of drunken sailors. And they had been at it all night. Had the world gone mad? Her grandfathers appeared content, enjoying their wives' attention, though they looked ready to fall over at any moment.

"So much for training today," Ethan quipped, noticing the sorry state the men were in. He didn't see any sign of Davin, guessing the armory master wisely checked out early, before seeing him curled up on the floor atop a pile of blankets.

"He fell asleep hours ago," Raymar said, noticing where Ethan was looking.

"Yes, the poor things are exhausted. Why don't you escort your grandfathers to their bed chambers, and Ander can do likewise with Master Davin and young Jered," Valera ordered.

"Yes, Mother," Raymar bowed as he and Ander cleared the chamber with their charges in tow.

"Sit, Ethan! You can join in after we finish this game," Porshana said, indicating an empty place beside her.

"The others claim you are very bad at this game." Caterina smiled as he took his seat.

"Who said that? I'm the one who taught them how to play," he said with a hurt look.

"They all said it," Valera said dryly before raising Corella five nuggets.

"Traitors," Ethan mumbled under his breath.

"Don't you have someplace to be, dear?" Porshana asked Alesha, who stood there in disbelief.

"Yes, as do we all, Mothers," she said acidly.

"You can treat with Lord Valnar on your own. It is a good test of your ability before your ascension to Queen Daughter," Valera said.

"Do not worry over your handsome husband, Alesha. We will take good care of him." Caterina gave Ethan a flirtatious wink.

"I am certain you will." Alesha shook her head, her response sounding more like something Ethan would say.

Ethan waved her bye as she gave him a look before stepping without.

"Give me two, and I'll raise you six," Porshana said, pushing Valera and Corella all in. "Ha! Full kitchen, queens high!" Valera declared triumphantly, placing down three queens, and two fours.

"Full kitchen?" Ethan made a face.

"Three of one kind, two of another. That is how Raymar explained it," Valera said.

"Full *house*, not kitchen," Ethan corrected.

"It can be a full castle for all I care, child, but it can't beat four of a kind," Porshana declared, setting her cards on the bench, all fives. The others groaned, throwing their cards in.

Two hands later and Porshana held all the nuggets. They redistributed them again and started anew, inviting Ethan to join them. He didn't last long, as in typical Ethan fashion he lost every hand. Since he was first eliminated, he replaced Raymar in fetching food and drink for the others. After his third trip to the kitchens, he swore to never play that *stupid* game ever again. He had to admit that playing poker somehow loosened those old gals up quite a bit. He couldn't believe these were the same women that he had to bow down to in their presence whenever they met.

By the end of the day, Ethan crawled back into bed with Alesha, worn out by the ladies who played all day.

"Did you have fun?" Alesha asked dryly, looking over a scrolled parchment while lying in bed.

"I spent the day as a glorified maid, fetching food and drinks for your mother and grandmothers. Just when I thought they were done, three more of them suddenly appeared, and joined in. Damn Ben and the judge for ever teaching me that horrible game," he moaned, lying beside her.

"Lost every hand, didn't you?" she quipped, not needing to look at him for confirmation.

"Yep."

*****

The following days returned to normal with Ethan and his motley gang continuing in their training and working in the armory. The queens left them alone but absconded with Ethan's last deck of cards. He didn't mind, and if he never played that awful game again, it was fine with him. The others looked on curiously one afternoon in the armory as Ethan gathered a pile of fist-sized pieces of marble.

"What now?" Corbin asked, looking over his shoulder as Ethan lifted a piece of marble that he shaped into a small figurine, with a faceless round head.

"We're going to play a new game, fellas, but I need to make the pieces. Can any of you replicate this piece?" Ethan asked, passing around the black marble figurine.

"I can," Davin said, examining it in his hand. He spent a year as a stone mason's apprentice before following his more gifted calling with steel.

"If you can, we all can." Raymar touched a hand to the armory master's forehead, extracting the knowledge, transferring it to the others.

"You can do that?" Ethan made a face, never hearing of such ability.

"I just did," Raymar japed, passing out pieces of marble and chisels to others to shape.

"That's convenient," Ethan quipped.

"If you think that is convenient, take a look," Raymar said, his right hand glowing red, bursting with intense heat while shaping the rock.

"That's still cheating, but I won't complain," Ethan said, thankful his new brother could hurry the process along. Mage power sure came in handy, he had to admit, considering the time he spent on that one piece.

"How many of these do you need, Ethan?" Darius asked.

"Eight black, and eight white."

"That explains the coloring of these stones, but what are they?" Ander asked, holding the finished one up to his eye.

"They're called pawns. They are pieces in the new game I'm going to teach you."

"A new game?" Jered asked, his eyes lighting up.

"Yes, little buddy, a new game. It's called *chess*." Ethan ruffled the boy's hair.

"Chess?" Raymar asked.

"Yes, Judge Donovan taught me to play when I was laid up in bed for all those weeks," he said, as they recalled the story of when he was shot in the back.

"I hope you are better at playing Chess than you are at poker," Raymar chuckled.

"I'm pretty good, Ray. I beat the judge as often as he beat me. Unlike poker, there is no luck in chess," he said.

Raymar was going to add that it was more than bad luck to explain why Ethan stunk at poker but allowed Ethan that illusion. After carving the pawns and the other pieces, and making a board, they went about learning this new game. Some took to it quicker than others, with Raymar the fastest learner, giving Ethan an even run after several games.

The following day, Ethan introduced another game he played in Astaria, with a large map board representing fictitious realms and pieces representing various military units. It was a game they could all play at once, a game of war, strategy, and shifting alliances. The others started the game by ganging up on poor Ethan and toppling his kingdom. He spent the rest of the game watching the others finish, shaking his head as they wisely attacked Raymar next, considering him the greatest threat. By the time they finished, young Jered was the last one standing, earning him everyone's praise.

As the days continued on, Ethan would introduce other games, as would Raymar and a few others. Oftentimes, one of the Lorian Mothers would observe their activities with interest, but for the most part, let them be. It was an early spring day when they gathered around the workbench, playing an Estasan dice game called Gold Rang, when Ethan noticed Jered off in the corner by himself, playing with his game pieces from his war game set.

"What are you doing, Jer?" he called out to the boy.

"I..." Jered looked up with wide eyes as if caught misbehaving.

"You were playing with the pieces. It's all right. So did I when I was your age. That's the nice part of that game. You can use the pieces as toys."

"I didn't know it was allowed. I am sorry, Ethan." Jered's sad face nearly broke Ethan's heart.

"Of course, it's allowed, Jer. Go ahead and play. Here, I'll play with you." Ethan got up from the bench and sat on the floor next to his little friend. The others looked at him strangely as he started setting the pieces up on the stone floor as if arrayed for battle.

"These soldiers will be the legions of the villainous King Magnar the Awful," Ethan said, pointing out the miniature men at arms with black and red crescents emblazoned on their shields. "Over here, will be the small kingdom of Weler and the beautiful princess named...I don't know. Do you know a pretty name for a girl, Jer?" he asked.

Jered reddened with embarrassment, lowering his eyes.

"You know a pretty name but aren't telling me," Ethan goaded, touching a finger to the boy's ribs, making him laugh.

"All right, stop." He giggled. "Sendra."

"Sendra. That is a pretty name. All right, Sendra it is. Here is Princess Sendra and her small kingdom, surrounded by the army of the evil King Magnar." Ethan pointed out the figurines set around the floor. "And here is the noble knight, Sir Jered, *the Bear Bane*." Ethan took a playing piece from Jered's fingers, a figure of a swordsman holding a great sword in both hands as if to strike.

"Bear Bane?" Jered scrunched his face, not understanding the word *Bane*.

"Bear Bane means killer of bears," Ethan said, patting him on the back.

Jered looked pleased with the moniker given his character.

"Who will you be, Ethan?" Jered asked.

Ethan picked up a large ogre figurine, setting it next to Jered's knight. "Why, I'll be your trusty sidekick, Krixan the ogre." He stifled a laugh, wishing the real Krixan was here to whomp him about the head for naming the ogre after him.

The others looked on as Ethan and Jered conducted a series of mock battles and adventures using the playing pieces. As their time came to an end, Jered gave Ethan a big hug, which was out of character for the shy servant boy.

"Thank you, Ethan. This was the best day yet." Jered hugged him fiercely, reluctant tears squeezing from his eyes.

"Really? After all the other fun things we do, you like toys the best?" Ethan smiled.

"I love every day with you, Sergeant Ander, Prince Raymar and the others, but I never played with toys before. It was fun." Jered smiled happily.

"What do you mean you never played with toys before? Why not?"

"I…" Jered's words caught in his throat.

"The boy was apprenticed here since his fifth year. His parents are peasant farmers," Davin explained.

"And you never had a toy?" Ethan asked.

"No, sir." Jered's smile was gone, his eyes lowered shamefully.

"And your parents are not here either?" He never asked about his kin, assuming they served in the palace like the servant children in Astaris.

The uncomfortable silence that followed, answered his question.

"Many of the child servants in Elysia are placed here by their parents, or are orphans. The crown takes them in, offering a better life than they might otherwise suffer," Ander spoke on the crown's behalf.

Ethan sighed, wondering how any parent would send their child away, even if it was for a better life. *It is easy for me to judge, considering the privileged life I've lived,* he scolded himself. Unless you were in those parents' place, how could you fairly stand in judgment?

*****

Sleep did not come easy for Ethan that night. He lay abed, staring at the ceiling as Alesha stirred beside him.

"What troubles you?" Her sultry voice asked, running her fingers along his cheek.

"Did I wake you?" He looked over at her, blue eyes meeting gold, the flames from the hearth flickering in her golden pools.

"Every time I fall asleep, I can sense your unease, and I wake."

"Sorry." He sighed.

"What is tormenting you?" she asked again.

"I was thinking of Jered. I didn't know he was all alone. His parents sent him here when he was five, and he hasn't seen them since."

"It was their choice, a choice for a better life for their son. Why does that bother you so?"

"A better life? I'd rather be poor and with my family than well-off and alone. And he isn't exactly well off. I've seen the servants' barracks. They are nothing to aspire to."

"Our servants are given a fair wage, a warm bed, fine clothing, and plenty of food. What more should we do?"

"I'm not blaming you or the crown. I was only saying that a boy needs his parents."

"You may feel strongly on the matter, but Jered's kin made that choice freely. Isn't freedom to choose one's path what you always claim you want?"

"I know, but they made a choice for him. It's not the same thing."

"A child belongs to its parents, Ethan. You must respect their wishes."

"Yes, but I don't have to like it."

"True, you are free to hate it all you want."

"Did you know Jered has never even owned a toy?" he said sadly, again looking at the ceiling.

"Most children don't. Most people in greater Elaria struggle meeting the base needs. Toys are luxuries they can ill afford."

"It doesn't take money to make a toy. You can make one out of anything if you have the time."

"Time that's often needed elsewhere," she reminded him. Part of her admired his concern for others, but another part felt put off, his remarks sounding accusatory, as if it was the crown's responsibility for providing everything to everyone.

"I have time," he said.

"What?"

"I have time. I will make him some toys."

"Jered is eleven, Ethan. He is nearing adulthood. I don't think he'll get much use out of them."

"Maybe, maybe not, but what harm will it do?"

"If it makes you feel better to be his Santa Claus, then you have my blessing. Can you go to sleep now?" She closed her eyes, resting her head on his chest.

"That's it!" he said excitedly, jarring her eyes open.

"What now?" She was losing patience.

"Santa Claus. Thanks for reminding me," he remembered telling her of the mythical bearer of toys that was a legend on Earth. He kissed her forehead and closed his eyes, going fast to sleep.

"What now indeed." She rolled her eyes, only imagining what he was going to do.

*****

The following morn

Ethan hurried the others through their morning drills, anxious to finish and head to the armory. Raymar commented on his unusual lack of focus. Ethan didn't answer, only grunting an apology, before moving on to the next drill. It wasn't until they retired to the armory that they knew something was amiss, as Ethan harshly ordered Jered to precede them, the boy shaking nervously. Ethan never raised his voice before, his tone causing the boy to lower his head sadly.

"Lift your head, Jered. Only cowards look at the ground!" Ethan ordered. The boy obeyed instantly, wondering what he had done to earn Ethan's disapproval?

"Is something amiss, Ethanos?" Darius asked, trailing him by half a step.

"You'll see," he mouthed wordlessly so Jered couldn't overhear.

Passing through the entryway, Jered stopped dead in his tracks, as three fist-sized figurines rested on the workbench. They were each soldiers, wielding swords in three different poses, each brandishing a shield, and painted in fine detail.

"Jered, the armory workbench is no place for your toys. Put them away!" Ethan ordered sternly, trying not to smile.

"But, they are not mine, Ethan," he said, not able to take his eyes off the beautifully crafted toys.

"You know better than to lie, Jered. I know those are your toys because I spent half the night carving them myself and painting them this morning while you were asleep."

"Truly?" Jered looked back at Ethan, his eyes wide as the ocean.

"Truly," Ethan said, his smile breaking across his face.

"Thank you, Ethan." The boy rushed into his arms, hugging him fiercely.

"Easy there, big fella." Ethan hugged him back, ruffling his hair as they parted. "The toys are yours, but you have to do something for me in return."

"Anything," Jered beamed proudly.

"Good. I want you to make me a list."

"A list?" Corbin asked, the others wondering as well as they gathered around.

"A list for what?" Raymar echoed.

"A list for our newest project. I'm Santa, and you're all my elves." Ethan grinned as his friends quickly asked what was Santa and what were elves. Before Ethan could explain, Jered was already at his workbench, cradling his newfound treasures in his arms.

*****

The following days found Ethan's motley band manufacturing toys out of wood, iron, and cloth. He made good use of the molds he purchased in Torval. Toy soldiers carved from wood or cast from molds, each painted in fine detail, were the most common. Princesses and ladies were the next most popular, with gowns of cloth draping their carved forms. There were horses in full regalia, kings, queens, knights, several ogres, and creatures of legend, each added as Ethan's ambitions grew.

"Let me see that list again," Ethan ordered as Jered fetched it from a shelf in the armory. Darius and Ander looked over Ethan's shoulder as he ran a finger down the list of names, stopping at a girl named Glinda, a chambermaid in the lower palace.

"What did she ask for?" Darius asked, unable to see through Ethan's fingers.

"A yellow unicorn."

"I'll start carving it," Raymar said from the other side of the table, after just finishing the final touches on a carriage, giving its wheels a spin before rolling it across the bench to Corbin, who was ready with the paintbrushes. His grandfather was quite skilled with the brush and coordinating the proper colors for each toy.

"Our second list is nearly complete. Well done, fellas," Ethan congratulated all of them, receiving hardy cheers in return.

"When do we give them their toys?" Darius asked, strangely excited by the entire enterprise. Jered gave them three lists of all the servant children in the palace, with each child's requested toy beside their name.

"We wait until the third list is complete. Saumbers day is in three days. We should be ready the night before. I want all the children to receive their toys when they wake on that morning," he explained. Saumbers day was the designated day of rest that happened every tenth day. It would give the children time to play with their newfound treasures.

They continued working for a time, exchanging lighthearted banter and telling stories to pass the time. Whenever one of them struggled with a task, Raymar would intercede, touching a finger to one who was skilled, and then touching one who was not, sharing their knowledge. It was by this means that Jered learned to read and write in a matter of moments, so he could make their lists. By that means, they all knew how to carve, paint, metal work, and design toys in equal measure, though each continued to do whichever task they most enjoyed.

"It is time that I retire for the day," Corbin said, removing the paint-covered smock he wore, setting it on the workbench.

"The day's still young, Cor," Darius said, using the nickname Ethan gave the elder gentleman.

"Yes, the day is young, but I am not, and I am required elsewhere." Corbin patted his son by marriage on the back, making his way to the door.

"Required elsewhere? By whom?" Darius asked.

"None of your business, young fella." Corbin grinned, using the language Ethan had infected all of them with. Even Ander was prone to use one of Ethan's figures of speech with increasing regularity, the former Astarian prince rubbing off on him.

"Oh," Darius's eyebrows rose in comprehension, realizing Mother Caterina was the one demanding his attention. Corbin and Caterina were acting more like awestruck lovers than queen and consort. If Darius was being honest, he and Corella were no different, their romance aflame like nothing he could remember. There was always a wall of formality between him and his wife, a wall that had fallen since Ethan's arrival. It was as if he saw Corella for the first time, stirring feelings he never knew he had.

"I should be making an exit as well," Darius decided, following Corbin for the exit.

"Stay on her good side, Dar." Ethan smiled, knowing where he was going. If Darius could keep Corella happy, then things would go easier for the rest of them.

*****

After finishing in the armory, Ethan made his way to the stables, paying his daily visit to Bull, bringing his friend a bushel of carrots. The spotted palomino stood comfortably in his spacious stall, eating carrots out of Ethan's hand.

"Are they treating you good here, pal?" Ethan asked, stroking Bull's neck with his free hand.

Bull brushed his tail side to side, answering his question.

"That's good. I asked them repeatedly to take good care of you. I'm glad they listened. I know you want to get out of here, but we'll have to wait a little longer. I keep asking to take you out of the palace for a ride, but the queen says no for some reason. Just bear with me, pal."

"Talking to your horse again, I see," Raymar japed from behind him.

"What are you doing here, Ray?" Ethan asked as he came to his side.

"Just seeing where you run off to each day after leaving the armory. I always thought you went running back to my sister's bed, but instead, I find you here talking to your horse, and what a handsome fellow he is." Raymar stroked Bull's mane.

"Well, now you know. I owe it to Bull to spend at least a little time with him every day. He is my fellow prisoner after all."

"Most prisoners aren't sharing a bed with their jailer." Raymar smirked, earning a punch in the arm.

"Oww," he mouthed wordlessly, grinning at Ethan.

"Go ahead and say whatever it is you've been wanting to say since I arrived. There's no one around to overhear," Ethan said.

"There is much I want to say, Ethan, but for now, I cannot." He sighed sadly.

"And why is that?"

"As much as I want to tell you how to be free of my mother's magic, there are other factors to consider, factors I cannot explain to you at this time."

"You mean factors that you *won't* explain. That is your choice, not mine, Ray."

"There is more to my decision than free will, Ethan. I am guided by the greater good, and for that reason, I cannot tell you."

"So I'm trapped here. First, I have you and Amanda warning me that my daughter will usher in an age of tyranny that must be stopped, but you don't know how I can accomplish this. Now you're telling me I have to stay here for the greater good. Maybe you can understand if I'm a little fed up with this whole mess?" He growled.

"I wish I could fully answer you, Ethan, but I will give you this. Your presence here has manifested drastic changes in Elysia that have been unforeseen. These changes might alter our predictions in a most positive way. Should you leave, these positives would quickly reverse."

"Changes? What changes?"

"My mother and grandmothers, they are…different now. You have seen it in my mother since Astaris."

"She's lightened up a little. A whole lot, actually," he admitted.

"A very whole lot," Raymar emphasized, before taking a deep breath, pacing around the stable with his hands behind his back, searching for the right words.

"Ray?"

"Your great-grandfather believed you were the Free Born. He spoke of this with you," Raymar said, looking at the floor as he circled.

"Yes," Ethan would ask how he knew but didn't bother since Alesha's kin seemed to know everything about him anyway.

"The Free Born prophecy is an age-old legend, heralded by some, and feared by many, especially House Loria," Raymar began to explain.

"So I've heard," Ethan said, his earlier conversation with Alesha coming to mind.

"What you don't know is the extent House Loria has gone to extinguish these beliefs in Vellesia and beyond. Those who adhere to the prophecy, the true apostles, have been driven underground, lest they be extinguished. There are so few of them left, and none as far as my mother's house is aware."

"You are your mother's house," Ethan reminded him.

"True, but I am also of my father's house," he said, looking intently into Ethan's eyes. The meaning was clear as the sunrise, House Menau adhered to the Free Born prophecy.

"That doesn't make much sense, Ray. If your father's kin believed I was the Free Born, why empower House Loria? Why would your aunts work to enslave me to them?" Ethan growled, his voice rising high enough to alarm Raymar.

"Lower your voice, you fool!" Raymar whispered harshly. There were ears everywhere, and each of the queens had spies reporting directly to them, and wherever Ethan went, many of them were certain to follow. Raymar was taking a grave risk confiding anything with Ethan, but Ethan needed to understand why he had to stay put for now.

Ethan calmed himself before nodding to Raymar to continue.

"What I speak of can never be spoken of by you to anyone. Avow it!"

"I avow."

"Very well," Raymar released a breath. "My father's house was the first to foresee your birth, long before House Loria. There was a great divergence in the interpretation of your birth, Ethan. House Loria saw only your power that could be passed on to their heirs, power that would make House Loria invincible, almost omnipotent. House Menau, however, knew your true purpose, as your legend is aptly named…Free Born. It is you who shall usher in a new age, an age of freedom."

"And how am I supposed to that?" Ethan heard all this before and thought it nonsense. "If you haven't noticed, Ray, I am a slave here. I can't free myself, let alone the world. And what does freedom for all the world even mean? Freedom from slavery? Freedom from hunger? Freedom from poor health?" He recalled the conversation he had with Elenna when they were briefly betrothed, where she used the same argument he was throwing at Raymar.

"Freedom from tyranny, absolute tyranny. It is the purpose of your birth, Ethan. You are the balance. House Loria has gathered unparalleled power unto itself. Despite what you believe, I do not hate my mother's house. As a son of House Menau, I feel a strong kinship to both of my parents' houses. Though I love my mother and her kin, I know that unchallenged power leads to tyranny. Even the kindest heart will grow wicked if given such power. No one is immune to its temptation. My unborn niece will have such power at birth. Who can temper her impulses should she go awry? Only you can."

"Me?" He challenged touching a hand to his chest. "And how am I supposed to do that? If she is as powerful as you all believe, there ain't much I can do about it."

"You can do what no other can."

"And what is that?" Ethan asked doubtfully.

"You can say *no*."

"You've got be kidding?" He shook his head. Was Raymar saying the purpose of his birth was to say *no* to a spoiled child?

"I would not jest on a matter so grave." He lifted his chin indignantly.

"All right, I'll play along with your reasoning for a moment. If I am the only one that can stand up to my unborn daughter, how can I do so without the queen's permission? If you hadn't noticed, I am bound by magic to obey her or my father's life is forfeit."

"There is a way around the magic."

"I know, but you won't tell me."

"Because you would be tempted to leave, and I can't have that," Raymar reminded him.

"And why is that? Because my presence is making your mother and grandmothers nicer people? I'm sorry, Ray, but their mood isn't my problem."

"But it is mine!" Raymar growled back, appalled with Ethan's selfishness. "I told you that your freedom isn't my concern, only the greater good. You weren't born to ride off into the wilderness to do as you pleased. You have a duty."

"Shouldn't the Free Born be free?" he growled back.

"To free others, Ethan. To free us *all*, not just yourself. Think of someone other than yourself for once!"

"What'd you say?" Ethan took a dangerous step toward him, his hands balled into fists.

"I said, think of everyone else instead of yourself," he repeated.

"That's all I've done all my life and look where it got me?" Ethan spat. "I put my neck out time and again, fighting for those less fortunate, with nothing but grief for the effort. I didn't accept the life of privilege I was born to, rejecting the pleasures it offered to help others throughout my time in Astaris. I spent my days helping old Yance chop wood or working in the smithy. I turned a motley band of peasants into a deadly light cavalry force, besting my father's armored knights, besting them on the battlefield. I received nothing but grief from my father for those efforts, but I proved that common men were as good as noble blood. I journeyed across the barrier to help Sheriff Thorton, risking my life several times over, because a good man needed my help. And in case you've forgotten, I broke my vow to my mother to never enter the Mage Bane to save your sister. There you go, my selfless act on her behalf and what did it earn me? It earned me a chain!"

"At least you slipped your chains at times. I've spent my life trapped in Elysia, captive to my mother's whims. If you left now, all our labors would be for naught."

"And what exactly have you worked for? Whatever it is, it didn't work because here I am. If my daughter is such a threat, maybe you could've warned me *before* I met your sister!"

"I tried." Raymar sighed, turning away. "I tried, but I was foiled at every turn."

"Your aunts," Ethan said, for no one else supposedly knew of Raymar and Amanda's plots but them.

"Yes. They hold to a different interpretation of the Free Born prophecy."

"One that required Alesha and I to wed," Ethan said, recalling his conversation with Sarella that night in the Gorgencian holdfast.

"Unfortunately, yes."

"So what now? Am I to just sit in my cage and wait?"

"For now. We must wait for Gabrielle to be born, and decide from there."

"Decide what, exactly? I'm not going to harm my own child. So where does that leave us?"

"You could take her away. Perhaps the Mage Bane or across the barrier."

"She would be vulnerable in either place. She could die, and I couldn't do that. Besides, the barrier is in Astaria, at the ruins of Plexus, well beyond our reach."

"There are other portals to cross the barrier, Ethan. The one at Plexus is one of many."

"And you know of another portal nearby?"

"I do."

"Where?"

"I can't tell you at this time."

"You can, but you won't."

"Yes, that is the right of it."

"So we wait. We don't know what we'll do after she is born, but we have to do something. If I stay after she is born, I doom the world to her tyranny. If I leave without her, I doom the world to tyranny. If I take her to the Mage Bane or Earth, I will doom her, as well as set the Lorian Order on a warpath that will doom the world to destruction, so I won't do that. So that leaves taking her somewhere else," Ethan said.

"I am uncertain if that is the correct action," Raymar said.

"Well, what else is there?" Ethan already lost patience with this situation.

"Give me time, Ethan. Prophecies are often tricky things, and this prophecy is the most important we have foreseen, its ramifications endlessly intertwined with the fabric of life itself in all of Elaria."

"Forget your prophecies. Think with logic and reason."

"Logic and reason? Is that what guides you, Ethan? I think not. You couldn't leave now if you were free and wanted to. You are helplessly bound to Alesha. The magic joining you is beyond my comprehension, but is all too real."

"You have me there. I am supposed to be immune to magic, but apparently not." He shook his head.

"I don't think it is magic that binds you and Alesha, but something more."

"Something more? Like what?"

"Fate. Destiny... Love." Raymar shrugged, not really understanding himself.

"It's magic, Ray. It feels like invisible cords wrapping themselves around me, forcing me to her. She is doing something."

"She claims you are doing the same. It is affecting her the same. You don't see it as clearly because you haven't known her that long."

"In what way?"

"She is different now. Ever since she returned from the Mage Bane, she has been...distracted. Since our father died, she has been cold, logical, focused, forever obsessed in claiming you for your power. Now, she is obsessed with just you. I fear what may happen should you leave her."

"I don't plan on leaving her," Ethan said, causing Raymar's eyebrows to rise.

"Then what…"

"I'm taking her with me," he whispered, even if he had to drag her kicking and screaming.

*****

"Drink," Corella commanded, offering her husband a goblet of wine.

"With pleasure." Darius smiled, losing himself in her silver eyes. They stood in the middle of her bedchamber, the light of the fireplace playing off their black, silken robes. He took a sip before offering it to her.

"You know that has no effect on me," she reminded him.

"You are not immune to its taste," he pointed out.

"Very well," she said, emptying the goblet and tossing it aside, drawing him into her embrace as the metal clanged off the floor. She kissed him fiercely with savage lust. The hunger for mage power was now a slender flame, replaced with a raging passion that was long suppressed. Their lips parted ever briefly, affording her time to lose herself in his piercing brown eyes. He was still a handsome man, despite his years, his taut, dusty brown complexion was without blemish. His coal black hair perfectly framed his masculine face. With her hunger reduced, it was like seeing him for the first time.

"Come." She drew him toward the bed. She was tentative when these new found feelings surfaced, fighting the urges that swept over her like a raging sea. It was Alesha who convinced her to give in to the overwhelming lust. Such a suggestion was unthinkable to a Vellesian queen. A Vellesian queen held absolute power over her subjects and realm, let alone her base emotions. Looking into her granddaughter's eyes, she knew it was hopeless. Alesha's advice was not from her position as a crown princess but from one who already succumbed.

Alesha was hopelessly smitten by Ethanos, and freely acknowledged it. Alesha was also stronger than her. If the most powerful Mage to ever live was overcome with lust, what hope had Corella? She quickly discovered that once you gave in, there was no turning back.

Corella and Darius made love through the night. Whenever his strength waned, she sent tendrils of power into his flesh, aiding his recovery. She held her controlling nature in check, allowing her husband's adventurous side to guide their actions.

Where had this side of him been hiding the last four decades? She closed her eyes, lying beneath him as another shudder rippled her flesh.

Whenever the fire began to die in the hearth, she would levitate another piece of wood into the flames with a flick of her wrist without breaking stride. The blankets were cast aside long ago, leaving them naked upon the bed. She opened her eyes, the flames of the hearth lighting the left side of his handsome face, and reflecting off the gold of his collar. She reached out a hand, running her fingers along its smooth surface. She recalled their wedding ceremony when she first placed it around his neck, binding his power.

Shame washed over her, finally realizing what Darius must've felt when his mage power was locked away. She couldn't imagine what she would've felt if her power was stripped away. She recalled the uneasy feeling whenever Ethan drew near, blocking her power while in her presence. Of course, that was only in Ethan's proximity, the collar was for as long as it was worn, and Darius wore it for forty years.

"Do you ever miss your mage gift?" she asked, her gaze trained on his collar before looking into his eyes.

He suddenly stopped his ministrations, her question catching him of guard. "My gift?"

"Yes, do you resent me for binding it?"

"Why not read my thoughts?" He smiled uneasily.

"I don't want to. I want you to answer freely."

"It...it is a part of me. Though it has been so many years since I felt it, I still remember running through the countryside faster than a horse. It was liberating and wonderful. But I...I understand why you did it. The protocols of the court demanded it." He smiled sadly.

"It was not court protocol," she confessed, staring intently into his brown eyes.

He tilted his head, reminding her of a curious dog, looking sideways at its master.

"The women of my family have bound their mates' magical ability to dull the hunger for their power. If you only knew how difficult it is to share a bed with someone who has something you so desperately crave and can never have."

He never thought of it that way. After four decades of marriage, they never spoke of such things, a lifetime spent together yet so far apart.

"Our collars were useless against Ethan, and Alesha felt no such hunger in his presence. She removed his upon their leaving Astaris, unable to bear seeing it upon him. Strangely, his presence has changed things here as well...," she said, reaching out, touching the tips of her fingers to either side of his neck, pressing them to the surface of the collar.

Snap!

"The hunger is gone." She smiled, withdrawing the two halves of his collar.

"Corella," he called her by name, euphoria coursing his flesh, his mage power restored in glorious rapture.

"Shh!" She touched a finger to his lips before reaching up to kiss him.

CHAPTER 18

The following days found Ethan and his motley band continuing in their endeavors. The armory was overflowing with toys. Piles of figurines were divided into knights, princesses, ladies in waiting, and many others. There were mounted knights with armored destriers brandishing swords or lances. There were archers with drawn bows in green livery and men-at-arms in chain mail brandishing axes and pikes. There were ogres, unicorns, and carriages.

As the night in question drew near, they gathered around the workbench going over their lists, matching each child and toy. They exhibited a sense of giddy excitement imagining the children's eyes when they beheld their treasures.

"One knight equals two archers or three men at arms," Darius reminded Ander as they assigned toys to the boys on their list.

Raymar, Jered, and Corbin gathered at the far end of the bench with a map of the palace rolled out over its surface, like generals planning a military operation.

"We'll start here and move from bottom up." Raymar tapped the floor plan of the subterranean levels of the inner palace, where the first servants' billets were located.

"We might need some help." Corbin eyed the mountains of toys surrounding them.

"Ethan's working on that," Raymar said, his eyes sweeping over the floor plans of the lower levels, mapping out their order of movement with military precision.

"Where has Master Davin run off to?" Corbin asked, looking around the chamber for the armory master.

"With Ethan, gathering more *Elves*." Raymar rolled his eyes at the moniker Ethan had given them.

"Any help would be most welcome," Corbin answered, warily eyeing the mounds of toys.

"We could have handled it ourselves if we limited one toy per child, but Ethan grew a little ambitious." Raymar snorted, following his grandfather's eyes to the mountains of toys.

"I think we were all a little ambitious." Corbin smiled, patting his grandson on the shoulder.

"What do you think, Jered?" Raymar looked across the bench where the young servant boy was studying the map so intensely.

"What do I think, Highness?" he asked, not understanding the question.

"About this whole operation. What do you think?" he asked again, waving his hands around the chamber at their handiwork.

"I...I think the children will be very grateful, Highness."

"Ease up on the Highness business, Jered. You may call me Ray when we are all alone here, all right?" Ray smiled with how Ethan was rubbing off on him.

"I..." Jered was perplexed by the suggestion. He was already calling Ethan by name, but that was different because...well...because he was Ethan. Raymar was a prince of the realm while he was but a servant.

"It's all right, lad. Think of our time here together as a secret order, a brotherhood if you will," Corbin said.

"A *Secret Brotherhood!*" Darius added excitedly, overhearing their conversation from the other end of the bench.

"Yes, a secret brotherhood!" Corbin pointed an excited finger at Darius.

"We would need a name," Darius said, looking at Ander for inspiration.

"Don't bring me into this, I am a mere sergeant in the queen's royal guard. I have duties elsewhere, Your Graces." Ander raised his hands in protest.

"Nonsense, Ander. Mother assigned you to watch over Ethan. We can't have a sacred order without one of its founding members," Raymar said.

"I..." Ander thought to refuse before Corbin interjected.

"And do you really believe Ethan would allow you *not* to join?"

"Very well." Ander sighed, knowing he couldn't win.

"So back to a name?" Darius asked, looking to the others for ideas.

"What about the Sacred Swords?" Corbin said elatedly until the others shook their heads, rejecting the silly name.

"Ethan's avengers?" Raymar suggested, receiving as little enthusiasm as the Sacred Swords.

"What do you suggest, Jered?" Darius noticed the boy deep in thought.

"It would be silly." Jered shook his head.

"We'll be the judge of that, lad, so out with it!" Corbin ordered.

"Well...I was thinking that Ethan has been calling us elves over the past few days. Maybe we should be the Order of the Elves. Though I don't really know what an elf is," he said, lowering his head, waiting for them to laugh at his suggestion.

"The Order of the Elves?" Corbin repeated, testing the name.

"Or, the Brotherhood of Elves?" Darius said.

"The Brotherhood of Elves!" Raymar declared, liking the sound of it.

*****

On the eve of Saumbers day, *The Brotherhood of Elves*, began their distribution, moving from room to room, delivering the toys. Ethan still couldn't believe they named themselves the Brotherhood of Elves, and his attempts to talk them out of it fell on deaf ears. He tried to explain that Santa's elves weren't mythical minions of great power, but little people with pointy ears and green hats. He eventually gave up and went along with it, especially when Corbin decided it was a great idea. Alesha's great grandfather had become the leader of their little band, and he reminded Ethan of Dragos in so many ways. The fact that Corbin held Mother Caterina's ear, gave him the most influence of the group, as Corella, Valera, and Alesha obeyed Caterina without question. It was her influence that allowed *the Brotherhood Of Elves* to move freely throughout the palace to complete these rounds.

The sounds of happy children filled the air the following morn when they woke to discover their treasures beside their beds. Word spread throughout Elysia of their mythical benefactor, a spirit named Santa and his merry band of helpers.

*****

Ethan and the others skipped their training session that morning, gathering instead on a balcony overlooking the feasting hall on the lower levels of the palace. Alesha ordered the hall steward to allow the children the use of it after breakfast was served, and the tables cleared away. The children gathered on the open floor below, playing with their toys and sharing them with each other.

Corbin ruffled Jered's hair as the boy stood at his side, overlooking the activities below. He looked up at Corbin with an ear-splitting smile, eyes beaming with joy.

"Do you want to join them, lad?" Corbin asked.

"Go on, Jered. We'll see you tomorrow," Raymar added, standing at his other side.

Jered bowed his head, and stepped away, but was called back before reaching the first step of the stairway behind them.

"You forgot something," Raymar said sternly, his harsh voice catching Jered off guard until the Prince handed him a heavy sack.

Jered loosened the bag's sinch rope before drawing two mounted knights carved and painted in fine detail. The work was disturbingly lifelike, down to the horses' wild eyes, and the links in the knights' chainmail. Of all the toys they constructed, these were the finest, and each of the men had a hand in making them as they were intended for their little friend. Jered's eyes bulged, looking straight up to Raymar and Corbin in disbelief.

"You've earned them, lad. Now go and play with your friends."
Corbin grinned, ruffling his hair before sending him off, but not
before giving them a fearsome hug.

No sooner had Jered's feet hit the stairway, Alesha stepped
through the archway behind the balcony, entering their midst. Ander
and Davin began to kneel before she bid them to stand. She regarded
each of them in kind, stopping at Ethan, who stared back at her with
those sea-blue eyes that seemed to see right through her.

"You all look very tired," she said, managing to tear her eyes
away from Ethan. They must have been up half the night delivering
the toys. Even then, she doubted they actually slept, anticipating the
children's reactions.

"'Tis only one night, my dear. We shall recover." Corbin gave
her an infectious smile, stepping forth to embrace her.

"Grandfather," she greeted him, returning his embrace.

"I am told we have you to thank for the use of the hall," Corbin
said as they drew apart.

"Mother Caterina can be very persuasive." She smiled, reaching
out her hand to his bare neck, where his collar once graced.

"She removed it last night," Corbin said.

"I am glad." She smiled, kissing his cheek. He was the last, as
Darius no longer wore his either. The need for the cruel devices had
long expired, for the Lorian bloodline was far too powerful to be
threatened by the meager abilities of their consorts. Their only recent
purpose was to curb the madness, which Ethan's arrival had dulled.

Alesha next hugged her grandfather Darius, joyed to see him
free of his collar.

"Beautiful." Darius smiled, taking in her lovely face.

"Careful, Grandfather, else Grandmother will grow jealous."
She kissed his cheek.

"No, she would be the first to agree. You are exceptional, my
child. Ethan is a fortunate boy," he said, giving Ethan a stern look,
which he returned with an acknowledged shrug.

She released the others to oversee the fruits of their labors, drawing Ethan away to the far end of the balcony, out of earshot.

He felt his blood race when she first stepped onto the balcony, wearing a silken white dress that hugged her inviting curves, and the small bulge of her growing womb. Her face was almost glowing, radiating a maternal femininity that only quickened his raging heart. She was always beautiful, but now it was overpowering. How did he ever live without this woman? He wanted to take her in his arms and never let go.

She didn't need magic to read his thoughts, but decided to playfully ignore the obvious. She held his hand while casting her gaze below. The boys and girls had segregated themselves to opposite sides of the hall, playing with their toys whilst ignoring the other side.

"It's always the same," she mused aloud, shaking her head.

"What's always the same?"

"The boys on one side, and the girls the other. They don't even look at each other."

"They're still children, give them a few years, and they'll do more than look." He gave her that smile that made her swoon.

"Yes, they'll do more than look, but it will be *war* nonetheless. Are we doomed to always be at each other's throats?"

"Are we talking about them or us?" he asked.

"Both." She sighed.

"There's no war between us, Alesha. You already won," he japed.

"Did I?" She looked at him doubtfully.

"I'm here, aren't I? You've locked me away and tossed the key."

"You're hardly a prisoner. In fact, I think you have usurped my throne."

"Really? And how do you figure that?" He wanted to hear this.

"You have somehow managed to win over every member of my family. My brother, the ever-dutiful son and prince, is now your partner in mischief. Whatever you suggest, he follows you blindly into battle."

"That's not true."

"The prince of the realm is playing poker with you into the late hours of the night. He never lifted a sword before your arrival and now trains with you every day. He helps the servants with their chores…"

"We all help Jered if that's what you mean."

"Yes, and if you knew my brother, this is not like him at all."

"He never complains about it."

"Because of you," she pointed out. "You were the one that offered to help Jered and volunteered all of them to join you." She briefly looked over to the others.

"They could've said no."

"And disappoint you?" She shook her head.

"I thought they liked doing it?"

"They do. That's the point. Raymar has a stupid smile painted on his face all day. My grandfathers talk of you constantly, and all the *wonderful* activities you do together. They've spent endless hours making toys because of you. They even call themselves elves!"

"The Brotherhood of Elves," he corrected her.

"The Brotherhood of Elves." She again shook her head. "Look at them. They are like little children."

"It's not my fault life was boring around here before I showed up." He shrugged.

"Do you wonder why my grandmothers allowed my grandfathers to join your activities?" She ignored his remark.

"To keep them busy?"

"Because I asked them to. I knew you would make friends with them as easily as you do with everyone, and I wanted you to be happy here."

"You did that? Thank you."

"Yes, and the Queen Mother and Grandmother Caterina thought it absurd but relented at my insistence. And now they, too, have fallen under your spell."

"They have?"

"Do you know what my mother and grandmother were doing last night while you and your band of elves were distributing toys?"

He just shrugged.

"They were playing poker."

"Really?" He made a face.

"You have no idea what you have done."

"You say that as if it's a bad thing."

"It's not bad, it's just…unexpected." She sighed.

"Unexpected, huh?" He scratched his head.

"Everything is strange. You wouldn't know because you weren't raised here, but this…" She waved her free hand across the chamber… This is not normal."

"I'm still not following. What are you getting at?"

"We are a strict monarchy, Ethan. The queens of Vellesia are near deities in Elysia. We are bound to formal protocols in all our interactions. To stand in the presence of the Queen Mother is a rare privilege, and commoners and nobles alike are never to look upon her unbidden."

"My sore knees can attest to your formalities," he reminded her.

"You have hardly knelt in weeks, Ethan. The queens have demanded little of you. The Queen Mother is revered throughout the realm, even the Queen Daughter must kneel in her presence. She has instructed me since birth on the expectations of my destiny. At first, she thought the idea of grandfather Darius training with you to be absurd and improper. A royal consort is expected to attend his wife, and quietly reside in the royal apartments. Do you care to know what she told me before coming here to see you?"

He just shrugged.

"She told me to *be kind* to Ethan."

"That was nice of her," he said innocently.

"Grandmother Corella is many things, Ethan, but nice isn't one of them. Since your arrival, she has removed grandfather Darius's collar, freeing his mage power, a power she does not possess. She has invited him to her bed, something she hasn't done in many years."

"Years?" He thought that a little extreme.

"Years," she reiterated. "She is the Queen Mother, a title that charges her to oversee all matters of House Loria. She seems uninterested in her duties, spending her days playing poker, and nights with her husband. My mother is even worse, leaving all matters of the realm to me."

He wondered where she was going with all this.

"I'm not scolding you, Ethan. I know that look on your face, and you can rest at ease. What I am trying to say is, that things are different now."

"Is that good or bad?"

"Very good." She smiled, pressing her hands to his cheeks. "The hunger is gone, Ethan. You have taken it away, and the possibilities are..." She looked out to the sea of happy children below... Endless."

"So you're happy that we made these toys?"

"It is who you are, Ethan, and I am pleased that my family now sees what I first discovered in the Mage Bane that you are more than a prophecy. And perhaps you can see Elysia as more than a prison," she said hopefully.

"See it as what?"

"A home."

"A home?" He shook his head. "How can it ever be that after..." He caught himself before saying anything more.

"After what?" she asked, drawing away.

He couldn't answer, knowing it would only anger her, and spoil her good mood, but one look in her eyes showed he already had. Why couldn't he just have made her happy?

"After what, Ethanos?" she asked again with her queen's voice.

"Astaris." He sighed, kicking himself for his ruining her good mood.

"I see," she said coldly, turning to leave before he caught her arm. A dangerous look passed her face, warning him that he went too far. One does not touch the crown princess in such a way, not even him.

"Alesha, wait."

She paused, looking disapprovingly at his grip on her arm until he released it.

"Forget what I said. You've done everything you can to make me feel at home here. You could've locked me away in the royal apartments like your ancestors have done with their consorts, but you didn't. Look, Elysia is not my home, not yet, but it doesn't have to be a prison either. In all fairness, Astaris didn't always feel like home either. It always felt like there was something missing, or...someone." He gifted her a smile.

Damn him, she thought, hating how he could disarm her so easily with that smile.

"Part of me wants to hate you for what you did, for using my father to force me to do your bidding, but I can't. Whatever this thing is that binds us together, it has dulled my anger. All I can think of now is you. It's maddening."

She didn't know how to react before he continued.

"One look at you and I'm lost. I can't control it anymore."

"Control what?" she asked warily.

He took her in his arms, pressing his lips to hers, fierce yet tender and all-consuming.

CHAPTER 19

Of all the things Ben Thorton and Andrew Donovan had seen in their long lives, nothing prepared them for the great palace city of Astaris. Even crossing the portal, as disorienting as it was, paled against the towering citadels of the inner palace that could be seen from afar. They were met at Plexus by Princess Ceresta and a host of royal cavalry, sent by King Bronus to escort them to the palace. Dragos frowned upon hearing that they were to proceed to Astaris posthaste, wishing to host his new friends at Plexus for a time. Instead, they all found themselves journeying on to the capital, with Dragos extolling the beauty of the Astarian countryside, with Judge Donovan on one side, and an annoyed Ceresta on his other. She quietly withdrew, joining the stoically quiet Sheriff Thorton, who trailed her grandfather several horse lengths. Ben found the princess to be the most striking woman he had ever seen, even lovelier than her sister, in a mature way that set her apart from Felicia's carefree nature.

"What think you of our fair land, Sheriff Thorton?" Ceresta asked, riding at his side.

"It's right pretty," Ben said, looking off to their right at endless rolling hills and pastures as far as the eye could see, and their left with forests of towering pines skirting the white caps of the Por-Shada Mountains gracing the horizon.

Ceresta stifled a laugh.

"Something tickle your gizzard, young lady?" Ben asked.

"Ethan said you were a man of few words, and your friend was a man of many. It seems my brother's assessment was understated." She smiled, lifting her chin in the direction ahead, where Dragos and Andrew were caught up in a nonsensical debate concerning bird migrations. The two of them chattered endlessly the entire journey on one subject after another.

"Aye, they do like to talk." Ben shook his head, though, in all honesty, neither held a candle to George Adams.

"I doubt they even know we are here," she said.

"No, reckon they don't."

"It does seem strange that you are such good friends, as the judge talks so much and you so little," she remarked.

"The world would be a dull place if our friends were too much like ourselves. I ain't much for speeches, and the good lord has seen it fit to pair me with those who are. My late wife enjoyed talking. She could go long in conversation without me sayin' a word." Ben smiled at the memory.

"My parents are like that in a way. Father is so large and gruff while Mother is graceful and well-spoken," she confessed.

"From what I've been told, he's a mite ornery. Men like that need a strong wife to temper them," Ben said.

Ceresta smiled, never hearing anyone brave enough to say that about her father or so bold. No wonder Ethan favored the sheriff so much. The man was brutally honest. "Do you speak from experience, good sir?"

"It takes an ornery old cuss to know one, Ms. Ceresta." Ben gave her as much of a smile as he was able, though it barely broke his lips.

"My father eagerly awaits you, Sheriff. We have all heard such wonderful tales about you, Judge Donovan and so many of your town folk, whether from Ethan, Jake, or Felicia."

"Stories tend to grow each time you tell 'em. Keep that in mind."

"I am aware. As much as my family is eager to meet you, I hope we meet your expectations as well."

"You're the third Blagen I've met, and I haven't been disappointed yet."

"Those that you have, feel much the same. Felicia speaks of you fondly, when she is not staring at your son with lovesick eyes." Ceresta rolled her eyes, recalling her sister's antics.

"He is equally guilty when it comes to that girl." Ben shook his head.

"He is more subtle than she, I assure you. In fairness to my youngest sister, it is she who was most informative when it comes to you and your people. Ethan spoke very well of you but was scant on detail, and Krixan was even worse."

"Krixan was never much for idle chatter. Your brother, on the other hand, asked enough questions to keep my brain working most hours of the day. Can't blame him for that since I'd have done the same if I arrived in a strange land."

"You are fond of him, I can tell." She sensed his admiration for Ethan by the tone he used whenever he was mentioned.

"Your brother's a good man. I doubt I'd be alive if he didn't show up when he did. I still recall the first time I saw him riding into town on Jake's horse. Thought he stole it before he explained what happened, though he didn't mention saving Jake's life. That's just like Ethan to leave something like that out. He was never one to boast, a rare thing in most men I've known."

"That is kind of you to say, Sheriff. Ethan said many good things about you, as well. He said you were the most honorable man he knew and brave. He planned on returning to visit you, but our Vellesian guests foiled that."

"In Texas, we don't call thieves guests," Ben growled, recalling what Felicia and Dragos told him of Alesha's betrayal.

Ceresta couldn't stifle her laugh, causing Ben to look at her curiously.

"*They hang horse thieves in West Texas, Valera, but in Vellesia they put crowns on their heads. That's all you really are, Valera, a thief!* Those were the very words Ethan said to the Vellesian queen in Astaris. He sounded very much like you," Ceresta explained with her mirth.

"The boy was quite impressionable. Glad to see he didn't change much."

"No, he was much the same even when he left. I hope captivity doesn't change that."

"Maybe we can do something about that. I'm not one for giving up on a man who's guarded my back more times than I can count.

This Queen Valera thinks she's won, but I doubt she counted on facing what we have in tow," Ben said, jerking a thumb over his shoulder where two Gatling Guns and three artillery pieces were somewhere in their long column, including many wagons of ammunition.

"You bring us a mighty gift." Ceresta heard much of their devastating potential from Jake and Jerimiah.

"A gift purchased with your father's gold. Let's just hope it does the job."

"All of Astaria knows what Ethan did at the Velo with one rifle and two pistols. If the great Ben Thorton says these weapons are many times more devastating, I trust that it is so." If Ben knew Ceresta for long, he would know she didn't make idle claims or flatteries.

"The great Ben Thorton?" He looked at her sideways. "You Blagen children have too high an opinion of an old broken-down cavalry captain who hasn't seen battle in many years. I'll try to live up to your expectations."

"You already have."

*****

It was midday by the time they came upon the gates of the city, where throngs of people gathered outside the city walls to receive them. Rumors spread far and wide of the legendary Sheriff Thorton and Judge Donovan, whose adventures were shared throughout the land. The story of their shoot-out in the streets of Red Rock was now well-known, becoming part of Astarian folklore, as nearly all of Ethan's adventures were. Joining Ben and the judge in the long procession were Long Paws and three other braves from his tribe, and Spencer and Gus Lawton, the last of which helped procure their heavy armaments. Long Paws was invited personally by Dragos, to scout out lands northwest of Plexus for his tribe to resettle. The region was sparsely populated with good farmland and plenty of game to hunt. The area was tributary to House Mortune and within his rights to gift to his new friends.

Andrew Donovan found the good people of Astaris a welcoming sort, never seeing so many smiling faces in all his life. The main gate of the city was open, and he noticed a large message written above the gate upon the blue stone of the castle wall, its lettering in Elarian script.

"That's a lot of words for a city's name," Andrew said, tilting his head, trying to figure out what it meant.

"It's not only the city's name, my friend, but a declaration." Dragos smiled, reading the words proudly.

"Astaris, where you kneel to no man, and no man kneels to you!" Dragos repeated in English for his friend's benefit.

Andrew thought about it for a moment. As an American, his countrymen had thrown off the yoke of Monarchy long ago, and no one he knew lived under its strict protocol. This was why Ethan so loved Red Rock, finding a place that reflected his values. He wondered if Ethan placed this greeting above the city gates or his father? Dragos could see him working it out in his brain.

"Ethan changed so many things. Bronus used to berate the boy for his *foolish* desire for freedom and his disdain for kneeling and such, but when the Vellesians placed that collar around his neck and made him kneel…well, you can guess how that made Bronus feel. When Krixan finally returned to Astaris and started to kneel, it was too much for the king to bear. Whenever he sees anyone kneeling now, it brings back that awful memory, and so no one kneels in Astaria. It is ironic, don't you think, that Ethan fought to gain his freedom to never kneel again, and now he is the only Astarian that kneels." Dragos shook his head.

"Not if we have anything to say of it. We'll get the boy his freedom, Dragos, if it's the last thing these tired old bones ever do," Andrew said.

"Old bones? My friend, we are in the spring of our youth, and the glories of Astaris await us," Dragos waved an open hand toward the city gates, just as a prestigious procession emerged from the city.

They eased their horses to a slow canter as King Bronus rode forth to receive them, with Tristan on one side, and Jake on the other. Bronus paraded forth astride a heavy black destrier, wearing thick black trousers and shirt, with a sword upon his left hip, and a holstered colt on his right. His short sleeves displayed his powerful arms in the cool spring air. His thick black beard and steel gray eyes reminded Andrew of a mountain man he wintered with in the Rockies back in '54, a bear of a man with the temperament of a starving grizzly.

Ben and Ceresta drew alongside them, as Dragos hailed his son by marriage, with the surrounding crowds looking on. Bronus took one look at Dragos and shook his head, regarding his and Ben's matching attire of dark trousers, tan collared shirts, dark vests, and six-shooters, with black Stetsons and stars pinned to their vests.

"Well, you certainly look different." Bronus snorted, bringing his horse to a stop, looking first at Dragos, before regarding the others, saving a smile for Ceresta and polite nods to Ben and the Judge.

"The Texas air has done wonders for this young man." Dragos smiled, removing his Stetson, and sweeping it across his chest to greet his king. "Bronus, it is my privilege to introduce Judge Donovan and Sheriff Thorton. Gentlemen, my son by marriage, and king of Astaria, Bronus Blagen," Dragos introduced them.

"Sheriff, I've heard many great things about you. And you, Judge Donovan. It is good to see faces for the names I've been hearing tell of for so long," Bronus said.

"We are equally honored to meet Ethan's father. I hope my son has represented us as well as your son did for you," Ben said, lifting his hat.

"Aye, he's a fine lad. He has been impressive enough that I plan on keeping him, or should I say, my daughter plans on keeping him." Bronus grinned, causing Jake to turn red, to the other's amusement.

"What of your badge, son?" Ben asked, knowing the pride Jake placed in wearing the star of a US marshal.

"If I have to choose between Felicia and the Marshals, I choose her." Jake shrugged.

"He has plenty of options in Astaria. He and Jerimiah would make excellent captains in our new ranger companies we are forming with the rifles you sent." Bronus smiled, regarding Jake proudly.

"You'll find no one finer than Jake," Andrew said.

"I've heard good things of you, Judge, if Ethan and Krixan told it true. They claim you're a fine-drinking man. I look forward to emptying many kegs with you." Bronus gave him a wolfish smile.

"Now that's the smartest thing I heard yet. Ethan was many things, but a drinking man wasn't one of 'em." Andrew grinned.

"My son was a cheater. Confessed to me his crimes before he was taken captive. All these years, he led me to believe he had bested me in the cups. Now the realm knows better, restoring me to my rightful place of drinking champion of Astaria." Bronus puffed his chest proudly.

"Well, enough of your boasting, lead on. We have feasts and celebrations awaiting us!" Dragos shouted.

"Aye, and two young rascals awaiting the marriage noose." Bronus grinned, giving Tristan and Jake a knowing look.

*****

"Your dress is lovely," Amanda said, touching a hand to the gossamer fabric gracing Felicia's sleeve. Her future sister by marriage stood before the long mirror in her chamber, testing the fit of her wedding gown, turning as the skirts swirled about her ankles. It was emerald green, with a bodice hugging her narrow waist, with billowing skirts draping freely below her hips. The swell of her bosom was tastefully displayed, revealing enough to entice her groom's eye while concealing enough to be modest.

"Do you think Jake will like it?" Felicia asked, turning away from the mirror, to look over her shoulder, examining the rear of the dress.

"He's not blind, Felicia," Arian said, standing at her other shoulder.

"His vision is as excellent as his taste," Amanda said, causing Felicia to smile. They spent the better part of the morning trying on their wedding garments, waited on by a dozen maids fussing with their gowns and shoes, and setting their hair in differing styles to find a match to their liking. Queen Gabrielle visited them several times, reminding them of their guests coming arrival, who they were expected to receive in the Great Hall.

"I would fear your impulse more than his vision," Arian said, considering the speed of her courtship.

"I do not refute what you say, Arian, but with Jake, I…I know he is the one I am to be with. I knew it when he first opened his eyes and looked at me after Ethan rescued him. It was as if I was staring into a part of me that was missing but is now complete. After all that time, he was all that I could think about, and he felt the same. Once father gave his blessing and permitted me to cross the barrier, I knew it was destiny. When you consider all that had to come to pass for us to meet, and then meet again, what but fate could explain it? Dragos had to discover the portal, Ethan had to cross it, and Ethan needed to find the stone and free Amanda for her to recognize and retrieve it. Without any of these events, Jake and I would never have found each other or been able to meet again. Even mother has warmed to the idea and given me her blessing," Felicia said.

"If Felicia is impulsive, I am equally guilty," Amanda came to her defense.

"No, you and Tristan are…" Arian tried to defend her but couldn't judge her less harshly than her sister.

"We are just as guilty of being impulsive. Our courtship was nearly as swift. It is all surreal. First, I was falsely betrothed to Geoff, and then Alesha betrayed Ethan, and I was set free in his place. Your father brought me into your family, and now I am to truly be your sister. If you only knew my life before. I only wish my family could or would share my joy. Despite their madness, a part of me always clung to the hope they might change. Perhaps that is just part of my father that still lives within me. He always believed mother could be redeemed, despite all that she did to him," Amanda said, with Arian and Felicia bringing her into their embrace.

"Our brother has chosen his bride wisely." Arian smiled, wiping a tear from her eye.

"Valera may have taken Ethan from us, but I am glad to have you in his place," Felicia added.

"My freedom is a gift I will forever be grateful to Ethan for. I wish he could be here for our weddings." Amanda sighed sadly. Though she only met Ethan briefly, she felt she knew him for a lifetime. While other maidens looked upon him with a romantic interest, he felt more of a brother to her, and now, he would be a brother by marriage twice over.

"He will be here in spirit. Mother plans for one of us to visit him in Elysia once Alesha gives birth. He will be pleased to learn of you and Tristan, and Felicia and Jake," Arian said.

Amanda's eyebrows suddenly lifted, causing the others to look at her curiously.

"Our sister has returned." She smiled.

*****

They were greeted by two dozen royal guards outfitted with rifles at port arms, upon entering the courtyard, the men standing at attention on the palace green, attired in black wool trousers and shirts, with matching rimmed hats. Jerimiah stood before them, ordering them to attention as King Bronus led his procession through the gate. The king broke off from the column riding up to Jerimiah, who gave him a formal salute, Bronus returning the earth gesture, finding it oddly humorous.

"Captain Hansen, are your men ready?" Bronus asked.

"Aye, sir." Jerimiah turned back to his troop as the others filled in around Bronus to view the demonstration.

"Company! Port Arms! Order Arms! Right shoulder, Arms! Right Face! About Face!" Jerimiah marched the men about the courtyard, ordering them through their drill and ceremony with almost perfect execution, impressing Ben and the Judge. Jerimiah's father taught his son much of his military training having served in the Union Army after escaping slavery in the summer of 1861. His father continued in his service, joining the Ninth Cavalry Regiment in the fall of 1866, which brought him to west Texas, where his young son would eventually encounter one Jake Thorton.

After concluding the brief demonstration, Jerimiah brought his men back to their starting point, the royal guards facing their King proudly.

"Captain Hansen?" Ben asked, regarding Jerimiah's new title.

"Commander, First Astarian Ranger Company," Jake answered for him, drawing alongside his father.

"For your view, Sheriff. The men were handpicked by Captain Marco and myself, each eager to prove himself with the weapons you helped us acquire," King Bronus said, waving a meaty hand across the assemblage. The men were a mixed collection of knights, nobles, royal guards, and those recruited from Ethan's famed light cavalry, including former slaves, commoners, and landed peasants. What they had in common, was proven ability, character, and willingness to work as a team in an entirely new military unit.

"If Captain Hansen is anything like his father, your new company is in capable hands," Ben acknowledged, having known the elder Hansen when Jerimiah's father served in the Ninth Cavalry.

"They are right pretty, but can they shoot?" Judge Donovan asked.

"They can shoot, Judge, and are improving every day," Jerimiah said.

"Very good. Gentlemen, let us continue on, my queen awaits you," Bronus declared, leading them on toward the inner palace.

*****

Queen Gabrielle received them in the Great Hall, where hundreds of courtesans, nobles, knights, and ladies joined her in greeting the emissaries of Red Rock. Long tables were arranged to either side of the cavernous chamber, where the servants prepared to serve a welcoming feast for their guests.

Guests? Gabrielle mused, the word greatly understating who they were awaiting. The name Ben Thorton took on a personally great meaning to the Astarian queen. He was father to her daughter's future husband, and Ethan's surrogate father during his time in Red Rock, a painful time when she wondered whether he was dead or lost, receiving no word from him for over a year. She waited in the center of the chamber with Felicia, Arian, and Amanda beside her when her husband entered, with their guests following, along with Tristan and Jake. The musicians in the corner of the chamber, greeted their guests with their own rendition of the Yellow Rose of Texas, which Jake helped teach them. The simple but lively tune reminded her so much of Ethan, reminding her of how much she missed him.

The room grew deafly quiet as the tune ended, with the entire court looking on as King Bronus presented their guests to his queen. Gabrielle was taken aback by Ben Thorton, his weathered face and narrow eyes more resembling a bird of prey than the man she pictured as Jake's father. Every wrinkle spreading from the corners of his eyes, looked more like the scars from a thousand battles, each telling a story. The holstered pistol on his right hip was a grim reminder of his deadly skill, a skill that was once alien to her, and now all too familiar. Like the others that haled from across the barrier, he was immune to magic, projecting a mageless void the permeated the air around him. It was terrifying to behold, even more so than Jake or Jerimiah, the man's presence unsettlingly powerful. If Valera and Alesha's magic was all-consuming, Sheriff Thorton's lake of it was terrifying.

"Ma'am, it's a pleasure to meet Ethan's mother," Ben said, his smile strangely comforting considering the face that wore it. She could tell he was once a handsome man, his age well carrying the masculine lines of his youth.

"Sheriff Thorton, your legend precedes you," Gabrielle offered her hand, which he kissed the back of.

"Well, it's as clear as a California sunrise where your daughters got their fetching looks, ma'am," Andrew said, following Ben in greeting the queen.

"You are most kind, Judge Donovan. We are honored to receive you," Gabrielle politely said after taking a moment to discern his words. Now here was a man that looked exactly as she imagined. His boisterous voice and large size almost equaling her husband's. Like the sheriff, he wore a pistol and was dressed in a black overcoat, holding a black Stetson in his left hand.

"It is I who is honored, my fair Queen. I have had the esteemed privilege of your father's company for quite some time now. Like his grandson, he has quickly grown on me." Andrew nudged Dragos in the ribs, causing the Lord of House Mortune to grin, which caught Gabrielle off guard. She hadn't recalled the last time seeing her father so happy. She could see Jake off to the side, shaking his head, the gesture earning the young man her appreciation.

They continue with the others introductions. Spencer Lawton professed his deep admiration for Ethan, telling Gabrielle of the gunfight in front of the jail when Sam Shade held him hostage, and how Ethan helped Ben kill the man, saving his life. The tale did little to ease her worry, realizing the danger Ethan was in with every tale. She started to wonder just how many gunfights he partook in Red Rock? Where Spencer Lawton was an awestruck youth, his great uncle Gus was an ancient fossil. He looked older than an ancient tome, his face was wrinkled as age-old leather, with more teeth missing than he kept. Despite his barbaric appearance, Jake reassured her that old Gus was well-schooled in the operation of both their Gatling guns and artillery and would gladly help train their people in their proper use. Next was Long Paws and his fellow braves. Jake was kin to all of them, each distant cousins on his mother's side. Dragos informed her that they would be settling on lands tributary to House Mortune, explaining their precarious position in Texas. Gabrielle went on to introduce her daughters and Amanda to their guests, as well as the rest of the court.

Bronus ordered the festivities to commence, inviting all to eat and make merry. The musicians played an encore of the Yellow Rose, followed by a few Astarian melodies, and a beautiful rendition of the *Streets of Laredo*, which impressed their guests with its rich tone. Queen Gabrielle and King Bronus began the first dance, with their guests and members of the court following in kind, each trading off partners, with both Gabrielle and Bronus sharing a dance with most of their guests.

At the midpoint of the festivities, Gabrielle found herself paired with Jake, providing her a clear observance of his dancing skills. Though unfamiliar with Astarian customs and dances, he managed well enough to not crush her toes. He reminded her so much of Ethan, especially with his gentle charm and easy confident manner. She could tell by his interactions with Felicia that he truly loved her, by the small mannerisms that most would overlook. Whenever someone said or did something humorous, she was the first one he would share a smile with. It was a minor gesture, but she knew that one always looked to share their mirth with the one they most trusted and admired. It was one of many small interactions that confirmed their love, without having to use magic to read his thoughts, which would not work on an Earther.

"I am grateful for your welcoming my friends and father into your home, Your Highness," Jake said as they moved across the floor.

"It is we who are grateful for their help, Jake. With so many threats surrounding Astaria, your people have given us the one thing we are sorely lacking...hope."

"Guns against magic. We'll see which will prevail," he said.

"Your weapons are impressive, but alone they can be overcome by magic. Rather, it is those of you from across the barrier that will tip the scales if we battle Vellesia. Even at the Velo, Ethan's bullets could not penetrate mage shields. Only when he passed through their protective bubbles could he render the fatal blow. Your weapons will help with the dragon though. Our projectiles that are magic driven fall harmlessly away when thrown against them. Only common weapons can avail them, and none that we wield can penetrate their flesh. We can only hope that yours can," she said.

"If our rifles can't, I am pretty sure the Gatlings or artillery will, if the beasts will stay put long enough, but your people can use them as well as us."

"True, but your people have a decided advantage that we do not," she said.

"We do?"

"Dragon fire is magical and just as our magical weapons cannot avail it, so its fire cannot avail you, or so Amanda believes. Of course, we cannot test this theory until the danger arises." She sighed.

"From what you all have said, these dragons are drawn to magic. If that is so, won't they avoid those of us immune to it, going straight for the strongest magic users first?"

Gabrielle paused, her eyes briefly out of focus before responding, a knowing look passing her face. "Why hadn't we thought of that? That is brilliant, Jake." She gifted him the most beautiful smile.

He wasn't sure they were thinking the same thing but nodded in agreement anyway.

"Enough talk of war and preparations. Let us enjoy this time of peace and friendship," she said. "After the battle of the Velo, just before he went off searching for Luke Crawford, Ethan played a lovely song when we were alone, just the two of us. His voice was so rich and tender, it brought me to tears," she recalled wistfully.

"What kind of song?"

"One of yours, a lovely ballad of a lover's lament to their true love who is departing their beloved valley, forsaking them to their loneliness," she explained.

"*The Red River Valley*." He smiled knowingly.

"Yes. You know it then?"

"My mother used to sing it to my brother and I when we were children, to put us to sleep. I remember it well."

"Would you sing it?" She hadn't heard him sing, but he did possess a handsome voice to match his face.

"I could, but there is another guest who would do it justice, far better than I. Shall I fetch him?" He asked.

"Do so." She smiled, seeing him off as he went to find Spence Lawton, giving way to his father, who took his place dancing with the Astarian queen.

"Sheriff Thorton, a most welcome pleasure," she greeted, extending her hand which he kissed.

"As I said earlier, it is my pleasure to meet the woman who birthed the finest young man I have had the pleasure to know." Ben smiled easily.

"Besides his recklessness, I do hope he was well behaved in your keeping," she inquired.

398

"I think you know better than to ask that. Is there a more kind and generous soul than Ethan Blagen? The boy accounted well of himself. His only flaw would be his terrible card playing," Ben laughed at the memories.

"Do you know he referred to Red Rock as *Home*? It took me aback, hurting me in a very personal way, though he didn't mean to. Your small village gave my son something we could not…true freedom."

"You needn't fret none when it comes to his affections. Ethan missed you terribly and oft spoke of his wonderful mother."

"Perhaps then, but if you had seen the look he gave me before leaving with Alesha." She shook her head sadly.

"I learned long ago to never take to heart words spoken in duress. I've said more than my share of foolishness, especially during the war. But the harshest words are said to those we know love us because, deep down, we know they will still be there when the dust settles and will forgive us," Ben said.

She smiled at that, his words a balm to her wounded heart. She understood then why Ethan admired this man so. He was good and honorable, and admired Ethan in turn for who Ethan was, not for the title he was born to. Sheriff Thorton only knew her son as his deputy and friend, not as a Prince of Astaria. These were men who fought and bled together. Such bonds were stronger than blood. She noticed his gaze drifting to his right, where several Astarian lords gathered along the side of the chamber.

"Who is that tall fella with the red and white cape with a mop of brown hair?" Ben pointed out the lord in the middle of the gaggle looking back at him.

"That is Lord Torrent," she said.

"Is he kin to Vancel?"

"Yes, his father. Vancel has been helpful, I presume?"

"Very helpful. He's one of my deputies. He and Krixan are helping Skeeter uphold the law until I return. He is a good man and getting pretty fair with a gun," Ben said, having taken Vancel under wing since his arrival in Red Rock.

"Lord Vancel will be glad to hear of it. He is most concerned since three of his four sons are across the barrier, considering the danger they could be in."

"The only danger to those boys is the marriage nooses the Adams girl are fixin' to wrap around their necks." Ben snorted.

Gabrielle had heard such, fearing Lord Torrent's reaction. The great fear she shared with Lord Torrent was the nature of the off-spring of such a union. Would their children be immune to magic like their earth parent or be able to wield it like their Astarian parent? They would not know until a child was born of such a union. She wondered what would become of her grandchildren by Felicia, if magic held no effect on them? Could they allow their offspring to pollute Elaria? If the earther bloodline was too powerful, then all people would be corrupted by it, and in a thousand years, no one would wield magic. Being immune to magic protected you from being harmed by it, but it denied you all its benefits as well. Any child born defected or became injured could now be restored by a mage healer. That would no longer be true. She raised this concern with her father earlier in the night, and he merely smiled and assured her all was well, and that any children born of a union of Elaria and Earth would be subject to magic if born in Elaria and immune if born across the barrier. When she asked how he could know this, he just smiled and mentioned *rabbits*. Whatever he meant by it, she expected a full explanation when they had time to discuss it.

It was then, that Spence Lawton began to sing, the palace musicians following in tune with his rendition of the Red River Valley. The young man's voice possessed a rich timbre that echoed strongly through the ancient hall. Gabrielle noticed Ben's eyes gloss over with a faraway look.

"Something troubles you?" she asked.

"Just remembering." He smiled wanly.

"The song. Your wife often sang it," she said, recalling what Jake had told her.

"She did."

"We must teach it to Felicia so she might sing it for our future grandchildren as well," she smiled.

"That is something I would love to hear."

The festivities continued late into the night, with many a song and story shared by Texans and Astarians alike. Bronus took a liking to the Judge, Ben, Long Paws and Gus Lawton in particularly, the old rancher knowing more cuss words than a man had a right to. Bronus took great delight hearing how Ethan didn't take so well to liquor during his time in Red Rock, further proving his place as the greatest drinking man in Astaria. As many of the guests retired for the evening, Bronus led most of the men to the palace tavern in the cellars of the castle. Tristan and Jake eventually gave up once they passed midnight, neither able to keep pace with the old men.

"Off to bed with you lads," Bronus taunted them, raising his tankard high in the air to send them off. Long Paws and his braves, soon followed with Jerimiah and Spence Lawton soon after.

Bronus made Captain Marco stand atop the bar telling his part in the battle of the Velo, where he and Dragos led the light cavalry charge upon the enemy rear. Another round of ale was downed with that telling before Bronus asked Ben to share one of his stories. He went on to explain his role in the Chattanooga Campaign, and his battles with the confederates, with Gus Lawton voicing his displeasure at any mention of the Union. It didn't stop either man from downing more ale, emptying tankard after tankard, before Judge Donovan shared one of his stories, about a whaling crew that was beset by a vicious whale. Ben accused Andrew of simply retelling the story of Moby Dick, but the judge set him straight.

"The book was based on the Essex, Ben. This is the true tale of what happened. When I was wee lad working as a shipmate, every sailor in New England knew this yarn," Andrew explained.

Bronus and the others listened as Andrew detailed the harrowing story of a crew lost in the middle of the endless expanse of the Pacific Ocean.

Dragos followed that story with a yarn of his own, about two feuding clans that dwelt in the Vecara foothills, one renowned fire casters and the other ice mages. As with all of Dragos's tales, a dark story always ended with a humorous twist, causing them all to down another tankard. Bronus went to explain their toy making and distribution efforts, crediting Ben and the judge for inspiring Ethan to begin the tradition here in Astaria. Both Ben and Andrew were impressed by the scale of their operation, which was many thousand times greater than their original efforts in Red Rock.

And so it went until the wee hours of the morning, setting the precedent for the Texans' stay in Astaris, with every day ending with drunken revelry and bawdy tales shared by old men who still thought themselves young.

*****

It was well past midday the next day when Dragos finally roused from his slumber, finding an irate Gabrielle awaiting him at the breakfast table in the royal apartments. His disheveled appearance looked annoyingly similar to his usual state whenever he peered into his orb, with silver hair sticking out as if struck by a lightning bolt.

"Now, Gaby, don't give me that cross look." He raised his hands in surrender before she could start yelling at him for not acting his age.

"It is difficult enough to instill discipline in my children when my father acts like a child," she remarked as he took his seat.

"Child?" He raised a bushy eyebrow, refuting that notion.

"Child!" She reiterated, looking directly at the Stetson resting high on his brow, which matched his Texan attire. It was all very strange considering he spent most of his life wearing his azure robes with stars and moons decorated along their folds.

"I'll have you know that my attire is not childish but appropriate for a young man my age. The widow Perkins repeatedly commented on my fetching appearance," he said defensively.

"I wasn't speaking of your attire, Father, but your late-night carousing. Bronus is still asleep, snoring loud enough to wake the spirits."

"Now, Gaby, the lad was just showing our guests the hospitality of Astaris. It went far in building trust between our peoples. I must say, I now understand why Ethan took such a liking to Red Rock.

The town folk are right decent. It certainly stands in contrast to the pomp and pretentiousness of court."

"I needn't remind you that as a member of the royal family, pomp and pretension are the natural order of our lives." She took a sip from her goblet.

"It is more a detriment than asset. I must commend your husband on the abolishing of kneeling. It was an antiquated gesture that I am most pleased to bid farewell. I have to wonder if Ethan wasn't so opposed to it, if Bronus would have reacted differently upon seeing him humiliated by Valera?"

"Yes, seeing Ethan forced to..." Gabrielle's voice tightened, recalling that awful sight of her son kneeling to Alesha, and that collar affixed to his neck. "It was too much to bear." She looked away, bitterly swallowing another sip of wine.

"Ethan accomplished much of his destiny without even realizing it." Dragos gave her an encouraging smile.

"How so?"

"No man or woman kneels in Astaria. That is something he can take pride in, something he values strongly."

"Yes. He would be pleased."

"Of course, Gaby." He patted her hand.

It was then she noticed something unique in his clothing, wondering why she didn't think of it before.

"Gaby?" He again raised a bushy brow, wondering why she was giving him a strange look.

"Your attire matches the sheriff, as does all our men who have returned from Red Rock. Even Krixan was similarly dressed when he and Ethan returned just before the Velo," she observed.

"Yes, why do you ask?"

"Why then, does Ethan's clothes look nothing like yours? His trousers are like Long Paws and his kin, and his shirt is a simple pullover garment. The only similarity he shares with you is the hat and the weapons," she said.

"Gaby, even in Red Rock, Ethan lacked conformity. Take heart that he did not single out Astaris for his fashion rebellion." Dragos snickered.

"That boy." She smiled wanly, shaking her head. Suffice to say, she doubted he was given such liberty in Elysia. She could well imagine the attire he was forced to wear in Valera's court.

"Father, last night when I expressed my concern over the magical nature of any offspring Felicia and Jake may have, you dismissed my misgivings with the utterance of *Rabbits*. Whatever did you mean?"

"Your father, in his infinite wisdom, anticipated this question, Gaby," Dragos said in a long, drawn-out explanation, emphasizing his brilliance all too smugly. "As you well know, anyone native to Texas and all points from across the barrier, are immune to magic, much like Ethan, but in a more subdued nature. This magical immunity extends to all living things, as Ethan's horse could attest. Raw materials and inanimate objects, however, are subject to our magical powers, which explains why Ethan couldn't simply shoot through the mage shields at the Velo without first personally penetrating their protective barriers."

"Yes, this I already know."

"Of course, but it failed to explain what would happen should those who are from across the barrier copulate with someone from Elaria. Anticipating this dilemma when Bronus gave Felicia his blessing in her pursuit of Jake, I brought with me numerous rabbits to Red Rock. Once there, I conducted my research, crossbreeding native Elarian rabbits with Texas ones. Some were bred in Texas while others were brought across the barrier to Plexus. Some were conceived on one side of the barrier, and brought across to give birth on the other while the rest gave birth on the side they were conceived," he explained.

"And?" she asked, curious of the results, which he annoyingly delayed in giving, enjoying the delivery of his brilliance.

"Those both conceived and birthed in Plexus were subject to magic. Those either conceived or born at Plexus were not, as well as those both conceived and birthed in Red Rock. We can only surmise that Felicia and Jake must copulate and give birth here in Astaria. The only unanswered question is the strength of the magic of their offspring," Dragos revealed.

"That's if the same applies to people," she said.

"True, but with what we know, I would guess that it does. Also of interest is this. Breeding rabbits that are both from Texas, but doing so at Plexus, resulted in the offspring being subject to magic, and conversely, rabbits from Astaria bred in Texas, resulted in offspring immune to magic."

Gabrielle was taken aback by the revelation, pondering its meaning.

"What this means, Gaby, is that humans originated in Elaria or Earth, and found their way across the barrier, most likely thousands of years ago. The origin of the portals is as much a mystery, one we can only guess," he said, forking a slab of meat onto his plate.

"And what does that mean for us?"

"In the long term, I don't know, but for the present, you can be assured that any grandchildren of Felicia's will be fine as long as she remains in Astaria until the birth. As for immediate priorities, we have new weapons to test, and men to train, and Gorgencians to prepare for."

*****

The following days and weeks continued with the demonstration of the Gatlings and artillery, with steadily improved aim of the men they picked to operate them. Three days after their arrival in Astaris, Krixan's father, Kraxen Kraglar, arrived with most of his large brood, joining Bronus and his guests in their nightly revelry. Dragos took great delight in introducing Poker to his fellow Astarians, where Tristan and Bronus proved Ethan's bad luck did not transcend to the rest of House Blagen. Kraxen was proud to hear of his son's exploits in Red Rock, especially with his position as deputy, and keeping the peace in Ben's absence. Word had spread far and wide of Krixan's legendary deeds across the barrier and the Mage Bane, with bards singing of his bravery. It came to pass that Kraxen was finding himself referred to as Krixan's father rather than his title as arms master of Vectus and Commander of the city guard. The stories went far in encouraging every young man in Astaria to volunteer to cross the barrier, seeking glory in that far off land called *Texas*.

As the days of the royal wedding drew nigh, Bronus grew saddened knowing his new friends would have to soon depart. Ben and Andrew needed to return to Red Rock, though Gus Lawton and his great nephew would remain to help train their Astarian host in marksmanship. Amanda was most helpful, transferring the knowledge from their best students to all the soldiers in their companies. Ben also helped impart his knowledge on cavalry tactics to the men, especially Jerimiah and Captain Marco, who were selected to lead the two Astarian rifle companies.

Dragos had already ordered his vassals to prepare the way for Long Paw's tribe to settle on his lands. Sheriff Thorton thanked his friend for the kindness, holding a deep fondness for his late wife's kin. There were many other tribes displaced in recent years by the US government, as Ben explained to Dragos, causing the lord of Plexus to invite them as well to settle their northern lands.

"There are Apache, Navajo, Pueblo and countless others. They were all once great nations, and are now few and scattered. It is a shame, really, and most of them deserve better," Ben said one night when they were all deep in their cups in the palace tavern.

"I can give them land to call their own. All I would ask is that they don't harm our people and join us in war should Astaria fall under attack. The only foes for them to worry about would be the wildlife native to the Por-Shada, and any wild men that manage to cross the mountains, but the mountain range north of that region is thickest there," Dragos offered.

"That's right neighborly of you, Dragos." Ben was touched by his generosity.

"Bah, think nothing of it, old friend. There was a time, not long ago, that I would have offered that because you are all Ethan's friends. Now I offer it gladly because you are also mine." Dragos lifted his tankard, with Ben joining him. They found themselves alone in the corner of the tavern while Bronus, Andrew, Gus, Kraxen, and the others were sharing bawdy tales and crass jokes in the center of the tavern.

"There was a time I would have volunteered to help your kingdom because you are Ethan's kin, and now I gladly help you because you too, are my friends," Ben added, causing Dragos to grin.

"I haven't told my granddaughter this yet, but I want you to know. I intend to name Felicia my heir. She will be the Lordess of Plexus when I am gone. Jake will be her marshal, not her US marshal, mind you, but her guardian and protector, and most of all, her beloved. It will be my wedding gift to them. It should also encourage Long Paws and his people to know their distant cousin's children will rule the lands nearby," Dragos said.

Ben shook his head, not hardly believing all that had come to pass.

"Family," Ben said, patting Dragos on the shoulder.

"Family," Dragos returned the gesture.

*****

The day of the weddings finally arrived with the great houses of Astaria gathered in the palace for the ceremony. Many eagerly came to see the Texans they had heard so much about. Others came to see the Vellesian princess that won the heart of Prince Tristan and who aligned with them against her cruel mother. Others were curious of the famed Jake Thorton, renowned friend of Ethan, who won the heart of the fair Princess Felicia. It was the stuff of children's tales come to life, and the entire realm was caught up in the wonder of it all. Felicia's wedding was in the morning, and Tristan's at midday, with the evening reserved for endless celebration. Jake asked Jerimiah and Long Paws to stand as his companions while Felicia chose Arian and Ceresta, who would do likewise for Amanda.

As King, it fell to Bronus to oversee the official union, standing upon the raised dais in the Great Hall, with the bride and groom standing before him, their companions gathered to either side. Felicia's emerald gown matched her eyes, both sparkling radiantly in the spacious chamber. Jake stood in dark contrast with a black collared shirt tucked into black trousers and boots, with a tie down holster riding his right thigh. His attire was simple, yet imposing, looking like a knight without armor, or the need of it.

"As king of Astaria, it falls to me to join these two in perpetual union!" Bronus declared before the crowded chamber. "I don't know all the words I am supposed to say, but the meaning is clear. Jake Thorton, do you take this woman?" Bronus asked bluntly, causing his poor Gabrielle to nearly place a palm to her face.

"Yes!" Jake couldn't stop smiling.

"Good lad! And you, my baby daughter, do you take him?" Bronus asked, causing Felicia to blush with his childish endearment for all the realm to hear.

"Yes, father!" She smiled, shaking her head.

"Then you are wed!" Bronus placed Jake's right hand in Felicia's left.

The crowd gave a raucous cheer as the young couple looked out to the sea of friendly faces.

"What are you waiting for, lad, kiss her!" Bronus encouraged.

There, upon the dais of Astaris, Jake Thorton wed Felicia Blagen.

*****

It was midday when Amanda and Tristan ascended the dais, with Bronus joining them in blessed union with the exact same words he used with Felicia and Jake, despite Gabrielle scolding him beforehand on his mangling the ceremony, leaving out entire oaths of fidelity, loyalty and virtue.

"Bah, no one remembers all that silliness. All that matters is they agree and say yes," he told her before ascending the dais and beginning the ceremony.

Amanda stood opposite Tristan, dressed in a shimmering silver gown with voluminous sleeves, and a tight bodice ending at her waist where her skirts billowed freely to her slippered feet. A jeweled tiara nestled in her coifed hair, matching the necklace and earrings adorning her. Tristan couldn't stop smiling, regarding his bride with loving pride. He forsook his traditional vestment of doublet and hose, matching his father's attire of black trousers and shirt, with a sword riding his left hip.

Amanda swooned looking into his gray eyes, bewitched by his princely charm, struggling to glance elsewhere, her spirit captive to his own. She marveled at the change in atmosphere in Astaria, which was always far more inviting than her native Vellesia, but was now far different from before. There was almost a joyous brother and sisterhood among the people, an outpouring of generosity and dare she say, *freedom*. Was it Ethan's capture that brought about this transformation? Or something else? It manifested most strongly in the king, and from there filtered to all the realm. It then dawned upon her, that Ethan's values were now shared by all of Astaria, especially his love of freedom, which he sacrificed to spare his people and kin. She need look no further than King Bronus to witness this metamorphous. He was forever changed after seeing his son abased, the bitter scene melting the king's heart in a way nothing else could. Though he was pained by the memory, he also embraced life to its fullest now, outpouring his love and friendship upon the realm and especially on those Ethan held dear. The people of Red Rock were thus embraced by the king, as if their friendship brought him closer to Ethan in some way. Krixan likewise felt the king's affection. He was always seen as a third son to Bronus, but what he felt now was many times that. His affections also went strongly to Torg the blacksmith and Yance the woodcutter, the latter of which enjoyed the king's companionship every morn, chopping wood. Looking at him now, she realized how much she truly loved him as a father, replacing all that she lost with her own gentle sire. Astaria was her home now, and what a wonderful home it was, filled with people who loved her. She was so lost in her musings, she barely heard Bronus declare their union or even hear herself say yes to whatever it was he asked.

"Amanda," Tristan said, drawing her from her thoughts, before taking her into his arms.

"Your future queen!" Bronus declared proudly as the couple kissed, an emollient embrace met with thunderous cheers.

CHAPTER 20

Red Rock, Texas

Krixan snorted, holding the barrel of his Winchester up to the window, before setting it back on the desk and running the bore brush through it for a fifth time.

"I think you done it enough, big fella. How much cleaner can you make it?" Skeeter said, shuffling a deck of cards for another round of solitaire while sitting across him at Ben's desk.

"Bah, with all the dust in this town, I'll need to do it again before sundown," Krixan grumbled, exchanging the bore brush for a cleaning pad dipped in bore cleaner, running the rod through the barrel.

"Maybe not, Krix, looks like rain this afternoon if those clouds are anything to go by," Vancel said, looking out the second window on the other side of the door. His foot rested on the sill with his right elbow on his knee, with his black Stetson pushed back on his brow. In his short time in Red Rock, Vancel Torrent came to love the town and its people, enjoying his place as deputy sheriff alongside Krixan. No wonder Ethan remained here for over a year. Vancel thought about staying even longer, if his father would allow it. Unlike Ethan's father, Vancel's had means of finding him. He also thought of Sara Adams, worried that his father would disapprove of their courtship. His objections would center on her ability to give him heirs that could wield magic, but Dragos assured him before he departed that she could. How Dragos knew that, he could only guess, but figured it had something to do with the rabbits he'd been breeding. Vancel also felt relieved to be out from his father's scrutiny. As the heir of House Torrent, he was expected to project the authority of a great lord, often failing to meet his father's expectations. Though he was large, he was also clumsy at times, losing as many jousts as he won, despite years of tutelage. He was grateful for Princess Amanda's transferring Javier's knowledge to him, but the results were only slightly improved, with him taking only one in four bouts with his old friend before departing Astaris.

Vancel's fortunes and outlook changed, however, upon coming to Red Rock. Here, he was respected deeply, striking up a friendship with the Sheriff, Judge Donovan and Skeeter. He also was a quick learner with a rifle and pistol, which was unexpected considering his early struggles with the sword and lance. It was almost as if he was born for this land and this life. He loved the role of deputy, and the way his colt revolver hung on his right hip. His friendship with Krixan also strengthened during his time here. Though a son of a much lesser house in Astaria, Krixan was still Ethan's best friend, and a favorite of the king, which made his friendship an asset. It was also strange having someone so much larger than himself. Vancel was one of the largest lords in the realm, but Krixan stood a full head taller. Vancel also understood Krixan looked to him to help ease Ethan's absence. The big man would never admit it, but he missed Ethan terribly, as did many others, but none were as close as the two of them.

Vancel caught sight of young Billy Wells running up the street, heading straight for the jail.

"We have a visitor," Vancel said just as the boy burst through the door, shouting excitedly.

"Skeeter, John Custis sent me to fetch you!" Billy said.

"Settle down Billy, you know better than barging in heres without as much as knockin'. Now what's all the fuss 'bout?" Skeeter asked, coming to his feet, his old bones nearly creaking as he did so. As acting sheriff until Ben returned, the safety of the town rested in his hands, with Krixan and Vancel his only deputies.

"Strangers in town, Sheriff, two men in dark coats and bowlers sitting down at the *Lucky Star*, as if waiting for someone or looking for somethin'. He also gave me this to gives ya." Billy handed him a folded paper.

Lucky for Skeeter, John wrote in large block letters for Skeeter's old eyes. His eyes scrunched up upon reading its contents, alerting Krixan and Vancel that something was amiss.

"What's it say, Skeet?" Krixan asked, quickly sorting out his rifle in case it was needed.

"Says here there's more strangers poking around at Caleb Miller's place," Skeeter said, scratching his neck, trying to decide what to do, when Krixan loaded his rifle and put his Stetson on his thick head.

"Where you going?" Vancel asked as Krixan started for the door.

"To see what these fellers want!" he growled.

"Hold on there, big fella. Let me get my hat and shotgun before you go and scare the town all by your lonesome," Skeeter said.

"You best stay here, Billy." Vancel ruffled the boy's mop of thick hair, following his friends into the street.

*****

Trent Stroud and Henry Bartlet sat in the back corner table of the *Lucky Star,* their backs to the wall as they carefully watched the front door. Rumor had it that they sat the table where Conrad Finch met his end at the hands of Sheriff Thorton. The two men were careful not to repeat the outlaw's demise. Both wore matching dark suits, with handlebar mustaches and black bowler hats. Their tie-down holsters indicated their vocation as professional killers to those with untrained eyes that failed to look a little deeper.

"Would you, fellas, like another round?" John Custis asked from behind the bar, eyeing the strangers warily. Something about the men felt off to the bar owner, their attire and cool demeanor standing in contrast to the locals. There were three other patrons in the saloon, a Lawton ranch hand sitting at the bar, well into his fourth shot of whiskey, and two Astarian soldiers sitting at a middle table, dressed in local garb of brown trousers, gray shirts and black vests, with holstered colts riding their right hips. He had to confess, the Astarians had come a long way in their ability to blend in, even picking up passable Texan accents.

"No whiskey, just a beer," Trent Stroud answered, keeping his eyes to the door. Neither man would take hard liquor when they needed their wits. They awaited their colleagues, who were scouting the surrounding area, reporting any strange activity. Things were most queer in this small Texas town, drawing their employer's interest.

Movement at the swinging front doors caused both men's hands to drop to their holstered pistols as Krixan filled the doorway, the floor boards moaning under his massive weight. They thought to draw down on him, but the star on his vest gave them pause. Trent Stroud had known many a large man in his life, but none rivaled the mountainous human staring at him with his rifle barrel trained in their direction. Krixan stepped to the left as Skeeter and Vancel entered, Vancel going right with Skeeter making a straight line toward them.

"Good afternoon, Sheriff. How might we be of service?" Trent said, his pale-green eyes drawn to the severe squint in Skeeter's right eye.

"Acting sheriff. Thomas Smith is my name, stranger. Might I have yours?" Skeeter asked, keeping his sawed off shotgun barrel trained on their table.

"The name's Trent Stroud. My associate is Henry Bartlet. Would you care to aim your shotgun elsewhere?" he asked, warily eyeing Skeeter's finger in the trigger guard.

"Just as soon as you place your hands on the table, where we can see them, mister!" Krixan growled, taking a dangerous step closer.

"Easy, Deputy, we have no cause against the law," Henry said as they complied, placing their hands flat on the table.

"That's good ta hear, fellas, but the last gunman to ride into town came for one of our deputies, before he was shot dead," Skeeter recalled Ethan shooting Miles Stanton, the hired gun sent by Luke Crawford to kill him.

"Miles Stanton was no friend or associate of ours, Deputy Smith, I assure you," Trent said. "I believe the deputy in question was one Ethan Blagen. Might I inquire his whereabouts?"

"He's out of the area at this time. Now what business have ya in town?" Skeeter asked.

The two men shared a look before answering. "We are agents of the government, sent to inquire on the events surrounding the demise of the Grierson family," Trent said.

"Government men, huh." Krixan snorted, circling behind them, before reaching into Trent's inside jacket pocket, fishing out his billfold with his badge attached to it, tossing them on the table.

Skeeter stepped forward to examine the badge as Krixan backed a step, keeping his rifle on them.

"What is it Skeet?" Vancel asked, Skeeter trying to read the inscription, before Vancel stepped near, lending his younger eyes. "Pinkerton Lieutenant," Vancel said, eyeing the badge with an eagle atop of it, with its wings spread. Vancel was unfamiliar with the detective agency, wondering their purpose, but doubted they were up to much good by the sour expression on Skeeter's face.

"What possible reason would Pinkertons have here?" Skeeter said with the clearest voice Krixan or Vancel ever heard the mostly toothless deputy ever use.

"As we already said, to investigate the demise of the Grierson family. We are…," Trent began, but Skeeter was having none of it.

"Griersons don't warrant Pinkertons. Who sent you?" Skeeter asked. By reputation, the Pinkertons were allied with the abolitionist movement, and hunted down criminals throughout the west, but also served the interests of the banks and powerful industrialists, often putting down working men, which raised Skeeter's ire.

"Our employer wishes to remain anonymous and has contracted with our agency to bring the outlaw Luke Crawford and his associates to justice, *alive*, to stand trial in federal court," Lieutenant Stroud said.

"Crawford is dead. Killed by Ethan Blagen. I saw it done, so you can be on your way," Krixan said.

"Did he produce a body? What prof have you other than your word?" Henry Bartlet asked.

"Your proof is his word, and I reckon you should take it," Vancel said with a Texas drawl, interceding before Krixan ripped the man's head off.

"Fair enough, we shall leave town first thing tomorrow morning," Lieutenant Stroud said, knowing they'd get no more answers, at least not in town.

*****

The next morning, Krixan and Vancel waited outside town, picking up the two Pinkertons heading toward the Grierson ranch, keeping well out of sight, with a dozen Lawton and Miller ranch hands, and ten Astarian royal guard trailing them further back. The Astarians were decked out in cowboy gear, with chaps and six shooters, following the ranch hands' lead. They held far enough back to stay out of sight but close enough to help should the Pinkertons turn on them. Krixan sent outriders to the barrier fortifications to warn the commander there and look for any sign of Pinkertons spying their encampments. Whatever story the Pinkertons were saying didn't add up. He was anxious for Ben and the judge to return, as well as the reinforcements the king promised.

Krixan and Vancel halted atop a low rise overlooking the Grierson ranch, keeping within a copse of live oaks, well out of sight. Whatever drew the men to the Grierson ranch, they could only guess. With Hank Grierson's death and his son Nate in prison for attempted murder of Ethan, the property fell to the youngest Grierson, Cole, who was barely a man. With most of the remaining ranch hands abandoning him, and Emmitt Cobb a fugitive in the Mage Bane, he was left with a fry cook and two wranglers. From his vantage point, Krixan couldn't see any sign of Cole or his men. The ranch house looked disturbingly quiet, with nothing coming from its chimney, and the barn doors barred. A handful of horses were tied off to the hitch post in front of the house, all saddled and waiting. He watched as the two men stopped and tied off theirs as well before

415

going inside. Whatever they were doing, it wasn't good, as much as Krixan could tell. He signaled the others forward, sending half of them in a wide arc to approach the house from the back, before moving closer behind a lonely oak, calling out to the ranch house from a hundred yards.

"Stroud! Come out with your hands high for me to see them!" Krixan shouted, his booming voice carrying well over the distance. The Miller ranch hands aligned to either side of Vancel with their rifles out, sitting their saddles, their horses shifting underneath them. The Astarians and Lawton ranch hands were in position behind the house. After several minutes, the front door slowly opened, with Trent Stroud steeping out, pistol in hand, his own rifle still tucked in his saddled horse off his right.

"What's this about deputy? You have no cause to question me!" Trent shouted back.

"Stand clear and bring out the Grierson boy!" Krixan ordered.

"He doesn't wish to speak with you, Deputy!" Trent shouted back, taking a step toward his horse, while two others emerged from the home, dressed in similar suits and bowlers, with tied down holsters.

"That's far enough!" Krixan warned before all three Pinkertons rushed toward their horses retrieving their rifles from their saddles while the three windows on the second floor of the house opened up.

Bang! Bang!

The sound of rifle fire broke the stillness of the morn, a bullet striking the ranch hand off Vancel's right, taking the man in the left shoulder. Vancel snatched the man's reins, ordering his men to take cover, with bullets flying left and right, and overhead.

Krixan's horse shifted behind the thick oak, bullets stripping bark off the edge of its trunk. He quickly dismounted, taking position behind the tree's opposite side, fixing his aim on the first target his sights found, squeezing off a round as the man was reaching for his rifle. The shot missed overhead, punching through the window behind the man. Krixan thought to aim lower but didn't want to hurt the horse. As much as Ethan was fond of Bull, Krixan felt affection for all horses. He had no qualms killing bad men or mean-spirited people, but horses and dogs held a special place in his heart, and he wouldn't shoot them unless necessary. He quickly worked the lever action of his Winchester, sending more rounds down range, one of them finding purchase in the man's left hip as he neared the doorway, trying to take cover. Other rounds from the miller ranchers behind him, struck the Pinkerton's back, dropping him in the middle of the doorway.

The crack of rifle fire sounded behind the Grierson house, signaling that the Lawton and Astarian men were now engaged. The responding fire from the house, made Krixan wonder just how many men were inside. He winced, a bullet striking the tree above his hat, showering his Stetson with splinters. His horse snorted loudly behind him, a bullet punching through its hindquarters. Krixan spared a glance, enraged to see his trusty mount sagging before another bullet took it through the breast, dropping it.

"Enough!" he growled, taking aim at the center second-story window, fixing his aim to the right where the shadow indicated his target.

Bang! Bang! Bang!

He worked the lever action, sending three rounds around the edge of the window, before shifting aim, unable to see his target slip to the floor.

Vancel grunted in frustration, trying to keep a high rate of fire to cover Krixan, who was far more exposed, squatting behind the lonely oak forward of their position. With his horse down, Krixan had no means of a hasty retreat. He could see the silhouette in the upper middle window drop, Krixan managing to hit him, when he was struck with an idea.

"Listen up, fellas! Everyone aim for the upper left window! Let's concentrate on one target at a time!" Vancel ordered, working his lever, striking the edge of the sill, the others showering bullets all around the window. There was inherent risk in such a strategy, for it allowed the other Pinkertons time to target them in turn.

After several minutes of heated fire, three Pinkertons burst from the front door, mounting their horses and riding off to the east, leaving several of their comrades behind, each laying down heavy fire, giving their fleeing friends time to escape. Vancel ducked behind the trunk of the oak, a bullet striking perilously close, sending splinters into the back of his right hand. He recovered, taking aim at the fleeing foe, his shots finding purchase in the back of one of them, the fellow leaning severely in the saddle, before falling off into the grass, short of a creek bed, his comrades continuing on without looking back.

"Keep up the fire!" Vancel shouted, mounting his own horse to pursue the escaping men.

"I'm with ya!" Joel Upton said, a lean, grizzled ranch hand, whose face looked older than his thirty years.

Vancel wasn't foolish enough to turn down his help, the two men racing far around the house, keeping further out of aim of the Pinkertons held up inside. Once beyond the creek bed, they were joined by five Astarian riders coming from the opposite direction. One of the Lawton ranch hands sped off toward the McPherson ranch, which was the nearest spread, to recruit help while the others kept up their attack.

Krixan growled a few expletives watching Vancel ride off chasing the others, the fool reminding him too much like Ethan with his recklessness. He would be sure to remind Vancel that he didn't have Ethan's luck. The last thing he wanted to do was explain to Lord Torrent how his son met his end chasing after outlaws or even outlaws with badges. Why Pinkertons decided to open fire on them was one question he wanted to know. There was obviously more to this than their claim of hunting Luke Crawford. He wouldn't be getting any answers until he ended this fight. With that in mind, he kept up his fire on the upper right window, his next shot striking a man in the elbow.

*****

Vancel leaned with the turn of his horse, a spirited appaloosa with a black speckled white coat, who was as obstinate a horse as any he ever knew. They skirted a line of scrub brush, the others hot on their tail, before coming upon a wide patch of open ground with a copse of trees up ahead, where their prey passed within.

Vancel had a sudden feeling similar to the Velo when they charged the Meltorian center, only to smack headlong into a shield wall, before greeting a host of fire mages tearing them to shreds. He didn't have time to order halt before rifle fire cut down Joel's horse off his left, the beast dipping head first in the tall grass, throwing Luke overhead. Vancel turned sharply right, a bullet grazing his appaloosa's tail. Another bullet took an Astarian trailing him, through the right shoulder, flipping him off his saddle, the fall breaking his other arm for good measure. Vancel dismounted, letting his mount run free. He made his way south, following an uneven terrain where the brush line met a high rocky patch that looked akin to miniature ridge. It allowed him to skirt the battlefield unseen as bullets flew back and forth to his immediate north, his comrades getting the bad end of the exchange. After a time, he chanced a peak above the small ridge, seeing the two Pinkertons positioned behind thick trees. The one furthest north was too well concealed, but the one closer knelt with his right leg exposed as he leaned around the tree.

Vancel recalled what Sheriff Thorton said about shooting, to aim at the center of whatever you could see. If it was only a hand, aim for the center. If all you could see was an arm, take the elbow.

"The knee it is," Vancel whispered, squeezing off a round.

The man immediately cried out, the bullet punching through his upper thigh. A second shot went through his middle as he writhed on the ground. Everything went quiet for a desperately long time until his comrades started making their way forward. Vancel slowly stood, approaching from the south, joining them as they entered the tree line. Once there, they discovered the still corpse of Henry Bartlet, the other Pinkerton gone, along with both horses.

"How many horses we have left?" Vancel asked Joel Upton, who was kneeling within the tree line, looking for sign.

"Two. The bastards shot the rest," the ranch hand growled, looking northeast where the tracks led.

Vancel sent one horse back to the Grierson ranch to fetch more horses, and the other to town with the severely wounded Astarian rider. Doc Wilson would have to patch him enough before transporting him back through the barrier, where several mage healers were waiting on the other side. The injured Texans would have to get by with the Doc's treatment. Vancel quickly searched Bartlet's corpse, finding a bundle of papers which he took.

*****

It was well past noon when Krixan approached the long silent ranch house, moving in concert with the small army now at his disposal, including ranch hands from the Lawton, Miller and McPherson ranches, and the Astarian cavalry. Gabe McPherson brought nearly two dozen men, along with his three sons. They pounded the ranch house with relentless fire until it grew deathly still. They were wary it was a trick by the Pinkertons, who could always open fire once they moved forward in the clear, but Krixan trusted his numbers, with dozens of guns covering the front as he moved forward. Gabe McPherson and one of his men stood to the left of the front door, and two Miller men to the right as Krixan kicked in the door, snapping it from its hinges. Both sets of men stormed through, each button hooking left and right, sweeping the main room as Krixan covered the middle.

Across the main floor, they found an overturned table and the bloody corpses of Stone Grierson and his ranch hands, each bound with their throats slit. Stone's body looked recently expired, severe bruising visible across his face. His shirt was torn open, with apparent burn marks dotting his chest and belly, most likely caused by cigar butts. Whatever the Pinkertons wanted, they thought Stone might know. They found the bodies of two Pinkertons on the main floor, and three more upstairs, one of which was still breathing, a man with light brown hair, who appeared midtwenties, with a neatly trimmed beard and haunting brown eyes. The man's eyes fluttered open as Krixan entered the second floor bedroom, staring in disbelief at the sheer size of the giant stepping near him, where he lie beside the window, his back against the wall, blood pooling through his shirt.

Krixan picked up the man's rifle resting near his feet, tossing it on the bed, before taking his pistol, and ripping his shirt open.

The bullet went clean through his side, but the amount of blood meant something vital might have been struck. Krixan wound the man's shirt around his middle, tying it off as tight as he could, before throwing him over his shoulder like a rag doll.

"Search all their bodies for everything, especially papers!" Krixan ordered the others upon descending the stairs.

*****

It was nearly dusk when they all returned to town. Doc Wilson was called to the jail to patch up their lone prisoner, the cell thick with chloroform as he tended the wound. Vancel already organized a posse to hunt down the one that got away, which they guessed to be Lieutenant Stroud, since he wasn't among the dead. Skeeter deputized several of the Lawton ranch hands until the Sheriff returned, however long that would be. He and Krixan waited for the Doc to finish his work, each sitting at Ben's desk when the bushy mustached Doc stepped from the back cell area of the jail, wiping the sweat from his aging forehead.

"How's it look, Doc?" Skeeter asked.

"We'll see if he makes it to morning. Just keep an ear out. He'll probably be thirsty. I'll be back after sunup. Any problems throughout the night, come and fetch me. I already said the same to Matt Davies," he said, regarding the Miller ranch hand that took a bullet in the shoulder. He did the best he could to patch him up. The bullet went clean through, but only time would tell if he made a full recovery. The wounded Astarian was patched up and sent on toward the barrier. The Doc shook his head at that convenience, constantly reminding the Astarians of their good fortune should their wounds not be quickly fatal.

*****

It was three days later when Sheriff Thorton and Judge Donovan rode into town with a sizable escort. Ben was already apprised of the situation upon clearing the barrier, making his way straight for the jail where Krixan and Skeeter were waiting. Vancel and the posse had yet to return. The telegraph wires were cut somewhere outside town before the battle at the ranch ensued, so no word could be readily sent to Abilene, El Paso, or anywhere else Trent Stroud might've fled to.

"You're a sight for sore eyes, Ben," Skeeter's voice whistled upon his entering the jail.

"Where is he?" Ben cut to the chase, with both men pointing to the rear corner of the jail.

"He ain't said but three words in as many days," Skeeter said, as they followed him to the back cell area of the jail, the prisoner resting in the one to their immediate left, staring back at them with his haunting brown eyes, and pallid lips. The man looked more corpse than a killer, lying motionless on his cot, with only the movement of his eyes proving he was still breathing.

Krixan handed Ben the man's badge and billfold, counting over eighty dollars, a sizable sum to be carrying about unless one had a long journey to take. He found a weathered identification card with the man's badge, identifying him as Charles Blake, a native of Chicago.

"Nothing to say, Charles?" Ben asked, his rough voice even causing Krixan to flinch. He'd never seen Ben so irate.

Silence.

Ben handed the documents to Skeeter before unlocking the cell door and stepping inside.

"I've known enough Pinkerton's in my day to know they wouldn't send this many of you all the way to West Texas to inquire about an outlaw they knew full well wasn't here. I can't see them ordering you to torture and murder the Grierson boy either," Ben said, his words having little effect on the man, so he continued.

"I met Allan Pinkerton back in '65. He was an honorable man, abolitionist and a good lawman. He would never sanction what you did if he was still alive, which means his fool sons did or are ignorant of who ordered it. Your agency has increasingly become the muscle of the railroads and banks, a far cry from true law and order," Ben said, knowing such monied interests were just larger criminal gangs with the law backing them, buying up judges, politicians, and prosecutors to serve their bidding.

Still nothing.

"Either you're doing what your bosses tell you or whoever hired you. I suggest you start speaking," Ben warned in a dangerously low voice.

Nothing.

"I'm figuring you think your Pinkerton friends, or whoever hired you, will have a federal judge they bought off send me a telegraph ordering your release or transfer to an agent in their employ. I have some sad news for you, son. Our telegraph is down, and even if it wasn't, you won't live long enough for it to reach us if you don't start talking. Your silence leaves me with two choices. One is an immediate jury trial, whose members are all kin or close friends of the men you shot or shot at. We can wrap that up in a matter of a day and hang you by nightfall. I'll have my deputy arrange the hanging, not the big fella here but that one." Ben jerked a thumb at Skeeter. "He is known to make mistakes from time to time. It would be a right shame if your drop wasn't arranged right. I'd hate to see you dangling there, strangling slowly. I seen that once, poor wretch kicked for five minutes before expiring." Ben let that possibility hang in the air before giving him the second alternative.

"The second choice is for me to get right careless with your security. It would be a shame if my late wife's Kiowa kin got ahold of you. They have creative ways for a man to die. Some are pretty lengthy." Ben let Charles's imagination do the rest.

"If I talk, I am dead anyway," he groaned.

"Not necessarily. You tell me what I want to hear, I know a place where you will be beyond the reach of the Pinkertons or whoever hired you."

"There is no such place anywhere between the Atlantic and Pacific," Charles grumbled.

"Maybe not, but that's not where you'll be going." Ben looked over his shoulder at Krixan, who crossed his arms, nodding in agreement.

"You offering me a prison, or freedom?"

"Let's just say you will be a *guest* of my friends."

"I have your word?" Charles asked.

"My word is my oath. If a man doesn't have at least that, he's not a man," Ben said.

"My word is also my oath, and I gave mine to my employer. Now my word is worth spit, but I'll take you for yours," Charles offered his hand, which Ben shook.

"All right, Charles. Let's hear it."

"We were contracted by a man named Anson Prescott, a financier from New York. He had an arrangement with Hank Grierson to partner over a silver mine located in this town, which the town folk knows nothing of. Since Grierson never shared its exact location, Mr. Prescott thought his son would know. If the boy knew anything, he'd have said so after the beating Stroud gave him," Charles said.

"Hank Grierson's been dead going on two years. Why come here now?" Ben asked.

"Anson Prescott is financially stressed as far as we can tell, though he was smart enough to make sure we were paid. He thought Grierson's silver story was likely a tall tale until the recent purchases of heavy armament to one Gus Lawton. Why else would a rancher need artillery and gatlings," Charles explained.

And there they had it. The recent purchases by the Astarian king raised prying eyes back east. This coupled with this yarn about a local silver mine made all too much sense why a wealthy financier back east would start snooping around.

"When we discovered the mine in full operation along the Pierna Mala, we knew the story was true," Charles's words froze Ben in place. The heavily fortified barrier entrance would easily be mistaken for a silver or gold mine. If word got out, Red Rock would be swarmed with prospectors and fortune seekers trying to make a claim. Once they stumbled upon the truth, Katie bar the door.

"Why hunt for Luke Crawford then?" Krixan asked.

"Because they believed he might know where this silver mine was," Ben said.

"What should we do, Ben?" Skeeter asked.

"We get him out of here. Dragos should still be at Plexus. Need to send word to Jake. If he's going to turn in his badge in person, now's a good time as any. Meanwhile, I want Gabe, Bill, and Caleb here before sundown. We have a lot to discuss,. Ben named the heads of the McPherson, Lawton, and Miller families. "Skeeter, fetch the judge while you're at it."

CHAPTER 21

Two moons hence
Elysia

Alesha sat regally upon the throne, her mother standing beside her, guiding her as she held court. She spent the better part of the morning dealing with petitioners, mostly nobles from different territories whose only recourse was through royal appeal. Most were petty but required the impartial hand of the queen to decide. The afternoon was spent with ministers of the realm. The minister of agriculture detailed the plans for the planting season, discussing crop yields, with plans to improve less productive regions.

The minister of health reported infectious outbreaks in the Celovar region. Alesha ordered additional mage healers to squash the disease before it could spread. The minister of trade followed, reporting successful agreements with Cordova and Valconar, both happy to establish ties with Ethan's new kin. Lord Darcannon, the Sea Lord of Valconar, provided a gift to House Loria of twenty casks of Polantis wine to honor Ethan and Alesha's wedding.

"Send Lord Darcannon our deepest gratitude. I remember well the friendship his brother provided myself and my consort during our desperate flight from the Mage Bane," Alesha declared, fondly recalling the charismatic Jorus Darcannon.

"Of course, Your Highness. I shall convey your gratitude and salutations." The trade minister bowed and withdrew.

Alesha ran her fingers over her growing womb, Gabrielle's power flowing through her, feeling its growing potency. Thoughts of her daughter one day sitting here as crown princess, whilst she sat as Queen Daughter, brought a smile to her lips. She wondered what she would look like. Would she have Ethan's sea-blue eyes or her golden pools? Would she favor Ethan's easy charm? Would she have Alesha's black hair or her namesake's auburn tresses?

You will be loved, little one, she mused. Thoughts of Ethan came to mind, as they always did when she touched her womb. Every night, he would rub her belly and kiss it gently, whispering to their unborn child. He would sing her lullabies every night, the sound of his voice calming mother and daughter alike. Alesha knew that she could never truly harm Ethan's father for his disobedience. She knew Ethan had come to realize this as well. Ethan was now bound to her with stronger bonds, bonds neither of them could escape. He was hopelessly drawn to her, and she to him, neither able to fight what fate ordained. Neither seemed to mind, apparently, each seeking comfort in each other's arms. Ethan might still long for his precious freedom, but his body spoke otherwise.

She wondered what he was doing at this moment, causing her to reach out to her grandfather Corbin, whom she knew was in his presence. She could see through his eyes, using a mage power that all members of House Menau possessed. She smiled, seeing Ethan and his *Elves* gathered in the armory around their favorite workbench. They were telling stories, by the look of it, while polishing armor, the sight warming her heart. The tranquil vision quickly soured when Lord General Faro entered the throne room, short of breath, his red serge cape billowing in his wake.

"My Queen!" Faro prostrated himself before the throne, pressing his head to the floor.

"What is the meaning of this?" Valera spoke sternly, stepping in front of the throne, shielding Alesha with her presence.

"My Queen, we received a missive from a border post along the Iona Divide," the lord general said, raising his head just high enough to speak.

"Rise and report, my lord!" Valera declared.

General Faro gained his feet, his armored boots making an audible clang on the mirrored stone floor. The man struck an impressive

427

pose, with thick auburn hair framing his steel jaw. He was dark of complexion, with a towering frame and build.

Alesha paled, reading his thoughts before he revealed the contents of the missive.

"The commander of the Iona garrison reports grim tidings, my Queen. A large host has crossed the boundary into Vellesia from the wilds."

"How large of a host?" Valera asked.

"They placed the number at over two hundred thousand, but it could be higher, much higher, my Queen," Faro said, though there was much more he needed to add to impart the gravity of the situation.

Valera could easily dispatch the number as any barbarian host likely had no mages in their disordered ranks. A sweep of lightning from her fingers could end them with ease. No, there was more to this report, and she ordered Faro to continue.

"They have a *dragon*!" Alesha echoed behind her, her words having the expected result on the court, as hundreds of voices erupted into debate.

"*Silence!*" Valera ordered, her thundering voice nearly sending the congregants to their knees. "How is this possible, Lord General?" Dragons could not pass into Vellesia without compromising the anti-magical barrier that guarded the realm for thousands of years.

"The barrier has fallen, my Queen. The barbarian host destroyed the barrier markers along the Iona Divide, opening a fissure large enough for the dragon to follow."

"If true, how were they able to bend a dragon to their will?" Valera's eyes burned like embers.

"The commander did not say, my Queen," Faro admitted sadly.

Whether the barbarians controlled the dragon or were merely following in its wake, they could only guess.

"The last portion of the missive states that the barbarian host had surrounded our border post," Faro added.

"Call a council of war, Lord General. Do so immediately!" Valera commanded, dismissing the court.

*****

News of the dragon swept through the palace like fire through dry grass. Only the Lorian Order kept the populace from panicking. Vellesia hadn't suffered an invasion in centuries and never faced a dragon. Oh, there was the occasional dragon testing the barrier along the northern border, but none met with success, save for the region of Carea, where part of the barrier grew weak overtime, allowing dragons to raid partially into the territory, and even slay the local baron during the previous spring. That was as far as any dragon threatened Vellesia in thousands of years since the mage lords of old constructed the barrier that guarded the mage realms.

The early evening found Alesha, Valera, and Corella gathered in the great room of Elysia, where their war council convened. Mother Evalena stood at the head of the map table, with her fellow mothers to either side. Lord General Faro stood halfway along the table to her right, holding an iron pointer, touching different parts of the map, reporting the disposition of their armies. The garrison General of Elysia and the entirety of Faro's war council, gathered around the map table as well, each answering the Queen Mother and Daughter's questions.

"The last report places the enemy host here," Faro touched his pointer to the fortress of Gallot, centered along the Iona Divide.

"Gallot has likely fallen, and we should plan accordingly," Corella stated coldly.

"They might endure if not for the dragon. Gallot was built to withstand a force the size of the one reported," Alesha said.

"Perhaps, but we must assume the worst. We must look to the next defensible position," Corella said, turning her gaze to the Lord General.

"Assuming the barbarians have control of the dragon, then Gallot is certain to fall. That would leave the Vang-Shar Mountains as the next natural barrier between them and Elysia," Faro said, running his pointer along the mountain range that ran along the north-west border of the realm.

"That is if Elysia is their objective," Corella pointed out, uncertain of the enemy's intentions. Once past the barrier, they could just as easily turn west toward Gorgencia, or southwest toward the sea, raiding the border regions of Vellesia, Gorgencia, and Sarcosa.

"We must assume the worst, that Elysia is their target," Valera said, drawing Faro's pointer from his hand, levitating it above the map, touching it to the two glaring gaps in the Vang-Shar Mountains.

"Castara is the nearest point to cross the Vang-Shar," Valera pointed out the palace resting in the Castaran Gap, northwest of Elysia. "Should the enemy seize it, the way would be open to the Salnar Mountains and Elysia. If not, then the next place to cross over the Vang-Shar is hundreds of leagues southwest at Lavera."

"We must marshal our strength and meet them before they advance into Vellesia proper. We must not yield any of our land," Mother Evalena declared emphatically.

"I would advise against that, Mother," Corella politely said. "Dragons are drawn to magic and would slay any mages within our army at the outset. Our armies are unprepared to fight without the guidance of mages. Meeting them upon the open plains south of Iona would be unwise."

"Would allowing them to raze our lands be preferable?" Evalena countered.

"We cannot openly face a dragon. Our powers are useless against it," Valera said before tapping the pointer over the Castaran Gap. "It is here, where we shall concentrate our forces. Perhaps…"

The sound of arguing and raised voices in the outer corridor interrupted Valera's explanation, annoyance showing visibly in her scowl.

"Out of my way!" a familiar voice growled, followed by a heavy thud sounding just beyond the door.

"Be still!" Alesha ordered the guards to stand down as they started to move to the door.

Ethan drew every eye in the chamber upon entering, clad in his buckskins and Stetson, with his holster tied down on his right thigh, and his father's sword upon his left. His strange attire and boldness caught everyone off guard, save Alesha and Valera.

"Ethanos, why have you come here unbidden?" Corella asked sternly, displeasure evident in her silver eyes.

"Kneel in the presence of the queen!" the guard nearest him ordered, his hand on the hilt of his sheathed sword.

"I won't be kneeling today," Ethan backed the guard up with a hard look in his eyes.

"Ethan, you don't belong here," Alesha warned, a sense of dread washing over her.

"I think I do," he said, his eyes sweeping around the table, the queens and mothers looking at him as if he'd grown a second head.

"Remove your holster and return to your chambers until I decide your punishment for this brazen act!" Corella ordered.

"I don't think so," he answered calmly.

"You don't think so? You assume much, child!" Mother Evalena snarled, her eyes ablaze with fury.

"Probably," he said, shrugging off the comment.

"Ethan…," Alesha warned before he cut her off.

"You know, for a House with a reputation for intelligence and cunning, you sure have your collective heads up your ass on this one." He lifted his open hand toward the map.

He felt the heated glares of everyone in the room bearing down on him with that flippant remark.

"You have managed to break every vow you swore to in Astaris in the moments since you entered this chamber, Ethanos. Need I remind you of the consequences of such insolence?" Valera warned.

"I know," he waved her off, the gesture only inflaming her further as he continued. "But any threat to my father won't really matter though if you go ahead with your current plans."

"Explain!" Mother Porshana commanded.

"None of you has any hope of defeating a dragon. They have anti-magic and attack any mage they see or sense. They will kill any of you foolish enough to lead an army against them. Once you are dead, the dragon will burn a path through Vellesia, with the barbarian host following in its wake. Without your magic, your armies will melt away. They haven't fought a war in centuries, and I'd bet they are completely dependent on your magic to win their battles."

"You dare insult your queens, Vellesia, and our armies?" Lord General Faro rose up in indignation, his nostrils flaring so hard, Ethan thought he might fly away.

"I've fought in many battles, General, have you?" Ethan's comment was like oil to flame, with General Faro ready to explode.

One look around the table forced Ethan to further explain himself before he ended up in the dungeon, or worse.

"It's not your fault, General, for not having experienced war. It's normally a good thing. Peace is wonderful, but these aren't normal times. None of you can face the dragon, but...I can."

His words stilled their anger, each reacting to his declaration.

"*ABSOLUTELY NOT!*" Alesha snapped.

"Alesha, I have to," he said gently, his blue eyes softening meeting hers.

"As your wife, I might indulge your bouts of mischief. As your crown princess, I do not. Guards, disarm my consort and escort him to my chambers. See that he remains there until I say otherwise."

"Belay that order!" Corella commanded, freezing the guards before they could take a step.

"Grandmother?" Alesha questioned the Queen Mother.

"There is merit to what the boy is saying. I will hear him out."

"Ethanos belongs to me. I have final authority on what he is or is not allowed to do," Alesha said in a dangerous voice.

Corella gave Alesha an icy glare that almost made Ethan flinch.

"You command Ethanos, and I command you, Alesha. Remember that. I will hear what Ethanos has to say," Corella said.

"I will not allow him to leave Elysia. His place..."

"His place is where I say it is, child!" Corella corrected her.

Alesha struggled to quell her pounding heart, visions of Ethan dying playing over and again in her mind. She turned sharply to Corella, tempted to enter her thoughts before stopping herself. She swore not to use her newfound powers on her family, but oh, how she was tempted. Even if she bent Corella's mind to her will, she would likely have to do so with everyone present, and that was something she was unwilling to do. Once you went down that path, there was no turning back. Instead, she sat there helplessly as Ethan explained his plan, winning converts to his cause with his every utterance. *Damn him!* she cursed.

"Send word to the armies in the field to *not* engage the enemy outright," Ethan continued.

"That will open us to invasion!" Faro huffed, taken aback by such preposterous counsel.

"Until you know their direction of travel and their control of the dragon, you cannot engage them head-on, General. Order whatever forces you have between Gallot and Castara to the east side of the Vang-Shar. Have them destroy everything in their path. Burn the crops, poison the wells, destroy everything of use to the enemy," Ethan said.

"Destroy our own lands?" Mother Veriana asked doubtfully.

"You have magic to restore your land. They do not. If the reports are true, the enemy host is massive. An army that size requires drawn out logistical chains unless they live off the land, so you must deny them the land, and attack their lines of supply. Do you have light cavalry or only heavy horse?" he asked the lord general.

"Two thousand light cavalry at Lavera, though they are newly formed," Faro said, Ethan's argument starting to sway him.

"How newly formed?" he asked, not liking the way Faro said *Newly.*

"Ninety days," Faro said.

"Ninety days? You must've thought of building a light cavalry only recently." He removed his Stetson, dropping it on the table while scratching his head.

"Your victory at the Velo convinced us of the wisdom of it," Alesha said, recalling the effectiveness of the light cavalry that her aunts reported on. It took Ethan years to turn his peasant recruits into an effective fighting force. This cavalry would be nearly useless at this stage unless...

"Are they ready?" He might as well ask.

"They are. Magic allows us to train men rather quickly," Valera explained, which meant they transferred memories from experienced

433

riders to their recruits, shortening their learning curve. That was a magical ability only House Menau possessed, though Dragos was able to do so in a limited capacity with language. Alesha's aunts were busy women by the sound of things.

"I would send them north, along the west side of the Vang-Shar. If the enemy breaks east for Castara, they will be positioned to cut their supply trains. If the enemy continues south, order them to split, with one half skirting the enemy host, maneuvering to their rear, while the rest destroy everything in the enemy's path," Ethan said, his plan earning approval, if the looks many of them were giving were an indication.

"I see the wisdom in your plan but cannot allow our soldiers to destroy our own lands," Mother Evalena stated firmly.

"It's not an easy choice, but it would be worse for your own lands to be used against you. If you drop a sword, isn't better for it to break, then be picked up by your enemy?" Ethan asked.

"Whether we agree with Ethan's plan or not, the important question that needs answering, is if the barbarians control the dragon or are merely following in its wake," Valera said, her eyes narrowed surveying the map.

"If they don't, the dragon could roam far afield. It would be free to attack anywhere in the mage realms," Mother Clarisa said.

"That would make it far more difficult to find and kill, but then you would be able to destroy the barbarian host quite easily with your magic," Ethan pointed out.

"As your father did at the Velo, once you removed the shield mages protecting the Relusian Army," Alesha proudly said, reminding everyone of Ethan's fell deeds. She recalled how impressed she was when she heard how he single handedly turned the battle to Astaria's favor. She hadn't yet met him, still plotting to bring him to heel. Back then, he was merely a name without a face, a name that grew more impressive with every outlandish thing he did.

"And if they control the dragon?" Corella asked coldly, wondering if such a thing was even possible.

"Well, it will make it easier finding the dragon." Ethan smiled, his attempted humor failing miserably.

"It would make our task nigh impossible," Valera said. "As Ethan explained, no mage can come near the enemy host without drawing the dragon's wrath, as I can fully attest. That means fighting the enemy without magic, something our armies are ill-prepared for."

"What do you suggest, Ethanos? You certainly can't defeat a dragon and an army by yourself?" Corella asked.

"Who said anything about just myself? Some of you are coming with me," he replied, a knowing smile on his lips.

"You just said that the dragon is drawn to our magic," Mother Vetesha pointed out.

"Not if I make you invisible," he said, enjoying this all too much.

"How?" several of them asked at once.

"You'll see, but I can only shield a few of you. When the time is right, you will destroy their army *after* I kill the dragon."

"Kill the dragon?" Alesha shook her head. "I will not allow it!"

"The queen says I can," Ethan pointed to Corella.

"I said you could explain your plan. I have not yet given my blessing. Do not presume too much, Ethanos!" Corella warned.

"No offense, Grandma, but what choice do you have?" he said, his jape receiving more than one dark look. The fact he was not soundly admonished, proved his point.

"If the odds favor the dragon, why are you so adamant on going?" Mother Caterina asked curiously. It was no secret that Ethan wanted nothing more than to be free of them, and yet here he was, willing to die protecting them.

"I don't like what you all did to me. I hated you all for it, to be honest. I probably won't ever forgive any of you for it either. Despite that, I can't sit by and let that dragon harm Alesha or those she loves, especially our baby. Protecting Gabrielle is something each of us can agree on."

The resigned looks he received proved his words true.

Alesha regarded him with a timeless look, touching a hand to her growing womb. He was risking his life to protect their child. She never loved him more than this moment and hated that she couldn't go with him. Despite all her power, she was still tasked with the onerous duty of child bearing. It made her feel helpless, despite the power coursing her flesh. Too bad, Ethan couldn't carry the child, she smiled to herself. If that was only possible, the world would truly be hers.

"It is settled," Valera declared. "Ethan and I shall leave for Castara tonight, joining our armies gathering there. Lord General, you shall provide us two hundred of your swiftest riders as escort. Have them outfitted with the lightest of mail. Heavy armor will only slow us down, and time is the currency of the hour," she said, catching Ethan nodding with approval.

"I shall assemble them immediately, my Queen," Faro bowed.

"Once that is completed, you will directly oversee the defense of Elysia. I want scorpions atop every redoubt and turret. The palace must be fortified!" Valera ordered.

"As you command, my Queen," the lord general again bowed.

"Mothers Mortava and Demetra, would you care to join us?" Valera asked.

The two women nodded in agreement.

*****

Ethan paused outside the door, taking a deep breath before entering. He couldn't decide what he feared more, saying goodbye or facing her wrath. He found Alesha in her bedchamber, staring out the window overlooking the Salnar Mountains ringing the palace in the distance. The view was breathtaking, with pillowy clouds lingering at the window's lip, as if the palace was placed in the heavens. She stood with her hand tucked into the opposite sleeves of her gossamer silver gown, not turning to greet him as he entered.

He didn't say a word, tossing his Stetson on the bed on his way toward her, wrapping his arms gently around her shoulders from behind.

"Are you angry?" he asked softly.

"I am not pleased, but you knew that before asking," she said dryly, girding her heart for what was to come.

"I have to go. You know that I am the only one who can do this."

"No, I am the only one who can, but we cannot risk Gabrielle's life if I am wrong."

"I don't want you anywhere near that dragon," he said.

"I can say the same for you," she countered through gritted teeth.

Ethan turned her around, staring intently into her golden eyes. "Allie, I will come back."

"You don't know that. You are too reckless with your own life to make such assurances. I thought bringing you here would finally remove you from danger, but here you are, rushing off to certain death with that stupid grin on your face."

"I'm not grinning."

"Oh yes, you are. Maybe not visibly, but you are on the inside."

"I'm not doing this for myself. I'm doing it to save you, to save your family and, most importantly, to save our child. Are we going to spend our last few moments together fighting?"

"Who's fighting? The argument is over, and you won."

"I won? All I won is the chance to fight this battle before it reaches our doorstep."

"Spare me your narrative. When you first heard of the dragon, you wanted to fight this battle. Ever since you saw Dragos's vision in Astaris, you wanted to fight a dragon. You were willing to rush into the wilds to do it before I put an end to such idiocy."

"Before you enslaved me, you mean," he growled.

"Enslaved you?" She rolled her eyes, turning away before saying something she'd regret.

"Allie, I didn't mean…" The sound of his voice set her off, and she turned sharply back to him.

"Does a slave have free run of the palace? You spend every day playing with the boys, sparring with swords, making toys, and doing whatever you please. Would any other consort ever be given such liberty? No! You have these freedoms because I begged the Queen Mother to grant them. And why? To make you happy, Ethan. Even though I couldn't let you leave, I still wanted you to be happy, happy and safe. I now know how your mother felt all those years, and it feels awful."

"Don't bring my mother into this," he warned.

"Why? Because it would make you feel guilt for what you put her through?" she growled, crossing her arms.

"She warned me about the Mage Bane, making me promise not to enter it, and I disobeyed her to save you. If I obeyed her, you'd be dead."

"The mage Bane was your destiny, crossing the barrier or entering the Wilds, was not. And if you didn't cross the barrier into Red Rock, Luke Crawford wouldn't have followed you back, and taken me captive. You wouldn't have needed to enter the Mage Bane to save me."

"And if you weren't spying on me in Cordova, then Luke wouldn't have captured you either. See, it goes both ways, Allie."

They stood there staring at one another for what felt like eternity. Neither of them wanted to spend these precious moments arguing, but were overcome with emotion, guilt, and hurt. Alesha thought how much she changed since coming to know him. The old Alesha would simply demand his obedience as his crown princess. He was her consort and bound to her authority, but they were beyond that now. She cringed thinking how petty she once was, obsessed with his power, and the glory of her House. Now she just wanted him for who he was. He was brave, kind, and so unlike anyone she ever knew. The thought of losing him filled her with trepidation. Her eyes drifted to his saddle packs sitting on the floor, filled with extra ammunition, knives, and a spare pistol. His rifle sat beside them, all ready to go, a stark reminder of his leaving.

Alesha stepped near, cupping his cheeks in her hands, kissing him fiercely.

"I'm scared, Ethan," she whispered, pressing her forehead to his chest, hugging him tightly.

I'm scared too, he wanted to say but couldn't let her know that, knowing it would only increase her worry.

"Hey"—he smiled, lifting her chin—"I'll be back before you know I was gone. I promise."

"I'll hold you to it." She laughed through her tears, overcome with emotion.

"Besides, I have to come back and see my little girl come into this world. Isn't that right, Gabrielle?" He winked before taking a knee, putting his face flush to her womb.

"Are you going to sing for her one last time before leaving?"

> There's a yellow rose of Texas
> I'm going back to see
> No other cowboy knows her
> Nobody, only me…

He sang softly, his voice causing the child to stir as if reacting to the melody. She loved the sound of his voice, and apparently, Gabrielle did as well. He started to rise after finishing before she put a hand to his shoulder, keeping him in place.

"You will return to me. That is an order."

"Yes, ma'am," he said with a Texas drawl, gaining his feet, before sweeping her into his arms, kissing her goodbye.

CHAPTER 22

They rode out in the dark of night, leading a long column of mounted knights, with Queen Valera, Mothers Demetra and Mortava, Ander and Ethan riding at the head of their small host. A dozen wagons bearing provisions, trailed the column, while Bull was placed in a separate, heavy cart. Ethan could not risk his friend breaking a leg, or pulling up lame on their journey, as Bull was immune to magic, and could not be healed with their mage powers. Ethan felt strange riding the spirited Varner bred light horse he selected from Queen Valera's stable, which she gifted him for the campaign. He hadn't ridden a horse other than Bull since the Mage Bane, and it felt wrong to him. Valera first offered up a white destrier, but Ethan explained the need for lighter faster mounts for the task ahead, choosing the plainest horse he found, which made him further stand out from the ostentatious knights in the retinue.

Ethan thought back to their final farewell on the palace green of Elysia, seeing the long faces of Raymar, Corbin, Darius and young Jered as he waved goodbye. The three men promised to look after the boy and to continue their training and work in the armory until he and Ander returned. Raymar had little time to speak with him, able to briefly say that he would be sorely missed. He could see the sadness in Raymar's demeanor, as if he lost the only friend he ever had. In some ways, that was true, but he couldn't let him feel so defeated. Ethan slapped him on the shoulder, reassuring him he and Ander would safely return, and they would all gather in the armory sharing their war stories, for the *Brotherhood of Elves* would demand no less.

"I fear the men might fall asleep and slip from their saddles," Ander quietly said, riding at his side as they made their way along the road that snaked through the Salnar Mountains. A sheer vertical cliff rested off their right, moonlight playing of its gray rock, illuminating their path. A deep chasm ran along the left side of the road, dropping hundreds of feet. Any man that fell asleep and drifted too far left risked a grizzly end. Valera could heal any wound, but couldn't bring back the dead.

"They'll have to keep an eye out for each other. Wish we could've waited until dawn, but we don't have time," Ethan said, looking over his shoulder to the men riding behind them.

"We'll need to stop and rest at some point, whether we can afford to or not," Ander said.

"Yeah, but not until we clear the mountains. I don't fancy pitching a tent near the drop of death," Ethan said in a Texan accent. Once they cleared the mountains, they could start making better time on the flat ground between the foothills and Castara. By then, they should receive clearer information on the enemy's whereabouts.

"It's a shame to leave behind many of our best knights. Some of these lads are green boys," Ander pointed out.

"Not much choice in that," Ethan said. They were forced to weed out any knights or soldiers with any measurable trace of mage power. Since the knights of the realm were mostly of noble stock, it was almost impossible find those without it.

"I never thought my lack of magic would be an asset." Ander shook his head.

"When it comes to facing a dragon, it certainly is."

"I hope your plan of shielding the Queen and Mothers Mortava and Demetra is a sound one," Ander said, wondering what Ethan had in mind.

"I can shield them if they stay near me or Bull, that's why he is in the wagon, to save him for when we need him." Between Bull and himself, they couldn't protect more than three, thus limiting how many mages they dare bring. All the mothers wanted to come, as well as Minister Mattiese, and the entirety of the queen's council. Ethan chuckled recalling the cold look Leora gave him when she found out she wasn't going. The greatest battle in Vellesian history was about to take place, and she couldn't participate.

"This shall be my first battle," Ander confessed, nervously wondering how he would perform.

"What about that Gorgencian village when we were attacked by the local Lord's idiots?"

"That was no battle, Ethan, just a skirmish."

"When you're fighting with men trying to kill you, Sarge, it's the same thing. You handled yourself pretty well that day, as I recall, and you've gotten much better with a sword since then. You got me pretty good on the chin the other day." Ethan ribbed his jaw, recalling the painful experience.

"Ha! For every blow I've given, you returned a hundred." Ander couldn't remember how many times he required a mage healer's touch after their sparring sessions.

"It wasn't that lopsided, Sarge. You are better than Dar and Corb."

"Only when they started. They're both nearly my equal now, and Consort Corbin is an old man."

"Corb only looks old. He's as spry as a spring chicken."

"Spry as a chicken? Where do you come up with these expressions?" Ander made a face.

"Judge Donovan used to say that. That man had more phrases than you could shake a stick at."

Shake a stick at? Ander decided not to ask where that one came from. He'd only get an answer filled with more phrases that didn't make much sense.

"That was one of the judge's too," Ethan answered anyway, reading his thoughts by the look on his face.

"Most of your phrases are from this judge you are so fond of," Ander said, pretending Ethan hadn't been talking about him and Sheriff Thorton since leaving Astaris. Part of him just liked hearing Ethan talk about them, as it put the boy in a good mood.

"Either them or Sheriff Thorton. My grandfather Dragos had some memorable ones as well."

"Lord Dragos Mortune, he is your maternal grandfather?"

"Yes. I see you've been paying attention to our conversations," Ethan was impressed.

"Partly, but every member of the queen's guards learned every member of your house before we visited Astaris."

"Oh," Ethan sighed as if he should've known.

"What phrase did Lord Dragos say that you remember?"

"*Ethan, my boy…,*" he mimicked Dragos's aged voice, shaking a finger at Ander like Dragos was apt to do… "*You can milk a bull all you want, but you'll only make him grin.*"

Ander winced at the image that popped into his brain.

"*Arguing with your mother is like picking your nose with your thumb, you just don't do it,*" Ethan quoted another of Dragos's stupid phrases, though that one had merit.

"Lord Dragos sounds very—"

"Crude," Ethan finished his sentence.

"Colorful, is the word I would choose," Ander said politely.

"That's the nice way of saying it. He is a character though. I do miss him, though," Ethan fondly recalled the many times he spent in Dragos's tower, helping with whatever research or project caught the old man's fancy. Sometimes he was just hiding from his mother or father, and Dragos found an excuse for him to do so, urgently requiring his *help*. He spent more time with Dragos than his own father. Whenever his mother tried to dress him in some ridiculous outfit or force him to partake in some awful activity like singing, poetry or dancing lessons, he would escape to Dragos's tower, where his grandfather shielded him from such torture.

"I see where you get much of your good humor from."

"You mean my foul tongue." Ethan grinned.

"No. You are not foul, Ethan, just blunt. It is quite refreshing from the practiced grace of most nobles."

That was surprising. Ethan wasn't expecting such honesty. Ander was usually guarded in his responses, ever mindful of his position.

"You're not so bad yourself, Ander. I'm glad you came along. It would be boring without you."

"I thought you were growing weary of me."

It was no secret that Ander was Ethan's shadow on behalf of Queen Valera, but it didn't stop Ethan from accepting him for who he was. What could Ander really tell the queen that she didn't already know?

"Weary of you? Who would I talk to if you weren't here?"

"Just about anyone. You are not shy, Ethan. You could strike up a conversation with a tree, and it would probably talk back and entertain you for half a day."

"Trees are good listeners," Ethan japed, causing Ander to smile.

They continued to talk through the better part of the night, doing their best to keep each other awake. Ethan broke off several times, riding along the formation to check on the other knights and soldiers. Few would engage him in conversation, merely acknowledging him as consort. Either they were afraid to speak with him or thought him an outsider. It was no secret among the palace guard that Ethan did not come to Vellesia voluntarily. The older knights merely grunted acknowledgments, paying him little heed. The younger knights were more apt to engage in conversation. He would ask about their kin and where they hailed from. He took note of those who were overly excited and those who looked deathly afraid of facing a dragon. It was his experience that you couldn't tell how men would react until the battle was upon them. A frightened man might suddenly becalm himself and display great courage. An apparently brave man might freeze in terror or flee. Or the opposite could transpire, where those appearing brave, actually are, and those frightened could be the cowards they appear to be.

"*Focus on the small things*," Lord Brax, his father's own lord general, repeatedly told his soldiers. It was good advice that Ethan took to heart, sharing with his own men that he recruited into Astaria's light cavalry, the very outfit his father often disparaged. Those light horse units proved their worth at the Velo, earning his father's respect. He would tell these same soldiers to focus on the small things before them, concerning themselves with their individual duty, and not be overwhelmed with the greater conflict. As Sheriff Thorton repeated the sentiment, if soldiers occupy their brains with task at hand, they won't have time to think about bravery or cowardice, they'll simply do their job.

*****

It wasn't until late in the next day until they cleared the mountains and were on the road to Castara. They were met along the journey by the local lords and vassals of each village they passed. People gathered along the avenues and road sides, greeting their queen, kneeling as they passed. Each lord they met gathered their vassals and followed the queen's entourage.

The third day after leaving the Salnar Mountains, they came upon the city of Delvar, a sprawling merchant hub that straddled the Delvaran Vale. The city was surrounded by lush forests to its north, and open farmlands to its south, with a curtain wall protecting the city proper. Sitting astride a red-spirited destrier, was the lord of Delvar, Tavis Ganelle, a barrel-chested man with curly black hair draping to his shoulders. He was dressed in resplendent shining steel armor, with his helm resting in his left hand, displaying his clean-shaven chiseled jaw, and steel gray eyes.

Lord Ganelle awaited Queen Valera beyond the city gate, with his heir, steward, and household knights in attendance. They dismounted as the queen's standard drew nigh, a golden rose upon a field of black, lifting strongly in the early summer air. Lord Ganelle and his entourage, knelt in unison as the lead knights bearing the queen's sigil broke off to his right, the queen following in their wake.

"My Queen, Delvar is yours!" Lord Ganelle pressed his head to the ground before she bid him rise.

"My gratitude, my lord," she replied, dismounting and tossing her reins to the captain of her guard, Jarvis Tolliver, a sour-faced warrior who guarded his queen fiercely, and couldn't hide his dislike of Ethan.

Valera stepped forth as Lord Ganelle grasped her fingers, pressing his lips to the back of her hand.

"Your beauty radiates like the morning sun, my Queen."

"Your words are kind, my lord. It is good to see your son again. Javon," she greeted, her gaze falling upon the dark-haired young man standing behind him, sharing a likeness to his mighty sire.

"My Queen." Young Javon bowed. He was clad in similar armor as his father, with a broad sword riding his left hip, and mace his right.

"A pretty lad," Valera said, regarding the boy. "You caught the eye of many fair maids at Elysia during your last visit," she recalled Javon dancing with several fetching maidens from the greater houses during the royal ball honoring Alesha's nuptials. Her comment had the expected result on the blushing youth.

"Mothers," Lord Ganelle again knelt as Mothers Demetra and Mortava rode to the front of the column, pulling up beside Valera.

"Lord Ganelle," Demetra regarded him cordially.

"Rise, my lord. I know it is rare to find mothers of the Lorian Order outside the walls of Elysia, but these are uncommon times," Valera said, introducing them.

"We are honored to receive them," Lord Ganelle said proudly. It was a great honor for any lord to host his queen, let alone members of the Lorian Order. The honor was even greater considering Delvar was a minor holding compared to the greater houses of Vellesia.

"Lords Crofton, Sulles, and Vemar, and their vassals, are accompanying us. You will find accommodations for them, and the other lords that shall be arriving in the coming days," Valera ordered.

"Of course, my Queen. We received your earlier missive. When shall we proceed to Castara? I am eager to feed the barbarian scum the point of my sword!" Lord Ganelle grinned, patting the hilt of his long sword.

"I am afraid you won't be joining us when we march, my lord," Mother Mortava said dryly.

"My Queen, my place is beside you in battle! I am a warrior, born and bred. With the enemy sweeping into our sacred lands, honor demands that I serve my queen in battle," the lord pleaded desperately.

"If you go, you'd only be dragon food," Ethan said, drawing up alongside Mother Mortava.

Lord Ganelle stared up at Ethan aghast, recognizing him right away, despite his off-putting garb. Consorts were to be seen and not heard. They were little more than pets. Why Consort Ethan was here was a question he needed answering, though someone else would have to do the asking, for the man seemed to have won over the queen.

"Ethanos!" Valera sternly warned, reminding him not to over-step his bounds.

Ethan lifted his hands in mock surrender, as if saying *he is all yours*.

"What my son is saying is that the dragon is drawn to mage blood. They are dangerous creatures that seek out mages to devour them. Magic is useless against them," Valera explained. At time like these, she wished she had Alesha's mental ability to simply implant information into another's mind. It would save her time she could not spare.

"All will be explained in council when the other lords arrive. For now, you will see to the hosting of the queen and her retainers. You shall also gather all your knights and soldiers, and those of your vassals, for my review," Mortava ordered, brokering no argument.

"Of course, Mother Mortava. When do you wish to review them?" Ganelle asked.

"Now. Here is as good a place as any." She cast a glance to the open grounds surrounding them.

"The royal army is gathering five leagues northwest of here. General Faro has informed you of their presence?" Valera asked.

"Yes, my Queen. We are apprised of the situation, and are deliv-ering the provisions he has asked.

"Very well. Let us proceed to the comforts of Delvar," Valera said, leaving Mortava and Ethan to their task.

*****

"Step away," Mortava ordered another soldier from the formation.

"I do not understand. He is one of my father's best warriors?" Javon Ganelle, the lord's heir, asked of Ethan. They followed Mortava up and down the line of soldiers and knights, as she weeded out one great soldier after another. The knights fared even worse, with fewer than one in ten remaining.

"Anyone with a hint of magic has to go," Ethan explained.

"I know the dragon is invincible, but the enemy host is just as much a danger. We will need magic to defeat them," Javon said, frustrated by the whole process. At the rate Mother Mortava was going, they would be left with an army of weaklings.

"We have a plan for that, but it won't be easy," Ethan said as the young lord gave him a look.

"We? Are you speaking for the crown?" Javon couldn't believe the queen would allow a mere consort such influence.

"I speak my mind, if that's what you mean. As far as the queen goes, she agrees with my strategy."

"And does that strategy involve stripping away most of our soldiers of rank? Will you truly rush into battle with so few knights? You have discarded most of our officers and sergeants as well. The men need leadership, and you have taken that away."

"That is your own fault. The high rate of magic throughout the leadership ranks proves they were promoted because of familial ties instead of merit." What Ethan said was true, as magic was passed down through rich bloodlines, with those in power promoting close and distant kin over common blood.

"It is the right of nobility to rule over our lessers. Why shouldn't our kin fill the leadership of our armies?" Javon asked indignantly.

"There's nothing wrong with it if you don't care about efficiency or facing a mage eating dragon." Ethan shrugged as Mortava dismissed three more soldiers.

"Will you purge the ranks of the royal army as well?" Javon asked, aghast.

"Yep."

"But there is more mage blood in the royal army than our own."

"Probably."

"And then what? Do you plan to fend off this barbarian horde with so few men, most of peasant stock, and hastily cobbled together?"

"That about sums it up." Ethan shrugged. There was far more to it than that, but Ethan relished allowing the young lord to think the worst.

"And who shall lead them?"

"I will."

"Y…you? You are a consort. What qualifies you to lead our armies?" Javon asked, nearly apoplectic.

"Besides having faced dangers and fought battles? Absolutely nothing." Ethan's sarcasm was lost on the young lord.

Javon knew little of Ethan, other than his being a prince of Astaria. His exploits at the Velo and across the barrier were known throughout Vellesia, but apparently, Javon hadn't heard of them. Of course, such news was only spread after he wed Alesha, with the tales of his deeds told throughout the realm. House Loria kept all knowledge of the Astarian prince a secret from the people until the trap was sprung in Astaris, guarding their interest in Ethan until he was fully in their grasp.

"And while you are going into battle, bathing yourself in glory, I will be relegated here like an invalid," Javon spat disgustedly.

"Glory?" Ethan gave him a look. "There's no glory in war, Javon. There's just horror, blood, and men dying, many of them your friends or you."

"You claim to have fought in battles?"

"A few," he said dryly.

"Was magic used in these battles?"

"In some."

"You lie," Javon whispered lowly. A prince of Astaria would never go into battle without a host of mages guarding him."

"You don't know me very well, do you?" Ethan laughed, shaking his head.

"What is to know? You were once a prince and are now the consort of our crown princess."

Ethan sought to set him straight but didn't bother. The fool wasn't worth the time, but Javon wouldn't let it go.

"Your silence is damning, proving your words false."

Ethan gave him another unimpressed look. "You got more mouth than brains. Unlike you, I don't need magic to protect me, which is why I'm leading this army, and you're not. Don't expect to stay here either. Your father will likely send you further away to keep you safe just in case the dragon flies right over us for tastier prey."

Javon didn't say another word, brooding in silence as Mortava finished culling the herd. She stood off to the side as Ethan took charge, calling out the highest ranking soldier that remained, an older knight of House Ganelle, Sir Guyan. Guyan quickly ordered the remaining men to close ranks, drastically shrinking their once respectable formation to a third its original size.

"My name is Ethan Bl…" He caught himself, before blurting his former name but not able to bring himself to claim the Loria surname. It was still emasculating to think about it. "My name is Ethan," he started over, addressing the men as Mother Mortava looked on, standing beside him.

"You're probably wondering why so few of you were selected. I don't think it wise to keep things from soldiers in my command if I can help it. None of you have more than the barest trace of mage blood. That would be detrimental in a world ruled by those who possessed it. With dragons, it is the opposite. You must forget almost everything you have been taught about battle and tactics to this point, especially those of you who are knights." Ethan gave Sir Guyan a hard look.

The thirty knights who remained, reluctantly acknowledged him, not liking what he was saying.

"Sir Guyan, gather up these men and march them northwest to where the royal army is camped. There we will organize our levies and prepare them for the battles ahead," Ethan ordered, Sir Guyan giving him a curt bow.

This was the third such speech he gave in the last two days to the winnowed ranks of disgruntled lords. His plan wasn't popular, but thankfully, Queen Valera believed in it. Nobles didn't appreciate having their power usurped, especially by someone they considered a barbarian, a notion only reinforced by Ethan's strange garb and blunt manners. Many of the lords he previously spoke with were gathered in Delvar. They would soon meet in the great hall for a council of war, a war few, if any, would partake. He could only imagine what would be said in his absence. Both he and Mortava would be with the royal army during the meet, preparing them for battle. Of course, the lords were wise enough to voice their displeasure in the most respectful way to Queen Valera.

Why couldn't mage lords give me as much respect? He shook his head. One would think they might give him the benefit of the doubt considering his deeds and experience, but he knew why they didn't.

"Because nobles are idiots," he mumbled under his breath.

*****

The following evening found Lord Ganelle hosting his queen and a dozen high lords of Vellesia, with Valera overseeing the gathering, receiving the lords one by one, each kneeling with their heads bowed before taking their place around the map table. Centered in the great hall. Valera stood at the head of the table, clad in black armor, with a golden rose emblazoned upon her breastplate. Mother Demetra stood her immediate right, and Selendra her left. All the lords recognized Selendra as the sister of Queen Valera's late husband, and a daughter of House Menau, whose reputation was second only to House Loria.

Selendra arrived early in the day, bearing vital news from Castara.

"My lords, we few who have gathered here represent only a quarter of our greater houses, but time prevents us from mustering our full strength. As each of you know, a large host has penetrated our northwest border with the Wilds, here at Gallot along the Iona divide," Valera said, light emanating from her outstretched hand, illuminating the northwest corner of the map.

"This host is rumored to have a dragon accompanying them. Selendra?" Valera called upon her to next address the assemblage.

Selendra's purple eyes swept over the gathered lords, taking their measure before beginning. "The enemy host had crossed into Vellesia

451

proper at Gallot, progressing fifty to eighty leagues. The host is numbered to be two hundred thousand, perhaps more. Few scouts have been able to get close enough for a full count. Lord Garvos, castellan of Castara, has sent several detachments to ascertain their strength, and all but one was destroyed to a man. Whether they were destroyed by dragon fire, or enemy swords, we can only surmise. The one that returned, suffered numerous casualties, beset by enemy scouts. The survivors claim to have seen the dragon in the distance, a juvenile creature that appears far smaller than the beast Queen Valera faced in Gorgencia."

The lords welcomed that last bit of news, grateful to not be facing a full-grown dragon.

"This is grand tidings indeed," Lord Sulles boasted, a tall lord with silver tainting his full dark mane. He was both a fire and wind mage, whose great-grandmother was a Vellesian princess and second daughter to Queen Elesha.

"Perhaps the threat is not as dire as we believed," Lord Ganelle added, Lords Crofton and Darluv nodding in agreement.

"Queen Valera is correct to consider the danger such a beast presents," Selendra continued. "Of all the detachments that Lord Garvos sent out, the only one to return was the one led without a mage. Not a single mage has come within ten leagues of the enemy host and returned to speak of it."

"Then how are we to combat such a beast?" one lord asked.

"How can these barbarians control it?" another said.

"The sightings we have received, claim a young woman rides upon the dragon," Selendra added.

"A young woman? How is such a thing possible? Dragons are hateful creatures that roam the Wilds, seeking human flesh," Lord Vemar asked.

"They do not seek human flesh unless it is mage blood. It is magic they devour. The peoples who dwell in the wilds have lived under the dragons' threat for thousands of years. Any one of them born with magic is quickly devoured, thus culling magic from their bloodlines. Perhaps the woman riding it, discovered it when it was a hatchling, and grew up alongside it. Or perhaps she has the ability to bond with a dragon that we are unfamiliar with," Selendra explained.

"If the beast is controlled by this woman, it will make Ethanos's plan easier to implement," Mother Demetra explained.

"The consort of the crown princess? Are we to march on his orders?" Lord Sulles asked indignantly.

"Mind your tongue, child. I'm not so old that I can't take you over my knee," Mother Demetra scolded.

"Yes, Grandmother." Lord Sulles bowed his head respectfully. Sulles was only three generations removed from the royal family while several other lords in attendance traced their family lines even further back. Demetra's third daughter wed one of Lord Vemar's grandfathers, many generations back. The lords present that were not her direct descendants, were descendants of Mother Evalena, making them kin all the same.

"Ethanos has a plan to deal with the dragon, a plan that is not without pain but sound. If it does not work, we have contingencies," Valera explained.

"My apologies, my Queen, but are we truly to remain here away from the battle? Our vassals will think us cowards?' Lord Crofton asked ashamedly.

Valera regarded him with sympathy. "There is no cowardice in obeying your queen's orders, my Lord Crofton. You may remind any vassals that disagree to bring their complaints to me."

"As Queen Valera has explained, magic is useless against a dragon. Marching off to engage it would only fuel its rage. Each of you shall remain here with Lady Selendra and myself, as well as Lady Thela Corval and her guild of healers who are currently en route," Mother Demetra declared.

"Further, you are to send your heirs to Brelar in the event the dragon evades us at Castara and strikes Delvar. Your houses must not risk extinction should you and your heirs be in one place," Valera emphasized, the eyes of the gathered lords drawn wide, realizing such possibilities.

"Ethanos and Mother Mortava are currently with the royal army and the soldiers they have selected from your bannermen. They must cull those with magic from the royal army as well, consolidating the forces that remain, and prepare them for march," Valera added.

"My Queen, they selected so few of my men. How can they hope to engage the dragon *and* the enemy host with so weak an army?" Lord Grolen asked.

"They will not be without magic. I will join them in battle," Valera sternly stated, her declaration drawing protests from her lords.

"No, my Queen! Send me in your place!" Lord Selles implored.

"Send me!" Lord Crofton pleaded.

"You cannot go alone. Send me in your stead!" Another added.

"ENOUGH!" Valera's voice boomed with magic, quieting the hall instantly.

"We can only send two mages into battle. Why this is so, I will not say. Mother Mortava and myself are the two that shall meet the enemy in battle, no more and no less. The fact the dragon has a woman rider has many benefits to our plan, providing that that fact is indeed true. A human rider means that the creature is in league with the enemy host. And should that dragon wander far afield, that great host can be destroyed by our magic. If the dragon remains close, then that will reduce its speed to that of the invading army," Valera said.

"Lord Ganelle, see to your city. As castellan of Delvar, you will retain tactical command of its defenses. Strategic decisions will require my approval," Mother Demetra said, Tavis Ganelle bowing respectfully before retiring with the other lords. As the last Mother of the Lorian Order to see battle, Demetra was chosen for this task, and would direct all Vellesian forces to support Valera's reconfigured army. Should the dragon be defeated, she would forward the remaining Vellesian armies into the fray.

"Selendra, inform the Queen Mother of our plans and disposition," Valera ordered her sister by marriage, who bowed and withdrew, leaving Valera alone with her grandmother many times removed. As a member of House Menau, Selendra possessed the magical ability to communicate thoughts over long distances, a power Valera was constantly jealous of.

"This is a dangerous plan, my child. A dragon is a dangerous and unpredictable creature," Demetra searched her eyes for any misgivings.

"What choice have we? The enemy host draws nigh, and we must give battle. And should the dragon wander, I will be positioned to destroy their army."

"And should it remain close, our army must be able to match them sword for sword and spear for spear. In this, I lack confidence in our numbers."

"We have Ethanos for that," Valera countered, not believing she was placing such trust in the one person who had so vexed her.

"And if it comes to that, they will have a dragon flying overhead, cutting swaths through our diminished ranks. Further, our *new* army will field few ranks after we dismiss two of every three, or is it three of every four?" Demetra shook her head.

"I will have Julius with us," Valera said, naming her most trusted general and commander of the Royal Army.

"Only if this stone can shield him." Demetra drew a finger-sized rock from her sleeve, hanging at the end of a makeshift necklace. It appeared as a nondescript gray rock of little note but was more precious than a mountain of gold. It was pure anti-magic, the rarest mineral in the world. That one small stone represented all the anti-magic in the Vellesian royal vault and their most cherished possession. The small amount of anti-magic stored within that stone equaled the amount dispersed in a barrier rock, the monuments able to ward off dragons.

"It will shield him. Julius is only a fire caster and a light bearer. The power in that stone should suppress them, making his magic invisible to the dragon," Valera said.

"And should we win the day, we may have to use that stone to repair the barrier monument these barbarians destroyed. If only we had more of it," Demetra lamented. House Loria spent hundreds of years gathering that small amount, and the thought of having to sacrifice it filled both of them with dread. Furthering their frustration was the fact the anti-magic stone Ethan gifted to Amanda was far larger than their pitiful amount.

"Perhaps, or perhaps not, but should we win the day, we may have more anti-magic than we could've ever dreamed," Valera smiled.

"The dragon," Demetra regarded her knowingly. "Perhaps, but you must kill the beast first, and I doubt you can."

"I cannot, but Ethanos can," Valera said.

"Perhaps, or perhaps not. Why do you think that he can?"

"Why else would our prophecies demand that he be oath-bound to defend Vellesia? It was for this moment, and if he does, we will have enough anti-magic from the beast's carcass to do what we originally planned to do."

"Alesha will not approve of that," Demetra warned.

"Alesha is the crown princess, not the Queen Daughter or Mother. She will do as she is told, just as she did in Astaris."

*****

Four days hence
Sixty leagues north of Delvar

General Julius Ortar sat astride a gray destrier, clad in resplendent silver armor, with a black cape draping his broad shoulders. His horse stood upon a small rise, overlooking the army setting camp for the night. Like all Vellesian nobles, he was clean-shaven, revealing a masculine jaw that appeared as if it was carved from stone. Ethan found the Vellesian nobles' exotic beauty unnerving, as if they intentionally bred such traits into their bloodlines.

Why not, enhancing their bloodlines is what mage lords and ladies are known for, he thought, shaking his head, sitting beside the stoic general upon his brown Varner-bred light horse. The general was obviously miffed that Ethan would set aside the beautiful white destrier the queen offered him, for the smaller mount he now rode. He was further dismayed when Ethan ordered three hundred of their remaining knights to trade their war horses for the Varner bred to match his own.

"You all right, General? You look a little green?" Ethan remarked, wondering if Julius might toss up his breakfast any moment.

"We are marching into battle with thirty thousand soldiers, against a horde many times their size, perhaps ten times as large. We need our heavy horse if we are to counter their advantage," Julius said as respectfully as he could manage. Ethan taking three hundred knights form their tally, left him with barely a thousand.

"Numbers won't win this battle, General. The royal army alone can field more soldiers than the enemy, but the dragon would decimate them. The barbarians made a choice in bringing a large army, and we will use that against them," Ethan said.

"There is logic in what you say, consort Loria, but as general of the royal army, I am loathe to give battle with only a pittance of my full strength. This entire plan is fraught with peril."

Ethan wondered if all soldiers were as stubborn as Julius and his father? What was it with the heavy horse that they were so hopelessly enamored? He recalled Sheriff Thorton telling him of his experiences in the Civil War, where commanders repeatedly used the same frontal attacks against withering fire, each ending in fruitless slaughter.

A good commander fits his plans to the situation, not the other way around, Ben Thorton often told him.

Was that what he was doing though? Was his plan shaped by the reality of the situation, or was it merely a wild guess? His plan was based on a key assumption that he could hide Mortava and Valera from the dragon's eye. What if he was wrong? Then again, what other viable option was there?

"What if your plan fails?" Julius asked, as if he knew what was on Ethan's mind. He hated how easily he was read.

"If all else fails, I'll kill the dragon myself." He shrugged.

"Can you do that?" Julius raised a skeptical brow.

"Who knows, but we don't have any other choice by the look of things."

"And if you fail?"

"Then we all die."

Julius snorted, unimpressed with that flippant remark.

"General Ortar!" His aide de camp heralded his lord, riding up the near slope of the hill, his charger kicking up clods of soil in his wake.

"Report!" Julius ordered as the young knight came to halt, dipping his head with a respectful bow.

"Sir Gorlun asks where you would like your pavilion, General?" the young knight asked.

"Pavilion?" Julius roared. "We haven't the time for such things. The enemy awaits beyond Castara, and I'll not waste half a day setting and folding such a luxury. Tell Sir Gorlun that we sleep under the stars tonight."

"As you command." His aide again bowed. "What of the queen, General? Should we at least prepare her majesty's accommodations?"

"No. I've already spoken with the Queen Daughter, as well as Mother Mortava. They are equally adamant as I in making haste," Julius affirmed.

Ethan admired a man who forsook comfort for the betterment of his mission. He hadn't met many lords who were similarly inclined. It seemed Valera chose wisely with his appointment.

"Have our outriders returned?" Julius asked of his aide.

"Two just returned. The others are still out, General."

"Once they have all returned, give them fresh horses. I want them to rest tonight and gone by first light. I want them to ride ahead, and clear the road from here to Castara. The last thing we need is to have our way blocked by frightened peasants fleeing the enemy."

"As you command, General." The knight bowed before hurrying off.

"A wise move clearing the road. I didn't think about that," Ethan said.

"You should have, considering the campaigns you've been in. I studied your father's campaign at the Velo extensively. One of his first standing orders before leaving Astaris was to keep the roads clear for his army. Much of being a good general is moving men and provisions from one point to another. He must have emphasized this with you long before you reached the Velo."

"I wasn't with my father at the outset, but I've been around him long enough to appreciate his attention to detail."

"Where were you if not with your father?" Julius asked curiously.

"I was across the barrier and didn't reach the Velo until the night before the battle."

"Why were you so late? A prince's duty is to protect his realm and serve as his father's shield," Julius admonished, regarding him disapprovingly.

"I didn't know we were at war. There was no way for my father to reach me across the barrier," Ethan tried to explain, hating the way he sounded making excuses. He went to further tell of his adventures in Red Rock, and why he remained there, though doing so kept him blind to what was happening in his native Astaria. Julius was rather unimpressed with is lack of respect for his father, pointing out that had he arrived a day later, the battle would have likely been lost.

Ethan never thought of it like that. Everyone thought him a hero for what he did that day, but he nearly brought his kingdom to ruin by his long absence.

"What made you return when you did?" Julius asked, finding it odd that Ethan would spend an entire year beyond the barrier, only to return when he was needed, and not a day late.

"I had a dream, a nightmare really." He sighed.

"A prophecy?" Julius perked at this information. "I was under the opinion that magic didn't work across the barrier."

"It doesn't. It was only a dream, not magic."

"Dreams of such importance are magic, Consort Loria," Julius pointed out.

"It wasn't magic, and please, just call me Ethan."

"That would be improper, Consort. We must hold to strict discipline. If I begin to refer to you by your given name, others might address you familiarly. Therefore, you are Consort Loria, and I am General Ortar."

Ethan let out a tired sigh, cringing whenever he was referred to as consort, or even worse, Consort Loria. He had to resign himself to the fact that in Vellesia, he would always be referred to as such before anything else.

Julius stiffened as Queen Valera and Mother Mortava ascended the hill. Mortava rode a black Varner while Valera sat strangely upon Bull, horse and rider making strange bedfellows. Ethan could tell

Bull's magical immunity engulfed his queen by the discomfort in her eyes. It was the same effect she had whenever she stood near him, losing all connection to her mage power.

"My Queen, Mother Mortava," Julius greeted them with a reverent bow.

"My Queen, Mother," Ethan removed his Stetson, sweeping it across his body, giving them a bow.

"Rise, my son, I know how that pains you," Valera said dryly.

"I've gotten used to it, I suppose," Ethan lied. He would never get used to bowing or concealing his dislike of it.

"I am sure." Valera shook her head, not believing him. "You may enjoy a reprieve of such ceremony. As of tomorrow, I am ordering a suspension of *all* formal courtesies as you suggested."

"My Queen?" Julius asked, looking back and forth between Ethan and Valera.

"My son has wisely pointed out that should his plan to conceal our magic from the dragon prove effective, our identity might still be revealed to the enemy by how we are revered. The same order is given to all commanders of rank. There shall be no bowing, saluting, or exaggerated deference. As Ethan suggested, every man should appear as similar to every other man," Valera exclaimed.

"But you are not a man, my Queen. You shall stand apart regardless," Julius said.

"I will be behind our formations, and at such distance, my armor shall make me appear as any other man."

"The order is even more important to your front-line officers, Julius. With most of our senior commanders removed from your chain of command, the few that remain need to be protected," Valera added.

"As you command, my Queen."

"Is Bull treating you well?" Ethan dismounted, stepping near, running a hand gently over Bull's neck.

"We are becoming acquainted," was all Valera would say.

"Bull and I have been all over West Texas and Eastern New Mexico together and across half the mage realms. He's as good a friend as you could want," Ethan said while fishing an apple from his saddle pack to give his friend.

"Don't you dare, Ethanos!" Valera warned, stopping him before he could put the apple in Bull's mouth.

"He likes them." He shrugged innocently.

"That might be true, but his digestive system doesn't," she scowled, knowing he fed apples to Bull on purpose so she could experience his foul odor.

The look on Mortava's face showed she was not amused with Ethan's antics. For all his fell deeds and wondrous abilities, Ethan was a child at heart. Like all the mothers in the Lorian Order, she was constantly taken aback by his behavior. They foresaw his birth centuries before, awaiting his coming with anticipation and fear. He was a powerful force essential to their aims but dangerous, wild, and unpredictable. For as much as they coveted his power and planned his capture before he was even born, they always feared what he was capable of. As his deeds and legend grew, these fears only intensified, fueling their need to cage and control him. When Alesha finally trapped him at Astaris, a sense of relief filled their hearts, finally setting their worries to rest. What they didn't expect, however, was his childlike nature once they actually came to know him.

Is this what we were afraid of? Mortava shook her head. He was not a malevolent force threatening to ruin their plans, he was something different altogether.

"I best check on the men," Ethan excused himself, tipping his hat to the ladies before riding off to see to his light cavalry.

"Your opinion, General?" Valera asked, their eyes following Ethan as he rode off.

"He is not what I expected, my Queen. Are you certain we should trust his judgment? If he is wrong, every one of us shall die."

"If we do nothing, then we shall die all the same. You have implemented most of his suggestions. Has there been any issues from that?" Mortava asked.

"The knights and commanders are none too pleased with the dining arrangements and the work details," Julius explained.

"The eating arrangements?" Valera asked.

"Commanders now eat *after* every subordinate. Some of our commanders take issue with their loss of privilege they feel they have earned through years of service or by right of birth. Consort Loria demands that each commander places the welfare of his men before his own. Whenever there is a meal, he and I eat last. Everyone pulls guard duty...*everyone!*" he emphasized.

"Yes. I saw Ethan standing post last night," Valera recalled.

"Yes, the very middle of the night, which is the worst shift, my Queen. He is not the pampered princeling that I expected," Julius acknowledged.

"No, he is not." Valera sighed. "And have the men acquiesced to his directions?"

"Most have. There was one who protested, but Consort Loria set him to rights," Julius said.

"How so?" Valera lifted a curious brow.

"A young knight of House Crofton took issue with standing post. Consort Loria snatched him from his saddle, armor and all, and threw him into the river. Ethanos retrieved him before he drowned, weighed down as he was."

"Did Ethanos say anything to the knight afterwards?" Mortava asked.

"*We are all in this together,*" he parroted Ethan's words. "He also told the men that you live or die by the courage and love of the man who stands beside you."

"He said this to the men, but to you, he said something else," Valera could read his thoughts, sensing something troubling the general.

Julius shifted uncomfortably before releasing a sigh, resigning himself to sharing what Ethan had said. "He said that soldiers fight hardest for each other, often giving their lives for the man beside him. I asked what of queen and realm and family. He said men are as likely to flee in the face of death than fight for things far away, even if they hold them dear." For Julius, there was no greater honor than laying down one's life for their queen. To suggest that men would likelier die for their comrades than their Queen was blasphemous.

"Perhaps he is right," Mortava stated. "I can read men's thoughts, but I cannot shape them. We haven't fought a significant war in centuries. Ethan, however, has fought in battles of varying scale. He understands the nature of men in such environs."

"Are you worried that Ethan is instilling greater loyalty in the men to each other over their Queen?" Valera asked sharply.

"NO...no, my Queen," he stammered, not willing to cast such aspersions. "He emphasized proximity in the motivations of soldiers. They'll more likely place themselves in danger for the man who fights beside them than the one who fights further afield. In fairness, he said the men are more likely to fight for each of you than the Queen Mother, Princess Alesha, or the other mothers of the Order because you are here while the others are far away."

"Do not trouble yourself with the boy's opinions, Valera. They are simply his beliefs on the nature of battle, and he was wise enough to share them only with Julius," Mortava reasoned.

"Very well," Valera said icily. She knew they could never change Ethan's mind on his opinion of their divinity while he was immune to their powers. *What did you expect when you loosened his bonds?* a dark voice whispered in her ear. Valera knew they needed to win this war, and even then, it would be a close run affair. And should they prevail, what favors would he ask of them for his service? He was entitled to nothing as he was sworn to serve them in any manner they chose, but Alesha would insist he be rewarded. She would face that dilemma in due time.

"Julius, we ask that you wear this during this campaign," Mortava said, drawing the precious stone from her satchel.

"As you command, Mother Mortava, but might I ask...why?" he regarded the simple gray rock attached to a chain.

"It will dampen your mage powers, perhaps completely. It is precious beyond imagining, and you must guard it with your life," Valera emphasized.

"It will hopefully shield your power from the dragon," Mortava added.

"And speak to no one of this, especially Ethanos," Valera warned.

"And if he should inquire? He must know I am mage born. Will he not wonder why?"

"He knows nothing of your power. And should he ask, you have none," Valera added.

"As you command, my Queen," Julius said, before riding off to see to his men.

Valera's eyes narrowed studiously as he drew from sight, her mind a whirlwind of thoughts.

"Ethan troubles you, child?" Mortava asked.

"The further he draws away from Alesha, the greater the hunger increases."

"I have felt it also. Being near him is almost maddening now."

"Unbearably so," Valera concurred.

"Except when I am fully within his aura, and then I feel…nothing." Mortava was thankful for that small mercy since much of this campaign required her to be close to him.

Valera acknowledged that strange paradox, Ethan causing insufferable madness in them, intensifying as they drew nigh, but then nothing once within his mageless aura.

"How did poor Alesha bear it when they parted the Mage Bane?" Mortava wondered.

They both recalled the sorry state that Alesha was in upon her return to Elysia after her first encounter with Ethan. But her anguish seemed more one of the heart, than physical torment. With the rest of them, this was not so. They suffered the insatiable hunger without ceasing until Ethan and Alesha were finally joined, and it lessened the longer they remained together. What they couldn't understand was why their hunger only abated when Ethan and Alesha were in proximity. Alesha was already with child, fulfilling Ethan's primary purpose. Their prophecies foresaw Ethan serving other purposes vital to the realm, which made sense considering the war they were now engaged, but what purpose did he serve being close to Alesha? Whatever the purpose, the fact remained, that they would never know peace unless Ethan and Alesha were forever near each other.

"We must win this war and return him to Alesha," Valera said.

*****

Two days hence

"What a beautiful view, wouldn't you say, Sarge?' Ethan asked as Ander drew up beside him.

"Of course. My home village lies just east of here," Ander said as the hill their horses stood overlooked a fertile river valley below.

"Sounds like a nice place to grow up. Does your family still live there?" Ethan asked.

"My parents have long passed, but I have two sisters who live just further east of it, and many distant kin who reside throughout the region." Ander sighed, fondly recalling his childhood, which felt so long ago.

"You know, I never did ask you how you came to be a member of the royal guard, considering you were raised this far from court," Ethan said.

"I was nine years when I came upon another young boy drowning in the river that cut through our vale. I was not large for my age but not small either, but being a good swimmer, I chanced the current and managed to bring him to the shore. He was sorely grateful, and as chance would have it, he was our local lord's son. His father rewarded me with a post within his household guard. Demonstrating a decent skill with a sword, I found myself moving quickly through the ranks, finding my way to the royal army, and eventually a place among the queen's royal guard, Queen Mother Corella selecting me personally for the prestigious post," Ander said with both pride and humility.

"She chose well," Ethan said, nudging his friend in the arm. "Well, Sarge, this looks to be as good a spot as any for our horses to graze," he said before dismounting. They stood upon a grassy ridge, their fellow cavalry filling in around them. A balmy northern breeze pressed their faces, rather brisk considering the season.

"How far do you plan to go before we set camp?" Mother Mortava asked as she dismounted off his left.

"Another twenty leagues, if we can manage it." Ethan removed his Stetson, scratching his head, annoyed with his lengthening hair. "I wish I could cut this. It makes my head itch," he groaned. Alesha had forbidden him from cutting his hair since Astaris, and it was now down to his shoulders.

"Don't you dare," Mortava smirked. Knowing how much he hated it somehow brought her wicked pleasure. *Why was that?* she thought. It was probably the same reason Ethan fed Bull apples to annoy them with his horse's foul gas.

The spirits take me, I am becoming just like him, she mused.

Perhaps I'll make a haircut one of my demands if I manage to pull this whole thing off, Ethan thought pleasantly. *That and the freedom to dress how I like and hunt when I want. I'll have to make a list.*

They were at least thirty leagues ahead of the army, scouting the lands between them and Castara.

"It seems we've drawn some attention." Ander lifted his chin toward the valley below, where a number of peasants working their fields, suddenly stopped working, looking in their direction.

"Better go and talk with them, Sarge. Don't want to scare them. Just reassure them we are passing through on business for the queen. Don't mention that Mother Mortava is with us, or they'll all start bowing and kneeling and wasting our time," Ethan ordered, but Ander already rode off. The sergeant had been around him long enough to know what he was going to say before he said it.

"He is very fond of you," Mortava said.

"He's kind of grown on me too." Ethan never thought he'd make a friend in this miserable realm, but Ander Jordain was a pleasant surprise.

"You are nothing like we expected," she regarded him, her golden eyes finding his sea blue.

"And what were you expecting?" he asked, unnerved by her exotic beauty, having to constantly remind himself that she was in fact Alesha's great-great-great-great-grandmother. Like most of the Lorian Order, she was many times older than everyone who ever lived.

"Whatever we were expecting, it wasn't you."

"Is that good or bad?" He grinned, not sure how to take that.

"It's not bad."

"That's not much of an answer."

"You are quite friendly, once one comes to know you. It took a while to see it at first with how angry you were when you first arrived."

"That's funny. I didn't think I was that angry when we reached Elysia. You should've seen me at Astaris."

"Oh, I know how angry you were there, but it was expected. I hope you now understand why we had to bring you to Vellesia. It is your destiny," she said with that timeless look that all of them used far too often.

"Yep, destiny in the form of a big, hungry dragon that will probably burn us all to a crisp. At least we're in this together," he japed, and for some reason, she returned his smile.

"You certainly don't dress like a Prince of Astaria," she said, looking over his buckskin trousers and moccasin boots, with his tied-down holster and a plain pullover shirt, topped off with his strange hat. The only princely thing about him was the way he carried himself, assured but not arrogant. That and his father's sword that rode upon his left hip.

"And how should a prince of Astaria be dressed?"

"In something less comfortable." She smiled, her perfect white teeth resplendent with her clear olive skin.

"And that's why I don't dress like one, at least when I am able to choose what I wear."

"As you have told us repeatedly. I am curious, Ethan. I know you resent us for bringing you here, but if you were free to choose your own path, what would you have done?"

"I would've returned to Red Rock and told Ben about Luke Crawford. Maybe spend some time with ole Judge Donovan. Of course, I would have had to deal with the dragon I saw in Dragos's vision at some point. I couldn't have it destroy Astaris."

She found none of this surprising considering Alesha told them of the great red dragon that Ethan saw burning Astaria.

"And then what, Ethanos? After you visited your friends and slew the dragon, what would you then do?"

"Be free." He shrugged. It was obvious he hadn't thought that far ahead. "I'm still the sheriff of Cordova, or at least I was. I'd have to return and continue my work there. Once they looked to be secure, I planned to find a place to settle down, someplace remote. I'd build a home, perhaps overlooking a lake surrounded by towering pines. I planned to ask Allie…Alesha, to join me," he confessed. Of course, all that changed in Astaris.

"You and Alesha living quietly in a cabin far from civilization," Mortava mused, picturing it in her mind. "Alesha would never have agreed to that."

"No, but Allie would have if she existed." He sighed sadly.

"If you are so angry with her choices, then why are you here? You asked to partake in this battle. Why?"

"Just because I hate her, doesn't mean I don't love her," he mumbled.

"That doesn't make any sense."

"Bah, I can't explain it." He snorted, confounded whenever he thought of his situation with Alesha.

"I think you can. You are drawn to her, as she is to you. Despite her deceiving you, you are helpless against the magic binding you together."

"I'm immune to magic."

"Not this sort. It is the magic of *destiny*. Against it, you are as helpless as she is. It is far more powerful than our prophecies foretold."

"I don't believe in destiny."

"Destiny does not require your belief in it. It merely is. And if not destiny, what do you believe in?"

"Freedom."

"Freedom?" she questioned.

"Freedom to choose my own path. Why must Alesha and I be bound by a destiny not one of you can honestly explain? Don't tell me about the deity of House Loria and your destiny to rule Elaria. That's not destiny. That's just greed." He winced, realizing he shouldn't have said that, but Mortava didn't seem offended.

"One might look upon our objectives as avarice, but is it not more selfish to hide away in the hills, denying the world your wondrous gifts? As much as you may hate it, Ethan, you cannot achieve the greater good without power."

"Just as much harm can come from unchecked power as good," he warned.

"Perhaps, but would it not be a greater sin to not even try?" she asked thoughtfully.

He hated that she had a point. She could see her victory in his silence. She saw little profit in gloating and decided to shift the conversation.

"So you came here to do battle because you love Alesha." She smiled.

"That and to kill a dragon before it destroys Astaria."

"This dragon might not be the one in Dragos's vision," she pointed out.

"True, but if I learn how to kill this one, it will help me kill the one I saw in the vision."

Mortava grew quiet at that comment. Did he truly believe they would allow him to enter the Wilds and hunt down the beast in Dragos's vision? They kept Ethan obedient by the threat to his father's life. That threat was meaningless if all of Astaria was threatened. They needed further leverage to restrain him, though, without it, he was still hopelessly surrounded by their armies and power. So much was their advantage, that even Ethan could not escape.

Their awkward silence was interrupted by Ander's return. He reported that the peasants working the fields below were ignorant of the war and therefore had little to say. He also discovered that one farmer's son was attacked by a mountain lion three days before and was abed in a cottage below.

"Is the wound mortal?" Ethan asked.

A sad nod from Ander answered his question. "He isn't likely to survive the day," he replied.

"Take me to him, Ander," Mortava said.

*****

She touched a glowing finger to the boy's forehead, her magic sweeping over his body in sudden rapture. Mortava straightened her back, staring down as the boy gasped, his wounds sealing instantly.

"Mother Mortava." The boy's mother dropped to her knees, tears of gratitude dripping from her tired eyes. The woman hadn't slept in days, a constant state of worry and work draining the life from her.

Ethan stood at the door of the simple cottage, observing the interaction curiously. The woman looked far beyond her years, kneeling with her head bowed, gray sweeping away her once lustrous black hair. She wore a simple brown shift with dust from the dirt floor swirling about its hem. The woman's eyes were bloodshot, with dark circles indicating her sorry state after tending to her stricken son for days without rest. What use were mage healers if you couldn't reach them when needed? Ethan remembered Alesha saying that the twelve mage healers that accompanied her to Cordova represented most of their guild in all of Vellesia. That put their true number, outside the royal family, at around twenty mage healers. With a realm as large as Vellesia, that left few to reach places as remote as this. What would've happened if they hadn't passed by? The answer was an early grave for the boy now rising from the bed.

"My child," Mortava spoke soothingly to the poor woman, touching a hand to her weathered cheek, her magic bathing the woman with its immense power, a golden hue glowing across her flesh.

"My Queen," she gasped, her hunched spine straightening, and the cracks in her weathered skin closing. Dark roots sprang from her head, pushing the gray strands out, her hair dropping below her waist before Mortava swept a hand over her head, cutting the dead hair away.

The woman ran her tongue over her mouth, finding new teeth rising in the former gaps that dotted her gums. Mortava helped her to her feet before stepping away, impressing Ethan with her generous act. He was impressed with the strength of their mage gift, able to not only heal wounds but restore much of what age had stolen. No mage healer in all of Astaria was able to do that.

"That was kind of you," Ethan said, following her outside where the villagers gathered around, dropping to their knees as she passed.

"Yes, it is kind, but more so my duty," she said, not stopping to greet the villagers, for time was of the essence.

"Duty or not, it is nice to see mage powers used to help folks instead of..." He stopped himself from saying *enslaving them*. But she could easily guess what he meant.

"Magic is a powerful gift, a gift bestowed by providence to those worthy to wield it. We wield it to forge a better world, Ethanos. That means a better world for *all*," she said as they passed beyond the village edge, several soldiers following, the others waiting just ahead where Ander held their horses' reins.

Every tyrant thinks they are serving the greater good. He kept that thought to himself. He had to admit, that even the poorest Vellesian peasant was well-fed and sheltered, which was far more than the other realms could claim.

As if reading his thoughts, she continued, "After these invaders are dealt with, I shall see that engineers are sent here to instruct these people on building proper floors, and enough wells for each home to have its own," she added.

"Ethan!" Ander shouted excitedly, pointing to the sky, his panicked gesture preceding a bone-shattering roar.

"Graghh!"

Ethan winced, the distant ringing paining his ears like garbled words scrambling his brain. He craned his neck, his eyes searching as a dark-winged form passed over the village behind them. The creature was the size of a house with leathery black scales covering its flesh. Fierce golden eyes fixed their gaze upon him, set above a large black snout.

Dragon. Ethan steeled himself as the beast drew near, its massive maw drawing open, bright white fangs jutting from its mouth like spears. He could just see the head of its rider peaking above its skull, a mass of red hair blowing wildly in the wind. The beast's eyes shifted back and forth from Ethan to Mortava, a volatile mix of fear, madness, and rage.

Ethan's eyes drew wide as the dragon's mouth opened to its fullest, revealing fire swirling in the back of its throat. He turned quickly around, wrapping his arms around Mortava, tackling her to the ground with a wall of flames passing overhead, igniting the ground around them in a blazing inferno.

CHAPTER 23

Two days before
Castara

"What devilry is this?" Lord Garvos cursed, standing atop the battlements of Castara. The fortress rested along the northernmost gap in the Vang-Shar Mountains, its towering walls running the length of the gap nearly one league to either side of its main gate. The walls were nigh two hundred feet high, with towering ramparts overlooking the Castaran Plain. Its northwestern face shielded the small city that housed its inhabitants with its sheer vertical stone surface.

"What could they possibly want?" His eldest son and heir, Lucis Garvos, asked of his father.

"Perhaps a parlay, my lord." Their master of arms pointed out, standing at Lord Garvos' opposite shoulder.

Nearly two hundred yards in front of the main gate sat three men astride of what appeared to be horses, though the beasts looked slightly built. The men were clad in furs and leathers, obviously barbarian garb with its utter lack of uniformity.

"They are beneath my station. I'll not treat with the likes of them," Lord Garvos sneered.

"Perhaps if they brought more men, we would deign differently." His son pointed out the measly forces arrayed behind them, counting no more than a thousand riders waiting some four hundred yards beyond them, all within ballistae range, let alone their mage powers.

"They'll not assail our walls with cavalry and certainly not with such scrawny mounts as those," Lord Garvos shook his head with contempt.

"What are they holding, my lord?" the master of arms asked, observing one of the fellows hoisting a pike into the air with a misshapen object affixed to it.

Lord Garvos possessed the gift of enhanced sight, fixing his keen gaze to the object in question. He immediately paled, recognizing the familiar face of the commander of Gallot on the severed head atop the pike, tar dripping from his greased hair and chin.

"My lord?" his master of arms asked as Garvos' back stiffened.

"KRALL!"

A piercing scream echoed overhead, driving men to their knees as if daggers were driven into their ears. Lord Garvos nearly stumbled from the battlements, his armored boots entangling with his son's, the terrible sound sending tendrils of pain back and forth through his skull. His eyes opened just as a stream of fire filled his vision.

The dragon swept over the fortress walls, flames spewing from its dark maw, igniting men where they stood. The beast made a quick circle above the main gate, its golden eyes fixed to the burning bodies of Lord Garvos and his heir, flames licking their charred flesh.

"KRALL!"

The dragon screamed at their thrashing bodies flopping upon the battlement below like fish tossed upon the shore before spewing more flames upon them. The intense heat melted the ramparts, removing any trace that the men ever stood there. The dragon suddenly shifted further along the wall, its attention drawn to the next strongest magic wielder, spraying fire along the battlements until reaching the mage, where an intense beam of pure white light shot from its mouth, the powerful blast bursting the mage into oblivion, chunks of flesh flying over the ramparts.

The intense light continued through the thick stone ramparts, blasting the wall to its foundation, throwing blocks of stone high into the air. The dragon closed its mouth, circling back to the main gate, and repeating the process there, blasting the wall apart down to its foundation. The bright light blinded anyone fool enough to gaze upon it. The stream of energy continued until a massive hole was punched in the wall of the fortress, leaving naught but melted stone and twisted rubble. The dragon continued straight into the fortress' center, cutting a massive hole through structure after structure, behind where the main gate had stood, before circling back again to the outer ramparts, sweeping back and forth along the wall, burning everything in sight.

*****

Karg sat astride his mount, staring intently as the dragon destroyed the Vellesian fortress. In the twilight of his fourth decade, Karg, Hammer Son, smiled with grim satisfaction as his young dragon rider brought another mage fortress to ruin. Karg Hammer Son, was a barrel-chested mountain of a man, with a thick black beard and bright pink eyes. He wore brown boiled leather mail over furs, with a crude iron helm that poorly fit his large skull. A bone necklace hung low across his chest, each a fore digit from a slain foe. He was certain to add several more necklaces after this campaign, the very thought filling him with morbid delight. He raked his fingers through his beard before touching his misshapen nose, where a cruel scar ran the width of his face, a terrible burn that fueled his hatred for the mage born, and the realms they ruled.

"Kai-Korub?" Gorbus Mammoth's Bane asked, sitting his left, a portly fellow with mismatched brown and green eyes.

"Aye, old friend, Kai-Korub," Karg affirmed, echoing their battle cry.

"Kai-Korub!" Gorbus hoisted the pike, heaving the severed head into the air, their cavalry repeating the battle cry before racing forth toward the smokey ruin where the main gate once stood. They swarmed through the break in the wall, branching off into the fortress proper once they cleared the breach. There was no longer anyone upon the battlements to answer their charge, just broken ruble and charred corpses. By now, the dragon swept over the eastern face of the fortress, laying waste to the few soldiers positioned there, before circling back to Karg, setting down beside him.

"It is done, my King," the flame-haired dragon rider hailed, dismounting from the black-scaled creature. She knelt before Karg, the barbarian monarch regarding her curvaceous form bulging against her leathers.

"You did well, Casandra. Let us hope your brother is equally adept. Attend me!" Karg promptly ordered, urging his horse toward the breech in the wall, the girl Casandra walking beside him.

The barbarians swept through the fortress, slaying nearly every man, woman, and child in their path. Most of their victims were hacked to pieces whilst others were made sport of before slain. Lustful men took their liberties with captive females, or males, if they were so inclined. A few survivors were gathered in the central courtyard of Castara, chained in a pen while their captors celebrated their victory. They recognized the head of Lord Garvos's aged mother being kicked around the yard by the foul-smelling wild men. The old woman was already dead when they found her in her chambers, crushed under fallen debris as the dragon clawed its way into the lord's apartments from above, drawn by her mage blood. Fortunately, the lord's wife and younger children were sent away when news of the barbarian invasion first reached Lord Garvos's ears.

The merriment continued deep into the night, the barbarians making use of captured stores of food and wine. More of them filtered into the ruined fortress throughout the night, as the thousand cavalry were merely the vanguard of a much larger host.

"You, wench!" One chieftain pointed at a comely captive maid chained in the pen, her arms pinioned helplessly behind her. She looked no more than sixteen years. Her rich lavender gown was torn to her shoulders, her pale-brown eyes staring frantically through her disheveled dark hair.

The chieftain stumbled toward the pen in a drunken stupor, a jug of wine dangling in his left hand. He opened the pen, snatching the girl by the throat, dragging her into the courtyard's center where his comrades cheered him on.

"Come here...lass," he managed to blurt out between a foul belch before planting a kiss to her lips, the girl struggling in his grip, tears pouring from her eyes.

"Easy wench or I'll tan your hide!" he growled.

"Teach her a lesson, Ord!" one of his men called out.

"I'll teach her right and proper. She's a spirited lass. I might take her to wife!" Ord sneered, drawing her close.

"Play with her, but cut her throat when you finish!" Karg commanded, stepping around the great bonfire they erected in the courtyard, his bright pink eyes sweeping the faces of his men gathered around, before stopping at Ord.

"I found her, and I claim her as is my right as chieftain of tribe Reven!" Ord protested.

"And as your *king*, I say not."

"Even a king must acknowledge chieftain rights!"

"The welfare of my chieftains is more important than their rights."

"But she's a fine-looking lass. What harm is there in making her mine?"

"She is tainted by magic. When this war is finished, the mage bloods will be scourged from the land. What good will it do you to welp pups from her when the dragons will burn them to ash, and probably you with them just to get to her?"

"She has no taint of magic. The dragon would've already slain her if she did." Ord snorted.

"She doesn't, heh?" Karg stepped near drawing the frightened girl from Ord's grasp. "She is too finely dressed to not share their noble blood, and we well know that magic is the source of all nobility in these southern realms." He ran a hand over her silken gown, the garment costing enough to outfit a thousand commoners.

"But if she was…"

"The dragon had bigger game to taste to be bothered with her, but now that their lord is dead, it will set its fire upon her." Karg dragged her away by the arm.

"If she had magic, she'd have used it to save herself?" Ord growled.

"Unless it's useless magic, like changing the color of her eyes or such." Karg threw her to the ground, ordering everyone to back away.

"Call your dragon, Casandra!" he ordered the red-haired dragon rider, who stood among the onlookers.

Casandra paused, sharing a sympathetic look with the frightened girl before obeying her king. The crowd grew quiet, drawing further away than Karg commanded, a large shadow passing over the moonless sky. Casandra extended her arms overhead, her green eyes clouding as the beast landed at her feet. The captive girl's eyes gazed up as the dragon swung its massive head from its human conduit to her, recognition alit in its golden eyes to her power. She was but a simple charm caster, and not a very strong one at that, but the dragon could sense it if he looked for it. She might've gone unnoticed if she wasn't brought before its searing gaze, but fortune forsook her. Her beauty and magic charm were enough to purchase her an easy life as her lord's mistress but did little good now.

Hot breath steamed from the dragon's nose, contorting her face and lifting her hair as she quietly pleaded mercy, rolling onto her knees, begging for her life.

"Please!" she cried as the dragon regarded her with an intelligence she didn't expect. The beast was clearly a young adult, its torso not much larger than a cottage, but it still towered over her small form. It had four, thickly muscled limbs with jagged claws that could rend a knight in half. Black scales covered its body, firelight playing off their glistening surface. She released a relieved sigh as it drew briefly away, thinking she survived its inspection.

Flames spewed from its mouth, engulfing her in a terrible inferno, her screams echoing briefly before she burst asunder. The dragon squashed her with its forelimb, grinding her charred corpse into the ground, dousing the flames.

"AGGHH!" the dragon roared in triumph before extending its black leathery wings, bounding into the air.

Karg walked over to where the girl once stood, shifting his boot through her burnt remains.

"She failed the test of fire!" Karg declared, his eyes sweeping the crowd. "Her impurity has been cleansed by the gods' sentinel, who renders judgment upon the wicked. Let this be a lesson to you all before we go further! The mage born are to be expunged from the land, from our sacred homelands, that they mock as wilderness, to the Aqualania Sea, from east to west, the Mage Realms shall be cleansed."

*****

Present time

Mortava winced, her face pressed against the ground as noxious fumes tortured her nose. She felt the weight upon her ease as Ethan gained his feet, then helping her up. She looked out of sorts, an unnatural dizziness overtaking her that could only happen in Ethan's presence. She attempted to step away from his overbearing aura to regain her senses, but his firm grip on her arm kept her close.

"You can't." Ethan coughed, holding her tight, his eyes fixed on the horizon where the large black wings passed from sight.

Mortava froze, transfixed by the unimaginable creature flying away, until drawn from her stupor by the cries of wounded men and the smell of their burning flesh. There, all around them, was a burning strip of land, gouged from the earth nearly ten yards abreast, running some two hundred yards in length. She and Ethan stood upon a small isle of green amid this sea of smoky ruin, a patch of untouched grass that perfectly matched his silhouette, where he shielded her from certain death. Several bodies littered the ground, their still forms charred beyond recognition. Several others writhed upon the ground where the edge of the strip met untouched grass, their bodies burned upon whichever side faced the flames. It was evident that anyone directly in the dragon's path could not have survived the intense heat of the fire.

"Ethan, I must help them." Mortava tried to step away to treat their wounded.

"I don't think you should. Your power is too great. The dragon was drawn to you. If you use your power, it will return."

"It is drawn to me, not you," she said, looking at him with wonder.

"That won't stop its fire from burning everything and everyone around me," he pointed out, looking at the carnage around them, wondering which of their men had perished. Sergeant Hawthar was stood beside him during the attack and was likely one of the charred bodies off his left. A relieved sigh followed as he spotted Ander coming down the hill.

"I have to do something, Ethan. I can't leave them like this." Mortava looked around at the wounded and dying men. Burns were terrible things, the pain a constant torment. These burns were so severe that she doubted any would live long without treatment.

"Can you heal burns from dragon fire?" he rightly asked. Dragons were anti-magic in nature, but was dragon fire the same?

"You are immune to their flames. If it were anti-magic as well, this would not be so," she said, her gaze drawn to a poor soldier suffering burns to the entire left side of his body, the flesh peeled away over half his face. It was a wonder he still lived.

"I need to at least try." She shook her head, her heart breaking for her people.

Ethan was taken aback by her empathy, considering the nature of her House. Was this the same woman who was once Queen of Vellesia, willing to risk her life to save common-born men?

"Wait, I have an idea," Ethan said, sending Ander back up the hill to fetch his rifle from his saddle, before ordering everyone else away from the wounded, while keeping Mortava close beside him.

"Are you ready?" Mortava asked, guessing what he had in mind.

"Ready as I'll never be."

"That's not reassuring," she playfully scolded him.

"It wasn't meant to be." He gave her that cocky grin that was irritatingly endearing.

"Then there is no time to waste," she said, stepping away to attend to the soldier with the burned face. It was rapture stepping from his shadow, her power returning as she passed beyond his aura. She didn't waste these precious moments, hurrying to attend to the wounded. A mere touch to the soldier's forehead sent a pulse of intense magic through his body, powerful enough to fully restore him. She paused briefly to see the results of her power, confirming if it could counter the effects of dragon fire. As soon as she saw the soldier's face begin its restoration, she moved on, running from one to another, touching a finger to each soldier she came upon.

Ethan didn't spare her a glance, keeping a look out to the horizon.

"Mortava!" he shouted, training his rifle on the dark silhouette appearing in the distant sky when a distinct ringing sound filled his ears.

*****

Casandra held tight to the spindles along the dragon's neck, the wind pressing upon her face as the beast turned sharply, racing back to whence they came. She felt the dragon's rage, the veins in its neck throbbing emphatically below its scales. She knew the source of the dragon's ire, drawn to the intense power radiating from a mage that somehow reappeared where they dispatched the other one, or was it the same one? It couldn't be the same, for no one could withstand the dragon's fire. What concerned her was the other source of strange magic in the oddly dressed man that stood protectively beside the mage. It wasn't magic at all, but the complete absence of it, much like the dragon, but in human form.

She could make out the scorched earth just over the rise, where they burned a swath over the enemy, consuming their mage, but the mage still stood, her power radiating brighter than any she had ever felt. The pain of the mage's presence sent crippling pain shooting through her brain, matching the agony of the dragon.

"KRALL!"

The dragon's roar echoed like thunder rolling across the sky, the mere sight of the mage kindling its fury, her intense power furthering its torment.

The mage was hunched over what appeared to be a wounded soldier when she caught sight of the dragon's approach, the intensity of her power glowing like a thousand suns. Then it was gone. A frigid cold permeated her soul as the mage's power simply…disappeared.

The dragon felt it as well as if the invisible cord connecting it to its prey was suddenly cut.

It made little sense. Casandra could see the mage standing beside the strangely dressed man. She was there, but for some reason, her power was gone.

"Something is wrong." She heard herself say as the man below pointed a strange-looking pole in their direction. Alarm rang in her mind, the dragon heeding her warning, turning just as a terrible sound echoed from below.

"*Nylo, we must leave!*" She pleaded with the dragon but could hear nothing but its garbled thoughts, its rage impairing their telepathic link.

The bullet grazed the dragon's neck, slicing several scales from its flesh as the beast roared in agony, its sudden shift sparing it further harm. Casandra urged the dragon to continue its turn, shifting its pattern as another bullet struck its wing.

"*NYLO!*" she screamed, feeling the dragon's pain, speeding away as the awful sound of the stranger's weapon sounded again like a crack of lightning.

"*I hear you, Casandra,*" Nylo spoke, unable to hide the pain in his silent voice. He pushed his labored wings to their utmost, flying countless leagues before setting down upon a hilltop beside a grove of pines.

Casandra slid off his back as he tucked his wings, blood dripping from his wound. She carefully examined it, tears welling in her green eyes.

"Oh, Nylo," she cried, pressing her head to his wing near the wound. The projectile passed cleanly through, but it looked painful nonetheless.

"*I just need to rest,*" Nylo said, setting his massive head on the ground, his golden eyes growing dim.

Casandra removed her fur cloak, wiping the blood around the wound. Fortunately, it didn't appear serious but wondered what sort of weapon could harm a dragon.

"*I could feel his thoughts,*" Nylo confessed, his weary eyes closing.

"*Whose thoughts?*" She came around in front of him, touching her slender fingers to his snout.

"*The human who hurt me. I could hear his thoughts.*"

"*How is that possible? Unless…*" She made a face.

"*He is like you, but also like me,*" Nylo said tiredly, his eyes still closed, as if he were unable to open them.

"*Who is he?*" she asked, fearful of the possibilities.

"*I don't know his name, but he called the woman mage, Mortava.*"

"*If you can read his thoughts, then…*"

"*He can read mine,*" Nylo answered.

"*Why didn't your fire kill him?*"

"*I don't know. That is a question we must find the answer to.*"

"*The king will not be pleased.*" She sighed.

"*Karg is never pleased,*" Nylo reminded her. "*Perhaps I should eat him,*" and give them a new king.

*****

Ethan staggered, the buzzing in his head slowly fading as the dragon disappeared from sight.

"Ethan?" Mortava asked, placing her hand on the rifle's barrel, forcing it down as he continued to look to the horizon.

"Finish treating the wounded, then I'll relax." He kept a wary eye on the heavens.

She hurriedly attended the remaining wounded before stepping back to his side. It was painfully evident that the time for them to remain in close proximity had come. It felt strange and unwelcome for her to be dependent upon another as she was now with Ethan. He held her life in his hands, her shield against the dragon. She scolded herself for such self-pity. It was beneath her. Besides, she knew their entire strategy depended upon their working in tandem, their powers complementing each other, much like he and Bronus did at the Velo. Mortava dispatched two of their soldiers to bury what remained of the dead before they continued on, blasting a hole in the ground with a burst of energy from her outstretched hand. 'Twas another power of House Loria that Ethan was unaware of, their list of mage abilities too numerous to catalog.

The late afternoon found them making their way north and west, scouting for signs of the enemy host. Mortava and Ethan shared a saddle, not risking a return of their winged nemesis. She sat behind him, wrapping her slender muscled arms around him as they passed under the branches of oak trees lining either side of the road. A flock of geese passed overhead, their calls giving all of them a sense of normalcy for a brief moment.

"You were right about the dragon," she said in his ear. It felt odd to be sharing a saddle with her granddaughter's husband, a part of her not sure how she felt about it. Though he was impossibly handsome, she did not feel attraction to him in that way but was pleased that he belonged to Alesha, who was an extension of her own flesh. He felt like her own child in a way. She knew he was resentful of the trickery used to lure him to Vellesia, but she couldn't imagine their realm or family without him.

"Which part?" he asked.

"That you could shield us from it."

"Well, we lucked upon that bit of information at the Kiernan Divide. Luckily, it wasn't a coincidence," he recalled that dragon's reaction to him when he saved Valera.

"Lucky indeed. Of course, lucky is one of your unique attributes, is it not?"

"Lucky? Me? You've seen me play poker."

"What is a silly game to life and death? And you, my child, have courted death on so many occasions."

"Being able to self-heal has saved me more than luck. I was stabbed enough at the Velo to die a hundred times over," he painfully recalled every cut and slice.

"I wasn't talking about the Velo. I was talking about Earth and the Mage Bane. Alesha spoke in great detail of your fight with Luke Crawford. You were spared by the slightest of margins, his bullet just missing your heart."

"Not his bullet. I killed Luke straight up. It was Emmitt Cobb who shot me right after. I still owe him for that," he growled, wondering what rock the outlaw had crawled under. That was another piece of unfinished business he'd like to address but was denied by his mistress. It was just another reminder that his life was not his own, even if they somehow defeated the dragon.

"The details are irrelevant. The fact remains you came within a finger's width of dying in the Mage Bane. Let us not forget the bullet you took in Red Rock."

He looked over his shoulder, giving her a quick glance. "Remind me to thank Krixan someday for sharing that." He shook his head.

"He is hardly to blame considering Alesha simply read his thoughts."

"Yeah, I know, but I'll still give him grief about it if we ever see each other again," he grumbled.

"You whine too much," she said.

"Probably." He didn't even deny it, which caused her to smile.

"I was meaning to ask, how did you restore that boy's mother back there in the village? I ain't ever seen a mage healer able to reverse the effects of aging," Ethan asked.

"*I ain't ever?* Your grammar is appalling. You didn't learn that from your royal tutors. You just love acting like a simpleton." She rolled her eyes.

"Who's acting?"

"You're impossible. No matter. To answer your question, the power to restore what time has taken is an advanced form of mage healing, but most mages lack the extra element needed," she explained.

"What element is that?"

"With every mage power, there is an advanced form, an ability to magnify its potency. This element is a mage power unto its self, and only by possessing both can you practice it. Most mages born with the power of magical enhancement are not born with any other power or just one. A mage possessing this power, and is also a light caster, will be able to cast light from their hands over a much larger area, perhaps a hundredfold or a thousand. To see them, you would merely think they were simply a stronger light caster, not realizing that they in fact were a light caster and a magical enhancer."

"And that's why all your family's magic is stronger than an average mage," he said. It finally made sense, explaining why Alesha's power was so potent. If this were true, it also meant all their powers were so enhanced, like their lightning. If his father could waylay an army, what were the Lorians capable of? Which begged the question, where and when did they gain this ability? For that, she answered for him.

"It was my father that possessed this power, making me the first queen of Vellesia with enhanced mage power with all her abilities. Think of the Lady Julia Forbis, whom you were acquainted in Cordova. She was a blinder, was she not?"

"She was."

"Yes, a very powerful one. She could hold several people sightless for much of a day, though it would tax her greatly, leaving her little strength for anything else. With our mage enhancement, myself being the first, we can blind a thousand, and hold them in darkness for years."

Ethan paled, again learning the scope of their power was far greater than he assumed.

"You can imagine the joy my house felt when my father was brought into their possession, giving me this great power. He wasn't even aware that he had it."

"If he didn't know that he had it, how did you?"

"Another gift we came upon long ago, long before Evalena was born. We have the power to sense the mage gift in others and its unique nature. It made collecting powers we lacked, that much easier."

"How convenient."

"Very mush so. Of course, we had no such need with you. As your birth was foretold long ago in prophecy."

"Again, how convenient," he said dryly.

"You can ill imagine the panic you caused our house when Alesha returned, relaying your adventures in Red Rock. Mother Evalena was nearly apoplectic with how close you came to death. We decided that we could wait no longer to fetch you, lest all our plans come to ruin by you getting your foolish self killed."

"All that fuss for little ole me." He shook his head.

"Yes, little ole you. You can now see how important you are to House Loria, far more important than simply siring our future heir."

"Yep, I'm your shield against the dragon. It's almost too convenient how I show up just before a dragon breaks through your barrier."

"Are you suggesting we knew this would transpire?"

"No, but it's just an unbelievable coincidence. Wouldn't you be suspicious if you were me?"

"That is irrelevant, for I am not you. If you are suspicious, then why are you here?"

"Being suspicious doesn't mean I'm unreasonable. I know you didn't plan all this to happen, and whether you knew it would happen or not doesn't lessen the threat of the dragons to Vellesia *and* Astaria. It looks like I was destined to face down a dragon no matter which path I chose, so it might as well be now."

"That is probably true. Like Alesha and your unborn daughter, you are a child of destiny. If this plan of yours is going to work, we'll be spending much of this campaign in each other's immediate company. How ever will you bear such a burden?" she teased.

"How will *you* bear it? It was either me or Bull as your companion, and you drew the short straw," he said.

"Short straw?" She wondered the meaning.

"Just something I picked up from Judge Donovan. It means you got the bad end of a deal."

"I did?"

"Yep. Valera got Bull, and you're stuck with whiney ole me."

"Bull is a handsome fellow, but I reckon I can manage," Mortava mimicked his Texas drawl, taking him aback.

"Not bad, Grandma, I'll make a Texan out of you yet." Ethan gave her that infectious grin that she was growing fond of. It was shocking how their casual banter had morphed into what it was now. If anyone had told her that she would one day be sharing a saddle with Ethan Blagen and that she would allow him to call her *grandma*, she'd have struck them dead. But here she was, talking with him like they were old companions riding the trail.

"So tell me about Texas," she asked, liking the way his eyes alit at the subject.

CHAPTER 24

Thirty leagues southeast of Castara

They waited within a copse of forest pines, watching as the foraging party passed, counting forty riders in furs and leathers. There were several women in the group, each as vicious as the men, their hair tied in braids, draping beneath their helms. They didn't have much in the way of armor, using boiled leather to guard their more vital regions. Few of the men sported thick beards, as most were little more than boys. The hardier warriors were placed in the fore ranks of the army, leaving foraging duties to the younger men and women.

Neigh! One of their horses stirred, causing everyone to look at the offending beast's rider, who sheepishly lifted his hands, confessing his guilt.

"The men grow restless. Give the command before we lose surprise," Mortava whispered in his ear, sitting behind him in the saddle.

Ethan agreed, giving the signal. Archers loosed arrows, taking several riders from their saddles. Horns sounded the charge as Vellesian cavalry burst from the trees, brandishing long swords upon emerging from their concealment, the bristling pines biting unarmored flesh. Ethan pushed through the brambles partially blocking their way, ignoring the pain as they cut his right arm. Mortava suffered far less, her finely crafted lightweight armor protecting her limbs. Bright sunlight struck her face as Ethan cleared the forest edge. Drawing his father's sword, he closed upon the nearest foe, a barbarian rider some ten yards away. The enemy quickly overcame their surprise, drawing swords in time to meet the charge. Ethan rode past the young warrior, the power of his strike taking the barbarian from the saddle. He circled about, his follow swing striking the prone man's knee as his back struck the ground.

The man cried out, his scream drowned in the din of battle. All along the road, men were cut down, overwhelmed by Vellesian numbers. Open meadows lined the opposite side of the road, a few barbarians racing straight in that direction, several stumbling in the high grass, their horses breaking legs on the uneven ground. Ethan set the ambush well, concentrating his men to the front and rear of the column, cutting off the quickest avenues of escape.

Mortava cursed the limitations of having to stay within Ethan's shadow. She could end this engagement with a snap of her fingers. Ethan was likewise limited, unable to move swiftly among the enemy as their movements required coordination. He was further limited by his use of weapon, favoring a sword over his guns to save his precious ammunition.

"Ethan!" she shouted in his ear, drawing his attention to their left, where a warrior rushed toward them afoot, wielding an axe.

Ethan passed his sword to his left hand, blocking the fellow's hurried strike. While Ethan held the axe in place, Mortava thrust her sword through the man's belly, stretching underneath Ethan's arm. Ethan backed their horse away, the fellow stumbling, unable to take a step without falling.

Ethan and Mortava dismounted in unison, better able to make use of their skills on foot. He caught sight of Ander approaching the wounded axe wielder from behind, running his sword across the back of his knees, face-planting the man before driving his sword through his back. Mortava drew Ethan in the opposite direction, where several foes were afoot, trying to form a protective circle, their round shields unsuited to the task. A Vellesian knight charged through their makeshift shield wall, breaking their formation.

Ethan saw one of the barbarians go down, trampled underfoot by the horse's hooves. The light horse was unsuited to the task, an axe finding purchase in its hindquarter, slowing its charge.

"Come!" Mortava said, rushing to help their comrade before they dragged him from the saddle.

Ethan struggled staying beside her, keeping her within his magical immune aura. He wasn't exactly sure how far his aura extended or if parts of her body stuck out if it would be enough to draw the dragon.

Mortava rushed forth, swords in both hands. The man nearest her met her initial strike with the flat of his shield, his counter strike meeting her second blade, while her first slid off his shield, striking off the wrist of his sword arm. She spun around him before his scream escaped his lips, chopping the back of his knee. The man tumbled in the dirt as she moved on, Ethan staying beside her, lowering his shoulder into another shield, the blow knocking the woman wielding it upon her back. Mortava took the woman's ankle, her blade cutting deep into the bone. Ethan followed, driving his sword into her breast.

Mortava marveled at the fluid ease with which Ethan moved amongst their foe. He was equally impressed with her sword handling. Even with her mage powers impaired, she was deadlier than any warrior he had known. All the mothers of House Loria spent several lifetimes honing their skills, using the gift of their unnaturally long life to its fullest. Ethan and Mortava learned to move in unison, never drifting apart. With each step, they grew accustom to how the other moved, picking up speed as they went. Ander followed close behind but drew back as they swept through their foes like a swirling wind, their blades spinning faster than his mortal eye could follow, lumps of flesh flying off their blades. They finally stopped with the last foes defeated.

Ander quickly set about organizing the men, taking stock of the wounded, and gathering prisoners for questioning. Casualties were light, with three dead, and several wounded. Only one of their wounded was serious, the soldier taking a sword to his stomach. Mortava wanted to heal the man, but they couldn't risk discovery by the dragon, for using her power was akin to lighting a bonfire on a moonless night. Her mere presence was enough to draw the creature, even without drawing upon her power.

The prisoners provided little information of use, each contradicting the others claims after Ander ordered them separated. Their stories varied, putting the enemy host between five and ten leagues north and west. Mortava ordered their throats cut before moving out, unable to bring them along. Ethan didn't argue the treatment of their captives after seeing the barbarians' treatment of the Vellesians they captured. They found several wagons laden with food stores, taking what they could carry and burning the rest, wasting little time before moving on.

*****

They came upon more burned out villages and farms in the following days, finding bodies hung from trees, or severed heads adorning pikes driven into the ground. Women and children were not spared their savagery, the macabre scenery stiffening their collective resolve. They encountered a band of outriders two days after their ambush, killing several after giving chase, keeping clear of the main host, not wishing to lock horns with the dragon until Valera arrived with her army. Meanwhile, Ethan used their light cavalry to strike and evade, killing their scouts, foragers, and outriders wherever they found them. They circled the enemy host throughout their campaign, drawing north of them. Each afternoon they would put many leagues between themselves and the enemy host, setting camp at a safe distance.

One late evening found them sitting around their cookfires, resting after another long day of riding. Ethan leaned back against his saddle, which rested on the ground, chewing on a blade of grass while staring into the flames, struck by a memory of so long ago.

"What troubles you, Ethan?" Mortava asked, sitting beside him. They had grown close of late, forced by necessity to nearly stay joined at the hip. They ate together, rode together, slept beside each other, and to their mutual discomfort, handled the other functions of nature in the other's presence. One false move and her power would draw the dragon to them. If the beast was drawn to an average mage, they could only imagine how the power emanating from a Mother of the Lorian Order would draw its ire? It would be akin to a thousand suns lighting the sky.

"Just thinking," was all he said.

"That encompasses a broad spectrum of possibilities, child. Do you care to elaborate, or must we suffer your morose disposition?"

"Oh, come now, Grandma, I'm not that sullen." He gave her that very smile that came so easily to him, leaning back against the saddle with his hands hooked behind his head, his hat high on his brow.

"Don't grow accustom to calling me that when we return to Elysia," she said, lifting his Stetson from his head, and putting it on hers.

"Don't worry, I'll be good if we manage to survive this. I'll say yes, my Queen, yes Mother so and so, yes my Princess, Yes, Minister Mattiese, yes…"

"All right, enough." She shook her head as he rambled off all the appellations that he hated repeating.

"Tedious, isn't it?" He goaded. "Maybe you all should just call each other by name and save us all the bother. It would be a whole lot easier."

"You seem to be the only one who has trouble with it. Perhaps we should assign you extra lessons on etiquette with Leora when we return," she teased, leaning back against their saddle pack beside him, lowering the Stetson over her face to hide her grin.

"That's just the kind of reward I'd expect from your family," he shot back.

"It's your family now too, Ethan."

"And what a family it is, spying on me since I was born, arranging wars to draw me back across the barrier, and tricking me into marriage." He couldn't help himself. To speak in such a way to a Mother of the Lorian Order was punishable by death, but Mortava and Ethan had grown close in their time together, forsaking almost all measures of propriety. She felt more like a friend, than Alesha's distant grandmother.

"I'm sorry, Mor. I didn't mean to offend you." He looked over at her, gauging her reaction.

"Had you said such things in Elysia I would have seen you punished. How things can change once you come to know someone." She smiled easily.

"Thanks," he said, taken aback by what she said. Could a Lorian Mother really be forgiving?

"I can forgive such outbursts, Ethan, because I know your heart. You speak harshly against our house when given freedom to do so, but actions weigh heavier than words. It speaks well of you that despite what we did to you, you are still here beside us, fighting to defend Vellesia. Despite the equal threat to Astaria, I believe you would still be here if that was not so. For one who claims to love freedom, you are bound by something far greater, even when you were free," she said, with a timeless look upon her face.

"Yeah, what's that?"

"Love." She sighed wistfully.

"Love?"

"Yes. You are bound by it and would suffer for it, forsaking freedom for the benefit of others. If you did not care for others, freedom would be a dull thing."

"Alesha said something similar after we escaped the Mage Bane," he recalled.

"And she was right. Despite what happened at the Velo, you could have taken your freedom anytime before then, if you so chose. Your father couldn't have stopped you from running off to live as you wanted. You stayed because you love your family. Just as you went to Red Rock to help Jake and stayed there to help Ben. You went back home to help your father at the Velo. You entered the Mage Bane to save Allie and bent the knee to her to save your father, forsaking freedom for his life. And even if you were not bound to us, you would still be here to protect those you have come to love, like Ander, Jered, Raymar, Darius, Corbin, and now myself. Do you care to deny it?"

"You know me too well." He never thought about it like that.

"All those years of studying you, and we missed that key point until Alesha used it to trap you. Love binds you, far more than any threats to your father, or chains and magical collars. But the one that binds you more than all the others is Alesha. You are as bound to her as she is to you. This is also something we did not expect."

"Yes, bound to her, but how can I love someone who betrayed me? And yet I can't bear being parted from her. It doesn't make any sense."

"It makes all the sense in the world, Ethan. You are both children of prophecy, following the currents of destiny that force you together. You can no more escape one another than the sunrise."

"There's that word I've come to hate, destiny. It is the bane of freedom." He shook his head.

"Freedom?" she asked. "Freedom will not bring you happiness, Ethan."

"How do you know?"

"Were you ever happy when you were free?"

Ethan thought for a moment, recalling the brief period that he was free. His time in Red Rock was one of the happiest in his life, but he always knew it was temporary, and he had to eventually return home. Once he earned his freedom, he spent all his time hunting down Luke Crawford. Before he could ever enjoy his freedom, it was gone.

"I was happy in Red Rock."

"Could you be happy there again?"

"Yes," he answered all too quickly.

"Without Alesha?" She raised an eyebrow.

His silence was all she needed to know.

"No, probably not." He sighed.

"We wouldn't be happy without you either," she confessed.

"For the greatness of your house, I know."

"Fool boy. It is more than that now. Since your arrival, the madness that is all consuming, has dulled. Before you disparage Alesha for her betrayal, you must understand what drove her to do so."

"The hunger, I know," he heard this all before.

"You know, but you refuse to understand. The firstborn of my maternal line is always female and is born with an insatiable hunger for any mage power they do not possess. It is all-consuming, driving some in the olden days to the brink of madness. There were times, even I was driven to my knees in crippling pain." She sighed.

"The olden days?"

"Over a thousand years ago, our ancestor, Queen Raella, wed a mage gifted with the power of regeneration, the very power that you possess. This ability to self-heal extends to the mind as well, preventing madness from overtaking us."

"The same power that gave you a long life?"

"Yes."

That meant the queens of Vellesia had been living for over three hundred years going back over a millennium.

"Now imagine living since birth with a hunger that can never be quenched. Then imagine the gift of extended life through regeneration, living many lifetimes with that hunger? In all that time, we looked for the day of your birth, Ethan, for your union with Alesha to fulfill our purpose. It was all we truly had to live for, the other pleasures of life doing naught to bring us joy. It was only recently we discovered a wondrous secondary benefit. Whenever you are in Alesha's presence, our hunger goes away."

Alesha told him as much but left out much of Mortava's passion.

"Do you see what this has meant, Ethan? We can now live, partaking the joys of life in ways we never could before, as long as you and Alesha are together."

"I'm not with her right now," he pointed out.

"Yes, and the hunger is returning." She sighed.

"You don't look hungry to me." He smiled.

"Being within your shadow has shielded me from many of its effects. The mothers in Elysia have no such protection. Even now they are likely succumbing to its terrible resolve. Only you returning to Alesha will assuage their suffering."

"That's a heavy burden to put on me." He shook his head. If this were true, they would never let him go.

"You were hoping to earn your freedom by slaying the dragon," she said, reading him as plain as an open tome.

"I know you would never grant it." He sighed.

"But you thought it."

"Yeah, I thought it," he confessed.

"I understand," she said kindly.

"You do?"

"Your love of freedom is all-consuming, like our hunger. When you were born, we only knew of your immunity to magic, the final piece to our dominion. When Sarella and Selendra sent us word of your peculiar nature, we thought it an inconvenience to our plans. We could hardly allow your pursuit of freedom to lead you away from us."

"True, chains and freedom don't mix."

"I am sorry you see what we offer as chains, but considering what drives you, I understand. At least now I do. It wasn't always so," she said sadly.

"Is that an apology?"

"No, merely an acknowledgment of what we took from you. To be sorry would mean we would not repeat our actions if given the choice, and we both know that is not so."

"Guess that's the closest I'll get to an apology."

"Whether I apologize or not, you cannot escape your destiny. You and Alesha are joined by omnipotent bonds drawing you together, and nothing we say or do will change that."

"You sound as if we would've been together no matter how things unfolded in Astaris."

"I believe so now but not then. I envy you, Ethan. You and Alesha." She smiled easily, staring into the fire.

"You envy me?" He made a face.

"Yes. Do you know how old I am?"

"Older than you look, that's for certain. You are a very beautiful woman, and I am not alone in thinking it," he said, causing her to blush.

"You are kind to say so," she said, though even she knew it to be true. She could tell by the men's reaction to her presence. Unlike Alesha, she could not mask her otherworldly beauty. "I am, in fact, 137 years. I have been widowed for 53 of those years, and should I reach three hundred, more than 200, I will have lived without my husband. What good is such a long life without someone to share it, someone worthy of you?" she said sadly.

"I hadn't thought of it like that." He sighed.

"Of course, you haven't. You were too busy whining," she teased.

"Fair enough." He smiled in good humor before she continued.

"My mother, Inese, is 159. My grandmother Porshana is 176, and Evalena is 292. Imagine living all those years without Alesha?"

Ethan couldn't think that far ahead, and doing so gave him pause.

"Imagine living for three hundred years, which you will, Ethan, and imagine if Alesha lived only as long as commoners? Could you bear living alone? Could you bear living with an insatiable hunger that could never be fully quenched? Then imagine the years you did have with her filled with that hunger, blinding you to the pleasure she brings you? That, Ethan, is the life I have lived. My husband was a decent man, a man I could never fully embrace, his power driving me mad with jealousy. Even when I placed that damnable collar around his neck, the hunger still persisted, though it was significantly dulled. I could never love him as he deserved, or I truly desired," she said, wiping a tear from her eye.

"I'm sorry, Mor." He touched her shoulder, giving her a gentle squeeze.

"Thank you, Ethan. You are a good man, and I am grateful for our time together. Just remember what you have with Alesha is beyond precious. Savor these years together. Perhaps it wouldn't be so terrible if the two of you lived elsewhere, raising your child from the tedium of court, sharing that cabin in the woods you once dreamed of," she thought wistfully.

"You mean that?" he asked, unable to hide his elation.

"I do, though the choice is not mine. I am but one voice of many. And Alesha still has a duty as Queen Daughter, a duty she cannot step away from, but time away from court would do each of you a great deal of good. But even if we allowed it, neither of you can escape your destiny. You are caught in its current, and must follow its course."

"Destiny." He shook his head, disgusted by the word.

"Destiny!" she affirmed. "You will find it is far stronger than your impulse toward freedom. You must balance the two if you are to find true peace of mind."

"I can't. Destiny and freedom cannot coexist. Destiny is slavery to events you can't control. Freedom is the choice to direct your own path."

"Do you deny the destiny that binds you and Alesha?" she asked, the evidence as clear as the sunrise.

"No, and that's the part that doesn't make sense."

"How so?"

"Why would the fates bind us together but instill in her a hunger for power, and in me, freedom? Why give us conflicting desires? For what purpose, other than a cruel joke?"

"I don't honestly know," she conceded. His love of freedom was overpowering, almost unnaturally so. There had to be a reason for him to be born so, but that reason was beyond her.

"My maternal great-grandfather believed in some screwy Free Born prophecy, thinking it was me," Ethan confessed. Raymar warned him not to speak of it to anyone, especially any of the royal line, but at this point what difference would it make? Besides, he already spoke of it with Alesha when he thought she was Allie. He quickly regretted his foolish utterance as Mortava grew deathly quiet.

"Mor, you all right?" he asked, looking over at her.

"I am...well," she struggled with her words, balling her hands into fists to stop them from trembling.

"Then why are you shaking?" he stupidly asked, realizing he made a grave mistake. Since Alesha already knew this story, didn't she share it with her grandmothers like she did everything else?

How could Mortava reply? How could she explain that the Free Born was a prophetic figure that would doom the Vellesian throne? How could she say that her house outlawed the adherents to that prophecy, hunting them to extinction? How could Ethan be the Free Born when he was bound to Alesha, bound to her by destiny? He couldn't be both their savior and their doom, could he? It made no sense, but then again, nothing about Ethan made sense.

"Mor?" he asked again, her silence starting to worry him.

"The Free Born is a thing best not spoken of," she said.

"Why? It's just a stupid prophecy, and if you hadn't noticed, I don't believe in them," he said, his light-hearted attempt at humor failing miserably.

"Prophecies and destinies are never to be taken lightly, Ethan. Since your destiny binding you to House Loria proves you could not be the Free Born, let us not speak of it again," she said, gifting him a smile that was more forced than genuine.

"Fair enough, I'm not much one for boring conversations about prophecies anyway." He grinned, trying to set her at ease.

It was then that Ander returned from checking their perimeter, setting his bedroll beside Ethan with several others following after, finding empty spaces around the fire to bed down for the night. They were saddle sore and weary, reminding Ethan of the posse he accompanied hunting down George Spencer in the New Mexico badlands. Too many hard days riding in the saddle wore down the hardest of men, and many of these men were little more than boys.

One soldier stood out from the others, a boy named Guston, who sat upon his saddle, on the other side of Ander, staring at the flames with a mournful look. This campaign was the first time many of these men had tasted battle, and it effected some far more than others.

"Is he all right?" Ethan asked Ander, looking over at the boy.

"The soldier we lost yestermorn was his dear friend," Ander whispered so the boy couldn't overhear.

There wasn't much he could say to that. He recalled losing many friends at the Velo. Nearly thirty of his light cavalry that he trained and lived with for over a year fell in battle. None were his best friend though. He couldn't imagine losing Krixan, Ben, Jake, or the judge. He could add so many others to that imaginary list, including his deputies in Cordova, let alone his family. Ethan reached behind him, fishing a pouch of jerky from his saddle pack, passing it to Ander.

Ander understood his intent, passing the pouch to Guston, who looked at him strangely before realizing what was intended.

"Thank you, Sergeant." Guston bowed.

"Thank Ethan," Ander said.

"My thanks, Ethan."

"You're welcome, Gus," Ethan said, taking a swig from his water satchel, happy Guston called him by name. After riding together for a while now, the men understood not to call him consort.

"It's never easy losing a friend, Gus. I lost more than a few in my time," Ethan said, staring into the flames, lost in a memory.

"Yes," Guston swallowed past the lump in his throat. "Tell me, Ethan, do you ever get used to it?"

"Used to it? You mean..."

"The killing," Guston said, looking at him now with soulful eyes.

Ethan released a tired sigh, not sure how to answer. He killed so many men he lost count. The first was a bandit from a band of ruffians that attacked him and Krixan during one of their hunts. It bothered him for a time, but the man tried to kill him and didn't give him much choice. He recalled the first man he killed with a gun, Stone Grierson. The terrible sound the pistol made matched the devastation it wrought. He could still see Stone on the floor of the Lucky Star saloon, writhing in agony, trying to hold his guts in as he cried for his mother. It was ghastly, but what choice did he have? Of all the men he killed, that one stood out the most.

"The first man you kill will stick with you for a time. Others, not so much, unless they stand out for some reason. You can kill dozens of men in battle and feel nothing when things are happening too quick for you to sort them in your head. It's when you have time to watch them die that sticks with you," he said in a faraway voice.

"I don't think it will ever leave my mind," Guston said sadly.

"The Texans have a song about a young cowboy dying in the street having lived dangerously until a bullet found him in the chest. It's a sad tale, almost hauntingly so, but beautiful," Ethan said.

"Why don't you sing it, Ethan?" Mortava asked.

"I wouldn't want to torture these poor fellas." He tried to squelch that idea at its inception.

"I've heard you sing, Ethan. You're not fooling anyone with that lousy voice excuse." Ander nudged him.

"Sing the song, Ethan," some others egged him on.

"It's kind of hard to do without my guitar," he explained, having left it in Elysia.

"Your voice will be enough, Ethan. Do it for them," Mortava said, pointing out the tired faces gathered around their fire.

Ethan knew when he was beaten.

As I walked out in the streets of Laredo
As I walked out in Laredo one day
I spied a young cowboy all dressed in white linen
Dressed up in white linen and cold as the clay

I see by your outfit that you are a cowboy
These words he did say as I boldly walked by
Come sit here, beside me, and hear my sad story
For I'm shot in the breast and I know I must die
It was once in the saddle I used to go dashing
Once in the saddle, I used to go gay
First to the dram house and then to the card house
Got shot in the breast and I'm going to die
So bang the drum slowly, and play the fife lowly
Play the death march as you bear me along
Take me to the green valley, there lay the sod over me
For I'm a young Cowboy, and I know I've done
        wrong

Please fetch me a cup, a cup of cold water
To cool my parched lips, the cowboy then said
But when I returned his spirit had lifted
And gone to his maker, the Cowboy was dead

So we banged the drum slowly and played our
        fifes lowly
And bitterly wept as we bore him along
We all loved the Cowboy, so brave, young and
        handsome
We all loved our comrade although he done wrong.

Ethan's voice carried well beyond their cookfire, his mournful ballad drawing others to gather round. Though few knew what a dram house meant or the significance of banging a drum for a funeral, they guessed the meaning. It touched their hearts, reminding each of their fragile mortality, and to embrace these precious moments of life. No one knew what tomorrow might bring, and could relate to the tale of a fallen comrade dying before them.

Once he finished, an eerie silence settled in, everyone's gaze drawn to the fire, lost in their own thoughts. Ethan kicked himself for singing that song, the tale having the expected result of depressing everyone, and that wouldn't do.

"Where do you hail from, Gus?" Ethan broke the silence.

Guston paused, wondering why he would care to know. "A small village called Casere. It is on the east bank of the Sorell, north of Corellis."

"Is there a girl in your village waiting for you?"

"Why do you ask?" Guston said.

"Just to remind you what you're fighting for. Don't think about death and dying, for life is too brief and precious to not savor its treasures. What is the name of this girl in Cesere waiting for you?"

"Galenda," Guston reluctantly offered up.

"And what color is her hair?"

"Brown." Guston made a face, wondering where Ethan was going with this.

"Brown, huh? All right, Gus, I'm going to sing a line, and you are going to repeat everything I sing, understood?"

Gus nodded uncertainly.

"That goes for the rest of you, as well," Ethan said to all of them gathered round, giving Ander and Mortava looks that meant them as well.

"Well, here goes…"

There's a brown-haired rose of Cesere
That Gus is going to see…

Ethan began, the others repeating after.

> No other soldier knows her
> Nobody, only he.
> She cried so when he left her
> It almost broke his heart
> And if he ever finds her
> They never more shall part
> She's the sweetest rose of color
> That Guston ever knew
> Her eyes are bright as diamonds
> They sparkle like the dew
> You can talk about your clementine
> And your Rosa Lee
> But the brown rose of Cesere
> Is the only girl for me.

They laughed and sang the merry tune several times before Ethan told them its original lyrics, "The Yellow Rose of Texas," which they asked him to sing as well while they joined in. He had to nudge Ander more than once to get him to do more than move his lips, the reserved sergeant needing constant prodding. Mortava laughed and clapped her hands like the others, enjoying the camaraderie that was unlike anything she felt before. Ethan soon goaded her to sing, knowing her voice was probably as lovely as Alesha's.

And so Mortava obliged, her silken voice echoing hauntingly in the night air.

> The sea, the sea
> Come away with me
> Across the still waters
> To lands far away
> The sea, the sea
> Come away with me...

It was one of those moments that would stay with them well into old age, comrades sharing songs beneath a starry sky. Ethan smiled at a memory, of another time sitting around a campfire with his light cavalry, all those years ago in Astaria. The stories, hopes, and fears were always the same, only their faces and names were different. He looked over at Mortava, hating how he was coming to like her. If only she was a conceited witch like he believed Valera was when he first met her, then it would be easier to hate her. He couldn't though, he just couldn't. He was struck by how different any of the Lorians were once he got to know them one on one. They were quite friendly and likeable once the madness was subdued. Was it really that powerful? He would never forgive them for what they did, but he understood it. If he spent several lifetimes consumed with such hunger, he'd probably have done the same thing. Their hunger was as powerful as his desire to be free, and their caging him would drive him to madness that would be as painful as their hunger. The fact that he would live for three hundred years, and do so as a captive in Vellesia, was unbearable. No, he would save them from the dragon, and plan his escape, if he could find a way around the magic binding his father, but that still left one problem...

Can I go without Allie? he asked himself. She so bewitched him that he couldn't imagine life without her. Well, maybe he could decide what to do later on. Perhaps she might be willing to...

I see him, Casandra, a voice said.

Ethan looked sharply in Ander's direction, then back to Mortava's, seeking the source of the voice that rang so clearly in his mind.

No. He is sitting beside that fire yonder, upon the hilltop, the strangely familiar voice spoke again. It was clear and calm, as if spoken in his ear, but it said *yonder*, as if far away. He stole a glance skyward, his gaze sweeping the distant horizon as he could see in the dark.

There, in the distance, he saw the dragon, black wings working in rhythmic grace as it passed along the horizon. Its rider sat its back, her red hair lifting in the night air.

"Ethan?" Mortava asked, alarmed by the look passing his face.

He sees us! the dragon's voice echoed in alarm.

Mortava followed his eyes to the horizon, cursing that her enhanced vision was blocked by Ethan's aura.

"What do you see?" she asked, her eyes returning to his.

"The dragon." He yielded under her gaze. He was a lousy liar, and didn't bother with a falsehood.

"The dragon? Where?" Ander jumped to his feet, his words stirring everyone to following in kind, panic threatening to overtake them.

"Easy," Ethan said, trying to settle them down, but they were having none of it. Men started to draw swords, though little good it would do them against a dragon.

"Stay calm, it's leaving," Ethan said as the beast flew away, disappearing over the horizon.

"How do you know, Ethan?" Mortava asked, studying his face.

"Because...I can see it."

"You can see in the dark?" Captain Golona snarled, staring at him from across the fire, wondering why he hadn't shared this information earlier.

"Is that true, Ethan?" Mortava asked critically.

"Yes," he sighed, finally divulging the one power he kept from them.

"You could have told us, Ethan," Ander said, the disappointment in his voice impossible to miss.

"It was not just us, was it, Ethan? No one knew of this gift, not even your family in Astaris," Mortava said.

"True." Ethan sighed. Had he told anyone, then Alesha could've picked it from their mind when she was in Astaris, let alone Sarella or Selendra.

"There is something else, isn't there?" Mortava could read him so easily.

His silence was damning.

"Speak it true, Ethan. All our lives are at risk," Ander said in a harsh tone Ethan had never suffered before.

"I heard...I heard its thoughts," he said.

"It's thoughts? The dragon's thoughts?" Mortava asked.

"Yes."

Everyone grew suddenly quiet, gathering closer to hear.

"How can you know what you heard was the dragon?" Mortava asked.

"I heard it say that it saw me in the distance. When I looked skyward, I found it along the horizon, over there." He pointed off to their southwest. "It then said that I could see them, as if it read my thoughts."

"You can speak to dragons?" one soldier asked, his eyes transfixed in awe and horror.

"How long have you known?" Mortava asked, the accusation hanging dangerously in the air.

"Known what?" Ethan asked.

"That you could speak to dragons. That you could read their thoughts?" Captain Golona growled.

"Just now, Captain!" Ethan growled back, taking a step toward the old soldier.

"What of the other times you encountered dragons? Couldn't you hear their thoughts then?" Mortava asked.

"The other times were different. I only heard a piercing noise in my head."

"Then why could you hear its thoughts now?" Ander asked.

"Good question." Ethan shrugged, unable to make sense of it. He was immune to mages reading his thoughts, so why could a dragon? And why now? Why did he hear nothing but a painful buzzing before?

"You *could* hear its thoughts before," Mortava said knowingly, suddenly realizing the mystery.

"I couldn't before. All I heard then was a terrible noise in my head. It was…"

"Maddening," she answered, knowingly.

"That's a kind way of describing it." He shook his head.

"Don't you see? The terrible noise *was* the dragon's thoughts. It all makes sense now," she said, a faraway look passing her eyes.

"Huh?" Ethan made a face.

"Mother Mortava?" Captain Golona asked with deep reverence, sharing Ethan's confusion.

"The other times you encountered a dragon, there were mages nearby, with full use of their powers. Not just any mages, either, but Valera and Alesha at Kiernan, and myself a few days ago. Tonight, however, there was only me, and my power was subdued." She looked at them to see if they were following, but they stared back at her with those confused looks about them.

"The dragons hate mages and attack those so gifted, hunting them to extinction, if they are able. Only the barriers protect the mage realms from such annihilation, and now we know why. Magic drives them mad, actually causing them pain," she explained, much like it caused her pain, if it was a magic she did not possess.

"You're saying the terrible sound is their thoughts?" Ethan couldn't imagine suffering that noise for long. If so, it was little wonder why dragons killed every mage they came upon.

"How is Ethan able to hear it?" Ander asked, the others looking at Ethan warily.

"He is probably bound to the dragon through his anti-magic," Captain Golona said, trying to make sense of it.

"Perhaps. Was there anything else you heard it say?" Mortava asked.

"Just a name," Ethan said.

"What name?" Ander asked.

"Casandra, whoever that is." Ethan shrugged.

"Casandra?" Mortava asked.

"I think it's his rider," Ethan said.

"His? The dragon is male?" Ander asked.

"Its voice sounded masculine, but who really knows. I never spoke to a dragon before."

"And this Casandra could hear the dragon's thoughts as well?" Mortava asked.

"That would be my guess," Ethan said.

"Could you hear hers?" she asked further.

"I only heard the dragon."

A human rider that could speak with the dragon was a dangerous thing. Mortava would've thought it impossible if the evidence
wasn't so damning. Was the rider fully able to control the dragon?
Was the rider immune to magic like Ethan? Could Ethan control the
dragon? These were questions she needed answers to. None of this
made sense. Ethan was the only one born immune to magic, their
prophecies were clear on that. If the girl wasn't immune, then her
link to the dragon was magical. If that was so, why didn't the dragon
attack her for her magic? Perhaps she was immune, just like Ethan. If
that was so, there could be many more like her in the wilds, all with
Ethan's abilities.

No. She shook her head. If that were true, one of them would've
tested the boundary by now.

"What should we do, Mother Mortava?" Captain Golona asked.

"There's only one thing we can do," Ethan said.

"And that is?" the good captain asked.

"We kill the dragon."

CHAPTER 25

Valera studied the map intently, running the numbers in her head over and over. Two hundred leagues separated her army from Castara.

Two hundred leagues, she reminded herself. Her scouts reported that Castara had fallen, and a large host was gathering there. If the rumors were true, the entire garrison was put to the sword, and the enemy host numbered in the hundreds of thousands.

"General Ortar, my Queen," the guard standing post at the pavilion entrance announced.

"Send him in!" Valera ordered, keeping her left hand pressed to Bull's neck.

Julius stepped within, his eyes taken aback at seeing Ethan's horse standing in the center of the pavilion.

"It takes time for your eyes to grow accustomed to such a ridiculous sight, Julius," she said, waving him hither.

"Odd but necessary if Consort Loria is correct, my Queen," Julius reasoned.

"If what the scouts reported on the dragon attacking Ethanos and Mother Mortava is true, then these precautions are wisely taken," she said.

"If Ethanos is immune to dragon fire, that gives us some measure of hope." Julius sighed, his eyes sweeping over the map.

"That and his apparent ability to shield Mother Mortava from the dragon," she added. That fact justified keeping Bull close, his power shielding her as Ethan shielded Mortava. The only problem was that her power was cut off while in the horse's presence. That grim reality meant that she was leading her army into battle without magic, while facing a dragon, an army reduced to a shadow of its former self, and greatly outnumbered.

"What news have you on the enemy?" she asked, following his gaze across the map.

"Survivors from Castara claim the fortress was taken by the dragon and a thousand cavalry."

"A mere thousand?" She was taken aback. Castara was a mighty fortress, built to hold back an army one hundred times that number. Could one dragon do that?

"A thousand was all they needed. The small force was merely the vanguard of the enemy host, numbering three hundred thousand strong. By now, they have passed through the ruins of Castara and are marching toward us. We continue to harry the enemy's advance, our cavalry wreaking havoc with their tenuous supplies, burning everything in their path, and slaying their foragers in great numbers. The dragon has taken its toll, however, slaughtering many of our riders."

"There is more?" She could tell when Julius had something more he wanted to say.

"We have a prisoner, my Queen. One taken by Lord Garvos prior to the fall of Castara. He sent the prisoner south just before his demise."

"A prisoner? Bring him here!"

Julius anticipated this, ordering the prisoner brought in from where he waited just outside.

Valera looked upon the wretched captive with contempt. He was a young man dressed in rough-sewn leather trousers and a wool shirt. His hands were bound behind him, and sullen blue eyes stared at her through disheveled blond hair.

"You stand before Queen Daughter Valera. Kneel or be knelt!" Julius commanded, his order not obeyed fast enough as he signaled his guards, who forced the man to his knees, driving his head to the dirt.

"Lift his head. I wish to see into his eyes," Valera said, keeping her hand pressed to Bull's neck.

The guards jerked the captive's head upward, forcing him to face her, though he looked off to the side, avoiding her gaze.

"Look at me, boy. If you do not, then I shall have my soldiers burn your eyes from your head," Valera warned with a deathly cold voice.

That got the man's attention, quickly looking at her, fearing she might bewitch him, but nothing would be worse than blinding, so he thought.

"Better. Now, child, tell me of your army?"

"I have already told your men," he managed to say, barely keeping his eyes on hers.

"You haven't told *me*. Let us begin with actual numbers. How large is your host? How many warriors? Of the women and children, how many are armed?"

"I don't...I don't know the true number. I can only guess."

"Then guess well." She narrowed her eyes severely, displeased with his stalling.

"I...don't know numbers," he confessed.

"You can't count?" Julius asked, not believing him.

"No, I can count, but not that high."

"Then guess!" she said sharply.

"Karg claims we have one million."

"Don't be ridiculous. I said guess, not make up fantastical numbers!" she growled.

"Who is Karg?" Julius asked.

"Our king."

"Tribes have no kings," Julius said, tired of his lies.

"The chieftains named him king to unify the tribes before we entered your lands."

"Entered? A poor choice of words. You enter where you're invited." Julius slowly circled the captive, drawing his attention as Valera coolly observed. Julius stopped in front of him, leaning down, his steel gray eyes staring intently into the man's dull blue. "Invasion is the appropriate word for your crime. My queen has asked you questions, questions you can better answer than you have."

The captive spent the next hour detailing what he knew about their army, their king, the dragon, and its rider. Three hundred thousand was the rough estimate of the barbarian host, their warriors comprising a third of that number. It was when he spoke of the dragon that Valera sensed deception. He claimed the dragon had a woman rider, which was confirmed by the reports she received from Mortava. If that was so, then where was the deception? Her instincts screamed that something was amiss. She needed to look into his mind, but to do so required her to step from Bull's protective aura to use her power. Her power would shine as bright as a thousand suns if the dragon was near, a risk she weighed against lacking the knowledge this captive wouldn't divulge.

So be it, she chanced it, stepping away from Bull, her mage power flooding back into her like a vessel being filled.

"My Queen!" Julius said alarmed.

"He is not telling us something, Julius. I need to risk it." She stepped toward the captive, touching a finger to his forehead.

"Tell us of the dragon. Tell it all and tell it true!" she commanded, her voice like quiet thunder, reading his thoughts as if they were her own.

He began speaking in a clear voice, obedient to her will, revealing the awful truth. When he finished, she backed away as if a dagger had struck her heart.

"We have to warn them!" Julius said, masking the panic taking his heart.

"Send riders out at once," she ordered, tempted to use magic to reach them, but it was far too dangerous at this juncture. She probably already exposed her location to the dragon, by stepping away from Bull. To reach out to one of Mortava's guards might be beyond her ability and would reveal a magical link between them. The dragon might see it and follow in either direction, exposing the army's location to the enemy.

If contacting Mortava was out of the question for her, perhaps someone else could, someone far more powerful. Before stepping back within Bull's protective aura, she reached out to Elysia.

*****

"They are coming, sir!" the young scout reported, drawing his lathered mount alongside Captain Golona.

"How many?" Ander asked, his spirited mount shifting beside the captain's gray courser. They stood below the shade of a towering oak, in the center of a wide open valley.

"Thousands, Sergeant," the scout blurted, eyes panicked.

"How many thousands, Soldier? Speak clear!" Golona ordered.

"Three thousand at least. They are approaching the valley in force. They'll be here shortly."

"Three thousand cavalry?" Ander asked.

The soldier shook his head emphatically, confirming the grim number.

"Any sign of the dragon?" Golona asked.

"No, sir."

"Very well. Rest and water your horse," Golona said.

"What do you think?" Ander asked as the soldier stepped away, his eyes scanning the ridge line to their west.

"Their number grows with every report. This morn it was five hundred, then a thousand. The next outrider will say ten thousand, I have little doubt," Captain Golona growled.

"The number is irrelevant at this point. We have a job to do. As long as they come up the valley floor, we should be all right," Ander pointed out.

"You are worried that they will flank us?"

"Aye."

"The western ridge is impassable on the far slope, with steep drops and thick pines and underbrush. The east ridge is equally impassable with boulders littering either slope, with a dangerous ravine just beyond your line of sight along the reverse slope."

"I'm not worried about here, but they could send a force several leagues to our west, sweeping around us, and cutting our escape. This isn't a mere foraging party. This is a large contingent of regular cavalry looking to finish us," Ander pointed out. Their hit-and-run tactics had finally drawn the enemy's full attention. Their dragon hadn't attacked them but clearly pointed them out.

"They could finish us with their dragon like they have with our other cavalry units."

"Unless they are worried about Ethan. The dragon has kept its distance since that first encounter. Ethan isn't sure his bullets can hurt the beast, but it hasn't tested us since."

"We'll soon find out," Golona said.

They remained in place until their last outriders returned with tidings that the enemy cavalry was fast approaching. They formed up across the valley floor, two hundred and seventy riders facing the barbarian cavalry, outnumbered ten to one. The barbarian mounts were a collection of light, swift breeds, bred for the open steppes of the wilds, but ill-suited for a frontal attack against heavy horse. Unfortunately, the Vellesians did not have any heavy horse in their contingent, as Ethan wanted only the swiftest of mounts. This changed the barbarians' calculations, drawing them to battle. Ander could make out their banners as their cavalry drew nigh, a black dragon upon a field of gray born by the lead mount, with another bearing a gray axe on a field of red. The men were clad in mismatched furs and leathers. Some wore iron helms, a few wore steel. They carried circular wooden shields and long swords or axes, with a few hammers and maces mixed in.

The Vellesians stood in stark contrast, with lightweight steel cuirasses and greaves over black tunics and leggings, with uniform steel helms and shields. Captain Golona paraded before their brave company, his spirited courser's legs trotting gracefully as he addressed his men.

"The enemy draws nigh, bringing the might of their cavalry to finish us, for our small band has bled them. Who among you will follow your captain into battle?" Golona asked.

"I will!" they shouted in unison, raising their swords into the air.

"Then charge when I charge, and run where I run, and the day shall be ours as we clip the invaders' wings!" Golona declared, drawing his long sword and turning his horse about, charging toward the enemy host.

*****

Gorbus Mammoth's Bane rode at the head of the barbarian cavalry, his mismatched brown and green eyes alit, finding the enemy charging across the valley floor to meet them. The troublesome Vellesian cavalry harried their advance, killing hundreds of their foragers. King Karg wanted them eliminated before their host advanced further into the Vellesian heartland, and assigned Gorbus the task, with twenty-seven hundred of their finest mounted warriors.

"They are attacking!" Ord, chief of Tribe Reven declared, pointing at the three hundred fools charging them across open ground.

"Then give them a northern greeting!" Gorbus hoisted his battle axe high into the air.

"Aye, Gorbus!" Ord snorted, hoisting his sword into the air before galloping off to their right, rallying his tribesmen.

"Kai-Korub!" Gorbus shouted their battle cry.

"Kai-Korub!" the others shouted in kind, the war cry echoing through the vale as they lumbered forth, thousands of hooves striking the ground like claps of thunder.

A wicked glee filled Gorbus's eyes as the Vellesian cavalry drew nigh, driving straight for the heart of his formation and certain death. Their king would be pleased for these troublesome raiders to be brought to heel so quickly. His glee soured like days-old milk, watching the Vellesians turn, racing back whence they came.

"Agghh!" Gorbus cursed, waving his axe toward the enemy, his men following as they gave chase.

*****

"It's time," Ethan said, staring out over the vale from the west ridge, his rifle resting over his shoulder as Mortava stepped from his aura, revealing her power in all its glory.

She took a deep breath, renewed by the cool air, her midnight black hair lifting in the breeze. The late-afternoon sun was at their back, casting its rays upon the valley floor where the barbarian cavalry was fast approaching their brave comrades. With her enhanced sight restored, she could make out the faces of Captain Golona and Ander Jordain from afar, leading the enemy host across her line of sight, just as Ethan had planned. Her eyes shifted to her right, catching sight of the enemy fast upon their heels, their numbers so vast that many were obscured in places by underbrush and trees blocking her line of sight. She focused on the riders leading the enemy host, in particular, a large-built man wielding a battle axe, whom the others seemed to follow.

Mortava outstretched her hands, lightning erupting from her fingers, streaming across the valley and striking the lead rider full in the chest.

Gorbus Mammoth's Bane's body lifted from the saddle, his head shaking violently. His dead eyes stared vacantly, lightning pouring through his tortured flesh, enveloping his head, the crackling light winding around his skull, stripping flesh from bone until exploding. Mortava swept her hands southward, her lightning spreading across the valley floor like cascading fissures, breaking off in ever-growing streams. Gorbus's headless corpse flew through the air, striking a rider trailing hundreds of paces behind him. The lightning grew exponentially, sweeping through the valley in deadly streams, unhorsing hundreds of riders in moments.

Mortava's left hand continued casting lightning, while her right spewed sickles of ice, the frozen projectiles riddling the enemy further afield. The icy spears struck with such force to pierce whatever they hit, passing through horses and men like knives through pudding.

Ord, chief of Tribe Reven, staggered, an ice spear grazing his neck, barely keeping hold of his sword as lightning flashed blindingly up ahead. The horse off his right dropped head first into the ground, two ice spears impaling its flank. Ord swerved, the dying beast nearly taking out his horse's legs. He winced, lightning flashing off his left. He barely opened his eyes as a body met him full in the chest, knocking him from the saddle, his neck snapping upon striking the ground as fire swept overhead.

*****

Ethan stood awestruck as Mortava bathed the southern end of the vale with lightning, ice, and then fire, converging in a maelstrom in which no living thing could survive. Fire erupted from both of her hands now, streaming into the valley floor with unnatural force, feeding a growing storm of swirling flames. She opened her mouth, wind issuing from the narrows of her throat, blowing the firestorm southward, away from their own small cavalry force.

Her power was unfathomable, many times his father's magical abilities, slaying three thousand men and horses with little effort. Mortava closed her fists, cutting off the stream of fire. She clapped her hands, lifting the firestorm skyward before dissipating in the air, revealing the scorched and tortured land below. It reminded Ethan of the Velo, where thousands of men lie strewn across the battlefield, burned by lightning, or piled in heaps where the mass of infantry collided. Here, it was fewer dead, but the scene appeared far more macabre. Horses and men were strewn across the valley floor in undistinguishable lumps, blackened and charred. Some moved, like fish thrown up upon a beach, their lives measured in fleeting moments.

Ethan scanned the horizon, his eyes briefly drifting to the northern end of the vale, where captain Golona reformed their cavalry, ready to finish any survivors, but he doubted there were any, or anyone able to fight.

"Ethan!" Mortava's voice rose an octave, as a piercing scream echoed in Ethan's brain, nearly driving him to his knees in pain.

"Mor, behind me!" Ethan winced, bringing his rifle to his shoulder as the dragon appeared in the eastern sky.

*****

Ander pulled back on the reins, his horse rearing up as the fires died away in the sky. The men filed into either flank, awaiting their captain's command as Golona drew up beside him.

"Mother Mortava did it," someone off his left said, a few others chorusing the same.

"*Ander,*" a familiar voice echoed in his mind, as if calling out from a great distance.

"*Who?*" Ander asked, looking over his shoulders.

"*Ander, it is ALESHA.*"

"Princess? Why..."

"Listen. You must listen, Ander. My mother has ill tidings that Ethan must know...," Alesha whispered desperately to his mind as the dragon passed overhead.

Bang! Bang!

The sound of Ethan's rifle echoed over the vale, drowning Alesha's voice in Ander's mind.

"Ander!" Her voice rang louder. *"Tell Ethan..."*

*****

Mortava stood behind Ethan, looking over his shoulder as the dragon drew nigh, flying nearly level to them across the vale, its large maw drawing open, fires swirling in the recesses of its throat. Ethan tucked the butt of the rifle to his shoulder, firing round after round as the beast drew closer, working the lever action in quick succession. The dragon shifted suddenly, a round glancing off its thick skull, a second piercing its mouth, causing it to dip violently, exposing its rider sitting behind its head. Ethan's third round grazed the top of the rider's head, a red-haired youth sporting a thin beard and light mail, the shot disorienting him.

Mortava's keen eye was drawn to a Vellesian rider breaking from their formation, hurrying in their direction with great purpose, waving his free hand excitedly. The hairs on the back of her neck stood erect, alarm ringing in her brain.

"Ethan! Behind you!"

CHAPTER 26

A second piercing scream echoed through his brain, nearly taking him from his feet. Ethan turned, his eyes drawn to a winged shadow fast approaching from the west.

"Crap!" he growled, reaching out to snag Mortava by the collar of her mail, pulling her back as the second dragon drew nigh, obscuring the late day sun, a blast of dragon fire spewing from its maw. Ethan dove out of the way, pulling Mortava with him, the beast's outstretched claws scrapping the ground where he stood. Ethan rolled to his knees, keeping hold of his rifle while releasing Mortava, tucking the butt to his shoulder as the dragon set down, its wings sweeping overhead.

Bang!

He fired into its side at the joint of its wing.

"*Agghh!*" He could hear the dragon's anguished thoughts, the bullet causing some damage.

Bang!

He sent a second round into its neck, just missing its rider's leg, a red-haired girl that he assumed was Casandra. He shifted aim to the dragon's eye as its massive head swung around, steam issuing from its nostrils.

Click!

Ethan cursed the empty chamber, dropping his Winchester, his right hand going to the hilt of his father's sword.

"*Nylo!*" Casandra warned, her eyes wild with fright as Ethan started to draw his sword. Nylo lumbered forth, reaching out his forelimb, knocking Ethan on his back.

Ethan managed to free the sword of starlight from its scabbard as the shadow of Nylo's forelimb closed overhead, lowering swiftly to grind him into the ground. Ethan tucked the hilt into the ground at his side, the blade aiming skyward as the massive claw came violently down.

"Krall!" Nylo roared, the sword piercing his paw, the rear portion of his foot coming down on Ethan's knees.

Ethan winced, the sound of his snapping legs echoing sickeningly through the air. Nylo pulled back his wounded foot, the sword still embedded in his tender paw, with the sword's hilt in Ethan's grip. Ethan's legs quickly healed as he was lifted in the air, his extremities dangling just beyond the dragon's anti-magical aura as he kept hold of the sword. Nylo snorted angrily, shaking his leg, trying to dislodge Ethan and the sword.

With Ethan drawing farther away, Mortava felt her power restored. The second dragon towered over her, venting its full ire upon Ethan holding tight to the sword, shaking him violently. Mortava gained her feet, drawing her arms together above her head, a ball of fire circling between her hands. She hurled it at the dragon's head, the ball disappearing before touching its flesh, swallowed by its protective aura.

"Rragghh!"

A terrible roar echoed behind her as her flames faltered. Mortava turned as the first dragon drew ominously close, having recovered from the bullet Ethan sent into its mouth. Her heart went to her throat as death stared her in the face, the dragon's golden eyes glaring menacingly back, her immense magical power fueling its rage. Her incredible power drew the dragon but was useless against it. The beast opened its mouth, fires swirling in the back of its throat, preparing to strike. She ran toward the other dragon, ducking underneath its thrashing wing, the first dragon's fire dying against the second dragon's aura. Here she was safe from dragon fire but in grave danger of being eaten or trampled underfoot.

Ethan's feet briefly touched the ground long enough for him to yank the sword free before Nylo pulled away.

"*Nylo, you are bleeding!*" the first dragon spoke desperately with a feminine voice, Ethan able to hear its thoughts as well, as he stood between them, Mortava coming to his side with her own sword drawn, her eyes darting warily from one dragon to the other.

"*Back away, Nyla. Let me finish him!*" Nylo swung his head around, staring directly into Ethan's eyes.

"*He is too dangerous!*" Nyla said as Ethan held his ground, the Sword of Starlight now alit with a luminous azure glow.

"Listen to Nyla, Dragon. I *am* dangerous. Leave this land and go back where you came. Let there be peace between us," Ethan said, standing a sword's length from the muzzle of the large beast, moisture glistening off its shiny black scales.

"What are you, human?" Nylo spoke aloud, taking Mortava aback by his ability to speak. She kept close to Ethan, which seemed to have a calming effect on the dragons.

"I'm Ethan."

"What is an Ethan?" Nylo's eyes narrowed severely.

"That is my name. And you are Nylo, I assume?"

"Krall!"

Nylo roared, angered that Ethan dare utter his name, his breath lifting Ethan's hair behind his head.

"Devour him!" the red-haired man sitting atop Nyla shouted, his green eyes staring down at Ethan with pure hate.

"He serves the Mage Realms. He must die!" Casandra shouted from atop Nylo. The two dragons stood side by side as Ethan backed a step, each staring intently at him.

"This one is different," Nylo growled, his dark lips twisting over glistening white teeth.

"He is a mage! Kill him!" The red-haired barbarian shouted.

"He is not a mage. He is something…worse." Nyla drew back her head, finding Ethan's presence unsettling.

"He speaks dragon. Only a mage gifted with Dragon Tongue can read our thoughts, but he is immune to magic. It makes no sense." Nylo shook his head.

"Only dragons are immune to magic," the red-haired man said.

"Then he is a dragon, Tomas," Nyla said, revealing her rider's name.

"We don't have to fight each other, Nylo. You can leave this land," Ethan offered, hoping the dragon could see reason.

"Perhaps in another place or time we might have been friends, Ethan, but you serve the mage born, and I cannot abide them," Nylo glared menacingly at Mortava.

"What is Dragon Tongue?" Mortava ventured, keeping within Ethan's protective aura.

"KRALL!" Nylo roared, his hot breath pressing upon their faces, lifting their hair.

"It must be my ability to read their thoughts," Ethan guessed, eying Nylo warily.

"I never heard of such," Mortava shook her head. Her house spent thousands of years binding every mage ability to their bloodline, never realizing that there might be one they overlooked, a very *important* one.

"Do not speak of it, mage!" Nylo snarled, his eyes shifting to her.

"Kill her!" the one named Tomas shouted.

"Touch her and you die, all of you!" Ethan warned.

"You can't kill a dragon, mage slave!" Tomas sneered.

"I can kill anything, dragon slave!" Ethan shot back, tightening his grip on the sword, noticing the blood pooling beneath Nylo's foot.

"It isn't possible!" Tomas said.

"Then explain his blood," Ethan pointed to Nylo's wounded paw, hoping it would give them pause.

All the more reason to kill him now, Tomas spoke to Nylo's mind.

If we can, Nylo countered. He was certain that he broke Ethan's legs, and yet he stood before them.

"If we can what?" Ethan asked aloud, unable to hear Tomas's thoughts, wondering to what Nylo was referring. Every utterance bought him time, time to reason with these powerful creatures to leave Vellesia. The dragons weren't what he expected. There was a reason for their hatred of the mage realms that went beyond the madness the magic invoked, but what? There was also a familiarity about them, one that he couldn't explain.

"There can be no peace between our kind and hers, Ethan," Nylo answered his thoughts, glaring intently at Mortava.

"Why do you serve her?" Nyla asked, looking deeply into Ethan's mind, discovering why he served House Loria, and his kinship to the mage born, both those of Vellesia and Astaria. But he possessed the Dragon Tongue as well, which fueled her confusion.

"I don't want to kill you," Ethan pleaded, sensing a kinship with the dragons, a natural bond akin to the one he shared with Alesha.

"She threatens your father's life, forcing you to do her bidding," Nyla accused, revealing Ethan's secret to the others.

"Stand aside and we can kill her for you," Nylo snared.

"Because she is a mage you would kill her?" Ethan asked.

"Every mage must die!" Nyla affirmed.

"My father and mother are mages. So is my wife. I can't let you kill them."

"You hate mage born. It is in your blood," Nylo accused.

"I don't hate them. I…" Ethan struggled putting his thoughts into words while keeping an eye on any sudden movements.

"You do hate them!" Nylo pushed.

"I hate the things some of them do but not all of them. Power is corrupting, especially with extreme power imbalances. Are you any different? How many of our people have you slain?" Ethan challenged.

"That is different. It is war. All who serve the mage born are our enemies," Nyla said.

"Are women and children your enemies? You've killed more innocents than soldiers," Ethan challenged.

"And what of our innocents, mage slave?" Tomas sneered, shifting atop Nyla's back.

Ethan gave him a look, annoyed by his slave reference, wondering what innocents he was referring.

"You privileged lords live high in your castles and keeps, atop the finest lands in all of Elaria, while our people starve! You live fat off the land while we are trapped in the lands you call wild. If that were not enough, your Mistress and her house call evil into our lands, forcing us to come here!" Tomas shouted, staring down at them.

Ethan made a face, wondering what evil he was talking about, when Tomas took it upon himself to end the discussion, hurling a spear at Mortava.

"No!" Ethan shouted, stepping in front of her while drawing his pistol, shifting his sword to his left hand, while drawing his colt with his right.

Bang!

The sound of the pistol rang out as the spear struck his chest, the bullet taking Tomas in the right shoulder.

"KRALL!"

The dragons roared, incensed by the affront.

Ethan stumbled, driven back by the spear, holstering his pistol, while yanking it free, stepping back beyond the dragon's aura.

"Kill them! Kill them all!" Tomas screamed, blood pooling beneath his shirt and mail.

Nylo's massive head lunged forth, his maw drawing open before Ethan fully gained his footing. Ethan stumbled as Nylo's jaws snapped, grazing his left hand near the hilt as he brought the blade across the dragon's jaw. Ethan winced, Nylo tearing off the last two fingers of his left hand. Mortava stepped forth, driving her sword into Nylo's chin, the blade snapping before touching his glistening scales, as if striking an invisible barrier.

"No!" Ethan shouted as the dragon's jaw closed over Mortava's right arm, biting it clean off above the wrist. Ethan snagged her by the collar with his right hand, gripping the sword with his left, ignoring the pain shooting up his arm while pulling her along. He ran along Nylo's right flank, shielding Nyla from attacking as she was to Nylo's left. Nylo shifted, trying to follow Ethan with his head as the sound of horns echoed over the din.

HAROOM!

*****

Ander drew his sword, charging across the rocky uneven ground, his horse's hooves swerving around knee-high boulders strewn over the ridge. Scores of Vellesian cavalry filled in around him, desperate to save Ethan and Mortava. His heart lifted into his throat when he beheld the dragon tearing Mortava's arm off. Within moments, Ethan circled underneath the beast's right wing as they sounded their war horns.

The sound drew the two dragons' attention, their eyes shifting suddenly in their direction. Ander stared in awe as Ethan drove his sword into Nylo's breast, the beast releasing a ghastly roar that pierced their ears like spear tips being driven into their skulls. A blast of wind pressed his face as Nylo's wings whipped overhead, with Ethan dangling from his side, his left hand gripping the sword embedded in Nylo's breast, and his right holding onto Mortava. Nylo swept along the ridge before breaking westward, disappearing over the horizon.

Once the dust cleared from the gust of Nylo's wings, Ander looked on with knowing dread as Nyla emerged from the settling dust, angling straight for them. Her massive jaw drew open, fire spewing from her maw. Flames erupted all around him, a blast of blinding heat scorching everything off his left. Ander shifted right, his horse throwing him after a sharp turn. The last thing he remembered was the sounds of men screaming in haunting torment.

*****

Mortava's screams died in the wind, unbearable pain shooting up from the stump of her right arm, the ground passing swiftly below them, her feet dangling freely as the dragon carried them off. They flew over treetops, the dragon swerving low to dislodge them from its breast. Ethan swung her with his wanning strength, avoiding the trunk of a pine tree, her back scraping against its upper boughs. Ethan winced, the pain in his left-hand straining holding onto the sword's hilt under their combined weight and his missing fingers, which hadn't regrown despite the time he was beyond the dragon's aura. His right hand held fast to Mortava, swinging her back and forth, avoiding directly hitting the tree trunks in their path.

Agghh! Nylo's anguished thoughts echoed in Ethan's brain, the dragon laboring with the wound, but strong enough to bear them to their apparent deaths unless Ethan could find a way to avoid it. He couldn't let Mortava go, for only his aura protected her from the dragon. Even if he released her and used his free hand to shoot his pistol, she might be slain by the other dragon, though Nyla was nowhere in sight, as far as he could tell.

Nylo's golden eyes went briefly out of focus, the horizon expanding and contracting as he grew dizzy. He drove his wings upward, pushing high into the air with Casandra holding dearly to the spindles along his neck.

A tingling sensation flowed up Ethan's legs as the treetops shrank below them, rising to terrifying heights. The valley below came into full view from one ridge line to the other, before passing over into the next valley beyond. Nylo never suffered a wound before, his flesh invincible against all weapons magic and mortal, or so he believed, yet Ethan hurt him twice, his foot and his breast, the sword digging painfully into his lung.

Green blood oozed from Nylo's breast, coating Ethan's hand, further straining his weakening grip. If he dropped from this height, it might take a day to recover or kill him outright, he thought warily, the ground seeming so far away, though he might heal as quickly as ever. He never tested the limits to his regeneration, and didn't plan to now. Mortava could float to the ground if her levitational powers worked from this height, but if he died, she would soon follow with no protection from Nylo.

"Ethan...Ethan," Mortava said weakly, her eyes growing heavy with the loss of blood, staring at the valley floor so far below.

"Stay with me, Mor!" he shouted in the wind. He wished to ask Nylo to set down and make peace, but that was beyond them now.

Nylo pushed higher, soaring into the firmament, bathing in the glow of the late day sun, his eyes closed before its brilliant glare. Then he stopped, closing his wings, tucking his head downward.

"Hold tight, Mor!" Ethan winced, the ground coming swiftly upon them as Nylo dove. The terrain below was open ground, a grassy meadow at the edge of a forest. Nylo extended his wings, breaking northward short of the ground, driving for a stream at the center of the vale.

With the ground growing lower and lower, Ethan realized Nylo's intent to scrap them from his chest on the rocky terrain ahead.

"Come to me as fast as you can!" Ethan said, releasing his grip on Mortava's collar, dropping her to the meadow below, where she tumbled in the grass, unable to break her fall, her powers impaired beyond his aura for some reason.

Ethan thrust his right hand into Nylo's wound, grabbing hold of the break in his scales, where the sword was embedded. He gripped the torn scales with all the strength he could muster while his left hand worked the sword free.

"KRALL!"

Nylo roared in agony, the sword wiggling painfully in his punctured lung.

Ethan cursed up a storm, unable to pull the sword free, his now mortal strength quickly draining. He stopped pulling and decided to push, driving the blade deeper, Nylo dropping suddenly with the rending of his lung, the shift nearly throwing Ethan off. He drove the sword fully into the wound before drawing his pistol, aiming between the open scales.

Bang! Bang! Bang! Bang!

With the fourth bullet, Ethan let go, falling away, his back breaking upon striking the ground, just where the meadow gave way to rocky terrain. Nylo roared in utter torment, dropping just beyond Ethan, his massive bulk coming to rest alongside a stream, his left wing dipping in the water.

Casandra slid down from Nylo's back, tears staining her cheeks. Once her feet touched the ground, she rushed to the front of his muzzle, staring into his fading eyes, pleading for him not to die.

"Oh, Nylo! What did he do?" she cried, her tears coming faster, dropping on his scales.

"Ca…Casan…dra…," he barely whispered, his labored breath growing weak. "I…am dying."

"But you can't die! Dragons are invincible," she pleaded, pressing her face to his muzzle, holding desperately to him.

"Go...go. Your brother needs you. So...so does Nyla." Nylo sighed, his golden eyes drawing dully open with his last breath.

"KRALL!"

A dragon roared dully in the distance as Nyla felt her brother's death.

"No!" Casandra screamed, rage suddenly overtaking grief. She pulled herself away long enough to see Ethan lying on the ground a short distance behind them. She wiped her tears, drying her hands on her trousers before drawing her sword.

*****

Ethan slowly gained his senses, his eyes fluttering open with a strange numbness in his legs. He could feel his severed spine slowly mending, the nerves stitching together far too slow. He lifted his bloody left hand, the last two fingers only partially regrown. He turned his head, sensing movement off his right.

"I wouldn't do it, Casandra!" he warned, training his pistol on her, still gripping it in his extended right hand.

"Murderer!" she screamed, approaching him with blood raged eyes.

"I still have one bullet!" he said, that detail having little effect. She probably didn't know what he was talking about, and he really didn't want to kill her. He had too many questions needing answers.

Bang!

The bullet struck Casandra's right knee, shattering the joint, causing her fall.

"Monster!" she cried, holding her knee, struggling to gain her footing, but the pain was too much. She crawled, dragging her leg behind her, intent to drive her sword through his gut.

That took long enough, he thought, jumping to his feet, his back finally healed. He holstered his empty pistol, stepping carefully around her. She rolled over, pointing her sword at him wherever he stepped. Ethan shook his head before approaching, disarming her with unnatural speed, taking her sword and walking away. He looked back where the meadow rested at the edge of the rocky terrain. He ran, looking for Mortava, knowing she fell somewhere in the knee-high grass. He found her sitting up a short distance away, nursing her right arm.

"Ethan!" she greeted him with a pained smile as he knelt beside her.

"It's not growing back, is it?" he examined the stump of her right arm, the flesh mending up to the wrist.

"Apparently not. And you?" she asked as he held up his hand, showing her his missing fingers.

"They're healed past the middle joint now. I broke my back, but that took a while to heal as well," he said, helping her to her feet.

"I can feel it healing, just very slowly. The dragon's bite must interfere with our powers," she guessed.

"Most likely. Now your healing will stop because you're near me. Sorry." He shrugged, knowing they couldn't risk her drawing the other dragon's attention.

"Sorry? You saved me, Ethan. There is no reason for you to apologize. You have become very good at saving members of my family, it seems."

"Forget about it, Mor. I owed you one back there. The dragon would've bit my head off if you hadn't distracted him. I'm not sure I could come back from that kind of injury," he japed.

"Let's not find out." She smiled.

Since her wound was now covered with fresh skin, they decided to check on Casandra, finding her still trying to crawl away, blood trailing on the rocky ground around her. Ethan quickly pinned her down while Mortava cut a strip from the girl's trouser leg, handing it to Ethan to bind her hands behind her.

"Get off me!" Casandra cried, kicking his back with her good leg before Mortava held it down.

"Keep still, girl," he said, tying a tourniquet above her right knee with a strip Mortava cut from her other trouser leg.

"Kill me and be done with it!" she spat as Ethan held her head down.

"If I wanted you dead, I would've already done it." He finished tying it off, blood still seeping through, forcing him to redo it, tying it tighter.

"I can try to heal her," Mortava said.

"It will draw the dragon," he pointed out.

"Either that or you carry her, and you'll need a better tourniquet to stop the bleeding, and a stick to wind it tighter."

"All right, we'll chance it." Ethan backed away, drawing his colt, reloading it from the bullets slotted along the back of his pistol belt, while keeping his eyes skyward.

Mortava closed her eyes, reveling in the restoration of her magic, and the tingling sensation coursing the stump of her right hand as it continued to heal, albeit slowly. She touched her left hand to Casandra's shattered knee, sending waves of magic into the wound.

"What's taking so long?" Ethan asked.

"The dragon's bite is interrupting my powers, but she is almost healed," Mortava explained, wondering how long this impairment would linger.

Ethan winced, a piercing scream echoing back and forth through his brain. Concern grew across Mortava's face, knowing the look. The other dragon was nearby. She quickly removed her hand from Casandra's knee, retreating to Ethan's side, the pain in his mind disappearing once she was within his aura. Ethan knew it was little wonder why the dragons hated mages, if that was what they felt in their presence. Once the pain subsided, he could hear Nyla's thoughts as clearly as his own.

*****

Tomas felt Nyla's anguish when Nylo fell, like a dagger twisting in his heart. He lost count of the Vellesians they slew, sweeping over the vale time and again, incinerating men and horses where they stood after Nylo flew off to the west. When he died, Nyla could feel it, releasing a deafening roar. He never felt her weep as she did now, fat tears running like rivers off her shiny scales. They broke off exterminating the Vellesians, what few where left, speeding westward through the firmament, drawn by Mortava's magical illumination that shone as brightly as the sun. They flew over the far ridge overlooking a deep vale, then another and another, continuing west until the horrible scene unfolded in the distance, Nylo's body resting beside a narrow stream, Casandra wounded and bound, and the one called Ethan standing over her.

The pain of Mortava's magic echoed in Tomas's ears, feeling the full effect through his link with Nyla. Once Mortava stepped near Ethan, the pain thankfully ended, allowing him to hear her thoughts.

"It's them. They have your sister," Nyla said.

"I warned you to leave. All this death could've been avoided," Ethan said, hearing her thoughts in the distance.

"Speak not to me, mage slave! You have forsaken your gift of Dragon Tongue for her kind!" Nyla growled.

"What did he say?" Tomas asked as Nyla broke off her direct path, skirting the eastern ridge of the vale, keeping her distance from the dangerous human.

She ignored Tomas's question, keeping her eye on Ethan, who stood defiantly beside his mistress, shielding her with his life.

"Kill them, Nyla! Kill them even if you have to kill me with them!" Casandra beseeched the she-dragon, pain shooting through her knee, though it was healed enough to use.

Ethan stood over her, following Nyla skirting the horizon, her golden eyes staring back at him, hate fueling her simmering rage. *"Go ahead, I've already killed one dragon today. Let's make it two,"* Ethan challenged, spinning Casandra's sword with practiced ease.

"Another day, mage slave," Nyla growled bitterly, turning away, her wings pounding the air, flying back whence she came.

"Better a mage slave than a child killer." Ethan shook his head.

"No!" Casandra cried as Nyla disappeared over the horizon, lowering her head to the dirt, her hands bound behind her, her tears staining the ground.

"Finish healing her," Ethan said, stepping away.

"What of the dragon?" Mortava asked, looking warily at the eastern sky.

"If I hear the noise in my head, I'll draw you close, but you need to heal and so does she. I don't feel like carrying her," he said, shaking his left hand, the wounded fingers now healed past the last joint, nearing full restoration.

Mortava finished, bathing Casandra's wound with her magic. It was disconcerting how the dragon wound impaired her powers. She would usually need only a touch of her finger to heal any wound instantly. Now she poured all her power into healing but a single wound.

"How's your arm?" Ethan asked.

She lifted it over her head, revealing the base of the hand fully restored, the palm slowly taking shape.

"The dragon's mouth must be poisoned." He shook his head.

"Most likely, or it's his anti-magic mixing with our blood," she surmised.

"That's as good a theory as any I can think of. Here, take this." He handed her the sword before pulling Casandra to her feet, marching back to Nylo's carcass.

"What are you doing?" Mortava asked as Ethan forced Casandra to her knees, leaving Mortava to guard her.

"Getting my father's sword back," he said, reaching his hand into the gaping wound on Nylo's breast, green blood covering his arm as he worked his hand further into the cavity until his fingers grazed the pommel of the sword.

"Unbelievable," he groaned, sticking his head in the wound, extending his reach to grasp the hilt.

Mortava cringed when Ethan emerged, blood soaking everything above his chest, his hair slick with blood dripping from his ears.

"Do I look that bad?" he asked, wiping the blade on his trousers before sliding it home on his left hip.

"You need a bath." She wrinkled her nose.

"I've heard that before."

"I am sure you have. I suggest we go upstream from this foul carcass," she advised.

Nylo's body lay partially in the stream, his green blood pooling on the ground beneath Ethan's feet.

Casandra knelt quietly, tears blurring her vision, her heart breaking staring at Nylo's lifeless body.

"You killed him." She lowered her head.

"He didn't give me much choice," Ethan said.

"You have the Dragon Tongue. He was of your blood!" she spat, lifting her hate filled green eyes to his.

"Just because I could speak to him doesn't make us kin. Maybe if he didn't invade this land and kill thousands of our people, I wouldn't have had to kill him."

"You had a choice, mage slave, and you chose her." Casandra gave Mortava a murderous look.

Mortava touched a finger to Casandra's temple, sending tendrils of pain through her skull.

"Do not speak of him with that tone!" Mortava warned, withdrawing her finger.

Ethan winced, never liking mages wielding such power over others, but his sympathy for Casandra was wearing thin. What did she expect? Waging war was a dangerous game, a game you had to be prepared to lose.

"By the way, how many dragons do your people have?" he asked.

She caught her breath, recovering from Mortava's agonizing touch, never suffering such pain in all her life. She closed her mouth, refusing to answer.

"Where is your army?"

"Who is your leader?"

"What is your relation to the other dragon rider?"

She shook her head with each question with smug defiance until Mortava opened her mouth.

"There were only these two dragons. Their main host is camped some thirty leagues to our southeast. The other dragon rider is her twin brother, Tomas. Their tribe found the two dragon eggs shortly after she and Tomas were born, each hatching when they were infants."

Casandra looked horrified as Mortava read her thoughts as clearly as if she spoke them herself.

"And how did they cross the boundary?" he asked.

"They discovered the barrier stone and disassembled it, allowing them to pass," Mortava said grimly, wondering how they had achieved that.

"Can you repair it?" he asked, wondering how many more dragons might pass through it.

"Perhaps, but not until we deal with their invasion." She failed to mention that Sarella and Mothers Vetesha and Ametria were each well schooled on the making and repairing of barrier stones, each working to resolve the issue once the enemy was defeated.

Ethan released a tired breath, looking off to the southeast, shaking his head at the task before them.

"How many more like you do they have?" Casandra asked.

"Lucky for you, I'm one of a kind."

*****

They made their way upstream where Ethan removed his leather shirt and cotton undershirt, washing the blood stains out in the river. He thought to wash his buckskin trousers too but decided against giving the ladies a show. Dipping his head in the water, he scrubbed his hands though his hair, cleaning most of the blood away.

"We should head back east and see if any of our men survived," Mortava said, trying not to look at his naked chest.

"Ask her if they could tell where we were when I concealed your magic?" he said, shaking the water from his hair, standing in the stream with his trouser legs rolled up past his ankles. He hated how long his hair had gotten. He thought to cut it, but Alesha gave him strict orders not to. Maybe he should cut it just to spite her. No, he put that thought from his head, knowing how adamant she was about it, going as far as directing Mortava, Valera, and Demetra to make sure he didn't.

Mortava didn't need to ask the girl that question before it was clear in her head.

"No, they cannot track us when you conceal my power."

Casandra hated the way the mage could pick apart her thoughts.

"But they can track us now, with your power lit up like the sun?" he asked, which she nodded affirm.

"How's your hand?" he asked, trudging up the bank where she stood upon the rocky ground, with Casandra kneeling beside her. He shook out his cotton shirt, before pulling it over his head, carrying his leather deerskin shirt in his hand.

"The palm is complete. Just waiting for the fingers." She waved it in front of his face. Her mage powers were coming back to full strength, especially her ability to read Casandra's thoughts.

They continued upstream before setting camp for the night, Mortava using her powers to snag fish for their supper, levitating them out of the water as Ethan gathered wood, which ignited with a stream of fire from her finger. They set their cookfire within a copse of trees along the east bank of the stream, planning to make their way back to the others come sunrise.

Mortava fed a piece of fish into Casandra's mouth, warning her not to bite. Casandra wisely obeyed, sitting beside her in front of the fire, her hands still bound behind her. The girl looked miserable, her bright red hair falling over sad green eyes. Ethan pitied her, even if she would gut him if she got hold of a knife. Mortava remained outside Ethan's aura, waiting for her hand to completely heal. The fingers were now grown to the last joint, almost able to wield a sword.

"You all right?" He asked, noticing her shivering. A Lorian shouldn't suffer the elements, able to warm or cool the air around them with ease.

"I am very cold for some reason." She shivered, warming her hands in front of the fire.

"Are you sick? I didn't think that possible." He could see Casandra's head lift at that observation, curious at his words.

"It's not possible, but I am feeling ill," she confessed.

"The dragon bite." He shook his head.

"Most likely. So this is how others suffer." She smiled wanly.

"Another new experience, like feeling pain," he recalled the injuries she suffered without her magic protecting her.

"A lesson I shan't forget." She wondered how he endured such agony through the years? Though he could regenerate, he wasn't immune to pain. She could only imagine the suffering he endured at the Velo. If the rumors were to be believed, he suffered enough mortal blows to kill a hundred men.

Ethan surprised her, getting up and placing his leather shirt around her shoulders. She appreciated the extra layer, finding the gentle pat on her back endearing.

"For what it's worth, Casandra, I didn't want to kill your friend," Ethan said, sitting back down across from them, not missing the miserable look on her face.

"You…" She couldn't put words to her thoughts, the narrows of her throat tightening as she bit back the tears.

It pained him to see her so, wondering why he felt guilty. She was the enemy. She and Nylo murdered thousands, and her flippant excuse that it was war was thin considering the destroyed villages they came upon. He never saw such mindless destruction, with whole populations put to the sword. All she could see were the injuries she suffered.

"It doesn't matter anymore, for you are doomed. We are all doomed," she managed to say, looking forlornly into the crackling flames.

"We are? How do you figure that?" he asked curiously, his relaxed demeanor shifting with the grim look passing Mortava's face.

Mortava reached out, bracing Casandra's head in her hands, staring intently into her mind.

"Get out of my head, witch!" Casandra screamed, squeezing her eyes shut, trying to draw away.

"Be still," Mortava whispered, causing her eyes to draw open, staring blankly ahead, obedient to Mortava's command.

"Wish I knew that trick." Ethan shook his head.

"Quiet," Mortava scolded him, staring deeply into the girl's mind. She lacked Alesha's powerful mental mage gifts but could still read simple thoughts, and complex thoughts if she looked deep enough. It didn't help with Ethan talking. Binding was no simple trick, and she still suffered the dragon's illness.

Ethan sheepishly shrugged his apology, keeping quiet as she continued her work. It sometimes frightened him how powerful each of the Lorians was, and he was immune to it. He couldn't imagine how frightened a normal person was, like Casandra, completely helpless against Mortava's ministrations.

"What is it?" Ethan asked as she withdrew, standing up and backing away, the firelight playing off the side of her face.

"We have to repair the boundary," she said, her eyes shifting slowly to Ethan, in a manner to raise the hairs on the back of his neck.

"We knew that already," he said, wondering how their plight could be more urgent.

"Yes, but…," her voice trailed.

"But?" He didn't like the sound of that.

"It might not be enough."

"All right, Mor, you're starting to worry me. What is it you saw?"

"Dragons. Red dragons."

CHAPTER 27

"Please, d…don't touch it, Maisel!" Tomas cried out as the old healer examined his shoulder.

"I must cleanse the wound, Dragon Friend," the old woman said, hunched over Tomas, who lay on the ground in the king's tent.

"Let her fix you, or I'll cut the arm off myself!" Karg growled, standing over them with his meaty arms crossed.

"You say it was a projectile weapon that did this?" Maisel asked, opening her medicine sack, laying out several instruments on a blanket beside him, along with various potions and tree moss.

"Yes, a powerful mage weapon," he faintly said.

"Magic doesn't hurt dragons, boy!" Karg snorted.

"It was! And he used it to kill Nylo," Tomas wept, a reluctant tear squeezing form his eye.

"And your sister? Where is she?" Karg snorted.

"He…he has her," he confessed, staring at the ceiling, his shoulder ruined.

"He! He! He! Who is *he?*" Karg growled impatiently. They were down one dragon, their best cavalry slain, and the chieftains were looking to their king for answers.

And so Tomas told him everything Nyla revealed to him, that Ethan was immune to magic and could heal himself. He told him that Ethan was the only one of his kind, a prophetic figure some believed was Free Born, but the Vellesians believed would give them ultimate power. Just as importantly, he revealed the power of the Lorian Order, that Valera was concealed by Bull's immunity to magic, and that Elysia held the most powerful mages in all of Elaria.

The grim tidings meant they were on perilous ground, and only Nyla protected them from certain annihilation.

"My king?" Maisel asked worriedly as he stood in silence for a painfully long time.

"Fix his arm. If not, then tie it down. He needs to be ready to ride his dragon," he commanded, stepping outside to meet his chieftains.

*****

"My king!" His people greeted him as he entered their midst. Most were hungry and threadbare, looking to him for hope.

"Kal!" He greeted them with the tribal salutation meaning *Friend.* They traveled far reaching this point, twelve years since naming him King and unifying the tribes to finish off the hordes that always plagued their peoples. He fondly recalled the day he slew the warlord of the Jangar, that fell deed rallying their tribes to destroy the horde that slew and enslaved thousands of their fellow tribesmen through the centuries. It was then they discovered two young children held captive by the vile Jangar, a boy and a girl, both chained by the neck and kept in cages. It was Karg that set them free, quickly discovering their special gift, the Dragon Tongue. Also among the prizes taken that day were numerous dragon eggs as well as two dragon hatchlings. How the Jangar came into possession of such treasures, Karg would never know.

"My King, when will the caravans return?" a young mother asked, holding her infant to her breast, a rough wool shawl shielding her from the cool night air.

"Soon." He stopped, placing a reassuring hand on her shoulder.

"Bless you." She kissed his forearm.

He gave her a gentle smile before moving on, his guards clearing a path as he moved through the encampment. He wanted nothing more than to see his people safe, fed and at peace, and that couldn't happen until the mage realms were destroyed, and the red dragons kept at bay. The red dragons couldn't be held back until Elysia was purged of its foul magic. His people were in dire straits, deep in hostile territory, surrounded by enemies, and supplies running thin. Vellesia possessed the strongest magic in all of Elaria, many times more powerful than the other realms combined. Their armies, if fully mustered, outnumbered the entirety of his vast host, most of whom were women, children, and elderly. Despite all this, they held the advantage in the form of dragons, the one weapon mages were helpless against, but that advantage was now cut in half by an interloper.

Farn! he cursed. This Ethan had ruined his plans, Ethan and the mage hag accompanying him. Nylo was dead, Casandra captured and his best cavalry slaughtered. He had to sort this out quickly, thinking of solutions as he made his way to meet with his chieftains.

They were gathered around a large bonfire at the edge of the encampment, beyond earshot of eavesdroppers. Representatives of the twenty three tribes awaited him, either chieftains or their designees. Several dozen warriors stood guard farther afield, with the shadow of the dragon passing over the full moon reassuring Karg that their protector was ever present.

"My King!" they chorused as he entered their midst.

"Chieftains and elders," he greeted in kind, his guards fanning out around him. He saw the worry on their faces, yet none dared putting voice to their fears, or whisper of the spreading rumors that froze their blood.

"My king, what news have you of our chieftain?" Niesa of tribe Revan asked. She was a grim-faced warrior whose weathered face belied her youth. She stood in place of Chief Ord, who led a cohort of their cavalry.

"He is likely dead. Tribe Revan must choose his replacement," Karg bluntly answered, not one to waste words in a war council. Only hard facts held a place here, and the facts before them were cruel.

"Dead?" more than one asked all at once.

"Yes," Karg affirmed, his thick jaw jutting prominently, daring anyone to contest his will, or cower in the face of what he was about to say.

How? Was the question each wanted answered.

"Our cavalry was decimated today. I don't know if any still live. Perhaps a straggler or two will come into camp tonight or tomorrow. They were destroyed by a powerful mage," he began.

"Why didn't the dragon stop her?" Plygar, chief of Tribe Aglar, asked, an aged warrior with graying beard and pox-scarred face.

And so Karg explained to them what transpired, the news of Nylo's death confirming their worst fears.

"What should we do?" several asked.

"Dragons are invincible," others said in denial.

"Can we turn back?"

"Kill the mage and her helper!" others advised.

"No! We need to move against their army while we can!" Wiser ones pointed out.

"Enough!" Karg silenced them, every eye looking to their king for direction. "There is no going back! Only death awaits us in our native lands. We must go on. We fight here or we die. The mage born are as evil as the danger we flee, but unlike that danger, we can defeat the mage-born scum. They've lived fat off this land, safe behind foul magic that kept the dragons at bay while we suffered and starved in the wilds, keeping the best lands for themselves. Should we forget how they treat our kind whenever one of us passed into their precious realms?" He waved his fingers dramatically across the scar that ran the width of his face.

"No!" several shouted.

"No." He nodded in agreement. "Should we repay the kindness they've shown our people?"

"Yes," Telvin, chief of Tribe Jutar, nodded.

Karg recalled the Gorgencian mage lord that slew his father and brother and burned his face when they passed over the boundary escaping raiders from the Butros Horde. "*Let your face be warning to your kind should they think to enter our lands,*" the lord declared. Karg was but a child and would never forget their *kindness*. He swore upon his father's life to repay the mage born their mercy.

"We still have one dragon, and now we know who and what can hurt her, and what and who can't," Karg said.

"What shall we do my king?" another asked.

"Prepare your people to move out at first light and give me twelve of your best warriors."

*****

"Red dragons?" Ethan asked, the vision in Dragos's tower coming to mind. That dragon was red, and he could never shake the image of the beast destroying Astaria from his mind. "All dragons are dangerous. How are the red dragons any different from the black, gray, white, or green ones?"

"Before this night, I would've believed so, but after looking into her mind, I see we were mistaken." Mortava shook her head, wondering how such knowledge escaped them for thousands of years?

"So what's the difference?" he asked, Casandra stealing a glance at him before looking back to the fire.

"Red dragons kill the others. They dwell in the far north, beyond any chart or map to our knowledge. They've kept to those fabled, far-off lands, never venturing anywhere near the mage realms until now," Mortava explained.

"They kill other dragons? Just how big are these things?" He made a face, not liking their chances.

"Many times Nylo or Nyla and far more vicious."

"More vicious? There wasn't anything gentle about Nylo."

"Which only proves their dangerous potential."

"All right, so what drew them from their northern habitat?" Ethan asked.

Mortava grew ominously still, her silence deafening.

"Mor?"

"We...we did." Her golden eyes stared sorrowfully into his sea blue. The crestfallen look on her face was heartbreaking. She looked like a woman whose whole world was coming apart.

"Huh?" he asked.

"The barrier stones were erected by mage lords of old, thousands of years ago to protect the mage realms from dragons. Their powerful spells dulled the dragons' anger, keeping them at bay while the mage realms prospered. When first constructed, the spells were strong, and mage powers were far more dispersed throughout the populace, less concentrated and powerful than today. As time passed, the barrier stones grew weak, while magic has concentrated into powerful bloodlines, bloodlines powerful enough to raise the dragons' ire, even from across the barrier. Over time, this caused the lesser dragons, those dwelling just beyond the barrier stones, to test the boundary," she explained.

"And now?" Ethan could guess where this was going.

"And now...the red dragons have invaded the wilds, drawing closer to the power rising in the south."

"Elysia," Ethan named the rising power.

"Yes. House Loria has grown so powerful as to draw the dragons unto it, especially now, with your union with Alesha."

"I'm immune to magic. How are they drawn to me?"

"You have the Dragon Tongue. And if you have it..."

"Our baby." He sighed.

"Yes. Just when I think I know everything about you, again you surprise me. You have the Dragon Tongue, a power we never knew existed, and it draws the red dragons as nearly as much as our own great power."

"Shouldn't the Dragon Tongue help control the dragon?" he asked, rightly thinking that Casandra, her brother or himself should be able to speak to the beasts.

"It doesn't work with red dragons. They devour those with the Dragon-Tongue, their power instilling madness in the red dragons, just as mage power causes madness in other dragons. Now the red dragons have entered their lands, driving them to invade Vellesia to escape destruction," she regarded Casandra briefly.

"So the barbarians are here escaping the red dragons?" he asked.

"It is far worse. They are here to destroy the mage realms, House Loria in particular, thus removing the primary source of the red dragons' ire."

It was ironic that the source of House Loria's power, their ability to bind all mage gifts to their bloodline, threatened to extinguish their line altogether. Ethan released a tired breath before scrubbing his face with his hands. It seemed there was no end to their troubles.

"Ethan?" Mortava couldn't miss the weary look on his face.

"I miss my hat." He gave her that infectious grin that seemed to put everything to right, making light of their troubles.

"I'm sure you will find it. It always comes back to you somehow." She smiled, not at all surprised he would say something so out of place. It was at that moment she realized she loved him as if he were her own grandson, and in a way, he was.

"Red dragons, black dragons, white dragons, and barbarian invasions, Alesha sure got her money's worth with me. You know, Mor, if we make it through all this, I have a growing list of requests," he japed.

"I'm sure you do." She smiled again.

With that, they decided to bed down for the night, Ethan taking the first watch after securing Casandra with tighter bonds. He stepped back from the fire, waiting inside the tree line, keeping one eye on Mortava and the other in the distance. The pale moon shone upon his face through the boughs of a towering oak. He wondered how his parents fared that very moment? Were they upon the ramparts of Astaris, gazing up at that same moon? Did they miss him as much as he missed them?

Stupid question, he scolded himself. They missed him terribly, and he spent so little time thinking of them. Ethan wondered if his own daughter would treat him as poorly as he treated his own mother and father?

I deserve it, he thought miserably, realizing he spent over a year in Red Rock without giving them a word, an entire year where they hadn't a clue if he was alive or dead. Oh, he sent messages but never confirmed if they reached them or not. He didn't think about how that must have tortured them. He could see his mother's smile when she first saw him upon his return, waiting for him at Plexus, a joyous rapture transfixing her face, happy that her boy was home and safe. All she ever wanted was for him to be safe and happy, only asking him for one thing, to not enter the Mage Bane. Even in that he betrayed her. If he hadn't, then Alesha would've died, but that is beside the point. He broke her heart. And after all that, he recalled how poorly he treated her after Alesha's betrayal.

She had every right to be angry, you fool. He shook his head, wondering if she forgave him.

"I'm sorry, Mother." He sighed, lowering his head, a lonely tear running down his cheek.

It was a short time after that he heard Mortava moan. He could see her shivering as he approached, curled up in front of the fire, clutching her arms tightly.

"Mor?" He squatted beside her, touching a hand to her shoulder.

"C…co…cold. So…cold." She looked up at him pleadingly.

"You're burning up," he said, placing a hand to her forehead. Something was wrong. She shouldn't be able to get sick, but the effects of the dragon bite were most certainly the cause.

"I…" She couldn't form the words, her teeth chattering.

He lifted her, wrapping his arms around her, pressing his warmth to her. He looked around for anything to cover her with, but all they had was what they wear wearing. All their gear, blankets, and horses were leagues away at the battlefield and probably destroyed. A sword, a pistol, and about twelve bullets was all he had, none of them much use to keep her alive if this went bad. She snuggled into his arms, stealing a glance at him from time to time, before fading back to sleep.

"Shh," he said every time she stirred, his soothing voice calming her spirit. And so it went throughout the night. Ethan closed his eyes from time to time, stealing whatever sleep he could manage. Come sunrise, they would make their way back to the battlefield and see if anyone was still alive, the spirits help them if they ran into the enemy host. He should be able to cut his way through them and escape or keep Mortava safe from the dragon, but not both with her present condition.

"*Where are you, mage slave?*"

Ethan sat bolt upright, jerking Mortava as her eyes sprung open.

"Ethan?" she asked, eyes struggling to come into focus.

"Rest easy, Mor. I heard something," he said, easing her to the ground before gaining his feet.

"*Ah, there you are,*" Nyla's voice rang ominously in his brain.

"Mor, the dragon's back!" Ethan said, her power igniting in all its glory once he stepped away, drawing his sword. Ethan winced, feeling the pain shooting through Nyla's brain.

Mortava looked skyward, her own ability to see in the dark slightly impaired by the dragon fever. She gained her feet, drawing her sword, her eyes sweeping the horizon through the branches of the surrounding trees.

"Ethan." Mortava pointed southeast, where a winged form grew ominously in the predawn sky.

"I see it." He winced before a deafening roar shook the heavens.

Fires erupted along the dragon's path, streams of blinding flame billowing from Nyla's maw. Ethan stepped in front of Mortava as the flames drew nigh, incinerating trees and exploding rocks where they stood. He held tight to his sword, braving the magical flames that could not harm him. Nyla closed her mouth, her belly smashing through the trees above, raining debris upon them.

Ethan pushed Mortava back, a thick branch smashing into his knee, driving his back to the ground. The sound of breaking timbers echoed above, his broken leg healing before pushing the branch off him, gaining his feet as Nyla's massive bulk dropped in front of him.

"KRALL!" Nyla roared, her breath pressing upon him like a winter gale.

"Ethan!" Mortava warned as men sprang from the dragon's back.

Ethan lunged forth, driving his sword at Nyla's nose, striking empty air as she drew back. She swept her right front leg, catching Ethan across his left hip, tossing him through the air, smashing against the trunk of a thick oak.

Mortava's power returned as Ethan was tossed aside, again drawing the dragon's fury, its feral golden eyes drawn instantly to hers. Her blood ran cold as Nyla's maw drew open; her gaze drawn to the swirling fires in the back of her massive throat.

"Agghh!" The sound of the men charging at her drew her attention away.

Whiff!

An arrow grazed her shoulder, sent by an archer standing beneath Nyla's right wing.

She outstretched her left palm, throwing three men back with a kinetic pulse. A snap of her fingers broke another man's neck, his axe dropping harmlessly at her feet, missing her by the barest of measures. Another came upon her left, a blinding spell sending his sword strike awry. He blinked his eyes, trying to clear his vision as she moved behind him, her sword cutting the back of his knees.

"Kill her!" Karg shouted, standing beneath Nyla's left wing.

"Our men," Nyla said as their men blocked her line of fire, the madness paining her ears.

"Kill her while you can!" Karg shouted, his order causing a few of his comrades to draw away from her line of fire.

Mortava levitated another man off the ground, a snap of her fingers breaking his arms, his sword falling from his useless hand. His eyes drew wide as he was lifted into the air toward her. She spun him around with a twirl of her finger, planning to use him as a shield against his fellows, but Nyla was having none of it, preparing to bath them in flames.

Bang!

Nyla's head jerked violently, a bullet striking the left side of her neck, green blood oozing from the wound, her head swinging back toward Ethan, who lay upside down at the trunk of a tree, his pistol pointing at her.

Bang!

The second bullet bounced off her skull.

Ethan's third bullet took a charging man in the gut, several others rushing toward him. His broken back healed as he rolled away from the tree, a large piece of bark sliding off the tree from the impact of his body. He holstered his colt, drawing his sword and gaining his feet in time to parry a hasty strike. Spinning around the man's strong arm, he drew his bowie knife with his left, punching it into his side, gutting him hip to spine, before sheathing the deadly knife.

Karg watched in horror as Ethan made quick work of two more, cutting them to pieces like a wolf amongst sheep.

Ethan fought the pain ringing in his ears that mirrored Nyla's, walking quickly toward the barbarian king, steel blue eyes staring from his bloodstained face. Karg backed a step, trying to work out how to deal with him in his mind, as Nyla bathed Ethan in fire.

"Nyla, we must leave!" Tomas warned, his left hand holding tight to the spindles along her neck, his right tied across his chest. He barely stayed in place, his vision blurring and skin pale from his ruined shoulder and the pain in his ears.

"He must pay!" Nyla growled as Ethan emerged from the flames unburnt, like a vengeful apparition.

"He can hurt you, Nyla. We can't risk you or we are lost!" he pleaded, caution replacing his earlier zeal.

"Forget him! Kill the mage!" Karg shouted desperately as Ethan kept coming, the dragon shifting behind him, its eyes shifting between the two threats.

Ethan strode quickly forth, closing upon the dragon as an arrow struck his left shoulder. He shifted his sword to his left hand, drawing his pistol with his right. The archer stumbled backward, the bullet taking him in the chest. Ethan holstered his colt before yanking the arrow from his shoulder.

"Withdraw!" Karg shouted, turning and running away, the survivors following their king through the trees to the open ground beyond. There was no time to climb upon Nyla's back with Ethan so close and the dragon shifting constantly.

Nyla backed away, her rump breaking several trees while keeping distance between them, the sound of snapping timbers echoing in their ears. He was closing faster than she withdrew, but the thought springing to mind brought Ethan to a halt. He barely glimpsed her intent through the madness caused by Mortava's magic.

Ethan sprang backward, moving toward Mortava as Nyla's jaws extended wide, flames spewing from her open maw. Mortava threw the soldier suspended in the air toward the dragon, his body igniting upon meeting the flames. She moved toward Ethan, dragon fire striking her back as she ducked her head, heat burning the flesh from her spine.

Ethan stepped into the fire's path before it consumed her, the flames bending around his aura like the tide breaking upon the shore.

Mortava slumped to the ground, her face planting in the dirt, unbearable pain coursing the back of her arms, the nerves on her back nearly burnt away. The dragon fire overwhelmed her magical immunity to pain but not her ability to regenerate. As soon as the fire shifted away, her tissue began to mend, pain running the breadth of her back where the nerves healed before her flesh.

Ethan stood between Nyla and Mortava, keeping his aura just beyond Mortava so she could heal. His eyes followed the dragon taking to the air, Nyla's powerful wings raising swirls of dust across the ground as she lifted higher, her golden eyes fixing him with terrible intensity.

Whoosh!

Nyla sped overhead, dropping down just beyond them, her claws snatching Casandra from beside their cookfire where she was bound. She again took flight, circling overhead before breaking in the direction of the others, leaving Ethan looking on as she set down in the distance, collecting Karg and their other survivors before disappearing over the horizon.

*****

Ethan squatted several paces from Mortava, resting his elbows on his knees as she convulsed in pain, her back healing painfully slow. She fought the tears squeezing stubbornly from her eyes.

"Hang with me, Mor. You can do this," he encouraged, keeping his distance so her magic could do its work.

"At...least my...healing powers are working. Not so mu... much my immunity to...pain," she managed to say.

"Too bad the healing wasn't working faster." He winced, seeing her face contorting in agony.

She shuddered, her breath catching in her throat as skin started forming over-restored flesh. Ethan quickly searched the bodies nearby, snatching a fur cloak from one of the slain. He shook it out for a good minute as she finished healing, before draping it over her naked back.

"You going to be all right?" he asked as she shakily gained her feet, clutching the fur cloak about her shoulders.

"The pain is excruciating." She closed her eyes, trying to put the memory from her thoughts but failing miserably.

"Pain isn't much fun, I can tell you that." He smiled, making light of the situation.

"I never thought of what you must've suffered at the Velo." She shook her head, trying to imagine his suffering.

"I can't imagine it either." He shrugged. "All I remember was that it hurt...a lot."

"How many wounds did you suffer?"

"At the Velo or overall?"

"Do I want to know?" she asked herself out loud.

"I can't answer for you." He shrugged.

"You're insufferable. How does Alesha put up with you?" She shook her head.

"I don't know, but I'm sure you'll ask her if we survive this," he said, loading his last few bullets into his colt.

"Are you going to answer my question, or continue stalling?"

"I couldn't honestly tell you, Mor. I must've been stabbed or shot with arrows over a hundred times at the Velo. When I awoke, I found myself under a pile of corpses with a dozen arrows and blades still sticking in me. I suffered thousands of injuries training in Astaris. I lost my hands more times than I can count. I got in a few scrapes with bandits and barbarians during my years in Astaria, not to mention a mountain wolf taking a generous bite out of my neck."

"Mountain wolf?" Mor lifted a brow at that.

"I had a run-in with a cave bear along the upper Torlin. I forgot about that one. Think I was fourteen at the time." He chuckled at the memory.

"Did the bear maul you?" She could already guess the answer.

"Not really, just took a bite of my leg. Krixan helped me finish it. We made a nice blanket out of its hide for his mother."

"If not for your recuperative powers, you'd be dead a thousand times."

"Not a thousand times." Je made a face.

"Nine hundred and ninety-nine, then?" She shook her head.

"Maybe seven hundred." He shrugged as if it was inconsequential.

"And you felt every one." She had to admire the boy's fortitude.

"At least with those injuries I could heal fairly quick. The dragon biting off my fingers hasn't been much fun." He looked down at his hand, wiggling his restored fingers, reassuring himself they were still there.

"Yes, with the dragon interrupting our regenerative powers to some degree. It will require further study should we survive this war."

"As awful as that was, it wasn't nearly as bad as the bullet Nate Grierson put in my back. I was lucky it didn't hit anything vital. Took me a good while to recover. I spent several weeks laid up in bed at Judge Donovan's home," he recalled, the nostalgic look on his face not matching the awfulness he described.

She recalled when they learned of that, as well as his duel with Luke Crawford, each shaking House Loria to its core, hastening their urgency in bringing him to heel before he got his fool self killed.

"Yep, took the bullet about right…here." He touched a finger to his lower right back. The scar completely disappeared upon his return through the portal.

"For someone who doesn't like pain, you're not very good at avoiding it," she said.

"Yeah, but that's not my fault. It's hard to avoid in war. I fought a war in Red Rock and another at the Velo and a third in the Bane. Thought I was done with them when your granddaughter dragged me off to wedded bliss, but here I find myself in a fourth one."

"You volunteered for this one," she reminded him.

"What was I supposed to do, Mor? Sit back in Elysia while the dragon kills all of you before making its way to me anyway?"

"As I said before, if we were dead, you would be free. Isn't that what you want?" Her weariness was making her more direct.

"Do you really think I could live with myself if I did that? Perhaps if you asked me back in Astaris when the betrayal was raw, I might've considered it. But now?" He shook his head.

"And now?" she asked.

"Now I know you. You had the right of it when you said what moved me. That's a weakness of mine. I get to like people, and I don't want to see them die. It's what kept me in Red Rock for so long. The thought of the Grierson clan or their hired guns killing Ben, Skeeter, or the judge was unthinkable. The same goes for Dar, Ander, Ray, Corb, Alesha, and the mothers, especially you. I couldn't bear looking in Alesha's eyes if something happened to any of you. I also don't want to explain to my daughter one day how I stood aside and let a dragon kill her mother's family, even if you all deserved it for what you did to me," he added the last so she wouldn't believe he was getting all mushy.

"Because you care, just as I said before. I am thankful you are here, Ethan." She cupped his face with her hands, pulling his head down to place a motherly kiss on his forehead.

He just looked at her for a time, staring into her tired golden eyes that looked so much like Alesha's. Ben Thorton once told him about the brotherhood one shares with those who fight beside you or sisterhood in Mortava's case. He felt it with his friends in Red Rock, with Allie and the Vellesians in the Mage Bane, with Krixan his entire life, and now with Mortava. They each placed their lives in danger for the sake of the other. That was something he would never forget.

"I'll get you through this alive, Mor, I promise you that much, and you'll see that new granddaughter come into this world," Ethan said with all his heart.

"I've lived many lifetimes, Ethan. If I have to choose between you or me to see her born, I choose you."

"You're not getting off that easy, Grandma. We'll see her together," he said, drawing her into a crushing hug that took her aback.

"Together." She smiled as they parted, marveling at the infectious optimism he drew out of her.

"Now all we have to do is find horses somewhere and make our way back to the army before Karg does." He started looking around, deciding which direction to take.

"We seem to have company," Mortava said, pointing out the movement to their east through the trees.

"Company? Any idea who?" He drew his sword.

"Ander." She smiled, a grin spreading across her face.

*****

The last thing Ander expected making his way across the open field was to see Ethan and Mother Mortava come running at him from the trees up ahead like two children chasing butterflies. Even more surprising was having Ethan throwing his arms around him, lifting him in the air before Mortava showered him with kisses all over his face. Ander stood there, dumbstruck as his fellow six companions looked on with equally surprised looks. The mothers of the Lorian Order were not known for emotional or affectionate outbursts, but that was before Ethan came into their lives.

"We thought you were all dead," Ethan said, looking at the seven men. They were all on foot, leading three horses, each packed with provisions.

"We feared the same for you," Ander said, Mortava's kisses leaving his cheeks an embarrassing red.

"Mother Mortava, we are so very pleased to see you well," the soldier nearest Ander said. He had a mop of black hair framing a youthful face. His gray mail was bloodstained and torn at the left shoulder, his helm missing and a severe dent imprinting his left greave. The others fared little better, each looking worse for the wear. They were tired, battle-weary, and hadn't slept since the previous morn. Ethan was pleased to find Guston among them, the young man looking to have aged a dozen years since yesterday.

"And I am pleased to see each of you alive, though I wish more shared your fate." She felt like weeping reading their thoughts, knowing the suffering they endured.

"I gathered the survivors. As you can see, this is it," Ander said, regarding his comrades sadly.

"Just seven?" Ethan shook his head.

"As far as I know the dragon burned the rest," Ander said. "We found your horses, along with a third wondering aimlessly about."

"My horse?" Ethan asked.

Ander nodded, relief washing over Ethan. His saddle pack contained sixty spare rounds for his pistol and another hundred for his rifle. Of course, his rifle was lost, so they did him little good until...

"Thought you might be looking for this." Another soldier stepped forth, presenting him his Winchester.

"How did you find us?" Ethan asked, taking hold of his rifle, working the lever action, confirming it was still functional and empty.

"We set out in the direction of the dragon, but that only started our journey. But then..." Ander's voice trailed off, uncertain how to continue.

"Alesha," Mortava gasped.

"Alesha?" Ethan made a face.

"The princess spoke to me, Ethan. First during the battle, warning me of the second dragon, but by the time I reached you, it was already too late."

"Not too late. Your war horns distracted the dragons and saved our lives," Ethan recalled.

"I hoped to reach you sooner. The princess was most fearful of the threat. She spoke to me again after the second dragon fled the battlefield after burning everything in sight. She told me to gather everyone I could and proceed westward in the direction the first dragon fled with you clinging to its side. She guided us throughout the night until we saw the area up ahead alit with dragon fire."

"How did you survive fighting the beast the entire night?" Another soldier asked.

"I didn't. The dragon that just flew off was the second one," Ethan said.

"Where is the first one?" Ander asked.

"Ethan killed it," Mortava said, the statement drawing the expected reactions of awe and disbelief.

"How?" Ander asked, taken aback. Dragons were thought to be invincible. If Ethan could slay one, what did it say about him?

"I got lucky, Ander," Ethan said tiredly.

Mortava snorted, dismissing that humble assessment. "Dragons are impervious to weapons wielded by mortal men, but Ethan is apparently able to penetrate this invincibility."

The others shared a look before she continued.

"Ethan is equally vulnerable standing within the dragons' aura, which makes the outcome of our coming battle precarious. Only Ethan can overcome the dragon, and only the dragon can defeat Ethan. Their duel will decide the fate of the realm."

"I didn't come along for my charming disposition and good humor." Ethan made light of the pressure bearing down on his shoulders, the others not sharing his optimism.

"Can you slay another dragon?" Ander asked.

"Who knows?" He shrugged. "I got lucky once, why not twice. I will need three things to make it even possible though."

"And they are?" Mortava asked.

"One, I'll need two of the horses. Two, I'll need you to contact Alesha again, if you are able. She needs to communicate with Valera and delay the battle until I arrive."

"And three?" Ander asked.

"I need my hat," he added for good humor, knowing it was likely gone for good or burned by dragon fire.

"It's in your saddle pack." Ander jerked a thumb to the lead horse behind him.

"Serious?" Ethan made a face.

"Found it blowing along the ridge where you dropped..." Ander couldn't finish before Ethan lifted him into the air with another bone-crushing hug.

CHAPTER 28

Elysia

Alesha stared out the window of her bed chamber at the Salnar Mountains ringing Elysia in their protective embrace. She ran her fingers over her womb, the child's power growing exponentially with every passing day, lending its omnipotent anti-magic to its mother.

"*Her* mother," she corrected herself, for the child was a girl, her precious Gabrielle.

"You miss your father, little one, I can feel the strains of his bond weighing upon your heart," Alesha's soothing voice was a balm to her unborn daughter's distress. She could almost hear Gabrielle whispering back in kind, putting voice to her lament.

"I miss him also." She closed her eyes, Ethan's face staring back, a projection from her memory, a cruel but kind reminder of what was missing. How she longed for this war to end and have Ethan returned to her.

She opened her eyes, reaching out with her mind across the great distance separating them, seeking any sign that would lead to him, his magical immunity still blinding her to his location. When her mother first called out to her, warning of the danger of the two dragons, it was as before, as a faint whisper vying with her many thoughts. It took great practice to hone this powerful gift of House Menau, able to communicate with another over vast distances. It was more like sensing their identity before calling upon them, their visage but blurry shadows far afield. This power was stronger with her than any other, as House Loria long possessed the power to control animals, seeing through their eyes. She would often use birds, flying them to areas where her connection was weak, granting her clear visuals to coordinate with a given subject. She used this to great effect spying on the enemy advance and relaying the information to Valera's commanders, helping direct the army. But now she no longer needed animals to see, able to find any individual for hundreds of leagues, calling out to their mind, whether friend or foe, human or animal, all except Ethan. Even the dragons she could follow, watching the world from their eyes, coursing the heavens in all their glory. Her own gift of flight was pitiful in comparison to that of a dragon, the magnificent and terrifying creatures speeding through the sky, masters of all they survey. Now, she was able to see as they do, joined to their minds, yet unable to control them. Would that power come as well? And where did it come from? Was the joining of Ethan's powers and her own that potent? And what of Ethan slaying Nylo? She knew he had done so when she sensed the creature's passing. Ethan was a dragon slayer, a fact she had difficulty comprehending. How was he able to do so?

She put such questions aside, focusing on Ethan's whereabouts once again. She hadn't slept all night, her waking hours spent guiding Ander to Ethan and Mortava. Whenever Ethan stepped away from her grandmother, she was able to sense their location through her, but something was amiss as if Mortava was afflicted with some malady. Her visage would illuminate and fade with painful regularity, preventing her from speaking to her. But she held enough connection to direct the others to them. It was through the dragon, however, that she could see much of the battle, especially Mortava's terrible wound. The only thing she couldn't see was Ethan, his visage an inky black shadow in her sight. Her heart broke for her grandmother, sensing her torment as she struggled to heal. It was the dragon's agony she felt even more forcefully, suffering in kind whenever a mage appeared before it. No wonder the creatures despised mages so, driving them into a murderous rage if one came remotely close to them. More importantly was why she could connect with the dragons at all. It was a power unheard of, one she clearly was given by Gabrielle. The fact their child would wield such power was equally breathtaking and frightening.

She again reached out, finding Ander just as he found Ethan and Mortava, smiling as she felt their embrace. Though she couldn't see Ethan, she was still connected to his overwhelming presence. Yet it was strange she could see the dragons but not him. Gabrielle's anti-magic allowed her to see the dragon, just as Ethan's allowed him to see one in Dragos's vision, but she could not see Ethan. How strange.

"*Alesha?*" Mortava called out to her, as if aware of her presence as she looked upon her grandmother through Ander's eyes.

"I am here, Grandmother," she answered.

"*You must contact Valera. Ask her to delay the battle until Ethan arrives. Tell her he slew one dragon, leaving only the she-dragon to contend with,*" Mortava said. Alesha was thankful Mortava spoke of the dead dragon. If she was forced to reveal that she knew, others might question how, and she desired that her newfound power was kept secret, even from her House.

"I shall. How is Ethan?" She needed to ask, frustrated that he was the only one she could not see, his presence obscured in shadow. She waited patiently, observing Mortava waiting upon his answer, not liking the look passing her grandmother's face.

Mortava shook her head sadly, before answering, torn by what he said.

"Grandmother?" she asked.

"*He asks that you prepare to leave Elysia in the event we lose. Should we fail, Elysia is doomed. Do not try to save anyone or give battle. Make your way south to the Mage Bane. Only there will you be safe from the dragon's fury, though other's dangers await you there.*"

The thought of Ethan dying was unacceptable, unthinkable. And who did he think he was talking to? She would not flee this battle. She will stay and give battle no matter the price. She would rather die defending her unborn child, her family, and realm rather than sheepishly run away.

"*Alesha?*" Mortava asked, wondering if she was still listening. She stood apart from the others looking skyward as if searching for her in the clouds.

Alesha steeled her heart, drowning any weakness in a sea of fortitude, lifting her chin in defiance. "Tell Ethan to win. I expect no less from a deputy of Ben Thorton's," she said, knowing the reference would kindle his spirit.

And with that she withdrew, standing before the window of her chamber for a time before reaching out to relay the information to her mother by way of whatever soldier was nearest her. Afterward, she continued to gaze at the surrounding mountain peaks, focusing on their minute details, from snow-capped summits to gray jagged ridges lining their slopes. Focusing on the natural beauty that surrounded her, helped be still her racing heart...for a time until thoughts of Ethan came flooding back twisting her insides like painful barbs. All she could do was wait, wait for a battle several days off that would decide the fate of the realm and their thousands of years of prophecy. The days would crawl painfully along, agonizingly slow and torturous.

A conversation in the outer corridor drew her from such thoughts, recognizing her grandfather's distinct voice speaking with her guards.

*****

"It is urgent that I speak with the crown princess," Darius said, standing in the wide-lit passageway, with several royal guards blocking his path.

"My apologies, Consort Loria, but the princess is not to be disturbed except by orders of the Queen Mother," Sergeant Valenous said, standing post outside Alesha's royal apartment, dressed in his formal palace attire of silver breastplate over a pristine white tunic and pleated kilt, with matching greaves and vambraces, a plume of blue feathers running the center of his helm.

"He may pass, Sergeant," Alesha called out from the archway of her door, her light-golden gown matching the hue of her eyes.

She gifted Darius a welcoming smile, taking him in hand, leading him into her chamber.

"I am sorry to trouble you my dearest, I know you have barely slept these past days." Darius's gentle smile matched her own.

"You are never a bother, Grandfather," she said, having him sit opposite her upon a settee, beside her large window overlooking the Salnar Mountains in the distance, pillowy clouds covering the greater city below. She regarded him briefly, noting the healthy luster restored to his face and build, his opened-collared black shirt revealing his masculine chest. Dark trousers and knee-high black boots completed his ensemble. She never before considered him handsome, being her grandfather as he was, but couldn't help but notice his dashing looks despite the silver tainting his dark mane. His eyes, though, bespoke a deep worry, which drew him to seek her out. She fought against reading his thoughts which was made difficult by how easily they were spilling from his mind. Her deep love and respect for him forced her to shield his mind from her, allowing him to speak for himself.

"I know you are anxious for this war to end and for your mother and husband to return. I, too, am fearful for their safety. These are dangerous times, and the thought of my dearest Valera facing a dragon's wrath is most troubling." He thought of his daughter leading their armies into battle.

"I trust them to bring us victory, Grandfather, but something else brings you here. What troubles you so?"

He grew uncomfortably quiet, looking down at his hands, trying to put his thoughts into words. "As you know, our lives were much different before…well, before Ethan arrived," he began.

"I know," she said, sending a tendril of comfort into his mind, setting him at ease. It was one of the few powers she would use on her family, giving them peace of mind.

"Ethan's arrival was like a cool breeze upon warm brows, a most welcome relief from the affliction of our House. Since the day I wed your grandmother, our time was measured by her insatiable hunger, tormenting her as she tormented me, an endless circle of misery. Ethan changed that, or more pointedly, *you* and Ethan changed that. With you sharing each other's company, the hunger was sated, allowing us a second chance to know each other. This precious gift is because of you and that boy."

559

"I know, Grandfather. It is a joyous thing, an unexpected boon of our union." She leaned forward taking his hand in hers.

"More than a boon, dearest one, but *life* itself. Forever the hunger was a wall between us, your grandmother and I, blinding us to a world we could never know. With its fall, we see the world anew, with all its possibilities. Imagine living with someone, but never knowing them, your mere existence causing them to despise you for the torment you cause them. Since Ethan arrived, that wall has fallen, allowing us to discover one another and liking what we found. And now..."

"And now it has returned with Ethan gone," she finished his thought.

"Yes. It is even worse, for she has seen what life could be, only for it to be taken away. The pain is excruciating, though she tries to hide it from me, sparing my guilt. The others are even worse, as you well know," Darius said, referencing the entirety of the Lorian Order. Such was their angst and hunger that a great pall had overtaken the palace, permeating the spirit of all that dwelled therein. Corbin was equally distraught, wanting to comfort Caterina, but his presence only fueled her pain. Raymar used his powers to comfort each of the Mothers, sending tendrils of ease and comfort to calm their minds, just as Alesha did with Darius. It was not enough, though, the curse of House Loria too great to long restrain.

Alesha closed her eyes, reaching out to the mothers of the Order, finding each in their own chamber, struggling to contain the hunger welling up within. Evalena sat her bedside, her head in her hands, silent screams running through her mind. Zelana stood upon the outside terrace of her chamber, sending lightning from her outstretched hands into the sky, venting her rage. Veriana sat crossed legged upon her floor, using meditation to fight the hunger, and failing miserably. Ametria lay abed, screaming into her pillow. And so it was with all the others, each coping in their own way, suffering Ethan and Alesha's physical separation as a blow to the head.

Alesha wept for them, guilt and grief rending her heart.

"Can you do anything for her?" Darius asked, drawing her eyes back to his. All his life, Darius resented Corella for caging him but now pitied her and all her kin, understanding a little of the pain they suffered, wondering why it was so.

"I shall do what I can, Grandfather, but the magic is greater than I." She wondered why this was so. What magical power was greater than anti magic? It made little sense. Why did their hunger abate when she and Ethan were together but return at their separation? Their powers were already joined through Gabrielle, which was the primary purpose for bringing Ethan here to begin with. There was also the need for their house to bind him to their throne for other purposes they did not understand, but didn't the sudden appearance of the dragons explain that? Wasn't Ethan doing what they needed him to do by fighting the dragons and sparing their realm? If so, why would the magic punish her Mother and Grandmothers for Ethan and her being separated when he was doing what their prophecies required? What else was he supposed to do beside protecting Vellesia and siring Gabrielle? Why did the magic demand they be together? Whatever the reason, there was nothing they could do but endure until Ethan returned.

"I would be eternally grateful, my dearest." Darius pressed his lips to the back of her hand, before they stood, drawing each other into a warm embrace.

"I will see to the Queen Mother and the others. Meanwhile, you and Grandfather Corbin should continue your training. Sergeant Bourvelle has agreed to aid in your instruction. I assume Jered is eager to resume sparring with each of you." She smiled, his eyebrows lifting happily with the suggestion. They had done nothing since Ethan and Ander departed, though he and Corbin still visited young Jered every day, helping him in the armory. It was their little ritual, a means of keeping the *Brotherhood of Elves* together, despite the absence of its most prominent member. Raymar joined them whenever he wasn't attending his grandmothers, trying to ease their torment.

*****

She waited patiently outside Mother Evalena's chambers for an insufferably long time before being given leave to enter. Alesha was tempted to use her new found power to expedite the matter, but decided against it, out of respect for her oldest and ranking grandmother. She found her in a miserable state, staring forlornly out her window, but seeing nothing but her own grief and troubles.

"Grandmother?" Alesha said, stepping nigh, the older woman turning sharply to greet her.

"You wished to speak with me, dearest?" Evalena asked curtly, a rare impatience when treating with her beloved granddaughter.

"I sensed you were troubled. Might I help?"

"We are all troubled, my dearest. The hunger has returned to us with a vengeful fortitude, as if exacting the agony we avoided since Ethan's arrival, tenfold with interest. The curse of House Loria is a cruel banker who charges usury upon its subjects," Evalena said, refusing to show the pain she was suffering.

"We shall put all things to right once Ethan returns, Grandmother," Alesha assured her, sending tendrils of comfort to Evalena's mind, flooding her with peaceful thoughts. Alesha swiftly withdrew them, taken aback by their ineffectiveness, the hunger greater than her anti magic and magic combined. How was this so? It indicated that the curse of their house was far stronger than any magic they possessed.

"Yes, put to rights," Evalena said with a faraway look, her mind already working out what that would entail.

"I bring good tidings, Grandmother, and as head of the Lorian Order, you are entitled to hear of it before the others," Alesha decided to offer positive news to lift Evalena's spirits.

"Out with it, child. You know I despise theatrics."

"Ethan has slain a dragon, leaving the enemy with one."

"A dragon!" Evalena gasped. "How?"

"The details are vague, but I believe it was with his sword."

"This proves our prophecies to be true. Why else would they demand he be bound to Vellesia? He was meant to spare us from these dragons." Evalena smiled intensely.

"Perhaps, but there is still the second dragon, and the barrier that requires repairing, lest other dragons follow in their wake," Alesha warned.

"It shall be done. Sarella, Vetesha, and Ametria are well learned in that art. And once the dragon is dealt with and the barrier repaired, we shall take the needed steps to ensure this never happens again," Evalena said, taking Alesha aback with the fierce determination in her ancient eyes.

*****

The early evening found Queen Mother Corella standing upon the outside terrace of her chambers, staring up at the starlit sky, her face bathed in the pale moonlight. 'Twas another day spent preparing Elysia for battle, every battlement and watchtower equipped with scorpions and trebuchets, along with companies of longbowmen. The skilled archers were selected from bloodlines with weak or little magic, hoping their shafts could penetrate the scales of a dragon, where those aided by magic might fail. Corella feared it would be all for naught, for how could one truly contend with such a beast that can reign fire from the sky with impunity, far beyond the range of their missiles and arrows to return the favor? Only Ethan seemed capable of such, and should the dragon come this far, then Ethan would likely be dead.

She kept matters of the realm foremost in her thoughts, lest the hunger consume her, but occupying herself with other things only went so far. She lamented her recent treatment of Darius, her poor husband suffering her rebuke for merely possessing a power she did not. She found it strange that she now felt guilt for such feelings that were as natural to her as breathing, but Ethan's presence afforded her that brief respite, allowing her to see the world as others do, without the curse of the hunger robbing her of its joy. Now he was gone, and the hunger was back, placing a cruel wall between Darius and her. It was too much to suffer his presence, his magic too much to bear. She thought of Alesha, her precious granddaughter. The girl visited her earlier, trying her utmost to ease her suffering, but it was for naught.

"Corella," Darius called out to her.

She turned, finding him standing in the doorway of her chamber. He finished bathing after a strenuous training session with the

563

others, wearing a long silver robe, his freshly combed hair swept behind him. He was strikingly handsome even in his advanced years. She regretted the years she let slip away, all but ignoring him, consumed with a hunger that could never be sated, and now it returned with a vengeful fury, again robbing them of their joy. It was even more so with his neck freed from the collar, his magic causing her intense annoyance.

He stepped nigh, his enhanced speed taking her aback, drawing her into his arms before she could refuse him.

"Darius, I cannot. I cannot suffer your presence, and I fear that I might harm you." She pushed him away.

"Could you suffer me if I was again collared?" he asked.

"Perhaps, but I won't do that to you. You deserve to enjoy your gift with the years left to you. I am sorry for taking that away for so long." She sighed, turning away, not able to look at his soulful dark eyes.

"I would be dishonest if I claimed to not care if I had use of it, but there is something far more important to me than the power of speed." He turned her around, drawing the hated broken collar from his robe, offering it to her.

"No, Darius. I will not do that to you." She shook her head.

"Just until Ethan comes back, then you can remove it for good. But I would not see you suffer needlessly in my presence, and my presence is necessary if we are to be together. What is my mage power compared to sharing a bed with my wife?"

His words broke her. All her life, she denied the existence of love, ascribing it to the emotions of weak-minded fools, and yet here stood her husband, willing to surrender all that he had, his one magical ability, to be with her. Could she shun his sacrifice and turn him away? With trembling hands, she took the collar and placed it about his neck, the broken halves fusing into one. The hunger slightly abated, but what remained no longer came from him.

"Why would you do this?"

"Because I love you, Corella."

With that, he took her in his arms, kissing his wife below the stary sky.

CHAPTER 29

Three days hence

Vellesian encampment. Thirty leagues north of Delvar.

"Easy, Bull," Valera said, easing the Palomino's gait while surveying the men finishing the entrenchments. General Ortar rode beside her, traversing the northern approaches of the Delvaran Vale. The valley was widest at its northern end, its opposing ridgelines several leagues abreast, before narrowing severely twelve leagues to their south, before opening up again upon the reaches of Delvar, the principle city that dominated the region, where much of the royal army awaited.

"I hope this is good ground, Julius," Valera said, circling Bull about, looking southward as Julius Ortar looked north beside her, each keeping a vigilant eye on the heavens.

"It is the best ground considering our situation, my Queen," he said with cautious authority. Gazing north, he could see the low ridge lines at the opposite sides of the horizon, each twisting along uneven rocky ground, with wide open terrain between them. A prominent stream meandered the vale, with dozens of now empty hamlets lining its banks, the populace removed south until the crisis passed. They stood at the edge of an uneven forest that followed the east ridge starting a league to their north before cutting across the vale behind them, before angling straight southward, leaving the western ridge barren. The valley stream meandered in and out of the forest throughout its course through the vale, with a prominent road skirting the western side of the forest.

Valera looked southward, observing the countless leagues of entrenchments lining the edge of the forest, which started to their northeast. Behind these strengthened earthworks, was the Delvaran forest, where much of their strength was hidden, and where those that would man the trenches could easily withdraw to.

"It seems risky," she shook her head with the madness of it all.

"At this juncture, every choice is fraught with risk. Weighing the positives and negatives, I see no better course, my Queen," Julius wondered how it came to this, their hopes for victory depending on delaying the enemy's advance long enough for Ethan to arrive. They preferred to move farther south, denying battle until Ethan arrived, but no other ground was better suited for his plan than here. The forest environ would cripple his ability to command and direct the army, but would give the enemy pause, and should they press their attack, it would cost them precious time. The plan was set, and it went against all military doctrine, deploying his men to a forest, where he would quickly lose control of the battle. In any event, many of his men would not survive the battle.

"You are certain they will come this way?" She asked.

"It is more like than not. They are moving too large a host to break east or west, the obstacles blocking those directions would spread them too thin. If they retained two dragons they might've chanced it, but only one forces them to concentrate their army. Should the dragon wander with their army close to a mage of your power, you could decimate them before it returned. By killing the second dragon, Ethan has effectively chained the remaining one to their horde."

"Yes, a most fortuitus turn in our favor," she said dryly. Word of Ethan's deed spread through the army like wildfire, lifting their morale just in time for the upcoming battle. She thought to keep it from them, always wary of fueling Ethan's legend, but times were desperate, and she would use everything to her advantage that she could.

"Your bringing of Ethanos to Vellesia has proven astute, my Queen. Who would have foreseen him slaying a dragon? I didn't think such a thing possible," Julius shook his head.

"Yes, who could have imagined it," she said, watching a company of Vellesian light horse performing drills along the bottom of the west ridge, some distance south. She lost count of the numbers assembled, more arriving each day from Lavera. Their skills with their composite bows were improving daily. Julius circled about, facing south to where she was looking.

"Aye, an impressive lot. Let us hope they match the skill of our foes," Julius said.

"Skilled, but not experienced. I am afraid Ethan was correct in his initial assessment of our readiness. We haven't fought a war in ages, and our men are untested," how she hated admitting the boy was right, especially about such a thing.

"Once the first arrow flies, they'll be experienced enough, battle does that to a man," Julius said. Of all Valera's Generals, Julius had in fact faced battle many times, volunteering in campaigns across the Aqualania Sea as a free sword in his youth, testing his mettle before bringing his war knowledge back to his native Vellesia. It was a unique apprenticeship that Valera intended many of her commanders to undertake as a substitute for their realm's lack of adventurism. That plan seemed useless now, considering all her soldiers would have war experience after this.

"Let us hope Ethan arrives before this dragon burns us all to a crisp," she shook her head, envisioning the beast sweeping over their ranks with impunity, setting them ablaze where they stood. If she could access her powers, she could read the unspoken fear plaguing her soldiers, the fear of dragon fire. Burning alive was a gruesome death, a painfully gruesome death. She well understood their fear, for she felt much the same. She gently stroked Bull's mane, thankful for his ability to shield her from such a fate. Of course, the dragon could still stomp both of them underfoot, or devour them whole, she reminded herself.

"I must confess my own misgivings, my Queen. Every general worth his repute envisions their own mastery of the battlefield, deploying their soldiers with stunning brilliance, smashing the enemy decisively. This plan does not afford me such vanity. If all goes to plan, we shall merely slow the enemy advance to a crawl, until Ethan arrives, where we must wait upon him to play his part," Julius said.

"If your plan is successful, Julius, the enemy host shall be crushed beyond your most optimistic calculations. Though you shall be the anvil to my hammer, the plan is still yours."

"You are kind to credit me so, my Queen, but you hold overall command. It is you that leads this army, and I am honored to serve beside you."

"Monarchs are the face of wars, but it is the generals that manage them. There is a reason I selected you for this most difficult task, Julius. You are the finest commander I have, and I trust none more than you to see us to victory."

"I am humbled, my Queen. I pray that I do not fail you."

"If you fail, none of us will live to know the difference."

*****

The next morn

Karg leaned forward in his saddle, gazing south from the western ridge overlooking the vale. A blanket of mist still hung in the morning air, fading slowly with the sunrise. He clutched the necklace about his throat, adorned with the fore finger bones of the men he slew. Today, he would add to the grizzly bauble, looking forward to taking his due from his slain foes. He knew a battle was afoot, the enemy cavalry herding his host to this valley, all other avenues of advance rendered impractical. Adding to the bait was the untouched farmland of this rich valley, as if they thought him a simpleton, following the only source of plunder left untouched by their Vellesian foe, like a mouse following a crumb trail. If this is where the Vellesian fools wished to offer battle, he would oblige them. His scouts reported sighting defensive works mirroring the forest that ran from the eastern ridge across the face of the vale before running straight south through the valley floor. They obviously expected him to follow the road skirting the western side of the forest, where they would spring upon his long drawn out host, cutting them to pieces.

"My King," Plygar, chief of the Aglar said, drawing his horse up alongside him, the aged warrior following Karg's gaze south and east.

"My King," Gurstak, chief of the Honlar greeted, drawing up along his left, the two men his ablest commanders after the death of Gorbus Mammoth's bane.

"Chieftains, today will give battle. The enemy await us below. They expect us to send Nyla to rouse them from their hovels and entrenchments, hoping to slay her with the foul sorcery of their fire sticks. That shall not happen. She will hold back until we discover the witch and the horse that shields her," Karg said.

"How can we be certain of this? Do you believe a horse can shield a mage's power from a dragon?" Gurstak asked.

"Nyla believes it true, having seen the thoughts of the mage slave," Karg said, sparing a glance skyward where the dragon circled above, keeping a watchful eye upon the barbarian host.

The word of the dragon was sacred and squashed their doubts.

"We find the witch and kill her. The horse is a strange breed, unlike any other in all of Elaria. Seek it out and kill it also. Once dead, she can be seen and killed by Nyla or kill her if she is near the horse, for her power to heal will be blocked," Karg explained.

"We shall lose many men fighting in the forest," Plygar said.

"Would it be wiser to circle around it, leaving them entrenched where they are?" Gurstak asked.

"That is what they expect of us. We kill their witch and their army dies. Once she is dead, withdraw. Nyla says the horse is the only one of its kind, and works the same as the mage slave, shielding mages from the dragon. Kill it and him, and the other mages will fall."

"What of the fire sticks?" Plygar asked, wary of Ethan's guns.

"There are only two, and they belong to the mage slave. He might be hiding in the forest, if he has rejoined them at all. If you see him, kill him, or take away his fire sticks. Without them, Nyla can crush him like the insect he is."

*****

By late morn, the sound of war drums echoed through the vale, the barbarian host sweeping down from the north, in fairly ordered ranks. The Vellesians manning the trenches along the northernmost end of the forest, looked on with growing dread as the enemy marched directly toward them. The banners of tribe Slotar aligned to the barbarian left, a white boar's head upon a field of black lifting strongly in the breeze. To their immediate right was the smashing gray fists upon a field of red of tribe Honlar, their chief Gurstak commanding the left wing of Karg's army. Lifting prominently in the barbarian center was the gray broken arrow upon a field of green of tribe Jutar. To the far west marched tribe Aglar, their chief Plygar commanding Karg's right wing. And in the skies above, circled Nyla, her golden eyes scanning afield for the slightest sign of mage power flaring. Tomas sat her back, his right arm bound in a sling, with Casandra sitting behind him, aiding him if needed, their distinct flaming red hair trailing in the wind.

Barbarian cavalry skirmished with their Vellesian counterparts along the slopes of the western ridgeline, exchanging volleys with their matching composite bows, before withdrawing to reform and strike again. The barbarians were frustrated that the Vellesians matched their strike and withdraw tactics, unusual for a mage realm to abandon its love of heavy horse. Without the Vellesians magic and the barbarian's dragon, both gave as good as they got, dozens of casualties suffered to either side. General Ortar observed the skirmish from the edge of the forest, some distance south of the approaching host. He was pleased with their cavalry performance throughout this campaign, the lighter and nimbler approach proving effective against the barbarian host. Like his contemporaries, he would prefer to deploy his heavy horse and sweep the enemy from the field, but such was folly when a dragon would torch any concentration of force. A few riders skirmishing here and there, however, was hardly worth the dragon's effort, which was proving true again this day. The only setback from this location was Julius's lousy view. When deploying your forces in a forest, your view was restricted to the ground in front of you. Standing within the tree line along the western flank, he was blind to happenings to his north, where the enemy was converging on his right flank.

The barbarian ranks stopped short of the Vellesian trenches, where the defenders manned the earthen works with leveled spears behind protruding stakes. More Vellesians were positioned behind fat tree trunks behind the trenches, namely archers and ballistae crews, holding their fire as the enemy drew nigh. The two armies stared at one another as the barbarians closed ranks, moving into final position within a hundred yards of the Vellesian palisades. At the appointed signal, the barbarian host formed a shield wall, advancing as the Vellesian archers and ballistae opened up, arrows, and stones tearing holes in the barbarian infantry. The tribes were equipped with an assortment of mismatched circular shields, wooden with iron or bronze covering their front, ill-suited for combating most mage realm armies. The barbarian archers responded soon after, trailing the forward ranks and loosing their volleys into the packed trenches. The barbarians stopped short of the trenches, refusing to advance, their archers targeting the Vellesians attempting to withdraw into the trees while others lobbed fire munitions into the trenches or open sacks with poisonous serpents in them, the irate creatures striking out upon landing in the enemy midst, most cut to pieces before slipping free.

A Vellesian fire munition struck a war chief of Tribe Honlar, killing the eldest son of Gurstak, the man engulfed in flames with three of his comrades. The Vellesian general commanding the northern trenches was mortally wounded, an arrow finding the weak link between his helm and neck. And so it went, both sides holding position, trading arrows and munitions, each waiting for something to break before the barbarians advanced or Vellesians withdrew.

To the west, the barbarian host swept around the open ground that stretched endlessly south through the vale, skirting the forest before striking the entrenchments along the western edge of the forest. Unlike the northern assault that held position, this attack was a full on assault upon the Vellesian positions.

"Kai-Korub!" The Barbarian war cry went out, men charging the palisades en mass. Dozens of ramps were brought forth, lain across the palisades, barbarians rushing overtop them, pouring into the trenches or advancing beyond. Several were dropped where the crews were slain short of the palisades before being taken up by those that followed. Elsewhere, men braved the trenches without the ramps, struggling to climb over protruding stakes and spears thrust to meet them.

General Ortar looked north from his position along the western edge of the forest, where the right wing of Karg's host turned into his flank. They poured over the open ground of the western ridge before charging into the forest to their east, their dark furs and iron helms melding in a caliginous sea of humanity. Julius tightened the strap of his helm before withdrawing deeper into the tree line, ordering a thousand reserves to follow him north through the forest to blunt the attack. His men cleared many paths through the dense forest in the last two days, enabling him to move troops from one point to another throughout the northern half of the forest. He was still mildly surprised the dragon hadn't burned them out of the trees as yet and happily accepted their good fortune.

Making their way north, Julius's men were greeted with a grizzly sight of barbarians flooding over their defenses, hacking their men to pieces along the trenches penetrating deep into the forest. The sound of dying and wounded men rent the air, a macabre symphony of clashing steel and howling torment. Julius broke his men up into ten man cohorts, with interlocked shields and short swords to maneuver in the narrows of the forest.

Julius drew his sword, leading his own personal guard into battle, following the sound of battle and movement through the well-spaced trunks of oak and pine, dodging low-hanging branches. The barbarians flooded the forest in an unbroken stream, crashing through underbrush and hastily erected defenses. Vellesian soldiers met them in places, their superior weapons matched by the barbarians greater experience. The northern tribesmen swarmed around pockets of resistance, attacking them from all sides, until they were subdued, and slain to a man, though suffering disproportionate losses in the exchange. Each group they fell upon slowed their advance until Julius's reserves appeared in greater numbers, stemming the tide.

*****

Karg stood upon the western ridge, observing the battle in the valley below, frustrated by the lack of progress. The day was drawing late, and his plans to sweep around the enemy's western flank was blunted for now. He could see his men trickling out of the forest, abandoning the hard won trenches along the western face of the tree line. Spirals of smoke drifted above the forest to his east, where fires were alit by munitions from either side. The trees were too moist for the flames to ignite a forest fire to their misfortune. Of course, one pass from Nyla and the thing would go up in a great fire, but he wouldn't commit her until the need arose, or the enemy mage and her slave were slain.

"Tell Plygar to reform his men and demonstrate along the western edge of the forest. The same order holds for Gurstak and the Jutar," he ordered his aides to relay the command to his three principle commanders. With night closing in, he would try a new tactic.

*****

By sundown of the first day of battle, the two armies held position facing each other along the trenches at edge of the forest, from the eastern ridge across the center of the valley and straight south. Small cavalry skirmishes persisted throughout the day along the western ridge and beyond the eastern ridge where the forest thinned, bleeding into open, uneven terrain, with deep ravines and boulder strewn fields. It was this area that Karg ordered tribes Vartop and Flugov to circumvent, striking the enemy from the east. It took much of the night for them to move into position, entering the unoccupied eastern edge of the Delvar forest while the Vellesians were kept in place by the barbarians demonstrating to their north and west. It wasn't until dawn that they were able to assail the northern Vellesian trenches from behind, though half their men were still lost somewhere in the forest, trying to navigate blindly in the dark.

The attack worked to some effect, the Vellesians manning the forward trenches caught between the attacking forces, once those to their front joined the fray. They rolled up the Vellesian northern flank, pressing south into the forest once clearing the trenches. The

Vellesians responded throughout the early morning, feeding rein-forcements into the forest from the south, the two armies entangled, fighting tree to tree, losing sight of their comrades, while battling wherever they came upon their foes. By midday, the barbarians made significant headway, driving the Vellesians south, continuing to roll up the entrenchments along the western edge of the forest.

Karg cursed as there was still no sighting of Valera, Bull, or Ethan. His army couldn't continue this battle indefinitely with much of his vast host holding to the north, waiting for clear passage through the vale, and the open lands beyond. He wanted to send Nyla to burn the Vellesians from the southern end of the forest but couldn't risk her until he had a fix on the threats that could harm her and his people. Nyla informed him of a large holdfast at the far end of the valley, many leagues south, where numerous mages were gathered, as well as the capital city of the realm that rested within a ring of towering mountains many leagues away. The mages were of such power to irritate Nyla from their lands in the far north, drawing her across the barrier.

"Elysia!" Karg whispered to himself, the name a source of such hate and misery to his people, causing the red dragons to invade their lands, driving them here, their fate resting on a knife's edge.

"KRALL!"

Karg looked skyward as Nyla roared, something drawing her ire. There in the heavens she flew overhead, her eyes fixed north, tormented by something in the distance.

*****

Smoke flared from Nyla's nostrils, her fury kindled by a familiar and unpleasant presence appearing in the distance.

Mage slave, she thought bitterly as Ethan emerged atop the western ridge, just north of their encampments, where their people waited for the outcome of the battle.

Tomas and Casandra followed her line of sight, unable to discern Ethan's visage from this distance, his body little more than a narrow silhouette along the horizon.

"Is it him, Nyla?" Casandra asked warily.

"*Yes!*" she snarled, her eyes blurred with hate. She thought he might have been hidden in the forest, wary to risk venturing there until it was cleared, but now she knew better. His power confused her. He possessed the Dragon Tongue, and yet he possessed magic, and anti-magic, combining the two great magics and the anti-magic of dragons. He was difficult to locate at times while other times she could see him clearly as she did now. She started to move in his direction, prepared to quash him beneath her claws, grinding him underfoot when Tomas drew her back.

"Nyla, he can wait. We must crush the enemy here and then turn back to finish him. His fire sticks are not in the forest, and neither is he," Tomas reasoned, winning her over.

"*So be it!*" she snarled, circling in the sky, before driving south, her black wings pounding the midday air.

*****

"So be it?" Ethan made a face, hearing Nyla's thoughts from afar, wondering what she meant.

"Ethan?" Mortava asked, sitting behind him upon the horse, wondering what vexed him. Ander sat the horse beside him, equally perplexed by the strange look crossing his friend's face.

"It's what Nyla said." He pointed south along the horizon where her silhouette looked little more than a small bird from this distance.

"If the dragon is there…," Mortava started to say, a horrified look crossing her face.

"Then so is their army," Ethan finished her summation. They rode for several days almost without cease, resting only to spare the horses, Ethan, Mortava and Ander, leaving the others behind. They brought only two horses, with Ander riding Ethan's pack horse, where his extra ammunition was stored, while he and Mortava shared a mount, shielding her from the dragon with his anti-magic.

"Ethan," Ander pointed, looking further south where spirals of smoke broke the horizon.

"We better hurry!" Ethan grunted, kicking his heels, spurring his mount forward.

*****

Valera looked upon Julius's war-weary face as he approached, finding her below a towering oak, with Bull dutifully beside her. Soldiers were gathered all around her, preparing to form a new line of defense in the thick forest as the enemy continued to press their front. Julius Ortar looked tired, his bloodshot eyes and bloodstained mail matching his exhausted state. Few men slept for the past two days, the endless battle taking its toll on all of them. Valera fared little better, keeping close to Ethan's horse throughout the campaign preventing her from ever lowering her guard. The damnable forest prevented her from seeing what was transpiring across the battlefield but also kept the dragon from locating her, though that protection would soon be lost once they were driven from the cover of the trees.

"How fares the battle, General?" she asked.

"If the new line is strong enough, we might last the day. Tomorrow, though, will be a close run thing, my Queen," Julius stated the brutal facts.

"Then make sure it is strong, old friend. If we can buy another day, it gives Ethan that much longer to find us," she said with as much ice in her voice as she could muster.

"Then I'll give him that day, my Queen," Julius said, proud to serve so brave a Queen. So few women he knew could endure what she had through this campaign, nearly chaining herself to Ethan's horse, suffering the elements with the men, while maintaining stoic discipline without complaint. The only doubt in his mind was Ethan, fearing the dragon might've already slain him. But if that was the case, why hadn't the dragon attacked them yet? Where was the foul beast?

Julius winced as a blast of flame burst behind him, a violent stream of fire sweeping through the trees north to south, before cutting west, where their last redoubts and trenches rested. Trees exploded on contact, chunks of wood and branches thrown through the air, each deadly projectiles, slaying men where they struck. Men in the path of destruction burst into flames, some incinerated in place, others lingering, flopping on the ground like fish spit up upon the shore. Others ran to and fro, flames covering their backs and limbs.

The dragon had answered Julius's question.

*****

Tomas shouted victoriously, as Nyla swept over the Delvaran forest, intense beams of energy spewing from her maw, cutting a swath through the enemy below. She coursed through the air, a harbinger of destruction, laying waste to everything below. The forest ignited into a blazing inferno in her wake. She sped west where the forest edge met the open slopes of the western ridge, blasting apart the remaining Vellesian trenches, cooking men alive in a torrent of swirling flames. Tomas looked back; his eyes drawn wide with wonder at the destruction she wrought, where a large gash was cut through the forest, Nyla's toxic breath cutting a deep channel throughout her trek, fumes, and debris spewing from its charred ruin. Nyla circled about, her maw drawn open, cutting across the southern end of the forest, gouging another line of destruction through the Vellesian ranks below.

*****

Valera leaned in the saddle, racing Bull through the trees, dodging a low-hanging bough of a forest pine, her back scraping underneath it, nearly tossing her from the saddle. Fires erupted all around her, a wall of flames following the dragon's course off her right, angling east. She cut south through the debris field, Bull immune from the heated ground, just as the dragon returned, its massive shadow barely visible through the foliage above. Bull suddenly halted, his way blocked by a downed tree in their path as the flames swept over them. Valera braced herself for the inevitable, dragon fire raining all around them before passing west.

Nothing.

She opened her eyes to a hellish landscape, the ground scorched all around them, save for a patch of untouched earth matching Bull's shape. She looked on through the now empty space above, watching the dragon disappear to the west. Bull had spared her a gruesome fate, his immunity to magic proving a great boon, and proving the merit of Ethan's original plan. Of course, it meant little unless Ethan arrived soon before the dragon found them. It wouldn't take much for the beast to crush them or devour them whole.

She took stock of her surroundings. Men were running in every direction, wondering if any path was truly safe, while others died where they stood, or hid in fright. She lost sight of Julius after the dragon's first pass. Flames were spreading from the charred channels marking the dragon's route of travel, igniting the forest ablaze. The only respite she could expect was the enemy withdrawing from the forest, lest the flames consume them in turn. She cursed the binding of her magic, wishing nothing more than to lift into the air above the treetops, spreading her own reign of destruction upon the enemy host. If the need arose, she would do just that, returning their favor before the dragon devoured her. Oh, but what a glorious end it would be. She swore that she would not die alone.

"KRALL!"

The dragon's roar thundered through the sky as if afflicted. Valera stared skyward, the treetops limiting her view. She wondered what ailed the dragon, failing to see it speed away northward.

*****

Ander raced his horse alongside Ethan, following the ridgeline northward as fires erupted in the distance. They soon came upon an impressive sight, a vast multitude encamped across the valley floor to their southeast, and a battle raging farther beyond, with the dragon sweeping over a distant forest, raining destruction wherever she passed, smoke and flames spreading across the treetops. His heart went to his throat, knowing their army must be in the forest where the dragon struck time and again, like a lion playing with its prey.

They were soon spotted by a cohort of barbarian cavalry rushing to meet them, the riders lifting their composite bows, preparing to fire as they drew in range.

Ethan eased his mount to a trot, setting Mortava down and moving a few paces away. She paused briefly, her eyes closed with wondrous rapture, her power flooding back into her in all its glory. Her eyes snapped open, lightning erupting from her fingertips, sweeping over the ridgeline into the approaching cavalry. The entire cohort lifted from their saddles, lightning striping flesh from their bones while soaring through the air.

The dragon roared in the distance, pained by her display of power and the magic coursing her veins. Ethan eased his horse alongside her, pulling Mortava back in the saddle, continuing south as they watched the dragon speeding to meet them. They rode apace, swerving around loose boulders strewn across the ridge, the barbarian encampment coming fully into view off their left in the valley below. Ethan eased his horse to a halt, the dragon drawing dangerously close. He dismounted in a flourish, Mortava joining him, drawing his rifle from its sheath and shooing the horse away. Ander tossed him a pack with extra ammunition before drawing away himself, snatching hold of the reins of Ethan's horse, taking it in tow.

"Don't get yourself killed!" Ethan warned him as he moved a safe distance away.

"The same goes for you, you crazy fool!" Ander shook his head, riding off.

"He's sounding more like me every day." Ethan grinned, watching his friend draw away.

"Yes. Your corrupting influence is most troubling, you insufferable rascal," Mortava slapped him on the back of the head.

"I'm wearing on you too, Mor." He gave her that mischievous grin before looking back to the approaching dread.

"You already have, you rotten brat. Now keep your eyes on the task at hand," she scolded as the dragon roared again, the intense stare of its golden eyes taking her aback.

"Krall!"

Nyla roared again, lifting high into the air before diving, speeding in rapid descent, her maw drawn open, the flames swirling in the recesses of her throat hurling forth.

Bang! Bang! Bang!

Ethan stood his ground, firing round after round into Nyla's open mouth as she descended, keeping the butt of his Winchester tucked tight to his shoulder, Mortava holding tight to his back, the flames funneling around his protective aura. Ethan dropped the rifle, drawing his sword in one fluid movement, Nyla's massive muzzle closing fast.

"The right!" Ethan shouted over his shoulder, Mortava following him as he shifted but not before Nyla's nose struck his left shoulder, knocking him flat as she landed in their midst. Her massive head followed him as he sprawled on the rocky ground before the pain rang through her brain with Mortava falling beyond his protective aura. She shifted away from Ethan ever briefly, spewing flames at Mortava just as Ethan gained his feet, diving in front of her, fire sweeping around him.

Nyla snorted her displeasure, drawing her right front paw overtop of him, trying to squash him underfoot. Ethan thrust his sword at the underside of her paw, causing her to retract it, shaking off the pain, her other feet shifting violently, nearly trampling him underfoot. Ethan wasted little time moving toward her throat, thrusting the sword deep in her flesh.

Ander kept his distance, watching as Nyla stomped about, trying to crush Ethan, while Mortava kept within the dragon's shadow, while avoiding being crushed herself. Ethan jabbed his sword into Nyla's throat a second time, the beast roaring her displeasure, blood issuing from the wound. Mortava stumbled, ducking under Nyla's left wing, only to be caught by her tail, sending her through the air, striking the ground some fifty paces away, well beyond the dragon's aura.

"Krall!"

Nyla roared, Mortava's power illuminating like the sunrise, briefly drawing her full ire. Ander looked on as Ethan took advantage, driving his sword through her side beneath her right wing, finding purchase between her ribs. She closed her wing, knocking him beneath her, before stomping on his left leg, snapping it in half. Ethan shouted in pain, rolling away just beyond her aura, the leg healing as he gained his feet, just as Nyla's head swiveled about, hot breath blasting his face. Ethan rolled underneath, driving his blade into her throat a third time, ripping it free in a large gash, opening a large fissure, blood pouring freely, soaking his head and arms. She drew up on her hind legs, releasing a gargled scream, her golden eyes wild with fright. Ethan stumbled, blinded by Nyla's blood coating his eyes, barely opening them as her massive maw lowered overtop of him. Ethan lifted his sword just as her fangs dug painfully into the right side of his chest, engulfing his shoulder, nearly tearing him in half before he struck the sword tip into her gums, preventing her from fully closing upon him.

"Ethan!" Mortava screamed as the beast thrashed about, tossing Casandra and Tomas from its back, with Ethan trapped in its jaws. Ethan managed to keep hold of the sword with his left hand, drawing his pistol with his right, the nerves in his shoulder still functioning by some miracle Mortava couldn't guess.

Bang! Bang! Bang! Bang! Bang! Bang!

He emptied his colt into her mouth, wincing as Nyla lifted briefly into the air before dropping dead. He lay there for the briefest moment, impaled on her fangs before darkness took him.

CHAPTER 30

"Ethan!" Mortava cried, horrified as he lay impaled on Nyla's fangs, draping over her slackened jaw. The dragon lay upon the rock-strewn ridge, its dead eyes staring vacant, its head titled on its side, lifeless wings drooping to the ground. Before rushing to help Ethan, she paused, looking off her left where Tomas and Casandra struggled to their feet from the high grass where they were thrown. A snap of her fingers broke their legs, dropping them where they were.

"Ander!" she cried out, rushing to help Ethan, cursing her inability to use her power to free him from the dragon's teeth. Ander rode up alongside the beast reaching him first, jumping from the saddle, cradling his arms underneath Ethan's back before lifting him. Mortava joined him, struggling to lift him from the sharp fangs protruding from the right side of his chest and lower right ribs.

"Don't die on us, you blasted fool!" Ander cursed, yanking with all his might, Ethan's body easing off Nyla's fangs. He slid on the ground, where they dragged him by his feet well beyond Nyla's waning aura, blood trailing in his wake.

"Ethan?" Mortava knelt over him, wiping the blood from his face, trying to clear his mouth and eyes.

"Why isn't he healing?" Ander growled, kneeling opposite her on Ethan's right side, looking at the terrible punctures running a circle from his right collar bone to his right hip, none of them mending. He could barely hear Ethan's labored breath, his right lung crushed and punctured.

"The dragon's bite is poison. It took a very long to restore his fingers and far longer for my arm. This"—she shook her head, looking at the right half of his chest nearly torn to shreds—"this may take a while," or not at all, she feared to say.

"What can we do?" Ander asked, looking desperately at her.

"Bind his wounds and keep him alive long enough for his body to extract the poison," she said when the sound of Tomas and Casandra screaming reminded her that there was still a battle to win.

"Go, Mother. I'll see to him." Ander nodded, knowing what she must do.

*****

Mortava stepped away from Ethan, lifting into the air, spotting Casandra and Tomas laying some fifty paces away in the grass lower on the ridge. Their pitiful cries fell deafly on her ears, an agonizing mixture of physical and emotional pain, with their broken legs and shattered hearts. She reached out, further neutralizing them with blindness, expending little of her power keeping them thus while directing her efforts elsewhere.

She moved on, sparing the barbarian encampment a cursory glance before moving on, noting little martial activity there. Another cohort of cavalry formed up between the encampment and the battle farther south. She floated through the air, closing the distance between them, before casting a stream of lightning, striking them dead in their saddles. She moved silently on as the dead horsemen toppled from their mounts. She pressed on, her steel gaze fixed to the battle beyond, the barbarian host swarming over the Vellesian trenches, from the northeast, wrapping around the forest edge running south through the valley floor. The barbarians would now suffer the full power of a mother of the Lorian Order.

*****

Julius gathered what men he could, leading them due west through the forest, following the tree markings his men used to direct his path. With fires spreading south and east, this was the only route left to them. They stumbled upon several small groups of barbarians, dispatching them in quick order before pressing on. The smell of burning pine tortured their senses, the flames drawing dangerously close. His sizable group quickly grew to over three hundred, scattering what enemy they came upon. He lamented losing sight of the queen, the dragon's deadly fire separating them in the chaos. He had to trust her safety to her guile, and Bull's immunity to dragon fire.

No matter their immediate fate, the battle seemed all but lost if the dragon wasn't stopped. He had no sense of the greater picture, reduced to battling on a tactical level of operation, trusting his men's safety to their own ingenuity and teamwork. He would despair if he hadn't seen their countless selfless acts throughout the campaign, a trait Ethanos favored over braggarts and pompous knights.

Daylight broke clearly through the trees ahead, meaning the edge of the forest was near. The sound of clashing steel and dying men proved the enemy awaited them in force, blocking their escape. Julius made his way forward, able to clearly see a large enemy host holding at the trenches they took from his own men earlier that morn. They were doomed, forced to attack a fixed position though they were outnumbered, or be devoured by flames. Julius resigned himself to the only option left to him. He removed the precious stone his queen entrusted to him to safeguard.

"Dadus, give this to Queen Valera should I die. Guard it with your life." Julius placed the necklace adorned with the stone, overtop young Dadus's head, his most trusted aide.

He stepped away from the stone, his magic returning, flooding through him in glorious bliss. Julius moved farther to the front, dodging an arrow passing overhead, outstretching his hands toward the enemy manning the trenches. Fire spewed from his fingertips, not the flood of flames the Lorians mustered, but a steady and deadly stream of unbroken flame, funneling into the trench to his immediate front. The cries of burning men echoed hauntingly over the din, flooding their narrow defensive works with a deadly inferno. He shifted to his left, continuing his deadly stream along the entrenchments, making his way south, lifting his aim every few paces, targeting those holding position west of the trenches. Barbarian archers concentrated their fire on him, their arrows filling the sky. Julius ignored the threat, keeping his deadly fire trained on the enemy infantry, knowing his audacious act would draw the dragon's ire. He was dead anyway at this juncture and was willing to give his life for his men to break free and reduce the enemy to his utmost. A feathered shaft found purchase in his right arm, and another his left hip, the rest bouncing off his sturdy cuirass and helm.

All of a sudden, a great tumult erupted in the enemy ranks, men breaking from formation, racing up the western ridge, fleeing the battle. His men looked on in dismay as others joined in flight, forsaking the fray, some dropping spears and stripping armor as they went. Then he heard the most beautiful sound, his men cheering loudly, proclaiming their savior...

"MORTAVA! MORTAVA!" They repeated in deafening praise before her thunderous voice declared...

"*THE DRAGON IS DEAD!*"

*****

Bull broke through the southern end of the forest, carrying Valera safely through, caught up in the stream of soldiers reforming in the open ground ahead. Men hailed their queen, looking to her for direction, which she obliged, assuaging their fears with decisive commands to reorder ranks. She was surprised to see so many in good spirits, eager to reengage the enemy. She could only guess how many were here, placing their number near ten thousand, maybe more. They were brave and stalwart, all treasured sons of Vellesia, and oh how she loved them.

"Prepare for battle! Let all know that upon this day we gave of our lives for Vellesia! For our people! For victory!" she shouted, wishing her voice wasn't limited by Bull's aura, but her men relayed her words, the smiles of her troops proving it was received.

Following that utterance, a strange look passed the faces of the men staring back at her, shock giving away to sudden elation and then shouts of joy.

"What ails them?" she asked the soldiers nearest her.

"Could you not hear, my Queen?" one asked of her.

"Hear what?"

"Mother Mortava spoke. The dragon is dead!"

She froze, the realization taking a moment to sink in before urgency overtook her. She dismounted in a flourish, stepping beyond Bull's protection, her power returning in all its glory. She ordered her men to remain in place and to safeguard Bull.

"Let not a hair on his back be harmed. Safeguard him at all cost!" she ordered before lifting into the air.

She sped north, floating above the forest spewing ice and rain upon the burning trees below before breaking west. There she was greeted with an advantageous view of the enemy breaking toward the western ridge, forsaking the battle. She coursed over their retreating ranks, spewing fire, lightning, and kinetic bursts through their ranks, the later snapping necks at will. The northern horizon was alive with a maelstrom of lightning, wind, and fire, with beams of energy spewing through the disorder, where Mortava was decimating the opposite end of the battlefield.

Valera smiled, unfettered by Bull's protection, able to access her full power and return these invaders the treatment they gifted her people. She swept north along the western edge of the forest, striking down the enemy with lightning and fire, sending beams of white energy farther afield along the upper ridge line. She cut back east, floating over the forest, soaking the burning wood with rain and ice, conjuring a storm above the forest pines. She zigged and zagged across the battlefield, first east then west, dousing flames and slaying foes with equal aplomb before spotting Julius standing amid his troops below. She made a large arc around him, dousing fires and finishing whatever foes remained, before landing in his midst.

"My Queen, you are spirit sent." He would have shed tears of happiness if he possessed the poor self-control of mortal men, his stoic countenance barely breaking with emotion.

Valera wasted few words, reaching out her hands, removing the arrows from his arm and hip with a flick of her fingers, before laying hands upon him, healing him in an instant.

"See to your men. Bring all the wounded into the clear. I shall quickly return."

*****

She found Mortava floating above the northern end of the battlefield above the open ground beyond the trenches, raining destruction on the barbarian host. The banners of Tribe Slotar rested below her, the white boars head upon a field of black, the standard laying upon a heap of slain tribesmen, the rest dead or scattered. The Jutar tribe suffered even greater loss, nearly five of six slain outright by Mortava's deadly barrage. The remaining tribes were equally afflicted, men slain in the thousands, others fleeing wherever they could. Some archers braved the carnage, firing uselessly as she hovered safely above their range, responding with torrents of lightning and fire. Others, she blasted with wind or snapped their bones with kinetic bursts.

Valera greeted, her elation souring with Mortava's grim demeanor as they floated above the charred fields of barbarian corpses, knowing something was terribly amiss.

"Mother!" she greeted, happy to see her grandmother among the living, but concerned by her sour disposition.

"See to Ethan. He lays yonder. Ander is with him. I shall see to the army," Mortava said.

*****

Valera came upon the horrific scene with knowing dread, the carcass of the dragon difficult to miss where it lay upon the ridge. She passed over several warriors making their way toward the beast, dispatching them with a wave of her hand, break their necks, their corpses dropping in the grass as she floated overtop of them. She circled the dragon before setting down beside Ander, who cradled Ethan in his arms, having bound his wounds with his own tunic, his naked chest stained with Ethan's blood.

"Queen Valera," Ander greeted her, holding tight to Ethan, looking up at her with the weariest face. The man hadn't slept in days, having accompanied Ethan and Mortava in their race to reach the battle.

"Set him back on the ground, Ander, so I might see him," she said, pulling back the remains of Ander's garment wrapped around Ethan's chest, and Ethan's shredded shirt beneath to inspect the wound. Three large punctures circled his torso from collarbone to hip along the right side. Easing him onto his side, she found larger indentations on his back where the teeth entered. He remained unconscious with labored breathing, and blood still oozing from the wounds, his wondrous regenerative ability struggling to produce blood to replace what he was losing. She briefly stepped away, setting her sword on the ground, bathing it in fire. Ethan's magical immunity would likely extinguish the heated metal, but she had to try. She quickly took hold of the hilt, pressing the heated blade to his wounds to stem the bleeding. It worked to some measure, slowly cauterizing the first wound on his back she pressed it to. She repeated the process time and again, frustrated by his magical immunity that dulled the heat. His compromised state still allowed enough of the heat to continue until all his wounds were sealed, the smell of his burning flesh torturing their nostrils.

"It didn't even wake him, not even a little." Ander shook his head, imagining the pain the burns must've caused.

"He needs time, Ander. Remain with him. The bleeding has stopped, for now, at least the bleeding externally. Whatever damage lies beneath we must trust to his own power to mend."

With that, Valera stepped away, briefly noticing that her power wasn't completely blocked in Ethan's presence, wondering what that portended. The sound of Tomas and Casandra's moans drew her attention.

"They were the dragon riders. They possess the dragon tongue," Ander answered her unspoken question.

Valera swiftly approached them; their unseeing eyes drawn to her as she trod through the grass where they lay.

"Who is there?" Tomas asked, his left hand reaching protectively in front of his face, the pain of his broken legs too much to bear.

"Your queen stands before you. Be thankful for your gift, children, for it has spared your lives. *Sleep!*" she commanded, touching a hand to their foreheads while mending their bones and Tomas's ruined shoulder while leaving Mortava's blinding curse in place.

*****

Valera and Mortava slew nearly every warrior they came upon, save for a few chieftains and commanders of significance they were able to identify, the most important of which was the barbarian king, who tried to take his own life, running his dagger along his inner thigh, before Mortava intervened, snatching hold of him, and healing the wound, handing him over to the Vellesian soldiers now flooding the field. The fires were quickly doused, hastening the search for the wounded who lay strewn through the dense forest, many dying before Mortava or Valera could heal them. Valera reached out to Sarella, who waited with the greater host of the royal army at Delvar, ordering all forces to converge upon the battlefield. Vellesian cavalry now emerged in force from the south and west, and another force from the north led by vassals of Duke Thandor, the lord of all the northwestern provinces that suffered the greatest harm from the enemy invasion.

The surviving barbarian warriors and leaders were rounded up and bound, leaving the greater number of noncombatants to deal with, namely the hundred and fifty thousand women, children, and elderly congregated in their camp. Valera dispatched the cavalry at hand to pursue any that escaped the battle, namely those that fled west. She and Mortava went about healing their wounded, moving swiftly among those gathered along the western edge of the forest, each placed in a continuous line, where Mortava and Valera touched one after another, restoring them fully. They lamented the many thousands that expired before they could heal them, though their sacrifice and bravery would live on in the annals of Vellesian history.

They moved Ethan to a wagon, sending him back to Delvar where he could mend in the comforts of the palace there, and be properly attended. Sarella and Mothers Vetesha and Ametria were dispatched immediately to oversee the repairing of the boundary. Each of the slain dragons was a likely source of anti-magic that they could extract to repair the barrier stones, or so they believed. Valera remained at the battlefield, sending Mortava and Ander back to Delvar with Ethan, planning to join them there once she wasn't needed, delegating much of the details to Julius, who set things in good order with impressive efficiency. She sent other cavalry units north to seek out survivors of Ethan and Mortava's contingent, gathering them together near the carcass of the first dragon Ethan slew.

Valera finished the day standing upon the western ridge, gazing northwest in the direction of the Iona divide, that lay countless leagues beyond the horizon, fearing another dragon might slip across before it could be repaired. She shuddered to think what would have happened had Ethan not stopped these dragons. What hope did they have if he died from his wounds or didn't fully recover? These weren't even the largest of the dragons, and he barely defeated them. She couldn't help but wonder if all their prophecies and planning were for naught. She sensed Julius approach, riding up the near slope of the ridge with apparent purpose.

"My Queen!" he greeted politely, drawing up alongside her.

"Something vexes you, General?"

"We have discovered something in the barbarian encampment, my Queen."

*****

Valera strode through the encampment, greeted by a sea of frightened faces drawing away as she passed through their midst. There weren't many men in sight, most having been herded away and secured. Those that did remain were children or the very old, though even these were dangerous, as their hateful thoughts projected. Even the women were deadly, each able to gut a man in a matter of seconds if given the opportunity. They were currently kept in place by her soldiers who moved freely among them, quashing any defiance. The slightest rebellion meant torturous death, as several examples were poignantly made before the assemblage. The unwashed masses were cowed for now. Valera would give them no reason to be otherwise.

Julius led her to a large pavilion cantered in the encampment, the former dwelling of their false *king*, presently guarded by a cohort of Vellesian soldiers. Julius led her within, where she was greeted by a massive wooden chest set in the middle of the floor.

"My Queen," he said, lifting the heavy lid.

Valera stepped closer, her eyes drawn to the objects therein. They were a myriad of faded colors, two black, two white, one each of gray, green, and red. They were a variety of sizes, from fist-sized to three times as big, the red being the largest by far. Though she had never seen their like, it was obvious what they were…dragon eggs.

Valera picked each of them up one at a time, studying their texture, determining if they were potent in any way. Part of her wanted to smash them to pieces, removing their threat for all time but couldn't pass up the chance to study them. She was ever thankful that Mortava managed to take their king alive and the dragon riders as well. She had many questions needing answers, answers she was certain to get.

"Pack all these up. Once reinforcements arrive, I shall be returning to Delvar with them in tow, along with our most esteemed prisoner," she said, referencing Karg. Tomas and Casandra were already en route with Mortava and the others. She would keep all three separated from their people.

"And the rest of the prisoners?" Julius asked, inquiring about the many tens of thousands.

"Remove them to Corellis. I shall confer with the Queen Mother before passing judgment," she said. The penalty for invading armies was death or enslavement. If the queen was feeling merciful it would be death.

*****

One day hence
The road to Delvar

His fevered dreams were a torrent of disjointed nonsense, each as ridiculous or annoying as the last. He found himself riding into battle at the Velo upon a pig, the poor creature's legs unable to keep pace with riders passing swiftly passed him. In another, he was in Crepsos again, facing Luke Crawford in the street as he had before, and again beating him to the draw, but for some reason, his pistol wouldn't fire. He squeezed and squeezed to no avail, the hammer refusing to fall. He was back in Astaris at the banquet where Alesha betrayed him, but for some reason, Valera sprang to her feet and danced around the great hall singing *Dance to My Lou*, the dance hall tune he heard sang in Red Rock. That strange image caused him to chuckle, only to be followed by another annoying dream. This one found him called upon by Lord General Brax during his instruction when he was a young boy, being tutored on the arts of war with many of his friends from noble houses of Astaria, including Vancel, Xavier, and Krixan. He was asked to repeat the lessons learned from the Balkar Campaign during the reign of King Elexar III. He didn't remember reading of it, and stared dumbly at his fellow pupils, suffering the lord general's withering stare.

I don't remember studying this! He wanted to scream, wondering why they expected him to know it. That painfully annoying dream was followed by the most ridiculous of all. He, at last, found himself back in Astaris having dinner with his family, including Krixan, but for some reason, Krixan and Bronus were dwarfs, neither taller than his waist, but both retaining their full-size heads. The two of them quickly got into a fight over a loaf of bread, rolling about atop the table, shouting curses with squeaky voices. Ethan laughed hard enough to wake himself.

"Ugghh!" His laughter died as soon as he felt the pain. It was as if the entire right side of his body was torn off, pain permeating everything around the right side of his chest. His arm was tied off to his waist in a makeshift sling. He was naked with only a wool blanket covering everything below his stomach. He found himself in a covered wagon, with a boxed roof made of wood.

"You're awake!" He heard Ander say with the happiest voice he ever recalled him using.

"Sarge." Ethan smiled weakly, finding Ander sitting beside him with the stupidest grin he ever saw. His throat was terribly raw, making his voice crack.

"Awake and alive. I had my doubts, Ethan, and am glad you have put them to rest." Ander sighed in relief.

"Yo…You called me…Ethan." Ethan smiled at that.

"Aye. You are my friend, Ethan, the finest friend I have ever had." Ander patted Ethan's leg, not daring to touch anything north of his knee, considering the many holes that were still mending.

A happy tear rolled down Ethan's cheek, touched by Ander's friendship. "And you are one of my best friends, Ander. Krixan is close as a brother to me, and Ben, Skeeter, and the judge...well, we fought many battles together. I count you among them now," Ethan said, reaching across his body with his left hand to grasp Ander's.

"I am honored to be named among them, Ethan," Ander said, fighting back a tear of his own.

"Where are we, by the way?" Ethan decided to finally ask, feeling every rut in the road despite the heap of blankets tucked underneath him to soften the blow.

"On the road to Delvar."

"Delvar? What of the battle? And the dragon?" He nearly forgot how his current condition came about.

"You don't remember?"

"The last thing I recall was stabbing and shooting the dragon so many times I lost count, even after it was trying to eat me. That's all I remember. Since I am here talking with you, something must've gone right." He tried to shrug, but the pain was too much.

"You are in a lot of pain. I can see that in your eyes, despite you trying to hide it." Ander shook his head.

"I've had worse," Ethan lied. Even the bullet he took in the back by Nate Grierson didn't feel this awful.

"You are a lousy liar, Ethan. Anyway, you killed the dragon, freeing Mother Mortava and Queen Valera to use their power. After that, it was pretty much over. Even a great host like that couldn't do much against their magic. They immediately ordered you taken to Delvar, which is the nearest holdfast. We attended to you the best we could. The queen managed to cauterize your wounds to some degree, but your regenerative abilities have done the rest, though it is going very slow by the look of things."

"So I'm getting better?" he asked as if he was ready to climb out of bed.

"Better, yes, but only in comparison to before. You still look awful."

"It can't be that bad," he reasoned, trying to sit up, but the pain was too much, his attempt sending tendrils of agony throughout his body.

"Don't go reopening your wounds or Mother Mortava will skin you like a beaver pelt, and me too for lettin' it happen," Ander said with the best Texan impersonation he managed yet, using another phrase he picked up from Ethan.

"She is here?" he asked, thinking she would still be with the army.

"Where else would she be? She refused to let you leave without her. Said you needed looking after. Between the two of us, we haven't left your side. Now you stay put, and I'll fetch her." Ander gave him one last smile and shook his head before climbing out of the wagon even though it was still moving.

A few moments went by before Mortava replaced him, settling herself down beside Ethan while Ander took her horse, riding alongside the wagon. Ethan was curious to have a look outside, hating being confined in the wagon like an invalid.

"Mor," he said, so very happy to see her.

"Hello, Ethan." She smiled, brushing his hair from his eyes, knowing its length was a source of annoyance to him.

"I am glad to see you alive. I wasn't so sure we were going to make it back there," he said, trying so desperately to hide the pain coursing through him.

"You did it, Ethan. Beyond all hope, you did what you said you would do. In all the annals of record, no one has slain a dragon, let alone two."

"That's because no one else had guns. It made all the difference, I assure you."

"You cut the dragon's throat with your sword, Ethan. Guns may have helped, but the deadliest blows were dealt by your hands."

"The guns sure came in handy, though. Speaking of which, where are they?" he asked worriedly.

"They are at the foot of the wagon, right over there, so don't worry yourself," she pointed them out just below his feet. His rifle rested atop his pistol belt, with his packs of ammo beneath them.

"And my clothes?"

"Are being mended. Valera thought they should be discarded, but I interceded, knowing your affection for the foul things. So you needn't worry about them either. We even have your hat, though I must confess to admiring it. I think it becomes me." She smiled, reaching for it, placing it upon her head. "How do I look?"

"It's hard to tell since you could make sackcloth look good, Mor."

"Never lose your charm, dear boy." She smiled, keeping the Stetson on her head. She would wear it until he asked for it back. But before she returned it, she would have it cleaned, for it had a foul odor, which he seemed impervious to.

"At the moment, charm's all I got," he japed, looking down at his discolored chest, and slung arm. He couldn't imagine his face looking any better.

She just shook her head and laughed. Sometimes he was just too much, and she wondered how they survived all these years without his good humor.

"Thanks for being there, Mor. It would've been a dull adventure without you. Same goes for Sarge."

"Despite the hardships, it was the best time of my life," she confessed.

Ethan smiled at that, recalling something Judge Donovan once told him.

"Something humors you, Ethan?" She lifted a reproachful brow.

"The judge once told me about a time when he was a young man working on a whaling ship. They were caught in a storm far from shore and weren't sure they'd survive it. It happened that the sailors he was with were a bunch of characters, telling jokes and humorous stories throughout the ordeal while taking turns manning the ship. He said it was the best time of his life. They were so caught up in having a good time, they never truly thought about the danger they were in until it was over. It was the same for me in Red Rock, during my first month or so there. I enjoyed the camaraderie so much that I didn't really think about the Grierson men trying to kill us at every turn. It was the same with you and Ander. I didn't really think about the dragons so much, now that I look back on it. I guess it shows that hard times aren't so hard if you're with good people."

"You think I am a good person?" She gave him a look.

"You're a good person, Mor. I'd bet my life on it."

"I would very much like to meet this Judge you're always talking about. The sheriff also," she said, never believing she could be so enamored with men she had never met before, only going by the word of the insufferable rascal lying beside her.

He was suddenly struck by the imagery of his last dream, and started to laugh, causing her to again raise an eyebrow at that. He went on to detail the vision of his father and Krixan in diminutive form, wrestling over a loaf of bread atop the dinner table. He laughed so hard it hurt, unable to conceal his pain.

"Don't reinjure yourself, else Alesha would never forgive me for not binding you tighter." She shook her head, laughing as well.

"Just remind her that you're her grandmother, and she has to bow to you," he reminded her.

"Perhaps I shall if she goes too hard on you."

"Thanks, Mor. You're a good friend." He couldn't believe he said it, or believe he meant it, but he did.

"Friend," she said with a faraway look. She never had a friend before, not in the sense most people do. She had a mother, grand-mothers, children, and grandchildren, but no friends. When she truly thought about it, all she really had was…duty.

"Mor?" he asked, wondering if he said something wrong. Of course, saying something wrong was a habit of his.

"You have had many friends, Ethan, and I have had only one, but I am glad that one is you." She smiled again, letting his Stetson rise higher on her brow.

It was then something broke in Ethan, his resentment and anger doused with forgiveness and pity. How he hated them all when he was betrayed and brought to Elysia, believing them all to be greedy, selfish witches, the whole lot of them. Now he had to wonder how

596

much of that was the damn magic and hunger driving them mad? With that in place, they were of one mind, like a hive working toward a singular goal. Once that was lifted, they were as different as any other family, each with their own desires and interests, and personality. He was suddenly struck by the fact that if he left now, that would be undone. He realized he could never truly leave, not without a part of him remaining in some meaningful way. He was connected to them by more than magical bonds and threats. They were joined by blood, marriage and friendship. He was as bound to Elysia as he was Red Rock, Cordova, and his beloved Astaria. Why couldn't they see that? Why must it be all or nothing? Then again, did it really matter when they had far bigger things to worry about.

"What are we going to do, Mor?"

"Do?" She wondered his context.

"The barrier? If these dragons overcame it, more are sure to follow. It's only a matter of time. And what if it collapses altogether? It was all we could manage to battle two, not completely grown dragons, let alone if we have to tangle with a red one, or dozens all at once."

"I don't know. It is much to think on. Sarella and Mothers Vetesha and Ametria are schooled in repairing the barrier. We shall see if their knowledge is sufficient."

"What if a dragon attacks while they are trying to repair it? They would be helpless. I need to be there."

"Be there? Ethan, you can't even stand, let alone fight another dragon. You need rest. That is something all of us agree on when it comes to a former Astarian prince who confounds us to no end, you insolent rascal." She ruffled his hair as if he were a child, which in some ways, he very much was.

"I'll be healed pretty soon. When I do, I need to be with them."

"There is time to decide where you are most needed once we attain Delvar. You need rest, young man."

"I'm wide awake since I've been sleeping for a day now. Besides, I don't have anything else to do right now but talk."

"True, but you are the one person who will talk himself out of bed when he should remain there. I still cringe thinking of the dragon biting you. I feared she tore you in two."

"It all happened so fast. I don't really remember. This may sound strange, but I feel regret for having to kill Nyla and Nylo. When they weren't angered by your magic, they were almost pleasant to speak to. It was like their presence was comforting in some strange way." He sighed. It was just as Nylo had said to him in another life they would have been friends.

"Yes, the Dragon Tongue. A magical gift our house has mysteriously overlooked. How convenient that the very power we lack is given to us through you. It seems the mysteries of Ethan Blagen have no end." She smiled, greatly understating the significance. She spoke very little of Ethan's newfound power with Valera. It would certainly be a source of heated discussion within the Lorian Order.

"A magical gift that doesn't help any when the dragon is trying to eat me." He chuckled, making light of it.

"Because you killed her brother. In a way, I understand her grief. Their riders are equally distraught. I would pity them if they hadn't committed such crimes against our people."

"Wait, are Casandra and Tomas alive?" he asked.

"Yes. They are at the back of this column, in a caged wagon, bound hand and foot."

"What are you going to do to them?" he asked, his voice filled with compassion.

"Their fate will fall to the Lorian Order. Their crimes condemn them, but they also possess much knowledge we must extract."

"We won, Mor. Perhaps mercy is a wiser choice than vengeance. Many in their horde are old and very young."

"Would they have been merciful with us?"

"No, they wouldn't, but…" His voice trailed, unable to refute her point.

"As Queen Daughter, Valera shall decide the fate of the greater masses. Tomas and Casandra's fate shall fall to the Order and the Queen Mother."

"There is much we can learn from them. Wouldn't it be wiser to spare their lives in exchange for information? I would like to know…"

"We do not require their cooperation to learn what they know." She reminded him.

"Oh." He forgot.

"But if I were to surmise the opinion of the Order, I think they shall be spared the headsman's axe," she said, knowing their unique power required intensive study. She could see the relief in his demeanor with that summation, taken aback by his merciful heart for those that intended to kill him.

"I wonder what reception we'll receive when we return to Elysia?" he thought aloud.

"You mean to say what reception *you* shall receive," she corrected him.

"I was just trying to sound less selfish." He shrugged, though only with his left shoulder.

"Things will be different from now on, I assure you," she said, her voice betraying that it wouldn't all be for the better.

"Different better or different worse?"

"You have done a wondrous service for the realm, Ethan. Without you, we would have been slaughtered, and the others will look upon you fondly for that." She left unsaid a deeper worry, which he could easily read in her expression.

"But?" he asked, knowing there was bad news to go with the good.

"But things will be worse in another way. Your absence has been difficult for the Lorian Order. As soon as you departed, the madness returned, and with it the pain, each many fold what they were before you came to Elysia."

"If you suffered so, why didn't you say something?"

"I didn't suffer, Ethan, not until after the battle when I spent more time outside your aura. Being near you protected me from its effects. Valera was likewise protected by Bull, but the others were not so fortunate."

"How bad were the effects?"

"As bad as you can imagine," she greatly understated.

599

"That's not good," he understated as well.

"Not good indeed."

"I have a feeling they will blame me somehow." Ethan sighed.

"Blame is not the word I would use," she said diplomatically.

"What other way would you put it? They always will find an excuse to restrict my movement."

"You sure like to whine." She shook her head. "As far as *they* are concerned, there will be no blaming you for their suffering. It was a necessary sacrifice for us to fight this war. We all had a part to play, and theirs was to endure the effects of your and Alesha's separation. And should the need arise again, they will have to suffer once again. Now you need your rest. We will be in Delvar soon enough," she said, making her way to the back of the wagon to step without.

"Mor?" he called out to her one last time.

"Yes, Ethan."

"I'd wager you were a great queen when you sat the throne," he said.

"Thank you, Ethan. And I would wager you would have been a great king of Astaria, whether you believe so or not."

"But no matter how good a queen you were, you are a better friend." He smiled.

"You too, Ethan." She returned the smile before stepping without.

CHAPTER 31

It was the next morning when their procession reached Delvar, Mother Demetra, and Lord Ganelle receiving Mortava before the main gates as the small column approached the city walls. They stood in stark contrast, with the lord of Delvar and Mother Demetra adorned in polished armor and helms, their hair combed to a bright sheen, whilst Mortava still wore her light-weight mail and leathers, marred from battle, her fierce countenance a reflection of the grim battles she endured. Mortava still sported Ethan's Stetson, wearing it proudly, drawing curious stares from Demetra and Lord Ganelle. Though each a mother of the Lorian Order, Demetra still looked upon Mortava as her great-granddaughter, recalling the day of her birth which heralded her own ascension to the Order.

"Mother Demetra. Lord Ganelle," she greeted them with a raised open palm, the formal greeting between members of the Lorian Order after a period of separation.

"Mother Mortava," Demetra greeted in kind while Lord Ganelle bowed low in his saddle.

"My Lord Ganelle, if you would be so kind to see to my men. The princess' consort is badly wounded. Please have him carefully moved to your most secure and comfortable apartments. And whatever he says, do *not* let him attempt to stand or move about on his own," Mortava ordered.

"It shall be done as you command, Mother Mortava." The stoutly built lord again bowed.

"There are also two prisoners in the caged wagon. I want them secured and kept *safe* from any physical or mental abuse. Am I understood?"

"I shall see to them personally, Mother Mortava. Delvar is yours." Lord Ganelle bowed a third time, before hurrying off to receive the procession while Demetra and Mortava moved off the side of the road.

"I am most pleased to see you well, Mortava." Demetra looked upon her with profound pride and admiration, though couldn't help looking at Ethan's hat resting on her head.

"It's quite fetching, don't you think?" Mortava asked bemusedly, her eyes lifting to its low brim shading her forehead.

"It is…different, though you are entitled to a little extravagance after a hard won battle," Demetra politely said. As the last mother in the Order to have seen battle, she knew well what Mortava must have endured.

"And I, you, grandmother. I was in constant fear of the dragons passing us by for more inviting prey," Mortava recalled her fears of finding Delvar in flaming ruin, brought low by dragon fire.

"Had the barbarians retained both dragons as they drew nigh, your fear would have proven prescient."

"Yes. Thankfully, Ethan removed that terrible possibility." Mortava would be certain to remind each of the mothers of his fell deeds.

"Yes, a most fortuitous intervention. His presence has proven the truth of our prophetic leanings. I do hope his injuries are not enduring?" Demetra asked.

"Hopefully not, but we are dealing with the unknown. The dragon's bite interferes with our regenerative abilities, even if we draw beyond its powerful aura. Ethan and I were wounded by the first dragon, he losing fingers, and I an arm. It took an inordinate amount of time for us to heal. The injury he suffered in slaying the last dragon was far more severe."

"May his restoration be hastened. Alesha did not receive these tidings well. She is currently en route, despite the Queen Mother's… misgivings."

"Misgivings?" Mortava doubted her objections were so mild. That Alesha departed Elysia in spite of them, proved the strength of her will on this matter.

"Perhaps it is for the best. Their separation has proven most troublesome for the Order and the Queen Mother," Demetra understated the extent of the madness afflicting them.

"Yes. Fortunately, I was spared much of it by my proximity with Ethan, though remaining constantly in anyone's presence for so long proved equally difficult."

"With the danger passed and a potentially large source of anti-magic in the form of two dragon carcasses, our good fortune abounds," Demetra referenced the anti-magic rumored to be found in slain dragons, though it hadn't reportedly been done for a thousand years.

"Perhaps, as long as we use the anti-magic wisely." Mortava meant to quash any notion of using it against Ethan.

"There is but one reason we have wanted it for so long," Demetra said.

"And that reason is misplaced. We have need of it in repairing the boundary and to create means of concealing us should another dragon breach it."

"Another dragon? Once the barrier is repaired, we shall ascertain our other barrier stones, correcting any deficiencies. After that is accomplished, we should possess enough to forever bind Ethanos to our house."

"You would do so after what he has done for us?" Mortava nearly spat.

"He has done his duty, Mortava, just as we all do. Ethan has fulfilled his destiny in delivering us from the dragons and shall fulfill his destiny in delivering us from the madness."

"You would reward his sacrifice by chaining his powers? That boy saved our lives!"

"And I am grateful, but the fact remains that he must be bound to us in perpetuity. That can hardly happen if he believes he is entitled to do as he pleases."

"Do as he pleases? He has kept to his vows, and you would reward him with treachery."

"I have lived one hundred and ninety five years tormented by our hunger. I'll not suffer another hundred years of torment if we have the means to prevent it."

"It doesn't require an anti-magical collar to prevent the hunger. Only keeping Ethan and Alesha in proximity shall accomplish that."

"This shall be decided by the Lorian Order once the crisis is passed. You shall have the opportunity to voice your opinion."

"I shall, and when the full council hears of the greater threat we are facing, they shall embrace my thinking most eagerly."

"Greater threat?" Demetra's curiosity perked with that bold statement.

"Oh yes, a much greater threat than what we just faced. One that overshadows all we have built, and one we cannot face without Ethan by our side."

*****

"Where are they taking us?" Casandra wept, sitting on the straw covered floor of the caged wagon, her hands and feet joined by thick manacles, her eyes staring sightless, still under Mortava's blinding power. They felt the wagon stop and continue several times in a brief span, the sound of voices gathering near seeming to be afoot. She had never felt such misery, suffering the loss of Nylo, and then Nyla, and falling captive to these demons.

"A prison or city, I suppose," Tomas said, trying to comfort her, but feeling just as miserable, his greatest fears coming to fruition. He always knew their invasion of the mage lands was perilous, but the coming threat of the red dragons forced their hand. He reached up, tugging the crude collar circling his throat. They placed that hateful thing on them yester morn, when stripping their clothes, replacing them with coarse woolen tunics that barely reached their knees, likely to ease their biological functions.

"Why don't they simply kill us? What do they want of us?" She sighed. Her earlier attempt to end her life met with an emphatic rebuke by their keepers, who were made aware of the knife she had hidden away by Mortava.

They couldn't see the crowd gathering about the wagon as it entered the courtyard of the inner palace, having already traversed the city proper, receiving the curious stares of a thousand onlookers. Many wanted to throw rocks or dirt at the passing cage but were sternly warned against it. Only when the door of the cage was opened did they realize their present journey had come to an end. They were briskly removed and taken to the dungeon, being led blindly through cavernous halls, feeling the damp stone floor of the subterranean passageways beneath their naked feet.

*****

Ethan awoke, finding himself abed in a spacious, richly furnished chamber, with white stone walls decorated with frescoes. A large bay window rested off his right, with a wide cedar sill, large enough for several people to sit. He could see clouds blocking the late afternoon sun in the distance, meaning he was facing west, his angle affording him a view of distant rolling hills. If he could sit fully erect, he would see the inner courtyard below and the greater city sprawling beyond the inner walls of the fortress. He was naked beneath the silken sheets and fur blanket, with the sling on his arm replaced with a much sturdier bandage that felt more like a shackle. He sighed, looking at the ceiling in complete boredom. He wondered where his clothes and weapons were, but a cursory glance around the room didn't find them. He couldn't remember how he came to be here, having spent much of the day lost in delirium, experiencing another bout of ridiculous dreams, save for the one of Alesha dressed as a salon hall girl in the *Lucky Star*, singing the *Red River Valley* while sitting his lap. That dream he wanted to revisit, but when he tried to return to it, he found himself and Krixan tasked with painting the walls of Astaris, all seven hundred feet high of them, with a brush no wider than his thumb.

"Stupid dreams," he growled, already bored after just a few peaceful moments staring at the ceiling.

"Well, enough of this," he said, forcing himself to sit up, pain shooting through his shoulder, though his chest was much improved. He lowered back down, his first attempt meeting with failure. How he hated feeling like an invalid and forced the issue a second time, preparing himself for the pain. After what felt an eternal struggle, he managed to work himself to the side of the bed into a sitting position with his legs hanging off the side, touching the floor. He looked around for something to wear, only finding a wardrobe along the near wall, and a chest at the foot of the bed, both closed. His first order of business was his parched throat, finding a pitcher of water conveniently upon the table beside his headboard, with a goblet beside it.

"What do you think you're doing?" He froze before moving toward the pitcher, turning his head to find Mortava standing in the doorway with her fists on her hips, and his Stetson upon her head. She was dressed in formal armor, with bright polished mail and greaves over black tunic and black trousers and armored boots.

"Hello, Mor." He sheepishly smiled, sitting back down, covering himself with his sheets and blanket, not wishing to give her a show.

"Don't *Mor* me, you rascal. Back into bed with you, and that's an order from this Mother of the Lorian Order." She stepped closer, shooing him back into bed over his weak protest. He was in no condition to fight a rabbit, let alone a woman of her power.

"I can't sit here all day, it will drive me crazy," he griped.

"Despite your many talents, Ethan, none compare to your whining. Here, I ordered the maids to clean this for you." She tossed his hat on his lap.

"Thanks. I've been meaning to do that for a while now, but..."

"Do not lie, Ethan, you're not very good at it. That thing hasn't been cleaned since you first put it on your fool head," she reproached, knowing the truth of it by the stupid look on his face.

"How about the rest of my clothes? Can't hardly go about naked, don't want to scare the locals."

"They are being washed and repaired. There are other clothes provided for you in the wardrobe once you are well enough."

"I can imagine what awful options are in there for me." He lifted his chin in the direction of the wardrobe.

"Nothing too terrible. I gave the steward your preferences. You'll find a fine pair of black trousers and shirt, all simple designs with no fancy adornments or collars on the shirts."

"I'm a simple man, so simple is good."

"You are only simple with complex matters, and complex with the simple ones, which only confounds us trying to guess what you will do next." She shook her head, tucking him back into bed as if he were a child running a temperature.

"Sitting in bed is good and all but there are other things I need to do, Mor," he said.

"Such as?"

"I really have to piss, and shi…"

"All right, you don't have to say it. I will send the maids, and…"

"I'd rather take care of it myself. Just send me a bucket."

"Very well. It will be nice for you to attend the functions of nature without being chained to me." She laughed, recalling all the times they had to manage that gross detail while on the campaign.

"I kept my eyes closed." He smiled.

"As did I, dear boy. Now if you'll excuse me, I have other matters to attend. Ander shall be here shortly to make certain you behave, and provide you company so you won't be *bored.*"

"It's a shame you can't stick around, Mor. You, me, and Ander could talk about our adventures and share some inappropriate jokes and stories."

"That actually sounds much more fascinating than what I have to do. Perhaps later, I shall return and do just that." She smiled. Never would she have believed in a thousand lifetimes that she would find such a thing interesting, but friendship does that sort of thing to people, and for the first time in her 137 years, Mortava had a friend. Actually, she had two, for Ander was a kindred soul, sharing the horrors of battle beside her. She looked one last time at Ethan before stepping without, almost tempted to look into his mind one last time, but deciding against it. She learned enough while healing him, though the anti-magic limited her power to fully heal him. The dragon's anti-magic somehow allowed her to touch Ethan with her own magic in some measure, just enough to hasten his recovery. It also allowed her to look into his memories, finding somethings troublesome, and others reassuring. She hoped he would heal soon enough before the others realized they could do the same, though with every passing day, his body extracted more of the dragon's anti magic, thus limiting their power to touch him.

With that, she kissed him on the forehead, like he was her own child, and stepped without.

*****

Tomas and Casandra were taken from their cells, bathed, dressed in clean leather tunics before being ushered into a windowless chamber, where they were knelt, their ankles chained to a shackle affixed to the stone floor, its rocky surface painful to their knees. Their sightless eyes stared blankly ahead, wondering if they would soon be tortured or slain.

"Would you like to see?" Mortava asked, standing before them with her hand resting on the hilt of her sword, riding her left hip, her wide stance in stark contrast to their kneeling forms.

"Yes," Tomas answered, hoping she would grant them that small mercy. Instantly, their vision cleared, though even the torches bracketed high upon the gray stone walls pained their eyes. He could see Mortava and Selendra standing before them, wearing matching armor, regarding him with piercing golden and purple eyes that unsettled him deeply. He felt Casandra's uneasiness beside him. He knew both women were powerful mages by their lack of visible guards.

"We have questions. You shall provide answers," Mortava stated flatly, brokering no compromise or defiant banter, which neither twin was capable of at present.

"How were you able to command the dragons?" Mortava asked.

"We have always been able to speak to them," Casandra said.

"The Dragon Tongue, explain it?" Mortava asked.

Surprisingly, they offered no protest, detailing what they knew of their strange power to speak their thoughts with dragons, a unique power neither Mortava nor Selendra had heard of before this war. Though neither twin knew the nature of their ability, Mortava could sense that it was of a different form of magic than their own, one that didn't come into conflict with dragons. In fact, it was the direct opposite their own, actually coming into accordance with dragons. That Ethan shared this ability came as a surprise to both Mortava and Selendra, raising more questions of his unique nature, and serious doubts in Selendra's mind of his true destiny.

They next asked how they came into possession of the dragons, which they answered, recalling what Karg and others had told them. They were prisoners of a barbarian horde called the Jangar, a brutal and ruthless clan that terrorized the steppes along the wilds. It was Karg and his tribesmen that rescued them, finding the dragon hatchlings as well. As for where the dragon hatchlings came from, neither knew.

"Be still!" Selendra stepped forth, touching a finger to their foreheads, before looking deeply into their memories. What she discovered shook her to her core, bringing into doubt all that she knew of their world. The twins were born of a people native to the far north, a people sharing their unique ability of the Dragon Tongue. They dwelt in apparent seclusion from the greater wilds, nurturing their connection to the dragons. It was then she discovered that a band of men snuck into their lands, stealing away the infant children and numerous eggs, gifting them to the Jangar. What she discovered next was equally surprising and terrifying, as the infants' hands were placed upon two dragon eggs, igniting them with an otherworldly light, before fissures spread across their unique surface, breaking apart as the hatchlings emerged.

"Selendra?" Mortava asked, curious of what she discovered. Only House Menau could peer into distant memories, extracting the most miniscule of details as far back as infancy.

"They hatched them." Her softly spoken words might as well have been spoken in a thunderous roar with their significance.

"Hatched them? Humans can do that?" Mortava made a face.

"Not only can but *must*. Only those with the Dragon-Tongue can hatch dragons, their very survival dependent upon those with the Tongue," Selendra said.

"If this is so, why didn't you hatch the other eggs Karg possessed?" Mortava asked of them, Valera having communicated the find to Selendra. The precious relics were currently enroute to Delvar ahead of the great host of prisoners, who were being sent in smaller groups to disperse them.

Tomas and Casandra refused to answer, though it didn't prevent Selendra from extracting the information.

"They tried and failed," Selendra said, before looking deeper into their distant memories, trying to glean whatever she could from their infancy, hoping to overhear conversations that might answer their questions. Mortava noticed her demeanor shift, realizing she discovered something.

"Selendra?" Mortava asked.

"They couldn't hatch them, for they can only hatch one. One dragon and one rider, forever bound." Her words striking the hearts of Casandra and Tomas, realizing that they would never have that bond again.

"And if one with the Dragon Tongue has not hatched a dragon?" Mortava asked.

"Theoretically, they should still be able to do so." Selendra realized where her line of thinking was leading.

Mortava waved her hand, reimposing blindness upon the two prisoners, before ordering them taken to cleaner and more secure cells. She instructed the guards to see to their comfort and that they were not abused in any way but ordered their limbs restrained, taking no chances of losing them.

*****

"I must advise against this, Ethan," Ander protested as Ethan managed to pull on a pair of trousers, struggling with only the use of his left hand. Fortunately, he had limited use of his right hand to help tie the drawstrings of the loose garment. The sling prevented him from pulling on a shirt, and if anyone took offense to his naked torso, they could go jump off the palace walls for all he cared.

"I haven't heard you say that in a while, Sarge." He grinned, stepping toward the door.

"Because you never listen." He shook his head.

"I listen, I just don't follow your advice." Ethan grinned, doing his best to hide the crippling pain coursing the right half of his torso, moving gingerly through the door.

"Where are you going?" Ander followed after.

"To stretch my legs and make our way to the palace tavern. Maybe have the kitchen maids bring us some food while we're there."

"I still don't think it a good idea, Ethan. Besides, Mother Mortava insisted that you remain abed."

"That was earlier in the day. I feel much better now."

"The spirits have mercy." Ander sighed, resigned to defeat. Trying to talk Ethan out of something was akin to talking a pig out of its slop.

They received more than one strange look as they traversed the corridors of the palace, some taken aback by Ethan's half naked appearance, others recognizing them, their admiration evident on their faces. They somehow managed avoiding any high lords, who would certainly object to Ethan's behavior. Ander could just envision what Ethan would say to them, thankful that he didn't have to play peacemaker.

The palace tavern was nestled within the cellar of the palace, with a layout similar to the one in Astaris, with a long bar upon its opposite wall, and a large open area where two dozen knights, warriors and lords were gathered, raising their tankards, celebrating the end of the war. Ander and Ethan took several steps before they were noticed, a hush falling over the crowd, all staring at them wondering what to say. By this time, every man in the palace knew of their fell deeds, their names bandied about with great reverence and respect.

"Can someone offer my friend here a drink. He saved my life more times than I can shake a stick at," Ethan declared, slapping Ander's shoulder with his good hand, ignoring the pain even that little motion caused.

"Ethan, I didn't save your life," Ander whispered, uncomfortable with undo praise.

"Oh, you did, Sarge, whether inadvertently or directly on several occasions. I can count them out one by one if you'd like." Ethan smiled, causing Ander to redden with embarrassment as the patrons gathered around them, slapping him on the back whilst shoving an overflowing goblet in his hand.

Ander didn't think his deeds were that significant, merely his duty, but Ethan saw it differently. From throwing himself in danger to protect Ethan at the Gorgencian village to the many times he distracted the dragon, sparing both Ethan and Mortava, he truly did risk his life time and again for Ethan. Here he was surrounded by knights and lords of the realm, giving him a hero's welcome as they were ushered toward the bar, where they were pelted with questions and handed one goblet after the next, with poor Ander doing his best to temper his consumption. Ander was thankful Ethan did most of the talking, but that brought its own set of problems.

"It was right then the two dragons were about to eat Mother Mortava and me when, all of a sudden, the sound of horns distracted them, saving us. And who was the source of this distraction? Ole Sarge here," Ethan pointed at Ander. "There was the crazy fool leading our men in a brave charge against the dragons. I wouldn't be here speaking with you fellas if he hadn't done that, and to my dying shame, most of the boys he led didn't survive the dragon's fire," Ethan finished sadly, recalling their sacrifice.

"To Sergeant Ander Jordain! The embodiment of a Queen's royal guard!" one knight bellowed, lifting his tankard high in the air.

"To Ander Jordain!" the others chorused, a round of hearty cheers reverberating off the stone walls.

The men continued asking of the dragon and the battle of the Delvar Vale, with Ethan only speaking of the dragon, barely recalling that engagement, whilst Ander completed the tale, having seen much of what followed. A few other warriors who returned with them were present to fill in more details. All marveled upon hearing how their queen and Mother Mortava destroyed the barbarian host once the dragon was slain. After a time, someone broke into song, singing a forlorn melody of a son gone off to war, never to return to his village.

> My son, my son
> Far away you go
> To battle for realm and queen…

The man was soon joined by others adding their voices to his, their song echoing through the lower palace, drawing more to fill the spacious chamber. Ander sighed, thinking of the men they had lost, sharing a look with Ethan, who felt much the same. He was certain of one thing, that war was terrible, and hoped it would never plague the realm again. Unfortunately, he knew what had driven the barbarian host to invade, Ethan and Mortava explaining the threat of the red dragons during their ride leading up to the battle. He also knew that without Ethan, they would have lost.

"Thank you, Ethan," he said, his eyes moist, overcome with emotion, which was out of character for the notoriously stoic sergeant. Of course, a few brews have that effect on one, especially after what they endured.

"For what, Sarge?" Ethan gave him a look as they leaned against the bar, their voices nearly drowned in the revelry all around them.

"Everything. For including me in your little adventures, like making toys and playing cards, and what not. Though I voiced displeasure with it all, secretly I enjoyed every moment. I could go on with your saving us all from the dragons and such, but what I enjoyed most was the little things. Of all the men the Princess could have taken as Consort, I am so very glad it was you," Ander placed a hand to his friend's shoulder.

"Thanks, Ander. I feel the same. Of all the men they could have picked to guard me, I am thankful it was you. You are a good man, Ander Jordain."

*****

It was still early in the evening when they made their way back to Ethan's room, and to their surprise, Ethan suffered some effect from the alcohol, his recuperative powers still impaired to some degree. He wasn't drunk by any means but was certainly affected, staggering briefly through the door, only to be greeted by Mortava waiting for them while sitting in the wide sill of the window, looking out across the horizon.

"Did you enjoy yourselves?" she asked, her bemused tone indicating she wasn't about to scold them.

"Yep," was Ethan's blunt response, making his way to his bed.

"My apologies, Mother Mortava. I am responsible for...," Ander started to say.

"You are forgiven, Ander. Few mortals can keep Ethan from doing what he wills. Besides, I knew where you were. Certain others thought to intervene, but they were reasoned with, allowing each of you some well-earned enjoyment," Mortava said, coming off the window, ambling toward the door.

"Thanks, Mor," Ethan said, knowing she intervened on their behalf.

"You are welcome. I am proud of both of you. You must rest now. Valera shall arrive in the morning, and Alesha tomorrow afternoon. We shall hold a council of war, which you may or may not be invited," she said before stepping without.

*****

By the next morn, Ethan was able to move his right arm, though with difficulty, managing to pull on a plain black shirt, trousers and boots to greet Valera upon her return. He didn't really care about seeing Valera as much as seeing Bull, regretting having spent so much time apart. He hoped Valera treated him well, considering he probably saved her life, hiding her from the dragons until they were dealt with, allowing her to destroy the enemy host at the opportune time. It was a pretty impressive feat by his Palomino, in his opinion. If he ever saw Jake again, he would be sure to remind him that he gifted him one hell of a horse.

He shouldn't have been surprised to find a small army of guards camped outside his chambers, shadowing him wherever he went. He couldn't tell if they were his jailors or protectors, but those terms meant the same thing since Astaris. A great crowd had already gathered when he reached the courtyard, and Ethan was content to hide along the periphery, perching himself near the stables resting just east of the main gate, where he found a nice pillar supporting an overhang that would conceal him nicely from view. That plan went out the window when Mortava sent Ander to fetch him, dragging him forward to stand behind Demetra, Mortava, and Lord Ganelle in the center of the courtyard just as Valera's procession entered the inner palace.

I should've just stayed in bed, he thought miserably. What he saw next made him rethink that.

The advance guard broke off upon passing through the gate, taking post to either side as Valera followed, still dressed for battle, her dark eyes finding him first as she entered, riding a red destrier, the visor of her helm lifted, affording her clear vision of the assembled host. If she was riding a destrier, then where was Bull? That question was answered by the wagon that followed her, drawn by a team of draft horses, with Bull standing upon the wagon while being attended by several servants. Ethan had to blink a few times to make certain he wasn't having another of his crazed dreams, but there Bull was, looking happier than Judge Donovan telling one of his stories. The servants had combed his mane into a bright sheen while feeding him an array of delicacies but no apples. Never in his wildest dreams would he ever have thought Bull be given a hero's welcome in Vellesia of all places.

The entire assemblage knelt as Valera dismounted and approached Mortava and Demetra, where she too knelt.

"Mothers!" Valera greeted with her mage voice, which echoed beyond the palace walls.

"Rise, my child!" Demetra greeted in kind, standing forward of Mortava as ranking Mother. She ordered the assembly to rise thereafter.

"General Faro awaits you in the grand council chamber. We have much to discuss on our post-battle operations," Demetra added.

"Indeed, Mother," Valera replied, following Mortava's gaze that went beyond her.

"How fares our guest of honor?" Mortava asked bemusedly, regarding Bull perched upon the wagon, an obvious attempt to spare his legs since they could not heal him should they falter.

"He faced battle as bravely as any horse of legend. He will be received at Elysia with full honors," Valera said loud enough for Ethan to overhear, regarding him with a knowing gaze.

"Yes, we have many heroes to crown. I have started a list and am certain your commanders have ones as well," Mortava added, turning to look at Ethan, who was uncomfortable with being praised.

It's better than being yelled at, I guess, he reasoned. He really just wanted to leave all this formal nonsense behind and go fishing, or hunting, or…he almost thought of poker, but quickly disavowed that stupid idea. That was one game he would never play again.

He was taken aback as Valera stepped nigh, touching a hand to his face, her stoic countenance unable to read. "Your plan worked, Ethan. Your friend was most helpful in our victory," she cast an appreciative glance toward Bull, who simply stared back, chewing a handful of oats as if he hadn't a care to the world.

"He's a charmer." Ethan shrugged, his flippant remark nearly causing her to smile…nearly.

"Indeed," she said before ordering the steward to attend to her men, and her many prominent prisoners, Karg the most significant. She issued a dozen commands, sending commanders and courtesans to and fro, before ordering Ethan back to his chambers to rest. It was her polite reminder that he wasn't to attend the war council.

Ethan wasn't really disappointed that he wasn't invited to their war council. Unless it was entirely focused on defeating the red dragons by any and all means necessary, then it was a pointless endeavor. The Lorians were no different from his father in one way, stubborn to change. He could've talked until his throat died from exhaustion before the battle of the Velo, begging his father to listen, and it wouldn't have turned him. He had to trust Mortava in making the others see reason, and that might be easier without him there to distract everyone. People seemed to have a difficult time looking past his overbearing presence, focusing too much on his demeanor and ignoring his words. He ignored Valera's command to return to his chambers and rest. Instead, he continued with what he planned to do from the beginning and followed Bull to the stables.

*****

Lord General Faro received Valera and Mothers Demetra and Mortava in the council chambers, with a deep bow, standing behind a vast map table depicting the realm in exquisite detail. A number of high lords joined them, including their host, Lord Ganelle, each taking their place around the table.

"You may forgo pleasantries, Lord General. I haven't the time or patience for such pomp with the state of things," Valera said, eager to commence.

"As you command, my Queen. At present, we have three armies of significance converging upon the upper Delvar. Duke Thandor's main host is presently west of Castara, ready to cross over the ruins of the palace, before turning south," Faro began, detailing the disposition of forces throughout the realm. Lords Sulles and Vemar were skirting the western approaches of the Delvar valley while the royal army was skirting the east and driving north through the vale, relieving the forces that Valera left at the battlefield. Faro detailed the position of the armies mustering across the realm, especially those along all the regions bordering the wilds. Duke Alose was strengthening his holdfast should any foe think to assail Brelar or Corellis.

"General Ortar shall reposition his army here at Delvar, where they will continue to drill and improve their coordination. Selendra will join Mother Elesha, inspecting every soldier in the realm for traces of mage gifts. Any found lacking shall be sent here and reconstituted in Julius's new army. His force shall be primarily tasked with countering any further barbarian incursions. Their lack of magic should make them less visible to any dragons loitering across the barrier," Valera explained.

"And the barbarian prisoners, my Queen?" the lord general asked.

"The leaders and the dragon riders shall be taken to Elysia. I want the rest distributed throughout the realm to every holdfast and palace. Their dungeons have plenty of room. There they shall remain until we decide their disposition," she added.

Most concerning was the speed at which the barrier could be repaired. Their unspoken fear was that Sarella, Vetesha, and Ametria would fall under a dragon attack before they could complete their work. Valera dispatched several cohorts to safeguard each dragon carcass, the one of Nylo resting far to the north. It was unlikely her men reached that point as yet.

Mortava looked upon the map with grave misgivings, knowing the precarious position they were in. The source of all their peril lay with the red dragons and what few options they had to deal with them, if any. They barely overcame the black dragons, neither fully grown, and far weaker than the red, if what they learned from Tomas and Casandra was accurate. Could Ethan defeat a monster of that size? Could he do so many times over? Mortava had her doubts. Also to consider was the magic of the Dragon Tongue, which the two riders possessed, a magic that she could not see in them. Since her house gained mage detection, they could look upon anyone, and determine if they possessed a mage gift, and what gift that was. Only in Ethan was that not possible, his anti-magic blinding them to whatever magic he possessed. That meant that their ability to detect magic was faulty or that the Dragon-Tongue was a different form of magic. Equally strange was that Ethan apparently possessed it as well. One would conclude his anti-magic was the source of this gift, but neither of the riders possessed anti-magic, their minds and bodies subject to her mage powers. Also confounding was the red dragons hunting those with the Dragon Tongue, as well as the lesser dragon species. If the Dragon-Tongue was required to hatch dragon eggs, then who hatched the red dragon eggs? Was there another category of Dragon Tongue they were unaware of? Or did the red hatch by other means?

Valera looked across the table to Mortava, guessing her thoughts. She, too, had many questions surrounding the dragons, their riders, and most especially…Ethan. The boy was a complete mystery. The more they thought they knew, the more they realized how little they did. Mortava had already spoken of his ability to see in the dark, a small mage gift, but one he managed to conceal from everyone until now. He also possessed the Dragon Tongue, which he was ignorant of. Could he hatch a dragon? That grim possibility was foremost in her mind. If so, then Ethan was dangerous to an extreme, far more deadly than they could have ever imagined. But if he had the *tongue*, would Gabrielle have it as well? Is that how she would eventually rule over all of Elaria, using dragons to conquer the Mage Bane and the Wilds? Or would she hatch dragons only for them to destroy Vellesia, dooming their house? The only thing Valera was certain about, was that she wasn't certain about anything anymore. Adding to her woes was Alesha. She was reportedly en route, forsaking her duties at Elysia to come here. What other than Ethan could draw her? Even Valera was thankful in a way for her coming, her joining with Ethan the only hope any of them had to quelch the pain their separation ignited. Only her proximity to Bull throughout much of the campaign spared her. Also to consider was their potential windfall of anti-magic, the very essence needed to forge a collar that could bind Ethan to them forever, but that idea seemed foolish considering recent events. They needed Ethan and needed him whole, and oh how she hated admitting that. Ethan was becoming more indispensable to their house every day, from his siring their future heir, to his removing their hunger and pain, to his protection from dragons. Just when she believed House Loria was all-powerful, destined to rule Elaria unchallenged, she now felt weak, their very existence resting on a precipice, where the lightest of breezes would send them to the abyss.

Mortava could read the doubt in Valera's countenance, her eyes betraying the struggle within. They all had much to discuss but not here. Once they returned to Elysia, they would reveal everything to the full Council of House Loria, the queens, and the Order. For the first time, she hoped they would see Ethan as a friend and not a slave to be bent to their will. If not, she believed they were doomed. She couldn't help but think about what she discovered looking into his mind when she touched him with her power, hastening his recovery. She expected to find his hatred for them, though she should have known better by the time they spent together that that wasn't in his nature. She was surprised to learn of Raymar's subterfuge and would have a conversation with her grandson when she returned to Elysia. What really took her aback was Ethan. Peering into his mind she was overcome with an intense feeling of...*love*. It was love for his family, Krixan, his friends in Red Rock and Cordova, and surprisingly so many of them. He loved Ander, Darius, Corbin, Jered, and her, so much so that it nearly made her cry. But most overwhelming of all was his love for Alesha. His love for her was so blindingly powerful, it forced her to withdraw from his mind, lest she lose hers in the exchange.

She recalled that moment so vividly, weeping uncontrollably upon her retreat, his love spilling out in abundance, overwhelming her senses. Fortunately, Ander was not in the wagon to see her in such a state. It was the most beautiful thing she had ever seen. It was then she felt shame for what they did, the hunger be damned. But then she paused, knowing that it was Alesha that magnified this love to unimaginable heights. A simpleton would ascribe such bonds to destiny. But there was something far greater going on than their simple prophecy. It was then she realized how much she loved that boy as if he were her own son, and knew even if they set him free, he would still return to Alesha, forever joined by unbreakable bonds that none of them could comprehend.

*****

"Did you miss me, pal?" Ethan stroked Bull's mane, the horse looking at him with a look that seemed like he wanted to shrug if he was able. *Could horses shrug?* Ethan wondered. Either way, Bull looked like he hadn't a care in the world.

"Of course, you missed me," Ethan told himself. "I'm a lot more fun to be with than Valera. But we have to keep that just between us," he said, stepping into the stall to run a brush over his friend's coat, though by the look of things, Bull's growing army of admirers had beaten him to it. It wouldn't hurt to do it again, Ethan reasoned.

"I hear you're a hero now. Just don't let it go to your head. I don't want you to be stuck up like all the horses in the royal stables. Just wait until Jake hears about this." Ethan smiled, wishing there was some way for Jake to learn of it, but with him here, there was no one able to open the portal to Texas. It was a fanciful dream though. He stayed there for a while, talking with Bull, sharing all his adventures as if the horse understood it all, and maybe he did, Ethan reasoned.

She stood outside the stall, listening as Ethan spoke to his horse, wanting nothing more than to rush into his arms, but couldn't pass up this opportunity to hear him speak so freely. It was endearing and reminded her why she missed him so terribly. Eventually, Ethan grew quiet, having said all he could think to say. He waited briefly, to see if anything else came to mind when he felt a familiar presence.

"Hello, Ethan," Alesha said.

His head and eyes went straight toward her voice, finding her standing in the doorway of the stall, dressed in riding leather trousers and blouse, her stomach bulging with child, her face glowing with a feminine aura that quickened his blood.

"Allie?" He wondered if he was dreaming until she stepped into his arms, her lips proving she was no illusion.

Ecstasy.

Her kiss sent tendrils of overwhelming love across his flesh, permeating his entire being.

He returned her fervor, kissing her lips gently, before succumbing, her passion fueling his own. She moved to his cheek, kissing him fiercely while he devoured her neck and then her ear, stopping at the top of her head, before pressing his forehead to hers. He forgot the pain afflicting his right shoulder, savoring this moment, not wanting to let her go, until realizing the pain was no more. He was restored instantly by her touch, bathed in her healing embrace.

"How?" he barely uttered, unable to put words to his question.

"How?" she asked breathily, brushing her lips across his, the question having many possible meanings, none seeming too important right now.

"You healed me, Allie. My shoulder was still recovering, and now…" His words died as she devoured him, crushing her lips to his, drawn by the seductive power that he was so stupidly ignorant of.

"I didn't heal you. Gabrielle did." She smiled, pulling briefly away, loving the happily bewildered look crossing his beautiful face.

She pressed her right hand to his chest, feeling the beating of his heart, her eyes closing with their foreheads again pressing gently together.

"I was so afraid of losing you," she whispered, savoring his embrace.

"And I, you. I feared the dragon would pass us by for Elysia," he said, keeping his eyes closed as well, wanting nothing more than to hold her forever and not let go. She hurried to reach Delvar, forsaking her escort along the way to hasten the journey, a fact that would earn her, her mother's rebuke, but she didn't care, for they spent long enough apart.

Their eyes drew suddenly open as Bull joined his forehead to theirs, running his tongue over their faces.

"Hey, get your own girl," Ethan said, wiping his face.

"That is no way to speak to a hero of the realm, Ethan." Alesha smiled, kissing Bull on the bridge of his nose, the spotted Palomino nodding happily with her gesture.

"I know, she loves you too." Ethan shook his head.

There, in the stables of Delvar, he again kissed his wife, savoring this precious moment, leaving their troubles for tomorrow.

EPILOGUE

Ethan wandered the corridors of the palace as if he hadn't a care in the world, Alesha's kiss still fresh in his mind. She hurried off to the war council, leaving him to explore the castle, somehow losing his guards along the way. The fact she healed him so easily still hadn't sunk in, but he was too happy to analyze it. Why ruin his good mood and fortune with a question that would only confound him? Her healing him was a gift from their unborn child, its love extending to him through the woman they each loved…Alesha. It was all so surreal, leaving him a lovestruck fool. And as far as not being invited to their war council goes, who cares? They would eventually come around to his line of thinking, and if not…well, they would all be dead.

These things will find a way to work themselves out, he reasoned. That was until he remembered that a lot of people he cared about might die. Then he cursed himself for such heartless remark.

He suddenly found himself in a long, impressively decorated corridor, standing before a massive archway, its door surprisingly open. There was something curious about the chamber that drew him in, and since the door was open, why not?

Ethan stopped upon entering, discovering a heavy chest centered in the chamber. He stepped closer, beguiled by it for some mysterious reason. As he opened the lid, his eyes were drawn to the seven oval-shaped objects resting therein; but only one called to him, as if whispering seductively in his ear. He reached out, placing his left hand upon the largest of the objects, its dull-crimson shell brightening as he touched it, as if renewed by his presence.

Flash!

His eyes went black, transfixed by the power of the dragon egg, visions flooding his mind like waves crashing the shore, coming one after another without respite. He felt his spirit lifting through the ceiling, through the uppermost battlements of Delvar, ascending high into the firmament until creation itself shrank below him. He gazed northward, his body jerking forward, speeding through the heavens like an eagle riding the wind. The lands passed swiftly below him, open fields, forests, rivers and mountains slipping by like points on a map. He continued north and east, passing into the wilds and over tribal settlements along the northern steppes. He could see black, white, and green dragons circling below, waiting to cross the barrier. There were gray and gold dragons coursing east and west, searching for mages to devour. Onward he went, passing into the far north, going beyond the known world to lands no one in the mage realms had ever seen, before coming upon a human settlement along the shores of a deep mountain lake. The people looked up, pointing skyward as he circled overhead, their distinct red hair lifting in the summer breeze. He continued on, passing beyond the lake to far-off lands before stopping, setting down upon a colorless plain with no discernable features. An eternity seemed to pass, but time was immaterial. His vision darkened briefly before light flooded his eyes, revealing a terrifying and glorious sight. There before him stood a mountainous dragon far larger than the one he saw in Dragos's tower, with the body of a gray dragon in its teeth. It dropped the gray carcass to its feet, its muzzle lowering, pressing to Ethan's face. Ethan stood statue-still, wondering why the beast hadn't eaten him, moisture clinging to its bright-red scales. A puff of air from its nostrils blasted his Stetson from his head, its black diamond pupils staring back at him, surrounded by a sea of red iris.

"*Come to me!*" the dragon beckoned, its split tongue gathering the slather dripping from its fangs, its eyes lowering to Ethan's hand, which was still pressed upon the egg, Alesha's face flashing before his eyes as the image faltered.

Then it was gone, the vision dissipating like mist in a summer breeze. Ethan stood there for a time, wondering if what he saw was real or another strange dream. He looked down, finding the egg brightly lit as if brought to life. No, not *if.* It *was* brought to life, and it needed to go home. Was that the message the dragon was sending, demanding the return of its child? Was that the reason for the red dragons' invasion of the wilds? Perhaps it wasn't the magic drawing the other dragons to invade but the threat of the red dragons looking for their lost egg. Why would one egg be so important? Couldn't they simply lay another? And how did it call out to him? Why not someone else? Was this his destiny, to defend Vellesia and Astaria from destruction by returning this egg to its kin?

"Ethanos!"

He turned, finding Valera, Mortava, Demetra, and Alesha standing at the doorway, staring at him and the bright-red glowing egg in his hand.

*****

Thus ends book 2 of *The Free Born Saga, Elysia.*
The saga continues in book 3: *Dragon Wars.*

APPENDIX A

Mothers of the Lorian Order

1. Mother Evalena: head of the Lorian Order
   Age: 292
   Power inherited from father: immunity to pain
   Similar earth racial grouping: fair-skinned Caucasian, Northern
        European

2. Mother Zelana: daughter of Evalena.
   Age: 271
   Power inherited from father: enhanced vision
   Similar earth racial grouping: mixed Northern European/East
        Asian

3. Mother Veriana: daughter of Zelana
   Age: 254
   Power inherited from father: levitation
   Similar earth racial grouping: mostly East Asian; slight Northern
        European

4. Mother Ametria: daughter of Veriana
   Age: 236
   Power inherited from father: voice projection
   Similar earth racial grouping: mixed East Asian/Southeast
        European

5. Mother Clarisa: daughter of Ametria
Age: 214
Power inherited from father: binding (compelling through touch)
Similar earth racial grouping: mostly Southeastern European

6. Mother Demetra: daughter of Clarisa
Age: 195
Power inherited from father: enhanced hearing
Similar earth racial grouping: mixed West African/Southeast European

7. Mother Porshana: daughter of Demetra
Age: 176
Power inherited from father: kinetic burst
Similar earth racial grouping: mostly West African

8. Mother Inese: daughter of Porshana
Age: 159
Power inherited from father: ice casting
Similar earth racial grouping: mixed West African/Arabian

9. Mother Mortava: daughter of Inese
Age: 137
Power inherited from father: magical enhancement
Similar earth racial grouping: Middle Eastern or Indian

10. Mother Elesha: daughter of Mortava
Age: 120
Power inherited from father: enhanced memorization
Similar earth racial grouping: mixed Middle Eastern/Celtic

11. Mother Vetesha: daughter of Elesha
Age: 96
Power inherited from father: eye color manipulation
Similar racial grouping: mostly Celtic Northwestern European

12. Mother Caterina: daughter of Vetesha
    Age: 74
    Power inherited from father: Aquatic mobility/enhanced lung
        duration
    Similar earth racial grouping: mixed Greek/Northern European

Royal Family of Vellesia

Queen Mother Corella: daughter of Caterina
Age: 57
Spouse: Darius
Siblings: Prince Alexar
Power inherited from father: sound mimic
Similar earth racial grouping: Slavic

Queen Daughter Valera: daughter of Corella
Age: 38
Spouse: Travin Menau
Children: Alesha, Raymar, Amanda
Power inherited from father: Enhanced speed
Similar earth racial grouping: mixed Slavic/Indian subcontinent

Crown Princess Alesha
Age: 19
Spouse: Ethanos Blagen
Power inherited from father: mental mage gifts of House Menau
Similar earth racial grouping: mixed Latin American/Indian
    subcontinent

ABOUT THE AUTHOR

Ben Sanford grew up in Western New York. He spent almost twenty years as an air marshal, traveling across the United States and many parts of the world, meeting people from a broad range of cultures and backgrounds. It was from these thousands of interactions that he drew inspiration for the characters in his books. He currently resides in Maryland with his family.

Other books by Author

Free Born Saga

Book 1 Free Born
Book 2 Elysia
Book 3 Dragon Wars (in production)

Chronicles of Arax

Book 1 Of War and Heroes
Book 2 The Siege of Corell
Book 3 The Battle of Yatin
Book 4 The Making of a King
Book 5 Battle of Torry North
Book 6 Fall of Empires (2024)

Made in the USA
Middletown, DE
27 October 2023

41384719R00378